Picture
Maker

Inuit

GREENLAND

Inuit

Sorqaq's
Village

Qisuk's Village

Western District

Halvard's
Greenland

Trader Island

Pine Tree Woman's
2nd Village

Pine Tree Woman's
1st Village

Naskapi

LABRADOR

Hawk Feather's
Town

Algonquin

Gulf of
St. Lawrence

Algonquin

Wide River

Doteoga

Ganeogaono

← to Oneida
← to Onondaga

Picture Maker's Journey

Picture Maker

Penina Keen Spinka

DUTTON

DUTTON
Published by the Penguin Group
Penguin Putnam Inc., 375 Hudson Street, New York, New York 10014, U.S.A.
Penguin Books Ltd, 80 Strand, London WC2R 0RL, England
Penguin Books Australia Ltd, Ringwood, Victoria, Australia
Penguin Books Canada Ltd, 10 Alcorn Avenue, Toronto, Ontario, Canada M4V 3B2
Penguin Books (N.Z.) Ltd, 182–190 Wairau Road, Auckland 10, New Zealand

Penguin Books Ltd, Registered Offices: Harmondsworth, Middlesex, England

Published by Dutton, a member of Penguin Putnam Inc.

 REGISTERED TRADEMARK—MARCA REGISTRADA

ISBN 0-525-94624-1

Printed in the United States of America
Set in Perpetua
Designed by Eve L. Kirch

PUBLISHER'S NOTE

This novel about a daughter is dedicated to mine.

Rasha Nechama Warshaw
and Tzivia Leah Wasserman

Acknowledgments

I have many people to thank for helping me get this novel written, beginning with my husband, Barry Spinka, who reminded me to save my eyes when I got carried away and forgot the time, to get off the computer and get some sleep. Thanks to my librarian brother, Gerry Keen, for helping me track down the Akwesasne Museum to find out how to say Picture Maker in "Mohawk." Thanks to Regina Ronk for reading and making suggestions. Thanks beyond words to Susan Kite for her tireless help and enthusiasm. My writers' groups, both the Hudson Valley Writers' Guild and the Phoenix area Writers' Roundtable—thanks for reading my chapters and giving opinions to keep me going. And, of course, thank you to my agent, Stephanie Tade, for believing in me and to Carole Baron and Laurie Chittenden at Dutton for making *Picture Maker* happen.

Contents

Picture Maker

Prologue

Before time began, before the Creator was born, pregnant Sky Woman fell out of heaven when she got too close to an uprooted tree growing from a cloud. She fell for many days and nights. When the animals saw Sky Woman falling, Loon told the others she could not live under the water. He asked Great Turtle to lie still on the water to be her resting place. Ducks and geese flew up to meet Sky Woman and lower her gently and while they did so, Muskrat dove to the bottom of the water to bring up earth to lie on Great Turtle's shell. This was the beginning of the world.

After Sky Woman came to rest, she walked the perimeter of Great Turtle's shell as she labored to bring forth her child. The earth grew larger with each circling, until it grew so huge, she could not cross it in a single day. When Sky Woman's daughter, Mother Earth, grew into a woman, she coupled with the West Wind. After nine moons, she gave birth to twins. The Creator was born first, in the regular way, but then the Destroyer burst forth from his mother's side, killing her. The Creator covered her lovingly with earth and caused all good things to grow from his mother's bones. Sky Woman raised her grandsons, but they grew up differently, always jealous and always competing.

When Creator grew up, he thought hard and decided it was time to create men to populate the world. Men multiplied and spread out over the surface of Turtle Island, until they became many nations. The Creator's brother also gave much thought to what he saw, and he wondered how best to create discord.

For many seasons, the nations on Turtle Island lived and prospered in their own places, but after awhile, men began to grow jealous of one another. Some had better hunting lands; others had better fishing or flint mines, or better groves of maple. Longhouse tribes established clans from what is now northern New York westward to the Great Lakes. One chieftain named Tododaho, from the center longhouse tribe, the Onondaga, decided that the longhouse tribes should be united before the Algonquin-speaking tribes conquered them.

Because he could see into the future, Tododaho saw even greater enemies arriving from across the ocean. He tried to convince all the longhouse people to come together, to form a confederation, with him as their great chief. This was not to be accomplished easily, for the longhouse people refused to give up their sovereignty and follow a single leader. Anger warped Tododaho, turning him into a fiend. He used his great powers to cause harm and instigate war among the very people he strove to help.

Across the ocean, the Crusades had ended. Three plagues devastated Europe, killing Europeans by the hundreds of thousands. During this time, the era we know as the Dark Ages, all knowledge was kept tightly in the hands of the clergy. The world east of the Atlantic had sunk back into ignorance and superstition. Because they were far from the mainland, Greenlanders and Icelanders, the descendants of Viking explorers, were not so easily controlled by European trends or threatened by its epidemics. Many had kept their old gods in their hearts. They continued to tell and write down their histories, reading them by firelight on dark winter nights.

Our tale begins as the northernmost territories of the longhouse tribes were changing in dramatic and irrevocable ways. While the longhouse people were locked in battle, the entire world was on the verge of new discoveries. A young girl named Picture Maker, born into the Wolf Clan, was about to learn that Turtle Island was not the only world resting on the ocean. She had new worlds waiting for her, and a destiny that she alone, of all her people, would be driven forth to discover and make her own.

BOOK I

Inuit

GREENLAND

◄ Qisuk's Village

Sorqaq's
Village

Inuit

◄ Western District

Halvard's
Greenland

◄ Trader Island

Pine Tree Woman's
2nd Village

Naskapi

Pine Tree Woman's
1st Village

LABRADOR

Hawk
Feather's
Town

Algonquin

Gulf of
St. Lawrence

Algonquin

Wide River

hunting trip
Doteoga

Ganeogaono

← to Oneida

← to Onondaga

— — Algonquin invasion by canoe
and on foot

*B*efore rumors of the war between the western tribes came, I had a dream that changed my name. In my vision, I saw myself—a charred twig between my thumb and fingers. I moved it over a flattened piece of white bark I had stretched between my crossed legs. Lines emerged from my charcoal as easily as water flowing, until I had drawn a mother wolf sitting on her haunches, alert to guard her cubs. I knew right away this was our clan emblem, the Guardian Wolf.

That vision had come two years earlier in spring when rising sap loosed last year's bark on the birches. Sometimes, bark falls off by itself when the new bark pushes away the old. Men collect the best curls from the forest floor to line their war canoes and repair the walls after winter's storms.

I had been considering my dream, as Grandmother always told us we must, while I walked to the newly turned cornfields. A stray gust lifted a curl of bark from an old birch and blew it against my knees. This was a sign from Orenda. It was so clear, I needed no faith-keeper to tell me its meaning. The Great Spirit had challenged me to repeat my dream, if I could.

Ganeogaono

Chapter

Lost, I cried out, "Spirit Orenda! Creator of the World! Don't let them take me. Father, where are you?" I thrashed and flailed, endeavoring to fight off my enemies before they did something unspeakable.

My father's strong hands seized my young body and held me very still. He kept my arms against my sides until I stopped struggling. When I gasped awake, confused and breathing as if I had been running, he pulled me close against his powerful chest. "It's me, Gahrahstah. You're home." His familiar smell of sweat, resin, and tobacco told me I was safe even before I could force the visions from my eyes. He pulled back just a little until I could see the hard angles in his face softened by the orange glow from the fire pit. I was home on my bed in Grandmother's longhouse.

No foreign warrior had dragged me away. No enemy braves bellowed war cries as they ran through our forest to attack and kill my people. I was Gahrahstah, granddaughter to Wolf Clan Mother, daughter to my mother, Glad Song, and my father, Dehateh, Bear Clan's first war chief. My older sister leaned over, asking what was wrong. My aunts and cousins came also, to see if I had been hurt. My mother calmly explained that I had had a troubling dream. She reminded them that children's dreams are often no more than dreams, and not necessarily visions. Children are too easily influenced by what they hear, she explained, and advised them to go back to sleep.

I was not so sure; it had seemed too real. The vivid pictures dragged themselves slowly to the outer edge of my consciousness as reality took over. I breathed in the sounds and smells of home in the deepness of night, grunts and snores, whispered conversations, fathers and mothers doing what they do to bring more children into our clan. I felt ashamed to have shaken with dread at the pictures my dream showed me.

My father released his hold, although my mother remained concerned. She smoothed my damp hair back from my forehead and combed it through her fingers. I leaned into her hands, relaxing. "Tell me exactly what you saw while you slept," she commanded. "Even though you are young, perhaps your dream did contain a message for our shaman to decipher."

"I saw many foreign braves attacking us at Doteoga. They were nearly to the stockade. I screamed out to warn you, but one of them seized me and dragged me away with him when our defenders came out to drive them off. You were there, too, Father." I looked at him to remind myself that he was solid. "You carried your war club and called to me that you were coming. You led the Wolf Clan warriors to bring me home, instead of running with your own clan."

"Why would I lead Wolf Clan when I always lead the Bears? Your mother's clan has its own war leaders." My father rubbed his chin. "Your dream is a puzzle to me. It would take a shaman to make sense of it."

I shook my head, trying to make sense of my dream, but my shame heated my cheeks and distracted me from the original problem. I roused myself to remember if there were anything more I could tell my parents. In case it might help, I added, "Our enemies wore strange war-paint designs."

"Naturally, they did," Mother said. "I will have to give this some thought." As soon as my mother loosened her hold, I moved back into my corner of the bed bench, ashamed before my sister and cousins that I had awakened them. "You can be sure no enemy will come here," Mother added softly. "Our lookouts would never let anyone catch us off guard. Remember that. Also remember that Ganeogaono girls don't cry out or show fear."

"I know. I should have fought off the dream in silence." I acknowledged my failure to do so. "I'll do better if it happens again."

She tucked me back into my furs and wished me peaceful dreams. Too excited yet to sleep, I listened as Mother discussed my dream with Father. "It's all that war talk the child hears," she said. "Orenda, bring down that Onondaga shaman. Destroy his power and remove him from Turtle Island, Great Spirit, before he causes more trouble. He won't carry his war east to us. We are safe here in Doteoga, far away from Onondaga Country, aren't we, Dehateh?"

My father spoke too softly for me to hear his reply. By then, my sister had returned to her sleeping place beside the wall and curled into her furs again. In his hanging cradleboard against the lodge pole, my baby brother slept again.

Seeing me awake, Father crept over and whispered into my ear, "Dream only good dreams, Gahrahstah. All our warriors are home. They will protect Doteoga." I vowed to be braver if ever I was sent a night terror again, but it was easier to be brave when I was awake.

Our village, Doteoga, looks like a porcupine from our cornfields, its walls of jagged spears of felled, sharpened birch and elm leaning outward to frighten our enemies. Inside stand fifteen longhouses, five for each clan. The Ganeogaono people, Possessors of Flint, have three clans: Wolf, Bear, and Turtle. I've heard other tribes have Otter and Deer and Beaver clans as well, but these three clans are what our elders decided, so three is all we have.

Wolf Clan's five longhouses belong to my family. Our women cultivate our portion of the corn hills while the men hunt and train our boys. Wolf Clan has its own war leaders, but when all the clans come together for councils and ceremonies, the elders make decisions for the whole of Doteoga. The Doteoga's faith-keepers keep track of time by the moon. They remind the people when to plant, and when to give thanks to the spirits of the strawberries, the maple, and, most especially, to the Three Sisters, Corn, Beans, and Squash. Braves and maidens of different clans meet on these occasions. Should their mothers agree to a match, the son moves to his wife's mother's longhouse. Any child who results from their union belongs to his wife's clan. A man will love the children of his sister or female cousins, because he remains of the clan he was born into. It is not that often that a father is close to the children he has sired. I felt fortunate that my father cared for us.

Although I had never been farther than half a day's walk from home, I had heard descriptions of the world. When we were closed in by high snows and dangerous winds, the hunters spoke about far places. I listened to the descriptions and thought about what lay beyond our forest. In the east, the realm of our blood enemies, Algonquin make their towns and villages. The Wide River separates us. We keep to the south of it, most of the time. Ganeogaono braves hunt north of the river only after the Algonquin leave their villages and move to their summer camps near the ocean.

Before rumors of the war between the western tribes came, I had a dream that changed my name. In my vision, I saw myself—a charred twig between my thumb and fingers. I moved it over a flattened piece of white bark I had stretched between my crossed legs. Lines emerged from my charcoal as easily as water flowing, until I had drawn a mother wolf sitting on her haunches, alert to guard her cubs. I knew right away this was our clan emblem, the Guardian Wolf.

That vision had come two years earlier in spring, when rising sap loosened last year's bark on the birches. Sometimes, bark falls off by itself when the new bark pushes away the old. Men collect the best curls from the forest floor to line their war canoes and repair the walls after winter's storms.

I had been considering my dream, as Grandmother always told us we must, while I walked to the newly turned cornfields. A stray gust lifted a curl of bark from an old birch and blew it against my knees. This was a sign from Orenda. It was so clear, I needed no faith-keeper to tell me its meaning. The Great Spirit had challenged me to repeat my dream, if I could.

I carried my sheet of bark home carefully. There, I washed it and pressed it with the tan inner side down against the ground and weighted it down with stones. I had to wipe it off again, but when it was done, I had a dry, clean surface on which to work. I chose several broken pieces of charred wood from the remains of an old fire and put them into a small splint basket to carry. With my bark tucked carefully under my arm, I wandered about the periphery of our cornfield. Between the working women turning over the muddy earth for the next planting and the stockade gate, where men and children wandered in and out, I found a patch of dry ground in the early sunlight. It was a little out of the way. Hoping no one would come to disturb me, I made myself comfortable in the long grass.

I rested my chin on my knuckles and wiggled my bare toes while I thought. Where was the best place to begin? It had been easier in the dream. After awhile, I touched my charcoal to the top quarter of my bark sheet and made the first curved line. I wanted her mouth open enough to show her tongue and her fangs. I made the first lines as lightly as possible, fixing and correcting as the outline grew. Little by little, as I became satisfied, I deepened the lines. When the outline was good, I worked on shading and strokes for fur and whiskers. I paid particular attention to her fangs and the slant of her eyes, for she had to be alert and ready if anything threatened.

After awhile, if anyone had looked, they would have known what my picture was supposed to be. Now, what would make it as good as my dream wolf? What did it need? I failed to notice when Grandmother walked up behind me. She watched silently as I worked. When I paused, my blackened fingers cupping my chin to appraise what I had done so far, she bent over to look closer. Her shadow fell across the bark and I, startled, looked around to see what had broken my concentration. "It is good, child," she said.

"Please. You are in my light," I said, annoyed. A half moment later, I realized my error. I knew Wolf Clan Mother always had to be treated with utmost respect, but I had tossed the words lightly over my shoulder. I dropped my charcoal and my fingers flew to my lips in horror, blackening the lower half of my face. I had been rude for no more reason than that I was spellbound by my own creation.

I began to get up and beg her pardon, but she would not allow me to do so. She pushed me back down firmly. "Since your wolf is not done, you must continue working on it. When it's done, give it to me."

"I will," I promised, glad to be let off so easily. It was not the owning of the thing that absorbed me, but its creation. Grandmother walked away, motioning my mother to silence and beckoning her to come away. The two returned to the gate and went inside. I had not noticed my mother standing there at all. Although I was troubled, my fingers worked over the bark, thickening the strokes I made with my charred twig to show each hair of my wolf's thick coat.

Later that same day, I talked my mother's young brother into giving me a small leather package of his red paint. He would not show me where he hid it or how he made it. It was war paint.

My uncle's name was Burns His Lips, for obvious reasons. He couldn't wait for food to be ladled into bowls, so he often ate out of the clay cook pots. He pretended to be fierce, but he was young, untested in war, and still wearing his hair in two braids, instead of a warrior's scalp lock. Burns His Lips was my favorite man in all of Doteoga, next to my father. I did not speak of this, since my uncle was my mother's brother, so we were of the same clan.

My uncle bade me stay inside the stockade while he went for the paint, saying he had it hidden in a special place. I did so impatiently, but I thanked him politely, since I expected I would want more on another day. As soon as he walked off, I ran for my bark to apply the paint to my wolf's eyes with a chewed willow twig. Next, I touched red to the inside of her ears, her tongue, and to the tips of her pointed fangs.

When the picture was dry, I took it to Grandmother. Holding it at the edges, she inspected my wolf. After awhile, she said Orenda had sent me both the dream and the skill to make it real. She used her awl to press two holes across the top of my bark and looped basswood cord through them. My neck and cheeks felt warm when she replaced the tattered old emblem that had hung over the larger doorway of our longhouse. Wolf Clan people strolling by turned to watch. Even Bear Clan and Turtle Clan people walking nearby paused while my grandmother fastened my emblem between the posts over the entrance.

Chapter
2

Green Corn Festival comes when the first ears ripen and we give thanks to Corn Maiden. That day, Grandmother fed our old clan emblem to the ceremonial fire in the central plaza. She covered it reverently with leaves of holy tobacco to send its essence to Orenda in the smoke. Thereafter, she declared I was to be known as Picture Maker, Gahrahstah. Later, after the dancing in the plaza, my mother told me Gahrahstah had been Grandmother's name before she was elected Wolf Clan Mother by our matrons when her mother died. Thus, I learned that Grandmother had drawn the first wolf emblem to hang over our door.

The morning after my dream about the attack on Doteoga, Mother spoke to our shaman, a wrinkled and toothless old aunt of my grandmother's mother's generation. This elder said my dream contained too many uncertainties to be instructive. Why would our scouts not have seen the invaders before a lone girl? Why would I have been out in the forest alone when the attack came?

This old aunt attributed my dream to my young and overstimulated mind. She had two solutions. First, the men must increase the guard to be sure we should receive sufficient warning in case of attack. Second, she commanded my mother and aunts to stop speculating about the western war and to produce dream-catchers. My mother made a dream-catcher for our family, looping twined basswood over the edges of a greenwood hoop. She attached feathers and shells to the spiderweblike pattern. She hung the dream-catcher over our portion of the bed bench. The idea spread, until all the longhouses had them hanging. If bad dreams squeezed through these catchers, the effort weakened them. None of us cried out in our sleep after this. If anyone else fought off bad dreams, they did not speak of them by day.

One day, we went out to forage, half a morning's walk from Doteoga, my mother and sister, my cousins and I. I remember Grandmother's hair had two streaks of gray, one on each side, extending from her temples halfway to the end of her braids. She walked lightly beside us as we collected our roots and herbs along the stream, pointing out various leaves and crouching beside several to dig up the roots. Grandmother was a healer, so as we walked, she explained which leaves and mushrooms to avoid, which were good for eating, and which had healing power.

All the young girls watched and listened with great attention as she dug the roots, which she intended to dry and powder for medicines, or to soak in warm water to make infusions or teas for stomachaches, to wash sore eyes, or to dull pain. She scraped willow bark to make a remedy for fever and pain. After gathering each root or leaf or piece of bark, she wrapped them separately and placed them in a pouch she wore on her back. There was so much to learn.

The forest was deep and full of mystery even at noon. The sun was mostly hidden in the foliage above us and no larger than the circle I could make with my thumb and first finger, when my cousin Brown Otter motioned for us to be still. She took aim with her bow. I listened and heard flapping. A green-throated duck flew at tree height above a large pool of water, an offshoot of our river. My cousin's back arched as she pulled back and pointed her arrow. She released it with a twang of her bowstring, her thumb and fingers coming to rest gracefully behind her right ear. The arrow whistled. I held my breath until I heard the splash.

"I'll get it," she said, and pulled her short leather dress off over her head, but she kept her underbelt around her middle to use when she towed in her prize. She left her dress, together with her bow and quiver, under a tree, then glided into the chill water with scarcely a sound.

"Wait for her, Gahrahstah," my mother said. "We will continue down the stream a ways for watercress. Take care to note where we go so you can bring your cousin to us. There's fog moving in."

A low mist drifted very quickly from the river to the stream and pond. It stole the pieces of sunlight that filtered down through the trees and overpoured the closer bank. It swirled around my feet until it erased my ankles. I wiggled my toes in old leaves and pine needles, amused at how my feet and the forest floor had become invisible. Fragments of fog swirled around my knees, making patterns with the remaining greenish light. I wondered how long it would be before the rest of me disappeared.

I turned my head to listen for Brown Otter's smooth arm strokes. She would have trussed the duck and had it dragging right behind. I wondered if the fog hid me from her view, but I feared to call out to her. Even in our own land, patrolled for invaders by our warriors, speech might attract unwanted attention or frighten game. I was thinking about trying a birdcall, when my aunt called me.

"Gahrahstah," she hissed. My name sounded like a twig cracking under autumn leaves. When I turned to the sound, I saw my mother's sister, Aunt Makes Good Soup, standing tall beside a sassafras shrub not far away, only her shoulders and head poking above the enveloping fog. She motioned me to climb a nearby oak to spy out our surroundings. I hooked my fingers over the first branch, then pulled myself up into the foliage. I climbed until I could see the place where the hidden pool must be. The tree smelled dank from the moss climbing its roots and the leaves dripped with moisture.

I pulled myself onto a strong-looking limb that stretched over the river like a pointing finger. A rough section of bark skinned the edge of my hand. As I had been trained, I clamped my lips to keep silent, then licked away the blood. I pushed aside a thick-leaved branch, hearing the sweep of leaves. My cousins foraged below, but even knowing where they worked, I could barely see them. They seemed like ghosts flickering in and out of a cloud.

The fog shifted like white smoke, curling around my tree's thick surface roots, creeping along the ground. Grandmother whispered to my mother, her voice lower than the wind through grass. Mother swayed as she answered, rocking my brother in his diagonal sling across her chest, his round baby face near her breast so he could suckle when he wished.

Brown Otter walked out of the mist, tendrils of it floating around her. She shook herself like a dog, rubbed the drops from her arms and legs, then squeezed out her hair. The water poured like a short waterfall. She stepped, quiet as a doe, through the glade. She had not noticed me yet, but her dark face became thoughtful in its concentration. I heard the soles of her feet press the grass as she found her dress, bow, and quiver under the tree. In another moment or two, I would proclaim my presence.

Brown Otter tilted her neck, and suddenly, she met my eyes. Her silent chuckle told me I was not hidden as well as I supposed. In moments, she had dressed again, slung her unstrung bow over her shoulder, and tied her quiver of arrows around her hips. "Where are they?" she whispered.

"There. Spread out along the stream. Come."

Pretty soon, we set out for home, wanting to arrive before the sky darkened. A small way north of the stream, we left the fog behind us. We walked in small groups, signing or whispering only when necessary. I turned my head at a nearby splash, to see a tribe of beavers guarding their river lodges. They seemed to notice our haste, take counsel, and decide that we were not a threat. Beavers live in tribes, just as people do, and work together to protect their dwellings and dams as we protect our villages.

We had covered more than half the distance and were padding through the soft mulch of last year's pine needles, when an arrow whistled nearby. It thudded into a tree some yards away. The small hairs on my neck and arms lifted and tiny bumps shivered down my legs. Mother yanked me into a close thicket and pushed me down into the shadows. My small brother sensed her desperation. He lifted his head, nostrils twitching and eyes slitted, opening his mouth wide as it would go. I tried to signal Mother, but, on guard for danger beyond our thicket, she did not notice. I pulled her arm and whispered, "Mushroom!" She turned to reprove me. For a moment only, he wailed. She reacted instantly, pinching off his breath with her thumb and forefinger.

My cheek pressed to the earth, I forced myself to take a breath. Mother must have done the same to me when I was an infant, to prevent me from crying out. A cry in the forest will attract danger, and it did. My brother's tiny face turned scarlet. When Mother finally released him, Mushroom's mouth opened again. Immediately, Mother's fingers came down over his nostrils and mouth.

He did not cry out again, but by then, it was too late. A twig cracked, and then a man's head and shoulders emerged from the leafy shadows, arrow nocked to his longbow. "Algonquin," my mother whispered.

Braids hung over his shoulders and his paint design was wrong. I had never seen a grown man without a scalp lock, but I had never seen an Algonquin. My throat tightened and, like a fawn sensing the crouched cougar, I froze. Mother untied the sling that held my brother, pushed him down between her knees, and shielded me with her body.

"*Mohowaugsuk squa!*" the man said, teeth showing like fangs. He drew back his bowstring, centering on my mother. I did not know the meaning of his foreign words, but I knew my life was over. I prayed to Great Spirit Orenda to not let me shame my people by crying out when his second arrow pierced my heart. I must die bravely, as befitted a daughter of Wolf Clan.

In a motion so swift that I could barely discern what had happened, there was a thud and a gasp. The man lay sprawled out on his knees, his head twisted sideways. Blood seeped into the dead leaves. His bow fell useless beside him, its arrow released, to slide feebly along the ground. It ended its slide at the base of a nearby tree. Other arrows whistled through the air. I heard heavy footsteps running, grow fainter, and then there was silence. When I stood, I caught a glimpse of my sister, Pumpkin Flower, and my cousin Brown Otter unstringing their bows. They bent calmly to retrieve their arrows from the undergrowth.

I helped my mother tie in my brother again, then swiveled around, in time to see Grandmother retrieve the small war club she carried in her belt when we went into the forest, just in case. "Come along now, Glad Song," she commanded my mother. She beckoned us all from our hiding places. "We may continue home."

It rained that night. To the sound of drips from the overhanging rafters splashing in puddles underneath, I heard my parents whispering into the night when they thought me asleep. "Tall Walker and I camped with Oneida hunters on one side of a bluff," my father said. "Their town has not yet been touched by the fighting, although it's drawing closer to them. The Onondaga shaman has subdued his chiefs with magic. From the tales, he intends to establish himself as high chief over all longhouse nations. He continues to rise in influence, this Tododaho." Despite my closed lids, I remained wide awake. Our troubles in the forest loosed everyone's tongue. People were nervous. Mother asked, "Do his own clan mothers do nothing to stop him?"

"He will not obey any woman."

Mother's breath came out in an exasperated sigh. "Then he's a fool. He'll have only himself to blame when he and his followers are destroyed. Tell me true, Dehateh, have we cause to worry here, so far from the Onondaga?" I held my breath for a moment, but when I could no longer keep from breathing, I turned my back to them and blew out slowly. At the same time, I inched closer to my parents to catch the rustle of their voices.

My father's whisper was deep and comforting. "Onondaga is no match for Ganeogaono, Glad Song. Even our women send fear into the hearts of our enemies. Our people will never bend to a foreign master."

"Shush. Remember the children must not hear war talk." My mother leaned over to tuck our furs snugly around my brother and me. She smelled warmly of pine resin, cooking fires, and bear grease. When she was certain we slept peacefully, she crept back to Father. "Let the shaman

satisfy himself with the Oneida. We have enough to do defending Doteoga
from Algonquin and keeping them out of our forest. War on both borders
would divide our strength."

"You would make a good war chief." Father chucked, a soothing rumble. "We're not Ganeogaono to them, but *Mohawk*. Whatever that means in
their foul tongue, their name for us makes them shiver in their beds."

"Mohawk?" Mother asked slowly, sounding it out. "What does it mean? I
don't like the sound of it, Dehateh."

"Perhaps a ghost of some sort, or forest demons."

"The Algonquin would have slain me and the baby for no more reason
than what we are. What could Picture Maker have done if he had wanted
to take her away? The child must never be allowed to walk into the forest
alone. It comes too close to her dream. We must guard all the children
from capture. Fortunately, my mother was there and her aim was good.
She killed him with her war club. Brown Otter and Pumpkin Flower drove
off the others."

"You see. Our old women and maidens are more than a match for Algonquin warriors." Father reached out to her and whispered something in
my mother's ear. I wondered what *Mohawk* meant for a while, but then
Mother crawled under Father's fur and their whispering was soon replaced
by other sounds. To the rhythm of their love for each other, I quickly fell
asleep.

The moons changed and the seasons flew by. My baby brother learned
to walk and then to run. I grew taller. During the growing season, I took
my place among the women in our clan's corn rows. One morning when
I had entered my tenth summer, Laughing Girl and I were working. She
helped me to pry sunchokes from under the soggy remains of last year's
corn rows with a digging stick. I enjoyed the warm mud oozing between
our toes while we turned over the earth for the delicious tubers.

Pumpkin Flower mixed mashed fish entrails into her planting hills. We
helped with the work. As the sun rose higher, it warmed our naked backs
as we bent to our task. My sister hummed, flicking away flies and mosquitoes while she planted her seed corn, content with her elevated status as
married woman. She had married Plum Stone, a Turtle Clan brave, at last
midwinter's festival. She would be a mother in the fall. Already, she ordered us around like an elder, flinging her braids behind her pink-brown
cheeks while she practiced looking stern.

The warble of courting and nesting bluebirds in the surrounding forest accompanied our work. Gray squirrels chattered, racing around tree trunks in their mating games. We rubbed handfuls of cool mud on our bodies and faces for protection against the thousands of gnats. Laughing Girl and I made a pact that we would never become so haughty as my sister, even when we had as many as sixteen years ourselves.

Brown Otter confided that she would not let marriage make her stern. Although she had avoided it so far, her maidenly state could not last much longer. "We could use another hunter in our longhouse. All this peace has its bad side," Laughing Girl explained knowingly. "Even if he has not earned his scalp lock yet, our mother will chose my sister a husband soon, or she'll be scandalized that she has no grandchildren."

The subject of our chatter noticed us and beckoned. "Bring your water skins and follow me," Brown Otter invited. She started off through the fields. We did as she said, and sprinted after her. Brown Otter's hips had become round. She no longer ran naked with us, covering her buttocks modestly instead with a small skirt. She tried to match her stride to the elders and walk with stately grace, but her best efforts failed. Her pert bottom attracted admiration whenever she walked past a young man. Laughing Girl swayed her hips suggestively behind her sister and rolled her eyes as if trying to make a young man notice.

While Brown Otter filled her water skins, Laughing Girl and I dove into the chill water, splashing and laughing. This was our creek, where we could make all the noise we wished. An old warrior who had fought his last battle years ago waved his arm angrily and shouted that we were disturbing the fish he was about to catch. More likely, we had disturbed him from his nap.

I dove to the oozy bottom, cutting through the water like a catfish. In the murky green, a large tadpole swam against my closed lips, then backed up for a better look. Its bulging eyes blinked before it scooted away. My loose hair streamed when I broke the surface. We made for shore, shivering and laughing while we wrung our hair and rubbed ourselves dry.

Brown Otter waited on the mossy bank for us to join her, then wasted no words. "If I tell you something, you must promise not to repeat it."

"Why?" Laughing Girl asked, growing serious

"We don't want to frighten the children. Give me your word."

"Of course, then. We promise," Laughing Girl agreed for both of us.

"Let's start back, but walk slowly so we may talk. Has anyone told either of you about Hiawateh, the Onondaga?"

"Hiawateh? No. A warrior? One of Tododaho's, no doubt." We were to hear news about the war. "What has he done?" I demanded.

Brown Otter's mouth turned down in sorrow mixed with revulsion. "Hiawateh was a shaman, not a warrior. He remained opposed to the war and tried to talk the others out of it." This was something we had not heard. Laughing Girl and I were rapt with attention.

"Hiawateh almost succeeded in having the chiefs put down Tododaho and declare peace. The clan mothers were ready to take the antlers of leadership from the evil shaman's head, when Tododaho threw a terrible spell at Hiawateh's family. His wife sickened, until her skin scorched the fingers of any healer who touched her. The Healer Society could do nothing. Everyone was too frightened to oppose the stronger shaman."

"The Evil Brother gives Tododaho power, doesn't he?" Laughing Girl's serious eyes were at odds with her wide cheeks and generous mouth.

"One would certainly think so. Even after Hiawateh's wife died, he persisted in speaking against the war. To punish him, Tododaho caused Hiawateh's elder daughter to sicken from a squirrel bite. She begged for water, but when her father tried to give it, she snapped at him like a mad dog."

We had crossed through the corn hills of the Bear Clan and Turtle Clan and were almost to our clan's rows when Brown Otter grasped our hands. "His last daughter's hand slipped while she skinned a raccoon. It was a mere scratch, but her whole arm turned black. She died in great pain."

We three stared at one another in horror of such misuse of power, which is why I did not notice when Pumpkin Flower approached us. I nearly jumped at the sound of her voice. "Brown Otter, stop telling tales immediately! People don't die of small cuts and squirrel bites."

Brown Otter corrected her. "It was Tododaho's curse more than cuts or bites. He did it to prove he was strongest. Hiawateh had to stop opposing him, because he went completely mad. There is more."

"Be quiet. Our shaman told us not to say the evil one's name." She blew through her first two fingers. "Do you want to increase the Onondaga's power and call his attention to us? Have you no sense of caution?" Her chastising tone might have belonged to a clan mother.

Brown Otter dipped her head contritely. Pumpkin Flower's status was higher than that of Brown Otter, who was a mere maiden. "I'll be careful of my words," Brown Otter promised.

That pacified my sister. "Think before you spread tales. You don't want to give children bad dreams again," she added, raising her chin before she

turned to walk away. My sister may have been proper to chastise Brown
Otter, but that she called us children irked me.

That night, I visited my cousins' section of the long bed bench. I
brought over my blanket of sewn squirrel furs and curled up beside Brown
Otter and Laughing Girl. As soon as my aunt and uncle were otherwise occupied, I whispered, "After that, what happened to Hiawateh?"

"You can't say," Laughing Girl reminded her sister. "You promised to be
careful of your words."

"I will be careful. Pumpkin Flower can't sneak up on us here." Brown
Otter spoke so softly, we had to strain to hear. "After the rest of his family died from the evil shaman's spells, Hiawateh lost all reason. He's quite
mad now. He lives in the forest, among the wild places and the snake pits,
preying on travelers who stray off the path. Human leg bones and skulls
have been found near his old campfires."

"Orenda, save us," I whispered. Brown Otter nodded, her nose and
chin touched with gold light by the embers of my aunt's fire pit. Laughing
Girl clicked her teeth together and licked her fingers. My stomach
clenched. "Don't do that!"

I tried to keep my voice low, but seven-year-old Spotted Pebble, who
should have been fast asleep in the next section, had been listening. She
crawled over. "Did he really do it?" she whispered. "Who told you?"

Spotted Pebble's mother crawled over, too. "This is worse than gossip,"
she hissed angrily. "Wolf Clan girls do not fear shadows, and Ganeogaono
warriors fear no one. Keep your tongues still." She pulled her daughter
back where she belonged, leaving us to huddle like whipped pups at the
scolding.

Brown Otter put her arm across the two of us and pulled us close.
"Shush," she whispered. "Never mind. Go to sleep."

Chapter 3

The cornstalks grew taller than I could reach and the pumpkins began to grow on their vines. We, both women and girls, hoed and weeded our ripening corn hills. My mother chanted as we worked, asking the Three Sisters, Corn, Beans, and Squash, to keep their promise and grant us a good harvest. I had climbed to a tall platform and lay in wait, my feet hanging over the edge. Whenever blackbirds dared settle and peck at our corn, I jumped up and waved my arms, screeching back at them and laughing at their loud complaints.

I was higher than the rest and able to see down to the bend in the river where the boys were swimming. When I was finished frightening off the birds, I took a final look to be sure no others lurked out of sight, so that I could let down my guard. There seemed to be some excitement by the water. I could not tell what was happening, but then boys started rushing toward us. My little brother was about five then, all eyes and excitement. He ran in the lead, his gang right behind. His hair clung and dripped as he pounded the path through the corn. What would make them hurry like that? "Mushroom is running this way," I called to my mother. "All the boys are running as if they saw ghosts."

"Climb down and stay close to me," she commanded. I did as she bade me, while my cousins and aunts crowded close to learn if something was wrong. One of the boys might have gotten hurt. If it was a broken limb, they might need Aunt Makes Good Soup or one of the other healers. The boys skidded to a halt when Mother, her arms folded across her chest, blocked the path between the green rows. "What?"

Mushroom sucked in air importantly. "Two men in a canoe. Oneida designs. Coming." He pointed, saving words. "Nearly to the tie-up. We have to tell the elders. Maybe the Oneida have war news."

"Hurry, then." Our mother stood aside to let them pass, and the boys rushed past us. This was no longer a time to bury our ears in our planting fields, ignoring the activity in the west. If the Oneida were on their way to us, a change was in the air. Bear Clan and Turtle Clan women strode with some haste toward the stockade. They would have seen the canoe first, being closest to the river. Mother brushed caked mud from her hands, arms, and legs. "We might as well learn what this is about," she said. Instead of making for the stockade, Mother led our clan women toward the landing to watch the strangers disembark.

Rocks and crossed birch stakes jutted out of the water at the tie-up. Several fishing canoes were moored there. Doteoga's light birch-hulled war canoes, each capable of carrying ten warriors with supplies and weapons, were not kept on the water like the smaller craft. They leaned against the inner stockade walls, safe from weather, but ready to launch at need.

The Oneida slipped rope loops over the stakes. When they stepped over the side of their canoe and climbed up to the bank, they left their paddles, as well as their bows and quivers. Laughing Girl and I looked at each other. "They demonstrate trust," Mother said. She nodded to her sister and cousins. "The Oneida put themselves in our power."

The younger visitor shouldered a rolled pelt as well as his pack. Ordinarily, it was impolite to stare, but until the strangers were acknowledged by the chiefs, our stares meant nothing. The two Oneida strode across our planting fields, not stopping until they reached the wall before the entry passage. There, they lowered themselves to their knees and bent forward, touching Mother Earth with their foreheads. "They show respect," my mother said with approval.

The two men whispered together, looking around but saying nothing to our people. They took council between them while they waited, seated with their legs comfortably crossed. We continued to whisper and speculate. "Their packs are too small for traders," Laughing Girl whispered. "So what are they here for?" She looked around, but no one came forward.

I watched the older man, examining him for details. I wanted to know how an Oneida differed from a Ganeogaono. In face and form, he might have been one of us, but a man his age would surely have earned his scalp lock by now. I wondered if he was a shaman or faith-keeper, a member of one of the societies that did not use strength of arms except in defense. If so, what business did he have with us in Doteoga? He could not be the infamous Hiawateh. A shiver raised bumps on my arms. No. It could not be.

A long green splint basket hung halfway down the elder's thigh, looped to his belt. Smoke seeped out between the splits. He retrieved two short-stemmed pipes from his pack and passed one to his companion. They filled the bowls with shredded tobacco, then lit their pipes with twigs from the live coals in the basket. They puffed and inhaled, letting white smoke curl lazily from their nostrils.

"They aren't warriors. No scalp locks," I whispered.

"I know that," Mushroom said, trying to sound as if he knew everything about warriors by virtue of being male.

Wolf Cub Mother, Mother's first cousin, had stepped up to us without taking her eyes from the strangers. She whispered, "It's more likely that they *are* warriors, Glad Song."

"Tell us why you think so, Wolf Cub Mother," my mother requested at once. Laughing Girl and I, thrilled by this cousin's superior knowledge, hushed to give her our attention. Wolf Cub Mother had traveled past our borders more than once, and had seen some of the world. Her husband, Walks Many Trails, was Oneida himself. He had been captured long ago in a border skirmish and adopted into our tribe before I was born. Wolf Cub Mother had gone with him to meet her mother-in-law in Oneida Country to show her their son. Tree Climber, that son, now stood nearby, watching the Oneida beside Uncle Burns His Lips. The two young men crossed their arms close to their chests. They kept their faces expressionless, except for the glimmer of excitement in their eyes.

"Ganeogaono warriors shave their heads after their first kill, except for the scalp lock. Oneida men, untried in war, must earn their war paint before they may use it. Notice the red stripes on their left cheeks? Even the young one? These are warriors, but they show the courtesy of experienced envoys. Soon, we will hear their message."

Wolf Cub Mother got her odd name when she retrieved her baby son from a wolf. The bitch had dragged him away by his wrappings while our cousin dug up roots with her digging stick a short way into the forest. With her back turned and the child trained not to cry, she did not notice what was happening until they were nearly out of sight. As she told it, she dared not risk a throwing weapon or shouting, but she ran toward them as fast as her legs would go. The wolf, forced to move slowly while she dragged the cradleboard, snarled a warning for the woman to keep back.

My mother's cousin explained to the wolf that they were sister wolves. Tree Climber was her cub. The female wolf did not dispute her, but backed off and watched until the female human had retrieved her cub. Wolf and woman shared a long look, each thinking her own thoughts, before the wolf trotted off to find other game. It was a story our cousin told often.

"When will the Oneida give their message?" Mushroom asked.

Wolf Cub Mother seemed to have all the answers. "After they're welcomed as our guests and fed. Keep close to your mother, if you want to hear. As Wolf Clan Mother's direct kin, you may stand behind her at the matrons' bench during the council."

A council? Something momentous was about to begin. When the cougar stretches, the forest holds its breath, wondering which way it will hunt. If it should choose our land, our Ganeogaono wolves would be ready. I closed my eyes, picturing our warriors like wolves. Brown Otter stepped up beside me. "Where did you come from?" I asked. "I did not see you."

"I was nearby. You should have known. You have not even the excuse of fog." I lowered my eyes, but she squeezed my arm with affection. "I don't say it to chastise you, but better me than an enemy. You were dreaming standing up again. An Algonquin might have snatched you up." She blew through her fingers to keep any evil spirits from hearing her.

To show me her rebuke was given with love and concern for my well-being, she touched my cheek with hers. "Stay alert. Learn young so that you will live to grow old." Every elder had the right to chastise a younger person to teach or guide. She was my elder, and therefore felt responsible to correct me for my inattention.

People gave way when Wolf Cub Mother's husband, Walks Many Trails, approached the visitors. After they exchanged a few words, he walked toward the gate, pausing on his way back to speak to his wife. "The elders sent me to learn what I could. Being Oneida first, I might have known them."

"Well?"

"They're not from my old village, but they are my brothers, being of Bear Clan. *Our* elders must be the ones to lead them inside." He walked off to the stockade to inform the Bear war chiefs, my father among them.

Soon, these important people came out. They approached the two Oneida, gathering themselves into a half circle around the strangers. The eldest chief gave greetings and words of welcome. When he was done, the younger Oneida drew something long and white from his pack. At first, it looked like a white snake, long as the man's arm. When he arranged it in a circle on the opened pelt, I saw three strings of fine white wampum.

"Is the fur winter ermine or white hare?" I wondered aloud.

"It's too large to be either. There are no seams," Mother replied. She had not moved closer, but her eyes were sharp. "It's not quite white, but it is very light in color. Perhaps it's from a winter elk."

Wolf Cub Mother said, "It seems to me that is the pelt of a bison calf, animals from the grasslands west of the Great Lakes. They are grazers and very plentiful where few trees grow to impede the grass. Their calves are normally brown. A pale one is born maybe once in ten generations. They are considered a gift from Great Spirit Orenda. The Oneida must consider their envoys' mission of high importance to have entrusted them with this sacred object."

Walks Many Trails returned to us to see how the welcoming was getting along. Mushroom pushed up to him. "Doesn't his white smoke mean peace? What about white wampum? Won't there be war?" Although he was young, like all boys, he already thought of the day he would take his first scalp.

"Yes, white smoke means peace," Walks Many Trails agreed. "These Oneida come to us in peace. If we decide on war, it won't be against them." He turned and pointed, leveling his index finger. "Look now."

The older Oneida unwrapped something and placed it within the circle of white wampum. I felt a shortage of air and my heart pounded harder in my chest. Inside the wampum lay a war club, painted red.

"Welcome to Doteoga," my own father said formally. "I am Dehateh." He held up his right hand, palm toward the visitors, to show he held no weapon. He introduced Swims the River, the Bear elder who was high chief to the three clans. A jagged scar like a lightning bolt ran across one of the high chief's dark cheeks, and three gull feathers stood upright in his scalp lock. "Welcome to Doteoga," he said. "You must refresh yourselves and take nourishment." Both visitors rose to their feet in one graceful movement. The elder Oneida handed Swims the River the white wampum. The chief took it from him, but when he also offered the red war club, Swims the River pushed it away.

"Later, we shall see," he said. "Follow me, now, to my home." The younger man made no expression at the chieftain's rejection, either of disappointment or resignation, but he wrapped the club back in its hide covering. He then rolled up the white pelt and draped it over his shoulder, around his pack, before he followed the other men into the stockade.

Swims the River's sister hurried first through the zigzag passage. She was Bear Clan Mother. "Don't stare," my mother rebuked us. "She goes to warm and ladle gruel, beans, and venison for these high-status guests. It is quite proper for a clan matron to serve such prestigious visitors herself. We may as well go home and eat, too. This will be a long night."

The stockade logs, like bristling spears, caught the late-afternoon sun's rays. They cast extended shadows over the central plaza before the Oneida pair and their hosts emerged from Bear Longhouse. People gathered from every longhouse to listen to the council meeting once the war chiefs and elders took their places. From babes in carriers to old men and women, our town must have held near to a thousand people. We filled the plaza and the spaces between the houses. If my cousins and I were not Wolf Clan Mother's own grandchildren, we would have had to watch from the back. As it was, I was close enough to hear every word.

Before the three clan mothers took their places, they lit the sacred council fire together with brands from each of their hearths. Callers were ordered to stand within hearing of the council to pass back the exchanges to the farthest reaches of the crowd. The youngest men, untried in war, stood back among the women and children. When all was ready, Swims the River introduced the elder visitor. "This is Running Fox of Bear Clan, Oneida Tribe, Town of Geneseo. Little Cougar is the son of his sister, also of Bear Clan. We await your message, Running Fox." Silence, as if we were in the forest, came over us.

The elder Oneida ascended the speakers' stump. As well as I can remember, this is what Running Fox said. His words have echoed through my memories these many years since that long-ago afternoon.

"Four days have passed since a party of envoys left our home in Geneseo, Oneida Country, to bring our message to the towns and villages of Ganeogaono Country. We thank you, people of Doteoga, for receiving us."

Our future hung on his next words. The Oneida spoke slowly and clearly, sending his voice far without apparent effort. "We won't deny that there have been border skirmishes between Ganeogaono and Oneida. We've taken captives and adopted them into our families, while you've adopted our men into yours. Yet, we come from a common root, given to us by the Creator. Most years, peace has prevailed between our two nations. We are brothers, the two eastern Haudenosaunee nations. Our shamans tell us brothers are most apt to recall their kinship when threatened by a common enemy."

The awaited words had finally been spoken. They were relayed at once to the farthest reaches of listeners. It was no longer a war between Onondaga and Oneida only. We, too, had been threatened by Onondaga. We would have to respond. My cousins Spotted Pebble and Laughing Girl pressed close. Spotted Pebble took my hand. She folded her smaller fingers tightly around mine. Brown Otter, who stood beside my aunt, kept her face blank, but I noticed her hands clenching and unclenching. To this day, whenever I see someone make this gesture, it reminds me. For once, Mushroom was not jumping or running. He stood still as an alert fawn, listening for danger in the tall green forest.

"Warriors of Doteoga," Running Fox called. "We need your help. Join with us. Help us hold back the flood of crazed warriors who fight a war of domination for their wicked master, the Onondaga shaman. The Evil Brother delights at his victories. The Creator needs us to take his part. Oneida men and women don't implore your help out of cowardice. For two years, we have resisted bravely, but we cannot prevail against our enemies alone."

"Why not fight magic with magic?" Runs the River asked when Running Fox paused to drink.

"His magic is too strong. Until a shaman can be found who is strong enough to subdue their master, we shall oppose Onondaga as warriors must, with spears and arrows. If we do not thwart them this year or next, they will bring their war to you. Will you wait until they pour out of destroyed Oneida Country like the Wide River in flood? Act now, my brothers, to halt them. Join forces with us before you lose your spirits and your homes to the Evil One."

The relays started again. A baby cried nearby. Its mother pinched its nose to silence it. While we waited, I pondered the messenger's word picture. A flood of warriors like a river in flood. The Oneida was a good speaker.

"Oneida envoys are presently visiting all Ganeogaono towns and villages. They go from the bitter waters of Saratoga, past the peaks of the Adirondack Mountains to Shenendehowa of the flatlands." He named a few places I knew of and others I did not. "While there's time, put aside our old differences. Little Cougar and I invite you to ally yourselves with us. Resist the Creator's Evil Brother and his Onondaga servants. Push them back. Join with us to keep both our countries free of one who would be our master.

"Warriors and clan mothers, that is all I have to say. Little Cougar and I await your decision." He descended from the stump and folded his arms across his chest. I felt a mosquito tickling my neck and reached back to scratch. My fingers came away bloody.

Now that we were free to move and speak, I did not know what to say. My brother's eyes glistened, lit from inside. He had drunk in the words of the speaker as if he had a great thirst and the Oneida's words were cold, sweet water. "The chiefs will decide for war," he said, and, feeling the solemnity of the moment, even he managed to keep his voice low. "They have to."

Many voices broke the silence, until the clamor around us grew louder. Everyone discussed the proposed venture. Mushroom, feeling the release of tension as the voices were raised to a din, ran to his age mates. The boys formed a circle, in which they pranced and jumped, practicing war cries.

My grandmother's brows grew close, deepening the creases over her nose. "Such clamor is not appropriate or disciplined. There must be proper discussion among the elders and war chiefs. They must call for quiet," she remarked to the other clan mothers.

"Why don't you tell them, Grandmother?" I asked, moving up to the bench. She was the highest authority inside the stockade.

She leaned back on the bench, her dark eyes on mine. "As the forest is men's domain, so are war and war councils. They stand to gain honor on the warpath and status at home, but they are the ones who must risk their lives in our defense. For this, we must defer to the men. Do you understand, Gahrahstah?" I nodded, assuring her that I did.

One of our elders ascended the speaker's stump and lifted his hands above his head. Conversations stopped immediately and silence descended, except for my brother's gang, which had not noticed. My sister walked over to them. "An elder has signaled for quiet," she said in her most matronly voice. "Do not shame Wolf Clan or our war leaders. Do you want these Oneida to suspect we have less discipline than Algonquin?" In a moment, it was quiet enough to hear a loon call across Wide River.

Pressed around the elders and chiefs, our warriors listened while the council continued their calm discussion, puffing on their pipes and scenting the air with holy tobacco. A chief gestured for those in the front to sit.

"We have questions. How many days' journey to the boundaries of the fighting?" Father asked Running Fox. He spoke loudly, in a voice to carry above a battlefield without seeming to holler, but the speakers dutifully repeated his question. I could imagine how my father encouraged his men in battle, shouting over the death cries, the clash of war spears, knives, and war clubs. "How many Oneida warriors remain? How many towns and villages have fallen to the enemy?" My father folded his arms to await Running Fox's response.

The Oneida's answer was unnerving. "When we left, the fighting was six days' travel by foot, half that by canoe. Towns have been emptied of people, their defenders, both men and women, drained of their will to resist the Onondaga onslaught. Of course, we have taken them in, but our towns are near the eastern border. The refugees brought what food they could save, but it goes hard. The standing corn was far from ripe. We must leave men behind to guard our fields, or no one will eat this winter.

"Before all of Turtle Island succumbs and we who resist are forced to live like moles underground, chewing roots for survival, we must press the attack back to the nameless shaman's own country. Defense is not enough. Great Spirit Orenda intends men to be free, to live under laws and keep His festivals. Shall men belong to other men? The Onondaga have burned cornfields. This is an abomination to the Three Sisters, Corn, Beans, and Squash."

One of our faith-keepers, a white-haired woman, called out, "Have they no respect for Mother Earth, from whose head and body our sustenance springs? It is a great wickedness to burn the Sisters."

"While the evil shaman rules them, the Onondaga have no regard for any law but his. If you join us, we will have to live off the land and the river. With so many men on the warpath, our usual game animals have fled. You must bring with you as much parched corn as Doteoga can spare. Also lines and fishhooks. Western Ganeogaono tribesmen joined us last summer. This year, more joined our war parties. We assemble at Geneseo. In a handful of days, we'll know how many warriors we have amassed and will plan our strategy from there. Little Cougar, reveal the map."

His nephew unfolded the pelt, exposing the inner hide, as pale as the fur. It was covered with markings and lines drawn in red and black. One on each side, they held the hide between them, turning it slowly for everyone to see. I noted the outlines of hills and houses, arrows, lines, and stick figures of men. Swims the River called for mats, so the pelt could be laid flat, without touching its white fur to the trampled earth. The chiefs crouched around it, their fingers tracing the air above the symbols, pointing and asking more questions.

"Explain for us," Grandmother commanded Wolf Cub Mother. "What is this thing the war chiefs study on the inner hide of the pelt?"

She explained. "It's a picture of a section of Turtle Island as if the Creator drew it from the sky. Thick lines mean rivers and thin lines mean trails. A longhouse is a village, two are a town. The last town on the right side, beside the thick line of Wide River, that is Doteoga. The man figures mean battles."

Grandmother thanked her. I thought how huge the world must be if Doteoga was the size of my thumbnail. It would take days and days to cross, maybe a full turning of the moon before one would find the far ocean.

My father consulted with the other chiefs, then mounted the speaker's stump. "If we decide for war, newly married men are to stay home to defend Doteoga." He stifled their protests. "They must also get their wives with child. This war has been going on for two years. It may continue for two more. We'll need another generation of men to make up for those who die in battle. Three men must stay home for every six who travel the warpath. We want Doteoga here when we return."

Torches were lit in the darkening plaza for the balance of the council meeting. The chiefs conferred with high-status warriors, then voted with open hands for peace or closed fists for war. I saw no open hands.

Formally, Running Fox offered the red war club again. This time, Chief Swims the River took it in both of his hands and lifted it high for all to see. We did not cheer yet. The moment was too solemn. His pronouncements might have been drumbeats, coming from a deep water drum that echoed and shook the trees.

"We have decided to align ourselves with Oneida," he said. "Young men, here is your chance to earn your scalp lock. Join us for your first war. Prepare your weapons. Experienced warriors, see to your nephews' spears and bows. Arrow makers, sharpen our arrowheads and straighten our shafts. Affix our spearheads well to bring death to our enemies."

Burns His Lips tugged his braids. He would finally have his opportunity to prove himself. Tree Climber squared his shoulders. He lifted his fist and brought it down as if striking a heavy blow with his war club. He grinned with delight.

The old war chief continued. "No less courage will be required of you who stay behind. Never forget our enemies across the river. In the morning, we shall dance and pray to Orenda. To those who will go, you have a first mission to perform. Lie with your wives tonight. Make more warriors for Doteoga. From tomorrow until we return home victorious, we save our strength to deal death." A loud cheer greeted his words. "Have the clan matrons anything to add before this council concludes?"

The three consulted before Grandmother climbed up beside Swims the

River on the wide stump. A hush came over all the people. "I speak to the women on behalf of the three clans. Prepare pouches of parched corn. Pitch the seams of your clans' war canoes so they will be strong. They need to carry our men to battle and back home again, when all who would threaten us are dead."

My brother and his gang resumed their dancing. Someone gave a great war whoop. Others followed, until the town rang and echoed with yells. My cheeks flushed hot with excitement. We were at war.

Chapter 4

No messenger returned from our men through that long summer. The sumac turned red. My sister, Pumpkin Flower, made and stocked a birth shelter in the nearby forest, well within our circle of protection. One day, without saying a word, she left us. Several days later, she returned to Doteoga with my new nephew strapped across her chest.

The maples turned scarlet, the birches yellow. Acorns littered the ground and yet not one man had returned from the war in the west. Preparing for winter gave our hands plenty to do, but nothing could keep my mind far from my uncles and father fighting the influence of the Onondaga sorcerer.

The days grew short again. Fall winds blew the leaves in circles and piled them against the stockade and the longhouses. Chill air soon penetrated our bark walls. Inside, we hung furs to catch the cold. We kept our hearth fires glowing and closed off our entrances with bearskins tied onto frames.

Snow would soon cover the trails, but it was useless to speculate about the men. I snuggled under my furs in the night, pressing against my mother's warmth for comfort.

One morning, after a rainy night, I found a thin layer of ice over the puddles. Strips of curling dried squash hung beside huge bunches of corn suspended by braided husks from the crossbeams. We had filled baskets of beans and stacked them under the bed benches. We were fortunate to have had a good harvest, since the men left behind to guard us were too few to leave on extended hunting trips.

We had little else to do than wait by the river for sight of our re-turning men, trying not to put our fear into words. Hunter moon fol-lowed harvest moon. By then, frost had killed the last of the pumpkins. Cold, gray rain streamed from the rooftops and the porch overhangs. We caught it inside in clay pots where the smoke holes let in water. My mother sang old songs about wives who wait faithfully for their men. We joined on the chorus, but our singing did little to ease our growing apprehension.

Warriors, two and three together, patrolled the periphery of the stock-ade and fields, while we mended clothing or gathered firewood in sight of the river, watching for canoes. When the sun filtered through the trees halfway down the western rim of sky, we returned home to prepare an-other meal.

At supper, no one felt much like talking. Quite suddenly, my brother stamped into the longhouse. "The men!" he announced to our startled ears. "They're coming around the curve of the river. They're almost here!" He spun on his heel and was gone, but his words echoed in the silent long-house. *They're almost here!*

A fly buzzed between the rafters and a chestnut popped near the fire. Grandmother rose to her feet, smoothing down the front of her stained doeskin dress. "Our scout brought good news. Let us not hesitate to greet our men."

Where the river dwindled away in the west, the last reflections of the sun-tinged clouds painted the water pink. As the canoes approached the landing, pink became red, then grew deeper, becoming the color of old blood. The red blended with the gathering shadows and was gone as the first canoes were tied up and their warriors climbed the bank. Stars ap-peared in the gathering dusk as more canoes glided silently home. Several women ran back to bring torches to light the banks and show us our way back to the darkened town.

Uncle Burns His Lips had his head shaved except for his warrior's scalp lock. He pushed a captive ahead of him. The man stumbled, ragged and downcast, his hands tied behind. Laughing Girl grabbed my arm joyfully when she saw both our fathers climb down from their canoe. "Look there!" I realized she had been holding her breath and only then, it seemed, had remembered to breathe. "They are coming up the bank."

Our warriors pushed and pulled their bound captives toward the stock-ade. Laughing Girl's fingers dug into my shoulder painfully. "Not so hard," I yelped, pulling away. "I'm Gahrahstah, not an enemy."

"Sorry," she muttered, removing her fingers from my arm. "I was so excited. There are the Onondaga captives!"

"I can see them as well as you can. They are not so fearsome, tied and helpless like that."

My father paused when he saw us. One of his legs was bound around with strips of stained leather and he walked stiffly. Mother strode swiftly up to him and touched his chest with her palm, fingers outspread, as if only touching him could make her believe in his presence. They leaned their faces close together, speaking private words. Father lightly caressed Mother's hair and cheek as they drew apart. "I must report to my elders," he said before he turned away and continued with his clan.

My mother composed herself before she turned around to look at us. "Let's go into the house. We have to warm the food again," she said, regaining some of her old brisk manner. Her lethargy was gone at last and her eyes smiled at her own words. "Your father will be hungry."

"In a moment," I said. Bright stars multiplied in the dark above the black water. My eyes were drawn up toward the figure of Sky Bear in the low eastern sky. The Four Hunters make a picture in the sky with their small sky dog. All summer, they pursue Sky Bear. In autumn, when they reach the horizon, they kill him with their arrows. Sky Bear's red blood and yellow fat stains the leaves. It happens every year, when the trees get ready to sleep. After spring, Sky Bear is reborn for the hunt to begin again.

Laughing Girl and I made our way home. At the entrance, we looked back to the line of captives passing by the dead fields. An elder standing near the stockade lifted his pine torch to look into their faces. They asked questions of our warriors, who led the captives by cords around their necks. Onondaga men kept their hair tied back with leather bands. Their faded green war paint and tattered clothing gave them the look of walking dead men. One broad-shouldered brute spit on the ground before his guards shoved him through the passageway, to show he had no regard for us.

"Onondaga vermin," I called after him.

"His flesh will be added to the stew, to flavor the corn," my sister declared. She walked away, until she was no more than another silhouette in the dark.

"Come. Our mothers are waiting," Laughing Girl reminded me. We walked into the town and crossed the plaza. Women ran to neighbors to borrow willow-bark tea and salves for wounds. Faces reflected the dancing flames from the torches. "Have you seen him?" This question was asked many times by women searching for their men. Now and then, a cry pierced the evening when a woman's fragile hope was shattered.

Fragrant smells from cooking pots wafted through the air. "Let's run home," I challenged Laughing Girl. We raced between the shadows and torch fires. The town seemed strange. Even the long, pointed stakes of the stockade walls flickered and swayed with the moving lights and shadows. War must not be brought into a house, so water was poured over each warrior's hands before he entered. A few faith-keepers waved damp baskets of smoldering tobacco leaves to purify the warriors, as well. When I reached our fire pit, Mother was stirring the stew while my aunt added chunks of a rabbit my brother had killed the day before.

Father soon entered. He held his hands in the faith-keeper's extended smoke, turned them front and back, then walked to our bed bench and sat down heavily. Mother filled his bowl and held it to him with both hands. It was odd to see him in his accustomed place, chewing his food slowly and thoughtfully, his lean hands cupped around his bowl. His eyes looked around the long hall. "A man on the warpath wonders if he will ever see his home fires again or if he will wake up beyond the clouds with Orenda. It is good thing to be back, Glad Song."

My mother seemed too full of gladness to speak. She watched my father eat, as if joy filled her better than food. When he was done, she took his bowl to refill, but he patted his sunken belly contentedly to show he had eaten enough. The lines of his face under the paint had deepened. He must have been close to forty that year. "That is all I want. I'm used to shortened rations. Just let me look at you and the children," he said to my mother.

I tried to hold his gaze when he turned to me, but I didn't want him to see my eyes, because they were tearing. I lowered them but smiled at him. "Picture Maker, you've grown. Your mother tells me you help provide meat for this house."

"My sister taught me to use a bow," I said, thinking of the hunting party I had joined for training. "Grandmother insisted we learn early. All the clan mothers agreed." Since he seemed interested, I explained. "We worked in teams. Wolf Cub Mother led my group. She taught us to read tracks a little, and how to stalk game. I can find my direction by the stars at night and by the position of the sun and the shadows it casts in the daytime. I can hunt, too. Once, I hit a duck on the water. Once, a goose in flight."

"My little girl. How peculiar to think of you tracking game instead of playing with your cornhusk dolls. Your grandmother is wise. It's good for women to learn such skills," he said.

"I haven't played with dolls for years," I retorted. "I'm almost a woman."

"I remember a few seasons ago, a girl who hid behind her mother's skirts when the False Face Society danced away an old uncle's toothache." I reminded him that was a long time ago. "I also remember when you saved your brother from that copperhead by the creek." He smiled, but I was glad when Father turned his attention to my brother, so he would not hear my heart beat faster at his praise.

"Mushroom. You have the bearing of a hunter. Your mother told me you provided the meat for this stew."

My brother said, "I'm Scout now, since Green Corn Festival. I saw the envoys first last summer and I was first to see canoes today."

"Scout is an excellent name." My brother stood a little taller. A war leader's commendation was the highest praise a young brave could hope for. "You'll be a warrior to contend with someday. Continue to live up to your name so your battle companions will value you in their brotherhood."

"I will, Father," Scout replied. His eyes glittered. "We practice already. My uncles taught us knife fighting and spear throwing and how to trip an enemy to kill him. You'll see, when it's my turn to go to war. I'll lead the Wolves someday the way you lead the Bears."

"Before you go to war, you have to grow up," Mother said to my brother. "Eat your supper." She beckoned my sister. "We have someone new to show you. Pumpkin Flower, bring your son."

Father smiled tenderly, saying, "Put him down here, next to me." Pumpkin Flower placed her son on our bed bench and opened his wrappings before she stepped back to see our father's reaction. The baby kicked strongly and circled his arms in the air. "Yes," Father said, "I can see this is a boy." His big rough hand, which so recently had wielded a heavy war club, softly stroked the baby's cheeks and legs. "What have you named him, daughter?"

"Red Leaf, Father, because the sumac leaves were tipped with red at the side of my birth shelter. He'll be a proud warrior for Doteoga."

"I'm sure he will," Father agreed, and closed his eyes, his face showing the fatigue I had seen there earlier. "I might as well tell you what I told the elders. The western war has paused for the winter, but it is far from over. Let us hope we won't need Red Leaf before it is."

My mother drew back. "Do you mean to say you're going away again in spring? Surely you were successful. Does the Evil One yet live and seek to control all the longhouse nations?"

"He does, and no one can get near enough to end his ambitions. They say he can turn arrows and spears away with his thoughts. We might as well try to kill the wind. Oneida warriors who were captured have fallen under his spell." We looked at one another, then back to him. "Yes, it is terrible. They are forced to fight their kinsmen and kill them if they can. Some of our captives are Oneida. Perhaps we may wash the webs of sorcery from their eyes, but I see no help for the Onondaga until a sorcerer stronger than their master can overcome him."

Just then, a high-pitched wail came from outside, from down by the river. I knew that voice. Her cry went up and up, like a wolf singing her moon song, pausing only to gather breath before howling again. My mother clapped her hand to her mouth, while Pumpkin Flower and I turned as one to the sound. "Wolf Cub Mother," I said. Other wails cried throughout the town. Wolf Cub Mother must have waited by the river a long time, hoping for a miracle.

"Which is dead?" Mother asked my father. "Is it Walks Many Trails or Tree Climber?"

"Tree Climber fell. It was late in the battle. Before he died, he won his warrior's scalp lock, so his mother has no cause for shame." Wolf Cub Mother showed few tender feelings, but it was known that she loved her son.

"Is his killer dead or captured?" Mother asked.

"He's one of the captives, brought back with us by Burns His Lips for Ganeogaono justice," my father replied. "They were best friends." I wondered if my cousin's killer was the captive who had spit at us from the line of prisoners being driven inside the stockade.

"Wolf Cub Mother shall avenge his death," my mother said. "I would not want to be in that Onondaga's moccasins tonight."

A sense of anticipation heightened my senses. When Grandmother entered the house, I ran to her, but something in her face gave me pause. Grandmother's eyes were ringed with red and she clenched her walking stick in her fisted hand. "Picture Maker," she said, taking notice of me, "you will be a woman before long. Stand with your mother tonight. I expect you to conduct yourself with Wolf Clan dignity."

"Yes. Certainly, Grandmother," I said, not knowing what was expected of me, but curious and determined not to shame my clan. "The men have eaten and rested," I reported.

"It is good," she said. "They fought to defend us from evil. All our injured have had their wounds seen to. None will die. Our dead sons and grandsons lie in foreign lands, but soon, we shall see to their killers. Glad

Song, Makes Good Soup," Grandmother said, holding out her hands to them when she reached Mother and my aunt. "Daughters, are you ready?"

"We are," they said together.

"Then, daughters and nieces, granddaughters and cousins, follow me." She walked at our head, the women of our house following. Watchers from the other houses alerted our clan women to join us. The plaza was lit with torches set around the plaza circle. The first had burned low, but new torches were added as they guttered. It would be a long night.

"Bring the prisoners out one by one," Swims the River commanded. Two guards soon returned, dragging a man between them. They pushed him to his knees before the matrons. "Who accuses this one?" asked Swims the River.

A Turtle warrior came forward. "I make the accusation," the man said. "I took him in battle, Turtle Clan Mother."

"Stand, captive," the clan matron ordered. Her hair was whiter than my grandmother's and her hands were arthritic from many winters, but when she spoke, I felt her power. With his wrists still tied behind him, the prisoner rose from the ground to face Turtle Clan Mother. In the torchlight, with his long hair hanging over his cheeks, I could not guess his age.

"What are you called, captive? State your name and clan."

"Flying Squirrel, Otter Clan."

Turtle Clan Mother nodded. "You are guilty of being our enemy and the enemy of our ally, Oneida," she said. "Tell me. Why have you attacked your neighbors? Did they force you from your hunting grounds? Have they stolen your corn? What did the Oneida do to your tribe that you left your own country to attack them?"

"They did nothing," he said. "Tododaho commands and we obey."

"Do you hate us as well as the Oneida?"

"I don't hate any Haudenosaunee tribe. War was declared by our chiefs and elders under the rule of Tododaho. I'm a warrior." His point was well taken. He could not refuse to obey his superiors without dishonoring himself.

Turtle Clan Mother paused a moment, looked around at our faces, then back to the man standing helpless but proud before her. "You have sent Ganeogaono warriors to the spirit world, to Great Spirit Orenda. These men were fathers and uncles, sons and brothers. Can you give me a reason why you should escape punishment?"

He did not hesitate. For a moment, I felt his valor. "Your warriors did not have to go west. If Ganeogaono had stayed home, your men would be alive now. I follow my war leader."

Turtle Clan Mother was just as strong. "As our warriors follow theirs. It is your war I question. Your fight was not to defend your borders, nor for food. Your master orders you to kill for sport. Oneida will not be enough to satisfy him. Ganeogaono is next in your master's plans. Do you deny it?"

"He does not tell me his plans." Swims the River drew his hand back to strike the prisoner, but Turtle Clan Mother restrained him with a sign. The Onondaga lifted his chin out of respect to the old woman. When she gave him permission to speak if he had more to say, he added, "A man does not hang back when he is ordered to fight. I'm not a coward."

"No," Turtle Clan Mother agreed. "I see that. Take him back to the guardhouse to wait for sunrise." Young men led him away.

One at a time, the captives were pulled out of the prison house for questioning. Two were interviewed and sent back before one was pointed out for a particular act of cruelty. "This Onondaga killed my friend Swimming Buck," the warrior said. "He scalped him while he still breathed."

A child's voice screamed. It was a Bear girl, my father's sister's child, Green Branch, who was eight that year. She ran up and shouted, "He's killed my father! Let me put his eyes out, Bear Clan Mother," she wailed, throwing herself on her grandmother's lap. I thought I knew how she felt. What if it had been my father?

"Control yourself, Green Branch," Bear Clan Mother commanded her sternly. Green Branch stepped back, her small chest heaving with her effort to do as her clan matron commanded, but her hands remained clenched.

Father's sister walked forward. "I ask you for justice, Bear Clan Mother," she said in a tightly controlled voice. "Give him to me."

"Have you anything to say in your defense?" Bear Clan Mother asked.

The captive made a sound in his mouth as if gathering saliva, but Swimming Buck's son, a boy of twelve, pushed through into the circle and struck him hard in the mouth, breaking a few of his teeth, so he spat blood. The blow sent him sprawling. Before the Onondaga moved, two warriors jerked him up between them and dragged him to a tall stake. "He is yours," the old woman said as the warriors bound him.

Each prisoner was made to kneel before the matrons. The old women sent them either to the guardhouse or the stakes. Any prisoner accused of special cruelty was taken to the stakes. More of these were erected even as we watched. A request from the dead warrior's family was sufficient.

The last captive was pulled forward by Walks Many Trails and thrown to the ground before the clan matrons' bench. Burns His Lips spoke as accuser. "Tree Climber was my best friend," he said. "This Onondaga might have killed him quickly, not little by little, with arrow after arrow, where it would bring death slowly and with pain. He told his companions he wanted to learn if Ganeogaono warriors are as brave as legends say, that they can suffer without screaming."

Grandmother asked, "And did Tree Climber scream?"

"Only at the first arrow, which took him by surprise. This Onondaga did not notice me come up behind him with my war club." All the time Burns His Lips was speaking, Wolf Cub Mother stood as if she were carved of wood.

Grandmother beckoned our cousin. "I believe this one must be given to you," she said. "He has discovered our valor. Now he needs to learn Ganeogaono justice." The captive caught sight of Wolf Cub Mother, how her eyes darkened and her mouth turned down like a Healing Society mask.

He tried to break away, which was a mistake. His guards held him fast. "No," he begged. "In war, everyone kills. Have pity."

Wolf Cub Mother hissed. "Wolf Clan Mother," she said, "everyone here knows I saved my son from a she-wolf with hungry cubs to feed. The wolf showed more pity for my son than this creature who begs in the shape of a man. She let me take my son back. This Onondaga gave no mercy; now he shall have none. Tonight we shall learn whether an Onondaga knows how to keep silent. Do I have your leave, Wolf Clan Mother?"

"Do as you think good, Wolf Cub Mother. May the taste of revenge be sweet on your tongue," my grandmother replied. "Tie him to a stake, friends of Tree Climber."

It was the first time I had seen such things as I saw that night. Flint knives peeled flesh; shell fragments cut off fingers joint by joint. Wolf Cub Mother thrust heated wooden stakes through her victim's eyes until they sizzled like meat in melted bear grease. The sounds from the prisoners became like nothing human. Branches were laid at their feet and melted fat smeared on them. Orange flames danced over the twisting bodies. I turned away, hoping the roar of the fires would drown out the other sounds.

Women and girls I had known all of my life participated. Mother and Grandmother, and even my sister and Laughing Girl, did this. I was excused because of my youth, but bile rose to my throat. I fled behind a tree to heave, but the sour taste remained. Burns His Lips found me trembling in the shadows of the stockade walls. "This is your first time. It takes getting used to. I felt the same after my first Onondaga."

"Killing in battle isn't like this," I protested. "There is no battle rage. The captives are helpless." I felt guilty for not enjoying the women's revenge. Was it only because I had not lost anyone I truly loved? "Green Branch is younger, but she didn't hold back."

"There is another kind of rage. Your cousin's grief for her father has hardened her." I leaned against his chest, smelling his sweat and smoke-tanned leather, glad he was home again.

"Picture Maker?" I looked up. "We're the fiercest of all Haudenosaunee. Tododaho fears to fight Ganeogaono in person. He sent his warriors to take or destroy the Oneida, but would he venture so far from his fire pit himself? Imagine him in the hands of Wolf Cub Mother."

The thought brought a savage smile to my mouth. "We'll fight his warriors until he has no place to hide," I said.

He pulled me to him for a quick hug. Then he walked me home, his arm over my shoulder. As we crossed between the houses, he said, "Tomorrow is the testing."

I didn't know what he meant, but I bid him a good night and tried to sleep with the bed furs over my head to muffle the sounds outside. At last, they faded, the others came inside, and I slept without dreaming.

Chapter 5

The plaza teemed with people by the time we arrived the next morning. Only six out of twelve Onondaga remained, and those were brought to await their punishment before the clan matrons' bench. Grandmother already sat on the bench with Turtle Clan Mother and Bear Clan Mother. These old women held no talking stick, wore no paint or any other insignia. Their dignity and stateliness and the deference people showed them was sufficient to know who they were.

The crowd parted to allow passage for Mother and Aunt Makes Good Soup. Pumpkin Flower, Brown Otter, Laughing Girl, and I walked proudly in their wake. My aunt and mother held highest status in Wolf Clan after Grandmother herself. We, her granddaughters, came next. At midwinter's festival, Grandmother had named my mother next in line for Wolf Clan Mother when she became too old or left us for the spirit longhouse in the sky.

As part of this procession, I held my head high, trying to demonstrate worthiness. I had nothing to fear but shame, if my conduct did not befit my lineage, so I cloaked my face and stance with dignity to await the testing.

Father was visible, his head higher than most of his Bear Clan companions. Scout was somewhere in the crowd with his friends. The remaining captives were helplessly outnumbered and naked but for their breechclouts. Armed warriors kept guard over them. Escape was impossible, but since they were still alive, hope must have dawned upon them that they might be adopted into our families.

"What will we do?" I asked Pumpkin Flower in a whisper.

Before my sister could answer, the people quieted. Swims the River climbed the speaker's stump and signaled for our attention. "He will explain to the captives and you will hear," she replied.

Our chief faced the remaining prisoners. His words were repeated for those farther back, but sitting beside my mother, I heard him well enough and will repeat what he said. "Captives," he began, "you are no longer subject to your former master. How you conduct yourself today shall determine whether you will live as Ganeogaono, be adopted and cared for as one of us, or die without status. If you try to oppose us, if you still harbor a desire for vengeance, we shall discern it in the next few moments. Your flesh shall fill our stew pots. The choice is yours."

By the morning light, I noticed the differences in the captives. One appeared resigned, hunching his shoulders and looking down. Another glared, defiant. The first man to be questioned the previous night looked heavenward, perhaps asking for courage to endure his trial. Either that or he expected to behold his dead comrades soon. It might go either way.

The chief continued his instructions. "If you can bury your bad thoughts, walk slowly through the line of women. Walk one at a time when I give the word. Don't make the mistake of underestimating these women. You shall be punished for opposing us. Any man too weak to endure or who thinks he can escape the whips will be killed instantly. Those who prove penitent, strong, and brave during this trial will be adopted. We will show you the kindness and affection we give our own, but in return, we demand your full loyalty. Are there any among you who do not understand the choice to be made and the conditions?"

I don't know whether they had expected better than slavery. It was a good offer. They whispered together. One who appeared to be their leader questioned Swims the River. "Our families are hostage to the sorcerer and they dare not defy him. Do you expect us to fight our own brothers and fathers in the spring? If you leave us behind, how shall you trust us not to destroy your town?"

It took me back to hear an Onondaga speak with logic and even eloquence. I don't know what I had expected, but it was not this. Swims the River appeared baffled by the question. He climbed down and beckoned to the elders for a decision. "The captive speaks just like us," I exclaimed.

"Well, what did you think?" asked my aunt. She crossed her thick arms. "They are Haudenosaunee just like us. Longhouse tribes always understand one another's speech, if not their actions. Those still have plenty to account for."

Bear Clan Mother expressed her view. "Shall we leave our former enemies warm and safe in Doteoga while our men risk their lives in foreign lands to free their families?"

"If we die fighting their former comrades and master, they inherit Doteoga, marry our women, and father the next generation of Ganeogaono," Turtle Clan Mother exclaimed. "We might as well surrender our will to their shaman now and save ourselves the effort of repelling him."

Laughing Girl's fingers clenched tightly around mine. Would all our young men die and would we become Onondaga by default? What would our grandmother say to this? "She speaks now, cousins." Brown Otter stood at my shoulder. Head turned to one side, she peered closely at the Onondaga who had asked the question.

"Let us give them a chance to prove themselves before we make that decision," Grandmother said. "Some of them may yet be saved." The final vote taken with a show of hands went with this suggestion, although Bear Clan Mother and several of the elders refrained from voting.

Finally, Chief Swims the River ascended the stump again. "Hear me, captives," he said. "If any of you cannot swear on white wampum before the eyes and ears of Orenda that you will keep faith with us, say so. Die now and spare yourselves further torment." When none spoke, he said, "The punishment shall commence. Let the first man ready himself to walk."

We women drew apart to form two sides of a path. Between every few women, a warrior waited with his spear or half-drawn bow strung and ready to loose if necessary. The captives huddled together before the first man, Flying Squirrel, began his walk. The women lashed out at him with braided rawhide whips and prepared green birch switches.

Excitement took hold of me, so that when my mother handed me a switch, I did my share willingly. The gauntlet between our lines was narrow enough that no one could escape without receiving many stinging and punishing blows.

The prisoner made no move to defend himself, but instead did his best to ignore the cords that slashed and tore at his back, chest, and legs. I noticed none of the women swung toward his face. The last of my loathing ebbed away as my lash cut into Flying Squirrel's back and legs. He bore it bravely. At last, I pitied him. I felt glad when he reached the farthest end of the gauntlet and was led away by a Turtle Clan mother who had lost her son. Her new adopted son would take the dead son's place to defend her and hunt and bring venison to her longhouse.

The second prisoner entered between the double line unsteadily. Before he was halfway down the line, he sank to his knees and covered his head with his hands. He was soon dispatched by a flight of arrows.

The ground became wet and slippery with blood, and the next man needed to place his feet with care so as not to slide, trip, and suffer more lashes. I managed to keep my face expressionless. Since this was part of Orenda's plan to restore our harmony, it was my duty to wield the whip as viciously as possible. It was my duty, as well, to observe either the forgiveness or the death of each man, as Orenda and each man's courage or strength determined.

The next few prisoners passed between us without event, but one stopped to curse us. "Tododaho will feed you to his dogs, Ganeogaono cowards!" There was no worse insult than that. Several warriors threw their spears at the same time and brought him down into the blood-drenched mud.

"You see what we had to deal with?" asked the warrior beside us. "They are mad!" He and three others walked to the twitching carcass in the red mud to withdraw their spears. One of our uncles and a Turtle warrior dragged the dead man out of our sight. There were no more outbursts and no more incidents. The last of the captives finished the course, was redeemed, and led away by his new family to his new home.

Life returned to its old routines. Shortly after our men returned, the last flocks of geese passed overhead, honking between the clouds. Bushy-tailed squirrels hurried up and down trees, their pouches full of acorns or dead leaves to make their nests snug. A group of hunters carried home a large-antlered stag. The women found a heavy layer of fat under his thick hide. By this, we knew a long, hard winter was almost upon us.

We dried and smoked the venison strips for jerky and gathered more firewood to keep our hearths glowing during the white season. Before winter's first snow, our clan's new men brought their share of meat and helped secure the bark walls of our longhouse against winter.

After the blizzards began, no one left the stockade without snowshoes. I had not thought it possible, but as the moons passed, the new men seemed to forget their former lives. They developed a loyal affection for the families who nursed them back to health. After awhile, their faces and personalities became so familiar, I could almost forget they had once been enemies. Eventually, they began to visit the widows and maidens of the other clan longhouses. Midwinter's festival saw several new marriages conducted. My cousin Brown Otter married Flying Squirrel. There was a time I would not have believed it, but she now considered him one of us.

The midday sun melted the snow enough to form long spears of ice against the roof overhangs and the porches. That year, our storytellers remembered stories they had not told for years. Gooseflesh rose on my arms at tales of monsters stalking travelers in the deep forest. In hidden valleys, waiting unseen, stone men preyed upon lone travelers. Serpents with horns and sharp teeth lurked underwater, waiting to burst through the surface ice to swallow the unwary who walked on the frozen rivers.

Since Uncle Wind in His Ears told his stories in his new wife's house, sometimes my grandmother's cousin came to visit our house to tell the stories she remembered. One night after the last meal, the old woman took the storytellers' seat. She tapped on her small drum while we gathered close around her.

Her voice crackled like old leaves. I listened to her legends with closed eyes, imagining that it was the wise autumn wind spirit, Ga-oh, who told the stories as he had once spoken to our uncle, by making the leaves whisper.

Winter storms circled the stockade, blowing new-fallen snow into hills against the stockade walls. Low skies blocked out the stars that used to peek through the smoke holes. Inside, sleepy and snug in our furs, by the glow of the fire pit's coals, we listened.

"In the wild parts of the forest," the storyteller began, "creatures with heads that look human but are twice the size of ordinary heads watch for humans to eat. The heads have no bodies, only arms covered with red fur. At the end of their arms hang strong, skinny fingers tipped with long claws like a bear's. Their small eyes cannot see well, but their noses are sharp and their teeth sharper.

"A young mother left her village to gather greens and mushrooms for a soup she planned. Her foraging took her far into the forest by the time she discovered by the sun and the gathering dark under the tall trees that the day was growing late. Her basket was full enough, so she found the trail again and began to trot back home. Her baby rode his cradleboard on her back.

"She had returned more than halfway to her village when she heard a whistling sound high in the tree branches. Three flying heads floated above the high branches, watching her and rolling their tongues over their crooked teeth, for they desired very much to devour the burden she carried. 'I see a tender, delicious baby,' one of the flying heads said to the other two. 'It shall be my supper.'

" 'I saw it first,' another protested, and the race began. The flying heads swooped down and began to fly after the woman, fiery hair trailing behind them like the tail of a comet. 'Wait, woman,' the closest head called out. Its voice hissed like water drops on hot stone. 'I want your tender-fleshed baby, not you,' it said reasonably. 'Let us make a bargain. Set it down and I won't harm you.' Of course, the woman had no intention of allowing them to have her son, so she ran as hard as she could for home.

"The heads flew closer and closer. Each time the woman looked back, she saw the head's teeth and jaws slavering in anticipation. This made her run faster, while the heads, red hair floating around them like a fireball, continued to chase her. Everyone knows that a woman with a baby can do things ordinary people can't." I thought of Wolf Cub Mother facing down the mother wolf and knew this to be true. The storyteller paused to tap her fingers on the skin of her drum, heightening the tension of what would happen next.

"The young mother arrived home two heartbeats before the leading flying head. She slammed the door shut so it could not follow her inside, but she forgot something. What do you think it was?" The old woman paused and looked about to see if anyone cared to guess.

"The smoke hole?" a little boy ventured. "He could get in."

"Exactly right. The flying head didn't see the smoke hole right away, so the humans were safe for a little while. In the meantime, the mother stoked up the embers in the fire pit to cook something for them to eat. She had some chestnuts, which she put into the fire to roast among the coals.

"While they roasted, she sang a song to her little boy. The song was like this. 'No head shall eat you. We're safe from the hungry monster. When you grow up, you will hunt him for me with your bow and arrows. When you catch him, we'll roast the head in our fire pit just like a big chestnut.' While she sang, she opened her dress and nursed her son. She rocked him and crooned to him, thinking they were out of danger, but they didn't know that the heads still hovered over the house and could see them through the smoke hole.

"The other heads grew tired of waiting and flew away, seeking different meat, but the hungriest waited. It thought that if it could squeeze itself up tight, it might be able to push through and into the room. The head planned that when the mother turned her back, he would fly down and seize the child.

"The mother bent over to snatch two chestnuts from the fire. 'We will eat these and get strong,' she said. She peeled a shell and pulled out the nut. Chewing one into small bits, she fed it to her babe while she ate the other.

"Of course, the flying head thought she was eating coals. 'Coals must be good things to eat,' it concluded. 'They make you strong, so maybe they are better to eat than small humans. I shall take a few for myself.' Deciding to make its move, it pushed and squeezed its way through the smoke hole. The woman screamed and grabbed up her child. She held him close to her breast and backed toward the wall.

"Before any of her tribe could answer her cry for help, the head plucked a clawful of burning coals from the fire pit and plopped them into its wide, drooling mouth. 'Aieee!' screamed the head. 'It burns! It burns!' The head sprang out of the smoke hole and on into the sky, still screaming, never to bother anyone in the village again."

We cheered at how easily the vicious, stupid enemy was vanquished. If only human enemies might be so easily conquered. I remember lying awake for a long time that night thinking over the story and trying to peer out of the smoke hole above and to the left of our fire pit. Like the woman of the story, I could not see out. Was there a flying head out there, watching us? It was good to have my family, so many of them, always with me. With our combined strength, we could vanquish any danger, no matter how frightening. I promised myself never to venture into the forest all alone. Years later, I still wonder if evil spirits heard my thoughts. They are more insidious than flying heads, in that they cannot be seen. If I had made the sign against evil, might it have changed my future?

I heard the cold drizzle spatter against our bark roof. Large drops penetrated the smoke holes, hitting the hard earthen floor. We hurried to place pots underneath to collect the water and keep our hide-covered floor from soaking. In my dreams that night, I felt a fierceness within as I dreamed of defending a child.

The yearly white dog, a female this time, was dispatched and sent to Orenda with our prayers at our midwinter ceremonies. We could almost forget the war while Doteoga and the forest were blanketed in thick snowdrifts and ice blocked the river. The winter moons passed, however, until the sun spent more time in the sky, and the seasons prepared to change again.

On the river, gray ice thinned and grew black and cracked. The water, trapped underneath for five months, bubbled to the surface. Boys and men

cleared the remaining ice from the cove, swimming and daring one another to stay in the longest. They practiced endurance, toughening themselves against weather and pain. Scout was seldom home. He spent his days
wrestling and practicing his aim, learning from his uncles about the strate-
gies of battle.

Uncle Burns His Lips led the group of Wolf Clan boys, who were
proud to take orders from an accomplished and proven warrior. Before
many more years went by, my uncle would be a Wolf war leader. The maidens from Bear and Turtle fell over themselves for glimpses of him when he
walked through the town. I imagine they had many conversations with
their mothers to sound out my grandmother about a match before the war
resumed.

In late winter, we made our maple sugar from the rising sap. Sweet
steam filled the air above the fast-disappearing snow. When the first green
fern heads and asparagus pushed up through the mud, we knew little time
remained before the warriors would depart. The women prepared venison
fat pounded with dried berries into pemmican for their trail food, as well
as dried hominy with maple sugar to give them strength.

Pumpkin Flower's husband, Plum Stone, accompanied the Turtle warriors this time. My father determined to make an end to the sorcerer this
year. He set out in the fore of his clan's fleet in his decorated war canoe.
The Wolf Clan and Turtle Clan warriors soon followed. I waved long after
they were lost to our sight around the southern sweep of the river, sending good thoughts after them.

Uncle Burns His Lips had been married at our Maple Festival. He lived
in Turtle Clan's longhouse with his newly pregnant wife, but he continued
to train the Wolf boys. His clan would never change. This war season, he
stayed behind in Doteoga, as did a third of our men. Of the four former
Onondaga, two chose to go, and two remained behind to help guard our
town and cornfields.

One morning while I worked among my corn hills, my mother called
me to her. "You will be a woman before very long. There are things you
ought to know. Collect your cousins and bring your gathering baskets. It's
time you learned about some of the herbs I have not explained before."

We walked into the spring green forest to the sounds of birds and the
joyous scampering of squirrels up and down the trees in celebration of
spring. Soft mosses cushioned our feet and tiny blue flowers poked up
along the side of the trail. The soft air stroked my legs and face like an old
friend.

I could not resist the urge to bound and race like a yearling deer. Laughing Girl and I grasped hands and ran together down the cool and welcoming path. Soon the others were left behind and we seemed to be alone in a great green world, away from men and wars and the confines of town. The threats and hidden dangers of winter's forest disappeared as mists lifted with the return of the warm sun. Laughing, we rested against the base of a willow near a swift-running stream. We cupped the cool water to drink, then washed while we waited for the others to catch up to us.

Aunt Makes Good Soup caught up to us first, her expression a disapproving frown. "How do you know an Algonquin wasn't waiting on the other side of that tree? You're both old enough to know better than to separate yourself from our band. Even a warrior does not do that without good cause." Our faces flushed with humiliation.

By then, I had learned a good deal from Aunt Makes Good Soup about which mushrooms were good to eat and which could kill, which leaves and barks were brewed to cure stomachaches, which could dull pain, and which prevented a wound from mortifying. She was the best healer in our clan. Laughing Girl and I discovered an orange-colored shelf fungus. We were worrying at it with our digging sticks to pry it away from the tree base when mother called us over.

"The shelf fungus can wait. I have something special to explain." She squatted beside a low-growing plant with deep green, dull leaves. "Here is a *woman's root* plant," she said. "Remember it."

Aunt Makes Good Soup showed us how to feel for the velvety underside of the leaves. "They grow low and spread out in marshy soil like mushrooms, but the roots go down deep into Mother Earth. The root splits into two parts and looks like a woman's legs with a notch above." It was easy to see why it was given its name.

My aunt dug away the rotted leaves and poked around with her flint knife to loosen the roots. She grasped it around the base and pulled it gently from the earth. When she passed it to us to examine, it did indeed look like the bottom half of a woman. "Every spring, woman's root blooms with small white flowers that become berries. The berries are poisonous; don't eat them. The leaves and roots contract your womb, which can be useful to a woman laboring to bring forth her baby. It eases a difficult childbirth."

It was a good plant to know. Mother placed the woman's root carefully in her basket, packing it with soil from the spot where it had grown. While she did this, my aunt explained further. "Before your last moon of carrying, brew a strong tea of the leaves. They are best dried and crumbled into the water beforehand, but the fresh will do if you tear it into small pieces. The dried and pounded roots are strongest. It would not hurt to keep them with you, since they might be hard to find in the dead of winter. Keep the tea in a skin bottle to take to your birth shelters. If your pains stop before the baby is born or your afterbirth is difficult to expel, sip your tea."

We nodded, thinking we understood. My aunt was not finished. "If rain doesn't come in its proper season and the corn is blighted, if Doteoga is in danger of famine, if meat is in short supply, or if a woman is too old to carry a new child safely for nine moons, drink a strong infusion of woman's root tea as soon as possible after you couple with your husband. That is no time to be making a new baby. Woman's root will keep a baby from planting itself inside you. There is another thing to keep in mind, Picture Maker. Daughter, you listen, too."

Laughing Girl gave her mother her full attention, as did I. "If ever a man forces you against your will, take strong tea made of woman's root. Even if a child has started to grow in your womb, a brew made from these leaves or roots will expel the unformed child."

"How could a man force me in our house?" my cousin asked. "I would call for help and all of you would come running to make him stop."

"Don't be stupid, Laughing Girl," said my aunt. "I'm speaking about rape. If the Onondaga win."

"That can't happen!" we both protested at once. "It will never happen," I added softly, making the words into a prayer.

"Shush," Aunt Makes Good Soup said, trying to comfort us. "Of course it won't. Our warriors will never let it happen. Remember my instruction anyway and hope you never need to use it."

Mother added, "Until our men report, we don't know how close the Onondaga might be. Never forget that our northern enemies, the Algonquin, have no fear of Orenda. No one knows how they treat women, but I suspect they would not treat one of ours kindly. Knowledge is strength. It's always best to be prepared. For now, let us dig up some more of these and plant them beside our corn hills." I touched the woman's root plant and shuddered.

Chapter 6

One late-summer day, we brought baskets into the forest to forage for herbs and mushrooms. We never went far, not since our lookouts had spotted Algonquin hunters in the forest less than a day's travel from Doteoga. When they gave their report, the elders concluded that the Algonquin were testing our strength. They could not fail to know that many of our men were on the warpath. We had not the number of warriors necessary to expel our enemies from our hunting and gathering areas or to retaliate for such intrusions.

When we foraged, Cousin Wolf Cub Mother and some older women carried small bows, even within our circle of protection, since our protectors could not be everywhere at once. I was squatting on the tree-shaded stream bank, intent on pulling up watercress, when an arrow hissed past my ear. There was a pained shout and I heard men's voices.

I whirled, looking around. At the same time, I drew my flint knife from the pouch of the small leather skirt I had taken to wearing since the start of my eleventh year. I knew there must be Algonquin in our forest, since no Haudenosaunee would attack gatherers. They had come south of the river again.

Makes Good Soup crouched protectively over Quill Worker, an older cousin, who lay bleeding on the ground, an arrow still quivering in her thigh. Three Algonquin stepped out from behind trees, bows drawn and arrows nocked. They might have easily killed Quill Worker, or any of us.

"This is our land; you may not hunt here," Wolf Cub Mother shouted in protest, but she kept her hand clear of her quiver. Her bow remained unstrung over her shoulder. She gestured in the hand signs she'd learned while visiting in the lands to the west, simple motions that even I could follow. "Leave this place; it is ours."

One Algonquin man pointed angrily toward the north and shouted to us in his foreign tongue. The motion needed no translation; he had ordered us away from our trail and this part of the forest.

I fought to control my anger, feeling that the older women might have resisted. My small cousin, Green Branch, whispered to Wolf Cub Mother, her voice so low, I could barely hear her over the rustle of the leaves, "Why don't we go around behind them and kill them?" She had suggested what I thought. We were many. They were three, and this was our land. How did they dare to order us away?

"And leave our bodies in the forest?" Wolf Cub Mother hissed. "There may be more we can't see." She motioned us closer, speaking softly as we gathered around to hear her. "We have pregnant women and children in our band. The Algonquin know the arts of war. Feel no shame in retreating, Green Branch. The time will come when our men return and our enemies will know grief."

Wolf Cub Mother turned to my mother. "Will you help me carry Quill Worker, Glad Song?" Mother helped lift our wounded cousin. They made a seat for her with their hands clasped over each other's wrists.

I put away my flint, placed the dripping watercress in my basket, and slipped silently to the trail, following the others. All the time we retreated, I expected an arrow in my back. After we passed the first three hunters, who had turned their bows to keep them aimed at us, more Algonquin stepped into sight. We had walked into a nest of them without knowing.

"How did Wolf Cub Mother know there were so many more?" I asked my mother as we trotted along beside the three of them.

"If there were not, would they dare to attack Ganeogaono women?" Mother asked. Her question needed no reply. "Remember that they are cowards and will not show themselves unless they think they have the advantage. They know our men are away. This war will bring more sorrow to us than it is worth. Wait until your father hears about this outrage. Our warriors will teach Algonquin to respect our trails and gathering places."

She made a disgusted hiss through her teeth. "They hunt on our land. Our warriors will put an end to that, but until they return, we dare not gather here again." She sighed. "No good has ever come from an Algonquin." She said no more, but all the way back, I pondered their intrusion into our lands.

Mother and Makes Good Soup related our experience to Grandmother. When the Council of Elders met, Uncle Burns His Lips stated his observations and conclusions. Since he had earned his scalp lock the first summer of the Great War, his status had been elevated enough to offer advice, unasked. "It would take all our defenders to attack the nearest Algonquin encampment and drive them off; yet, we must not leave Doteoga undefended. The women and girls must keep closer to the stockade. We must shorten the perimeter of our patrols until winter sends the remainder of our men home." The elders agreed with this plan.

Afterward, we foraged close to home and watched the river. Quill Worker's leg wound healed. Our remaining warriors took turns, several on patrol day and night, signaling with loon calls for safety, owl-hunting cries for danger. Each time I heard an owl call after its kill at night, I shivered unless a loon cried soon after to tell us that it was really an owl.

Only the tips of the sumac leaves were red, although the birch leaves had already faded to yellow over their silvery trunks. Most of our corn was harvested and the beans dried for winter. The acorn squash and pumpkins still ripened on their vines beside the brown cornstalks.

We were not expecting the men to return yet, but that did not lessen our rejoicing when the boys came running to say they had seen our canoes. We left our harvesting and hurried to greet them. I raced down to the river, hoping to glimpse my father. Warm water lapped against my feet, so close did I stand to welcome the returning canoes, and I wondered whether the Creator had sent a first snow early to save our men for a different purpose.

Pumpkin Flower's husband, Plum Stone, strode toward her. They looked at each other without touching. Their little boy could stand now, but he looked at his father as at a stranger. "Snow ended the last battle," he said. A touching glance passed between them, warm and loving. "We slaughtered all our captives; there was no food to spare. War spooked the game. Only hungry wolves prowl the trails now. Even so, the war is not over. The Onondaga shaman still lives." He turned to follow his Turtle comrades to his chiefs and elders.

Women searched and waited for more canoes, asking for lost fathers and brothers. Their wails began even before we cleared the fields and reached the winding entrance to the stockade.

We saw my father at last! He sent us a weary smile. Before he came to us, he helped his crew carry their boat out of the water and bring it to high ground. Coming up to us, he touched my mother's cheek gently with the back of his hand. "I must go to Bear Longhouse first," he told us. "After-ward, I will come home to eat."

When he entered our house, my mother and father finally embraced. He held her for a long moment. For him to do so before others already inside was not seemly, but the war and close brushes with death seemed to have changed the men. Father had aged more than a season. The frost of age whitened his temples and shadows haunted his eyes. I started to approach him, to tell him how glad I was to see him, when I heard him whisper to my mother, "I dreamed my own death, yet here I am. What can it mean?"

"Some dreams mean nothing. It was your anger that this war has taken so much from us. Orenda meant you to come back to us, or you would not be back," Mother said sensibly. "You need to rest. You have more to do before you leave us. Eat and rest now. Regain your strength to kill more of our enemies before you tread the spirit trails at the end of a long and hon-ored life." They stood for a moment, gazing into each other's eyes, until I felt I had no place there.

Father turned his head. "My Picture Maker," he said to stop me from backing away. "You are nearly a woman now. I will never again make the mistake of mentioning your dolls." He held out his arms for me and I ran back to hug him.

My brother hurried over. Scout had seven summers then and his legs were the longest part of him. "How many Onondaga scalps did you take?" he asked excitedly, looking up boldly and grinning.

"Four, but I'd rather it were none, and that this war had not begun. You've grown again, Scout," Father said. "In a few more years, if this Great War does not end, it will be your turn to paddle a war canoe."

"Have you left me any Onondaga to kill?" my brother asked quite seri-ously, sounding almost like a warrior already.

"Too many, I expect," he said. "I have given my place as Bear war chief to Cougar Teeth. Next year, I shall remain home with the elders."

Mother paused in the middle of handing my father a bowl of corn and beans flavored with squirrel meat. "Dahateh!" she exclaimed. "You're not old enough to be an elder."

"It's time," he said. "What strength and speed remain to me will be best used in defending our Doteoga." He took the bowl from her hands, scooped food into his mouth, and chewed slowly.

Uncle Burns His Lips came over to join the discussion, squatting beside the hearth and helping himself from the cooking bowl as usual. "When spring clears the trails, I think we need to let the war go on without us.

There have been too many deaths and too many widows raising boys without their uncles and fathers to teach them."

"What do you mean?" my grandmother asked. She had walked over after hearing the other reports. She, too, looked older after hearing the war news. "Are we giving up the fight?"

"The Oneida between us and Onondaga Country grow weaker. We're losing too many men away from home. I think it's better to wait here. We must stop sending our warriors to die in foreign lands."

Father's jaw tightened when mother told him about the Algonquin and their attack upon us in the southern gathering places. "Perhaps this new threat is why Orenda forced us to return early. I see that winter has not touched you yet. There are enough of us now to give the Algonquin a surprise. I think I must bring this up at the council meeting tomorrow."

"Look at this pot of corn and beans with squirrel meat," my uncle complained. I noticed he said it without pausing in his chewing. "We need venison and bear. Let's hope the Algonquin have not killed off all the game in our forest. We shall have real meat soon."

All the talk of war in our longhouse weighed upon me. I wanted to experience the freedom I had expected to feel on our warriors' return. I left them to their talking. The day was still young when I crossed the longhouse to my cousin's bed bench. "Let's go gather the wild grapes on the hill by the big hickory trees," I said. "We ought to be celebrating our men's homecoming."

"You want to go into the woods?" Aunt Makes Good Soup asked. "I'm not sure that's safe. Don't go past the fields."

"But grapes don't grow in the fields. You know the hill where the tall hickory tree stands alone above the river? It's in sight of the stockade. No one can hurt us with our men back." I felt more confident than I had in months. The trails were ours again, for all the Algonquin thought they could take them from us. "We'll be back before you miss us."

"Very well, but no one enters the forest alone. Even though our men are back, we keep our rules. Take a group with you. Fill your baskets with nuts and grapes and get home," Mother said.

Late-afternoon sunshine warmed my cheeks as we crossed through the fields. Gray rain clouds piled in the eastern sky, too far away to concern us. A breeze flipped the yellow birch leaves over, revealing their silver undersides. The boys of our band ran on ahead. When my girl cousins and I turned into the hickory grove, they were already filling their mouths with the grapes. We set down our baskets and began to pick.

On the dark hill, the old hickory tree waited. "Look how many husks. They're already brown. The tree knew we were coming," I shouted to Laughing Girl, and raced up the shady slope. Spotted Pebble, Green Branch, and Laughing Girl ran right behind me while the boys plucked grapes and filled the baskets, eating half of what they picked.

The old tree seemed to have spread out since we had visited it last. Its leaves were bright crimson, orange, and late-summer green against the dark blue of the sky. I greeted it like an old friend, rubbing its rough bark. I pulled myself up to a low bough, then shimmied up to the next strong limb. With my basket left below, I scampered up, limb after limb, into a canopy of leaves. My two cousins set to work to pull the bottom nuts down. "I'm going up high to shake the branches," I said. "Stand back."

At last, I broke through the leaves. It was dizzying to be this high. When I looked down, I could see all the way to the bottom of the hill, where my cousins worked among the grapevines. Their voices blurred and only fragments of conversation made it to my ears. I shook the branches and the thick four-lobed husks rained down. Spotted Pebble ran down the slope to bring the others closer with their gathering baskets.

While they chased the rolling husks, I climbed out on the highest limb that would support my weight, held on to the bough above for balance and pushed aside the leaves to spy on the world below. There were our swaying cornrows, yellow and full, and there, the pointed wall of the stockade. The air was clear enough to see thin plumes of gray smoke lift into the bright sky above Doteoga's longhouses.

When I turned my head, the afternoon sun glimmered off the Wide River's ripples in sparks of movement. Willow leaves seemed to float lazily along the river, swimming closer, walking on legs. Willow leaves. I realized I could not see leaves on the river from this distance. The shapes moved southwest, against the current. I rested against the branch, closing my eyes a moment to adjust them to the shifting light. When I shielded my eyes and looked again, horror caught in my throat. As far as I could see, the eastern reach of the Wide River held a fleet of canoes such as we had just seen that morning, only these canoes came from the east. Algonquin.

I blinked the glare from my eyes and shook my head to make my thoughts stop bouncing about inside. My cousins still chattered below, gathering in the nuts. Past them, past the hill and the vines, was the trail that led away from Doteoga, to the east, where our women never gathered. There, lines of men snaked along the trail between the trees. Algonquin were invading in force, on land and water, and in all the world, I was the only one who knew. This must be why Great Spirit Orenda guided me to the top of the tree on the hill, I thought, for I had surely been drawn to this spot and up into these branches to give warning.

"Scout!" I cried as loudly as I dared. I did not want to be heard by the invaders. "Laughing Girl! Spotted Pebble! Get Scout!" I began to descend through the branches, but I was only halfway down when Scout appeared.

"What do you see?" my brother called up to me.

"Algonquin swarming on the river and running through the forest toward Doteoga. Run home as fast as you can. Signal with the owl call. Tell Father and our uncles to meet them in the forest before they reach the town. Run. Warn Doteoga." He took off. The others left their gathering baskets where they were and ran after him to the safety of the stockade.

Laughing Girl called sharply to me, "Hurry, Picture Maker! We have to get home. I'll wait for you." The hill was already deserted, the children running after my brother. Only the two of us remained.

"Don't wait for me. Go!" I scrambled madly through the branches, almost dropping from one bough to the next. She hesitated. "I'm right behind you. Don't wait for me. They might catch you."

With a last glance, she left the base of the tree and ran for the enclosing curtain of vines. She was gone before I reached the last branch and lowered myself to drop to the floor in a crouch. I stumbled over some husks beneath the tree, then righted myself and streaked to the trail.

The warriors ran silently, their moccasins like the soft pads of a mountain cat, but their numbers caused the very ground to pulse. Now that I was down, I realized my error. I might have remained in the tree, waiting quietly for them to pass. In my panic, I had not been able to think further than warning our men. After that, I did as the others, as my cousin had demanded. I did not turn, afraid to see how close they were, but ran homeward with all my might. War yells from the stockade told me Scout had arrived in time and that the men were rushing out with their weapons. At least my brother and cousins were safe. My Wolf warriors would come soon. They would not let me be taken.

Only moments must have passed before there were shouts and yells everywhere. The circumstances had reversed now and the Algonquin had to regroup for battle. They had lost their advantage of surprise. War whoops filled the fields as the defenders burst through. The stockade walls loomed before me. I thought I was safe, until a hand grabbed my shoulder and yanked me back.

"Let go of me," I screamed to the one who held me. This must not hap-

pen, not when I was so close, I thought. "My father will kill you," I threatened, as if the Algonquin could understand. The man pushed me back behind him. There were sweat-slicked Algonquin hands reaching, grabbing
for me. They were everywhere. I could smell them and their hunger for
my death.

I had promised my mother I would return shortly with the grapes. I
wanted to joke with my uncle, tell my father I was proud of him, tease my
brother again, pick more strawberries for my mother. I twisted and
kicked, trying to reach my knife to destroy the man who held me, but
someone pulled it away from me.

Bear and Turtle warriors streamed to the river, to our canoes, which
were still tied up at the landing. They launched them at once to repel the
invaders who came over water. Wolf Clan warriors brandished their war
clubs and spears and bows, howling their war cries as they ran down the
trail to my defense. Scout must have told them where I was. I saw my uncles and cousins with the red Wolf Clan streaks on their cheeks. My father,
instead of racing for the river with Bear Clan to fend off the enemy canoes,
had run with Wolf Clan. He was coming to save me.

I struggled, managing to free myself from the warrior who held me,
but another pulled me back. I could not get loose. "Father!" I screamed,
hoping he could hear me over the din of war yells, death cries, and the
thuds of arrows on hide and bark shields.

Above the yells, and the running, I heard my father's voice. "Gahrahstah! We are coming for you." I tried, but I could not escape the hands that
held me.

The advancing warriors, yelling their war cries, joined in battle, blur-
ring together in their speed and the clash of their war clubs and shields. An
Algonquin advanced on Burns His Lips with a raised war club. "Uncle!" I
screamed.

My uncle blocked the blow with his shield. When his antagonist raised
his war club again, Burns His Lips shoved the edge of his shield under the
other's chin, half-cleaving his head from his neck. He finished the Algonquin with his club, dropping him to the earth. Before another moment had
gone by, a cousin had his Algonquin pinned to the ground with a spear
through his ribs. I watched how he pulled it out and how the blood spurted
and stained the ground. Another cousin skidded in the blood, his unexpected rush catching several men and dashing them to the ground in a confusing tangle of limbs and weapons.

My father engaged two Algonquin at once, but Uncle Burns His Lips was turning one of the men away from my father with his side attack. I could not tell who had the advantage of numbers, but we knew the land and were fighting for Doteoga, while they had expected to find mostly women defenders.

Men rushed to one another's defense, until it again became difficult for me to see what was happening through the confusion. Blood spattered everywhere and the smell of death came strong on the breeze. The man who imprisoned my arms backed up from the worst of it, still holding me securely.

From the new site, my view was better. I saw former Onondaga fighting beside our Wolf Clan men, wearing splashes of red paint on their browned cheeks. They were on our side now. Seeing their fearlessness and hearing their terrifying war yells, it was good that they no longer fought against us. Horror flowed and the battle eddied around me like whirlpools around a standing stone in rapids. Men were killing and being killed while I waited for the outcome, locked in the strong grasp of my enemy.

The Algonquin had intended to destroy Doteoga. They might have kept their advantage long enough to make a difference if our warriors had been taken by surprise, but the Ganeogaono had been warned. My face burned as the realization struck. Because the approaching men and canoes were seen by a girl in the top branches of a hickory tree on a hill, our men had had time to take their weapons and meet the Algonquin in the forest, not at our very walls.

I suspected even then that the enemy knew I was responsible. A good number of them had been cut down and would fight no more. Slowly, the Algonquin were being driven back, pulling me with them. The short hairs on my arms stood up straight and my throat grew tight.

Our foes shouted in their foreign tongue—whether cursing or planning their retreat, I could not guess. My father had brought an enemy to his knees and bashed in his head. An older warrior cried out in anguish as if he were the one struck down. It might have been his son or a nephew my father had dispatched. The older man's cry rallied more enemy warriors rushing in to attack my father.

My uncle and the others tried to drive them off in a wicked clash of shields and spears or war clubs. Again, my father started for me. I held out my arms. "Father, I'm here!" I screamed again, and kicked back hard at the legs of the man who held me. He yelped and swung at me, but I managed to slip out from under his sweaty hand.

Another Algonquin caught me, a bigger man. I kicked and scratched with nails clawed like a wildcat's, but I could not get away from this one. He grabbed my braids tightly with one hand and both my hands with the other, until I could no longer struggle. "Let me go," I cried. At least I was keeping him too occupied to fight, but in my effort to free myself, he had turned me around, so I could not see what was happening.

I tried to turn back long enough to see if my father had evaded the raised Algonquin war club swinging toward him, but I felt a blow on the right side of my head. Everything darkened as I slipped to the ground. The sounds of the battle around me floated away, and for a while, I knew nothing.

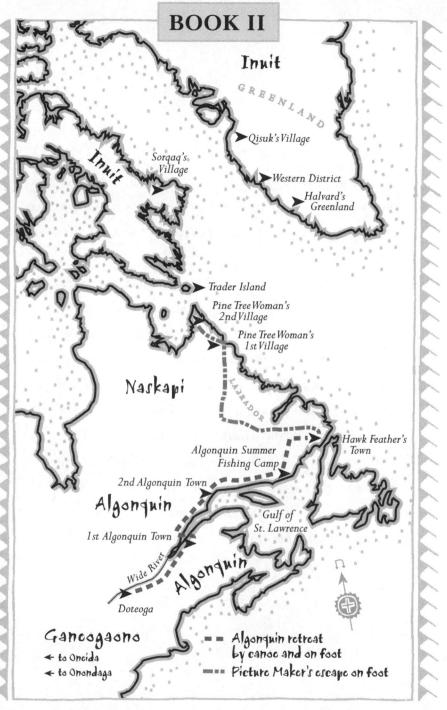

BOOK II

Inuit

GREENLAND

Qisuk's Village

Sorqaq's Village

Western District

Halvard's Greenland

Inuit

Trader Island

Pine Tree Woman's 2nd Village

Pine Tree Woman's 1st Village

Naskapi

LABRADOR

Hawk Feather's Town

Algonquin Summer Fishing Camp

2nd Algonquin Town

Gulf of St. Lawrence

Algonquin

1st Algonquin Town

Wide River

Algonquin

Doteoga

Ganeogaono

← to Oneida

← to Onondaga

- - - Algonquin retreat by canoe and on foot

····· Picture Maker's escape on foot

"*I* had a daughter once," the storyteller woman said. "She died. Life is hard." I believe she was saying there was no hope for me to return to my own country. I nodded slowly. "I think you will not see your home again," she added. "They will look for you to run south. Don't."

Then she did a strange thing. She came close and put her arms around me as a mother or a grandmother might do, then placed her old moccasin beside my ragged one as if measuring the difference. Her voice was softer than a breeze between summer leaves. "When you can no longer bear it, there will be a warm coat, moccasins, food, and a knife in a hollow oak tree three oaks east of the first bend on the northern trail. If you run, go north, but cover your trail as you leave. It is your only chance." She took her arms from me then, but the warmth lingered even as I saw her walk away. She became small in the distance as she made her way among the wigwams and entered her own.

Algonquin

Chapter

A robin sang nearby, but I did not trust myself to open my eyes. Through the wisps of pain and dizziness that circled my head, I cracked my eyes open very slowly. All I could see was the trail and running legs. After awhile, my captor set me on the ground and pushed me along ahead of him.

I turned, stumbling along among the warriors, looking to find an opening, a way to escape. My legs buckled, still asleep and weak as a toddler's. My thoughts were far from clear, but I imagined that if I broke away, they would not follow. I realized they must still be retreating from our warriors. Father, running with Wolf Clan, would be close behind, just down the trail. Turtle and Bear warriors had taken to their war canoes. I had had time to see that before I was clubbed. Soon, they would arrive to destroy this war band and take me home. My mother would worry if I was late.

The pace of the retreat soon returned my legs to normal. I watched for my chance, then darted to the side between two men and off to a break between the trees. My captor was on me in an instant. With one large hand grabbing my braids, he twisted me around and struck me sharply across my cheek with his open palm. His blow made me see stars again and knocked me hard to the ground.

Dried pine needles and twigs scraped my knees and legs. I rubbed my hands free of grit and touched my stinging face. How foolish I had been to bolt like that, without a chance of success. If my head had been clear, I would have foretold the outcome. Perhaps I would think of some plan in the night, when they were asleep. The Algonquin gripped my arm and yanked me to my feet, saying something that made the others laugh, finishing with "Mohawk" and another word I did not understand.

Hordes of painted warriors, naked but for their breechclouts, leggings, and moccasins, filled the trail before and behind. They laughed at my humiliation. My face stung and my nose swelled under my fingers, dripping blood. I took several long breaths through my mouth and pushed myself to my feet. The slap was nothing much, merely a promise. Worse would be done if I tried again. The Algonquin nodded, seeing how I lowered my head in submission.

We continued, the Algonquin and I. He pushed me roughly back to the trail. A glance behind confirmed no rescue party was hurrying to my defense. The next moment had us swiftly on the move again. My break for freedom had taken only moments. We were on a trail near what must have been a tributary of the Wide River. It narrowed and flowed rapidly eastward, gushing and bubbling around rocks. This was a part of the river I had never seen.

The sun slid down the western slope of the sky. It had not far to go before leaving us behind in the dark. At least, my mind was free. I was certain Doteoga had won. Had we fallen, the Algonquin would be celebrating their victory, not running home. The invaders would have slain our remaining warriors and probably all the boys older than seven. The clan matrons would have resisted slavery, I was sure, setting the example for courage, dying rather than submit to enemies. My own submission shamed me. I had disgraced myself.

As though they could hear my thoughts through the miles, I vowed not to bring more shame to my mother and grandmother, and all the women of my line who had labored to teach me our ways. As Orenda created the world and all that is good in it, I vowed to remember who and what I was.

The wind watered my eyes and worsened the pain in my throbbing head. My legs ached from such prolonged running and my breath grew ragged. Laughing Girl and I had promised each other we'd be brave, keep expressionless as a warrior if ever we fell into enemy hands, whether Onondaga or Algonquin. As recently as this morning, I had not expected to have my resolve tested so soon. Sniffling, I rubbed a grimy hand across my mouth and nose while my own legs moved me farther and farther away from Doteoga, from home.

The war chief, a man my father's age or more, ordered a stop at the side of a stream. When I ceased to run, shivers ran through me and my stomach clenched. My fear became obvious to my enemies as the contents of my bowels poured away to the earth until there was nothing left. I buried my head in my hands while the warriors laughed, calling me the name I was to carry from that moment, as long as I remained among my people's enemies. They called me "the Mohawk Girl." These were words I did not understand, although I was to later learn their meaning.

While I had the opportunity, I dabbed water over my wounded forehead and nose, washing the vomit and excrement from my dress as best I could. The water was cold, making my teeth chatter. I rinsed my mouth and spat the soiled water on the ground. My wound had reopened. Fresh blood oozed from the shallow cut on my scalp. They might have killed me so easily. I could not imagine why they hadn't.

The men opened the pouches on their belts and withdrew pemmican and parched corn. My guard bit off a piece of his pemmican and threw it to the ground before me. In spite of everything, I felt hunger, like an animal was gnawing away at my insides. I picked the food from the ground, washed it, and ate. It was not much, but I could not have held down much in any case. I drank water to fill part of my stomach's emptiness, thinking nothing would ever fill my heart's emptiness again if I could not get home.

The chief shouted orders again, and the men got to their feet. Someone pulled a short cord from his pouch, yanked my arms behind me, and tied my hands at the wrists. I ran again when they pushed me, but I stumbled often without my hands for balance.

When we entered the Algonquin town, women and children with tribe elders close behind swarmed around their men while I, like a rock in the streambed, remained in with but not part of them. I took the man-high bark-covered humps for temporary shelters, and I wondered why so many camped together. It seemed their real homes must be elsewhere, for I saw no longhouses.

Talking, wailing, and dog yips filled the air all at once. Leather-faced elders exchanged sharp words with the warriors. I gathered from the sounds and expressions given that the returning men had made excuses for their failure. The expedition they had planned so well had ended disastrously. They pointed to me several times. Of course, they had planned on the majority of our men still being away in the west.

The elders' anger soon turned to panic. I rejoiced, for that meant they feared retribution. Perhaps I yet had reason to hope my people were coming. My guard wandered off, leaving me on my own. While no one watched, I might melt into the dark woods and find my way back to Doteoga.

Before I could take stock of my chances, a large-framed woman, fierce-faced with anger, pulled me away from the tumult. "Mohawk Girl," she said. She pointed to herself and said a word I took for *mistress,* for it was not her name. I was to call her "mistress" ever afterward, so I have forgotten what sound the others used to get her attention. She pointed toward one of the shelters, a small rounded affair covered with bark and hides. Realizing that I understood none of her speech, she pushed me ahead of her.

There, she removed the cords around my hands and shoved me down to crawl inside. In the dim light, I saw a clay bowl of cooked beans resting on a flat stone hearth beside a fire pit. Bed furs rested along the bark walls. My mistress ignored the food, but she set about collecting clothing, awls, twisted cord, bowls, cups, and spoons. She plopped these into a burden basket. Next, she wrapped the cook bowl and shoved that into the basket, too.

My confusion cleared up abruptly. The Algonquin were moving their entire town, people, dogs, food, and belongings from this location to another, too far for Ganeogaono vengeance. My mistress motioned to tell me what to do. I dragged the basket through the low entry flap, then hunkered down to lift the deep burden basket by its straps, affixing the forehead band, and struggled to my feet.

My mistress managed the corn sheaves and a smaller burden basket. With words and shoves, she directed me to follow the others down to the river. Family groups waited for the rest of their canoes along the bank, beside piles of their hastily packed burden baskets filled tight with belongings. We returned once more to the house for another load and took it to the river.

At the water's edge, I squinted into the dusk at Algonquin canoes, many carrying wounded men. More boats paddled up to shore as we watched. I wondered why no Ganeogaono fleet paddled into view. I realized our wounded must have been carried back home before the warriors could follow our retreating enemies—in order to give them to the healers. There must have been many wounded, and those would take precedence over a captured girl. However, that would not to take too long. I continued to believe that our men were coming, my rescue imminent.

If only I might hide to escape being carried farther away. How long would our warriors follow, leaving Doteoga undefended? It would take more than a war party to face the entire might of the Algonquin in their domain. During the loading, I backed away. A few steps into the forest, and

I might hope to blend in with the darkness and steal away home. Unfortunately, a child shouted and pointed. "Mohawk Girl," she called.

A man loped after me easily, caught me around the waist, and pushed me back to my mistress, who slapped my face hard. I was made to sit between two women with children in the canoe. Its captain gave his command. With a heave from those left on the bank, the canoe glided away from the bank. We were swallowed soon by the darkness under the overcast sky.

Babies cried and children muttered to one another, but after awhile, the young ones slept, lulled by the rhythmic dip of the paddles and the cold drizzle. Men and women whispered. The crickets on the shore were more comprehensible. Someone lit a torch from a pouch of live coals and set it into a holder by the raised prow. Each boat came alive with its flame, until all across the Wide River, yellow torches flared like campfires floating in air.

The canoes followed the current eastward until orders were called out. The warriors pulled hard to turn the canoes north. We banked and disembarked, taking up the bundles before the men lifted the canoes out of the water. The women found a likely place among the trees to set up their camp.

Before long, they had cooking fires going. My mistress had me carry bundles and set out mats beside her fire. I wondered whether I might be able to steal one of the fishing canoes and a paddle. I'd do better to cross the river and try to run back on the south shore, rather than cover the distance we had canoed, for I would be alone against the current. If I could not find a small canoe, I was determined to try the north shore. I'd find a way back across if I had to swim, or drown in the attempt.

While the others slept, I crawled away as if to relieve myself in the woods. Smells of wood smoke and food were quickly lost behind me at the river. There was no moon, nothing to see by the starlight but the lapping of the black wavelets and the silhouettes of cattails. A frog croaked. Near a tree, I found a woman's craft, light enough for me to manage alone. I had no food, no weapon, but I felt sure that once I set out on the water, I could manage to return home.

I lifted the canoe knee-high and set it at the water's edge, when shapes stepped out of the black to snatch me back and pull the canoe from my grasp. A sharp whack shoved me full length into the cold water. They dragged me back, dripping and coughing, to throw me at the feet of my mistress.

A man's voice said something and laughed lightly. The first words were unintelligible. The next were "Mohawk Girl." I had heard these words several times by then and was beginning to wonder what kind of name they had given me and what it meant.

I pulled off my long jacket with the antler buttons and set it beside me to dry. My mistress lifted it up. The next morning, she threw me a torn leather hide with a cord with which to cover myself, for my fringed jacket had been given away to her friend's son. I saw it many times afterward and remembered how my mother had made it for me.

Early the next day, we left the river, hurrying north. The men carried the canoes, six to each boat. We passed white water—rapids over rocks in the riverbed. The river broke up, separated by small islands into channels. We walked until we came to a wider and deeper stretch of water. The boats were set in the river and loaded again.

When the shadows grew long, they pulled to shore to make camp and cook the evening meal. I decided to learn the meaning of the name: Mohawk Girl. "What does 'Mohawk Girl' mean?" I asked, using my words mixed with the unknown sounds. She scowled, but repeated the phrase, spitting on the ground.

The old chief watched. From his cruel smile, he seemed to find this amusing. Adults milled around, children, too. They stopped to watch this exchange. From their expressions, I expected I was the butt of a joke, and would soon be beaten. It had to happen sooner or later, when they found time, so I asked again, my hands palms up and my face questioning, "Mistress? Mohawk Girl?"

She called a girl over to her, a child of six or seven. The girl looked at me warily, as though I were a fanged snake. "Girl," my mistress said, explaining my first Algonquin word.

I repeated it. "Girl." Now that I knew one of the words, I realized it was not a name; it described something about me. Could it mean the "captured girl"? "Enemy girl"? I had yet to discover the meaning of the name Mohawk. I repeated the word again, demonstrating my continued bewilderment.

The child picked up a stone and hurled it at my legs. It hardly hurt, for the meaning of the word began to penetrate. Another child pitched a second stone. I covered my face, knowing the word generated loathing. When the stones stopped flying, I lowered my hands. A small boy came close enough to kick my shin before he ran off.

Words were spoken around us, harsh words, and I turned, to see some warriors spit on the ground. Did the words mean "hated girl"? I nearly had it right. My mistress pretended to eat an invisible piece of meat, holding it in one hand, taking bites and chewing long, as if the meat were tough. Then she pointed to a man who stood close by, saying something to make the others laugh.

The meaning finally became clear. Their name for us was Mohawk, meaning "man-eater" in Algonquin. At our victory feasts, this practice was a cleansing of our souls, a restoration of our harmony. It was a balm for the hate that would have destroyed us. Only those who killed our men with extra cruelty met that fate. I pointed to myself and said, "Girl," the Algonquin word. "Ganeogaono Girl," I said, identifying myself by tribe. If they must use my people's name, let them say it properly, as we called ourselves.

"No!" my mistress exclaimed, disgusted, it seemed, at the stupidity of her slave. "Mohawk Girl." She slashed the air with her hand as if to tell me I wasted her time. In that instant, I knew as long as I remained among enemies, I should remain the Mohawk Girl. "Ganeogaono," I cried out in spite of myself. "Not Mohawk! I'm not Mohawk Girl!"

The children cavorted around me, aware I understood now. Their taunts stung as much as their stones had, for they chanted over and over again the terrible name.

Chapter

Before winter, I managed to gather enough castoffs to keep from freezing. In the garbage midden, I found torn moccasins, which I wrapped with scraps of hide to make them fit. Among the bones, broken baskets, and pots, I found a discarded stag horn and tied a handle to it to use for an awl. There was a discarded beaver parka, nearly hairless. I covered myself with this when I went outside to pull in firewood from the pile or to butcher what the hunters brought back from their expeditions. Whenever I held a knife to do this work, I was especially watched. My mistress would not allow me into the woods.

With inner basswood fibers rolled against my thigh, I produced thin lengths of cord. I used these to sew my pieces of leather and scraps of clothing into a patchwork dress and coat. Also, I made better-fitting moccasins for myself. All were too ugly for anyone else to crave.

During the last dusky days before snowfall, hunters brought in several stags and even a young moose. A grown walrus had been discovered inland, on the bank of a salt river. When they dragged its bulk up the hill to the village, I hardly knew what I was seeing. The women exclaimed over its tusks and hide. I gathered that this was an ocean animal and wondered what it was doing so far from home. Then again, we might have been closer to the encircling ocean than I knew.

Children stood guard with long staffs to keep the dogs away while the strips of meat dried on birch frames for winter. Low, thick clouds grew and spread, until the sky was like slate as far as the horizon. The strong, tangy odor of snow came in the north wind's breath. Before nightfall, the waiting ended and the first snow began to fall. Lazy flakes drifted down silently. People hurried to pull in the meat and divide the fuel, bringing in all they could fit inside. They stockpiled the rest under hide shelters between the wigwams.

Soon, the snow came hard enough to reduce the wigwams to gray shadows. I was glad to be able to wrap my rags close around me and sit inside by the low fire. The blizzard continued through the night.

Next morning, when I pushed away the snow and crawled out, the sun glistened off rounded piles of snow. "Well, don't just stand there," my mistress squawked. "Use the broom and push the snow off the wigwam, before I decide to use it on your Mohawk hide." I took the broom and set to my work.

Until after the sun climbed to its zenith, the sky remained blue. A wind came out of the north as the day progressed, bringing new clouds. Before night, it snowed again. The second storm in as many days lasted longer. For several more days, the north wind blew, bending fir boughs low with wet, heavy snow. The wind whistled through skeletal branches like malicious spirits.

I was patching clothing by firelight when my mistress said, "Mohawk Girl, we need more wood. Get an armful and bring it inside." In a way, I was grateful to go outside to the impartial wind. I tied my wrap around my shoulders and left the wigwam without a word, crossing to the snow-covered woodpile. My fingers felt half-frozen even before I reached the wood.

It was a struggle to loosen a few logs while new gusts of wind pelted me with flecks of ice. Mostly, the wind played with the tops of the high trees, whooshing and whistling like the flying heads of legend. I imagined all the horrors of our stories in the swaying treetops. "Brother Wind, I'm only a slave. Don't freeze me," I whispered. "Be my friend. Tell my family I'm alive and I'll try to get home to them as soon as I may." My old uncle had made a friend of the wind; why not me? I had no one else to talk to who would understand. With an armful of branches, I hurried back to the smoky wigwam.

My mistress's children were grown. Quite often, she visited them. Otherwise, she slept or ate the day away. My master seldom stayed in the wigwam, so I was left alone a good deal of the time. The snow and cold guaranteed I would stray no farther than the woodpile or the midden to empty the refuse or throw away the bones.

Toward spring, I needed to bend farther to crawl into the wigwam's low entrance, which told me that I was growing. Sometimes at night, I awoke, wondering why odd thoughts came into my head of men and women mating like otters, the male biting and grabbing the female's neck with his long, sharp claws. My unrestrained imagination filled me with apprehension. The morning I discovered blood on my bed, I knew the reason for my worry. As long as I remained a girl, I had some protection. The blood flow made me a woman.

My master had gone out, but my mistress continued to snore softly under her bed furs. I ran for snow to wash out the stain, then took up a scrap of leather and filled it with dried moss to soak up the blood.

After eating, I set out for firewood with a sling over my back. I snowshoed far enough into the woods that the village was out of sight, but I knew there was no escape in winter. I could only pretend to be free for a little while. Before long, I had to return.

That night, under my furs, I stroked my budding breasts, wondering why my body would betray me like this in the midst of enemies. It did not take me long to learn how to walk hunched over to hide my increasing breasts and height. I wrapped more coverings over me to conceal the outward signs of my womanhood.

In Doteoga, women in their moon-flow times slept in a special section at the far end of the longhouse, curtained off from the others. They did not mix with the rest of the community during that time. It was harmful to gaze at a man or his weapons at such a time, and no woman wanted to hurt a hunter's animal luck.

If this had happened to me at home, my clan would have made a feast in my honor when the first time was finished. My mother and aunt would have cooked corn cakes and I would have danced with the women to celebrate my changed status from girl to maiden.

I hoped to keep my emerging womanhood from my mistress. Mostly, though, I hoped to keep it from my master, for I feared he might find another use for his Mohawk Girl.

During the first winter of my imprisonment, I observed the differences between my people and these Algonquin. We made our fires with flint. They used fire drills. They called Orenda by a different name, which sounded like Manitou. Algonquin women lowered their voices and deferred when in the presence of men. Although my familiarity with their speech grew, I was careful not to speak more than a few words, in order to keep them from knowing how much I understood.

One evening after the fire had died down to glowing coals, the old conversation began again. "Stop your worrying," my master's gravelly voice said to his wife. His throat had been damaged by a blow during battle, which made him sound older than he was. "I told you we killed enough of their braves that they will not come into our territory north of the Great River. When the trails are clear again, we'll drive them out of our southern lands altogether."

"Do you think their men will leave their town undefended next summer, after your attack? Before you waste more of our own braves, you ought to spy out their strength." Whether or not Algonquin women shared in decision making, my mistress was certainly not silent.

"We are aware of that. Remember that war is our affair, not yours. We know how to do it. If your slave hadn't warned them, their lands would be ours this winter, along with their flint beds. We knew how few defenders they left to guard their women. Our scouts had counted their men just that morning. How were we to guess the rest would return from the west that very same day?"

I couldn't mask the gleam of triumph in my eyes before my mistress noticed it. "Damn the girl! I *thought* she understood us. You'll sleep in the cold for that look, Mohawk Girl, and be glad I don't give you to someone who would use you properly, as you deserve."

I wrapped my mangy bed fur around me and slunk outside before she could think to keep me from taking it, then rested my head against the bark of their wigwam. A little of the fire's warmth seeped through where the bark layers and hides didn't quite overlap. I put my ear near the crack, watching and listening. "I wish one of our shamans could tell us whether their war leader died."

I held my breath, thinking he might have meant my father, although each clan had a war leader. If the chief engaged our warriors on the trail, he would have seen my father with his war leader feathers and paint. "That one will never fight again, in any case. When he killed Little Elk, we rushed him. It took three of us to bring him to his knees, although his men stopped us from finishing the task. He gave us a good fight to get to the girl. She must be his daughter. That's why we had to take her, to punish him for Little Elk."

It *was* my father they spoke of. I moaned out loud. If he had died, it was for trying to save me from the Algonquin. But I still did not know. He might be alive. That is why the braves had not come. They'd had to take him and the others to the healers first. If they had come after us later, we were already gone, but I would never know.

"Little Elk has been avenged."

My mistress said, "I've heard Mohawks get their clan and status from their mothers and grandmothers. If that's true, the war leader must have been her uncle, not that it matters, so long as he's dead or disabled. You would have been smart to kill her, too. What did you bring her to me for? I see my son's death each time I look at her. What good can come from this girl in our camp? I'm surprised she can cook and sew at all. I hear Mohawks teach their daughters to hunt."

"One more summer and their land will be ours, as in the days of our grandfathers. In the meantime, the presence of Mohawk Girl strengthens our hate. We must never forget what we have suffered at their hands, how they stole our southern lands. When they see her walk among us, our young men's hands itch to crush Mohawk skulls."

"Are you sure they're not itching somewhere else? Are *you*? The girl has become a woman, although she thinks she has us fooled."

"Me? Touch a Mohawk? I'd as soon desire a she-wolf."

Now I realized why they kept me. They had taken me to punish my father for the chief's son. One for one; me for a warrior. It saved my pride a little.

Sleep was a long time coming to me that night. Under my furs, I burrowed into the snow and found it kept me warm. It occurred to me if I died of cold, I should no longer suffer the humiliation they heaped upon me. I intended, however, to make good on my next escape. More than five months had passed since the Algonquin attack on my people.

On a night near to spring, when the frigid winds stopped, I pulled away the door flap and crawled from my mistress's wigwam. The moon looked like a slender bow hanging between the trees. Clouds swam through the sky, obscuring most of the stars. Since I often washed in the snow during the night, there was nothing remarkable for them to notice about my absence.

I followed the trail south to the river path at a trot. With my inside pockets filled with parched corn and dried fish, I considered I had enough of a head start actually to get away before hunger forced me to hunt or spend an extra day to lay traps for my food. Going hungry did not concern me. I had been trained to live off the land or do without food for a few days if I had to. I knew how to wiggle my fingers like fat worms just below a pond's surface and flip out a fish. If need be, there were beetle and grubs hiding below tree bark and under stones. Nothing mattered more than escape.

Little snow remained. The ground continued hard enough in most places not to take my prints. I managed my thirst that night with snow and ice, then sucked my hard corn until it was soft enough to swallow, not making a fire, for the smoke would have given me away.

Threading the bracken and clumps of weeds to the river's edge, I surveyed the distance between the banks. The river was still wide, but narrower here than near Doteoga, before it curved away to the west. An opening beckoned between the brittle reeds and frozen cattails. The river of stars across the sky paled the ice, showing the way. If only the frozen surface could hold me this one night and melt with them on it tomorrow.

I set my foot on the ice gingerly, ready to withdraw at the slightest crack. With each step, I listened, alert for the trickle of water and the brittle sounds of ice shivering apart. Predawn light illuminated the river as I crossed. Cattails and marsh grasses showed where the tributaries split away. Thick trees grew on islands midstream.

My feet felt like stones as I stumbled over an exposed root. My arms and legs had grown almost numb with cold and fatigue, but I continued along the ice through the early hours of the day. I knew there must be somewhere I could take shelter, somewhere cloaked enough with reeds and old snow that I could hide myself. A marsh loon made its lonely cry from a nearby tree as I limped along, trying to keep from being seen in the river mist.

All this time, no human footstep had sounded on a dead leaf or a twig. Small animals skittered around the marsh, lapping up water in the melts. A beaver slapped its tail down on thin ice when a bobcat scrambled down for a drink. A fawn moose followed its mother back up the bank, safe on the other side of the marsh. I spied a batch of pale and brittle feather grass on the southern bank, the most likely place to take shelter and rest so far. I rolled myself up in my worn sleeping fur, hoping I looked like a fallen log or a patch of brown mud.

A black bear or cougar might see me in its rambles for food and water along the shallows. I had to chance it; my eyes would no longer serve me, nor my legs. I bent and pulled some ice from a high root to wet my mouth, letting it melt on my tongue and drizzle down my throat until it slaked my thirst. With a few parched corn kernels on my tongue, I snuggled down into the shadows, tucked my ragged pelts close, and slept.

The grass grew soft and green again. I found myself beside the familiar Wide River, returning home at long last. There were our cornfields. I sprinted effortlessly along the trail between the fields and stockade. Dogs barked their welcome. My longhouse clan emerged, exclaiming in their astonishment at seeing me alive and well.

I flew the last few paces to embrace my family. They crowded around, touching my cold cheeks, warming me with touches and grateful tears. "Can this be? Is this our very own Gahrahstah given back to us?" my mother asked joyfully. "I give thanks to Great Spirit Orenda for protecting her."

Uncle Burns His Lips embraced me, saying, "We never thought to see you again. Your warning came to us barely in time to meet them outside the stockade walls. We could not prevent your capture, even though you saved us."

That was not quite accurate. "It was my brother who brought you the warning," I pointed out. "I was too high in the tree. I told him only that I saw them coming. It was terrible to be so close and not be able to break away. I'm so glad you lived through the fighting."

Scout was there, too, brown and wiry, with shining eyes. "If you didn't tell me, I would have had no message. Many more would have died," he said. "You were brave to escape our enemies this time, and run so far alone. When I was very small, you killed a snake on the riverbank to save my life. You have always been brave, my sister."

My face grew warmer when Grandmother told me how often they had prayed that Orenda would send me back. "We dared not lose more of our men. So many were injured. Still, we never gave up hope we would see you again."

My cousin Laughing Girl stood beside Grandmother. She broke away to hug me. "Picture Maker," she cried. "I should have waited. I should have shared your exile. They call me Girl Who Weeps since you were taken from us.'"

"You can ask Grandmother to change it back again," I told her happily. "I escaped on a dark night and ran over the river and many days more."

Grandmother shook her head, dark eyes sad within the wrinkled folds of skin. Why would she not change it back? What did she know that I didn't?

When my father walked out from the stockade behind the others, they did not seem to notice him. Even when he paused near my mother, she did not acknowledge him. He was hazy, as though composed of moon-light. "Father!" I exclaimed, walking toward him. I held out my hands to take his, elated to see him again after thinking he had died. His fingers felt like ice. "What happened to you when I could not see, Father?" I asked.

"The Algonquin chief thinks he killed you. I have waited all this time to know."

"My spear pierced the Algonquin just as he brought down his war club. We died at the same moment, he and I, Gahrahstah." Father's tone remained calm and accepting, but my eyes stung with tears at his revelation. "Don't be concerned. A warrior expects to die in battle. It was a fitting death and one that will be spoken of around the campfires. What matters is that Doteoga was saved."

"If I had not gone to gather grapes and nuts . . ." I trembled.

The Algonquin had already been on the trail and on the river. There was nothing that could have prevented their coming for us. "If you had not gone to the hill, our enemies would have reached the stockade and set fire to it. If we hadn't had time to arm and meet them on the forest trail and the river, it would have been worse. My spirit rides with the wind now, with Great Spirit Orenda. You will see me again when you need me. Meanwhile, be brave." My father smiled at me before he faded away.

No one else appeared to have heard his words to me or mine to him, but my grandmother continued to shake her head sadly. My uncle comforted me, as had my father, with almost the same words. "We had time to take up our spears, our bows and war clubs. I wanted to come for you right away, but we needed to get the wounded back inside. The next morning, we chased our enemies all the way to their camp across the Wide River. When we saw their dwellings deserted, we burned everything there, their shelters and fields. We blackened wampum with soot and hung it from their trees. We shall not allow them to return."

"Let's go inside," I said. "I missed you all so much."

I was so deep within my dream that it took several kicks to jar me awake. The glare of the sun on the frozen river almost blinded me. It touched down and glinted from the melting pools in the gray ice. Again, one of the men kicked me. "Get up!" The silhouettes became two Algonquin and a dog standing over me.

"On your feet, Mohawk Girl." He bent and jerked me upright.

"No!" I screamed, my rage startling a flock of resting geese who fluttered together into the sky. One of the men patted his straw-colored dog, praising him for finding me. The small beast wiggled his back end and leapt madly at his master's petting and praise.

I rose unsteadily to my feet, looking for flowing water to throw myself into, to end my life rather than return. There was time for me to take only a few paces toward the steep bank before the Algonquin yanked me back.

"No, you don't, Mohawk Girl," the other said. "You are going back where you belong." He tugged my arm, spun me around roughly, and pushed me ahead of him, following closely behind. My head slumped with reality as I pointed my feet back to the north side of the Wide River. I hoped the ice would break and carry us all to our deaths, but it held.

We had crossed a third of the river when the second warrior suddenly said, "Wait." I thought he heard the river ice crack, and I listened hard to see where I might drag them down with me. The only sound was a gurgling too far below the surface to matter.

"You go ahead with the Mohawk Girl," he told his companion. "I'm going to check on our summer village." It was as though he were saying he could return home even though I could not. The first Algonquin grunted his approval and pushed me ahead of him again.

The yellow dog trotted beside his departing master. They reached the south bank, leapt up, and disappeared into the reeds.

My captor did not speak to me again. When he decided to rest, he gestured for me to crouch until he was ready to resume. The journey back was as bad for me as it had been the first time. I had been so close to freedom, but I had not considered that they would hunt me down with a dog. Without it, the two warriors might have passed only paces from my hiding place without noticing me.

My mistress bared her teeth when she saw me again. "Worthless slave," she ranted. "Not worth the corn she eats. I'll take it out of her hide." She thanked the warrior before she led me away to beat me.

She left me tied to a post outside the wigwam, bare after the whipping, while the blood ran down my back and legs, forming small puddles at my feet. Somehow I managed not to cry out and shame my people. Someone cut me down, carried me inside, and threw a fur over my bruised body. My mistress crouched near me when I opened my eyes again.

"Food in pouches sewn into your clothing," she hissed. "Sewn well, too. You aren't worth keeping. Someday, you'll remember your days in my wigwam and wish you were back."

I dragged myself to my knees and crawled to the water pot, where I dipped the gourd. My lips were cracked and my tongue swollen. When I had slaked my thirst, I reached toward the cold gruel. "Eat," my mistress allowed, "but don't think to fool me again."

Her husband walked in while I was licking the last bit off my fingers. I noticed how he stared at me, puzzled. "None of our girls would dare to go

into the forest alone," he said to his wife. "You'll never tame her. She de-
fies us, this Mohawk Girl. She's not like a female at all."

Soon I was able to sit up and tend the fire again. While I worked, I
thought about my dream. Dreams are sent by spirits. Perhaps I had really
spoken to my father's spirit. Perhaps I had actually spoken with the dreaming spirits of my family and all they told me was true. I would learn when
the warrior with the dog returned.

I was working somewhere outside when he entered among the wigwams. He stalked angrily about, shouting, "Where is she? Where's the Mohawk Girl?"

Someone pointed. I stopped pounding corn and stood, unflinching, returning his glare with as much insolence as I could muster. People walking by stopped and gathered around. Someone ran for my master and
mistress.

"What's the news? Tell us," the chief demanded.

The younger man spoke. "Our homes are burned to the ground and
the ashes are scattered. Black strands of wampum hang on the trees
around the clearing. Our Mohawk enemies destroyed our dwellings and
fields. We must go back now and kill every Mohawk south of the Great
River and east of the Great Lakes. This one must die first, for the trouble
she caused."

There were shouts of anger and outrage while my accuser pointed. To
my surprise, I remained calm. The shouts of "Kill her! Burn the Mohawk!"
elicited no fear in me. I thought, I shall not have to tolerate them anymore.
Death will free my spirit. I shall welcome it.

The chief raised his hands, speaking gruffly. "The Mohawk Girl will live
and be our slave, as I ordered. *You will not free her to death!* I shall discuss
returning to the south with our shaman and the elders. Wait here." The
muttering continued when several gray-heads followed him into his wigwam. Savage looks followed, but no one moved to harm me.

Soon, my master returned. "We've lost too many of our young men to
return yet. The time for the final battle between the Mohawk and the Algonquin must be delayed until we are stronger. We'll go to the ocean to
fish and plant our corn. The day will come when we shall take revenge for
the outrage in the south." The people complained bitterly while they
walked back to their wigwams, but no one challenged his decision. I was
allowed to resume my work.

As my uncle had told me in my dream, they had truly destroyed the Algonquin village east of Doteoga. Knowing my vision to be true, I no longer

doubted my father's death. My capture had brought about the razing of the Algonquin village. Enough animosity existed between my people and our enemies on both sides of the river to set ablaze all the lands between the Great Lakes and the ocean. I wondered whether the Creator knew when all the wars would end, or how many more had to die.

Chapter 9

When the women broke winter camp, I learned the swiftness with which they had packed and left their summer town had come from practice, not only fear of Ganeogaono retaliation. I could scarcely believe how quickly several hundred people, including children, could dismantle their homes, load up their dogs, and get moving. Had I not seen them do it the previous fall, knowing our men were after them, I would have thought it an exception. Algonquin tribesmen seemed not to stay in one place very long. But then, I supposed they had become practiced in the art of retreating.

Lodge poles were soon harnessed to their dogs, and hides tied between to form travois. The men conferred with one another while the women piled each with as much as it would hold. The men carried only their weapons.

My mother spoke truly that Algonquin women were closer to slaves than equals, even in their own lands. Fortunately for them, they knew no better, but walked with infants in back carriers, balancing baskets on their heads, gossiping and laughing.

Several men had left earlier with the canoes, probably to fish and hunt, and choose the evening camp. I slipped behind bit by bit, thinking to slip away and lose myself between the trees. To my dismay, the children kept me in sight every moment. Even when I relieved myself beside the trail, they remained with me until I rejoined the column.

We trekked northeast, seldom stopping long to rest. Each night, when the women and children arrived, campfires welcomed them with the

smells of roasted salmon. The nights grew mild enough that the people
slept without erecting shelters, with only their sleeping furs between
them and the stars. On the way, the travelers came to a village, only six
wigwams, with a small cornfield already planted and growing. The elders
and chiefs of the village welcomed the travelers. While the men met and
smoked, the women set up camp beside the cornfield. Before sleep, several people wandered between campfires.

A crone, bent under the weight of at least fifty winters and thumping
with her walking stick, led a gang of unruly children. She screeched to her
companions, "Where is the Mohawk Girl? I want to see her."

"There she is. Look at her," shouted the group of children appointed by
my mistress not to let me out of their sight.

By the way the ancient woman looked at me, I might have had antlers.
I doubt that she or any of the villagers had ever seen one of my tribe. "Do
you talk Algonquin, Mohawk Girl?" a child asked loudly.

"No," I said, and refused to say another word.

After corn gruel at sunrise, we picked up camp and continued. We did
not need to carry water, since the streams ran high with snowmelt from
the mountains. The nightly camps were always pitched beside running
water. I overheard my master say he intended us to set up the village by
the ocean, where we might remain for a year or two.

Several maidens kept close by me on the trail the next day, whispering
among themselves. From time to time, they taunted me, but I refused to
respond. I did not know, nor did I care, whether they reckoned I understood their words. When two of them crowded me, as others did to show
they had first claim to the road, I turned sideways to allow them to pass.
"Do it now," one said. One knelt behind me and the other shouldered me
backward over her back and into the brambles.

The sudden move took me by surprise. I cried out, unable to suppress
my anger and shock. When I regained control of my emotions and returned to the trail, my arms and legs were red with thorn scratches.

"The Mohawk Girl bleeds," one said.

"She feels pain, just like any animal does, even if she tries not to show
it," the other answered. "Since she won't talk, she doesn't need her tongue.
We might cut it out for you, Mohawk Girl," the speaker threatened.

They set on me again, trying to make me run from them. Instead, I set
my back against a slippery elm, feet apart, eyes narrowed, preparing for
their next attack. "My father died because of you," the shorter girl said.

"People say Mohawk girls think they're as good as men." I brushed my long, loose hair away from my eyes with my fingers, refusing to dignify her taunting with a response.

"Why won't you speak? Is it just that you're too stupid?"

"Maybe we can teach her to talk."

"She's too dim-witted," the second girl responded scornfully. "She's a Mohawk." She laughed. I suspected they were gathering their courage to shove me again, so they could brag of my easy defeat to their friends.

Before they could think of more taunts, I called up the Algonquin words I had learned and put them together, but purposely not too well. "You father taste bad. Too stringy." I grimaced at them like a fright mask, licking the points of my teeth. "You fatter. More easy to chew, I think."

The girl yelped and bolted, screaming for her mother. She streaked down the path. Her friend hesitated, undecided, but not for long. I tried to gauge how much of a head start I might have, even in daylight. How soon would they notice I was gone? A small way off the trail, I might disappear among the leafy trees. I hesitated, considering my chances. There was no nearby stream in which to throw a dog off my scent. I picked up my bundle and returned to the trail.

The girls received permission to punish me for my insolence to them. To my chagrin, I moaned at each descent of the birch, my breath hissing through clenched teeth. I tasted blood on my lip, then realized I'd bitten it in my effort to remain silent as a warrior.

Eventually, the oaks and maples thinned, giving way to spruce and pine. The earth at my feet became coarse and sandy. Seagulls floated on the air currents and salt air teased my nose when the wind blew east through the trees and marsh grass. We were nearly to the ocean. We neared Earth's edge.

There was one grassy hill left to climb. A few scrub pines and twisted oak trees bordered the sandy path. A thin copse of white birch bent toward us in the moisture-laden wind. Then there was nothing but pale green sea grass in the sandy earth all the way down to the surf and the blue horizon.

The first of the long column reached the crest and waited there for the others to catch up, pointing and talking. A boy whistled and exclaimed, "See how the ocean moves. The water piles up into lines of white mountains and rushes forward like warriors to attack the rocks and sand."

I had imagined a river stretching far into the distance, moving as rivers do. Even our legends had not prepared me for the white-topped green humps that gathered speed until they tumbled onto the beach. As if it lived, the water breathed in and out, leaving behind vanishing islands of foam, seaweed, and crabs. Seagulls rested lazily on the wave crests, rising and sinking. From the heights, it was possible to see distant lines of white rushing toward us. The ocean really did go on without end.

"Move. Get out of the way, Mohawk Girl." My mistress grabbed my arm and pulled me back. "Don't you see the shaman and the priests?"

The town priests, who had carried their fire baskets, built a small fire on the hill. They laid dried tobacco leaves on the flames and called down Manitou's blessings for their new settlement. After the ceremony, they put out the fire.

The Algonquin did not erect their wigwams very near the beach as I thought they might, but on the plateau behind the cliffs, safe from tides and wind. The travois became lodge poles again. Women climbed onto one another's shoulders to fasten the bark and hides to the houses. I unloaded packs and hauled supplies while the women cooked their cornmeal mush in pots over several fire pits.

The next day, the work to clear new ground for cornfields began. I wondered how well the sandy soil would hold the corn. I was allowed to prepare the hills, but my mistress set the dried corn kernels, the squash and bean seeds into the ground with accompanying prayers and tom-tom beats.

In the morning, there were tide pools to be searched out to provide urchins and crabs for the stew pots. I saw my first live seals sunning themselves on rocks. The males were larger than big dogs. A hunter ran at one and speared it through. The others scattered and escaped into the water, moving clumsily on land, but graceful as fish when they reached the water.

Whenever I could get away for a little while, I looked for excuses to be near the beach. I dug up clams, swept the tide pools and gathered seaweed, watching the ocean all the time. Its vastness imparted a sensation of being free, unstoppable. I wanted to know it. Often, I woke before light just to watch the sun climb the rim of earth and leap into the sky above the water.

Storm clouds blew up soon after we arrived. The water piled into black waves three times their normal size. They covered the beach, foaming angrily and lathering white against the slate-colored sky halfway up the cliff to the wigwams. Lightning forked down into the water when Heno, Thunder Spirit, searched for sea serpents to destroy with his fire sticks. Wind and thunder made the cliff tremble, but I did not fear Heno, and Ga-oh, Wind Spirit, was my friend. I stood in the drenching rain, my hair blowing behind me like seaweed, watching and feeling almost free, as if I were a bird that could leap into the air and fly away.

I was soaked to the skin when I returned to the fire of my mistress's wigwam. "Where were you, little fool?" she asked.

"Cliff," I said simply.

"Do Mohawks have no sense at all? The ocean might have swallowed you." I shrugged, wondering why it would matter to her.

Once, when I took my gathering basket through the marsh grass to dig out cattail roots and pick cranberries, an Algonquin boy came looking for me. He looked a bit older than my brother, Scout, ten or so by my reckoning; I had begun my thirteenth year. "Mohawk Girl," he said. "The hunters have a moose for you to butcher." He cocked his head toward the town and ran off, only glancing behind once to be sure I was following.

I climbed back up the hill behind him, feeling my homesickness like a lump in my throat. My breasts had been swelling and aching. Suddenly, my legs cramped and I felt a wetness between my legs. I waited a few moments, making sure my face would not reveal the sudden fear that chilled me more than a cold wind. I found some dry seaweed to catch the bleeding. How many of them had guessed that I had become a woman? Fortunately, I had the moose to butcher. Its blood mixed with mine on my stained clothing.

No man here could want me for his wife, but the young men might remember me when their wives were not available. The Mohawk Girl might be used to ease the swelling their manhood was subject to. Would a child I bore be a slave, too? I hoped they felt as my master had, when he said he would as soon fornicate with a she-wolf. If an Algonquin turned from me in disgust, it would serve my desire to be left alone.

In desperation, I devised a plan to get away. It would take me more than a month to return home, but what was a month when compared to a life among enemies? I might be able to manage one of the women's canoes alone, if I could get it over the waves and go south. Once I returned to the Wide River, I would avoid every village and hide from hunters. Nothing would stop me.

I discovered that a canoe does not do well in ocean water. A swell turned it easily as a twig, and it was a long swim back to the shore. The canoe's owner was angrier than my mistress, because the canoe I stole broke apart on the rocks. If I had drowned, my mistress declared, she would have been well rid of me. Stripped and under her lash, I could no longer deny I had become a woman.

Early one evening, I remained alone on the beach. The last moon of summer had ended its cycle. Most of the harvest had been taken. The air felt soft and warm, although gray clouds gathered. The tide flowed in, making wide overlapping arcs. I ran back and forth through the foam, laughing and splashing, kicking up the water, waving my arms like a bird. Feeling the pull of the ocean, I stripped off my dress and stepped into the surf.

Past the lazy waves, pelicans slept with their funny bills tucked under their wings. I turned over onto my back. The brightest stars were already visible in a sky deep into dusk. While I floated, storm clouds hurried from the east, covering up the pale stars over the town on damp, warm winds. Pretty soon, they blotted out the eastern sky. This did not disturb me in the least, since the water enveloping me felt warm as my mother's embrace. I loosened my braids and ran my fingers through my long hair until it floated around me like seaweed.

When I finally returned to the beach, my dress was not where I had left it. The tide had not reached up this far, so I guessed one of the boys from the town had been sent to fetch me and was enjoying a prank. Unworried but slightly annoyed, I continued to look, darting my eyes here and there, watching for my dress, angry at not being able to punish the boy.

I passed by a grassy dune, when someone stepped toward me. In the gathering darkness, it was hard for me to make out his face, but I knew he was not from the town. In my innocence, I did not suspect danger, only wondered how long he had been there spying on me when I imagined myself alone.

"Who are you?" he asked. There were none among the town's folk who did not know me by sight. Something about his voice set my neck hairs on end. "Don't be afraid," he said. "I'm visiting from another town, north of here. We knew there was a new settlement. You swim as well as any boy." My eyes had adjusted to the dark and his face told me he could see quite well that I was no boy. "Where did you learn to swim like that?"

I turned my head, trying to muffle my voice so he wouldn't hear my accent. "On the river," I said. The wind was rising. I backed away from him as if I felt shy and was still looking for my dress. He moved swiftly beside me and locked his hand on my wrist.

"Shall I take you to your father up on the hill?" He pointed with his chin in the direction of the town. "It's going to rain."

"Give me my dress. They'll be looking for me."

He pulled me closer to look at me. "Who'll be looking for you?"

I wanted to say my father, my brothers. I wanted to frighten him into letting me go, but I was too scared to find the right words. "Let me get my dress," I said. I knew I put the words together wrong, but I was afraid and becoming more so.

His smile was menacing. "You don't speak properly. No Algonquin girl swims like that. Neither would one be alone on the beach at night. You're not Algonquin at all. What are you?"

"Let me go," I demanded, and broke his grip with a twist of my hand. I ran toward the trail that led up the hill, but before I was halfway there, I heard his feet pounding the damp sand behind me. His hand closed over my shoulder and he spun me around to face him.

"You're not one of us," he declared angrily. "Who are you? What are you?" I knew I could no longer convince him I had people on the hill who would punish him if he harmed me. I had nothing with which to fend him off, and he had no reason not to harm me. Desperate, I gambled that if I told him my tribe, he would turn away from me in disgust, not wanting to defile himself.

"They call me Mohawk Girl," I said.

I saw from his grin that my gamble had failed. "It's only a Mohawk girl," he uttered. "Fair game for anyone." He grabbed me. With his other hand, he loosened his breechclout and kicked it away as it fell.

"No," I shouted. Twisting away, I turned and pulled with all my might to escape, but he was too strong for me. When I raised my knee sharply, aiming for his groin, he caught my leg effortlessly and flipped me over. Sand entered my mouth and tiny bits of shell scratched my cheek and breasts. He dropped onto my back, laughing, and pulled my body up to meet his.

"Fight," he laughed as I struggled. "Algonquin girls are too gentle; they bore me. A Mohawk woman ought to be like a wildcat. I'll tame you the same way I tame my dogs."

He stopped talking then and concentrated on what he was doing. Somehow, I managed to keep from crying out loud while he violated me, biting the inside of my cheek until I tasted blood. My torn flesh was nothing to my anger. Tears of helpless rage burned my eyes and dripped into the sand.

When he was finished, he rolled away. I had turned to look at him, wondering if he would let me go now that he was done. He picked up my dress and threw it over me. Instead of taking it, I ran blindly back into the ocean, silent tears flowing down my cheeks. I followed the sound of breaking waves in the dark. A few stars peeked through cracks between the blowing clouds. There was thunder; then a flash of light lit the sky pink for a moment.

I shall give myself to the ocean, I thought. It will wash away the foulness that the Algonquin put into me. My spirit will flee this place and all my hurts. I shall float up between the clouds to rest with Great Spirit Orenda, clean, I thought. I shall be done with my captivity.

So thinking, I slipped between the crash of one wave and the rise of the next. When the water was up to my mouth, I lowered my head and waited for the next wave to wash over me and carry me away to my death.

Something pulled at my hair, but not the water. It was the man's hand. The rumble of the waves and the thunder had prevented me from hearing him follow me. He dragged me back through the waves. When we reached the sand, he pushed me ahead of him, for I was stumbling and too weak to resist.

My dress lay where he had thrown it. "Pick it up," he ordered, and I did. He made me walk ahead of him, back to the wigwams, naked, hair dripping and covered with seaweed. Someone saw us. "The Mohawk Girl comes up the hill with a stranger. Get the chief. Hurry!" By the time the first drops of rain pelted the earth, a crowd had gathered. I stood, raising my face to the rain, letting it wash away the seawater and the filthy touch of the stranger.

"I am an emissary from my chief," he said. "We have learned you are here. He sent me to learn if you are friendly, if you wish to be good neighbors." The chief invited the visitor into his wigwam.

"You get in here, Mohawk Girl," my mistress ordered. She pushed me into a dark corner. I placed my sodden dress near the fire to dry it a little. While the chief and his visitor talked, I pulled some meat and beans from the stew pot. If I had to live, I had to eat. The wind rose, blowing the rain hard against the bark walls and roof. From time to time, crashes of thunder shook the wigwam.

"My Mohawk slave knows no better than to stand naked in a rainstorm," my mistress complained. "She's done it before. Don't mind her."

"I don't," the man said. My mistress offered him food, corn cakes and roasted elk meat with spruce-needle tea. After he had eaten, she filled a pipe for him and moved herself into the shadows while the men talked. Water dripped into the ditch around the wigwam and drained away.

"I'm Hawk Feather," the visitor said, giving his name at last. His was not a name I chose to remember; but rather, one I was unable to forget. "My town is three days north of here, on the coast. Our hunters and fishermen noticed your men in the forest and your wide canoes on the water. When they reported to Red Squirrel, our sachem, that new people had settled here, he wanted me to find out who you were, to learn your intentions and if you want to trade and make marriage arrangements with people of our town."

My master spoke when Hawk Feather paused. "Your sachem may have forgotten. We've lived here before, although we don't come every summer. Since he is to be our neighbor and I am sachem here, I accept his greetings. I speak for my people. We came here with peaceful intentions, as we do whenever we return to our summer fishing camp." He scratched his head as though thinking. "If the hunting is as good as I remember from past years, we might stay a few years this time. I would like to visit your town with a party of my people, to meet Red Squirrel in friendship."

"When I found that female on the beach"—Hawk Feather pointed at me with his thumb—"I wondered at first if our new neighbors were Mohawk."

"The girl's tribe encroached on our southern territory. She gave warning when we arrived to take it back. We have reason to think she was daughter to one of their war leaders." Hawk Feather looked at me with raised eyebrows.

"Her father won't meet us in battle again; he's dead now. We took the Mohawk Girl captive during our last battle, before we left for our winter home," my master explained.

"What's it like having a Mohawk slave? Does she use men's weapons?" This new Algonquin sounded as if he knew nothing at all about us but rumors, although he was quite prepared to believe those rumors.

"As if we would let a slave touch weapons." My master laughed. "My wife says it's difficult enough to teach her women's work. She's run away several times, and although my wife whips her, she has not learned to be obedient." This was bargaining talk. The thought must have occurred to him to trade me.

"I don't know," Hawk Feather said. "She may have a use that has not occurred to you. If you were to offer her as a gift to my sachem, it would convince him that you and your people mean to establish friendship between our town and yours." I listened in horror, wishing I had managed to give myself to the ocean. They were speaking of handing me to Hawk Feather.

"I will think on your offer. My lesser chiefs and our elders will agree with my decision in this matter and all others. In the morning, I'll tell them what we discussed. This is no night for visiting." Rolling thunder followed his words by several beats. The worst of the storm was over.

"So? What are your thoughts about the girl?" Hawk Feather asked, his tone seeming to be curious, but not especially anxious.

"I must speak to my wife, since the girl belongs mostly to her."

If that were so, they would have discussed it before the bargaining began. I was as good as given away. It would do no good to plead or to tell them what he did to me on the beach. What happened in one Algonquin town would happen in another. Hawk Feather walked away to a raised bed in the farthest corner of the wigwam while my master and mistress discussed my future.

"It's not as if you don't constantly complain about her. You can't tame the Mohawk Girl anyway," my master said. "Some of the people are angry I insisted she be kept alive. Since we're not going south again soon, it makes no difference. It would do us greater good to offer her to Hawk Feather's sachem."

"I suppose you're right, husband, but if she runs away from them, they'll have no slave and will think we traded dishonestly."

"We both warned him. *He* asked for her. It's not as if he doesn't know what he's getting. Besides, sending her north puts more distance between her and her people. She's more fool than I think if she tries to escape again."

He turned back to Hawk Feather. "What gift did your sachem send for us? If he sent you to us as his envoy, you must have gifts in your pack. Not that I doubt your word or his, but I want to see proof of his good intentions."

"He sent a fine gift for you. He hoped your settling here would be a good thing for all of us." The visitor brought over his pack, withdrew a pouch, and opened the flap. "Look at this," he said, lifting out three fine strings of white-and-pink wampum. He held them beside the hearth, where they caught light from the orange flames.

"Mmm!" My master grunted appreciatively at the wampum's pale purity, lifting the shell strings one by one to measure their length. "This is a splendid gift. White wampum means your word is good. Therefore, I accept your chief's offer on behalf of my people. Tell him we shall plan a visit shortly to help you celebrate your harvest. We had to plant late this season, so if our new neighbors wish to welcome us with gifts of food, we will be pleased to accept. We'll bring our eligible daughters and sons, who may find favor with your people, to the benefit of both our towns. Sleep now. In the morning, we'll inform the others together. Give him a good blanket, wife."

Hawk Feather smiled at his hosts and wished them a peaceful night, but when they had turned away in their furs to sleep, he moved his bedroll closer to mine. I closed my eyes, pretending to sleep, but my lashes fluttered when he touched my arm, so he knew I was awake and listening. He muttered, his voice a purr. "You must learn to be docile, Mohawk Girl. I'm your master now. Be sure I shall teach you many things. Don't think to escape me."

I pulled the ragged old pelts I used as a blanket over my head and turned my face to the wall. At least it was the last night I would have to sleep among the people who had killed my father.

Chapter 10

Sometime during the night, the rain ended. By dawn, cloudless blue peeped through the smoke hole. The storm had matched my mood the night before. It did not seem fair for bluebirds in a nearby tree to be chirping and repairing their nest as though last night's devastation was no more than a temporary annoyance. On my way to empty the night baskets, sunshine glistened off raindrops clinging to branches and leaves, creating tiny rainbows. Children splashed noisily through the bright-lit puddles.

The storm had left other tokens of its passing; torn bark fragments and broken branches littered the earth between the wigwams. Women scurried to repair their homes, laying woven mats to replace the torn and hanging bark and hides. Some of the things damaged during the night could not be set right again.

An oak tree in the near cornfield had taken a direct lightning strike, which had split it halfway down the trunk. Cracked, black, and charred, one side leaned to the right. The other side clung to life, its leaves still green. The leaves did not know they had been cut off from their source of life. Fortunately for the tree, it could not think and remember.

After morning gruel, the chief escorted Hawk Feather to a council meeting with the town elders. While they were gone, my mistress gathered up corn cakes and dried meat from her stores and wrapped them in cornhusks. She also packed a small basket with two mugs, one inside the other, then added basswood cord, sinew thread, bone needles, and awls, arranging all in a leather pouch.

Mumbling to herself about repairing Hawk Feather's canoe, if he had one, she strode around the circular room. As she had not ordered me to do anything, I pulled up my knees and rested my chin against them, watching her silently.

"What will Hawk Feather's chief think of me if you arrive like that? You look like a drowned wolf cub. Comb your hair at least, Mohawk Girl. Try to braid it and look like a decent maiden instead of a wild Mohawk. If Hawk Feather's sagamore likes you, he'll think better of us and we'll get better trades."

Lying in a basket beside her bed, there was a jagged oyster-shell comb alongside strips of hide and feathers she used for decoration. I had never dared to touch her personal belongings. "Go on. Get the tangles out, if you can; the rainwater should have softened it."

While I worked at my long, matted hair, she left the wigwam. She must have hated me if she thought my father had killed her son, but she had not really used me as harshly as she might have. She'd never denied me food. I tried to imagine how her heart must have ached for her son whenever she looked at me.

By the time she crawled back in, I had parted my hair and tied it into two thick braids fastened at the ends with strips of rawhide. She dropped a pair of moccasins into my lap, not good ones, but better than the ragged shoes I had worn the previous winter. I had planned to make another pair for myself sometime before winter came again, but in summer, it was easier to go barefoot.

"Here's a better dress," she said, taking if off her arm and holding it out to me. When I didn't move, she dropped it on my knees. I stared at her hard, wondering at the unexpected gesture. "Well, put it on," she commanded. "One does not send a shabby gift. You ought to have learned to talk decently by now. I suppose he'll think you can't understand his commands. You're way too quiet. Don't sit there like a dummy; put them on."

I pulled off my rags, following her commands one last time. After I had the dress on, I said, "You are not *too* bad, for an Algonquin." After awhile, she remembered to shut her mouth.

Hawk Feather thanked my former mistress warmly for her hospitality and the extra pack of food for his journey, which he promptly gave to me to carry. After words concerning the agreed-upon visit, and directions, he departed, flashing a last white smile to his hosts. No one spoke to me.

I followed him from the wigwam and through the paths between the other homes until we reached the trail down the hill to the ocean. My new master was half a head taller than I, well muscled, and not unpleasant to

look at. His neatly sectioned braids hung straight down his back, interrupted only by the bend of his unstrung bow. His full quiver slanted against
his shoulder. He strode with smooth, silent steps in his soft moccasin
boots.

I kept my eyes ahead, looking neither to the left nor right as I trudged
behind him with my burden basket. Of course, I could not avoid seeing the
others standing and watching near the still-dripping trees. They mumbled
to one another as Hawk Feather led me away. Among them were warriors
who blamed me for their defeat and women who blamed me for the deaths
of their men. After a year, the children of this town still saw me as the
enemy.

In my longhouse, mothers had warned us of fiery flying heads with
sharp teeth and perverted appetites. It seemed Algonquin mothers scared
their children into obedience by threatening them with Mohawks. Hawk
Feather's village was farther away from my land. I hoped the sachem to
whom my master sent me might perceive me as merely a friendless captive, unlikely to cause harm.

The women paused in their hoeing and filed out of their cornfields to
watch us. Before long, the hill above the ocean held all the people of the
town, just as when they had first arrived the previous spring. It seemed
destiny insisted I travel farther north. Hawk Feather glanced back at me
from time to time. When we were beyond the people's hearing, he
stopped and turned. "You speak better than you would have them believe.
Keep silent unless I speak to you. Do as you are told, if you expect to keep
your skin whole. What I say or do is not for you to question. If you ever
contradict me . . ." he paused, not bothering to finish.

After that, he seldom spoke at all, which was quite acceptable to me. I
hoped he would not force himself on me again, for I was still sore from his
first attack. Perhaps his sachem would appreciate his gift better if he
thought I was untouched by another man. Even after the previous day, I
was foolish enough to believe Hawk Feather's spoken intentions.

On the beach, the stones and sand were strewn with seaweed and broken shells from the storm-driven waves of the night. Between them, gulls
fought with bills and claws over stranded fish and crabs. I plodded after
Hawk Feather most of the morning, until we came upon a small freshwater stream that emptied into marshlands beside the ocean.

"Stop," he commanded. He stretched out to take long swallows of the
clear, cold water. I, too, cupped my hands and gulped noisily, splashing and
rubbing the water over my parched skin. Some water remained in our

leather bottles, but it was hot by then and tasted of leather. I refilled the water bags with fresh water, holding the bag under the surface and watching bubbles rise.

I took a corn cake for myself before he claimed the rest. When the last was eaten, he ordered me to dig clams. Glad for the excuse to be away from him, I took a small basket and ran down to the shore.

The tide had gone out by then. Saltwater pools remained on the wide stretch of damp, gravelly sand. Where gray bubbles oozed in the sand between long hanks of seaweed, I dug down with my fingers. Before long, they encountered the rippled bivalves. I piled the largest into my small loose-woven cord basket, filling it halfway to the top. Just beyond the low breakers, I bent to let seawater wash them clean and then returned to the shore. Hungrily, I pried one open, severed the muscles with a shard, and swallowed down the meat inside, then ate another.

Hawk Feather would grow angry if I took more time than necessary. I was hunkering over, feeling for more clams, when I sensed him creeping up behind me. I started to jump up, but he moved too fast for me to evade. Clutching my elbows behind me, he pushed me down again and lifted my dress.

"No!" I cried out, twisting wildly and curling my sandy fingers into claws. He grabbed both my hands with one of his, then flipped me back into the sand. "You held white wampum. You said I was for your sachem, a greeting from my old master," I gasped in helpless rage. "The Creator, Manitou, heard your promise. He knows you are false; he hears and sees how you lie."

"They said you could barely speak. They lied, too. Remember who your master is now." He slid between my legs, forcing them apart with one knee, then closed the space between us. I stopped struggling and fell limp, for struggle was of no avail.

"What? Why have you stopped fighting me, Mohawk Girl?" he gasped through his teeth in the process of ravishing me. "This is too easy. Have I conquered you already?" I tasted blood on my tongue from my broken lips and bitten cheek, but I remained limp. I moaned each time he slammed into my body with great heaves and grunts. Finally spent, he washed in the ocean.

Later, while he feasted on the clams, I rose to my feet shakily. Far away, the green water met the blue-green horizon in a long, flat line. Low waves rolled in, breaking gently over my feet, bathing them in foam. I walked through the surf, continuing until the water touched my breasts. Hawk

Feather called to me. "Don't try to drown yourself again. We're leaving soon."

I backed toward the shore, not looking at him. The cords I had bound around my braids were lost somewhere in the sand. Even as I stood there, a gust of damp, salty ocean wind lifted the tangle of my hair. It whipped the long strands about wildly, like hissing black snakes. "Ga-oh, Wind Spirit," I cried, for the god was there in the wind. "Hear my words." I raised my arms over the ocean. "Take my message with you to Doteoga, to my Ganeogaono home by the Wide River. Please, tell my grandmother I shall not use my name, Gahrahstah, Picture Maker, again. I am as good as dead to my people, so she may use my name for the next picture maker of our clan. Also tell my mother, Glad Song, that although I live, it is as slave to Algonquin, which is worse than being dead. Tell my brother, Scout, to grow fierce, to avenge our father and me, to take many Algonquin scalps."

I heard splashes behind me and spun about angrily. Hawk Feather had followed me. "Stop saying Mohawk words," Hawk Feather snarled. "No one understands them."

"I talk to Ga-oh, Wind Spirit," I shouted, outraged that he would interrupt a prayer. "He understands." I used the Algonquin word for Wind Spirit, but Ga-oh was his name in my tongue. I did not know how the Algonquin called him.

"You'll speak my language or not at all." His fist smacked against my jaw. I heard a crack but hardly felt it because of the shock.

My fingers came away with blood when I touched them to my lips. "Kill me. Go ahead. Leave me here in the ocean."

"No more talking! Shall I cut out your tongue? It is of little use. Get the basket. Now." I left the water to do as he commanded.

A trail appeared on the fringe of the woods, past the sandy hills that led into the cool shade of the summer forest. The coast curved away far to the east. The track we trod remained narrow, barely visible. The leafy canopy above allowed a little sunlight to filter through. When Hawk Feather halted by the stream, I slipped out of my burden basket and knelt down to cool my pained jaw and lips and wash away the blood.

Nearby, an old willow trailed slender leaves into the water. Hawk Feather paced along, peering up into the branches. "Ah. There it is," he said to himself. The tree had a low-hanging limb, which he seized with both hands. In a moment, he was into the tree. His legs dangled, then disappeared into the green. Something dark dropped to the ground before

Hawk Feather's legs appeared again. A paddle, another, and finally a small black birch canoe descended prow-first.

We paddled past small islands in the stream, some only wide enough to hold a slim tree or two. After the islands, we paddled northward for two days. Then, the stream turned again to the east. Other streams joined it, until it became a narrow river rushing toward the ocean again. Then we turned into another northbound stream. The banks grew so close that little light penetrated the overhanging branches, making it hard to be certain which branches belonged to which side. The river seemed cavelike, darkened by tall shadows.

Leafy bushes hung over the bank, their roots half-exposed in the river mud. One such was laden with clusters of bilberries. Moss and pine needles gave a spicy scent to the damp air. Green oozed upon the smooth rocks below the canoe. We bumped into them, but, being smooth, they did not tear the craft's shell. Hawk Feather pulled to land, holding his craft still while I removed all the berries I could reach, packing them away in my gather pouch.

The river widened and deepened. Its surface appeared calm, except for the ripples and slaps against the bark sides of Hawk Feather's craft. There was the faint sound of the paddle's descent and the small drips as it rose again. Night insects began to buzz as they became more active. I slapped a mosquito away. A red-winged black bird darted by, showing a flash of color before it disappeared into the reeds under the gathering darkness. A pair of loons, unseen in the gloom, began their night songs. I continued to ply my paddle, numb with fatigue. A black mother bear and her cub watched the canoe until it drifted out of sight.

I was thinking we would have to stop soon, when my ears caught a new sound above the dip and swing of the paddles. A solitary cougar lapped water amid the shadows. As we passed close, he lifted his head, jaw dripping. Intelligent yellow eyes peered into mine, curious, perhaps, about the strange creature our craft seemed to be, floating on water with two legs and two heads. The cougar had not yet moved from the spot when the canoe turned the bend.

The first stars sprinkled the sky when Hawk Feather said, "Keep the boat steady and away from the current." The water pulled heavily against my blade, but my arms had strengthened from pounding corn. I looked behind and saw my master squint, peering through the undergrowth as if watching for a familiar place. I fought down the urge to bring the paddle down over his turned head. "Here," he said, his voice coming out of the near darkness, startling me. He propelled us toward the bank, tying the canoe rope to a convenient tree.

Before sleep, Hawk Feather had me kneel with my head upon my arms. Although I remained silent, my fear gnawed at me. If his sachem complained I was already with child before I became his, would Hawk Feather claim I had tempted him? If I ran again, he had no dog to smell me out, but he had frightened me too thoroughly with his descriptions of what he would do if I tried to escape. Sure he would do as he threatened, I made no attempt. My former mistress had been right. Compared to my new master, she had been kind. This one made my flesh crawl even before he touched me. In any case, I was no longer a foolish girl. There were too many enemies between myself and my home.

When he was done with me, I crawled into the shallow stream and allowed the cold water to rush over me. If only I could ride the current south like a twig or a fallen leaf, I thought. Something brushed by my leg, a frog or a snake. I shivered, pulled myself out, and dressed again. The cold cleared my mind, alerting my senses, for I could see almost as well by the full moon through the tall trees as I would have by the predawn sun.

I wandered the perimeter of the campsite, looking for raspberry leaves to brew for tea. Ferns brushed against my legs as I walked. I paused and sniffed at familiar-looking foliage. Garlic grew beside large orange mushrooms. I gathered them into the apron of my dress.

Against dark clumps of jagged deer fern and milkweed, I recognized the distinctive leaves of woman's root. I greeted it like an old friend. It could help me now. All of my aunt's instructions returned to me at once. Exulting in the one bit of good fortune that had happened to me since the day I was captured, I gathered the plant up carefully, tenderly, saving every leaf whole, and tucked it inside my dress.

At first light, I blew up the fire and set a clay bowl over the coals to cook our morning meal. I had crumpled woman's root leaves in my mug, preparing to steep it in the hot water. "What have you got there?" Hawk Feather asked after a morning swim.

"Food things," I said.

"Let me see." I showed it all, hoping he would not recognize the woman's root leaves between the garlic and the mushrooms.

"What is this one?" He picked out the unusual leaves with their oddly shaped root and lifted it.

"Woman's root," I said in my own language. "Good for eating. Good for tea. Like mint."

He lifted one arm, the side of his hand ready to descend. "Say it in my words or be quiet. You'll taste anything you cook before I eat it. Remember that."

I couldn't have said the plant's name in his language if I'd wanted to. "Mint?" I asked. "I don't know your word."

He snorted but left me to my task. I chewed a small bit of root and spit it into both mugs for good measure, pouring simmering water over them. While it steeped, I cut the mushrooms and some dried meat into a wide-lipped clay pot. To this, I added cut garlic leaves and bulbs. I let that cook and reached for my tea mug. Hawk Feather watched me suspiciously.

"You drink first." The tea was strong and bitter, like brewed willow bark, which fights pain and cools fevers. I had not known how it would taste, but I breathed in the steam as though it were pleasing. I sipped, then downed half my tea before he tasted his.

"That's not mint; it's Mohawk piss!" he exclaimed, and spat it out. "Never give me this again. Get me plain water."

I dipped his mug into the stream and brought it to him. After that, he would not suspect the tea I'd made was poison. I kept the leaves and made the same tea several more times, brewing it strong. I wrapped fresh moss around the roots to keep them alive and dampened them often, since I intended to plant them alongside his town. We continued upriver for another day, coming to a small village toward evening.

To their questions, he replied, "She's my Mohawk slave." He warned the villagers that people from a recently established settlement several days south would pass their way shortly, probably within the month.

A woman stared at me boldly. "So that's a Mohawk," she mused, reaching up to cup my bruised chin. I was taller than she. Her son reached out to touch me, then hesitated, looking toward his mother for permission.

"Go ahead," Hawk Feather coaxed. "She won't hurt you. I've tamed her." The children laughed and poked while I did my best to ignore them.

That night, Hawk Feather did not touch me. His hostess gave me corn gruel in the morning. Only one more day's travel need be endured. Still believing I was to be turned over to the sachem, I consoled myself that an older man might not be as cruel as Hawk Father or have need to brag about taming me.

His home cornfields were visible before the wigwams. Alert dogs ran up to us, barking their warning. They soon recognized Hawk Feather and sidled up to be petted, pushing their noses into his hands. They sniffed me curiously, but no longer showed their teeth, for I must have smelled of him. Hawk Feather's was a large town—four hands of dwellings—in a clearing as large as Doteoga.

A stocky man with gray-streaked black hair approached through the gathering people, walking directly to Hawk Feather. His buckskin leggings with fringes flapped as he strode over. Looking through his colored quill-decorated open jacket, I saw scars crossing his chest. His painted and dignified face spoke for him. Here was an elder and a chief, what these people called a "sachem," or "sagamore."

"Welcome home, Hawk Feather," he said. "Sit beside me and tell me about your journey." He lowered himself to the ground and sat cross-legged while the people backed away to give them room to converse. Hawk Feather sat also.

I backed almost to the people. "Thank you, Red Squirrel," the younger man said. "The new town is three days south, quite close to the southern end of the peninsula. It was a long journey, shortened by traveling cross-country along the river. I completed your mission successfully."

"So? What did you learn about the newcomers?"

"I spent a night with their sachem, Lone Stag. His people lived beside Long River. They say they've been here before," he said. "Lone Stag accepted your wampum and his elders agreed to your offered peace. When they visit in two hands of days, Lone Stag claims he will trade with us. They hope to make matches for their young women looking for husbands, and to meet our maidens. To seal the friendship we offered, they will bring gifts for you at that time."

"That is good. Why did they leave their former home?" He was keeping the conversation to generalities and had not mentioned me yet. My new master appeared to be a patient man, more patient than Hawk Feather, who was almost imperceptibly fidgeting under his sachem's scrutiny.

"They were recently attacked by Mohawk warriors. With great valor, they chased them back across the river." The people pushed close to hear the news.

"So why did they leave, then, since they were victorious?"

"Too many died to risk another battle soon. Also game fled the area. The elders seek a new beginning, for their families to raise their children away from marauding Mohawk warriors, who, as all know, are thieves and killers. They intend to stay several years."

Red Squirrel nodded. "I see. It was good that I sent you to visit these neighbors. Lone Stag sounds like a thoughtful man who sees to his people's welfare. Have you nothing to say about this quiet girl who listens so intently?"

Hawk Feather cleared his throat. "She's a Mohawk girl. I found her on the beach beneath their hill and took her up the hill to show to Lone Stag. It turned out she was his captive, caught in the war. She has no name, but she answers to 'Mohawk Girl.' She's hardly worthy of your attention. Lone Stag said she was a worthless slave to his wife, lazy, barely able to speak. He gave her to me for delivering your message of peace."

I gasped. He had lied, saying I was his. He made no mention of the deal he had made with my previous master. Hawk Feather attempted to bring the conversation back to the awaited visit, but Chief Red Squirrel's eyes bored into mine. I discovered I could not look away. I hoped he would accuse Hawk Feather of lying. It was so obvious.

"I see," Red Squirrel replied. I know he saw more than Hawk Feather had told him. "So. They will bring gifts when they come. That explains why they sent nothing now to seal the peace between our two towns."

I looked to Hawk Feather, wondering how he would twist his words next. He dared not make an enemy of his sachem. "That is right. They had nothing prepared because they did not know I was coming. I'm sure they will bring many gifts when they visit us."

The older man's eyes narrowed. Warmth rose into my cheeks at the false words I heard, but I dared not speak. "So," Red Squirrel said softly. "I thought you found a wife among our neighbors, but you took this Mohawk slave to get her off their hands. She's quite young, just a girl, by her appearance." He rose to his feet and stepped closer. "Do my eyes fool me or is she a woman?"

Hawk Feather could do nothing while Red Squirrel touched my face with one finger, drawing it lightly across the scabs. "Don't be afraid of me. I won't harm you, child," he said. "Have you learned to speak our words?"

"A little," I replied.

"What is your name?"

"The Algonquin call me 'Mohawk Girl.' "

"You have no name?" I lowered my head rather than answering. His gentleness was too unexpected and threatened to bring water to my eyes. "Or none that you wish to tell. I understand. Answer a different question, Mohawk Girl." He was actually talking to me, not to Hawk Feather. "When were you captured?"

"A circle of seasons ago, when the leaves started to turn."

Red Squirrel nodded. "Rumors tell of a war between the longhouse people. We hear many have died, too many to bury. It is said that Onondaga, Oneida, and Mohawk are killing one another. The rumors say our enemies will be dead in another circle of seasons. Is that true, Mohawk Girl?"

"No," I cried. "It can't be so."

"Would you touch white wampum and give me the same answer? I wonder." I saw now what the others must have seen. Red Squirrel had not been fooled. He knew his envoy had handled the white wampum he sent for a present and peace offering.

"I could not lie touching white wampum," I whispered. Though Hawk Feather would beat me for it, I had to speak the truth as far as the question Red Squirrel asked me. "There must never be an end to the Haudenosaunee."

"What is 'Haudenosaunee'?"

"Longhouse people. My people. Those you call Mohawk and the others. Fighting between us must end. The longhouse people together will fight and kill all Algonquin." I put my hand to my mouth in horror, for I had said more than I'd intended and had imparted a warning for the future he might not have guessed.

"I will punish her for saying that, Red Squirrel," Hawk Feather said.

Before Hawk Feather could lead me away to his wigwam, Red Squirrel said, "Don't be too hard on her. She's alone among enemies, but brave enough to speak what she perceives as true. I value honesty in those I lead. Since you have already taken your reward, I need not give you more." He turned away and left Hawk Feather standing there.

My master clutched my elbow and pulled me angrily away from the throng of people. They made a path for him, stepping out of his way. "Hawk Feather." A gentle-voiced woman stepped up to us.

My master stopped short. "Mother."

It hardly seemed possible he had a mother, but there she was, soft-featured, and with a long gray braid over her left shoulder. "Welcome home, son," she said. "Have you taken a wife from the new village?" She could not have heard the conversation.

"The southern sagamore gave her to me. She's a captive Mohawk, a savage who barely speaks our language." The lie slipped off his tongue. "She is called Mohawk Girl. She's lived with them a year and still knows next to nothing. They were glad to be rid of her."

The woman glanced at me again, then looked at her son and pursed her lips. "In any case," she said, "it's good that you're home. I made a new breechclout for you, and leggings and a parka. Also moccasins. Yours must be worn after your journey. I left them on your bed. Why don't you put them on and come eat in my wigwam. There's enough rabbit and pumpkin stew for your slave, too. Red Squirrel's sons brought me meat while you were gone."

Hawk Feather nodded and told her he would join her shortly. When we reached his low wigwam, he gestured me to get inside. "You speak our language too well," he said angrily. "I ought to beat you for what you told Red Squirrel, but there's no time now. My mother is waiting. Be glad you said nothing more."

I consoled myself by thinking that when Lone Stag and his people came, the truth would have to surface. They would tell Red Squirrel of Hawk Feather's deception.

My master hung his weapons and pack on the wall. I found a hook and, after emptying my burden basket, did the same. There was only the one bed in the small wigwam. I laid down my bedroll opposite his on the floor and waited. He removed his leggings and kicked out of his breechclout, then slipped on his new clothing. I wondered if he was inclined to leave me behind, but before he ducked out of the low entrance, he said, "Be careful what you say, even to Down of a Duck, or you'll hurt for it. Follow me."

I crawled out of his wigwam and walked behind him to his mother's. People greeted him, asking questions. Apparently, little of what was spoken before had been repeated. He recited the same lies. People nodded pleasantly and walked on to their destinations.

His mother was a widow and shared her small home with two other old women. The other two were out, but I saw their beds and belongings. No weapons hung from the walls. We had barely entered before Hawk Feather poured out his complaints. "Red Squirrel didn't invite me to eat and smoke in his wigwam. He had more to say to this slave than to me. Is that proper gratitude for the days I traveled, for the risks I took?" His mother made no reply, merely ladled meat into his bowl and handed him a carved spoon. He blew over his food and ate.

"I am called Down of a Duck," she told me, half-filling a second bowl and handing it to me with a wooden spoon. I glanced down, then back to her. She smiled, answering my unspoken question. "I have already eaten, Mohawk Girl."

The stew was as good as anything Aunt Makes Good Soup might have cooked. Comfort and warmth emanated here, where I had expected nothing but harshness and loathing. Algonquin mothers must have little to do with raising their sons, I thought. I licked my empty spoon and she gave me more.

The following day, while I was pounding corn, several young women exchanged confidences nearby. I did not wish them to know I understood, so I did not look up. I attempted to make out their words over the thumps of my pounder. One said, "Since he brought the Mohawk Girl, he won't ask my father again to give me to him. He's not a person a woman can live with. Look at that poor girl. Her nose is swollen and her chin is bruised. Both of her eyes are black. I wonder if he's knocked out any of her teeth yet."

Of course, I kept up the pretext of not understanding and continued lifting the pounder and bringing it down hard. The dried corn kernels became meal and sifted through the holes on the bottom of the hollow log to the mats around it. From time to time, the girls gathered the meal into sacks, then returned to their gossip. As before, I pretended not to be listening.

After awhile, one of them said, "If you married him, his slave would belong to you, too. You wouldn't have to work so hard. She'd cultivate your corn hills for you and pound cornmeal in your place." Her friend added, "Your father was good to give you a choice, though. I was afraid Hawk Feather might ask for me when you refused him." They spoke as though I could not understand a word of their conversation.

"No decent woman would live with him. It's better that he have a slave to serve his needs. Hawk Feather has a temper; that's sure. Did you hear he kicked his hunting dog when it tasted the deer it helped him bring down? Poor thing. It was hungry. He broke its ribs and ended up having to kill it."

"He's a liar, too. Everyone knows it now, but no one calls him on it."

I managed to hear most of that sentence before I lifted the pounder again, but I missed the next few words. "The Mohawk Girl is the best he'll ever get. If the southern village knew him better, they wouldn't—" They glanced my way, but I kept my eyes downcast and continued pounding.

"Of course they would. Even if it's Hawk Feather, she's still a Mohawk girl. Surely, it's no more than she deserves, coming from those people. I wouldn't want to fall into the hands of such savages." I kept pounding.

Still, these young women looked at me with more sympathy than hate. I kept working. "Poor little Mohawk Girl," one of them said. "It's best that she can't understand. She's still so young. It must be so hard to lose your family and everything you know." To be pitied by my enemies was nearly as bad as being reviled, but I kept pounding, as though I hadn't comprehended their words.

Chapter 11

To the people of Hawk Feather's town, so far from Ganeogaono Country, my people populated tales of terror. I doubt they imagined that their first "Mohawk" would be a slim young woman, rather than a ferocious warrior with dripping fangs. At least I was easier on their eyes than the other would have been. After their first surge of curiosity was settled, no one was cruel to me, except, of course, for my master.

One day, while I harvested cranberries at the salt marsh, a handful of children confronted me. Pressing together for courage, they whispered and poked each other, until a boy of perhaps six summers spoke. "Are you *really* Mohawk?" His voice squeaked a bit on the hated word.

With none but children to hear me speak, I replied as well in his words as I might. "Mohawk is a bad name." I refused to define myself by one terrible horror of war and its retribution. "We are Ganeogaono, Possessors of Flint." I gave them the exact translation into Algonquin of the name Ganeogaono.

"She says she's not a Mohawk. Maybe Hawk Feather is wrong about it," one little girl commented to her companions.

"I never heard of Ganeogaono," an older girl said. "I wonder if they live near Mohawk Country, so Hawk Feather mistook her for one."

"Did the Mohawk warriors eat all your people?" another child asked, wide-eyed and sympathetic. "Is that why you were alone on the beach when Hawk Feather found you?"

"There are no Mohawk," I persisted. "We are Ganeogaono. My people live in clans. Our houses are large enough for many people to live together."

The first boy curled his lip and pouted, gravely disappointed and miffed. "Everyone says you're Mohawk. I thought you were real." He stuck his thumb in his mouth and began to suck, consoling himself.

They *wanted* me to be Mohawk. For the first time in so many moons that I lost count, I felt myself begin to smile. My shoulders shook at the irony. I turned my face so they would not see me lose control, but soon, peals of laughter bubbled up out of my throat. I snatched a peek at the children's shocked expressions. They did not know what to make of my mirth, or my gasps for breath. It seemed improbable that I could ever laugh again after so long. My cheeks hurt.

The first girl backed away at my helpless efforts to control myself. They must have thought me odder than before. Then she giggled, and soon, the rest joined in. My sides ached. "You *want* me to be Mohawk!" I gasped. When I gained control and could speak normally, I asked shyly, "Do you want to help me pick cranberries?" They all helped.

Soon, both my leather carry pouches were full. With the children's sympathy, even my labors did not seem so bad. Of course, missing my family still stung. If only there were a way for my master to lose himself on a hunting trip, to fall into a crevice or a cave where he might be eaten by a hungry bear, I might have been able to tolerate my life.

We left the marsh, climbing the twisting trail up the hill. When we reached the clearing, the children said good-bye and scattered to their different dwellings. The sight of Hawk Feather's small wigwam brought back the gnawing feeling to the pit of my stomach, as if a bird had pecked at it from the inside. My scalp twitched. He was away, but soon he would return.

His long bow and quiver had been taken from their hooks on the lodge pole. I sighed in relief, grateful for some time by myself, free from his demands and punishments. I set my pouches of cranberries down, arranged the furs and baskets neatly, and swept the floor. In the fire pit, embers still glowed faintly in the banked coals under a powdering of pale ashes. I built up the small fire to prepare the evening meal, adding cranberries to the cornmeal mush in a baked clay pot. I stirred in maple sugar and water, swallowing a few mouthfuls, then set the gruel to bake. The nights were short. I had begun my work in the fields at sunrise and gone cranberrying afterward. Tired, I curled on my bed to rest.

"Mohawk Girl. Come out here!" Hawk Feather's voice called from outside. My eyes snapped open. I shook the sleep from my head and dropped to my hands and knees so as to crawl through the flap.

My master and his friend, One-Eyed Snake had just gotten there. Each man carried one end of a spear shaft on which a slain yearling elk had been impaled. They set down their burden. "I need you to butcher it," Hawk Feather said. "Go borrow my mother's skinning knife and hurry back."

I made haste to do as he commanded, running to the other wigwam. "Down of a Duck," I called at the flap. "It is Mohawk Girl. May I enter?"

When I told her the purpose for my visit, she handed me the knife without hesitation. "I'd best walk you back to my son's wigwam before anyone thinks you took it without permission." Down of a Duck paused to get her walking staff, moving slowly. The joint disease made it difficult for her to walk without it. I was grateful, but anxious that I would not be fast enough to avoid a beating.

Hawk Feather changed his expression when he saw his mother hobbling beside me. "Greetings," he said formally.

"You had good hunting, my son. My friends will be pleased for the meat." She nodded appreciatively at the carcass. "It's a young buck."

He nodded. "One-Eyed Snake gets a third. I'll bring you your portion and your knife in the morning," he said.

"If you send Mohawk Girl with the cleaned hide, I'll sew you a warm shirt and leggings for winter. Good night." She nodded, then hobbled off.

"Divide it, Mohawk Girl," Hawk Feather said as she walked way. "Be careful not to damage the hide." The carcass had already been split from neck to crotch and the offal removed. The elk had not been dead long, less than half a day. Perhaps its spirit remained nearby. While I crouched to my work, my master and his friend entered the wigwam.

The large glazed-over eyes stared pitifully and the tongue protruded from the open mouth. I closed its eyes, brushing away flies and whispered to the elk's spirit. "You are free to go now."

While I carefully stripped away the hide, Hawk Feather and One-Eyed Snake scooped food out of the cooking bowl. The smell teased my nostrils, almost covering the smell of the blood. I should have eaten more while I could. Through the open flap, I saw them eating the cranberry and maple—flavored gruel, then playing over a marked game tray at the plum stone game.

Before I was finished carving the meat into sections, One-Eyed Snake and Hawk Feather came out to watch me work. Another of his cronies sauntered over and idled with them. The sun had sunk low between the trees. People wandered home from forest and stream, pausing to watch, then continued on home. The good smells of supper were in the air. This was the first time Hawk Feather had let me use a knife. His shadow fell cold across my shoulder, cutting off my light. From time to time, I glanced around, wishing that he would go away.

One man left, but Hawk Feather and One-Eyed Snake remained near. Each time I glanced over my shoulder, he was intent on my bloody arms and hands. His breathing quickened when I severed a tendon. His eyes followed when I moved to the other side. I bent again to my work, but I could not fail to see in the corner of my vision how his tongue played over his parted teeth.

By then, my dress and all my exposed skin were sticky with blood and gore. It was on my face as well, since I'd scratched my cheek and brushed flies from my nose. I tried to hurry, for the sky grew dark. I wanted to take the chunks inside and go to wash in the stream. The meat needed to be kept away from the dogs, or they would gulp it down before I could hang it to dry in the morning.

I dragged in the butchered meat, wrapped it carefully, and made ready to run to the stream, when I heard talking just outside. "She's done, and she didn't tear the hide," One-Eyed Snake said. "She's going to the stream now to wash. Why don't you come inside so we can finish our game?"

His friend's voice startled Hawk Feather, but he continued to wait, arms crossed over his chest. "Do you know that Mohawk women fight alongside their men? She might have come from a battle covered with Algonquin blood, looking as she does right now." His friend gave him a long, doubtful look. "It's quite true," Hawk Feather continued. "The stories say so. Show us a Mohawk warrior's dance, Mohawk Girl," he commanded.

"I am not permitted. I am a woman," I said at once. My hand tightened around the grip of Down of a Duck's butchering knife.

"I said women are warriors among the Mohawk. The men plant the corn. Don't contradict me. I have given you a command. Dance." If I were not so frightened, I would have asked if men bore the children, as well. At first, I might have fooled him with a woman's dance, but it was too late for that. I'd already told him I could not comply. Hawk Feather often pretended I had given reason to justify his punishments, but of all his tricks, this was the worst.

I remained still, poised to run for the stream, as though I had not heard. He baited me, waiting for me to refuse. I could not think what to do to avoid a new beating. "Yes, dance for us," agreed his friend. "I would like to know how your people dance for war."

When I shook my head desperately, Hawk Feather panted. He was working himself into a rage. No matter; I must refuse. "No, my master," I said as with as much deference as possible. "I can't."

"Did you say 'No'?" Hawk Feather's voice rose as he stretched out the words. He slapped my face with his open hand. The shock forced me to let go of the flint, which my hands yearned to plunge into his purple face.

He might have seen my fingers clench, sticky with blood, for he hit me again. The blow knocked me to the ground. Without thinking, with no knowledge of what I intended, or any plan at all, I ran. I needed to be away from pain and humiliation. Somehow, I found myself at the opening to the sachem's wigwam, with Hawk Feather and One-Eyed Snake almost at my heels.

With no invitation, I ducked and then crawled into the large wigwam. Red Squirrel's wives stared. Visiting men exclaimed and protested my intrusion. The chief, who sat near the fire, talking to another man, rose instantly at the commotion. I had breached etiquette, if nothing else, by barging in like this. I was a slave, someone with no status and no right to his protection, but if he would not aid me, no one could. No matter what Hawk Feather did, I would not dance a man's war dance for the amusement of my enemies.

My master called from outside the entry flap. "My Mohawk Girl seeks to escape her punishment. May I enter, Red Squirrel?"

"Come inside, Hawk Feather," said the sachem. "What is the cause of this tumult on such a peaceful evening? If we are at war, why has no one informed me?" He gestured toward me, all covered with gore and dried blood, where I knelt in a supplicating posture at his feet, then looked to my master.

"My slave was disobedient. It is nothing at all. I will take her away."

One-Eyed Snake had followed my master inside the large wigwam. Red Squirrel glared at both of them. "Does it take two warriors to chase down a helpless girl?" he asked. His gentle voice seemed more powerful for its softness. A moment had not passed before One-Eyed Snake wisely ducked out of the wigwam. "Tell me what happened, Hawk Feather," Red Squirrel said.

"A sachem does not rule between warrior and slave. The girl disobeyed me; that's all. She needs to be taught to do as she is told."

"You are here now, and I would like to know what is going on in my home and in this village. What was it you ordered her to do, Hawk Feather?" he asked. "She has never disobeyed you before, has she?" I had not moved from the spot, nor had I uttered a word out loud, but Red Squirrel was defending me.

"She has been slow and insolent before. This is worse. I commanded her to dance to amuse me. She refused."

Red Squirrel saw the splattered blood and gore, even on my face. "Did he do this to you, child?" he asked, his mild voice exuding quiet authority.

"It is only elk blood, Great Sachem," I replied.

"Rise and tell me what happened, Mohawk Girl," the sachem ordered.

I got to my feet, teeth rattling as I tried to piece the words together correctly. "He told me to do a Mohawk war dance. I am a woman. I must not do a man's dance." I did now know the word for *forbidden*.

Red Squirrel's wives and visitors waited for the sachem's decision. That he was judging between us elevated my status. Hawk Feather was not pleased at all. "A slave is for work, not dancing," Red Squirrel stated. "Remember that, and don't ask her to do a man's dance again."

So he had understood after all. He judged in my favor. To me, he added, "You have been butchering meat. Go and cleanse yourself, Mohawk Girl." I lowered my head respectfully, ducked out of his wigwam, and ran to the stream.

Hawk Feather followed a short while later. I saw him from the water. He did not speak a word to me as he stalked past, carrying his weapons and a sack of food. He did not return for two days.

The Algonquin planned an early harvest celebration. When the delegation arrived from the southern town, they were ready to receive them with new corn, beans, squash, and cranberries. My former master had led a small multitude to the northern town, several elders and warriors, perhaps as many as fifty people. During the visit, maidens and young men looked one another over. There was eating and speech making. Friendships were formed and gifts were exchanged while we ate turkey and corn and sweet maple sugar mixed with cranberries. During that time, Hawk Feather made himself scarce.

If anyone ever asked Red Squirrel how he enjoyed his new slave, I was not there to hear it. Of the visitors who remembered my time with them, there were none who showed any particular anger toward me now. My former mistress had not made the journey. Those who looked for me found me working silently among the other women. I went about my work quietly, serving and replenishing the bowls of meat and succotash.

After the visitors left, more of the harvest was brought in and prepared for winter. This town did not pick up and leave their cornfields. Being near the shore already, they were in the best location for the fish and seafood of spring.

Once the crops were in and all the meat dried for winter, even before the first snow, storytellers began to entertain the people at night. I was allowed to sit against a far wall and listen. Hawk Feather allowed me to attend, since he did not like leaving me unwatched.

One old storyteller brought her hand drum to the sachem's large wigwam, where there was plenty of room to gather. Many people crowded to hear her tell the stories and legends. Mothers carried small children wrapped in their blankets. Although everyone else pushed close, I kept alone in my dark corner. When she tapped her drum and began to speak, I closed my eyes so as to be able to "see" her stories as moving images.

My understanding of Algonquin words had increased. Listening to a legend-speaker reminded me of Grandmother's hearth in Wolf Longhouse and old Uncle Wind in His Ears. Even the stories were similar, though I needed to listen more carefully to the foreign words.

One night, the story had nothing to do with creation, the sky people, or how brave mortals defeated monsters. It concerned people who lived in her grandmother's time, she said, when Mohawk tribesmen first encroached on Algonquin lands. She had it backward, but I listened closely.

She began. "Not many have heard this tale. It happened during one of the many wars between the Mohawk and our ancestors; an Algonquin warrior was captured by Mohawk warriors in battle. He was young, handsome, and very brave. Because it took three Mohawk warriors to subdue him, he earned the respect of our enemies. The Mohawk chiefs decided not to kill him at once, but to save his killing for a festival to honor their Manitou. They intended to torture him by fire and eat his flesh, as everyone knows Mohawk do."

Many of her listeners in the close-packed group turned to me. I huddled in my small corner, trying to make myself invisible. I tried to slink even farther back into the shadows.

"The Algonquin was kept well guarded. His captors gave him the respect they reserve for the best of men. They provided him the softest of bed furs. Two times each day, the most beautiful woman of the village, a daughter of their war chief, brought him the best tidbits of meat."

I moved closer when she said "a daughter of their war chief." I was also a war chief's daughter. Had the storyteller woman learned something of my history from their visitors?

"The Mohawk maiden had fine, smooth skin, without blemish, and hair like a black curtain, down to her hips. Her eyes were like river-polished slate. The maiden and the warrior began to learn each other's words.

Sometimes, she lay with him in his furs, for he was supposed to enjoy life, so as to miss it the more when it was gone. When the maiden entered the place of his captivity, his eyes lit with joy, as if she brought the sun and his freedom as well as meat.

"She was proud of her beauty, proud that she was skillful enough to please him so well. One of her assigned tasks was to taunt him with how he would be burned, but a strange thing happened to her. The Mohawk woman's heart was moved by the prisoner. When she returned to her longhouse, she could not sleep. She thought only of his voice and his eyes. She could not help thinking the handsome Algonquin should not have to die. Her family would kill her if they suspected her thoughts, but she decided to free him.

"As the day for the festival and the Algonquin's death approached, the Mohawk maiden watched every moment for her chance. On the final night, she brought his guards a sweet berry drink, into which she had seeped sacred datura root. Soon, the guards slept, dreaming their magic dreams and paying no attention to their captive.

" 'They will not awaken until you are many miles away,' she said. 'I have drugged their drink. Come with me now and you will not have to burn,' she said, opening the flap to his wigwam and showing him. 'I'll lead you to freedom and we will live with your people. Do you think the Algonquin will hate me very much for being one of the enemy?'

"He put his arms around her tenderly, saying, 'They will not hate you, because you are good and beautiful, but if your father catches us, he will kill you for betraying your people. I fear for you. Better let them think I escaped myself.'

" 'My people will kill me in any case because of the sacred drug I gave your guards,' she protested. 'Even though you are my enemy, I love you. Don't you see that I must go with you? Let us leave now, or my death will be for nothing. If we run, we may yet escape the runners my father will send after us.'

"So they ran. At daybreak, when the priests came to take the Algonquin to the stake, they discovered the sleeping guards and the empty wigwam. The cry went up. Pretty soon, the Mohawk warriors and their tracking dogs were after the escaped brave and his Mohawk lover. The two ran until night. They were exhausted, and when they stopped, they discovered they were on the top of a cliff.

" 'Give yourselves up. There is no escape,' the Mohawk war chief called to them from below while his warriors closed in. 'We will give the Algonquin an easy death and permit the girl to live. She was befuddled and did not know what she was doing.'

" 'Go back to your father, beloved,' the Algonquin pleaded with the maiden. 'Save yourself. I will jump off the cliff before I let my enemies take me again.'

" 'No. I won't leave you,' she said. So they held hands and jumped over the cliff together. Their bodies were found in the morning, crushed and broken on the rocks below. They were still holding each other. The Mohawk war chief and his braves gathered up the lovers' bloodstained corpses and took them back to their village. When the priests heard how they had died, they agreed to bury them in one grave." She tapped her hand drum briskly. "That is how the story ends."

One girl, sitting near the storyteller, sobbed. She wiped her tears with her bed fur. Even some of the boys sniffed. Old women, who might have heard the story when it was new, shed tears at the sad ending. Several men appeared disturbed at this tale of enemies finding love together. I had never heard of a story where the heroes died. Even so, this had been successful storytelling. The listeners' reactions left no doubt of that.

I wondered why the old woman had chosen to tell such a legend. A boy and girl crept over to me in the corner. The girl draped an arm over my shoulder and touched her cheek to mine, as though I were the war chief's dead daughter. At last, I realized what the storyteller had done. She had used her words to gain sympathy for me, but I could not begin to guess why.

The storyteller woman sipped tea from her mug. Then she told another story, this time a familiar favorite. By then, since the children were beginning to yawn, she said it was enough. Hawk Feather left after the first story and had long been gone by the time the others picked themselves up off their mats and hides. The visitors withdrew, returning home to their warm beds. Before she left, the old woman motioned to me. I followed her out of the cozy wigwam and over the frost-covered earth. The moon hung low over the naked branches about the village. We stopped under the moon-cast shadow of a large spruce tree.

I never learned the woman's name. She was old, older, perhaps, than my grandmother, and had gaps between her teeth. Her white hair was tangled as last summer's bird nest, but her wrinkled face and creased eyes spoke of wisdom. "Mohawk Girl," she said. "You understood every word of my stories. The children tell me things they don't tell their parents. I know."

"Yes," I whispered. "I understood."

"Speak to me, then."

I did not know what she wanted of me, what she expected me to say. "My master is cruel, not good and brave."

"Cruelty on both sides is why our peoples hate each other. If good is spoken as well as bad, perhaps that can change. Think how my people cried at the story. Many here wish you well, but we can do little for a slave, except perhaps to allow you to escape."

At the word *escape,* I held my breath, not daring to hope it would happen. The old woman stroked my hair with her rough, calloused hand. "He's not likely to change his ways, but no one else here will trouble you. You are his to command, except for dancing. Everyone has guessed you were not meant for him, but Red Squirrel won't interfere. It would detract from his dignity."

"This is a bad dream. I want to wake up in my mother's longhouse," I said, my eyes stinging and growing moist with unshed tears. Her sympathy reached out and covered me like a warm cloak to keep out the cold.

"I had a daughter once," the storyteller woman said. "She died. Life is hard." I believe she was saying there was no hope for me to return to my own country. I nodded slowly. "I think you will not see your home again," she added. "They will look for you to run south. Don't."

Then she did a strange thing. She came close and put her arms around me as a mother or a grandmother might do, then placed her old moccasin beside my ragged one, as if measuring the difference. Her voice was softer than a breeze between summer leaves. "When you can no longer bear it, there will be a warm coat, moccasins, food, and a knife in a hollow oak tree three oaks east of the first bend on the northern trail. If you run, go north, but cover your trail as you leave. It is your only chance." She took her arms from me then, but the warmth lingered even as I saw her walk away. She became small in the distance as she made her way among the wigwams and entered her own.

A few days later, when I returned from gathering roots and cranberries to cook with the evening meal, I found Hawk Feather feeding my dried leaves and roots of the woman's root plant to the fire. "Give me the rest of them, Mohawk Girl," he demanded. He had found my hiding place. My feet had grown roots and I could not move. He grabbed my shoulders and shook until another leaf slipped out of my dress.

He pulled the dress over my head and threw the leaves that fell out into the fire. "I showed One-Eyed Snake what you use to make your tea. He said it makes your woman's blood come. You're a worthless Mohawk slave. You are mine to do with as I wish. I decided to breed a son out of you. Do you think an Algonquin isn't good enough to start a baby in your belly?"

His face grew purple, like a summer plum. Given the heat of his wrath, I thought it would catch fire. This was not like his anger over the war dance. He wanted to force me to bear him a child, and without my special tea, I had no protection. I backed to the wall of the wigwam and sunk to my knees, with my arms covering my head, knowing what was coming.

Lifting his longbow from the wall, he began to cudgel my back with it. I curled, rolling sideways. He kicked me once in the stomach, then rolled me to my back with one foot. He would not kill me or destroy that part of me he wanted to use. I could not keep from crying out, for the pain burned like fire, taking my breath. As I twisted and writhed, the blows descended upon my breasts and shoulders. His next blow slammed me into the wall.

"Mohawk Girl," he shrieked, and dropped to the ground to press himself into me. "You'll not kill another son of mine, do you hear?" Each time he spoke, he smacked his hips against my bleeding back and buttocks. At last, the sounds faded away. I had sunk to the floor, senseless.

He must have taken me many times that night, but everything seemed as if it were far away and happening to someone else. Gray, fuzzy light drifted all around me like a thick fog. A flute played a haunting melody somewhere, reminding me of my youth. My father appeared before me and lifted me into his protecting arms.

"This is how the warriors stay silent, isn't it, Father? I always wanted to ask you. Have I discovered their secret?"

"This is how the warriors do it, Picture Maker. They visit the spirit world and feel nothing of what is done to them."

"But am I only visiting? I have died, haven't I, Father?" I asked. The fog lifted and the sun shone golden light all around. Fat meat sizzled on a nearby spit and berries the size of plums grew close at hand between the heavy limbs of bent trees. "This is what it is like to be with Great Spirit Orenda."

"Rest with me here a little while. Soon, your strength will return," my father said. "That much, Orenda will grant—for your wounds to heal quickly. You must return to life. It's not time for you to die."

"But I want to stay here and be with you, Father," I pleaded. "Why must I go back to my enemies?"

My father smiled dangerously, his teeth brilliant white in his dusky face.

"The man who used you so badly deserves to die. Never forget that you are my daughter and the granddaughter to Wolf Clan Mother. That man has forfeited his right to live. Great Spirit Orenda charges you to perform the deed. Go back now. I will lend you my strength to do what must be done. You are an instrument of justice."

When my eyes opened, I found I had returned to Hawk Feather's wigwam. The pain from my cuts and bruises was already lessening and my teeth felt tight in my jaws. I hurriedly put on my dress, leggings, and moccasins. I set my master's small bow and quiver of arrows beside his back carrier.

Hawk Feather slept several paces from where I had lain senseless. His slumbering breaths came in ragged growls as his chest rose and fell. I guided myself by touch in the dark to where his leggings had fallen in his fury. His flint knife remained in its sheath.

The banked coals and hazy moonlight over the smoke hole were enough to see by. I had never killed a human, but my mind was calm. More than my own strength was in me. The flint's wooden grip fit well to my hand. I touched the blade lightly with my thumb to find its cutting edge. With care, I crouched, positioned it, and made deep slices, two times, to be sure. I backed away as air hissed from his throat and blood spurted out of the artery in his neck.

Hawk Feather's eyes opened. His mouth contorted with pain and words he could not say. With his last strength, he jumped to his feet and started toward me, but I was beyond his reach. Like a falling tree, he fell full length to the floor, over the banked ash-covered coals in the fire pit.

He writhed, trying to push himself away, but he did not get far. The noises he made as his life bubbled and hissed away might have troubled me if it had been anyone else. Down of a Duck would mourn him, although I doubted even she would blame me. Red Squirrel's sons would hunt for her. I wondered if I could pity a man I had slain. The answer came easily. Hawk Feather's cruelty deserved justice as much as any of those captives tied to the stake when our men returned from the Great War.

No matter how I might have gained the sympathies of the Algonquin, they would follow me to the edge of the earth. I might elude them at first, but eventually, they would hunt the northern lands and the legend of this night's deed would follow me. I would be in jeopardy anywhere their tongue was spoken.

If the storyteller woman's promised supplies were not yet in the old hollow tree, winter would kill me almost as fast as any pursuer. I had not yet come to my fourteenth year. I had little time to make preparations, needing to put as much distance between myself and this enemy town as soon as possible before they began the search, but I looked around the nearly dark wigwam.

I made a bundle of as much parched corn as I could find, placing it into Hawk Feather's back carrier. I took his leathern water bottle, which I could fill as needed. With weapons and carrier secured, I listened with heightened senses, then ducked out of my hated prison.

Still in my crouch, I paused at the flap of the wigwam. Dawn was far off, but there was frost in the air. No one walked in the dark emptiness between the wigwams. My master's body lay behind me in a spreading pool of blood. Before he was found, I must be long away. With a shudder at what I had done, and what I had yet to do, I left Hawk Feather's wigwam one last time.

Chapter

An upward glance revealed pale clouds floating over the clearing and the forest. One large cloud cast a veil over Grandmother Moon's face while I passed silently among the wigwams. A dog lifted his head for a moment, sniffing, as I padded by, but it did not bark. Only the sounds of crickets in the marsh and brush of an owl's wing could be heard as I entered the forest.

I had to move slowly through the darkness, feeling for the third oak east of the bend in the trail north of the town. A shiver danced along my spine, and cold sweat trickled under my ragtag fur. What if Hawk Feather *had* gotten me with child? The thought of bearing an Algonquin baby, his in particular, sickened me with a loathing more intense than any beating.

I drew in deep gulps of frosty night air to slow my racing pulse. Hawk Feather's last moments returned, raw and ugly, in my memory. My eyes had pierced the gloom of the small wigwam. Again, I could see his lips move while his black blood spurted and pulsed from the false smile below his chin. Be proud of me, Father, I thought grimly. Your youngest daughter killed another snake.

No thump of running feet pounded down the trail. I sent a prayer to Great Spirit Orenda and to my father to keep me from harm. Once more, I considered circling the town at some distance west, then turning south to look for the river. If nothing hindered me, I could be home in a month, two at most, before midwinter.

The storyteller woman had bought me time, and I dared not refuse her gift. As if we had spoken at length, I knew she would convince them I had run south. She had realized it would come to this, that I would have to kill him. Therefore, as she had bidden me, I would flee away from my country, rather than toward it. None would suspect that I had gone north, not with winter coming.

I found the third oak, knowing its rough-feeling bark, its skeletal broken limbs black against the gray night. The tree had once been great enough that a tall man could not reach around it and still touch the fingers of his other hand. Now the top half had fallen and rotted away. Dim, misty light helped me find the shadowy gap, chest-high on the decaying stump.

I reached into the hole cautiously. A tickling sensation against my hand and wrist told me I had disturbed some small many-legged creatures. When I snatched my fingers away, something dropped to my feet. It was too dark to see what it was, spiders or a family of mice. Something crawled away through the fallen leaves. My heart thumped louder in my chest.

Again, I reached in, prepared to pull back the instant my fingers encountered a snake or rodent. Instead, I felt the edge of smoothed, curved wood, with taut hide strips woven between. "Orenda, bless the storyteller," I prayed in an earnest whisper. "Give her long life, honor, and much meat." It was the heel end of a long snowshoe. Using both hands, I worked it loose. Its mate came out more easily. They had been tightly pressed against the inner surface of the tree.

When I reached into the hollow space again, I felt a strap secured to the inside on a jagged stump of inner bark. This, I pulled up, hand over hand, until it drew forth a soft hide-covered bundle. Feeling no more, I stashed the bundle in my carrier and fled northward up the trail.

The misty clouds uncovered the moon's face and vanished behind the southern trees. I followed the steady North Star, putting distance between myself and the place of my captivity. An hour or so of walking brought me to a split in the trail, one going east, the other north. Since I knew Algonquin tribes liked to winter near the coast, I determined to follow the inland trail. So deciding, I turned and headed north into the barely illuminated forest.

The reds and golds of the leaves on the autumn trees became visible in the morning light. Crisp breezes tore these from their perches, hiding any footsteps that might betray me. Somewhere, I had to find sanctuary before the searing cold of winter began in earnest.

My thoughts became jumbled and my legs ached too much to go on. I had to stop to catch my breath and rest a little. A short way off the trail, a doe and her fawn emerged from a sheltered thicket. I was downwind, where she could not smell me, but I was curious how close they would come toward me before the doe sensed danger. She lifted her nose and twitched her ears alertly, ready to run. With a bark and the stamping of her forehooves to warn her fawn, the pair bounded into the orange and gray shadows and disappeared.

A moment later, I had made myself snug under the leaves in the soft deer thicket, my wrap pulled up over my mouth and nose. No images of home and family teased my sleep this time. Neither did I behold an Algonquin warrior standing over me when I awoke. The noon sun poured warmth upon my blanket of leaves. From my sanctuary, I listened, like the doe had, for the sound of men. I lacked the eyes and ears of a deer, but the doe had not spied me until I was within killing range. The thick forest was my ally, if Orenda willed it. Having been allowed to live thus far, I suspected I might live longer.

Before I left the thicket, I pulled open the pack the storyteller woman left for me. On top were a pair of moose-hock stockings stitched to moccasins. I kicked off my ragged moccasins, setting them in my pack. I might have a long walk ahead of me. The winter boots fit perfectly. So that was why the old woman had put her foot next to mine.

The hide she had used to wrap the bundle could make a windbreak for my lean-to shelters. The warm parka she had promised was next. The pale fur was mink, an otterlike creature, with soft, warm fur. I thrust my arms through the sleeves, closed the ties, and pulled up the hood. At the end of the sleeves were leather thongs attached to mittens. The old woman could do more than tell stories. Inside the parka were several packages wrapped in cornhusks. On opening them, I found pressed berry cakes, shelled nut meats, parched corn, cord and fishhooks, and a skin of water. I drank and ate and drank again.

The final package was flat, wrapped well, and heavy for its size. Inside was a parfleche sheath with a knife. I withdrew it, staring in wonder at its oddness. Between grip and blade, it was a third the length of my forearm. The pale yellow grip took warmth from my hand, but I could not tell whether it was carved of horn or polished bone. Strange black designs were carved into it.

If the grip was odd, the blade was odder. It was fixed within the grip of the hilt. It seemed as though hilt and blade blended into one. The substance of the blade was another mystery. It felt colder than stone. The point and edge were sharp and slippery, neither chert nor flint. As I held it out toward the sun, the blade appeared opaque, with a gray sheen. I struck it across its surface with Hawk Feather's flint knife. Sparks flew, dying before they landed. There was magic here. I settled the knife pouch on its cord between my breasts, under my dress and parka, and slipped my flint knife into its sheath inside my sleeve.

While I walked along swiftly through the falling leaves, I strained to hear the sounds of men and dogs. Hunters would be out on such a day, but I saw and heard nothing. I could not keep from wondering about the knife blade. Wolf Cub Mother owned bracelets the color of oak leaves in autumn. They were copper, a substance that leaks out of rock when it is heated in hot fire. Western and southern nations know how to do this. If my knife was copper, this was another kind, for it was gray, like old ice.

Why had the storyteller woman given this treasure to me, a friendless Mohawk girl? Because her daughter was dead and she felt for my mother's daughter. I held her gift to my cheek for a moment. As though alive and responding to my thoughts, the blade turned warm.

All that day and the next, crossing creeks, running over fallen logs and around hills, along any trail that led northerly, no dog came to sniff me out, and no hunter found my hiding place when I slept. On the third day, it snowed. About midday, when the snow was past my ankles, I tied the snowshoes onto my boots and continued, keeping warm enough with the exercise.

I was able to take a winter-coated hare with my short bow and kill a goose with a broken wing during the next few days. The goose would have died in any case. I had saved it from a colder death and starvation. I thanked whichever spirits guarded this forest, and the animals who fed me, as well. That night, I lit a small fire for the first time since my escape. I hoped the smoke and light would not attract humans, but no one entered my camp. Before leaving, I buried every sign of my fire and raked a dry branch over the marks of my lean-to.

Between one full moon and the next, my arrows were spent, either broken or irretrievably lost. Without arrows, I thought, my death will come soon. My snowshoes kept me on the surface of the deep snow. Halfway through the following morning, I found a caribou doe trapped deep in the iced-over snow. She was half-frozen, waiting to die. With my knife's sharp edge, I ended her waiting. "Go to Orenda and be warm again," I whispered to her hovering spirit. "Please forgive me for killing you, but I am hungry."

Since I could not carry all the meat, I cut and packed what I could, leaving the rest for mountain cats and forest wolves. This became my habit when I hunted, always to leave some behind as a gift to them and the spirits who protected me. Perhaps it would suffice and the wolves of this northern forest would not attack me as I walked through their home. None did, although I heard soft growls from time to time, as though they were discussing me.

My small fires pushed the black world away. Throughout my travels, I never saw any of the monsters of legends I heard populated the forests. I never doubted they existed, but they did not fly out of the trees as I once thought would happen. Sometimes I saw reflecting yellow slits from behind the flames, and wolf silhouettes circling back into the nothingness behind a tree. Perhaps my clan spirit talked to these wolves, for it almost seemed that they protected me. I found paw prints on those mornings.

A moon's cycle passed. Although I saw snowshoe tracks, none was quite fresh. My father's spirit must have watched over me, keeping danger away. I told myself stories as I walked, whispering them just to hear my own voice, to remind myself I was human. I needed more than an animal's alertness to escape danger and find my next meal. It seemed to me I was alone in the world, having passed all the places of human habitation. I dreamed no memorable dreams during my journey, only wisps of faces and old conversations that faded with the day. Sometimes, I wondered if even the spirits had forgotten my existence. Only hunger and cold, as well as my unquenchable fear, pushed me to keep going.

I spied the black of a cave partway up the side of a mountain. My snowshoes gripped the surface, making it possible for me to climb high enough to see over the tops of the trees. The distance stretched out before me the way the Creator must see from the clouds. White land spread down and out from the mountain to the horizon, with fir trees the size of twigs stretching out in every direction. Clearings of emptiness, like islands in a river, told me people lived in this northern forest.

I climbed higher, watching for any dry-fall—a fallen bird's nest or a twig I might snap—to make a fire, for I sorely needed to rest. The distance confused me. By the time I returned to the cave ledge, mist and fog banks rose like wraiths from the valleys and crevasses of the mountain. It was hard to be sure whether I was seeing smoke or patches of fog. I set up my lean-to with the branches I'd kept, covering them with the hide the storyteller woman had provided. Grandmother Moon waited near the horizon. Only a few stars lit the sky, but bands of color hung close like curtains in the northern sky. Before the Moon of the Darkest Month appeared over the plain, I had built my fire.

I ate and rested for two days, waiting to regain some of my strength while snow continued to fall. When it ceased, I continued. At last, the time approached when I could go no farther alone. I had to find a village, a sign of habitation, or hunters on the trail. How I yearned to see another human face.

On the fifth day after my rest in the cave, I crossed the low eastern meadow of a mountain. Another snow began. I just had time to find the shelter of a huge pine and huddle under my skins on the lee side, out of the wind. There was no time to make a fire, nor had I caught or found anything to eat since the day before.

Snow blotted out the sky. When I awoke, I could neither see nor feel. Everything was gray. I thought I was dead once more, but my breath felt warm on my wrists. My stomach felt like a knot inside me. Since there is no pain or hunger in the spirit world, I realized I was alive. With a great heave, I pushed up and struggled to break through the snow. It shuddered, cracked, and opened, falling around me. The snow itself had kept me from freezing to death.

The graceful curtains of the northern lights draped closer. They were smaller at home, a blue or green smudge between trees. In the spruce forests of the north country, trees stood farther apart. Here, the lights moved across the sky, changing colors and vying with the moon for attention. Since the days were so short, I used their light to travel. The trails had been hidden under snow, but wherever there was a break in the forest growth to the coast, I used it.

After the blizzard, I lost track of time, sleeping often because of my hunger and fatigue. When I woke, I did not know whether night had come and gone again. The effort of walking with no food in my belly sapped my remaining strength. One time when I paused to rest, I dug under the snow with my hand, looking for fallen branches, but I found a snake instead. It seemed dead, frozen stiff. Some animals sleep through the worst of winter. I had not intended to stop for the day and make a fire, but I needed to eat. My coat hung loosely and I had hardly the strength to move my feet. I broke off the head as easily as snapping a branch. Inside, between my breasts, the snake soon thawed enough for me to penetrate it with my teeth. I saved half for the next day.

Even when I found food to eat, nausea threatened. I feared I was becoming sick. The cold and exhaustion were further weakening me and the loneliness was like nothing I had known. "Where is everyone?" I shouted.

A new storm began when the echo of my voice died away. I did not rest, but struggled instead, through the wind and the falling snow. The sky was the yellow-gray color of flint. Nothing intruded on the emptiness. I had not eaten since the day before and had no hope of finding food. Night was coming again, although it seemed the sun had barely cleared the southern horizon. Perhaps I was losing all sense of time. I gathered dead-fall, stretched the worn deer hide over the branches, and built a small fire.

The sky grew black again and the winds died away. The old crescent moon swam through the departing clouds. This was to be another night without food. I heard wolf song nearby. "Wolf Clan of this place," I said softly. "Let me live until morning." I wanted to see the sun once more, but if the wolves made a meal of my body afterward, I could accept my death with no complaint.

Exhausted, I slept. In my slumber, I heard the northern lights sigh and hum. I had not known that they could do that. The pack wolves sang, too, their voices weaving like strands of bark to form a basket.

In the morning, the sun cast rainbow lights against the crystallized snow. I was light-headed, but for once my stomach did not trouble me. Perhaps, it was used to not eating by this time. I washed my face with snow and swallowed some to ease my thirst before I slid into the straps of my pack. Wrapping the deer hide over my parka to add warmth, I turned to where I thought I had seen smoke rising. Dizzy and weak as I was, I needed to find people, no matter what language they spoke.

I walked against the wind, holding the skin in front of my mouth and nose to warm my breath. The searing cold had begun. I continued with only my eyes uncovered. I tripped and fell forward. My hand touched something soft and warm, a white hump hardly visible against the snow. Frozen blood stained the whiteness. It was a snow hare, its throat bitten through. The scarlet blood trail told me the hare had been dragged. There were wolf prints beside it in the snow.

My knife was out of its sheath in a moment. The stomach and liver had been torn out—a thing I had not noticed at first glance. The wolves had taken them and left me the rest, returning the gift of food I'd left for them earlier. Grateful, I lifted the small creature and silently thanked the Creator, the spirit of the hare, and the wolves, then cut deep into the flesh with my knife.

My fingers were almost too cold to move. With my teeth, I pulled my mittens away, warming my hands inside the hare before I bit into the raw meat. With my stomach full of rabbit, I felt a glimmer of hope that I would find shelter after walking alone for two moons and several days more. I gathered up my belongings and continued to where I thought I would find the coast and people to take me in.

Before the sun reached its zenith, I spied a frozen river and smoke rising from a small community of wigwams. If this village was Algonquin, I could hardly explain why I was wandering alone, and must not try. Only let them give me food and shelter, I prayed.

I stumbled up to the nearest dwelling. People at last. Several came to look me over. I sat on the snow and held out my hands to them to show my need.

"Who are you? Where do you come from?" a boy asked. His accent sounded different from those in Red Squirrel's town, but only as different as Onondaga is from Ganeogaono. The words he spoke were Algonquin. This knowledge hit me like a stone.

"It's a forest spirit," a girl said. "Maybe she was raised by bears like the boy in the story Grandmother told us. Do you think she can talk, Mama?"

"If she belongs to the bears, they must take her back," the woman declared. I thought they would leave me then, but the woman felt my face with her hand and looked into my eyes. "I suspect she's human, but she is so thin. Perhaps she's a ghost or a walking corpse." Fearfully, the children backed away.

"Don't go. Help me," I pleaded, forcing the words out. An older woman moved from behind the others and approached me. "I'm cold," I murmured, calling on my last strength to keep from fainting at her feet.

The woman touched my cheeks and neck. "Poor little one; you are like ice. She's not a spirit," she said to the others. "Let us take her inside. Build up the fire and pour some soup for her. We must make the poor creature warm before she slips away from us. Hurry!" I could hardly walk, but they helped me to my feet and led me into the nearest wigwam.

Naskapi

Chapter 13

I awoke slowly and painfully, bewildered at my surroundings. My toes and fingers ached in the surrounding warmth, the kind that occurs when heat reflects off walls. It slowly came to me that I was no longer lost in the forest and that a heavy fur had been pressed around me.

Embers in a stone-encircled fire pit glowed close by, and smoke plumed in a blue haze that rose toward an open patch of blue. The scent of spruce hovered in the small room, teasing my nostrils, sweet and sharp at once. It mingled with the scent of unfamiliar foods simmering over the hearthstones of the fire pit. Where food cooked, people were near. I feared to make any noise, unsure how I would explain myself.

I recalled white cold and the wind whistling through spruce trees. I had been closer to death than I knew, and now my memory returned in small pieces. There had been the excited voices of children, speaking together and pointing. The ringing in my ears must have muffled their words, for I could no longer recall them. A middle-aged woman, who seemed very like a clan matron, had practically carried me toward a low group of houses and fed me warm food. I must have slept after that, for I could recall no more.

A young woman tended a clay pot on a hearthstone beside the hot coals. She looked in my direction and let out an audible breath. "She's awake!" Sure enough, her words were Algonquin, although accented differently from those spoken in Hawk Feather's town. Warmth ached against my toes and fingers. I curled to look at her squarely, knowing I could no longer delay facing the people who had saved me. The woman hurried to where I lay. "I am called Still Water," she said. "What may we call you?"

My mouth opened, but in my confusion, I could not think how to answer. In spite of the trek that had almost killed me, I had not escaped Algonquin Country. "Maybe you'll find your voice later. You've slept long enough in any case. We thought you'd never get up," Still Water said. She hunched down and uncovered my feet, gently holding her fingers around my toes. "How do you feel now? Do they hurt?" She squeezed them gently.

"I . . . A little." My voice came out oddly and my throat felt tight in my chest. I waved my hands as if to indicate it was difficult for me to speak.

"You haven't stirred for more than two days. When you came, Mother said we might have to take off your toes. They were almost all black, but they turned pink again. You're lucky." I did not respond, my mind in a jumble as to how I ought to speak to her and how much I dared to say.

Two days, I thought. Another day in the forest would have cost me more than toes. The smell of food brought with it pangs of hunger. "Don't try to move yet," Still Water said, covering my feet again. "I'll be right back." She pushed aside the flap of the wigwam and ducked outside to the white world. "Mother. Come quickly. She's awake," I heard her call.

The older woman entered the wigwam and stood up from her crouch. She was tall and sturdy, smelling of wood and snow. She approached my pallet. "I'm Pine Tree Woman," she said, crouching down beside me. Her face was the color of bark. "Who are you?" she asked.

When I did not answer, she continued to gaze at me steadily. Her eyes burned like two flames, like the wolves on the other side of the fire. They put me in mind of the guardian wolf emblem I had made for Grandmother that long-ago spring. I tried to frame a question, to ask her where this village was, when I recalled what I had forgotten in my fatigue and desperation. In spite of the warmth and kindness of these villagers, I dared not stay. The silence in the room stretched out, except for the fire's crackle. I reached out to touch Pine Tree Woman. My fingers closed gently around her wrist; then I reached up to trace the lines of her cheek. She reminded me of the women of my longhouse. In spite of my training, I found my eyes had become moist.

"Are you feeling better, little one?" she asked, breaking the silence herself. When I nodded, she asked, "Are you ready to get up and take something to eat?" My thoughts must have been muddled. Without feigning, I managed to convey my confusion, but when I attempted to get to my feet, my stomach lurched. "Wait," she suggested, and brought me the covered basket. I let her help me to it gratefully. In spite of the gray streaking her braids, Pine Tree Woman looked younger than my grandmother. "Can you understand me?" she asked.

"Yes," I replied. I had to speak. She deserved no less. I knew her language, although I despised it.

"Did you lose your way among the trees when the storm came?"

I shrugged my shoulders and bit my lower lip. "I must have, but I don't remember," I said. My powers of speech and reason remained sluggish, for I could not think of a convincing story. How could I tell them I was an escaped Mohawk slave? I didn't know how to answer, so I remained reticent. I wanted to look outside, to see how many wigwams were in the village. How soon would word come north concerning the slave who had slain her master? It was true that my experience in the forest had clouded my mind, but I needed to tell them something about myself, and soon. I implored Great Spirit Orenda's direction to guide me in what I ought to say to these people.

"The girl's still dazed," Pine Tree Woman remarked to her daughter, who had taken the basket from me. I tried to get up, to follow her. "No, child. Don't try to go outside. I have marsh gruel heating. It will settle your stomach. After so long without eating, you need nourishment."

I did not know what kind of food she meant. While I reclined, watching her move about the small dwelling, she selected a small clay bowl from a shelf, then scooped something into it from the wide cooking pot on the hearth. It was gray and black, not cornmeal mush.

"Thank you," I said slowly, grateful she no longer pressed me for answers.

"Eat," she commanded. "We will talk later." I breathed in the steam from the food, wondering what sort of food it was. At my hesitation, she encouraged me. "The seeds came from my own bundles on the lake, where I gathered them into my canoe. The husks are scorched and winnowed well, so you won't find grit in your teeth. There are dried blueberries cooked with it." I took a bit off the spoon and rolled the black-and-gray food around on my tongue, trying to judge the flavor. "Surely you know cooked food when you see it. My grandchildren wondered whether you were raised by bears. No bear made that fine parka for you or fashioned the framed pack you carried, worn and torn as it is. They look to have been made by Naskapi hands." She poured water into a clay mug and put it into my hand for me to drink.

I took more food, eating slowly, in hopes my stomach would not cramp. When it did not, I spooned up more, finding the seed food curiously good. While I ate, Still Water returned to the wigwam, followed by a man who seemed to be her husband, and the children who had seen me stumble out of the forest.

They dropped their gathering pouches, piling branches and cones next to the wall, then removed their mittens and outer clothing. The girl and boy blew on their hands and rubbed them while their mother removed her loose-fitting parka. A baby rode in a sling across her chest, waving its tiny hands and squinting into the dimness, trying to look around.

"I see our 'bear girl' woke up," said the man.

"She's not a bear girl, Crab Eater. Mother was right. She's just a poor lost girl. The cold must have dulled her wits. Did you find out who she is, Mother?" Still Water lowered herself to her bed furs. When she lifted her shirt, the babe turned its cheek to nurse.

"Not yet," Pine Tree Woman said. "She'll talk later, won't you, Little One?" she asked me, saying the last words like a name this time. The wind played over the smoke hole, sounding like a shrill flute. The whistle and the sucking and smacking sounds of the nursing baby felt like home. Someone tapped heavily on the bark outside and a man's voice requested permission to enter. Pine Tree Woman told him to come in.

The visitor crawled through the flap and stood up. He was a tall man with loose gray hair. His brows were still dark and his nose crooked. When he turned, the fire illuminated his sunken eye socket. It seemed it must be an old wound, for lashes and scar tissue closed over the place where his eye had been. His remaining eye gleamed with intelligence, grasping everything within the wigwam. The family showed him deference and made room. "I heard that your forest girl has come out of hibernation." He smiled faintly at me.

"Little One," Pine Tree Woman said, "this is our headman, Gray Wolf Eye. He has been waiting for you to wake up."

Wolf was part of his name. Was my clan totem watching over me? I remained respectfully silent and waited for him to speak first. The chief crouched across the fire from me, pulling his warm knee-length parka down over his knees. Crab Eater filled a pipe for him and, in a smooth movement, carried a reed of fire to the pipe's bowl. He sat on his heels and puffed until the dried leaves glowed, then handed the pipe to his guest.

Gray Wolf Eye pulled deeply on the pipe. Smoke curled lazily from his lips and nose, drifting through the smoke hole above us. The pipe's bowl was not a hollowed corncob like some I'd seen further south. I wondered what it was.

After several puffs, Gray Wolf Eye turned to me. He phrased his sentences quickly, and I had to listen hard to understand. He reminded me how I had been found at the edge of the forest with the worst month of winter coming on. He reminded me of what Pine Tree Woman and her family had done to nurse me. "Let us help you find your way home," he said. "It improves our standing with Manitou to give aid to strangers. Tell me, Little One, where is your family?" He and the others sat back on their furs while the wind whispered around the smoke hole.

My throat tightened and burned until I wondered if I could make words come out. I disliked to speak falsely, although I had learned that there were times when, as much as I wished it were not necessary, a small untruth was best. "I lost my people," I said honestly. "Many times, I tried to find my way back, but each path was the wrong one. Many days passed. Then, the whiteness confused my eyes, for I could not see the sun. I had food when I set out from our camp. When it was finished, my wolf sisters left a rabbit for me to eat. Here is the fur." The bits of skin were still poked into my dress and my torn parka. I spoke the truth without giving more to them than was prudent.

"Try harder," Pine Tree Woman prompted. "Remember how you asked me for help when you came out of the woods? How many days has it been since you saw your family? You'd been going in circles, but your tracks started inland. Where are you from?" She said names I assumed were nearby villages. I shook my head, bewildered at how to answer so as to avoid detection. Even in winter, the rumors of my deeds might have passed me and come this far.

"Who is your father? Your chief?" When I did not answer, she added, "Where did you intend to go when you set out?"

"I was looking for my family," I admitted. I dared not say my home was south, or they would take me to Hawk Feather's village in the spring. His companions might still be looking for me. In each village they passed, they would give the people a description of the Mohawk slave girl who had murdered her master. "My home is over the North Ocean," I lied. All I knew for certain was that I must go farther north, where there were no Algonquin-speaking people, where my past could never catch me.

"That's impossible. No one lives north of Naskapi Country except the Eskimo. You're not one of them. You couldn't have come so far south from their islands all alone." I thought she then asked me if I ate raw meat. What were Naskapi?

"Ask her to say her name," the boy suggested.

"What may we call you?" Pine Tree Woman asked politely.

I could not say my name was Picture Maker, for the words of my name were Ganeogaono. I didn't even know them in Algonquin. Besides, I'd renounced that name so Grandmother could give it to another. Nor could I tell them I had been known as the Mohawk Girl. The last time I admitted that, it got me ravished on the beach. Since the words meant "girl child of the man eaters," they would think me a monster. "I don't know," I whimpered. "How is that possible?" I looked to them as though they might explain it to me.

Still Water said, "The cold has dulled her wits like it froze her toes. Couldn't we keep her here, Mother? My children like her."

Before Pine Tree Woman could reply, Gray Wolf Eye said, "No one can travel until the bitter cold breaks. Little One will stay with us for now. I heard of a man who left his village to hunt. Running through the forest after elk, he became separated from his companions.

"When his friends found him, they had to surmise what happened from the tracks they found and the bump on his head. He could not remember his own name or what he had been doing. They took him home and his wife cared for him, but he did not recognize her or their children for many cycles of the moon. One day, he awoke, and it was as though he had just left to go hunting the day before. It seemed to him that his children had grown taller overnight. Perhaps the same thing happened to this girl. Until we learn more about her, she will stay here with us."

Pine Tree Woman picked up the food bowl from the mat beside my crossed feet. I looked up into her kind eyes, loathing myself for misleading these good people. "You are kind," I said, stating the obvious. "All of you."

Pine Tree Woman's grandson persisted in trying to learn where my home had been. "Is your village near a mountain, or a river, or the coast? Are you sure you can't remember your mother?"

I lowered my burning face, afraid my thoughts would be seen if I looked up, when Chief Gray Wolf Eye commanded, "Stand and let us look at you."

I did as he bid me, finding it easier to stand now. My clothing was little more than clinging rags with bits of uncured rabbit fur stuffed into the moccasin boots, dress, and parka. No doubt, I seemed like a scarecrow set among corn hills, thin and filthy, with fingers and nose black from frostbite. My hair hung around my face in long and matted clumps.

"Her middle is swollen," Chief Gray Wolf Eye said.

"If a person goes without food for a long time, that can happen." Pine Tree Woman stroked my cheeks with the palm of her warm hand, then felt the skin of my belly, which was tight and round below my bony ribs. Her expression changed, and she pushed at the taut skin with her fingers. She looked at me with sympathy before she turned back to Chief Gray Wolf Eye.

"There is a baby in there. The girl is older than she seems."

"No! It can't be," I wailed. The ground shifted beneath my feet. As I collapsed, Pine Tree Woman rushed forward to catch me. *No. Please don't let it be,* I prayed. Not Hawk Feather's baby. *Let me die first.*

"Little One," Pine Tree Woman said. "Try harder to remember your village or the name of your chief. Your husband must be mad with worrying about you."

If only she knew. I struggled up and crept to the door. With one hand pressed against a lodge pole, I stood, gathering my strength, breathing hard. Then I rushed out into the icy winter.

The midday sun's brilliant light reflected off the snow. I had been in darkness so long, I could barely see. It was cold and there was a wind blowing, although the sun shone. I listened to the wind sighing in the tall evergreens that seemed to stand guard over the village. A clearing beyond the village led to a lake, white, with frozen reeds at the edge. The lake would not be my friend, not allow me to drown myself in it. Even the ocean would not take me, having allowed my enemy to pull me away from death.

Hawk Feather's child grew in my womb. Raw cold bit into my skin. Defeated, I knelt to the ground, hands over my head, and swayed side to side, keening softly.

"Where do you think you are going, Little One?" Pine Tree Woman asked. She lifted me and, wrapping me in a cloak, still warm from the fire inside the wigwam, tried to lead me back to her wigwam. "Try to remember the direction to your home," she insisted.

I twisted away, looking for the sun. "That way." I pointed. "North. I must go north," I said, remembering the storyteller woman's warning. "I'll be safe in the north." I managed a few painful steps on the crusted snow before I collapsed. Crab Eater's strong arms lifted and carried me back inside to my pallet, where they heaped me with furs again. Pine Tree Woman rubbed my naked feet with melting snow, then cleansed my scratches with a dampened bit of hide.

Although I was scratched and bleeding again from where I had fallen against broken branches, my keening dwindled down to a soft, miserable moan. I heard myself, as though the sounds emerged from some other source. "Shush. Rest now," Pine Tree Woman said soothingly. She held me close to ease my trembling with her warm body, stroking me with her strong hands. "When the ocean opens to allow our canoes to ride it again, our men go to trade with the Eskimo on the traders' beach. The Eskimo will know whether one of their hunters' women is missing. They'll take you back to your home." She settled me down and tucked the furs closer around me.

A girl crawled near and sunk to her heels beside my pallet. She gazed at me with bright, curious eyes. "Don't be afraid of Marsh Lily," Pine Tree Woman said to me. "This is my granddaughter, Little One. You won't mind if she sits with you and tries to put your hair in order, will you?"

The old woman took my silence for acceptance and brought a clamshell comb from her own pallet to hand to the girl. "Go ahead. Try to fix Little One's hair," she said. "Use my bear grease." The girl smiled at me shyly, then set to work on my matted hair. It hurt as she struggled with the knots, but I closed my eyes as I felt her soft palms and gentle touches.

Pine Tree Woman moved back and spoke quite softly with the others, discussing me as though I could not understand their words. Although my eyes were closed while Marsh Lily worked, I strained to catch every word. "She must be Naskapi, even though she talks oddly," Chief Gray Wolf Eye declared. "Possibly her father traded her to an Eskimo. All she remembers for sure is that her home is north of Naskapi Country."

"She carries a child in her womb," my protector reminded him. "She's older than she seems. What if she accompanied her husband and a hunting accident befell him? She could have been trying to get back to their village."

"It's possible. They build their dwellings anywhere, even on the ice sheet. In winter, they build them out of frozen blocks of snow," Crab Eater allowed.

The chief nodded, adding, "It's true. They move more frequently than we do, following after the white bear in the winter and the seals in the summer. I wonder if this young woman walked over the ice from one of their islands."

Still Water, who had not spoken up until then, said, "Did you notice there are scars on her back and legs? They're not very old. Do you suppose she might have been a slave, instead of a wife?"

"Would she want to go back to them if they beat her?" Pine Tree Woman asked pointedly. "Her scars could be from a fall into brambles while she was lost. I think her husband is Eskimo. If he still lives, he and all his village will be looking for her. She could be carrying his son. It better be a boy she carries. They don't care much for girls."

"They can't despise girls altogether, or none of them would have mothers. Let her choose a new husband among our young men. My brother needs a wife." They continued like this for a while, drinking their mint tea.

There was a hum of subdued conversation. After awhile, their voices grew faint. When I awoke, Marsh Lily remained, although the others were no longer sitting by the fire. She crawled close and whispered into my ear, "I want you to be a bear girl. Don't go away from us when spring comes."

"Hush, Marsh Lily," her grandmother said from her bed near the other wall. "She will stay with us until the ice breaks and the trees come alive again."

During the next few days, I ate and slept, until I began to feel stronger. When someone came to visit, Pine Tree Woman told them my possible history, adding that the terrible events I might have witnessed and the loss I had suffered must have driven all memories from my mind. Village people accepted her theory as truth. While the heavy winter winds moaned around the small village, I regained my strength, knowing I must depart for the north eventually, just as I must one day bear the child of the man I had slain.

The village children found me amusing and often visited with me, one or more at a time. The last time I had lived in a secure home, I was a child myself. I had become an adult among my enemies, and now I waited while an enemy child grew inside me. It amused the children that I possessed no memory and no real name. They laughingly practiced their storytelling for me. I encouraged them, since hearing their words helped me become more fluent in their language.

I had not forgotten the skills I possessed for basket making and mat weaving, sewing or cooking, so I did what I could to be helpful to Pine Tree Woman and her family.

After the coldest month of the year, when the cold snapped limbs off trees and people's breath turned to ice, a break came in the cold. Several men left the village to hunt, returning with a half-grown brown bear and a mountain sheep that must have wandered from its hilly refuge into the lower lands. The meat roasting over a wood fire made the inside of my cheeks grow damp in anticipation. My arms and legs had rounded over the last month. When I rose to my hands and knees in the morning, my belly protruded to the furs beneath me.

The families shared their meat and firewood, as our clans do. Pine Tree Woman showed me how to hull the scorched lake-grass seeds that made up the bulk of their diet. She explained how, in autumn, water-grass seeds ripened in purple plumes by the lake edge and also in the marshes. "We paddle out on the lake to tie off our bundles. When the seeds are ripe, we knock the grains into our canoes. You do remember your mother doing this, don't you?"

"I'm not sure," I replied. "Tell me more."

She couched her questions carefully, trying to bring back my memories. "Doesn't any of this seem familiar?"

"Perhaps," I said, wanting to please her. "I do remember my mother and aunts gathering herbs and mushrooms, digging for cattail roots and shoots."

"I told you so," Pine Tree Woman said to her family. "She was born one of us. She's no eater of raw fish and she's far too pretty and tall to be an Eskimo woman. They are like chubby children, so short and squat."

"If she is Naskapi-born, that doesn't give us the right to keep her, not if she's wife to one of their hunters," her son-in-law reminded her. "Eskimos are touchy. Her family would not take it well if they learned we kept her. Even if her husband is dead, his family has rights. If she carries a son, they'll want it."

Still Water, who had been quiet during the exchange between her mother and her husband, asked, "How will they know she lives here if no one tells them? It's said Eskimo women have little status, even though women make all their fine clothing. No one knows how one of their tribe thinks."

When they argued like this over my future, I ached inside. They talked around me as though I were still a child. Under the circumstances, I did not mind too much, as long as they allowed me to go. After what I had lived through, though, I might have had twice my years.

One day, I could no longer fight down the urge to ask Pine Tree Woman why they didn't grow maize.

"Little One, if you remember eating maize, you were born in the south. I've eaten trade maize meal and seen a dried ear of it. It won't grow here. The ground is too hard and the summer too short. We have our lake-grass seeds to cook. How far you must have wandered in your short life to know of this food. Yet you persist in believing your home is north of Naskapi Country."

"My family traveled," I said. "I remember many homes." The second part was true. "I know you are trying to help." Tears of shame sprang to my eyes. How I longed to tell her the truth, but if I told them my true origins, they would shrink from me.

Pine Tree Woman patted my arm. "Poor Little One. I fear you'll never find your home again." In this, she was right. I never would find my way back home, not with Algonquin warriors whispering the tales of my deeds in the land between my country and hers.

The following day, I felt stronger. When the others went out to search for broken branches and twigs, I went along. The ice storm had snapped many branches, leaving the trees broken, limbs hanging crookedly. I discovered a wide scrap of birch bark, not much torn, and tucked it carefully inside my parka, against my skin, to work out the curl.

Back in the house, I choose a cold piece of charred wood from the ashes. I scraped the bark clean and laid it across my knees. Pine Tree Woman's granddaughter stood at my shoulder. "What are you going to do with that, Little One?" Marsh Lily asked me.

"I'm not sure," I replied. An intense expression that the girl had been taught to respect in elders must have crossed my face, for she left me to help her grandmother and mother with their tasks. The others walked off as well, leaving me alone with the piece of bark laid across my knees and the charcoal stick poised in my hand. I touched my stick to the bark and began to draw.

My coal pushed along the bark, leaving lines that spoke to me. Still Water and Pine Tree Woman approached silently with March Lily. I lifted my head to acknowledge them, then resumed my work.

Under my fingers, the outlines of a man in a canoe took form. Turkey tail feathers appeared above the earflaps on his fur cap, and the markings of a war chief decorated his cheeks and nose. My father plied his paddle, making his canoe fly past a cloud. I added more clouds and the sun in the picture, although it might have been the moon, being only a circle in the sky. I imagined it was my father gliding through the sky river to take me home. All that I saw in my mind's eye became a picture on the bark.

"What is it?" Still Water's eyes grew large as they peered at the bark.

"A man in a canoe," I replied.

"No. I mean what do you call it—what you have done on the bark?"

"I don't know the word," I said. I had not seen any such things as pictures in any Algonquin village.

"It's a picture," Pine Tree Woman informed us. "A likeness made flat with coal on a bark or drawn into sand."

I questioned her to be sure I understood she did not mean any of the individual representations within the picture, but the entire thing I had drawn on the bark. "A picture," I repeated quietly.

"Girl Makes Pictures." Marsh Lily said my name in Algonquin. The adults pointed, fascinated. Apparently, no one did this among them. "Where did you lean this magic? Is it a shaman trick?" the girl asked me.

"No," I replied. "I made pictures for my grandmother when I was small. When she was young, she made pictures also."

Pine Tree Woman's eyes narrowed. "I told you the girl belongs with us. There's no birch bark wide enough on Eskimo islands. No real trees grow there. She's Naskapi, like us, no matter how she got involved with the islanders."

During the rest of winter, when wind rattled against the bark and hide of the wigwams, I heard that families gathered close around their hearths and speculated on my supposed history. I did little to encourage them, but my drawings became a way to pass time and give something back. The wigwam children searched out barks and wide pieces of shale or leather scraps for me to make pictures on. Children from the village encouraged me. I attempted to draw them at play, but the village faith-keeper came while I was working. He forbade me to put their features on the bark.

"Do you want to capture their souls and cause them harm?" he asked roughly. His eyes pierced my thoughts, and I hoped they would hold my secrets inside.

"Oh, no, I would never do that," I assured him.

"Make pictures of animals."

"Yes. I will," I agreed, glad to do so. One time, without thinking, I had forgotten to be careful and had drawn my longhouse. "What is this?" Pine Tree Woman had asked, almost pulling the picture from my fingers. I had not noticed her walking up behind me.

"It's a beaver house, isn't it?" I quickly added lines to the smoke rising from the smoke holes to make them into bare winter trees. Anything about my life before I came to them would betray what I was to the sharp eyes of my benefactors. I took care never to draw my longhouse again. Neither did I draw corn, beans, or squash while I waited for spring to melt the ice in the ocean. Once the wide seaworthy canoes could travel north, I would go into a boat and leave my world of Turtle Island. I would be parted forever from all I had ever known.

Chapter 14

The sun rose higher above the horizon each day, and the days grew longer, until the northern lights faded. Winter released the lake from its frozen hold. Sheets of thin ice floated free past the coves and the reed-filled shoreline. Each day, the water flowed more swiftly into the steam-fed lake and out of it again. Snowmelt gushed down from the mountains, turning the crusted snow to slush.

The village's winter supply of dried meat dwindled, and their reserves of parched lake-grass seeds were almost gone. It was time to hunt. Men tied new bowstrings to their bows and fletched new feathers to newly-made arrows. The smells of spring seemed just beyond our noses.

Gray Wolf Eye came to visit Pine Tree Woman's lodge. I withdrew into a corner, thinking he wished to speak to the others, but Pine Tree Woman beckoned me. "Come closer and listen. Gray Wolf Eye wishes to consult you about something important." She must have known what he had in mind, for she disappeared behind us and returned shortly with mugs of sweet-smelling sassafras root tea. Still Water and Crab Eater, her husband, ordered the children over to them, leaving me sitting alone across from the chief.

I tried to be courteous, keeping my eyes on his nose, rather than letting them stray to the place were his missing eye should have been. He threw his head back and laughed heartily. "You don't have to do that. It makes your eyes cross, Little One," he said. "Don't be afraid to look at my face. I'm used to this." He pointed to his sunken eyelid. "Men take pride in hunting wounds, or in war scars received in the defense of our people. It is an odd name we call you. I wish we knew your real name." When I did not reply, he went on. "You have been our guest most of this winter. I have a favor to ask of you."

"What I can do, I will. Of course," I answered without hesitation, but I hoped what he had come to request of me was within my ability to do.

"Walks in Shadow tells us that your pictures hold magic. He knows how to release that power for the good of the village."

Walks in Shadow was the shaman. "How can my drawings hold magic? They are only charcoal on bark."

"Did you not notice how your summer pictures made us all feel warmer? Thoughts put into form can help bring the thing itself. The caribou lead bull sends scouts ahead to seek out the best pasturage for their summer browsing. We have our own scouts searching for them, but none have been seen. Who knows where Manitou will send them to graze this time? We can only hope that they have not begun their migration in some other direction. We will need to journey to our summer home by the ocean soon, and we must have meat.

"Even a holy man cannot always foretell where animals will go. Walks in Shadow says that if you draw caribou on bark or shale for him, he can pull the magic from the pictures to call them toward our valley and our river."

My pictures had contained no magic for Grandmother. Our faith-keepers would have told me if they had. Still, I had to do as the shaman required. "My pictures have never been used to call animals. At least not that I can remember," I added cautiously. "But certainly, I shall do whatever you and Walks in Shadow request of me, as well as my skills will permit."

Gray Wolf Eye nodded solemnly. "It may be that there was no shaman in your village who knew such magic, or game was plentiful enough. Then again, to my knowledge, Eskimo don't think of women and hunting luck together. The sap rises in the nearby elm trees. Already, their bark loosens as they stretch and prepare to bring forth their buds and leaves. Walks in Shadow has the young men looking for the best and largest bark pieces now to repair our canoes. We will soon have enough for you to make pictures for us."

His request had been a formality only, for he and Walks in Shadow had naturally assumed my compliance. I would do anything to help them get along with their lives in peace and plenty, except stay among them.

Later, when Gray Wolf Eye entered Pine Tree Woman's lodge, the old shaman accompanied him, bark sections under his arms and charcoal sticks in a bark-strip basket. "Build up the fire so she can see," the shaman ordered. The family and both powerful men left me to my work.

I closed my eyes and searched back in my memory for caribou, moose, and elk running or grazing among the trees. I wondered if indeed there was magic in my pictures and thought how peculiar it was that our shamans would not have known. If it were true, I might have drawn the sorcerer of the Onondaga bitten by one of the snakes of his own hair. If only our shamans knew the magic to make pictures into reality, they might have stopped the sorcerer and his war.

With the point of my charcoal, I drew the outlines of caribou, as many as the pale side of the bark would hold, fat and sleek. Many times, I had to hold my bits of half-burned bone or wood in the fire again. When I filled a bark, I leaned it against the wall and reached for another from the pile beside me. With the side of another piece of charcoal, I shaded my picture animals' winter coats to make them look rounded and fat, as though they could jump off the bark sheet. I added antlers afterward. Last to add were their legs. "Does he want the caribou to be running or standing still?" I asked, for I could draw lines to make their feet seem to be in motion.

"Swimming." The shaman had returned silently and sat on his haunches against the far dark wall. I turned at his voice, thinking I had been alone. His lips widened and his few teeth showed. "Swimming," he repeated.

When my pictures were completed, I gave the barks sheets to Walks in Shadow. He carried my pictures outside to see them in sunlight. I followed him out of the wigwam and saw him nod, tracing the outlines of the caribou without touching so as not to smudge the work. He reminded me of my grandmother and how she had once traced the lines of my Guardian Wolf picture, which might still hang beside our longhouse entryway. The village's hunters gathered around, observing my drawings and waiting for their shaman's commands. By that time, I knew most of them by name. Gray Wolf Eye waited with the others for the words Walks in Shadow would speak.

I began to walk away. A men's hunting conference is no place for a woman, but Walks in Shadow stopped me. "We shall have the ceremony in my wigwam. Come, those who will hunt and this Woman Who Makes Pictures."

An involuntary gasp jumped out of my throat and I shut my eyes tightly to hold back the salt water that threatened. He had spoken in Algonquin, but he said my name. When I opened my eyes a moment later, the men were already walking off, my pictures in their hands.

I hoped no one had seen my reaction, but I knew Walks in Shadow had seen and heard. He had waited for me. "Pine Tree Woman," Gray Wolf Eye said, "have the women prepare our canoes." She nodded and walked off to tell them.

I followed the men. The shaman's wigwam was twice the size of Pine Tree Woman's. Its floor was covered with hides, enough to spread across the packed-earth floor. The hunters sat cross-legged. I crouched by a wall to observe.

Walks in Shadow propped my barks open and fastened them to the curved walls with spruce gum. Then he evoked Manitou, raising his arms and shaking his turtle shell rattle. After this part of the ceremony, we filed out again. He commanded a fire to be lit on the clear space between the lodges. When it was burning well, he and several others brought the pictures and set them reverently on the flames, as though they were offering leaves of holy tobacco. Walks in Shadow spoke to the Creator while my pictures cracked and blackened. The bark sheets turned to ash and smoke. Lastly, he placed fragrant leaves over all.

I was permitted to take one of the fragrant leaves home afterward. It was not our kind of tobacco, but another aromatic leaf, long and tooth-leaved. These leaves must have served the same purpose as tobacco leaves did in Ganeogaono Country—to carry prayers directly to the Creator. Pine Tree Woman observed how I turned the leaf over and sniffed at it. "The sweet smoke carries our prayers to Manitou, the Great Sky Spirit," she explained.

"Yes, I know," I replied.

Her expression changed. "Your memory is returning. Before long, you may tell us how you came to be lost and your real name."

"Walks in Shadow knows my name," I said softly, "but I must not pronounce it. Please forgive me that I cannot speak of certain things." At that, she sighed a very deep sigh. I was sure she knew all the time that I was holding back secrets.

The lake fed a medium-sized river. The water flowed fast with rain and snowmelt, causing white-topped wavelets to dance and shiver across the water in the wind. The women readied their wide, flat-bottomed canoes, stitching the supple bark with sinew thread and coating the hulls in and out with thickened spruce sap to keep the bark watertight. We packed provisions for the whole village to camp beside the river where Walks In Shadow dreamed the caribou would cross. It was cold and dark as we set out. The stars winked out as the sky paled. I pulled my collar high around my neck as we walked in single file. The men led, carrying their canoes and weapons on their broad shoulders. Next came the women with packs of food. Dogs pulled drag ropes of tanned hides to make lean-tos. The children scampered around, trying to keep their excited high-pitched voices low. It was the first time they had left the village in many moons.

By midday, we reached the indicated location. The women set up camp among thick trees on high land, where the herd was not likely to run. Small campfires were soon lit. The families gathered around each fire, eating as soon as the food could be prepared. After we ate, the men scattered. Their signals were to be the call of night birds in the day, the call of day birds in the evening, so we would know when the herd was sighted.

Pine Tree Woman took charge of the women. "Keep knives in your belts and stay close," she commanded. "Keep the dogs quiet. If you must speak, use whispers or signs. We may not see the men until they're ready to have us come to them. Impress upon the children that they must not raise their voices above a whisper. The caribou must not hear us."

The sun was high when I heard a night owl's hoot. The call sounded so true that if I had been unaware of our signal, I would have thought the owl had its day and night confused. A hunter appeared at the edge of the clearing and motioned. Silently, the women crept along behind him. Before he took another track, he motioned us toward the great rocks high above the river. We took our places among the bushes and watched how the hunters laid their ambush.

Half the men carried harpoons and cordage into the canoes. They set out, paddling in the shadows of the high banks. The remainder of the men and boys found places to wait behind trees near where the river widened, to give chase and frighten the caribou back if they turned away from the ambush.

When the herd came pounding into view from among the tall trees, my eyes grew round. Even the older village women put their hands over their mouths at the sight of so many caribou at once. The stags led, then the does with their fawns at their sides, hooves pounding the ground, nostrils snorting white into the chill air. The boys waved their shirts and shouted, howling war yells to drive the caribou to ford the river where the canoes waited. The caribou moved downriver and bounded into the water.

They churned the water white. Ice floes forced the frantic caribou into more confusion. Their barks and bellows rang out while the chasers shouted, running and waving. The herd needed to swim against the current without slipping underneath the ice. The hunters in the canoes were ready for them, although the swift-moving water and ice sheets created difficulty for them, too. They pulled alongside the scattered fringes of the massed animals to isolate their prey. Two men managed each canoe: One wielded the harpoon; the second managed an extra looped rope to drag the wounded beast to shore, where they could more easily finish it off.

Two canoes maneuvered one large male between them, leaving it little chance for escape. The men almost had it, but then the stag tried to throw himself into the canoe. The boat flipped over, turning the men into the water. The stag bit and tried to gore them with his small spring antlers, until it was impossible to see if the blood came from animals or men.

Another canoe drew up beside the overturned one. One hunter let fly a flint-bladed shaft while the other threw his loop and pulled their prey off the struggling men. A third canoe pulled the nearly drowned hunters out of the roiling water. In its driving swim to get through, a heaving animal scrambled over the deserted canoe, thrashing it with his hooves until it sank. The uncertain flow of the ice made swimming for man and beast treacherous. A floe shifted and sliced the water, its edge thin as a blade. It cut off retreat and might have sliced into necks, as well. It happened again several times, farther out, as the herd thrashed and swam for the southern bank. There, animals staggered to shore, bleeding and crippled, to die soon after.

One young man from a third canoe balanced on both knees, drew back, and let fly his harpoon directly into a male's bellowing chest. When the animal floundered, another hunter sent his spear after the first. The injured buck stopped struggling, his blood spreading through the water while men looped ropes over its neck and dragged it to the bank, where the waiting men hauled it from the water.

Crab Eater beckoned to the cliffs with a wide swing of his arm. "They are ready for us," some of the women shouted. We ran forward to butcher the meat so we could drag it more easily back to camp.

One hunter floated dead in the water. His companions pulled his mangled body from the mud at the shoreline, after the last of the herd had crossed. He was so trampled, I thought his mother would not recognize him. Of course, she did; her keening and wailing filled the air. The young man's father carried him to high ground, arranged his broken limbs, and wrapped him gently in hides to carry back to the village burial ground. Still Water told me the hunter was not yet married and that this was his first hunt. A village maiden of about twelve or thirteen knelt beside the mother. If she was not his sister, he had been betrothed.

"I'll be back," Pine Tree Woman told us before she left to comfort the family of the dead hunter. I looked after her, wondering if there was anything at all I could do to help.

"Keep working," Still Water advised. "We have much to do before we can leave for the camp." I continued to slice up the meat with my flint knife. Some of the young men paddled off in their canoes to retrieve caribou that had died on the other side of the river.

We worked until dusk. Shoulders and haunches were placed on spits over campfires. There was enough food here for much of the coming summer if they smoked what they could not eat fresh. But the food came at a cost. Almost every hunter would carry the scars of their day's work.

While we worked, a young man approached the women, blood still seeping from a gash on his cheek. Still Water carried her sewing supplies in a pouch at her side. "Let me see to your cheek," she said. She took him aside and tended to his cuts. I glanced their way from time to time, wondering how to treat such a wound. I'd heard of sewing skin flaps together but had not seen it done.

First, Still Water mopped away the fresh blood to inspect the gash. Another man approached them to ask her if his friend must be held down.

"I won't flinch," insisted the injured one. He glanced up and noticed me watching. I turned away from his curious eyes to my work, but I glanced back from time to time. The man had lain down, hands clenched at his sides. Still Water removed something from her pouch, then chewed and spit it out into her hand. Holding the flaps of his cheek together, she smeared it on the raw edges. He closed his eyes and seemed to pray silently until his breathing slowed and his hands unclenched.

When her bird-bone needle pierced his cheek, he did not move. I could not help but watch, impressed by his control as she drew the sinew thread through. When she was done, Still Water covered his wound with dampened astringent leaves and bound rawhide over his cheek, strapping it around the back of his head. The hunter would carry a scar across his right cheek, almost to the inner corner of his eye.

As darkness descended, the smell of roasting caribou and the sounds of chewing filled the night. We gathered around the campfires' glow to keep warm in islands of light. "Bucktorn likes you," Still Water whispered to me out of hearing of the other young women. "His name had been Stag Hunter, but his friends renamed him Bucktorn because of his cheek. He said his spirit was drawn to yours, when I sewed his cheek." If he felt me judging him, he has the makings of a shaman, I thought, but I said nothing of these thoughts. "I have a feeling he's going to ask you to stay with us and be his wife."

I turned my face to see if I could pick him out from the other hunters. He sat on his side of the fire with his friends and family, but he glanced toward us at the sound of his name. I flushed and turned away. "I can't do that. He knows I must leave soon. How can he want to marry me?"

"Wait and consider," advised Still Water. "If you were born one of us, you have no obligation to return to your dead husband's people." I had said nothing to discourage the assumption most of them made. "You may still change your mind before the men leave for the trading." I could not answer her.

The evening after we returned to the village, Gray Wolf Eye entered Pine Tree Woman's wigwam. We worked around the fire pit, making buttons, awls, hooks, and arrowheads from caribou bone. I would have moved back, but the chief motioned for me to stay. "Be still, Little One. Listen to me, and before you speak, think well how you will respond. The day after tomorrow, we leave for our summer village beside Ungava Bay. Only a few days afterward, our traders will set out on the ocean for the traders' island. Bucktorn, whom you know, has requested that I give you his message. He desires for you to stay and be his wife. If you agree, we will adopt you into our tribe. I will convey your answer to him."

"What about my baby?" I asked, both hands over my bulging belly, as if staying were possible. I detested my hesitation, and knew it for stalling.

"The village needs more children," he replied. "The Eskimo have no way to learn you are living here with us. Does your question mean you are considering Bucktorn's offer?"

"Stay," Marsh Lily pleaded. "Be my older sister."

"I can't." My voice came too loudly in the small room. I felt torn in half, wanting to stay around familiar things, but too frightened to remain on the mainland. "I want to, but I may not. Tell Bucktorn I can't. I must go north to find my family," I concluded sadly.

Gray Wolf Eye bowed his head once, accepting my decision on behalf of Bucktorn. "The trading island is four days north of Ungava Bay. We shall trade with the Eskimo for our pipes and for tools fashioned of ivory. They are skillful carvers, better hunters than any Turtle Island tribe, even than Naskapi, since they are connected with animals more closely than we are. They have a taste for our tobacco, and they need strong wood with which to make their paddles and harpoon staffs, green wood to bend for their bows and arrows."

"Wood?" I asked. Hadn't Pine Tree Woman said something like this? "Why do they trade for wood when trees grow everywhere?"

"They have none. No trees grow so far north. Small birch or willow saplings do for their small bows and arrows, good only for hares and weasels, but such trees wouldn't reach my chest. They have no oak, no spruce or elm. The ground where they live remains frozen underneath all year through. No real tree can put down roots."

No trees? What kind of people could live beyond Great Turtle Earth?

As if she heard my thoughts from beside the fire, Pine Tree Woman said, "Eskimo ways are hard and their customs are strange. They eat nothing but white bear and seal and fish. They carve walrus tusks and whale teeth, so they must know how to kill even those monsters."

"Give me the meat of caribou and brown bear," Crab Eater said. "Let the monsters of the sea keep far away from my canoe."

"If they kill even whales," his son said to me, "you won't go hungry in the north, Little One, but if you miss corn, will you be content with nothing but meat?"

"Is it true?" I asked, turning to Gray Wolf Eye, who had known Eskimo. "Do they really eat nothing but meat?"

"What do you imagine you'll find away from the world?" he answered gruffly. "Part of your memory seems to have returned. Do you remember that the world exists on the back of Great Turtle?" When I nodded my head, he continued. "Our northern village sits on the right flipper of the Turtle as it faces north. Eskimos paddle walrus-hide boats to islands beyond the world. They build wigwams of stones and turf. An Eskimo will trade his toothless old wife for a good sled dog. What kind of status do you expect to have among them?"

From his question, I knew I must not expect much. "But they need women, or they can't have sons. Every boy has a mother." It couldn't be as bad as he imagined. "Their hunters can't nurse their sons."

Gray Wolf Eye raised his chin, staring down at me with his one eye. His brows drew together and a frown line formed over his nose. "Yes, they have uses for women. Go north, since you insist. Clever Hands will lead the expedition. He'll tell the Eskimo headman about how your pictures brought us hunting luck. If your talent works for them, I expect they'll take you, whether or not they know your husband's village."

"Thank you," I said, grateful to have someone else ask for me. Another thought came to me. I should have inquired before now. "Do they speak the same words as the Naskapi?" I asked, and waited for his answer. So much depended on what he would say.

"Don't you know? Don't you speak their tongue?"

If I had lived among them, I should know their words. I felt as if ice were cracking beneath me.

"Perhaps I did once, but not now."

Gray Wolf Eye turned from me to Pine Tree Woman and back to me again. "I know a few Eskimo words, and their headman knows several of ours. We trade with hand signs. I'll send Clever Hands to Pine Tree Woman's wigwam to teach you to sign, if you like."

"Yes, please," I agreed. "That will help me remember, I'm sure."

Whether or not he believed me, he added, "Most certainly, their words will come back to you after you've been with them awhile, as ours did. I see now that the Great Spirit sent you to us for four moons only. During that time, you've repaid what we've done for you many times over. Since you continue to feel your destiny lies in the north, we won't hold you back. Though if you find you are unhappy off Great Turtle Earth, remember that the Naskapi of my village would have kept you with us. We never turned you away."

"I will remember."

Gray Wolf Eye departed from Pine Tree Woman's wigwam. If he guessed the truth about me, I was certain all his kindness would end. The Naskapi would not tolerate a murderer. Certainly, they would not have given refuge to a Mohawk, who might kill them in their sleep and eat their flesh, as the Algonquin believed of my people. If the Eskimo tribe rejected me, I was lost. No matter what the north islands held for me, I had to go there. In Eskimo Country, Algonquin was not spoken. No one from Hawk Feather's village would come to point me out as a slave and a murderer. Never again would I hear my people called "Mohawk." I would be safe at last.

Chapter 15

Marsh Lily climbed onto her mother's shoulders to unwrap and drop the hides and bark from the upper wigwam. Pine Tree Woman and I worked below, gathering them up and deciding which were undamaged enough to take. My belly protruded too far for me to climb easily. When only the scaffolding remained, the women worked in pairs to take down the birch lodge poles and the bark cord that wound around them. We fastened the poles to the dogs' harness straps, for the supplies would be dragged behind in net-covered travois.

Gray Wolf Eye and Walks in Shadow led the long procession. As we walked the narrow trail, the breeze carried fragments of their conversation back to us. Next, the hunters, walking in pairs, carried their great canoes between them on their shoulders. Mothers followed, papooses peeking back over the trail. Older women and maidens steadied bark baskets on their heads with one hand. The nubile girls moved with sinuous and graceful dignity, sharing jokes and stories as they walked. I would miss the kindness of the Naskapi.

The children guided the dogs along the path by their harnesses straps. Other hunters brought up the rear, weapons near to hand. When I looked back to the clearing where the village had stood, there was nothing to see but piles of stones and the scorched earth where the fire pits had been.

Gray Wolf Eye's lookouts were to secure an area for our overnight campground. The chieftain scanned their markers and led the procession from one trail to the next. I soon learned that even the youngest knew what to watch for. "Look there!" exclaimed Marsh Lily, as she gestured toward a young birch tree. On one side was a broken branch that pointed unnaturally. "We're to turn north at the next crossing."

When we paused beside a fast-moving brook to dip our water bags, dead branches, upended, stuck up out of the muddy bank, pointing again. It was a short rest, for we had far to go. Before we moved on, Gray Wolf Eye removed the stakes.

Our last beacon, three puffs of smoke, urged us on. We made camp beside a wider stream, which rippled into a mossy pond. The sun cast long shadows through the budding trees. Dusk brought night sounds. Loons called from across the water. By the time we made our lean-tos, the hunters had meat propped on stakes around the campfires, roasting it. Pine Tree Woman led some of us off to the nearest trees to gather kindling, as well as peat moss to dry for diapering. We lined our moccasins with peat moss, as well. Since winter, none of the women had done any long-distance walking.

I crouched beside the water, inspecting the new growth. We bent with our flint knives to collect watercress and new cattail shoots. The women dug up several sprouting plants with their roots. In the gathering dusk, the evening air felt chill. The forest smelled of spruce and fresh, rich earth, black and fertile. Frogs croaked, invisible on the black pond, and birds chirped in the tree canopy.

At our campsite, two young women complimented the unattached young hunters on the choice of our campsite and the wonderful smells coming from the fire. Their muted voices spoke of anticipation. After supper, like shadows, couples melted into the surrounding darkness. No one called them back. Their mothers nodded to one another, probably remembering when their own matches were made. Blessings would be asked for all the new families at the next festivals, with hopes of babies being born for the tribe.

Spring meant courting and renewal. It held a different meaning for me. The trails were clear to the Algonquin now. I recalled with anguish the pain and humiliation Hawk Feather had inflicted upon my youthful soul. I was not rid of him yet, for I carried his child. If I stayed on the mainland, my son's hand might someday be turned against my tribe. Even if I was safe, I could not allow that to come to pass. My child must never hear the name Mohawk and think us his enemies. If he lived with those who spoke Algonquin, I could not be sure that this would never happen. As for me, my memories of Hawk Feather's abuse would forever warp any hope I might have of coupling with a man again. What the other young women sought with joy and anticipation, I dreaded.

I still feared recapture. Every crack of a twig behind me on the path reminded me. What if I had left prints on the path before the snows came?

In Pine Tree Woman's lean-to, I sat up with her and the children, talking over the day before sleep came. Still Water and Crab Eater lay in their own shelter. "It is good to have a tribe, to choose a man," I commented, knowing my own thoughts on the latter, but imagining how it was for the others. Pine Tree Woman's eyes closed painfully and she wiped at their corners. "Forgive me," I added hastily. "I did not mean to remind you that you are alone, too."

"I have good memories," she said. "Perhaps you'll find where you belong and what you require in the northern islands. If not, return to us. I have wished you would choose to stay with me and be one of my daughters. The winter was far less tedious with your pictures to amuse us."

During the time I remained with the Naskapi, I realized I had grown to love Pine Tree Woman as much as I loved my real mother, who was lost to me forever. My fright and needs confused me, but I pushed my feelings down as I had been taught to do, focusing on the present. "What is that you're sewing?"

"The second of two leggings with straps to tie onto a belt sash under a dress. My daughter gave you hers, so she'll need another. We must sleep now; it's too dark to work anymore." She set aside her work and pulled her bearskin, fur side down, over us.

The children cuddled beside us. Our bed rested on fir boughs and hides, quite comfortable in the spring night. The tang of spruce sap filled my nose. Marsh Lily's soft arm rested across my cheek while her fingers played with my hair until her breathing grew even. Before I slept, flute music drifted on the wind and shadows stole past the campfires. Before long, sighs of delight and suppressed laughter drifted on the breeze, along with the fluttering of new leaves.

The scouts found another good stopping place the following evening. While light remained, Pine Tree Woman worked on Still Water's dress, pushing her awl to poke holes through the stretched and softened doeskin. She decorated the sleeves with dyed quills, stitching the reds and greens into patterns on the shoulders. "It grows dark," she said when I tried to admire her designs. She folded her sewing and put it away. The campfire died down to glowing coals before we retreated to our shelter.

Pine Tree Woman spread her fur over us. Marsh Lily crept from her parents' lean-to into ours, resting her arm over my belly and her cheek on my breast. She looked up into my eyes, blinking through her long lashes. "If you stayed, I could take care of the baby when you wanted to be somewhere else." I said nothing. "I wish you could stay with us, Little One," the girl whispered.

By predawn light, we harnessed the dogs again and picked our way along the trail, eating cold meat as we walked. We did not hurry, stopping often to forage in good places. Aside from sprouts and shoots, there were new spring herbs for flavoring—mint and licorice root, fawn's foot, onion and garlic.

Pine Tree Woman scraped inner willow bark, stuffing the fragments into a small sheath she wore on a cord around her neck. I remembered my aunt telling me willow was good for fever and pain. I had not learned enough to be a medicine woman, but I knew the healing powers of many of the herbs and roots women gathered. I knew what to use for fever or indigestion or the healing of wounds. I wondered if the same herbs grew in the northern islands. I knew nothing of Eskimo and wondered if they would even let me live with them.

Near the stream, I used my flint knife to cut curled fern heads. Bending forward, I noticed a clump of woman's root plant. I had not seen it in so long, I bent to sniff the leaves to be sure.

"You are familiar with squaw root?" Still Water's voice startled me. I had not known she was so close, and I straightened guiltily, remembering Hawk Feather's fit of anger when he discovered my use of the plant. But he was dead and my fear unwarranted here. I rested my hands over my swollen belly.

"It will be useful when I have the baby," I replied, amused at the Algonquin words for it. My mother simply called it woman's root. No wonder Hawk Feather had exploded in anger when he learned I used it to keep from conceiving.

"Yes, it does help in birthing," she said. She knew as well as I that it prevented conception when used soon after copulation. "You should carry some with you to help when your child comes." She set to work with her digging stick to gather up the plant, which we wrapped in damp moss. If I had found these particular leaves on my trek north from Hawk Feather's village, I would not be expecting his child.

Although I hadn't wanted it, I would not attempt to loosen its grip now. It was my child, too, my mother's grandchild. Pine Tree Woman must have sensed my thoughts, for when she looked my way, warmth spread over my neck and face. Nothing had been said, but I believe we understood each other.

The dense forest thinned. Birch and pine replaced thick oak and slippery elm. The earth grew coarser, lighter, with more pebbles. There was no high ground here, only dunes and rocks. Streams blended with others, gathering into a reed-filled marsh full of cattails and feathery marsh grass, the same grasses the Naskapi women harvested when their seeds grew full.

The bay widened, gray under low clouds. Its beach was rocky, with enough coves for tide pools when the water retreated. I had learned to know the ocean already. We would have no trouble discovering urchins and crabs.

Marsh Lily slipped her fingers between mine. Together, we looked out over the endless water. Broken ice floes floated out of the bay toward the ocean. Small waves lapped into the shore and the air tasted of salt. Above us, seabirds glided through the damp wind, fishing and squawking over prizes, grabbing fish from one another. My hair blew around my face like smoke in the wind. This was the northern edge of the world.

"We're here," the children shouted, jumping in their excitement and looking for familiar rocks and trees. It was a homecoming for them. They dropped their packs, raced down to the water, and jumped into the foam. The dogs, finally loosed from their harnesses and drag poles, ran to romp and chase the seagulls and terns while everyone worked to put up the wigwams before dark.

"Where is the ocean?" I asked of my companions.

"There," replied Still Water, pointing through the thin copse of blue-green spruce. A cove had created the bay, separating it from the ocean. The bay's coast curled around to the larger water. "Listen." I heard the distant rumble of crashing waves and could make out the foam-flecked humps of green. Still Water took pleasure explaining the lay of the land to me. "We build our village by Ungava Bay, across the small woods from the ocean. Our fishermen and traders don't put out into the waves, where they would overturn or be torn by the rocks. We'll have eggs to steal from the cliffs soon; the birds are fighting over nesting sites."

"I hear them," I replied.

"Look how the trees bend away from the wind."

Indeed, the few scrub pine and birch that grew in the loamy soil closest to the ocean's strong winds were crooked and bent.

"Do you come here every year?"

Still Water smiled. "Most years. It's our summer home. I was born here and married to Crab Eater here. It's easier to live by the bay, but the ocean is interesting to watch. You have to climb down rocks to get to the water. There's no beach to stand on, but it's worth the trouble. On a clear day, you can see dolphins jump or a whale spume in the distance."

We set up the summer village far enough from the bay so that most storms would not be a problem. The women entered the clearing beside a sweet-water stream, nodding and smiling in their gladness.

"It's good to come home again," Pine Tree Woman said. She leaned her head against the trunk of a tall pine. "This tree is my namesake, Little One," she informed me, adding, "It shaded my mother's wigwam the day I was born. Come and help me put our house in order."

The next morning, I awoke ravenous. It was becoming harder to rise. My belly lifted my shift in front when I stood. When I returned to the wigwam after relieving myself, Pine Tree Woman handed me a wooden bowl of gruel made from ground lake-grass seed.

"Enjoy it while you can," she said. "This is the last of it. We'll be eating fish for breakfast until we return to harvest more lake grass when the leaves turn color. But by then, you will be far away in the north, eating raw fish."

I said nothing, knowing the only reason for her taunting was to try to change my mind so I would stay.

Later, when Still Water and the other young mothers hiked through the woods toward the ocean, I went also, although slowly. The children ran on ahead. The ocean sounds increased, until finally we came out of the forest above the steep rocks that sloped to the narrow beach. The others scrambled down to look for crabs among the rocks while the children hunted out nests to steal eggs.

I picked my way carefully and sat on a wide stone to watch the others. With the flat of my hand shading my eyes, I gazed above the waves to the horizon. What we had heard the evening before was not merely the roll of the waves breaking against the rocks. Not so long before, the ocean had been an ice field. Welcome as spring was to us, safe on land, it had changed the ocean's face. Great chunks of ice pushed and clashed against others, rumbling and crackling. A great white wall lifted, stood high, then slid with a grating noise under the black water. The wave caused by its sinking was larger than the others. Saltwater droplets, carried on the wind, wet our clothing and faces.

The children and women backed away, laughing. Still Water ran up to see if I had suffered any harm. Droplets dripped from my face. "It's too dangerous to take the canoes fishing or to travel yet," she said. "In another few days, Father Wind will blow the ice south. Then the route will be clear to the traders' island." She looked at me wistfully.

"What's it like out there, after the world ends?" I asked, speaking half to myself, half to the ocean. It seemed alive, able to hear me and answer.

"Well, don't you *know*?" Still Water looked into my face. I don't know what she saw there, but she walked away soon to rejoin the others.

I asked the spirit of the ocean itself, speaking as though the water were a living thing. "Who are the Eskimo who live on your islands? Are they your own special people, like we on Turtle Island belong to the Creator? Will you accept me when I go to them and teach me how to live off the world?" The clash of two colliding ice floes answered me. A great spout of water gushed high into the air. It fell with a retreating rumble and the black waves covered the floes as if they had never existed.

Under Grandmother Moon's silvery light in the village center, Walks in Shadow made a ceremony fire of driftwood. When it was going well, he placed fragrant leaves on the leaping flames. "We thank you for bringing us home, Great Spirit Manitou. Allow us to find good foraging and fishing in your land and water. Give healthy children to the families of this village."

The villagers danced to the piping of a youth's bone flute while an older man beat a tom-tom with the leg bone of a deer. *Tom-tom* meant "beat-beat" in the Naskapi language. *Tomahawk* was "beat-a-man," the Algonquin/Naskapi word for war club. So *hawk* meant "man." *Mo* meant "eat," which is why the name Eskimo meant "they eat raw fish" and Mohawk meant "men-eaters." The words became clear when my last days among Algonquin speakers could be numbered on the fingers of one hand.

Bucktorn and Cloud Flower danced among the other new couples to honor the Creator and entreat His good will. I could have been dancing with Bucktorn, but instead, I sat awkwardly beside the married couples and elders, who sang while the young folk danced. The music and dancing continued until the fire burned down to warm ashes and coals.

Although Bucktorn built a new wigwam for himself and Cloud Flower, he, too, planned to join the trade voyage. While we waited for the ocean to clear, Clever Hands practiced Eskimo hand signs with those who intended to accompany him. I was the only woman who attended these lessons. I hoped it would not inconvenience the men to bring me along, awkward as I was and little able to help.

Several older women replanted the fragrant plants they had brought with them from the forest. When the moon turned full again, the leaves widened. They gathered those the Eskimo liked best to smoke and to make tea, wrapping them in hide containers. Pine Tree Woman gave me crushed squaw root to add to my tea when I felt my birth pangs begin.

The villagers shaped saplings of green wood for longbows, good for bending, and strong paddles for moving over the water. They prepared stone-tipped, fletched arrows for themselves, and unfinished arrow wood for trading. The Eskimo would finish these, but the wood itself was needed. They bound sheaves of arrows together with basswood cord. Packs of leaves were added to the long bundles on the floor of the canoes. The women packed journey food and filled skins with freshwater for the traders while the men painted pitch on the inside seams and hulls of their wide-bowed seagoing canoes.

Since the day I stumbled out of the winter forest at Pine Tree Woman's feet, not once had I opened the sheath I kept on a leather thong between my breasts, under my rags. While I'd been asleep, anyone might have seen it, but it seemed to me that my secret had not been violated. No one asked me what lay hidden inside. Perhaps they assumed from its length and narrowness that it was a special fetish, a bone of an ancestor. Pine Tree Woman never suggested I show her what my pouch held.

What would they think if they saw my knife, which reflected the sun, rang and made sparks when struck against flint? I could not explain the magic even though I possessed it. Because of all Pine Tree Woman had done for me, I had decided to give her a piece of the truth. I owed her that at least.

"Come with me where we can speak alone," I said softly. She asked no question, just put down her work and followed me into the small islet woods. The sun slanted between the spruces, highlighting each pebble. I gestured for us to stop. "There is something I want you to see." Pulling out the pouch with its thong from beneath my dress, I slipped the cord up over my head. I held the pouch on my hand, where she could see it.

She averted her eyes. "Your fetish? Be careful. Its magic may dissipate if you show it to anyone."

"No, Pine Tree Woman. It's not a fetish. It is a special kind of knife. I think there may be magic in it, but I don't know. I've been afraid to show it. Please look." I drew it out and handed the knife to her, bone-colored hilt first, with the carved designs upward. "Perhaps you can tell me what it's made of and what the black lines mean."

Pine Tree Woman stared, touching the designs, then the gray blade. "How did you acquire such a knife?" she whispered, although none but the two of us could hear. "Did your people give it to you?"

"I have no people I can speak of. A southern friend gave me this knife for a parting gift, but I never had the chance to ask her about it. She pointed out my path to me and bade me go north." I saw Pine Tree Woman struggling not to ask me questions. With great effort, it seemed, she refrained.

"I can't say more, except that she was as good a friend to me as you have been. The Great Spirit sent you both to me to save me from . . . death or possibly worse." Had I said too much? "Do you think the knife is Eskimo work? Have you ever seen one like it?"

"Never," she said, handing it back to me. "Put it away. It might tempt people who would use its power for evil. It seems to me that such a knife must hold much power. The maker of those designs may have tied them to spirits as I sew prayers into the colored quill designs I make into clothing. I might pray for hunting luck if I sew a shirt for a man, or an easy birth if I fashion a woman's dress, but I can't guess what those designs mean. The hilt feels like ivory, the long tusk of a walrus, or a whale tooth. The hilt might be Eskimo, but I've never seen such a blade. Did you really marry an Eskimo man?"

I dropped the knife into the sand and threw my arms around her, trying hard to steady my trembling. "I can't tell you more than I have already done. Please don't ask me to."

Pine Tree Woman returned my embrace. "I'm sorry, Little One. I shouldn't have asked that." She lifted the knife out of the sand. "The blade is truly strange. It was warm a moment ago, and now it's cold. Look! Look how it reflects the sun." She moved it back and forth. "I don't know *what* it is."

Having shared knowledge of its odd properties, I felt free to examine the knife again. "The blade is like copper, a substance I have seen in armbands traded from the western tribes. Copper is the color of human skin and bends more easily than this. This blade is heavier. Listen to the sound it makes when I strike it." I took out my flint knife and struck the hilt of one to the blade of the other, one forward and the other away.

"Oh!" Pine Tree Woman said, as the blade rang and sparks flew. "It has fire in it. Perhaps if you show it to Walks in Shadow—"

"No! No one must see it until I'm gone."

After a moment, she asked me the obvious question. "How will the knife be here to show him when you're gone?"

"You returned my life to me. You took me in and gave me food when I thought never to feel warmth or see another human again. If you hadn't taken me that day, I would be bones under the leaves. I want you to have my knife."

Pine Tree Woman did not hesitate to reply. "No. You are wherever Great Spirit Manitou wants you to be. If He wanted you to die, He wouldn't have sent you to me. That knife is yours for a reason. Whatever magic it holds, it is part of your destiny. You must take it with you. Its meaning will be made known to you at the proper time."

She stopped my protests, pressing the tips of her fingers to my lips. "You have a hidden self, not only from us. It seems that you don't know who you are. Continue along the path that opens to you. Someday, you'll find out what the designs and the strange blade mean." She slipped the blade back into its sheath and handed it to me. I slipped the thong over my head and tucked it inside my dress, next to my skin again.

I had thought escape was all that the storyteller woman had promised me, if I managed to travel beyond Algonquin territory. Could there be more reason than that to keep running? Now, I had to cross the Great Water to islands in the north. I'd been across many waters already, beginning with Wide River. Since then, I had crossed streams and rivers. The ocean itself awaited.

Pine Tree Woman led me back to the trail. Soon we would be among the others, with no further chance for private words. "You will not let me leave you anything. I have nothing else for you to remember me by."

"You gave us something to wonder about during all the moons you lived among us. We'll tell stories about you to our children, and they will continue to tell the story of a girl who came out of the forest to make us magic pictures. The story will end with how she went out of the world to find her destiny. Maybe you are like Earth Mother and the baby you carry was sired by the Father Wind, like hers."

I almost laughed. My baby's father was not Ga-oh, Wind Spirit. The Creator and his evil brother were both born from the joining of Mother Earth and Ga-oh. Pine Tree Woman and I knew the same story. By this, I knew the Algonquin Creator must be the same as ours, only with a different name.

"It's getting dark here under the trees, Little One. Still Water must be preparing the evening meal. We'd best return to the village now. Marsh Lily and I have something for you. We mustn't disappoint my granddaughter." She smiled in a secretive way and touched finger to lips. "Not another word."

The others were watching for us. When we entered into the wigwam, I crouched upon my bed fur; Still Water and Marsh Lily told me to hold my hands out in front of me and close my eyes. "Don't open them until I tell you," the girl commanded, sounding like her grandmother.

I heard Pine Tree Woman step away, lift a basket lid, and return. She placed something heavy across my arms. Tears seeped from under my closed lashes when I felt the soft doeskin with its quill designs. I realized what it must be as soon as I touched it, but I had not guessed it was for me.

"Open your eyes now," the girl said. My sense of touch had not prepared me for the beauty of the sleeved dress with its fringe and intricate colored quillwork. There was a martin-fur parka with a hood, and mittens, too. "Grandmother worked on this mostly when you were learning the Eskimo sign talk. She made the parka big enough to keep your baby covered, too. While he's small enough, you can carry him on a sling underneath so he can nurse whenever he likes."

I set the parka down on my pallet and held the dress out by its shoulders to look at it. It was the most beautiful dress I had ever seen. Words deserted me, but I hugged Pine Tree Woman, showing the emotion I felt.

Still Water said, "She's forgotten how to talk all over again, just like when we found her." The others smiled, knowing I'd not forgotten, but that I simply could not think how to express my gratitude. Gladness and sorrow clouded my eyes, and "rain" threatened again.

Ganeogaono are trained from infancy not to cry. A baby's cry might alert an enemy, as my brother's once had. Teardrops trailed lines down my dusty cheeks. I thought about how I must have weakened away from my own people. "I will wear it and think of *all* of you!" I said. When I held the dress close, the fringed hem almost touched the toes of my calf-high moccasins.

In the morning, Still Water helped me wash my hair in the stream. Marsh Lily rubbed beach sand with both her hands into the strands of my hair to carry away the grease of two seasons of smoke and sweat. "Now lean back." Suddenly, they ducked my head underwater. The cold made me gasp. Laughing and dripping, I rose up and pushed the small girl's head underwater, too. We both laughed and squirmed.

"Into the stream with you!" Still Water commanded. "We'll never get the sand out any other way. If you weren't with child, Little One, I'd say you were hardly old enough to have a husband." When she bent over to scrub my neck, I yanked her in also.

"You need a bath, too." I laughed and they both joined in. We allowed the sun to dry us on the wide boulders, with our hair spread out to dry. I savored the warmth and their company.

Later, Still Water used a shell comb to part my hair, plaiting it on both sides and tying my braids to hang down in front of my shoulders. Marsh Lily tucked shining green duck feathers into my hair. "They look nice," she said, sitting back to admire her work. "The green catches the light." She gazed at me for a while, then sighed. "It's time to eat." The villagers gathered together that night, sitting around a driftwood fire and eating our evening meal. Clouds moved across the twilight sky and covered the moon before we slept.

After the sun rose in the southeast, the traders loaded their canoes. A last filling meal was quickly served to the travelers before we cast off. I tied on my leggings and slipped my new dress over my head, tucking the leggings into my wide-topped moccasins. I almost hated to cover the beautiful dress with my parka.

"You are so beautiful," Marsh Lily whispered. "I'll never forget you." I hugged her and said my good-byes to the many villagers who had been kind to me. Finally, I heaved my bundle to my head and walked with the other families down to the bay shore.

Walks in Shadow chanted a prayer, asking Manitou to bless the traders and bring them home safely. He had a private word for me before I boarded Crab Eater's canoe. "Girl Who Makes Pictures," he whispered. "This is your private name. No one else knows. Gray Wolf Eye hopes you might come back to us, but your path will take you elsewhere. I pray the Great Spirit to guide you well. We will remember you in this village as Little One of the Naskapi."

I clasped my hands together and bowed my head. His shaman powers had told him I was escaping from something evil in the south. He knew my name, yet he kept silent. Shaman power could be terrifying, as my own people knew, when it was used for evil. Walks in Shadow used his magic for the good of his people. "Peace to you and all your people," I said, then turned away and climbed aboard, crawling into my place beside Crab Eater in the wide seaworthy canoe.

There were four men in each of the two canoes; eight men altogether—and me—with our trade goods. The shoreline fell away and the captain told us to turn east, heading for the open sea. The waves rolled and crested white and the wind blew fresh, scattering clouds across the sky's face. Spray dampened my cheeks while the men dipped their paddles. Gulls, pelicans, and others birds, whose names I did not know, skimmed the water and dove for fish, screeching and squawking around the canoes.

The men spoke little, sweeping their paddles deeply. I had little to do but think. Resting my hands on my rounded belly, I thought again of my unborn child. It had no family to protect it—no father, no village, only me.

"Baby," I promised silently, "I'll do my best to care for you. I'll teach you your heritage. You will grow up with off-worlders." I sent comforting thoughts to my child. "But you won't be a stranger like me. You'll learn to manage a skin boat and to hunt with a harpoon. You'll never taste corn, so you won't miss it. You'll never climb a tree." Nor would I, ever again.

Before dark, we put into a cove and pulled our canoes ashore. Clever Hands knew of a spring on the island where we could drink and refill our water bags. We collected driftwood for a fire to bake the fish our lines had caught along the way.

After we ate, Clever Hands had us practice the hand signs he'd taught us. "Sorqaq is their chief. Since last year, who knows? He's an old man, for one of them, perhaps over forty winters. Remember, don't call the island people 'Eskimo' to their faces." I listened more closely.

"They don't know we call them Raw Fish Eaters. By now, they may have figured out our name for them. Listen well, Bucktorn. This is your first trip." The young man looked toward him. "Their word for man is *inuk*. They call their tribe "Men," *Inuit*, in their language. It's best to speak only with the signs I showed you and only about trading. They are a touchy people, and we wouldn't want to make them angry by saying a wrong word."

"How do you mean?" Crab Eater asked.

The leader seemed to search in his mind for an example. "What if I said, 'You are a fish,' instead of 'That is a fish'?" He followed his question with a grin.

"I'd laugh," Crab Eater replied, and the other men smiled.

"An Eskimo might take it as an insult and skewer you with a barbed harpoon. He'd claim it was an accident to his chief, that you looked like a seal from behind. Therefore, let us take our trade goods home with our skins intact. Eskimo have fine goods, but be cautious around them."

"You joke. No one can take offense that easily," Crab Eater objected.

"I'll stick to hand signs just to be sure," Bucktorn said nearby. I turned, to see him watching me grimly. "Be careful among them, Little One," he cautioned. "You were not born to their ways."

"I'll be careful," I agreed. "Thank you for your concern."

"We'll need our rest for tomorrow. We have most of another day to go."
With that, Clever Hands pulled up his blanket and we all tried to sleep.

On the third day, we reached the island. It was barren and rocky and
had a small hill. It was good that we had brought water. Driftwood littered
the beach. The men collected it and began a fire. When it was going well,
they covered it several times with a damp hide for a moment. A series of
dark puffs rose to the sky.

"Is the smoke to help them find the island?" I inquired.

"It will tell them we've arrived, but they need no help to find us. Eskimo know every island in this north ocean better than we of Turtle Island
know the trees in our village."

I climbed the slope, using my hands to pull myself from rock to rock.
Finally, I sat on a low-lying boulder, watching the ocean and the clouds.
The salt wind dampened my face. All around the island, the gray ocean
continued as far as I could see. High clouds left from last night's downpour
gathered toward the south. Rain must still be falling over the Naskapi
camp, I thought, and looked north again. Three small black lines appeared
below the horizon.

The lines grew larger, until they turned into gray boats riding over the
rolling waves. Nearer they came. Instead of seeing silhouettes against the
rise and fall of the waves, I began to make out different faces of men
dressed in glistening coats with close-tied hoods. Three slighter figures sat
astride the bundles, dressed differently. I wondered whether the Eskimo
had brought women with them.

I got to my feet to see them better, my heart racing. In less than a day,
I would know whether or not they would allow me to join them. The figures in the boats gestured and pointed at me, until a few of the Naskapi
men looked my way. Awkwardly, I descended back down to the Naskapi
camp on the gravel beach. "Make ready," I announced. "I see them coming
in their wide boats. The Eskimo are almost here."

BOOK III

Inuit

GREENLAND

Ice Sheet

Sorqaq's Village

▶ Qisuk's Village

Inuit

▶ Western District

Halvard's Greenland

▶ Trader Island

Pine Tree Woman's 2nd Village

▶ Pine Tree Woman's 1st Village

Naskapi

LABRADOR

Hawk Feather's Town ◀

Algonquin

Gulf of St. Lawrence

Wide River

Algonquin

Doteoga

Ganeogaono

← to Oneida

← to Onondaga

--- to Sorqaq's village

--- Qisuk's crossing by dog sledge

"*Do what is needed to restore balance. The world cannot exist without it. Wherever your destiny leads you, you must restore balance. Orenda requires it of you.*" Grandmother's words were sibilant, crackling like fall leaves or the last breath of a dying flame. "*You will find what you need across the water.*" The smell of tobacco smoke lingered a moment longer; then it, too, was gone.

I rested somewhere warm. In the dance of the firelight reflecting upon stone, between light and shadow, nothing was solid. From a little above, my spirit eyes observed the solidness of my body leaning against piled furs on the illeq while the lamp fires warmed the air. Voices almost penetrated my reality, but not quite, for I could not comprehend the lifting and falling of the words.

Where was I? Quite suddenly, I knew. Just as suddenly, I realized what had happened during the moons my spirit had slumbered.

Inuit

Chapter 14

Since the day the Oneida envoys tied up their canoe at our landing on Wide River, I'd found the idea of new people intriguing. Traveling to meet them had not been my plan, but since my destiny had brought me this far, I wanted to learn all I could. Questions crowded my thoughts, but much more than idle curiosity compelled me to study the travelers in the skin boats. At my grandmother's knee, I had learned never to despise knowledge and skills. Whatever I could learn from these strange people would help me survive in their world.

Would their words be too difficult to pronounce and remember? How did they cook and heat their dwellings without wood to make fires, or did they truly eat only uncooked meat and fish? I hoped their name was an exaggeration. Without birch or elm trees for structure and bark for a covering, what did they use to frame and protect their homes? Was it possible to use the bones of great white bears or even those of whales? Since Clever Hands had told us that Eskimo built their homes from blocks of snow, I did not know whether to believe anything he said.

While the Naskapi hurried to set out their trading goods, Crab Eater observed me sprinkling mint and sage leaves into pots I had filled with freshwater and set to simmering on stones beside the fire. He approached me there, when a sudden gust of wind blew up sparks and stinging smoke. Driftwood fires are difficult to control, being so dry, but we had nothing else to burn.

I moved around to the other side of the fire, coughing. "Do I do right to make tea to greet them, Crab Eater?" I asked. "Will they want tea when they land? Will they like this? Do they drink the same teas we drink?"

"Who wouldn't want a warm drink after being out on that?" He pointed toward the ocean. The water was deep, dark, and choppy. A new puff of wind brought cold spray with it from the last wave. "After a day with them, you'll know more than I do about them. Serving them tea will show the Eskimo you are industrious. From what I've been able to understand, the island people consider all things in terms of their usefulness to them."

"Then they are not like the Naskapi, who took in a wanderer with nothing to give back, but out of kindness only," I added.

He regarded me silently, wondering, surely, at my demented desire to go away with the off-world strangers. "Yes," he allowed. With his eyes on the approaching boats, he lowered himself into an easy crouch beside the fire. "Little One," he said just above a whisper, "Gray Wolf Eye and Walks in Shadow ordered us not to ask you again, but I will disobey. No one can hear us. If you change your mind, I will say they turned you down, refused to take you with them. Even if you once lived here, your heart is with us back on Turtle Island. Come back now, and dwell with us."

I blinked and swallowed back my emotion. "If only I could, Crab Eater." I turned away so he would not read my face. "But I can't." He clasped my trembling shoulder, then released it before he walked a little way down the beach to join the other men in welcoming the northern traders.

As soon as they reached land, the Eskimo lifted their dripping boats to carry them onto the beach. Sorqaq was the name of their headman. I knew him by the description Crab Eater had given me. He was not the tallest or the strongest, but his air of command and intelligence told me it was he. Sorqaq strode forward, looking with slanted eyes from one side of the beach to the other. His thin black beard and mustache held wisps of gray. When he pushed back his hood, long hair fell past his shoulders. His fingernails were black and he stood no taller than the shortest man of the Naskapi.

"Sorqaq!" Clever Hands ran up to him, his arms outstretched. The headman walked into them and hugged him affectionately. Stepping back, he spoke some words and signed the rest so I was able to follow. "My father, Gray Wolf Eye, sends greetings to you and your Inuit."

A big smile spread over the older man's face. *"Go da!"* the Eskimo exclaimed loudly and Clever Hands responded, *"Go da!"* just as forcefully, using real words, not signs. I had expected only hand language.

Silently, I crept over to Crab Eater. "What did the Eskimo chief say?"

"He bid us welcome to their island," my friend explained in a whisper. "All the off-world islands are theirs." While he spoke, he had laid out clay bowls and mugs as well as bundles of herbs, arrow shafts, bows, and paddles, arranging them neatly on the caribou hide. "Try to remember what Clever Hands told us about their words."

"If Clever Hands knows Eskimo talking words, why didn't he teach them to us?" I felt unsure of myself, noticing I had forgotten to use the name Inuit once again.

"*Go da* means 'greetings,' no more than that. Clever Hands knows very few spoken words and I know fewer. Each year, we need to be reminded of their hand signs. Their words are difficult for us to speak, hardly worth the trouble for a day of trading. You knew their words once. They'll come back to you."

"Yes," I said. "Of course they will." I dared not vary my given tale, needing to perpetuate the lie I'd lived with for the last two seasons.

The new arrivals sniffed the sage and mint tea wafting toward them on the breeze. Several Inuit approached me, holding their mugs out. I dipped them some tea, which was steaming as I poured it. Most of their fingers were frost-blackened. The men warmed their hands on the mugs, blowing away the steam. They sipped almost before the tea had ceased to bubble. One man noticed me as I crouched beside the fire, studying his fingers. He bent down and peered into my face, his small black eyes dancing with laughter. I looked away, embarrassed. Even the women smiled at my error. After that, I kept my eyes low.

The three women kept together, pointing and talking among themselves with quick words and high-pitched voices. I gestured to them, indicating the tea, inviting them to have some. "*Iyeh*," one of them murmured, and the three approached with their mugs. Their hands, more delicate than the men's, held the mugs and blew away the steam.

One woman—I could tell she must be young—pushed back her glossy hair, and her curious black eyes wrinkled as she smiled. One of her companions grinned to me before she raised the mug to her lips. She sipped slowly, breathing in the fragrant mint steam. "*Ti*," she said, smiling. She looked me over curiously. I wondered if they had ever seen a Naskapi woman. Probably not.

"*Iyeh. Ti,*" I repeated, saying my first words in their language. We explored one another with shy glances. Their parkas ended at their knees, with the fur outside. They wore them partly open, exposing the swell of small breasts. One of the women sat and hiked up her parka. Her leggings ended at an apron, which protected her loins and covered her all the way up to her waist.

I felt their eyes inspect my clothing and face, noticing my parted hair, which was brown, lighter than theirs, and tied in feather-decorated braids. Their hair, black as their small slanted eyes, was pulled back from their faces into high buns. My skin was more coppery, theirs more the color of faded brown leaves. The warm tea and the sun beating down on the beach increased the warmth that heated my neck under their scrutiny. I slipped out of my short Naskapi parka.

One of them touched my dress with two fingers and let the fringes pour over her hand. I told her my words for fringes and dress. Then I asked questions about her parka, and how to say the word in her tongue. She gave me the word *anorak* for the parka, *kamiks* for high furred boots. Crab Eater was right. In the time it took us to drink our tea, I had learned four words.

Using signs, I asked about the garment that covered her loins. It looked like fox skin. She explained in her own words, and I repeated them. The men wore white fur leggings that joined where their legs met and were tied below the knee. I asked for their word for this.

"*Kraslik. Nanuk.*" I was to learn that was their word for bear-hide pants. She touched her chest proudly, indicating she had made them.

"Fine work," I signed, a phrase I learned for the trading, although only the men would actually trade merchandise. The woman seemed delighted with my compliment, then said more words together and much too fast for me. She touched my middle.

"Baby?" she asked in sign language. She had not asked whether I was pregnant, which was obvious. She was seeking information. I repeated her word to learn it.

"Where's your *angut?*" I tried to show I had not understood. "*Inuk?*" she signed. "Where is your man? Which Naskapi is its father?" She pointed toward the mainlanders, waiting for me to indicate one of them.

"No father," I replied sadly. "Dead." The women clicked their tongues.

Meanwhile, on the mats above the beach, the trading continued briskly. Mostly, the men used signs or pointed, offering suitable trades. Everyone was anxious to go home again while the fine weather held. The Inuit women and I walked closer to see the trade goods. On seal hides, the Inuit displayed hooks and harpoon heads, pipes and carved statues smaller than my hand, all carved from antlers, walrus tusks, or possibly whalebone.

One small figure of a bear looked so real, it might have been the animal in miniature. I leaned forward to inspect the work, seeing each hair and each tiny claw carved perfectly. I lifted it. One of the women let out a shrill cry. Before I could respond, an *inuk* rushed forward and pulled the thing out of my hand, scowling and shouting many words. I had not meant to take, only to examine. Confused and fearful that I had angered him, I backed away.

Clever Hands saw what had happened and hurried over. "You touched a hunting charm. Women may not touch them. They think it will lose its power."

"I didn't know."

"Little One meant no harm," he signed to the object's owner, trying to pacify him. Sorqaq ambled over to see what had happened and the three of them talked with both words and signs. It took some time for the first *inuk* to calm down. Clever Hands signed: "Wait." When he returned, he held a good longbow up and offered it in trade for the bear effigy, even though I had touched it. The *inuk* examined the bow, strung it, and drew it back. He seemed partially satisfied, but he signed again to show he wanted arrows, too. He held up five fingers. Clever Hands considered and countered with two fingers. The *inuk* hesitated, looked around, whistled a bit.

Clever Hands looked skyward, as if to say he was wasting his time with someone so greedy. After all, if the bear token was injured, how could its owner reasonably expect more? At last, the *inuk* settled for the two arrows Clever Hands added to the bow in trade. My blunder may have cost Clever Hands a bow and two arrows, but I feared it had cost me even more. Eyes downcast, I walked back to the driftwood fire. Clever Hands walked away with Sorqaq.

Crab Eater, who had watched the incident without interfering, walked over to me again, holding out his mug for more tea. As I poured it, he whispered. "Clever Hands is going to tell Sorqaq how your drawings called the caribou herd to our river. That should undo the harm you did by touching the bear fetish."

"Do you really think so?" I asked hopefully, although doubting it.

"Think about it. The fetishes we traded for last year lost their power, or Walks in Shadow would not have needed your pictures. By touching that one, you might have added to its power, rather than taking away from it. At least, that's what Clever Hands is attempting to make Sorqaq think." That put a new light on it. Crab Eater apparently knew how Clever Hands would bargain.

A thought came to me. "An Inuit shaman must have put the hunting magic in the fetishes. If a woman must not touch hunting things, what will they think of a woman who claims to be stronger in animal magic than their shaman?"

"But you have not made that claim. Clever Hands will simply tell Sorqaq that you made pictures at our shaman's request. He'll say how Walks in Shadow used them. He's not saying you are a shaman, only that you can make tools for a shaman to use, *if* he's clever enough. Let us see how good a trade he can make for you, my little friend." His smile flashed white. "With luck and Clever Hands' trading skill, you should be worth at least three pipes, two silver-fox furs, and an excellent pair of mittens."

"Trade?" I asked, startled. Was I a slave to be traded for?

"I was teasing you. I think he'll tell him the truth," Crab Eater said. "That you are wife to an *inuk* who may have died hunting, and you walked to us alone, losing your memory from an injury in your wandering. He'll say you are looking for your husband or his family in the north. That is the truth, isn't it?"

I was saved from having to answer. Clever Hands approached with Sorqaq, saying both our names aloud to the Inuit headman. He signed "Little girl" to Sorqaq to interpret my name. The headman threw his head back and barked out a laugh, then signed too quickly for me to follow his meaning. I looked to Sorqaq. His dark eyes held mine immobile while Clever Hands translated his words and explained why he had laughed.

"He says a little girl is unlikely to have such a big belly." The Naskapi trader signed, watched the *inuk,* then translated again. "I told him you were hurt in the head and forgot who you are before you arrived in our village. I said you believe you have family through marriage with his people but that you can't remember his name or village, or how you came to be in our forest. I asked if you may return to their lands with them to search for your husband's relatives."

Sorqaq walked around behind me as if looking over a dog. I stood very still, hardly daring to raise my eyes to his face. The manner of the other women with their men told me this was proper courtesy from woman to man among his people. He stopped in front of me. By his features and bearing, he was older than any man on the island, about the age of my father. If he gives me leave to stay among them, I thought, no one will oppose him.

"Mikisoq," he said. Sorqaq seemed to be speaking to me, not to Clever Hands. I repeated his word, making it into a question.

"The woman's name is Mikisoq." He signed Little One or Little Girl, in his words, giving me back my Naskapi name but in Inuit, which told me he considered taking me. Sorqaq continued speaking and signing at the same time. "Mikisoq, Clever Hands"—he said the foreign name slowly— "says you can make pictures of animals. Will you make them for our *angakkoq?*"

"Angakkoq?" I looked to Clever Hands for the word's meaning.

"His shaman. I don't know whether *angakkoq* is his name or if it means shaman, but he makes their ceremonies and holds their magic. He would have wanted to talk to you if he were here. You'll meet him when you get to their village on the northern island."

"I see. *Iyeh,* Sorqaq," I replied for myself, having turned to face him.

The headman nodded. "Good," he said. "She talks like an Inuit woman already." He signed: "Your pictures will call animals to our hunters?"

"I don't know." I shrugged, afraid to say yes. "Not always. Sometimes. As the Creator decides." I could not sign well enough to tell him that myself, but Clever Hands translated, pointing to heaven and the ocean to make the sign for the Creator. What if I make pictures and the animals do not go where the hunters can find them? I wondered.

"Sometimes is good," Sorqaq said. "It is always as Nerrivik wills. Mikisoq is a fine woman. I give her permission to live with us." I understood his signs and grinned to show him my appreciation. Clever Hands turned away to see how the packing was progressing, which is why he was not watching when Sorqaq signed his next words.

"Your baby." I understood what he said so far, having heard that word from the women. He pointed to my middle to be sure I understood.

"My baby? *Iyeh?*" What did he want to know about my baby?

"Is his father Inuit?" he asked in his words.

"No father," I signed. "Dead."

He pointed to his head, indicating he already knew that. Sorqaq repeated his question. "Is he Inuit?"

This seemed to be an important issue to him. Of course Hawk Feather was no Inuit, but why would that matter? Since I was supposed to have lost my memory, I shrugged.

"Then I will take you. The baby must have Inuit father."

"Iyeh," I said to show I understood. He would give my baby to a man of the tribe to adopt, to teach him proper skills as he grew. That was good.

I signed to Sorqaq, thanking him, then thanked Clever Hands for helping me find a place in the Inuit wide boat and a home in Sorqaq's village.

After both men nodded, I stepped back, leaving them to their final words together. It was time to tell the women I had permission to return to their village with them.

With my pack of supplies, I returned to the women. "I'm going to stay with you," I signed. "Sorqaq said yes." The tallest pulled me close, pressing her cheek against mine. I imagined I might be happy with them, when I learned their customs. I wondered, though, why she made clicking sounds in addition to her welcoming embraces. She rubbed the caribou hide of my long dress above my belly and made a sad face. Yes, it would be a hard life in the north, but I thought all would go well. We have been accepted, I thought, my child and me.

"I am Mikisoq," I said, pointing to myself.

She laughed at the name but accepted it. "I am Meqqoq." She pointed to her hair. I discovered later that her name meant "hairy." Meqqoq did have a thick head of hair. She pointed to one of the Inuit and signed 'Father,' lifting her chin proudly. He was a small, serious-looking man with a great pile of trade goods on his mat. From this, I gathered status came to daughters from their fathers. My child would have no status, then. A small doubt tugged at me, but I pushed it back. Meqqoq led me closer to the other women.

"I'm Padloq." Padloq laughed merrily. I learned later that her name meant something like "lazy," but, once I knew her, I realized that it really meant the opposite. She was very industrious. "Hello, Mikisoq. We will be friends."

"I am Aama." Aama grinned at the sound of her name. In spite of her short stature and small features, Aama's eyes were delicately shaped. Her tiny, flattish nose led down to perfect lips and a fine, strong chin. Even to my foreign way of seeing, Aama's beauty was obvious. Later, I learned Aama meant "again." No wonder her name made her smile. I thought, How peculiar I must seem to them, a woman tall as most of their men, with wide eyes and a straight nose. Will they think my foreignness unappealing?

Meqqoq gave me a slab of cold dried seal meat to eat. "Come with me to sleep after eating," she signed, motioning to indicate eat, then sleep and come, ending with herself. She indicated the small women's tent. "We are leaving early." The signs were not difficult. Learning Inuit words would take much longer.

While we ate, the sky cleared, leaving the heavens a brilliant blue with wispy clouds. I discovered that none of the young women were married. However, they were nubile, and, therefore, ready to choose their husbands. They had come along to examine the hunters in close quarters, to make their selections. They had more to say in choosing their husbands, if the men agreed to their choice, than did a young woman of my people. Each woman's father was there. There were five young men and five fathers to make marriage arrangements, should a young man and woman decide to couple off.

"My father is Ululik," Padloq informed me, pointing to the oldest-looking of the traders next to the headman. She pulled me closer and turned us away from the others. With signs and words, she confided, "I like Sorqaq's son, Qisuk. He is very handsome." She pointed to him, cradled her face, and tried to look handsome in a manly way, strong and brave. I had to laugh at her talent for mimicry. "He has a wife, but she is my sister. Maybe he will like me and take me, too. Then Sorqaq will be my father-in-law." I had to guess some of what she meant, not having enough signs or words. She blushed and grinned at her confession.

"We go to sleep now. Come," she said, linking her arm with mine. In the tent, she kept me at her side and pulled her bear fur over us, covering her mouth and nose. Even before I had found a comfortable position to lie in, she slept.

When we awoke, Padloq took my hand, leading me to the place in the cleft of the hill where Aama and Meqqoq had gone. We relieved ourselves, away from the eyes of men. I found the Inuit women's shyness and modesty perplexing. It would be less simple on the voyage, but when it was possible, women preferred to be private about such matters.

I tried to emulate their actions, the better to fit in. I did not see their men as being handsome, nor did I see the women as pretty, except for Aama. Everything must be gotten used to and will seem odd for a while, I cautioned myself. When I had learned their words, their ways, and how to behave, it would be easier.

We did not take time to make tea, but each took another slab of dried meat before we lifted the bundles to carry them down to the wide boats. We waded through the surf. As we handed the bundles over, the men took them and tied them down. I asked the word for boat, stroking its rough yet pliable surface.

"Umiak," Aama said, her gesture taking in all three vessels. Touching the material of the boat, she signed: "This—walrus skin. Strong." As she signed, she pretended to pull something resistant between her hands. "Not let water in." She stroked one of the ribs that held the walrus hide. "Sorqaq." She giggled, then demonstrated something huge and swimming. So I learned that Sorqaq's name meant "whalebone." I repeated the new words.

"Good," Aama said. "You learn a little."

The Naskapi traders packed their canoes, preparing to depart. Sorqaq and Clever Hands walked up to each other for the last time this year, their respective traders standing nearby. The leaders embraced as they had when they greeted each other the previous day. It had been a good trading session. "When the ice blows away—next year," each said in his own words for his men to hear, repeating in signs. It seemed to be a ritual of leave-taking they all knew and expected.

People on both sides called out their farewells. "Good travels, Little One," Crab Eater said. I waved sadly to him and the others.

"I'll remember my time with you," I called. "Give my love to Pine Tree Woman and the others." He nodded and turned away to his canoe.

We climbed into our umiaks, crouching, with our knees on either side of the bundles. One *inuk* shoved the boat, running beside it, then leapt in. Most of the men used paddles, but several in the stern used longer, wide-bladed oars. When we passed the island, I looked back. The last I saw of the Naskapi canoes were small silhouettes in the distance, heading south, back to Turtle Island. An *inuk* put a paddle into my hands. I did my best, as did Padloq, Aama, and Meqqoq. Every hand was needed.

The trading island vanished into the green-blue water behind us. After a while, more islands appeared on our left as we moved over the rolling water. Dolphins leapt, seeming to laugh at the fast-moving umiaks, but the Inuit made no effort to catch them. Thick clouds gathered, covering the sun, but the rain held off until we had put into land for the night and set up our tents.

The next day, we passed small hilly islands, rocky and uninviting. After the next sleep, we saw a pack of black-and-white whales, small, but larger than the umiaks. Wondering if the whales might tip over the boats, I pulled my paddle across my knees so I could aid my speech with signs. "Padloq, are the men going to hunt them?"

"No. They are orcas. Too smart. Maybe they will hunt us." We rowed with great energy to put distance between the whales and ourselves. From the size of the bones that lined the umiaks, they came from larger whales than orcas.

The following morning, Qisuk reached for his harpoon and throwing board. With knees spread wide for balance, he stared into the water, following a ripple with his eyes. He took aim, still as a statue, one arm poised back for the throw. The harpoon flew from his thrower and the barbs stuck. "Good," the others complimented. Someone fished the shaft out of the water. The struggling animal pulled the umiak, strongly at first. After awhile, it tired, weakened from its struggle and the blood it had lost. While Qisuk worked to pull his bleeding and wriggling catch in, more men grasped the rope to help pull.

It was a strange animal, unlike any I had seen before. A twisted horn protruded from above its mouth. I could not say if it was fish or porpoise, but it was big as a man and fought well. Bloody foam lapped against the boat's side. The beast thrashed from side to side, but the line held. When the animal ceased fighting, the boat drew beside it. The other two boats waited nearby while Qisuk and two others dragged it over the side, still gushing blood.

I asked Padloq for its name. "Narwhal," she said. "Small whale. Very good to eat. Horn very lucky." The men patted Qisuk's back. The narwhal might still have been breathing while Qisuk and his companions butchered it, handing out shares to the teams in the other boats, which had drawn up close.

Sorqaq held his hand high in a fist and waved it up and down, a sign for a job well done. He called to his successful son, nodding, and pointed to me. I imagined he said something like: "Maybe the Naskapi woman brings us hunting luck already." At that, several Inuit turned measuring eyes toward me, as though to gauge my worth. My being among them had nothing to do with it; it was Qisuk who had spied the narwhal and killed it. His skill as harpooner and the strong arms of the Inuit had brought in the beast.

Sorqaq nodded to me, inclining his head, and showed his teeth in what looked like a smile. Those close enough to do so clapped his back, showing enthusiastic approval for his decision to bring me. He accepted their praise, then motioned for us to continue. So far, having me along had proved lucky. I supposed the men thought of me as a sort of hunting charm, something like the ivory statuette I had not been allowed to touch.

Chapter 17

Between islands, an ice mountain drifted into our path. The cold wind gusted, blowing crystals off it and into our faces. No one else seemed particularly concerned about the deathly cold ocean pressing only a palm's width beneath our knees. The men's strong arms propelled the umiaks where they, not the wind and waves, chose. Qisuk whistled three shrill notes. Within moments, our umiak slowed. We waited for Sorqaq to make a decision while the men dragged their paddles against the water to halt our forward motion.

Sorqaq rose up, his knees wide for balance as he tested the wind's direction and took our bearings. His thin black beard blew about while he sighted the floating mountain. Apparently satisfied we could cross its path safely, the headman gestured for us to stay on course. The men dipped paddles.

As we closed on it, the mountain of ice rose from the waves like a blue-and-white thundercloud. It loomed over us, blocking our view of the crescent moon hanging low in the light summer sky. An animal that enormous could have swallowed all three umiaks. The low sun's reflection glared off meltwater running down the ice fissures and cracks. Scattered rainbows flickered into existence and then out again. At the beginning of time, Sky Woman had been gently lowered by helpful birds to the back of the Great Turtle. I never suspected that land other than our pleasant, tree-covered Turtle Island existed below heaven.

The floating ice mountain vanished as the men put distance between it and ourselves. The moon drifted like a sky boat from behind clouds. Summer days at home were long, but in this northern sea off the world, the sun did not set at all. It remained opposite the moon, just above the horizon, painting the low clouds in the western sky gold-red.

After our second sleep, Meqqoq had paired off with Salluq, a young hunter of about sixteen. Aama chose Taaferaaq. He seemed older, possibly as old as twenty summers. Taaferaaq could hardly contain his happiness that the prettiest woman preferred him. I wondered if he had been waiting for her to grow up. It made me smile to see their happiness. Impatient, no doubt, to get Aama alone under his furs, he set the pace for the other rowers. Qisuk remained oblivious to Padloq's longing glances and continued sleeping alone.

After Aama and Meqqoq had moved to sit and sleep beside their chosen men, I found myself together with Padloq most of the time. "He thinks only of his wife, my sister," Padloq complained, motioning to help me understand. "After her baby is born, he must sleep away from her until her bleeding stops." She smiled coyly. "When he has no woman to warm him between his legs, he'll think of asking my father to send me to his igloo. I won't mind being second wife to my sister's husband. An *inuk* has need for a woman, especially in the spring."

Padloq spoke more boldly than I would have expected from her demure manner. She blushed and lowered her eyes whenever Qisuk happened to glance in her direction. Although she assumed the role of my teacher, she continued to make herself available to Qisuk in case he might return her interest. I didn't see how he could fail to notice her. She must have been quite young when he married her sister, if he still regarded Padloq as a child. Perhaps the love he felt for his first wife was too strong to allow interest for another, but I guessed he was too full of himself to notice Padloq's adoring glances. It seemed to me his main concern was trying to impress his companions and to gain their esteem.

In Doteoga, a woman might choose to live without a husband, since she had her clan. Her uncles and brothers would hunt for her, and her children as well, should she bear any without marrying. In these off-world islands, a woman required a protector. Sorqaq had offered me sanctuary, but I disliked having to impose on his family for long. I could see that once my child was born, I would need to choose a husband to provide for us. Fortunately, that was a decision I did not need to make right away.

The seemingly tireless Inuit covered more distance than the Naskapi had in the same length of time. On the third day out from the trading island, the smell of grass came to my nostrils on the briny wind. Even before the brown-and-green land appeared against the sky, we were slapping at mosquitoes.

"Home!" Padloq pointed. The umiaks entered a long blue-green inlet. Gray strands of pebble beach framed the green hills. A village appeared soon. It consisted of about ten or twelve turf-covered homes set against the green hillside like beaver mounds. Some of them were built right into the hills. Instead of flaps, supports lined entrance tunnels into the low dwellings. They looked like standing turtles with their necks stretched out.

"I see my igloo!" Padloq shrieked. "My mother sees us! She's calling the villagers to come out and welcome us!" In her excitement, she jumped to her feet. Her movement rocked the umiak. Qisuk rounded on her, not saying a word, until she sat back with lowered eyes and dipped her paddle. She looked like a whipped dog. Such subservience turned my stomach. The women were not slaves here, but their deference to the men made them seem hardly more.

Villagers poured out of the igloos and gathered on the beach to watch our approach. Children climbed the larger hill behind the village for a good view while the umiaks covered the last waves and pulled up on the beach.

The village men helped pull the boats up onto the sand. Large thick-coated dogs with long muzzles yipped, barking a welcome to the returning traders. Women pointed, chirping like birds in quick, high voices. They wore blue-fox *kapataks,* summer jackets. Quite a few carried infants riding in their *amaaqs,* the hoods behind their *kapataks.* The babies leaned forward to peek out at us, making the mothers look as if second, smaller heads grew from their shoulders. The women as well as the men were shorter and stockier than the tribes I had known, with broader faces and smaller features. The women hurried to help carry or drag the heavy trade bundles up the slope while the men carried their skin boats up into the village.

In the commotion, Padloq remained near enough for me to keep her in sight. When she beckoned to me, I followed her lead to the center of the village. Sorqaq disappeared among the people up near the igloos. Believing he had gone to explain my presence and to make arrangements for me, I expected he would return soon. After being on the water so long, my legs felt peculiar and unsteady. My belly, bulging out in front, set me off balance. I reached out to Padloq's shoulder to steady myself, when Aama, who had been on one of the other boats with Taaferaaq, ran over to help me, too. Between them, they guided me toward the igloos. "Soon, baby come out," Aama said.

"Iyeh," I agreed. It could hardly be soon enough for me. I wanted to feel like myself again, but I hoped I would have sufficient time to prepare warm wraps for my infant and find enough of what Inuit mothers used for diapering.

Padloq and Aama had not let me lug any of the heavier packs, but I managed a pouch of tobacco leaves and my own pack, which I had strapped over my shoulders. The dogs nudged and nosed me, forcing me to a halt while they smelled my clothes. Ululik, Padloq's father, spoke to them, his voice soothing and commanding at once. The dogs dropped to the ground. "They know you now and will not menace you," he assured me. That was a relief, but I still did not know where I was to stay.

"Wait here," Padloq said. I had learned most simple commands by then. With effort, I was smart as the dogs. While I waited just outside the igloos, several short women with quick eyes and moving hands chattered among themselves and pointed me out to the others. Padloq took Ululik's arm, pushing him a little farther away so that I could not hear what they were saying. Nor would I have understood if I had, since they spoke very fast.

Ululik went over to talk to Sorqaq, who had appeared again beside the largest igloo. When he returned, Ululik nodded to his daughter and grinned. Padloq ran back to me, stopping herself with an excited little hop. "Sorqaq does not mind. You can stay with me in my father's igloo. You will be like my sister. We will be together all the time!" Her smile flashed white in her walnut brown face. So that's what they had been arranging.

"What will your mother say?" I asked. "Will she mind?" I hoped I'd made my signs correctly, but Padloq knew what I intended to ask.

"She must do what my father decides. Don't worry. I know she will like you. Come." She hurried me along past drying racks, where long slices of fish dried in the wind. Children holding sticks guarded the meat from the dogs. Sledges rested beside the igloos. The umiaks, which had been brought up to the village, were covered with hides to protect them. Small, narrower boats leaned against a cliff. "Kayaks," Padloq said in answer to my question.

Standing in front of Ululik's igloo, I noticed something about the walls of the stone I had never seen on a hide- or bark-covered wigwam. Several stones were set apart on purpose. I could see how light and air entered directly through these spaces. Through this opening, I beheld Padloq's mother.

Padloq dropped to her knees to crawl through the tunnel to the room inside. I crawled behind her, down and then up again, passing bundles piled against the stone sides. I assumed this was where their food was stored. "Here we are," Padloq said. As soon as we got to our feet, she pointed to me. "This is Mikisoq, my new friend. Father says she can live with us. Mikisoq, my mother is called Maki." Padloq's mother sat atop a fur-covered platform, from which she tended a cooking bowl propped over a fire. The flames rose from several plugs floating on what seemed like clear water. There was no wood. Instead of a hearth in the floor, there was a raised rock with a depression filled with what appeared to be water. Tongues of flame burned at the ends of twisted moss wicks. The small flames burned evenly and silently, making smoke plumes that left through vents where the overhead stones did not meet.

Maki narrowed her eyes at me without speaking or welcoming me, or even moving to welcome her daughter. I smelled meat roasting. A moment later, Ululik ducked and crawled through the stone tunnel.

Husband and wife said, "*Go da,*" to each other. Their eyes met through the steam of the tea Padloq's mother dipped into a bowl and handed to Ululik. I wondered whether I should have waited outside while they told her about me.

Padloq embraced her mother. "Mother, my friend Mikisoq comes from the Naskapi tribe. She's looking for her dead husband's family. They say she lost her memory, but she thinks she was wife to one of our people. She's going to have a baby."

Ululik added, "In the meanwhile, I decided to let her stay with Padloq. Our daughter likes her."

I understood little of their actual words, but I got the main thrust of their conversation. Maki looked to her daughter, eyes frowning and mouth twisting. I imagined she thought, Here's another mouth to feed.

When I found an opportunity to ask about her cooking fire, Maki's expression stated what needed no translation. Why had they brought such an ignoramus into her home? I felt like a simpleton, but never in my fourteen winters had I seen such a sight as that of fire sitting on water.

Padloq touched the water with her finger and had me do the same. When she tasted it and indicated I was to do likewise, I discovered my mistake. It was clear, melted fat. Next, she pointed out the islands of flame floating in the fat. "Wicks," she explained in her language. "Haven't you ever seen a wick before?"

"No," I said, and repeated the word. Where there was wood to burn, what need would exist for such a thing? They turned their attention to the food, as did I. Meat and roots simmered in the stone bowl standing on a tripod of flat stones set around the fire basin.

"For cooking, Mikisoq," Padloq said, indicating the whole affair, the tall rock, basin-shaped cavity, fat and wicks, and cooking bowl. "She has forgotten our words, Mother," she said to explain my difficulty. "The Tobacco Growers say she might have been hit on the head." The older woman ladled stew into a clay bowl of Naskapi design and handed it to Ululik, who took it and climbed up on the bed platform to eat.

"Mikisoq," Maki muttered, as though tasting my name. "It's an odd name for a grown woman." Since the name meant "little girl," I had to agree with her, but I could offer no explanation. My swollen middle under the caribou-hide dress spoke for itself. "Stay then, since Padloq wants to keep you."

I gathered she did not welcome me with a whole heart, but supplicants can't choose their welcomes. "Thank you," I said in the Inuit tongue.

"You may call me Maki," she said. Her face was round, an older version of Padloq's, plain but lively. Her brief smile made her face almost pleasant. "Eat now," she said. She served out food to us, heaping Padloq's bowl with boiled meat chunks, roots, and broth.

"Come sit with me on my *illeq*," Padloq invited, pulling me behind her over to her platform. "We'll eat out of the same bowl." I did as she directed, making myself comfortable on the furs and taking a piece of steaming meat with my fingers. Hunger added all the seasoning the caribou meat needed.

While we ate, Ululik discussed his trading, bragging about how much tobacco he possessed. When his bowl had been emptied and he would take no more, he belched softly. Maki smiled at the compliment to her cooking.

Ululik then filled his pipe and carried flame to light it with a strip of hide. While he puffed, Padloq added to the conversation, telling her mother which men Aama and Meqqoq had chosen for their husbands. She finished by adding how skillfully Qisuk had harpooned the horned sea beast.

Maki bobbed her head, approving of the matches made on the voyage. "Does no one but Qisuk meet with your approval?" This led to conversation spoken more quickly than I could follow. When we finally prepared to sleep, several stars twinkled through the small openings in the stone walls. Padloq's bed furs on her *illeq* were warm enough. She curled close to my back, stroking my hair with her hand. It was good to be able to sleep lying down again on a bed that was not bobbing on the waves.

The following day, we visited the other igloos to meet the villagers. I found the women's faces blending one into the next, their names too hard to pronounce and remember. So many new words and names spun through my head, it made me feel dull and stupid. If only I might make myself useful in a corner, instead of visiting, but I knew no task well enough to do it properly. Even the Inuit lamps and cook fires were beyond me.

As people spoke, quite often a sentence sounded like one long word. Tired from travel and confusion, I wanted to curl up somewhere and sleep. Eventually, Padloq took me back to her igloo. "Rest, Mikisoq," she said. "I'll see you later." She left me alone in the empty igloo.

When I woke, she was beside me again. I wondered whether it was time to begin a new day, but I had no way of knowing that by the sun's odd position. I felt more rested, although still somewhat uncomfortable. Maki was cooking again. There seemed to be a continuous feast of welcome going on for the returned traders. Once more, we made the rounds of the igloos. I hoped this time, I might remember names. In every home, the women offered us food. I never saw any people who could eat the way they did.

Between eating, everyone, men and women, puffed on pipes. Even some of the children enjoyed the sweet smoke. It seemed tobacco held no ritual significance to them as it did among my people. They used holy tobacco smoke merely for pleasure. As far as I knew, their shaman had yet to offer prayers for the traders' safe return, unless Padloq had not awakened me for that.

The fumes made my stomach queasy, so I could not taste the food that was offered me. After awhile, my back muscles tightened. I tried to stretch, thinking I had felt less cramped in the umiak. I smiled at my hostess and made a motion to indicate I must excuse myself. They nodded, seeming to understand when I ducked down to crawl through the entry tunnel to the outside.

With my big belly, it was not easy, but I managed, gulping great swallows of fresh air not heavy with tobacco smoke, sweaty people, baby urine, and cooking smells. Padloq had come out, too, her face showing concern for me. Sorqaq saw us walking between the igloos. Maki came up to me, but before she could speak, Sorqaq asked, "Mikisoq, are you feeling well?"

"Iyeh," I replied, trying to make my face seem pleasant as I attempted to keep from gagging. I breathed deeply, striving to hold back nausea.

"Watch her, Padloq." He waved me on and continued his visiting. Maki noticed how I was tiring. My back tightened and I pressed my fists into the hollow above my buttocks to ease the strain. She and Padloq gave me their arms to lead me back to Padloq's *illeq*. They left me there to sleep again.

During the night, the baby must have shifted, because I awoke with a feeling of uneasiness. Distress tugged at my mind, evoking my mother's calm face. She seemed to remind me that I had not felt well since we made land. My own sense of logic spoke to me with my mother's voice while I answered in the tones of a small girl.

If you are exhausted, why do you not sleep?

Everything is new here, the food and the people.

Was everything not new in Algonquin Country? Did you not sleep well when you ran for your life?

Yes, but. . . .

It is time to ask the women where to go. Your baby begins to come soon. Be ready for her.

You are right, Mother, as always. I will ask. Determining a course of action, my lids grew heavy at last. I slept.

The next afternoon, the family began another round of visits. Several hunters returned to the village, dragging two slaughtered musk oxen behind them. The women ran up to begin the butchering. The animals' fat glistened with their summer grazing. The women took their crescent moon–shaped knives, which they called *ulus*, and began to skin the shaggy beasts, trimming the inner fat from the thick pelts to render later.

At Maki's direction, the children ran down to the bay to find driftwood. Both animals would be cooked at once. It did not take long before black smoke rose, mixed with the scents of roasting fatty meat. The village women sliced away portions of ox as it cooked, returning the raw sides to face the heat.

There was plenty of meat in Ululik's igloo, but I found that I had no appetite. I nibbled a few bites, at Padloq's urging, then tried to keep out of the way while the igloo filled with people. Qisuk came with his wife, Aleqasiaq, Padloq's older sister. She was bigger in the middle than I, although it may have only seemed so. She was more slightly built. Qisuk hovered over her. When their eyes met, I felt emotion pass between them. Qisuk doted on his wife.

While the men ate, Aleqasiaq sat with Maki and Putu, Sorqaq's wife, her mother-in-law, on Padloq's *illeq*. So many people filled the igloo, I found no room to sit. I moved close to one of the narrow windows for air.

The cooking odors combined with sweat and smoke, making me dizzy. The new words I had learned jumbled in my head and the walls pressed in on me until I felt I had to go outside in order to breathe. I got up, looking around for Padloq. She was talking to her mother. Hoping no one would think me rude for walking away, I left the house.

As I got to my feet outside the tunnel, I pulled in some shallow breaths, clear of smoke. It made me feel slightly better, so I did not leave the area around the igloo, but watched through the window as the people devoured the slabs of meat. They gulped mouthfuls of the boiled meat, chewing and swallowing loudly, smacking their lips and complimenting the hunters. While Maki and Putu loaded mats with more meat, the men drank broth, belched, and ate again.

I noticed how Aleqasiaq's breaths came quick and shallow, and how she was barely touching the food Maki had brought her. It occurred to me that she should be the one to answer my questions about where women went to give birth, and tell me what I must prepare. I wondered if I could make her understand me and if she knew sign language. There seemed to be no way to speak to Aleqasiaq alone. Both mothers fussed over her, chattering with worried and nervous movements, touching her hair and her face, trying to make her comfortable.

Suddenly, I realized her labor had begun and she was not telling them. Why would she ignore her body? Was it rude to leave in the middle of a feast? The signs were so obvious, I don't see how they did not guess. Qisuk continued eating with the men, joking and laughing. When the men lit their pipes, Aleqasiaq's sagging eyes turned yellow and her sallow face flushed. Sweat beaded above her lips and her jaw tensed. I thought she was going to be sick.

A small round-faced boy of about six years came up to me dressed in caribou trousers and a long shirt, with short boots to protect his feet from the cold ground. "I'm Sammik. Qisuk is my father. Who are you?" He was the first of the children who had spoken to me. He waited for my answer with round, curious eyes.

"They call me Mikisoq."

The boy laughed at the meaning of my name. "You're a grown-up. Why aren't you talking with the grown-ups?"

I guessed what he meant, but I did not know how to explain with the few words I knew. Since Padloq could not help, I did my best. She sat inside beside her sister, fanning her. Hoping he had learned some of the sign talking from the men before they left to trade, I motioned: "I come from

Turtle Island." I had to say in my own language the name of the animal whose back gave rise to my world.

The boy looked at me sideways. "Why do you speak strange words, and what are you doing?" he demanded. I touched my mouth and made the sign for hand talk. His expression told me he did not understand.

"Padloq. Help me," I called desperately.

She ran outside. Immediately, she realized my problem and explained to Sammik why I was trying to use hand signs to talk to him. "Mikisoq is Naskapi. She doesn't know how to talk properly," I believe she said to him. He nodded sympathetically. She motioned, saying, "Sammik is my sister's son. Qisuk named him Sammik when he learned . . ." The rest of her words were unclear. When I shook my head to show I had not understood, she paused. "Why don't you show Mikisoq the hand you use best, Sammik?" she asked the boy. He lifted his left hand high and wiggled his fingers. "Sammik," she said, touching the hand and then pointing to the child. I gathered that the boy's name meant "left-handed."

Sammik looked me over, touching the quills on my shoulders and the soft fringes of my hem and sleeves. He touched my braided hair and ran a finger down my longish nose. I almost forgot my aching back when I laughed. He walked around me, hand rubbing his chin like an old man, then stopped in front to poke my middle. "Your face is skinny, but the rest of you is fat like my mother," he said. "Are you making a baby in there?"

"*Iyeh,*" I replied, understanding some and figuring out the rest. I did not mind at all when he changed the subject.

"Come and see my new dog. He's right outside by the door, waiting to play with me. I had enough to eat."

Padloq encouraged me to go with him. "The wind and sun will be good for you. Go ahead with Sammik, but don't stay outside long or wander away."

Sammik and I walked a short distance. A sturdy half-grown pup scampered up to the boy. The two bounded together up the hill behind the igloos to a grassy ridge. "We're going to kill a big bear," he yelled down to me. The two were stalking and leaping, pretending to stab a bear. I was forced to laugh again. He reminded me of my brother when he was that age. Sammik squatted. His pants opened so he could relieve himself without pulling them down.

Suddenly, my abdomen tightened. The pressure made me want to follow Sammik's example on the hill, until I realized its cause. *Not yet,* I pleaded. *I'm not ready. Give me more time!* Mother, I prayed silently. I could almost see her shake her head sadly. She could not help me with this.

Sweating with strain and fear, I made my way back to Ululik's igloo. There had been no time to collect diapering or to make small blankets. I had erected no birth hut, nor would I know how without saplings and soft leaves. I did not know where to turn in this village of strangers. Sammik paused in his play when he saw me. He stood there uncertainly, then ran down the hill toward me, his dog barking playfully at his heels "What's wrong with you, Mikisoq?" he asked.

As I tried to think of what words I could say, a sharp scream came from the passageway. Sammik's face paled. The next moment, he had run to the entrance and dropped to all fours. Before he could begin the crawl to his mother, he had to push aside the now-frantic puppy.

Just then, the passageway darkened with people. Qisuk backed out first, with Sorqaq managing the other end of a hide. Sammik's mother was lying on it, being carried. They dragged her through the tunnel and out of the igloo. She hardly seemed to breathe. The hide under her was wet and colored with blood. Both Maki and Qisuk's mother followed behind.

"I want my mama," Sammik screamed. "Mama! Get up!" He tried to be with her, running beside them, but Maki pushed him away.

He tore away from his grandmother and tried to throw himself onto the hide carrying his mother, but his father grabbed him, shoving him out of the way. "Stay with Padloq," Qisuk snapped. "Your mama is busy now." The boy crouched, his mouth trembling while his mother was carried toward a small igloo above the others on the hillside.

Padloq came over to me. With her eyes, she followed her sister, mother, and brother-in-law out of sight. Sammik moved hesitantly toward his aunt, who crouched down and pulled him close. "I want my mama, Padloq," he insisted tearfully, burying his head between her breasts.

She hugged him and stroked him and licked the tears from his chubby cheeks with the tip of her pink tongue. "Your mama has to push her baby out of her belly. He's ready to be born. Remember, we told you this would happen. Be brave while she is away from you. Stay here with Mikisoq while I go to the birth igloo to help your mama with her new little boy." She spoke fast, barely noticing my presence beside them.

I had neither the breath nor the words to ask why all babies must be boys to the Inuit, until they are born. My back tightened again and I leaned forward, trying to catch my breath. When Padloq turned to make sure I understood, her eyes opened wider. "Sammik," she ordered briskly. "Mikisoq can't stay with you, either. Go to Salluq's mother and tell her she must care for you until I return to get you. Take your bed furs to his igloo. Mik-isoq needs to come with me."

Sammik's small chin trembled in reaction to his father's sharp rebuke. He raised hopeful eyes to Padloq as though she might bring order back into his world. His mother's face as she was half-dragged, half-carried, away from him had been as gray as a snow-bringing cloud. Blood stained her clothing. Almost as unsettling, his father had snapped at him, told him to get out of the way.

Although I longed to help Padloq comfort him in his confusion, I was caught up in my own. My pulse pounded in my ears like the waves pounding the side of an umiak. I breathed as though I'd run up a hill.

"Go now. Do as I tell you," Padloq said, giving Sammik a loving squeeze and a push to hurry him along. "I'll get you later." With a sniff, he hurried away. As soon as he was on his way, she took my hand. "Come with me, Mikisoq," she said. "We have a birth igloo all prepared for you and my sister."

Chapter

I let her lead me to the birth igloo. We followed after Maki and Putu, Qisuk's mother. By then, Qisuk had lifted his wife and was carrying her in his arms as one carries a child of five. Cradling Aleqasiaq, he spoke to her tenderly, making soothing sounds as he hurried to the isolated igloo. Between them, they got Aleqasiaq down on the hide again to drag her though the slanted entrance tunnel. I hesitated before the igloo, undecided. "What's the matter?" Padloq asked.

"A woman should be alone when she gives birth," I replied, not knowing if I had said it right. Padloq looked at me without comprehension. "Too many people," I said, hoping to make my concern understood. "A mother ought to be alone when she gives birth. Only the Creator's spirit, Orenda, should share the birth hut with her until the baby emerges." I guessed at the signs but then gave up. There was no way for me to express so many complicated thoughts.

She looked at me sideways. "Don't be silly," Padloq said finally. She pushed my head down for me to enter into the igloo. There was nothing else for me to do but proceed as she directed. When we came in from the tunnel, Putu had just begun a fire. She lit several of the wicks, which had been plunged into the lump of congealed tallow in one of the tall stone lamps. Double layers of dried membrane in the windows permitted light to enter the room through thin openings set in the rock and turf walls.

Maki endeavored to make her daughter comfortable on the *illeq*. Qisuk stood in the room of the birth lodge, where no man should be, watching but doing nothing. If a man of my tribe ever entered a birth lodge, he'd be ridiculed by the men and banished by the mother's clan. Off-world customs turned everything upside down. They expected every child to be a boy. They even allowed men in the birthing hut. My grandmother would have been furious.

I worried for Qisuk's wife. She must have been laboring long before she let on. I could only imagine that she did not recognize her pains for what they were. Even if she had recognized them and come sooner, I don't know if it would have helped. Her spasms had sapped her strength, leaving her unable to squat properly to expel her baby. Maki removed her daughter's pants and opened the ties of her anorak. While the laboring woman gasped between contractions, Maki stroked her daughter's abdomen, using circular and downward motions.

"Why are you here and not with Sammik?" Maki demanded of her younger daughter, looking up without ceasing her movements. Her glance crossed to me. "Oh!" she exclaimed. "I see."

Padloq guided me to the other *illeq* and helped me remove my leggings, motioning for me to recline. "No," I said. I had heard my mother and my sister, Pumpkin Flower, say that pacing helped. An upright position guided the baby's head down. I tried to recall every instruction, every warning, every prayer. Birthing was women's purpose for existence, as war was men's. A woman must be trained as carefully as boys are trained for battle. This was to be my first "war."

"At least take off your pretty dress. I'll take care of it for you." Padloq made me understand, pointing and showing me what she meant for me to do. My Naskapi dress must not be stained and destroyed. I allowed Padloq to help me. She laid old bare caribou hides over my shoulders to keep me warm. While I waited for my body to tell me what to do next, I continued to pace from one gray side of the birthing hut to the other, between the *illeqs* and the tall lamps.

Maki instructed Qisuk to climb behind his wife and grasp her around the shoulders, his legs below her rib cage, to help her push the baby down. He wrapped his arms securely around her armpits. Here, at least, the man took orders, and did as his wife's mother directed. He crossed his legs over her belly, above the baby, as if the couple would push the baby into the world together.

What an odd notion, I thought, for Inuit men to assist their wives to give birth. Unfortunately, Aleqasiaq could not do much to help herself. She seemed unable to take a deep breath. Her cries were weak, and she grew paler with each spasm. I would have prayed for her if I had known how or what god to beseech. Her child seemed not to want to come out. Already, too much blood had pooled and dripped from between her legs to the hides she lay on.

Keeping as far from the poor woman as my pacing would allow, I could barely hear her moans above her mother's prayers and Qisuk's mother's directions. Even so, I perceived how Padloq's sister twisted in agony, how her eyes fluttered. I recalled captured warriors tied to stakes, withstanding the worst tortures bereaved wives' could inflict on an enemy. Just as they did, Qisuk's wife attempted to withdraw into her spirit to escape the pain. Pretty soon, I thought, she would escape too far to return.

Water skins, clean rags, and oil to anoint the baby waited next to seal-hide wrappings to swaddle the infant. Maki sat behind her daughter on the *illeq,* directing Qisuk and beseeching her gods while Putu crouched between her daughter-in-law's spread knees. Aleqasiaq suddenly took a ragged, gasping breath, then screamed.

I stopped pacing, holding my hands on both sides of my bulging middle as if I could prevent my unborn infant from taking fright at the sound. Padloq's sister still breathed when Maki dipped her finger into a water skin to wet her daughter's parched lips. I saw Putu draw her woman's knife from her pouch, and I turned away, not liking the desperate look in her eyes.

Maki gave terse directions to Qisuk, who leaned his wife forward with his legs until she was almost vertical, but Aleqasiaq cried out again, her whimper more feeble as her eyes closed in helpless agony. Maki patted her daughter's cheeks and called her name. Padloq, who had kept out of the way in a corner, jumped to the *illeq* and listened to her sister's labored breathing. She pulled her mother aside, whispering, gesturing angrily. Who was there to blame if the child was too big to be born? What taboo had her sister forgotten to observe?

I needed to direct my thoughts and efforts to *my* body, to discern what it demanded of me. With closed eyes, I drew forth calm and strength from those who had shared my ordeal and lived to name their children. I called upon the spirits of my mother, grandmother, all mothers, especially Mother Earth, who had given life to the Creator, although birthing his evil twin had killed her.

When my next spasm seized me, I panted, one hand resting against the wall of the hut for balance. Padloq hurried to my side. "Don't you need to squat?" she asked, gesturing. "There is room on the other *illeq.*"

"Soon," I managed to say. Everyone was so concerned about Aleqasiaq, I felt like an intruder. "What is wrong there?"

"Baby. Bottom first." In her anguish, Padloq forgot to sign. She caught her lapse and pointed to her own bottom. Sometimes women who left the stockade for their birth hut in the forest never returned. I remembered my longhouse, how sometimes my cousins and I listened to newly menstruating maidens and young matrons whispering behind the menstrual curtain about birthing and what they went through before they first held their babies in their arms.

Women sometimes died in their birth huts. The young women said a baby might be cut from a dead mother's belly if it was found soon enough. Mostly, it was too late by then. Besides, what dead mother would leave her infant behind? Death hovered inside the birth igloo. I couldn't see him, but I felt his glance and hot breath brush past me as I paced, before he turned his attention entirely to the laboring woman on the *illeq*.

A spasm seized me with such force, I gasped and dropped to my knees. The room and all within it vanished, until there was only pain. When it let up, I took a deep breath, then turned my head and listened. Padloq wept softly. Maki had moved to her eldest daughter's head, while Putu, still squatting on her haunches between Aleqasiaq's knees, watched her gasping daughter-in-law give up the struggle. Part of the child's body had emerged, the bottom part. The rest of him was trapped inside. Putu's lips formed a determined line.

Qisuk screamed an order to his mother. "Save my son," he cried. "I want him." Maki turned away to compose herself, then leaned forward and touched her cheek to her daughter's. My blood pounded in my ears, drowning out other sounds again while waves of pain racked my body, doubling me over. Warm water gushed from between my knees. Padloq helped me move to the *illeq*.

"He's coming, Mikisoq," she cried. When the pain started again, the ache welled up, tightened, and pressed, until I thought it would squeeze the life out of both me and my baby. I took a few deep breaths and gripped Padloq's wrists.

"Now!" Padloq screamed. I pushed as I knew I must, first breathing deeply, as though preparing to swim underwater. My final push brought my baby's head out far enough for me to see the black hair between my parted knees. I reached forward, turning its head to ease its shoulders out. Once the head emerged, the rest followed more easily. Sagging in relief that the worst was over, I rested a little, my breaths quick and shallow.

A blood-slippery female infant lay on the soft hide between my knees, crying her first cry. Dear Mother, I thought. My months of anguish were over. I had not produced the son of my enemy, born to be a warrior who would kill my people. I had birthed a daughter.

Elation washed over me. Before I regained the strength to do it myself, Padloq broke several strands of my long hair and tied it around the cord, close to the baby. When the cord drained of blood, she severed it with Maki's moon-shaped *ulu*. I murmured my thanks to her and tried to smile.

"It's only a girl," she said sadly, lifting the child and looking her over front and back. Padloq wiped the baby's back clean of birth blood, then sighed. "She's not of Inuit blood," she muttered and clicked her tongue. "Very sad."

What did that matter? Padloq placed my infant in my arms. When I touched her soft cheek, my newborn turned her head to my fingers. Her breath smelled like strawberries, fresh and sweet. When she rooted until her tiny lips found my breast and latched onto my nipple, my soul soared. Hawk Feather, I thought triumphantly. You wanted to make a son; you thought to vanquish me. Instead, I have vanquished you. My daughter held no essence of her father. New and innocent, she belonged to me alone.

I hardly felt the passing of the afterbirth in my joy of having given life to a girl. Padloq wrapped the afterbirth in a bloody rag and kicked it to the edge of the tunnel. My trial finally over, a great exhaustion came over me. My eyes fluttered, heavy with sleep. Before I gave in to it, I lifted my daughter from my breast and examined her tiny face. Framed by damp black hair, her eyes blinked, unseeing. For one moment, they seemed to look into mine. "You are a child of Turtle Island," I murmured, cradling her, smelling her. "I'll teach you your heritage. I'll choose a name for you tomorrow."

I placed her again at my breast and pulled the furs higher. Fatigue overtook me and I had begun to doze off, when a terrible scream pierced the room. Padloq stood between me and the other *illeq* so I could not see what happened. Had Padloq's sister given birth at last? The odor of blood filled the room. I heard the tiny mew of another baby, its infant wail increasing, demanding attention. It was all right, then. My child turned toward the sound only a moment, letting go of my nipple, before she latched on again. With her mouth warm against my breast and the back of her head with its soft black hair pressed to my arm, I slept.

Sunlight poured through the window when I roused and stretched. A child was still under my arm, tucked against my breast. "Daughter," I sighed, lifting her and smiling. To my horror, it was not the same child. Where its legs met, there was a penis.

Padloq hurried to me, tenderly pushing my hair back from my face. The other *illeq,* where Sammik's mother had labored, was empty. Padloq's sister was gone, but the two older women remained, and they were gazing solemnly at me. "What happened while I slept? Where is my baby?" I whimpered.

"My sister is dead. Your girl is dead, too, for she was too little and could not breathe. Don't grieve too much; she was only a girl. You have the honor to nurse Qisuk's new son."

That was not possible. My child was *not* weak. She had cried and sucked strongly. What did the Eskimo woman mean, saying my child could not breathe? Padloq gazed into my face sorrowfully. What had they done to my daughter? "I want my baby," I insisted. "Give her to me."

Padloq conferred softly with the two grandmothers. Afterward, she spoke to me again, gesturing slowly and patiently so I could not fail to understand. "You have no man. Sorqaq told you if your baby was not Inuit, it must die. She had no blue mark in the small of her back like an Inuit child. You are to nurse this baby instead. It's a *boy.* Much better. Understand?"

She encouraged me to remember, as though I knew but had merely forgotten what had been told to me. The older women clucked over me, as the three young women had on the traders' island. Then I remembered.

On the island, Sorqaq had touched his nostrils with two fingers when he spoke of the baby if it were not fathered by an Inuit. I supposed he had meant for me to keep my baby from crying, that it would not be as valued as one of their own. I never suspected he meant it must die. Or had I? It was Hawk Feather's baby. Hadn't I wanted it dead? No, part of me protested. I had accepted it. I had promised to care for it.

Pressure constricted my head the same way my body's contractions had squeezed my middle. This pain was as terrible. No amount of breathing could relieve it. It would never stop. Too late, I realized that my baby was never intended to live. With a shudder, I realized what I agreed to on the traders' island. I had assented to my own daughter's death.

"No," I whimpered. "I didn't understand right. Don't let it be true. Oh no!" The outside world clouded over. I pretended to have lost my memory when I dwelled with the Naskapi. In the small igloo where my firstborn daughter breathed her first and last breath, I had lost everything.

Chapter 19

I sank gratefully into my cloud of nothingness, allowing it to enfold and swallow me. There was no pain or cold in my life. I felt neither hunger nor the passage of time. People became shapes, colors, and sounds. When someone put food into my mouth, I ate. When someone pressed a mug to my lips and tilted my head, I drank. I think I must have gone outside or to the clay-lined basket to relieve myself when that was needed. A small shade guided me, slipping smooth, warm fingers into mine. Only the shape of a small boy penetrated my dreams through the fog.

From time to time, a small, hungry being appeared in my cloud with me, my shirt having been tucked up to expose my breast. The creature sucked and grew heavier. Other shades entered my fog, but they were like smoke in fog, without faces. I turned away at voices, for their words held no meaning. All I recalled were the words of my youth and homeland, but no one spoke my language except for my visitors, the ghosts.

I raised a hand to acknowledge the shape of my father. I had not seen him for a long while. I seemed to recall that he was dead, although he appeared strong and vigorous. "Picture Maker," he called. "Listen to me. I've been waiting for you to wake up."

"Why, Father? Have I been asleep?"

"Look around. Where are you? Do you know?" I did as he bid me. There was nothing aside from ourselves to see, although I felt the closeness of walls around us. All else was fuzzy, like the pale inside of a cloud.

"No. There's nothing here to show me. Where are we?"

He reached out and took my hand. We rose through the low roof together as though it were formed of mist. "Behold!" My father pointed down at the fog. It thinned until I could see. We hovered over a frozen inlet where humps, half dug into the hills and covered with snow, huddled in a group. Wisps of smoke spiraled above each of them, blending with the remnants of the fog. "It's winter. Those are off-world houses you see in the place you chose to dwell."

"Yes. It comes back. I remember now," I said. "Then it must be true. Strange little men brought me with them in a wide skin boat to a treeless land north of Turtle Island. People really do live off the world. I never would have dreamed of it." My father looked at me sideways. Had I forgotten something? Why did he appear so sad? "I had to go with them, Father. It was the only way to escape the Algonquins. You see that, don't you?"

He nodded. "Yes, I do see. Your grandmother wishes to talk to you. It's a long journey from her bed bench in Wolf Longhouse. I will guide her spirit to you here, but first, I must ask your permission."

I could hardly remember the face of my grandmother. "I want to see her." My heart pounded fast.

"She will visit you soon. Be strong, Picture Maker." He faded away.

I tossed about. In my stupor, a small hand stroked my face and neck. Someone talked to me, but I could not understand the words. Harsh winds blew outside, whistling over the smoke vents as they did above my grandmother's hearth. It might have been the same day or a moon's cycle later when Grandmother materialized before me. Her loose hair had changed from gray to white and it floated behind her like a cape of snow. I smelled the holy aroma of tobacco smoke.

"Are you alive, Grandmother?" I inquired.

"I still live, but I'm very old, Gahrahstah, our own little Picture Maker of Wolf Clan. You see my spirit as my body looks to others. I shall be young again when I join with Great Spirit Orenda. I won't tarry much longer on Turtle Island. Too many of my loved ones have gone over to Orenda already. Your daughter's spirit has cried out to me. Why did she die before she lived? I have seen her wandering through the shadows, homeless."

With horrifying intensity, my memories returned. As if they were happening again, I could see what had occurred around me that summer day in the birth igloo. Grandmother and I floated above it, the roof clear as water to our spirit eyes. Maki lifted my baby from under my arm without waking me. The child never even whimpered when Maki's two flat fingers pinched off her air.

"They smothered her, and I didn't stop them," I sobbed. "But I didn't know. Grandmother, tell my daughter I didn't know what they would do."

"She says you did know." Grandmother gazed at me steadily, her hooded eyes probing my soul. "You must convince her yourself." She faded, until I could barely see her outline, but her warmth remained along with the sweet smell of burning tobacco.

"What shall I do?" I cried in a panic. "Don't leave me yet. I'm afraid."

Her voice answered in my head. "Ganeogaono women ignore fear and do as they must. You came to this strange treeless country, where people practice strange customs. You must accept what has happened and move on. Speak to your daughter. Her spirit waits. If you don't rise to life soon, you will be lost, as well. Restore harmony to yourself and others. This is your purpose. Give release to your daughter. Only you can do it."

"What do you mean, Grandmother?"

"Do what is needed to restore balance. The world cannot exist without it. Wherever your destiny leads you, you must restore balance. Orenda requires it of you." Grandmother's words were sibilant, crackling like fall leaves or the last breath of a dying flame. "You will find what you need across the water." The smell of tobacco smoke lingered a moment longer; then it, too, was gone.

I rested somewhere warm. In the dance of firelight reflecting upon stone, between light and shadow, nothing was solid. From a little above, my spirit eyes observed the solidness of my body leaning against piled furs on the *illeq* while the lamp fires warmed the air. Voices almost penetrated my reality, but not quite, for I could not comprehend the lifting and falling of the words.

Where was I? Quite suddenly, I knew. Just as suddenly, I realized what had happened during the moons my spirit had slumbered. They had taken me to live in Qisuk's igloo. The young hunter had blamed his mother for his wife's death, although she was not to blame. Aleqasiaq would have died in any case. Putu had saved Qisuk's son, as he had ordered her to do, and she had done it the only possible way. Both mother and infant would have died without her intervention. When no other choice remained to her, Putu had cut open her daughter-in-law's womb and removed her living grandson.

After the first deed was done, Padloq's mother, Maki, closed my baby's mouth and nostrils with her fingers. What I did not know yet was that without a father to hunt for them, even Inuit girls may be smothered. How much less chance had a fatherless foreign child? My milk was needed for

Qisuk's new son to thrive, so they cared for my soulless body, keeping me alive. Aleqasiaq's death had caused strain between Qisuk and his mother, allowing disharmony to enter the village. I was given to know this, but I had yet to grasp why.

The small hairs on my neck shivered when one last, small ghost approached through the mists. My throat tightened at the sight of my daughter, floating and wrapped in hazy grayness, as she appeared that one day of her life. It hurt to look at her, knowing how well I deserved her reproach.

"You killed me," she accused, floating closer, drifting before my face in her flowing grave rags. At least they had not buried her naked.

"No, daughter," I protested. "I did not kill you. In my ignorance, I allowed you to die."

"You wanted to destroy me. You know you would have killed me yourself in the beginning."

I could not lie to the ghost of my child. It was true I had never wanted to conceive her. If I'd known sooner, if woman's root had been available, I would have washed her away in blood. I could not lie to her, and would not. "I might have done so once. As you grew inside me, I vowed to care for you and teach you about our people. I would not have abandoned you. You were *mine*. I meant to raise you, to give you a name. It is the truth."

"You never loved me, Mother." Her gaze pierced my heart, breaking it.

"You're wrong. I thought I could never love you as a mother should, yet when I held you and touched you, I knew better. Before they took you away from me, I loved you. I've been grieving for you since they took you away. Look into my heart," I challenged her. "You will see that my words are true." I felt her doubt as if it were a solid thing. She judged my soul, deciding whether or not to believe me. "If I had known what would happen, I would have remained with the Naskapi, even if the Algonquin came for me."

I waited, hoping she would feel what anguish I suffered when I realized I had lost her forever. When I could breath without sobbing, I felt my daughter forgive me at last. The last band of ice that pressed against my heart melted. Her specter floated toward the smoke in the updraft of the fire lamps. When she approached the vent, she paused. She did not know where to go.

"We are of Wolf Clan, daughter," I told her. "We have our own spirit longhouse in the Great Spirit Orenda. My Father is of Bear Clan, but he'll guide you there. Call for your grandfather, who is my father. He will come to you." She hovered for a moment longer, then floated away with the smoke.

Quite suddenly, I felt the furs piled around me over the stones of the *illeq.* Padloq was humming a tune. Seal oil burned in the lamps, and the walls of the igloo solidified. More of what had happened while I was trapped in the twilight world between life and death became clear. I understood that Padloq had taken her sister's place and become Qisuk's new wife, though she would not have chosen the method. I nursed his new son, but only she could care for him.

Left-handed Sammik was the child who had watched over me all these moons. I learned later that special taboos applied to a woman who had lost her baby through miscarriage. The Inuit treated me as such a woman. So as not to cause angry ghosts to plague the village, they had not allowed me to eat certain foods, such as the front paws of a bear or walrus. Nor had I been allowed to watch hunters depart or arrive, because it would curse their hunting luck. I might not touch a knife, even a woman's *ulu,* or eat by myself. A child must put bits of food in my mouth. Their taboos were observed in vain, for ghosts had visited the village and this house.

I tucked my legs to one side, making myself more comfortable on the *illeq.* It was then that I noticed I was clothed with the same short seal-fur shirt and trousers the Inuit women wore. When Sammik moved to adjust my furs, I noticed that he had grown. His unfastened anorak rested on his shoulders. Beyond the seal gut covering the one window in the curved wall, it was dark. Several wicks burned in the lamp. What had happened to summer? How long had I slept while the seasons turned?

"She's looking right at me," Sammik said. "I'm sure she sees me."

"She doesn't really see anything. Her soul isn't in her body all the way since your brother was born. Only a bit of it is left. I already explained that to you." Padloq's voice sounded tired and listless. Standing at the side of the *illeq,* she cleaned the baby and oiled his bottom and legs, then wrapped him up again. "Remember how Qalaseq's eyes moved before he got big enough to really see? Mikisoq's the same now. Her eyes move sometimes, but that's all."

"Only come look and you'll see for yourself, Padloq," the boy insisted. To my surprise, I understood the meaning of their spoken words. I wasn't guessing or interpreting signs, but actually understanding.

Qalaseq began to fuss, which is why Padloq did not hear when I said, "You're getting big, Sammik." I spoke quietly, not wanting to alarm him, but I could not keep from smiling when he stiffened and shook his head to clear it.

Suddenly, I realized I had uttered my words effortlessly, in Inuit. I could barely remember the sound of my own voice. Sammik's small nostrils dilated and his mouth hung open. He gathered his feet beneath him, preparing to run, when I reached out and grasped his wrist. His skin felt like ice. "Don't leave," I protested. "Stay with me. You are getting so big; soon you'll kill a real bear with the hunters, like you said when I first came. Don't you remember?"

It seemed only yesterday that I watched him run and play on the green hill behind the village, romping with his puppy in the summer grass while his elders smoked their pipes and ate great amounts of food in Ululik's igloo.

"Padloq!" he called. "She's talking!"

Poor Padloq could no longer deny it. She heard, too, and trembled as she took the few steps that separated us. She moaned, holding the baby and backing away. "It's an evil spirit, a *toornaq,* that puts words in poor Mikisoq's mouth. Run! It will kill us and your brother."

"No it isn't! It's really Mikisoq," he insisted.

"A ghost speaks with Mikisoq's mouth," she cried. "We have to get Minik to drive it out of her. Sammik, come away from the ghost."

"It really is me," I insisted. "Please don't run away." She stopped, midcrouch, in the act of ducking into the passage to the outside. I thought fast when she turned to look back. "Don't you remember how you sat next to me on the umiak and became my friend? Remember how Qisuk got angry when you stood up and almost tipped the boat? This is his boy, Sammik." I let go of his wrist and lifted his left hand.

He wiggled his fingers and flashed a grin. "A ghost wouldn't know that. I told you it was Mikisoq!" He believed me and was no longer afraid.

My soul had slept, but my body had been moving all along, thanks to Sammik. Still, when I stood up for the first time on my own resolve, I held out my arms for balance. I stretched, yawning. "It's cold. Why is it so cold? Isn't there anything to eat?" I walked over to look in the pot above the flames.

Padloq crept toward me, muscles taut, ready to run. "Ghosts don't eat," she said, watching me cautiously.

"So I'll eat and prove I'm not a ghost," I said, laughing, and snatched up a piece of seal meat heating in the broth. I popped it in my mouth, chewing noisily.

Padloq clenched her hands and moved her head from side to side, gulping air. "You really are Mikisoq, aren't you?" she asked with less uncertainty. "After so long! You've really come back to us. I wouldn't have believed it."

"Iyeh," I said. "I have. Believe it."

She approached, holding both arms wide. I stepped into them and hugged her enthusiastically. "Your spirit went away when . . . when my sister died," she mumbled into my hair. She did not finish the sentence the way she had begun it. She had meant to say when my baby was killed.

"My daughter's ghost has forgiven me for not protecting her. I didn't understand when Sorqaq told me she was supposed to die. If I had, I would have gone back to Turtle Island, not come with you to this village."

"You didn't know?" Padloq's eyes blinked several times and tears appeared in her eyes. "You really didn't know?" When I answered, she shook her head and said, "Our poor Mikisoq."

It seemed so long ago since I had come to terms with my daughter's death that I had to remember what Padloq must first be feeling. I tried to think how to comfort her. "Inuit words and signs confused me. That was a long time ago. We can't change what happened. At least my daughter's spirit is free now. Since she forgives me, I forgive your mother for killing her. It's no good to stay angry. I'm fine now. Please, don't cry, Padloq."

Suddenly, she backed away from me, wary. "How can you say so much if you are Mikisoq?" she demanded. "Mikisoq doesn't know how to talk, not more than a few words. You must be an angry spirit come to avenge her baby. You are the ghost of the dead girl in your mother's body."

I plopped another piece of food into my mouth. "She's eating," Sammik said. He hugged me. "I believe her. It will be so funny when Qisuk finds out Mikisoq is back. Don't tell him. I want to see his eyes pop when he hears her talk." The little boy laughed at the joke he planned.

Padloq seemed somewhat mollified, but she remained confused. "How did you learn to talk, then? How can you speak so many words now?"

"I don't know," I said with a shrug. With great suddenness, it came to me. Sammik! "It must have been Sammik. All the time he was with me, he kept talking, so I learned without trying. If I tried, after all this time, I would still not speak this well. Sammik, you did it. You taught me how to talk."

"Well!" Padloq exclaimed. "Whoever heard of such a thing? Stories will be told of it. Did you say you are hungry? Qisuk said you must not go hungry. I'll get you something to eat."

"I can move around by myself now," I reminded her. "Sammik, you don't have to hold my hand and put food in my mouth anymore." Only a few pieces of meat lay in the cook pot; it was mostly broth. "Is there no more food than this?" I asked, noticing Padloq and Sammik were thinner than when I had last seen them.

"We have two packets of seal meat left, stored in the tunnel, and a little fat. Enough for two days, three if we stretch it." At my dismayed expression, she explained. "This is the worst winter we have had in many
years. For a long time, no hunters could leave the igloos to hunt. One old
man crossed between igloos. They found him frozen hard as a stone. Until
yesterday, the wind blew bits of ice like knives, cutting into our skin. The
wind stopped this morning. Our men must find meat again or no one will
live to see another summer."

"Oh no," I said. The village had suffered and changed much since my peculiar sleep shut me away from life.

"The seals and the caribou must have changed their feeding grounds,"
she said. "From time to time, a hunter harpoons a seal at its breathing hole.
This is a time of sorrow, a famine. The old folk have gone away to die and
the children grow weaker each day. But I shouldn't be telling you sad
things. You don't know that Qisuk took me to his igloo to be his wife so I
could care for Qalaseq and Sammik. I prepare their clothing and cook for
them. He hunts and protects you as well as me, because you make milk for
his son." The baby boy still rested on her arm and looked to me as if he
knew me well.

"What! Am I his wife, too?"

"Of course not," she replied with a hint of a giggle. After all she had related, I was glad to hear she could find humor in something. For myself,
not being Qisuk's wife was a great relief. "You can't agree to take an *inuk*
for your husband while you are sleeping. When the hunters return, if
they've caught little or nothing, Sorqaq must ask Minik to make a 'going
out of his body' ceremony. He'll ask Nerrivik herself what to do."

"Wait." I held up a hand. "You're saying more than I know. Who is
Minik? Who is Nerrivik?" I asked.

Sammik danced around the room impatiently. "Minik is *angakkoq* to our
village. He makes magic and talks to Sea Woman for us. Tell her the story
of Nerrivik while we wait for my father, Padloq," Sammik begged, excited
at the prospect of a story.

Before she joined us, she set a fresh twisted wick in the lamp fat, ladled
out three mugs of broth, and handed one to Sammik and one to me, along
with thin, flat slices of seal meat. "Here, tuck the furs well around us. We
might as well be warm while I tell you the story." Padloq sat across from
me with the baby and Sammik, the three huddled close for warmth. I took
a bite of meat and sipped my broth.

While we sipped and ate, she explained. "First, you must know what an *angakkoq* does. He can see into people's thoughts and speak to spirits. He can chase evil ghosts if they threaten the village. He can send his soul out of his body and ask Sea Woman, Spirit of Life, what we must do to appease her. She can tell us where to hunt and what to do. Am I speaking too fast for you?"

"Your Great Spirit is called Sea Woman?"

"Her name is Nerrivik, but she *is* Sea Woman. I'll tell you how she became Spirit of Life. This is the story as I heard it from my mother and she heard it from hers. The story has been told from generation to generation, back to the days when people and animals could talk together."

Padloq glanced toward me to make sure I understood the concept as well as her spoken words. I nodded. "Of course," I said. "It was the same in my country at the beginning of time."

"This is the story, then. A maiden called Nerrivik was courted by a large bird, like a seagull, but much larger. Birds were bigger in the old days. She thought he would make a very good husband because he had no trouble finding her family plenty of fish to eat in famine. So she agreed to marry the bird, with the arrangement that he would continue to supply her family with food. The bird and Nerrivik went away to an island to make their new home.

"After the marriage, the village hunters made several good hunts. Nerrivik's mother and father forgot how much they depended on their son-in-law. The two parents decided one day to set out in their umiak to visit their daughter. When they arrived, their son-in-law was out fishing. Nerrivik served them a fine stew, full of shellfish, tuna, and whale meat. Even while they ate the food he had provided, the foolish mother told her daughter how people laughed at her for having a bird son-in-law. 'You could have done so much better. We have several fine hunters in the village who can supply your igloo every bit as well or better than your bird husband. You should leave him and return home with us.'

"Nerrivik had no reason to complain of her husband and said so. 'You eat the food he caught, even here in his own igloo, yet you want me to desert my loving husband.'

"Her father also tried to convince her to come with them, but he used different logic. 'You'll probably never have children with that bird. Even if you did, you'll give birth to eggs and need to sit on them to make your children hatch. In addition, your children will have beaks and feathers. People will say they are ugly. Now, desert your husband and return home with us.' She was an obedient daughter, too polite to remind them that they arranged the match for her in the first place, when they needed food for their hungry village.

"Seeing his daughter hesitate, he hurried her along to make her escape. 'Gather your things,' her father said. 'All the single young men back in our village want to marry you. They'll fight over you like rutting caribou bucks over a doe in heat. They'll give me presents for you. You can have a real man for your provider, but you must hurry and leave now while your husband is away. He won't really mind. I'm sure when he sees you've left, he'll find himself a bird wife.' So they talked until they had convinced her. The three of them got into her parents' umiak and paddled toward the mainland.

"As soon as the bird husband returned to the igloo, he guessed what had happened. He'd been expecting it sooner or later. Well, he became very angry and flew after them, flapping his great wings and looking over the ocean with his sharp eyes. He found them before they reached land.

" 'Give me back my wife,' he screeched. 'Give her back or I will turn over your umiak and feed you to a whale.'

"Now the parents became very afraid and sorry that they had influenced their daughter and interfered in her life. 'Go back to him,' they ordered.

" 'I won't go. You insisted I come with you. What happens now is your doing,' " Nerrivik said. Her father had never heard her speak to him in that manner, and he became angry. He decided he'd better throw his daughter into the ocean, so he told his wife to help him. He picked her up and threw her overboard, but Nerrivik swam to the side and wouldn't let go. The skin boat rocked with her efforts to climb back in. Not only that; the bird was diving and clawing at them from the other side and screaming from the air to let his wife go.

" 'I'm trying to,' the father insisted. 'She won't let go of the boat. Don't hurt us. Leaving you was her idea.'

"Nerrivik hung on to the side of the umiak, but her father chopped off her fingers with his big hunter's knife. She hung on with her bleeding knuckles, crying pitifully all the while, but he cut those off, too. Her mother sat still and did not try to help her. Nerrivik cursed them both before she sank under the waves for the last time. 'I will tell the animals to keep away. You will go hungry now and no one will help you. You will starve, as you deserve.' "

"Is that the end of the story?" I asked. It was a horrible story, and I still had not learned how Nerrivik became Sea Woman.

"Tell her the rest," Sammik said. "Why did you stop?"

Padloq licked her chapped lips. "First, bring me some broth to drink. My mouth is dry and my tongue won't work."

The boy did as she bid him, then sat beside me, his chin resting on his up-drawn knees, intent upon his aunt. "Go on. We're waiting."

"When Nerrivik sank, she didn't drown. She got bigger and bigger, until she was Sea Woman, god of all living things and bigger than an iceberg. She may decide to let us all starve, as she did her father's village. If Minik sends his spirit down under the ocean to her, maybe he can learn how to appease her, for she seems to be very angry. He'll comb out her hair and arrange her home neatly for her. Remember, she can't do it herself, because her arms end at the wrists. If she is grateful for the favor, she'll be kind to us again and tell Minik where our hunters will find caribou or seals to hunt."

Having finished the story, Padloq sucked up the last bit of her broth loudly; then she leaned back on the *illeq* and pulled up the bear fur until it was up to her nose. She curled on her side with the sleeping baby. "Didn't the Naskapi say you brought hunting luck to them? Maybe you can help us."

"Me? How can I help?" Did she expect me to go under the ocean with Minik to speak to Nerrivik?

But she did not answer. Telling the story had tired her out. "I'm sleepy," she said, her voice muffled. "Why don't you and Sammik go outside and see if the hunters are on their way back. Maybe they caught seals." She was half-asleep by then, and soon she began to snore.

Chapter 20

Eight months had vanished since I'd seen the village, the sea, and the sky with knowing eyes. Afraid I might have withered away in all this time, I looked myself over, assessing my body objectively. My arms and legs were thinner than they had been before; my belly was soft, but flat. I stretched my arms out, standing on my toes. It might have been worse. During these past months, I must have walked and possibly even carried bundles.

When I told Sammik I wished to go outside, he handed me a knee-length parka lined in fur, with a hood I could tie closed at my neck. It was as though I saw it now for the first time. The thick fur appeared to be that of blue-fox pelts, taken and skinned in deep winter and sewn with great skill.

"Here is your anorak," he said. "The wind stopped, but it's still very cold out." When I took it from him and passed my fingers over the smooth, thick, yet almost seamless garment, I had to admire the skillful tailoring that had produced such a fine piece of work. "You've been wearing it all winter. Don't you remember it, now that you are awake?"

"No." I stroked the soft fur against my cheek and sniffed it.

His question did not disturb me. I knew I had been insensible for many moons, so naturally I did not remember it. "It used to belong to my mother."

I pushed it back toward him. "She will be angry at me for wearing her . . . her anorak. I must not put it on."

I feared to touch the thing again, until he said, "You nurse her son and she nurses your daughter. You and my mother's spirit should be friends."

He had been able to put his mother's death in the past and had ceased grieving, as I had tried to do with my loss. Although the memory would be with me as long as I lived, he was being wiser than I. I tapped my temple and said, "You are right. I had not thought of that."

My praise brought a bright smile to his face. "Put on the anorak so we can go outside. Padloq is no fun anymore; she sleeps too much." I did so, finding, to my surprise, that it fit me perfectly. Sammik's mother must have been taller than Padloq. As I slid my arms through the sleeves, it occurred to me that it and the shirt and trousers I wore, even the mittens, must have belonged to the dead woman. "Put on your *kamiks,* too. You put the hare-skin socks on first, fur side in, to keep your feet from getting wet and rotting. Then you slide the *kamiks* over them." Sammik looked toward me expectantly, waiting for me to lace the high boots, anxious to be outside. Even if he felt no disquiet seeing me in his mother's clothing, I sensed the oddness of it. It seemed almost that I had taken her place, living in her igloo, nursing her baby, being sister to her sister, playing with her elder son.

"Come on," Sammik urged, already dressed for the cold. "Let's go!"

"I'm right behind you," I said, and dropped down to my hands and knees to crawl after him through the tunnel. The sun hovered brightly above the southern horizon, casting long shadows. Its brightness lit the expanse below the hill down to the inlet. Waves no longer lapped at the shore, for the ocean itself had been stilled by winter into a sheet of ice.

Sammik carried a wide scrap of fur under his arm. While I waited below, he climbed the round hill behind the igloos. He kicked toeholds in the snow and used his mittened hands to keep from sliding backward. At the rim, he positioned himself. "Here I come!" he shouted, and pushed himself off, laughing in pleasure as he sped down. He reminded me of one of our miniature iceboats during midwinter's festival, racing down the prepared slope all the way to Wide River.

How wonderful it must be to feel the wind in your face, to rush down the hill without a care. I had to do it, too. I ran to meet him where he had glided to a stop. "It's my turn," I insisted. Sammik let me take the hide. After so long, I surprised myself with such anticipation and energy as I felt, climbing with little effort up the white slope.

Reaching the summit, I remembered that the last time I had climbed a small hill, it had been to watch his people approach the traders' island in their umiaks. Last summer, I had been slow and awkward, carrying my child inside. Now my young body belonged to me alone, along with my almost forgotten agility and grace, a gift from my tribe. Grace and balance were part of our nature.

From my vantage point atop the hill, the land's starkness was dismaying. The wide inlet curled against the land like a sleeping cougar. I knew rivers often froze. Even the bay around the Naskapi peninsula had frozen, but how could the entire ocean be held still under a field of solid ice? I wasted no more time, but set down the hide and sat upon it, my legs in front of me. Pushing myself off, I whizzed down the hill, holding tightly to the edges while the wind stung my nose and eyes, until I came to a gliding stop on the level plateau.

People ran from their igloos, alarmed, calling to one another, but I cared not at all. I wished my ride could last twice as long. Half the village women waited, looking down at me. Meqqoq and Aama, my companions from the voyage, stared in amazement. Except for them, Padloq, and Sammik's grandmothers, Putu and Maki, the others barely knew me. They must have known of me, however, by their amazed and horrified expressions.

Curiosity drew frightened women toward me, but fear kept them back. Like waves, advancing and retreating, they approached, holding their amulets for protection against ghosts. "What are you? Why do you possess the Naskapi woman's body?" Putu asked, facing me bravely. Her status as wife to Sorqaq made her most senior of the assembled women. "If you are a ghost in Mikisoq's body, Minik will force you to depart."

"It's me, Putu," I said. "It's only Mikisoq."

Sammik, annoyed that the villagers had interrupted our game, explained more brusquely. "It really is Mikisoq. When she woke up, she knew how to speak. Her daughter's ghost forgives her for letting you kill it, Grandmother, so—"

Maki, Padloq's mother, screamed before he could finish. "Don't kill me," she said, and fell to her knees, arms crossed over her head, as if that could protect her.

Putu challenged me boldly. "If you are indeed the Naskapi woman we know as Mikisoq, you knew what would happen before you came to our island. You have no right to complain now."

"I didn't know your language yet, Putu," I explained. "I asked for refuge for myself and for my unborn baby. When Sorqaq told me in signs what would happen, I misunderstood. If I knew my child must die, I would not have come to your village." My words took Putu by surprise. She backed away, palms up, openmouthed and gasping.

Aama stepped up to me hesitantly, offering me her mittened hand. I took it and touched it to my cheek. At that, she embraced me, weeping great tears from her lovely eyes. Meqqoq approached, still apprehensive. I reached my mittened hand toward her and beckoned. The three of us huddled together, when I heard the crack of a whip and the distant sound of barking.

The sudden screech of bone runners on the windswept ice field turned all our heads to the frozen inlet. More villagers emerged from their igloos at the noise. "The hunters are returning!" Sammik screamed above us. He had retrieved his scrap of hide and climbed up the hill again, while the women's attention centered on my return to life. "The hunters!" he yelled. "I can already see my father." He plopped onto his hide sled and pushed off in a blur. It did not take him long to travel all the way down to the ice field.

The men were still dark silhouettes on the gray ice field. Three sledges approached the village, coming in fast, each with a hunter riding on the back, pulled by a blur of running dogs.

"*Assut!*" came the voices of the hunters. "Faster!" Their shouts carried across the distance to our ears. The dogs strained at their harnesses, expecting meat when they finished their task. They needed little encouragement. The hunters raised their voices and cracked their whips in the air to alert the women to prepare for their return. Even before they reached the village, it was obvious the sledges were too light, too empty. It had not been a good hunt.

Sorqaq and the other men hurried from their igloos when the hunters' calls went up. We women, along with Sammik and the other children, ran down to the bank. Sammik pointed to the men, telling me, "My grandfather Sorqaq and his friends came back from hunting inland yesterday. They found a few hares and a couple of seals breathing at their *allut*. Not enough to fill our stomachs at all. They want to see if the ice-field hunters did better. *Ajorpaq!* It's useless. You can see they haven't, so we will go on being hungry."

The returning hunters stepped off the back of their sledges and trudged beside their dog teams up the hill to the igloos. We stood back while the men released them from their *anuit*. The large dogs panted and whined, awaiting their food. Their masters threw them each a few chunks, aiming high to make them leap. The dogs caught the meat on the fly and swallowed without chewing. When the dogs, still hungry, clamored for more, a few kicks and shouts sent the exhausted animals whimpering away to sleep.

Qisuk and the others were so encased in snow-covered fur, they might have been snowmen. Their hide boots met the fur of their trousers below the knees. Hide masks covered their eyes and the tops of their noses as they looked through tiny slits. Even their hoods were frosted with white. Only the men's wind-darkened cheeks remained exposed to the icy air.

There were several small bundles left on the sledges. Until her husband was done with his dogs, Aama waited near me. The noise must have awakened Padloq from her sleep. She ran up before the men finished feeding their dogs, with Sammik's baby brother peeking out of her long hood. Qisuk extended a mittened hand toward her. She welcomed him, taking his hand and pressing it to her cheek.

The hunters unloaded the last bundles from their sledges and parceled out the meat. Not until the last share was taken away by the villagers did Sorqaq give vent to his anger. "We've had more than enough of poor hunts and being hungry. Let the hunters warm themselves and rest. In the morning, everyone will come to my igloo. Nerrivik may explain why we find no food. It's obvious she withholds her favor from this village. Maybe Minik can learn from Sea Woman herself why we're going hungry and where the caribou and the musk oxen are hiding themselves."

Loud approval greeted his suggestion before the tired men walked to their igloos. The setting sun shone red over the ice field. Behind the village, the sky deepened to a dark purple. Stars, visible since the sun's descent, glowed and sparkled above the hills as delicate drapes of colored light wavered and shimmered in the sky like dancing rainbows. When we reached Qisuk's igloo, I ducked into the tunnel after Sammik.

Padloq set the baby on the fur-covered *illeq* and placed another wick in the melted tallow. She lit it and added more rancid fat to the lamp. We might have eaten the fat, I supposed. Warmth and light, or food—that was the choice.

"Help me get these off, Sammik. My feet are like ice," Qisuk said, sitting on his *illeq* and holding out one foot. I perched on the bed while Sammik hurried to help Qisuk remove his short men's *kamiks* and his bearskin pants.

Padloq put chunks of seal into her cooking bowl over the fire. "Food will be ready soon," she said. "The water is already simmering. It's good to have you home again." She tried to hide her worried face from Qisuk, holding her head low while she crouched to rub his feet. "Are you feeling them yet?" she asked tenderly, her fingers making circles on the dark soles and rubbing his toes.

"*Iyeh*. Oh! The feeling is coming back. What a hunt!" he complained. "Two days out from the village in the cold and the wind picked up again. It blew against us all the way back, but not as bad as it was blowing before. The seal holes were all closed up in the usual places. Before I harpooned even one seal at its *alu,* I had to kill the weakest of my dogs to feed the rest. Where did the seals go? Why has no one caught a bear yet this winter? Have the caribou all gone away? Maybe Minik will tell us to move, but it's hard moving in winter."

Padloq and Sammik made appropriate sounds. "The men who hunted inland had no more success," Padloq reported. "They killed nothing but small animals. Nerrivik must relent if we are to live." I remained quiet, remembering Sammik's instructions.

"Last winter, we found caribou and a couple of bear. No one went hungry. Grass grew on all the islands, so the caribou increased. Since the dark came this year, there're hardly enough seals to feed my dogs."

While we waited for the meat to cook, Qisuk related the details of his hunt. He had crouched over the open *allu* for half a day before a ripple alerted him that a seal was underneath. With lightning speed, as he told us, he plunged down his harpoon and wrestled our meal out of the black water.

"You are the best of hunters. So patient, so enduring," said Padloq, complimenting Qisuk while she prepared his pipe. She lit it for him from the burning wick, puffing a few times to make sure the tobacco in the bowl remained lit, and handed it to him. She encouraged him with more questions. "How was the trip home? How did the dogs do?" She went to stir the simmering water, which finally smelled like soup, to fish up warmed chunks into a bowl. "Here," she said, handing it to her husband.

She also handed some to me and to Sammik, taking a little for herself, which she finished quickly. Sammik soon finished, tilting the bowl for the broth. I did not touch mine, since I was supposed to wait for the boy to feed me, as usual.

With nods and grunts in appropriate places during his narrative, Padloq set to work cleaning the seal skin, scraping off every bit of fat and meat and adding them to the pot while Qisuk talked and ate. He talked more than he ate. Teeth to a good-sized chunk, he pulled back and sliced the rest away. In this manner, he gave more to Sammik and Padloq. Padloq said, "Make her eat, Sammik. She has to make milk for your brother."

"Eat," Sammik echoed when I hesitated. He put a piece to my lips as he must have done many times before. The meat was practically raw. Was this what they had been feeding me all along? "Take it," Sammik encouraged me. "What are you waiting for? Chew."

I took a small bite. The aroma of the meat cooking in its broth made my mouth water in spite of myself and my stomach's emptiness craved food. At last, I was able to swallow the lump in my mouth and take another bite.

Padloq was smacking her lips over her small portion, chewing long and well. "We'll save the rest for tomorrow," she said. "I'll add water and we'll have broth for many days. May it give us strength to wait until you find more."

"There are too many people in the village; that's the trouble," Qisuk said, still chewing. "Too many old, worthless mouths to feed when there's not enough food for those who are young and useful."

I sat back, no longer hungry, for Qisuk's words had started me thinking. Was the village so crowded with people, and was there so little food that the Inuit had no choice but to live this way? If so, more than tradition had killed my daughter. The Inuit must have surrendered to necessity, whatever that necessity might be, so that the rest of them might live.

"There are no old people left," Padloq protested. "The last of them walked away toward the northern lights on the ice field, the grandmothers whose teeth were too worn down to chew, along with the grandfathers too bent with so many winters to go on a hunt. They won't hunger anymore. May Nerrivik accept their sacrifice and help us find meat for the children."

"I did not know. May the old ones' spirits forgive me for doubting them. They had the good of the village uppermost in their hearts," Qisuk responded, contrite. "My mother; what about her? Did she go with the old women?"

I heard two sides to his question. One side hoped she was gone, the other that she lived, for he loved and hated his mother at the same time.

"No, she didn't go with the old ones. There are more than two hands of useful years left to her, if we could find enough food. If Nerrivik is willing to show our hunters where to look for caribou and seal, I mean."

Qisuk bowed his head and even Sammik stopped eating. I could see for the first time that Qisuk was young to be Sammik's father. He must have been hardly more than a boy when he married Padloq's sister and hardly sixteen or seventeen winters when she bore Sammik. Although I was no shaman, I easily guessed why Sea Woman withheld her favor. Qisuk's anger at his mother for killing his wife had angered her. Although he himself had commanded Putu to save his son, he refused to realize she had committed the act at his order.

The conflict and hurt in this village had gone on far too long. That's what was killing the villagers. I took another bite of the nearly raw seal flesh and then another to make milk for the baby, but my appetite was gone. Padloq handed Qisuk more broth. He sipped the flavored water, warming his lips, both hands clasped around his bowl.

At last satisfied, he crossed the floor to lift his youngest from the *illeq* where the eight-month-old played on the soft fur. Qisuk examined the baby's legs and tickled him to make his baby giggle. A slow smile spread over his face.

"Little *inuk,* little man," he crooned tenderly to the baby, picking it up and rubbing its nose with his. The brave hunter kept a soft place in his heart for both his boys. "You're growing," he said. "Even in the last few days, you've gotten bigger. Mikisoq's milk continues to flow well. I am pleased," he declared. "Make sure she keeps eating, Padloq."

"I've had enough," I said, putting down my bowl. "I don't want any more. Give it to Padloq."

Qisuk's eyes popped, just as Sammik had said they would. He raised both hands defensively, palms outward. "Did Mikisoq talk, or are my ears playing tricks on me? Is it a ghost? Does Minik know about this?"

Sammik giggled. Even Padloq's tired face managed to smile.

"I can speak," I said slowly. "I woke up a little while ago, Qisuk. Now I understand what people say."

"It's a miracle, a sign! It must be a sign! Minik must be told about this. Maybe he can explain what it means," Qisuk said, cautiously lowering his hands. He looked me over carefully. "When did this happen? Why did no one tell me?"

"It happened today, only a short while ago," Padloq confessed. "Besides, Sammik wanted to surprise you." The boy had checked his mirth, but he still appeared to find his father's alarm amusing.

"Well, you've had your joke. I say Minik has to know, but it can wait until later. I'm tired now. Everybody will go to sleep. When we wake up, I will go to my father's igloo for the ceremony." He leaned back on the *illeq* and pulled the furs up to his nose. In a moment, he was gently snoring.

We pulled the furs over us and huddled close for warmth. With Padloq lying against me on one side and Sammik on the other, I felt warm enough. Qalaseq lay tucked under my arm to nurse as he wished. In spite of my scrambled thoughts, I, too, soon slept.

The next day, a number of people had already assembled in Sorqaq's big igloo when we arrived. Two stone oil lamps with several wicks each made it uncomfortably warm inside the stone house. I found myself a place to watch from against the far side of the igloo and sat down with the baby on my lap. Fortunately, little Qalaseq slept. If he cried, I feared they would make me leave. I held no status, no rank even to *be* in the headman's igloo, watching an animal-calling ceremony. With luck, no one would notice me.

While the villagers entered and chose their places, I had time to observe the shaman Qisuk called Minik. If he could do all Sammik said, he was a sorcerer of the first quality. His open-necked ermine shirt was decorated with fine shells and colored stones. Many ivory amulets descended to his chest from a multitude of leather thongs around his neck. Tattoos covered his cheeks, his chin, and even the backs of his hands. I assumed they were to bring luck or help him make magic. Black hair darkened his upper lip and a line like basswood cord hung thinly down from his chin in a scraggly beard.

His hair, combed smooth and glossy, lay like a sealskin cape over his shoulders. He turned his head slowly, as if counting the people within the igloo. His eyes bore into this or that hunter's as though determining something of the man's inner thoughts. I lowered my eyes, not wishing him to discover I had been staring at him, but then I felt him touch me from across the crowded room. I already guessed his power over men was not such as Sorqaq's, but the kind that comes from the spirits, and very strong. I wondered if he would have been a match for the Onondaga shaman, whose name my people feared to say. I had seen spirit power in our holy men, but only from afar. I had been a child.

Minik's presence probed my soul. I defended my innermost thoughts, erected a stockade around them. Our two souls touched behind my eyes. "Let me learn of you," his said. My soul, wary at first, gave in to his gentle touch, allowing him to enter. He learned I no longer lived among the shadows. When he departed, his touch left a warmth behind, like a promise given by a friend.

Sorqaq motioned for silence. "Minik must have room to walk, to prepare his body to keep breathing while he's gone. We must keep the room warm. Anyone who can't sit still, leave now." He waited while some women took small children away. Qisuk told Sammik to leave. With a sullen glance, he joined the other children. I suspected he would not go far.

To those who remained, Sorqaq said, "This is powerful magic and the last hope of our people to find food. If Minik dies on his spirit journey, we shall all die." His admonition could not be denied. No more inducement needed to be given. "While Minik walks, we shall chant to give his spirit strength for its journey, and then again to guide him back to us in this igloo."

When the chanting began, the remaining children crammed into the passageway to make room. The song, if that is what it was, seemed to be one word repeated softly over and over again, more of a sound than a word. *"Aja-ja"* is how it sounded. Nothing moved but the small flames flickering in the seal-oil lamps. There was only the chanting. Minik's eyes went all white suddenly, and he collapsed, falling backward onto the arms of those men who waited to catch him. They lowered him gently to the *illeq* and laid a fur over him. The chanting continued, very softly.

While we waited, black smoke plumed off one of the lamps. Putu fished out the wick and lit another, standing it in the fat she added to the lamp's stone depression. I concentrated on the bearskin-covered heap in the center of the room. After awhile, the breathing sounds of many noses and the orange flicker of the flames made me sleepy. The room closed in. I rubbed my eyes, determined not to sleep. A sudden cry startled me alert. "Minik has returned!"

The *angakkoq* was helped by his son, a boy of about ten winters, to sit up on the fur-draped platform. Sorqaq poured Minik water, tipping the mug to the other man's lips and holding his head back so that the shaman could drink. Minik's complexion was ashen and his breaths came one after the other, like a woman in labor. A deep sigh lifted his chest and escaped his lips and his entire body quivered violently. A small woman, Minik's wife, as I learned later, crouched to rub his feet while his son rubbed Minik's hands.

At last, the *angakkoq* cleared his throat and spoke in a hoarse whisper. When he used words I did not know, I thought I had forgotten how to speak again. I mentioned this to Padloq. "He talks in *angakkoq* words," she whispered in my ear. So they were words of mystery and magic.

Sorqaq translated. "Nerrivik says anger between members of a family has seeped down through the ice field and made the water too salty. Her seals have moved their breathing holes far to the southeast. The bears have followed them." In so small a village, everyone knew or thought they knew the reason and who was angry. A few of the men glanced in Qisuk's direction. He compressed his lips.

Not far from where I sat holding Qalaseq on the *illeq*, Putu, Qisuk's mother, hid her head under her folded arms. Maki looked at me. When I noticed and returned her scrutiny, she lowered her head. I wondered whether she felt partly to blame.

The women whispered among themselves. Children's voices came from the passageway before Sammik's head poked in. Someone must have told him that Minik's discovery concerned his family.

"No talking," Sorqaq commanded. Minik spoke again in the special language while Sorqaq continued to translate. "He says the southern woman is no longer mind-sick." The people turned to look at me. Sorqaq had not heard about this yet. "How long has this been true?" he asked.

Putu called out, her voice strangely like a cry. "Since yesterday." She, his own wife, had not told him I had returned from the spirit world. He had ordered my child's death before she was born, but Maki had carried it out. Putu killed Qisuk's wife to save his son. What complicated and sad circumstances.

Sammik had told me Qisuk forbade him from visiting his grandmother Putu since the day his brother was taken live from his mother's opened body. There was truly much discord in this village.

"*Iyeh,* it is true I woke up yesterday," I answered for myself. Many a hand reached for and held firmly to a neck amulet at the sound of my voice, which had been unheard by any in this village for so long.

Minik rose to his feet, his fur dropping from his shoulders. He spoke for himself now, in the ordinary language, having come completely out of his trance. His finger pointed me out to the others. "Nerrivik felt Mikisoq's grief for her daughter. The southern woman did not understand the conditions Sorqaq gave before he agreed to bring her to live with us. She didn't understand your hand signs, Sorqaq." The headman opened his mouth as if to speak in his own defense, but he must have changed his mind.

"She didn't know she agreed to her child's death by coming to us," Minik concluded, watching the others to see how they accepted this information.

Many voices rustled like the whisper of the fire. Maki made a terrible moan deep in her throat. Nerrivik was angry at the village. Was this entirely because of my ignorance? If I had not come to them, I could not have caused this misfortune that was destroying the village. My cheeks burned with guilt.

Sorqaq spoke, not to Minik and not to the Inuit, but to me. He said, "I should have made sure you understood. You answered too soon, but I accepted your answer because you can make animal-calling pictures. I apologize, Mikisoq. The fault is mine."

I held no status here. I was no more than a stranger with milk for Qisuk's son, yet the headman of the village had humbled himself to apologize to me. "My daughter's ghost visited me. She forgives me now, and she has gone to the resting place of my country, to be with Great Spirit Orenda, across many waters." Whether the others understood what I had said or not, Minik did.

He interpreted, explaining for the others by saying, "The southern woman uses her own word for Nerrivik. She calls her *Orenda,* spirit of all life to her people. Am I correct, Mikisoq?"

"Iyeh," I replied. It was as though he and I were having a private talk. He motioned for me to go on. "Padloq's sister died because her baby was wrong inside of her. That could not be helped. It is good I was here in time to make milk for Qalaseq. Perhaps it happened as Nerrivik planned. Could that be?" Being a stranger, I hoped I had not spoken too familiarly. I had no right to speak for Sea Woman, but Minik didn't reprimand me. Discord had caused Nerrivik's displeasure and led to the salting of the sea. Too many tears had been shed. When Orenda is out of balance, the same thing happens on Turtle Island.

"Mikisoq," he said, "you awoke now because we need your help."

"Mine?" I rose and walked to him, still holding Qalaseq in my arms. People made a path to let me through.

"Nerrivik will provide meat to our hunters if they can see the animals they wish to find, not amulets or carvings this time. She wishes you to make representations of bears, seals, and caribou. We have need of your pictures. Will you make them for us after what we did to you?"

"She wants me to draw pictures?" This was so little. I knew well that my pictures by themselves had no magic. Minik nodded calmly. Then, as if he had said it in words, I knew. If Nerrivik had told Minik she required pictures, she would provide the magic. The Inuit trusted Minik's power, which derived from Sea Woman. "Of course, I will do as you require," I replied, "but I must heal myself completely first. My hands won't obey me until my harmony is restored."

"What do you need to restore your harmony?" Sorqaq asked patiently. "Do what you must." Perhaps he thought I meant to pray to my gods first. The Inuit waited for me to voice my request or see what I would do.

With Qalaseq in my arms, I walked between the people to Putu, Qisuk's mother. I held her grandson out to her. The baby clung to me for a moment, then held out his arms to be taken. Putu hesitated, her eyes darting toward her son for permission. Sorqaq had made it easier for him by apologizing to me, setting an example. If the headman could admit he was wrong, Qisuk could do the same. It was a time for healing.

He spoke. "I was unjust to blame you, Mother, and wrong to keep my sons from you," he said. "I apologize. You did nothing wrong. My wife would have died anyway, and you saved my new son, as I requested. Please take Qalaseq. You, of all people, have the right to hold him. He would be dead but for your action." Finally, she reached for the baby, holding him close and swaying with sighs as she stroked him.

A moment later, Sammik came tearing into the room. "Grandmother," he screeched happily. "I missed you so much. Hold me, too!" He plopped himself into her lap beside his baby brother, almost displacing him, and hugged her neck. All around us, people laughed gladly, appreciating their reunion. It was much more than the humor of it that lightened the feeling in the room; it was a release. Although I had been in the private world of my own troubled soul, I felt sure that laughter had not been heard in this village for far too long.

Padloq glanced toward her mother, then back to me. She did not have to speak for me to note her hesitation, and the worry that went with it. Padloq knew. She had been there in the birth lodge. One last thing remained for me to complete my healing. I went over to Maki and crouched in front of her. "It was my misunderstanding that killed my daughter," I whispered. The words hurt to say, but this last mending had to happen between the two of us. "My daughter's ghost has forgiven me. As much as her death grieved me, what happened is over. It's in the past." I held my hands to her, offering friendship.

"I regret that I have caused you grief," she said, taking them. She bent her head low. "I don't know how to ask for forgiveness."

"You acted according to your custom. It's different from mine, but proper in your world. My daughter never blamed you; she only blamed me." At that, Maki rose to her feet and wrapped her arms around me in a tearful embrace.

The burden of my resentment and hurt lifted away from me like smoke leaving the vents. Accord had been returned to the people and I had been its instrument, restoring balance, as Great Spirit Orenda required of me. "Now, I'm ready to do as Minik asked me, as Nerrivik commands," I said.

Chapter 21

All but a few people went home to rest after the ceremony. Minik sent his elder son on the errand. He returned shortly, carrying several pale slabs of stone. "I got them from an empty igloo," he told his father. Minik took them from him and stood them against the wall, but their eyes met. The older man's eyebrows lifted in question. The younger man held out his hand, palm down. I guessed what the symbol meant. He added, "The owners won't need these stones again."

If any villager supposed that my lines in the shapes of animals could end a famine, they were wrong. It was up to Sea Woman to do that, although I would do the part Minik had assigned to me. I might have asked for cleansed hides, since these were usually light in color, but stone was my first thought for a surface, and Minik had approved.

Putu brought me a supply of charred bones in a basket and set a clay bowl of soot-blackened grease on the *illeq*, next to my feet. "Thank you, Putu." Although I spoke normally, my voice sounded loud, as if silence were now required after the crowd, the chanting, and Minik's soul-sending ceremony.

A long time had passed since my first days with the Inuit. I had forgotten how to use the strange lighting method they employed. My next request displayed my ignorance, but I saw no way around it. "I have not learned how to manage the lamps. Will you light more wicks so I can see better to draw? Not enough light enters through the window."

Silently, Putu withdrew some twisted moss wicks from a storage basket. She plunged them into the waxy tallow in the waist-high stone lamps.

The surface of the wick stuck out of the fat, about the length of the first joint of my thumb. She lit them with a stiffened long wick dipped into tallow and then allowed to harden away from the flame. The small lamps burned almost silently, producing steady spots of light that neither flickered nor waved like a wood-based fire. Thin plumes of gray smoke rose to the vents where the roof met the wall. I thanked her. She nodded, backing away. When I looked again, she was gone.

The earlier warmth from children and adults packed together into one large room had dissipated. This time, the extra flames did not make me sleepy. I flexed my fingers, hoping they had not stiffened from disuse. With my palms open and resting on my thighs, I prayed, asking the spirit of these people to tell me how I should begin. "Make a bear," Sorqaq suggested from behind me. I jumped mentally, as if he had heard my thoughts and answered them.

"A bear," I repeated, picturing it in my mind before I touched charred bone to stone. Help me make it good, I prayed. I drew the first lines. The lines joined and grew until a bear emerged, standing on its hind legs, furry arms outstretched, ending in great curving claws. The open jaws exposed sharp teeth ready to snap a spear in half or crush a dog. That put me in mind that the bear ought not to be shown triumphant, but ready to give itself to the hunters. Curved lines became dogs snarling at the bear's feet, readying themselves to leap. I drew the outline of several hands casting thick spears flying from the outer edge of the stone toward the bear's heart.

To my great relief, the special ability Orenda imparted to my fingers still remained to me. I intended to lay the first painting aside and pull a second slate up to the *illeq,* when a hand touched mine, quite gently, so as not to startle me. "I will keep the first by me," Minik said. "Here is another." I looked around, stretching out my legs, curving my back to get out the kinks.

Only Minik and Sorqaq remained within the igloo with me as I worked over the drawings. The headman had been trimming the wicks to keep them from smoking. If memory served of my first days among the Inuit last summer, men did not trim wicks. It was woman's work. Yet Sorqaq did this for me while Minik attended to my needs, resting the completed pictures against the *illeq.*

I sketched a representation of a musk ox next, with wide horns, his herd suggested behind him. On another, I drew a seal, fat and glossy underwater, swimming up to its allu while a silent hunter crouched above the hole on the thick ice, his harpoon poised to strike.

My work absorbed me so completely, I hardly noticed when several people crawled inside. Voices whispered and fingers pointed to the completed pictures standing against the walls while men discussed them in undertones. I yawned and stretched, looking around. My eyes watered from extended use.

"May I ask you a question?" came a hoarse whisper. I turned away from the slate and found it to be Ululik, Padloq's father.

"Of course."

"Tell me. Did an *angakkoq* among the Tobacco Growers teach you this magic?" His question surprised me, since his own people carved amulets in animal likenesses that surpassed anything I had seen in the south. A flat painting was simply another form of the same thing. It took a similar skill.

"No *angakkoq* taught me this. When I was a child, I made a picture of a wolf, my clan's totem, in a dream. The next day, I lifted my hand to learn whether my dream was true or false. This is when I discovered the Creator had given this talent to my fingers and my eyes. If I can see something in my mind, I can make a picture of it on rock or hide or bark. Great Spirit Orenda gives such gifts as He chooses." I looked skyward to try to indicate Great Spirit Orenda to them, the part of Himself the Creator left behind on the earth to guide His people when He flew back to the sky for the last time.

"She says her dream and skill came from her people's Sea Woman," Minik said knowingly. Ululik nodded.

"Shall I continue making pictures? Do you need more?" I gestured toward the unused stones in a stack beside the *illeq*.

"This is enough. You are tired. We must not overuse your powers. Better go to Qisuk's igloo to eat and sleep." When I thanked him, Minik added, "I understand how your work has drained you. Refresh yourself. If Sea Woman is contented, these images will be enough. If she is not, no amount of pictures will drive animals to give themselves to our hunters' spears and harpoons. Another time, if your customs allow, I hope you will tell me about your people's gods and how your shamans speak with them."

"I only had twelve winters when I was stolen away from my people, but I'll tell you as much as I know. I will tell you our stories, as well. Our spirits don't mind if we wish to talk about them." I covered my mouth politely, unable to hold back a huge yawn.

Minik smiled reassuringly. "That would make me glad. You've done very well today, *Gahrahstah*."

A small scream jumped out of my throat. "My old name! In my people's tongue! How could you know it?"

He patted my shoulder to soothe me. "It is what you are, what you can do. Men call me an *angakkoq*. Nerrivik puts words in my head just as she puts pictures under your fingers. Go back to Qisuk's igloo and rest, but first tell him to gather all who will hunt tomorrow. Tell Qisuk they must bring their sleeping furs and weapons here. Tonight, they will sleep with me in Sorqaq's igloo in the presence of your images."

Ululik walked me to Qisuk's igloo. The village lay white under the violet sky while the stars flickered like spirits' campfires. Pale clouds drifted across the full moon's face. The colored drapes of lights floated directly above us, unfolding and changing in their mysterious dance. "Eat. Then sleep, Mikisoq," Ululik said, leaving me in front of the passageway.

Qalaseq's angry wails increased when I entered. "The baby," I said. "He hasn't been nursed; he must be hungry." I remembered my responsibility, seated myself, and reached for him. The boy crawled up to me, pulling at my shirt. "Poor Qalaseq. Come here." I took him up onto my lap and got him settled.

When he was sucking contentedly, Padloq handed me meat and broth in a bowl. "We're all hungry," she commented. "It didn't hurt him to wait. What you did was more important."

I had almost forgotten. "Qisuk," I said. "You must gather the hunters. Have them all take their furs and weapons to Sorqaq's igloo to sleep there tonight. Minik told me to tell you."

The hunter eyed me curiously. "Mikisoq gives me orders?"

I flushed. "Not I," I replied, correcting him. "Those are Minik's orders. I would never . . ." I closed my mouth, the roots of my hair seeming to burn my scalp.

He laughed. "I shall do as you bid me," he said, bowing slightly. "You are a very important person in this village today. Minik gave you more status than you know." He gathered his bed furs off the *illeq* and slung his weapons over his shoulders, his spears and whip and bolas. He laughed again before he ducked into the tunnel and walked off into the night.

"And if the hunt is no good, who will they blame?" I asked Padloq.

"Only themselves." Putu had come to visit while I tended to Qalaseq. I had not noticed her. "They won't blame you."

I looked again and noticed another woman who had crawled in behind her. When she lowered her hood, I recognized her face from the ceremony. Of all the women who had been there, only she had remained close to the *angakkoq*.

"I am Inuteq, Minik's wife," she said, smiling at me. "I will stay here tonight because a woman's presence would weaken men's dreams of hunting prowess and strength. You have done all human power may do. For tomorrow, it will be as Sea Woman allows. We must keep one another warm so we can save the wicks." She pinched out all but two of the flames while we drew the furs over us on the *illeq.* The others respected my exhaustion, but later, when they thought I slept, I heard whispers.

"I have the feeling a lot more is going to change," Minik's wife whispered.

"What's this about changes?" Maki asked. "What are you talking about?"

"Sorqaq and Qisuk are father and son, but do you notice Sorqaq always chooses to hunt inland, while Qisuk takes his companions out over the ice field?"

"They don't like to be in each other's way," Maki said.

"Exactly. As you know, there can't be two leaders in one herd, nor two headmen living in the same village. Qisuk grows too big and important in his own eyes to be a follower, even if the leader is his father."

"Do you think my husband will challenge Sorqaq, Mother?" Padloq asked, forgetting to keep her voice soft. I stirred, unable to help myself, and blinked my eyes open.

"Shush," Inuteq commanded. "You woke Mikisoq."

"What will happen? Will they fight?" Padloq asked. My fears pushed me alert. I rose up on one elbow to follow the conversation better.

"No. No. I do not think so. Sorqaq is strong and has the respect of the men," Putu declared, but she wavered in her certainty. "You don't think Qisuk would challenge him, do you, Inuteq?"

As Minik's wife, Inuteq possessed the same high status as the headman's wife. "Not directly," came her reply. "Qisuk loves his father. We are Inuit, not musk oxen or walrus. Something is going to happen, though, whether this hunt succeeds or not. The hunters divide already, each group with one leader. The tribe has too many hungry mouths, and too many opinions. Perhaps there are too many for one village. If Qisuk won't content himself to wait for Sorqaq to get old, events will be interesting." She did not elaborate.

The women looked at one another. Inuteq left the conversation to squat over the night basket. That was as good as telling us the discussion had ended. Sammik lifted his head. "Padloq, are the men back yet? I'm hungry. I dreamed I had food. So much food."

"Shush. Soon you will. No more talking for now. Everyone, go to sleep," Padloq said. This was her igloo.

Sammik cuddled closer, lying against my back. He grew warmer as sleep returned. "The bears can smell the seals out on the ice field," he said. "When my father comes back, I'm going to eat a bear. Afterward, if I'm still hungry, I'll eat half a musk ox. And if I'm still hungry, I wonder. Do you think anyone will kill a walrus?" He paused to think about what else he might want while the women curled up to sleep.

Shafts of light poured through the membrane-covered window above the tunnel, brightening the interior of the igloo. Children's voices called out, "The hunters return." I ran out to see, having to shield my eyes from the sun's reflection against the whiteness. Dazzle changed the sky over the ice field to gold, lighting the teams. "Look," the villagers shouted. The sleds were piled high.

We heard the stories as the Inuit feasted. Out on the ice field, a bear had been cornered and killed, with only one dog lost. Several men had come upon seals scuttling over the ice. While the women worked to pre-pare the bear for cooking, Sorqaq, who had led his hunters inland, as usual, returned. Their sledges dragged butchered musk oxen packed in their own hides.

Minik declared the day a holiday, for prayers of thanks to Nerrivik and to the ghosts of all the animals. Freshwater was placed respectfully upon the killed beasts' lips. Aama's husband, Taaferaaq, placed not only water but a pipe with burning tobacco into a bear's mouth. "If we honor him suf-ficiently, his spirit will return to his mountain cave and be born again. In three years, more meat." The hunters slapped him playfully on the back for his good idea.

Sammik tried to keep his word until Padloq warned him about leaving meat for another meal. It felt good to be full. The women saw me stop eat-ing, and they encouraged me to take more. "I can't," I protested. They con-tinued feeding one another meat dripping with fat. They danced between the igloos long into the night. Several of the hunters nodded with rever-ence to me as well as to Minik, giving me part of the credit.

Before many days, the Inuit were fat and happy once more. One day, Qisuk came home and he said, "This village is still too large." He let Padloq help him off with his *kamiks*. "We are full now, with plenty in reserve until the ice melts and we can take out our kayaks again. That's good for a while, but I think we'll have problems again next winter or the winter after. The old folks are gone, but there will soon be more children who need to eat. When a village has too many people, there are always problems."

"But the hunting was poor because people were angry with one another," Padloq reminded him. "Nerrivik's not angry now."

"There will always be disagreements when there are so many people. More than one hunter will lay claim to the same kill and will both expect the arms and hide. More than one man will want to be headman."

He had finally said it. "Has your father decided he is too old to lead us?" Padloq asked, as if the thought were completely unexpected.

"He hasn't said anything of the kind, but some of the younger hunters want to follow a younger leader. Sorqaq's hair is streaked with gray. He will be old in a few more years."

The break was already coming. Padloq waited for the rest of his news while I nursed the baby and listened, keeping my opinion to myself. Living with the Inuit as an accepted foreigner was one thing, but I knew I could never think as they did. Nor would I ever be less than a foreigner, as I always thought in my own ways instead of theirs. I was a woman from a land where women ruled, living in a land ruled by men.

"I'm the father of two boys. No one can dispute my skill and my luck. I won't fight my own father over leadership, but as long as we keep together in a big village with more babies on the way, there are going to be shortages. I have given this much thought and I have decided that now is the best time for us to leave."

"Leave?" Padloq looked at Qisuk as though he had gone out of his mind. "Leave for where? It's still winter. Where would we go? To another island?"

He smiled for an instant before answering, as though he knew his answer would amaze and stun us. "I shall take us to the village our fathers left before we were born, back across the ice field. We will drive east to the land on the other side of the ocean."

I almost choked on my broth. "There is land across the ocean? But this is an island in the encircling sea. There can't be any land in the east. No one has ever heard of it, Qisuk."

He laughed. "Your people know so little on your southern mainland. You think you live on a giant sea turtle and the turtle became the entire world. How can you know anything when you've never traveled? Our grandfathers boated here in their umiaks when my father was still a small boy. Your father came, too, Padloq. You must have heard him speak about our eastern lands. If they could cross one way, we can cross back the other. Our hunters are every bit as brave and lucky as the Inuit of my grandfather's time."

"The ocean. Qisuk. You're talking about crossing the ocean," Padloq pointed out, still protesting. "Our grandfathers came because they had to. My father said it was dangerous in the old land because of a curse. People kept dying. A quarter of the village died in the crossing. The old land was haunted by *tupilat*, angry spirits. Why don't you go west or north if you must separate from Sorqaq? There are other islands. Not over the ocean."

Sammik's mouth hung open as if he were drinking in his father's plan, and his small eyes glowed with anticipation. "Will we go by dog sledge, Father?"

"*Iyeh,*" Qisuk said.

I saw Padloq shudder.

Sammik shouted for joy, jumping up and down. "It will be so exciting. We'll chase bears on the ice mountains. I'll be the bravest hunter in the village, after you, of course, Father. We'll have so many stories of our crossing, we will tell them for years. When will you tell Grandfather Sorqaq?"

Qisuk patted his son's head and smiled. "Soon. We'll have to go before the ice field melts. We should leave half a moon or more for the journey. Come along with me. Now is as good a time as any." Padloq and I exchanged glances, saying everything with our eyes.

"What did Sorqaq say?" Padloq demanded when Qisuk returned.

"He said to have a good trip. He also said to hurry, before we find ourselves living with Nerrivik."

"He doesn't care?"

"He does not really think we will do it, but he won't try to stop those who choose to go. Inuit are Inuit."

That was the same as saying, "each man to himself." Sorqaq obviously thought the idea foolish, but he would not interfere.

Padloq interjected her thoughts. She had no choice but to follow her husband's orders, but at least she would tell him what she thought of them. I was glad to see she was no longer the child who thought Qisuk could do no wrong. "Just like that? You'll say good-bye to your father and mother forever?"

"You will, too. How soon can you be ready?"

Padloq did not answer his question, but instead, she buried her head in her bed furs and squeaked, "You've taken leave of your senses! You left them out on the ice field. They fell down an *allu* in the ice and a seal swimming underneath swallowed them."

He ignored her outburst. "How soon?"

"Two days. Maybe three."

I was part of Qisuk's household, so it was assumed I would go, too. Each day brought us closer to readiness. There was more to do than the dividing of food stores and the readying of the sledges and dogs. Families would be broken in half. Friends would have to say last good-byes to friends. Single men and women would decide whether to couple or be lost to each other for good.

"Minik is leaving his elder son here to be *angakkoq* for Sorqaq," Qisuk related. "The boy is almost a man and has many of his father's powers. Minik was born here, but all the talk about the east has him curious. He said he wants to see our first land before he grows too old to travel, so I decided to take him." He smiled broadly at his announcement. To me, he resembled a ruffed grouse posturing before its mate. Minik was doing him the favor, possibly at Sorqaq's urging, to try to calm any evil spirits we might encounter along the way and beg Nerrivik's blessings for the travelers.

They did not need me on this expedition. I was far enough from my homeland as it was. I was certain Sorqaq would let me remain here if I asked him. Qalaseq could do without my milk. He could live on chewed meat mixed with broth. If I stayed behind, I would have to find a new family to live with, and accept an Inuit for my husband. I tried to puzzle out my best course of action. Padloq had become like my sister. As crazy as she believed her husband to be, she had to go where he led. I felt torn, but I did not say so. Padloq, Qisuk, all of them simply assumed I would remain with them.

Padloq and I visited Aama. "Of course, Taaferaaq and I are going," Aama stated, "although my baby will come soon. I hope we make land before then. Meqqoq and her husband are coming, too. If she has a boy and we have a girl, or the other way around, we already decided to promise them to each other." She appeared to be happy at the prospect of living in a new village. Both their mothers had died in the famine.

I followed their example and tried to be cheerful. We repaired clothing and *kamiks,* harnesses and kayaks. "We'll leave the umiaks behind," Padloq told us. "We can't carry them, so we'll make new ones there. Kayaks can be carried on the sledges. The men will need to hunt seals when the ice field melts."

"Aren't you afraid?" I asked, finally saying the words. I hoped it was not against custom to talk about fear with women.

"We can take shelter in a blizzard, or build an ice igloo. I'm more frightened of the sun returning and melting the ice. What if the hunting is not good? We might run out of food before we get there," Padloq admitted. "Sorqaq should have tried to convince Qisuk to go north or west, any-thing but east. Going east across the sea ice is so stupid. When Sorqaq said to hurry or we'll find ourselves underwater, he knew. Every day gets longer. In another month, the ice breaks up." She shuddered.

"We give ourselves to Sea Woman's protection," Aama said piously. That much was always true. I continued to help them prepare for the trip. For once, the frigid winds felt comforting.

Only three days had passed since the decision. Sorqaq and Putu came to watch the bundles being tied onto the sledges. Sammik ran to his grand-mother, where he was caught up in a swift embrace. They would soon say good-bye.

"Qisuk?" a deep voice said.

"Iyeh?" Qisuk stopped tying bundles to his sledge and rose to face his fa-ther. The two men had become equals. They stood leader to leader, neither lowering his eyes.

"Remember what I told you about the light-skinned foreigners whose hair grows greatly on their faces. Their hair is the color of the sun or fire. These monsters dwell south of our eastern village and build their houses farther inland. Even if they speak like men, be wary of them. They are not to be trusted."

"The Qallunaat?" He used the Inuit word for Big Eyebrows as though giving a name to a strange tribe.

"Iyeh. Watch out for them. Their kind came to our eastern land from a place even farther east. Their people have stolen our land since the days of my grandfathers' grandfathers. Their boats are larger than ours, many times larger, and their weapon points are harder. Avoid Qallunaat if it is possible, or kill them if they come into Inuit land. Leave the south to them and go elsewhere to build your village. They kill or make slaves of children who are not of their tribe."

Qisuk laughed. "My spear can go through a man more easily than through a bear. I'm not afraid of the hairy Qallunaat. If another Inuit tribe has taken our old village, I'll deal with them as Minik advises. Qallunaat may not challenge our right to return to our own lands. We'll feed them to our dogs like seal meat."

Sorqaq pressed his lips together. Finally, he said, "Take my warning se-riously. You laugh about the hairy people with the white skins, but don't forget their weapons. Their knife and spear points are harder than ivory. Their arrow points are sharper than flint. The Qallunaat don't think twice about killing people and carrying off their children."

"Thank you, Sorqaq, for your concern. I'll remember."

It was good of Sorqaq to warn his son. The men were trying to keep peace. If Sorqaq refused permission to any of his villagers who wanted to go east with Qisuk, new resentments might incur Sea Woman's renewed anger. He and his son would separate the village, but they would leave as friends, not under a cloud. The men embraced. It was a good thing.

I wondered if Qisuk possessed half Sorqaq's wisdom and leadership qualities. It pleased me that Minik had decided to go along to advise him. I hated to think anything might happen to Padloq and the others, but the more I thought about it, the more I realized that I would not stay behind. The destiny Grandmother saw for me waited in an entirely new direction. She had said I would find what I needed across water.

"Come eat with us," Putu said to Sammik. She and Sorqaq walked the boy to their igloo. I heard them talking as they walked him away, the grandfather and grandson discussing the hunting of white bears. While Qisuk strode off to inspect the packing elsewhere, Padloq and I returned to the igloo to warm ourselves and drink broth.

Our conversation led to how much we could take without overburdening the dogs, without weighing down the sledges. I remembered the knife I wore beneath my shirt and thought of Sorqaq's warnings. When Padloq undressed me that day last summer, she must have seen the pouch where I kept my knife. She had never asked me about it, nor the scars on my back, respecting my privacy just as the Naskapi had done. My Naskapi dress was now packed in one of the bundles. Padloq told me to keep it for my wedding festival and to show to my children when I had some.

"I have thought it over and decided to go with you, Padloq," I said.

Her mouth hung open for a moment. "Did you think you would not? You never spoke about staying behind."

"Sorqaq gave me shelter. I never decided Qisuk was my headman. It is because of you and Sammik that I will go."

My friend shook her head in amazement. "Women are very different where you come from. Imagine women making their own choices where they will live! Well, then, I'm glad you decided you're coming with me."

Padloq's father was the oldest man to ask to join Qisuk's expedition. Ululik and Maki decided they could not bear to have their only remaining child, Padloq, and their dead daughter's children leave without them. I was in the igloo, checking over the dogs' harnesses, when I heard Qisuk ask, "How many winters have you, Ululik?" Ululik blinked and raised his chin at the insult. It upset me to see an older man have to humble himself before a younger one.

"Two more than forty," Ululik said. "But I can still handle a kayak and harpoon as well as I've done for years. I did my share in the hunt. My eyes are still sharp. No one knows the eastern land better than I, except for Sorqaq, and he's not going. I lived there until I was Sammik's age. I offer to be your guide. With a guide and an *angakkoq,* you'll have a much better chance."

Qisuk nodded, recognizing the wisdom of Ululik's suggestion. He would have been a fool not to take someone familiar with the land. "It will be good to have you with us on the journey and in the new village," he admitted.

Ululik smiled, but his eyes remained hard, no doubt remembering the insult and that he had needed to humble himself to do Qisuk a favor. Something told me we had not heard the last of it. At least, with him and Maki going, Sammik would get to keep one pair of his grandparents. Putu, of course, had no choice but to stay behind. After tomorrow, her two grandsons would go where she would not see them again in this life. My heart ached for her, and for Sorqaq, too.

Before we left, Putu and Sorqaq piled presents on their departing family, toy weapons for practice and warm underclothing for the children. "Remember me, Sammik," Putu said, giving him another hug. "Tell Qalaseq he has another grandmother and grandfather across the ocean, thinking about him."

We ate and slept a final time in the igloos that had sheltered us, lying close together on the old *illeq.* When gray and pink gathered like the inside of an oyster to chase the black from the southern sky and mist rose from the ice field, we tied the final bundles onto the travelers' sledges. The Inuit fed their dogs lightly, then harnessed them into their traces, leaving the spare animals to run beside us.

I counted seven sledges, loaded high. Fourteen couples had joined the expedition, with six children and two on the way. The wind picked up over the ice field. I pulled my hood tight and laced it higher, covering even my nose for warmth. Only my eyes were uncovered while we watched for the sun.

Far out where the frozen inlet met the ice field of the ocean, strange formations of waves seemed frozen in motion from when the ice had buckled during the freeze. Like bent fingers, the ice beckoned us toward the dawn.

"Masks!" Qisuk directed when the first rim of the sun transformed the ice field from gray to blazing white. I lifted up my carved ivory mask, adjusted the thin slits so I could see, and tied it in place. The slits cut down on the glare. Last hugs from friends and families were shared before the remaining villagers moved back from the sledges. Last words and final touches.

"Aak! Assut!" Giving the order to his team to make forward, fast, Qisuk snapped his whip over their backs. "We go!"

The big dogs crouched, pulling hard against their harnesses. The men helped them get started. White wind blew past my cheeks as we sped down the hill and onto the ice field. The village was soon left behind. I shrank deeper inside my hood and long winter anorak, trying to believe that another world awaited us on the other side of the ocean. It would be a long trek. I prayed the ice field would not melt before its end.

Chapter

Where the inlet met the ice field, we confronted the first of the frozen hummocks. Up close, those beckoning fingers were no longer beautiful and mysterious. On the ice field, I saw them as dangerous obstacles, as did the Inuit who hunted the white bear with their dogs. To my astonishment, Padloq took the reins and grasped the crossbar, keeping the sledge from tilting while Qisuk helped the dogs haul themselves and the sledge over the jagged piles.

Scaling the hummocks took most of the first day. Padloq appeared to be caught up in Qisuk's adventure, finally. Even if she was only making the best of it, she moved more quickly and laughed often. The crossing was a daring thing to attempt. I supposed the excitement affected all of us, keeping our spirits high. The ice would not melt for at least another turn of the moon. After the hummocks, we set up our first night's shelter on the sledges. We cooked over our fire bowls, warmed ourselves with food, and huddled close under the furs to sleep.

After a breakfast of cold walrus slices, we set off again, striding beside the heavy sledges, lifting and pushing to ease the dogs' burden. Uneven ice slowed our progress. I wondered how much help the Inuit could reasonably expect from Minik, aside from his role as a spirit talker. It seemed his powers were not limited to the spiritual. He knew how to hunt and work his dogs, too.

During the brief nights, he looked toward the star animals as they floated across the heavens. Once, when we had pulled up to change teams, he measured the sharpness of the air by removing his hood and counting on his fingers how long he could withstand the discomfort. With his long hair blowing out behind him, he might have been Ga-oh, Wind Spirit.

As we progressed, the moon changed from full to new, then began again. It was never far from my mind that winter might give way to spring before we found land. Minik used his staff to measure the thickness of the ice around a seal *allu*. When he called out to tell us it was safe, Padloq breathed more easily. She had been hiding her worry.

"I think we reached the midpoint of our journey or a little beyond," Ul-ulik said. He, too, had been counting the days and watching the moon's changing face as we traveled. There was no sign of land yet, only a field of ice as far as the farthest-sighted of our party could see.

The sun had not yet set when Qisuk ordered, "Pull up. Make camp." With shouts and whistles, the Inuit ordered their dogs to draw the sledges into a huddle. We tied heavy hides into place to make our tents. Maki and Ululik pulled close to us, so all of us made one shelter together. Aama, Meqqok, and their husbands made the tent next to ours, and Minik, his wife, daughter, and youngest son slept with the last two families. Our camp seemed like a large tent with three compartments. With the sledges lashed together and the weighted hides holding out the wind, we lit our oil stoves. Our sleeping shelters became cozy with spots of light and all of us close enough to keep in our warmth.

While Qisuk fed his team, I spread extra furs on the flat of the sledge for our bed. "When you're done with that, would you pack away the rest of the tinder while I get snow melting in the pot?" Padloq asked. She added thin slices of meat. "It won't be long before we have warm meat and broth."

I realized why Qisuk had called for an early stop. Our food supplies were running low. The dogs needed more to keep their strength. The constant work was wearing them away. We had little time to rest, so we needed more food than when we were sleeping half the winter away, under our furs back at the village. He and the men searched to discover if any seal *allut* might be in the area. No one was quite sure how long this journey would take, since even Ululik had to rely on memories more than thirty winters old.

Once the men were out of hearing, Padloq asked, "So? What do you think, Mikisoq? Would your Tobacco Growers make such a journey? Is there any so brave as the Inuit in all the world?" Maki and Inuteq had come to visit. At Padloq's question, they turned to me, wondering, no doubt, how I would answer.

"If I could tell them what you do, my people would think I made up a story to amuse children. We never heard of a land across the ocean." I still almost doubted it. "They would not believe in these sledges of caribou and walrus bone lashed together. Even the ocean is foreign to us. It's like where the spirits go, a place to think about only. My people have never seen it."

"Never seen it? Your hunters may not travel on it like we do, but they've seen it and been on it. Your village sits on a bay. Your people trade with ours every year," Maki said.

"I came to them only last year. I have told you they're not my people. They helped me on my journey. My people live farther south, where many trees grow tall, and so close that their leaves cover the sky. When we think about the ocean at all, we think it's like a river with only one bank, that it flows like a river, hugging the land."

Maki exclaimed at this. "How can people be so ignorant?"

I wanted to tell her how ignorant she was of forests and clans and the great wars that destroy men and how women grow corn, but instead, I said only, "We know different things. It is true that your dogs are larger and stronger than dogs of my world. Inuit make the best hunters and the bravest. They cross between worlds." At their questioning glances, I added, "I've lived with different peoples, and I know there are no others who would dare what you have dared."

Maki looked at me with narrowed eyes, which made me wonder whether she took my praise as flattery. After all these moons, I still doubted myself among the Inuit. My Naskapi friends were right to warn me how unknowable Inuit are to those not raised among them.

I raised my chin and she lowered her eyes. She was not challenging me. I think Maki found it odd that I admired their bravery and skills as I did, thinking them ordinary and expected. "You never told us much about your country. You talk to Minik about your spirits, but not us. If women may speak of them, tell us your stories, too. Do you know about Nerrivik in your land? What kind of houses do your people live in? Why did you leave your home to travel alone when you were so young? Tell us while we wait for the meat to cook."

I meant to tell only a little at first, just enough to answer Maki's question. I had held tight to my secrets for so long. As I decided what to tell them, memories flooded back to me of my carefree youth in Doteoga, my friends and cousins in our protecting forest by the Wide River. For a long time, I had barely thought of home.

I spoke for myself as much as to satisfy the women. "I lived in a large village beside a river," I began, "with my mother and father, an older sister and a young brother. Many people live in my house, which is made of the trunks of young trees tied together with birch bark to cover the framework. The houses are narrow and long, with a doorway at each end." I described our bed benches and our four fire pits dug into the earth down the middle line of the house. "Many families live in one house. We are all related through my grandmother's mother, except for the husbands. My mother's mother makes all decisions."

At this, Maki's eyes narrowed. "Wait. Are you telling us an old woman like me gives orders to your people?"

"My grandmother is much older than you. Her hair is all white now. I know this because her spirit visited me when I was sick. She rules inside the village for her family, our clan. The men rule outside, in the forest."

"Explain 'forest,' " Inuteq said.

Every statement brought another question. It would be impossible to explain it all. "You remember trees? I explained them before." They nodded. "A forest is land covered with trees, too many to count. It is where animals make their homes, away from where people make their villages. We cross forests to go to other villages the way you cross bare land or water."

I feared the women did not see the picture I tried to paint in their minds. "Go on," Padloq suggested. "Tell us more."

"I will explain how I became lost from my people. Our men went away for the warm season. We women took care of our ourselves."

"Your men went hunting?"

"Something like that. In my twelfth summer, while the men of my family were gone, bad men came. They wanted to kill us and to take our homes and hunting grounds for themselves."

"They did?" I had not seen Sammik crawl close.

"*Iyeh.* They did." Especially because I wanted to please Sammik, who, like the rest, enjoyed the dramatic, I decided to make my story more sensational. I crouched, both hands before my face, peering through my spread fingers. It was a game we played with young children at home. We called it "Now you see me; now you don't." I made my eyes grow wide. "They thought they were going to surprise only the women and the children. But . . ." I paused and looked around. There wasn't a sound in the tent. Every face was intent on my next words. "They did not know our men had returned that very morning. They were going to surprise our warriors, but we surprised them instead and chased them away."

Sammik jumped up and cheered. Suddenly, a thought intruded on his joy. "Then why are you here?"

"I saw the Algonquin warriors, the bad men, sneaking through the forest. I was watching from a high place, in one of those trees I told you about. My little brother was the fastest runner among the boys. I ordered him to run back and warn the men, but I couldn't climb down fast enough. The warriors saw me and knew I gave the warning." I paused, thinking how different my life would have been had I stayed hidden in the boughs of the hickory tree. "The bad men took me away with them when they ran back to their own country."

"Poor Mikisoq!" Sammik threw himself onto my lap, hugging me and sucking his thumb to comfort himself.

"Sammik, wait." I attempted to console him. "If it didn't happen that way, I wouldn't be here with you. You wouldn't be my friend. Who else had milk to nurse Qalaseq? Maybe Nerrivik planned that I would come to you." I had not thought of that before, but anything could be possible if both our great spirits wished it so.

"Sea Woman sent you to us to make pictures, to give the hunters animals to kill," Sammik said. He hugged me again, then lay with his head on my lap while the women encouraged me to go on with my story.

"This may be true," Padloq said. "Now, get off of Mikisoq's belly, Sammik, so she can finish telling us her story. What happened then?"

"What about your father and the others?" someone asked me. "Why didn't he save you and take you home? What about all the men of your village?"

"They tried. Many men died. My father died, too, trying to save me." My chest tightened and I could not speak for several moments.

"How awful!" Padloq said. "Go on."

I did so, touching briefly on my captivity and how I was traded to a northerner who used me harshly. I told them I escaped, but I left out the part about killing Hawk Feather. By the way Maki crinkled her nose and Padloq leaned back, her mouth sagging, I believe that they guessed.

"But if your enemy's seed made that child, then why did you care about it?" Aama asked. She must have seen my face. "Forgive me, Mikisoq. I didn't mean to bring up unhappy memories. I only asked because it confuses me. How could you care about the baby of a man you hated?"

"It wasn't the child I hated; it was the man. Besides, among my people, the child belongs to her mother, and her mother's clan. A husband moves in with his wife's family. Children belong to their mother's clan alone. The child is only of the mother, not the father."

The women discussed this back and forth in quick, soft voices. It was a strange concept to them. While they talked, little Qalaseq awoke and began to fret. Padloq changed his diapering and handed him over to me to nurse. Sammik moved over a little. The sound of Qalaseq's sucking and the small flames licking the cold fat blocked out the frigid emptiness of the ice field. The fat itself gave a good smell to our tent. "You say your house holds many families, but all of you are one family clan?" Maki asked.

"*Iyeh.*"

"We here are not all of one blood, but we are like a family. This sectioned tent is like your longhouse."

I had been feeling that, too. "Let me show you how our houses look," I said, thinking I should have drawn a picture for them earlier and saved myself words. I pulled away the hide scrap that made our flooring, took up a sharp-ended bone, and began to scratch out a picture on the white ice. I drew the outline of a longhouse with smoke emerging from appropriate places along the roof. When they had seen, I rubbed away the image with the side of the bone.

"Do you think it's safe to do that, to rub out the likeness of your house?" Meqqoq asked, worried. "If your pictures hold power like an amulet, what will happen to your family's house?"

"No *angakkoq* put magic in this picture. I cannot do so myself." Minik's wife, Inuteq, agreed with my explanation. When the food was ready, Maki portioned it out to each of us. The other women left for their own fires, but a few of them returned with their bowls to continue our talking. "Is your shaman very strong?" Inuteq inquired. "As strong as Minik?"

"Our shaman has the power to send my grandmother's spirit to me. She counseled me in Sorqaq's village when I was mind-sick, although my father's ghost helped her make the trip. He came first to ask my permission to bring Grandmother. My home is more than a year's journey from Sorqaq's village, so our shaman must have powerful spirit magic."

Inuteq asked, "Do you speak to ghosts and spirits often?"

"No. Or rather, I may speak, but it is seldom that they answer. I see those I love and miss in dreams. Is that not true for everyone?"

Inuteq shook her head slowly. "My husband can send his own second spirit on a journey to spirit realms, but I never heard of an *angakkoq* sending another's to a far place. Yet, your shaman doesn't appear to know picture magic for hunting. How strange."

Maki had a question. "If your women make the decisions in your clans, how do the men know their status, and which must obey which?"

"By their courage and skills. Also, the eldest, who have kept their honor in war, command the younger men. My own uncles taught me many things. In war and hunting, our council chiefs rule. If a chief does not do well, the clan matrons take away his command and replace him. There is a ceremony for this."

"And you say Inuit live off the world!" Padloq exclaimed. "Everything is upside down in your country. I'd like to see such a place for myself. Better not tell the men about it, Mikisoq. They wouldn't like it."

Later, the hunters returned. They announced that they'd cornered a bull walrus by an ice hummock and killed him before he could make his attack. "Wake up. Bring your *ulus*," Qisuk roared to the women. We quickly pulled on our anoraks, fastened our hoods, and slipped on our mittens.

The walrus had been dragged to camp. "He's a big one," Maki said, whistling with appreciation and rubbing the great beast. It was bigger than a man. "Plenty of blubber for more fires. Meat for half a moon and more ivory!"

The men rested, eating while the women worked. We loaded up the sledges again. Qisuk decided to have the women drive, since the men needed sleep after their hunt. All the women knew how to handle the dogs, but only did so with their men's permission. Despite the bumpy ride, Qisuk soon slept among the bundles on the sledge while Padloq guided the dogs.

Ice formed over the runners after our next stop. The air felt warmer. That was very bad, for winter must not depart while we were on the ice field. It took many twists and turns on the handholds to jerk the runners free. The dogs slept and ate in their harnesses. There was no time to waste. A flick of the whips and shouted orders sent us flying over the ice again.

Snow fell on our next camp. When I awoke, I peeked through the hanging furs and could not see the dogs. Qisuk opened the furs wider to slip past me. He walked some distance away to urinate. "Where are the dogs, Qisuk?" I called to him. "I don't see them."

He pointed to lumps under the snow. "Don't worry. They know how to keep warm." He raised his voice to tell everyone to get ready, then walked down to the humps of snow to dig his team out. The dogs helped, paws and jaws working and tearing at the half-frozen crust above them. They emerged white, sending a shower of snow flying when they shook themselves.

Mostly, we ate while we walked or ran beside the sledges, holding chunks of walrus meat in our mouths until they thawed enough to chew. The Naskapi name, Eskimo, suited us more often than not, for the meat was raw.

We had been twenty-one days on the ice field when the free-running dogs cornered a bear against the foot of an ice hummock. The hunters seized their harpoons and ran in pursuit. Salluq and Taaferaaq brought down the giant and dragged it up to the women by its hind feet. Minik sprinkled freshwater on the bear's tongue and thanked its spirit. Since the hunters hadn't gone looking for it, he felt Nerrivik favored our chances. If only the sun did not grow warm.

Maki had given me a round-edged *ulu* earlier, which I now used to help with the butchering. I kept my special knife in its pouch between my breasts. When I lifted my wide shirt for Qalaseq to nurse, the sheath showed a little, but the Inuit respect for privacy was strong. No one ever asked me about it. Since my escape from Hawk Feather, only Pine Tree Woman had seen it unsheathed. I thought that if we reached land, I would someday ask Minik if he knew what the designs on it meant.

Both Aama and Meqqok expected their babies to be born soon. They often rested on the sledges with the smaller children. Such a journey had to be a strain for them, but they did not slow us. Each day, the sun rose higher and stayed above the horizon longer. Warmth on my eyes frightened me. It hastened the thaw, death-giver to our traveling village.

We camped near an ice mountain. When wind whistled eerily through its crevices and peaks, I held Qalaseq closer, for the sound bothered him, too. He reached for my breast with both hands, pulling it to his mouth to comfort himself. I felt the beat of his heart. Sammik's breathing came from my other side. Padloq and Qisuk huddled close on the *illeqs* we made of our sledge floors, whispering before they slept. Maki and Ululik lay opposite us under their pile of furs. Soon, fatigue overtook me and the sounds of the mountain died away.

I was startled out of sleep when one of the men lifted a flap of our tent. Aama's husband stood beside us, looking frightened.

"Maki!" Taaferaaq said tightly. "Aama says her baby is coming. Please come help. I don't know what to do." His lips were white with fear in his wind and sunburned face. Since Aama never complained, he never would have heard her moan before. Without a word, Maki crawled from under her sleeping fur and slid her arms through the sleeves of her anorak. In a moment, she had her *ulu* and a clean hide. She followed him out of the tent.

I started to rise, reaching for my anorak, when Padloq pushed me back. "My mother will take care of Aama and her baby. We need to go back to sleep."

"But how can we go on? Aama will not be able to catch up."

"She'll be on her husband's sledge. When her baby comes, her son will ride in her hood. We go on today like every day. The moon is still low over the ice mountain," she said, peeking through the hides. "Try to go back to sleep."

Aama's baby had not yet arrived when Qisuk gave the order to start. The men shouted commands and the dogs pulled, while Aama, laboring on a lonely sledge, with Taaferaaq and Maki attending her, grew smaller in the distance. Every snap of the whip made me think the ice was cracking.

Shortly after we stopped to change dogs and feed them, Taaferaaq's sledge was observed approaching the camp. Runners scraped against the wind-blown ice; they screeched to a halt. Maki climbed off first. Aama's tired, happy smile greeted us from beside the bundles under the great white bearskin from the last hunt.

"Look!" she demanded, lifting her infant, "Behold the first child of our new home." She held it up against the sheltering warmth of her fur-covered anorak. There was a small hide wrapped around its bottom. She unwound the wrapping and turned it around, exposing its tiny backside to the people. There, above the crack, in the small of the infant's back, was a dark blue mark the size of a thumbprint. So that's the mark of an Inuit, I thought. I had learned every child born to their tribe is given this sign at birth by Sea Woman. It is a mark of her advocacy. An infant born without one is likely to die, as I knew too well. "It's only a girl, but Taaferaaq is happy anyway. My next one will be a hunter. I'm a little tired. Is there enough meat for us?"

"You did well," Qisuk said. "We'll need every child in our new village, even the girls." Minik made a hand motion over the baby as if presenting her to Sea Woman.

The wind increased. I pulled my collar high over my nose, and my hide mask shielded my eyes. The fur of my hood caught my warm breath and made frost on the outside. As much as the cold hurt, I was glad for it. The wind blew the snow in clouds of white around us and dried the ice field. Our sledges moved more easily, but the runners screeched as if monsters pursued us.

The sounds affected us all. Maki and Padloq talked about evil spirits, *tupilat,* waiting on ice mountains to pounce down on our procession. It reminded me how little power we possessed, riding the breast of Sea Woman and praying for her favor. We tempted fate and the sun, trying to do the impossible. Wide green and pale blue drapes of color flamed and crackled in the blue-gray sky, becoming violet and red as we raced across the night.

"How much longer will it be until we reach land, Minik?" Qisuk asked when we stopped.

"This is your journey," the *angakkoq* answered. "I never came this way. You have to rely on Ululik for answers. You should ask him." Subtly, the *angakkoq* had reminded Qisuk of Ululik's resentment at having had to ask to be included. Ululik never spoke of it, but sometimes I saw how he looked at Qisuk when the younger man wasn't watching.

A man's cry came from one of the sledges behind us. "It's Meqqok's turn," Maki said. "I must go see if she needs help."

As we continued, the wind blew out of the northeast. Snow crystals stung our uncovered cheeks as we walked into it. The wind soon covered the sounds behind us. I heard later that Meqqok gave birth on the sledge. Maki arranged the bundles so Meqqok had room, then slit the young woman's trousers enough for the baby to come out. Between them, they shielded Meqqok from the wind.

After we had the tents set up for the night camp, Salluq's sledge caught up to the others. "It's a boy," he shouted. Everyone was joyful. Salluq was ecstatic, bragging and strutting around. Meqqok lifted her son for us to see, unwrapping him to show his blue mark first. Then she turned him around to display his penis to the admiring Inuit before bundling him and tucking him into his sling under her long anorak.

"We're off to a good beginning," Qisuk said inside our tent as we ate. "Two new children, no dogs lost, meat found along the way. It should not be much longer. What do you say, Ululik? When?"

Padloq's father took another sip of broth. "Don't tempt the spirits. Wait to celebrate until we set our feet on land again," he replied gruffly. "The wind from the east doesn't smell like land yet. A few warm days and the ice field will start to break apart. Our weight will turn it over with all of us on it."

Qisuk frowned. "Don't make gloomy predictions. What was the trip like when you left your village in the east when you were a boy? Can you remember?"

"I remember it well, but I didn't count days. I was Sammik's age when we left. This is entirely different, since we journeyed during summer in umiaks, our whole village with the dogs. It felt like a month, but it might have been more. One of the boats turned over in a storm, losing all who rode in her. Each storm wave took us up into the sky. It was like riding up one side of a mountain that lifts by itself, then sliding down to the base of another. My best friend and his father were in that umiak we lost. The father had a new wife. His first had died in childbirth in our village."

"Like my first wife." It was the first I had heard Qisuk speak of his earlier loss, and I realized how he must still mourn for Padloq's sister. He patted Padloq's arm, for they both missed her sister.

"My elder daughter," Ululik reminded him.

"*Iyeh.* Of course. Tell us more, Ululik."

"We ran out of drinking water. Some of the elders died of thirst, giving their share to the hunters. Until it rained, we lost a pair of babies, too, when their mothers' milk dried up. During a second storm, we barely kept the umiaks afloat. We caught fish and drank their blood for water. We killed dogs and ate their meat raw. We had few dogs left when we finally reached land."

"What do you remember about our home in the east?"

"There are high mountains inland, covered with glaciers. We'll see them from the ice field. We were a few days out before we lost sight of them. There are many islands, but the true coast has a narrow beach, only rocks and high cliffs, and very difficult to climb. There is a cleft where we can climb to the headland. The coast juts into the ocean in many places."

"Our fathers lived there, so the land must be good when the spirits are not angry. If we don't find our old place, will we have trouble finding a stream or a spring? What about the animals? Are they the same as those we know?"

"The springs are hot, sometimes. Glacier melt swells the rivers into torrents. You'll find bear and seal. Musk oxen and caribou live inland among the valleys where an *inuk* can hunt, but he must use great care. The land is treacherous. It shakes sometimes. Your footing can disappear suddenly. The next thing you know, you are alive in your grave, with only a crack of sky to remind you of the earth you left behind." I shuddered, wondering if the length of the journey and the sound of the wind gave everyone such morbid thoughts.

"What else can you tell us?" Qisuk demanded, scowling.

"Watch out for Qallunaat settlements, as your father warned you. Keep to the north and the most western reaches of the long inlets. Beluga whales swim close to shore there. We may hunt them from the umiaks with poison-tipped harpoons if we can find the right plants inland to make the poison. I remember one summer our fathers caught two. We had enough to last the winter."

"Were there other villages near our fathers' village?"

"There is one village close enough to visit. We traded with them. I remember a stream and a spring behind our old village. The spring bubbled hot and steamy, and it poured into a pool. The water tasted odd because of the yellow rocks, which smell like old eggs. You will see, if we ever get there. Let me sleep now." So saying, Ululik pulled his fur over his face and was soon breathing rhythmically. We all curled in our furs and went to sleep.

When Qisuk was out of hearing the next morning, I asked Padloq if Ululik remained angry. "I don't doubt it," she replied. "It is known my father had to ask to be included. Qisuk depends on him, but he won't acknowledge Father's importance. A man's pride and skills are the most important things he possesses. No man makes less of another's pride and expects to keep his goodwill. My father won't speak of the insult, but he remembers."

"If Qisuk did not invite him, why did your father ask to come?"

"He asked because he's my father, and he's Sammik and Qalaseq's grandfather. My mother did not want me to leave without her. My father asked to come because of my mother and me, and the boys." I nodded, feeling I knew Ululik better, and also the reason for Padloq's apprehension.

In the morning, Qisuk said, "When we are close enough, look for the cliffs you know, Ululik. If our old village is still deserted, we can claim our igloos."

"Only if the *tupilat* are gone. We'll know our old village by the star that fell out of the sky and now rests in the ground behind the two hills." I wondered what he meant, but it was time to go.

It rained that day. The ice became slippery under our feet, giving the dogs trouble. Qisuk called for a council. The seven men huddled to discuss our situation. Afterward, Qisuk commanded us to travel day and night, for the wind had stopped and the sun strengthened. "The women drive while the men and spare dogs sleep on the sledges. We shall sleep in shifts, the way the dogs pull. We will make no more camps and no more fires until we have reached land."

I slept on the sledge with the baby. When I awoke, Padloq's voice floated back to me, calling to the team, encouraging them. Qisuk slept beside me, wrapped in furs. Sammik straddled him, looking like a boy riding a bear, asleep, his head on his father's chest.

We stopped only long enough for the men to unharness the exhausted dogs and hitch the new ones into their traces. One of the bitches dropped a litter of six pups. Qalaseq curled up to sleep with them on the sledge. No matter what, we kept moving. My legs had ceased to hurt. I could no longer feel them.

Ululik shouted, "Look. I see land!" Against the seemingly endless expanse appeared small white clouds that were not clouds, but the tops of mountains covered with snow. The sun broke the light apart like a rainbow over the mountains. It took my breath away. The sight set the Inuit cheering. "We aren't there yet," Ululik remarked.

The journey had to end soon, but whether we were to live remained in doubt. The sun beat against the ice. Salluq drove the lead sled. He had gotten well ahead, when there was a sudden lurch. The other drivers pulled up their sledges and skidded to a halt. Salluq was too far ahead and his team was moving too fast to stop. The ice lifted upward in a huge sheet, tipping sledge and dogs backward. Meqqok and her baby held to their sledge as it lifted higher than our heads. She screamed, trying to get her feet under her and jump off.

Padloq pulled up our own dogs and yanked them wide of the gap. Indecision would have taken us in next, but Padloq thought fast, driving us to safety while Qisuk, jarred awake, jumped from the moving sledge to try to help Salluq's family from the water.

Three of Salluq's team struggled, trying to pull back, but their paws found no purchase on the slippery sheet. The other three dogs already floundered, whimpering, in the black water. Two more men leapt from their sledges, landing at a run as they pursued the dogs and the sledge, trying to help. The remaining dogs were in danger not only of sliding in after them but of choking on their harnesses. They yelped and howled their fear, thrashing, leaping back on their hind legs.

One moment they were on the ice; the next moment, a splash of black water covered them. No! I thought. I beseeched Sea Woman, or any benevolent spirit, to save them.

Ululik circled with his team and tossed the tail of his whip to Meqqok and Salluq. I thought they would be too much in shock, too frozen to move, but Meqqok, who had entered the water last, grabbed the leather. With her son in her *amaaq*—the extra hood carrier in her anorak—she was too heavy to pull herself forward to the firm, unbroken ice, but she got the whip handle to Salluq. He managed to hang on to the whip with one hand and on to Meqqok with the other. They could not last long in the freezing water.

Ululik ran toward them with the extra harnesses and traces. Salluq's face and one arm lifted above the water in his struggle. "Get away," he shouted. "The ice won't hold you!" Then he saw what Ululik offered. "Throw!" he screamed. Ululik had looped one end of his harpoon rope over his sledge. He heaved the other to Salluq. Together, all the men dragged the half-submerged sledge with its team and people high enough for the others to pull them to thicker ice and safety.

When they were back on the surface, Maki and Minik grabbed the furs off their sledges and dried the victims. "The water will freeze them if we don't get them dry," Padloq explained as we worked. The baby was driest of all, but in shock. Salluq and Meqqok were blue and shaking.

"Rub hard," Qisuk yelled, rubbing the trembling Salluq himself with dry furs. "Salluq! Can you hear me?" he screamed. "Get them to move. I don't want to lose them!" Salluq moaned and water spilled from his mouth. Maki and I rubbed Meqqok while Ululik, Taaferaaq, and the others dried the wet dogs to keep ice from forming under their fur.

Qisuk and Minik helped carry Salluq and Meqqok and set them on their sledge under thick piles of furs. Qisuk drove to thicker ice while I trotted behind. As soon as they stopped, Minik's wife, Inuteq, lit her oil stove and set it between Meqqok and Salluq. "Strip them," she said. When we had done that, she piled dry furs on top of them. I rubbed Meqqoq under the furs, harder and faster, hoping to warm her while Aama rubbed the infant. Their blue skin turned red with the rubbing and they felt pain again, a good sign. They would live.

Qisuk drove Salluq's dogs, and Padloq drove ours. This was no time to rest, while the ice melted around us. After the sun went down and it was cold again, we stopped for a while to rest and make a fire. We could not stay the night, but it felt good to be still for once. I offered to nurse the new baby, but Minik's wife told me it would do Meqqok good to suckle her son. We warmed some food over the fire. Qisuk sat unmoving as a mountain, his legs out before him on the bed of his sledge.

"Come eat," Padloq invited. "There is warm food." He did not seem to want to rise, withdrawing farther away among the bundles. Minik and Inuteq went to talk to him while we meted out the portions.

At last, Qisuk approached the rest of us. We had all been given a fright, but Qisuk had taken it the hardest. He would not take the food Padloq offered him; instead, he crouched, making himself lower than Ululik. "We almost lost three lives, not counting dogs. If I had not broken away from my father's village, if I had not talked everyone into this journey, you would be safe at home." No one said anything, and Qisuk continued. "Ul-ulik knew what to do. I didn't."

The older man lifted his chin, eyes shining. He said no words, however, waiting for Qisuk to finish speaking. For the very first time since I had come to the north, I heard humility in Qisuk's voice, and saw him lower his eyes. "You have been guiding us since the weather turned. You should be our headman. If the others agree, I won't contest your leadership." Qisuk leaned his head forward, his arms resting against his knees, and waited for Ululik to respond.

Padloq's father would not be hurried. Sometimes, I felt Ululik's resentment seething just beneath the surface, like the ocean under the ice. When finally Ululik cleared his throat, Qisuk did not change posture, but he lifted his head. "I will speak my thoughts plainly," Ululik said. "You were too young, too inexperienced to take so many lives into your hands. In your head, two sons made you a big man. You seemed to forget my first daughter died to give you your younger son. Now, you have taken my second daughter into your care, and you have my grandsons to protect. You meant to take them out of my life without even consulting me, your father-in-law. You forced me to lower myself. I begged to be included in your expedition to be near my last daughter. You, in your unbounded pride, thought me too old to be useful. If you were not Padloq's provider, I might have taken your life."

Ululik's stark honesty astounded me so, I could scarcely take a deep breath. No one moved while we waited. Qisuk did not rise, remaining lower than his father-in-law. Finally, he spoke, but we had to listen hard to hear him, because his words came out softly and with difficulty, as if they were hard to say. For Qisuk, I am sure they were. "I wronged you. With more pride than wisdom, I wronged all of you." He looked around, at all of us. Sammik stood at the fringe of my vision, his mouth hanging open at his father's words.

Qisuk continued, focusing again on Ululik. "I couldn't challenge my father and take his leadership away from him. He has been a good leader, and I love him. My only path was to leave, to find another place for those who would go with me. Ululik has more sense than I ever did. We won't reach land before the sea breaks in on us. Ululik, kill me and give my body to Sea Woman. Perhaps she will relent and let the rest of you reach land before she opens her mouth to swallow us." Padloq paled as she clutched her amulet and waited.

The older man backed off at Qisuk's offer. Padloq's eyes moved between her father and husband, then back again. Every *inuk* had a surplus of pride. I had grown used to that. For Qisuk to humble himself like this, his despair must have shaken him to his soul.

"No one questions your courage." Ululik's next words came slowly and gruffly. "I say this to all our community." The men gave him their complete attention, as did the women. "Qisuk has grown in wisdom during our journey. I think it's time for us to continue, but that is our headman's decision." So saying, he gave Qisuk back his dignity without relinquishing any of his own.

"I would be a fool not to learn from our most experienced member," Qisuk responded. "We have no time to linger. Let us put out our fire and go." Padloq sighed in relief while the men lifted their fists in silent approval. The ice had closed in solid again over the bottom of the sledges. The men tugged back and forth on the back braces to break the frozen runners free. After the rest and food, Salluq could manage his dogs again. The men shouted orders to their dogs and we took off, making our own wind as we raced toward land.

We dared not stop. Every whip crack above the dogs reminded me of the splinters of water piercing the ice field. At last, we entered the long, dark shadows of the high cliffs. In my weariness, I could barely place one foot before the next, but everyone—men, women with their babies in their long *amaaqs*, even the children—climbed out of the sledges to help push. Our weary dogs did their best. Sniffing and smelling land at last, they began to yip and bark, straining in their harnesses to reach it and finally be able to rest.

We pulled and dragged, not cheering or even speaking, but saving our breath to help drag the sledges up onto the narrow beach. It hardly seemed possible, but we had crossed the great water. Here was land, solid land, under our feet at last. Gratefully, I rubbed my cheeks against the earth and the rough stones of this stark and barren land under the rutted gray cliffs of the new world.

Qisuk's Village

Chapter 23

L ike a bear on its hind paws, the cliff rose over the narrow beach where we made landfall, appearing to touch the sky. Its overhang blocked our view of the headland. From the rock face, several large gray-and-white birds with long hooked beaks threw themselves into the air and swooped low, screaming to protest our arrival. More birds squawked from the stony crags and filled the air, circling and diving to defend their eggs and newly hatched chicks. High above our heads, small tufts of their nests peeped out of recesses and ledges.

"I know this beach." Ululik's gruff voice sounded soft for the first time, and his small eyes seemed to look inward. "My feet have walked on this land." He stood like that, chin raised, the black hair of his beard streaked with gray and blowing in the wind. No one interrupted his silence. The younger people showed respect for the older man's memories. I wondered if he heard the voice of his mother calling him to come back from the beach, beckoning him home.

After awhile, Ululik returned, blinking and focusing again on the Inuit of the present. He pointed. We followed the direction of his arm. "There's a way to the headland. I almost remember how to recognize it."

"Where?" Qisuk remained subdued.

"Not far. Less than a day's walk north." He yawned. "Let us rest for a while. I may see the place in a dream as I saw it many summers ago." Qisuk motioned to the stretch of black sand and gave word to set up camp. With the white sheet of ice at our feet, we settled there for the night.

The smell of simmering meat awakened me. It was daylight. When I

yawned loudly, Padloq grinned. "Our first morning on the eastern land,"
she said cheerily. "We may want to sleep, but the children are hungry."

I would have shut my eyes again, but I realized that I needed to urinate.
I disengaged Qalaseq's small hands and managed to find a suitable place.
When I returned, Padloq offered me breakfast. I waved her away, wanting
to crawl back into the warmth of our sleeping place, too tired to think of
food. "Not yet," Padloq said. "You might as well drink this broth while I
change Qalaseq." She sniffed her nephew's sealskin-clad bottom. "I'm sure
he needs it."

She poured a mug of soup for me with chunks of walrus meat. While it
cooled, I sipped and watched as she attended to Qalaseq. He complained
angrily, twisting his legs and kicking as she firmly smoothed protective oil
on his fat bottom and tucked in fresh dog fluff before she closed his pants.

She handed him to me. He settled comfortably on my lap and watched
me impatiently until I had tucked up my shirt. He grabbed for my breast
and was soon sucking noisily. He nursed as much for comfort as for nourishment now, since he had begun eating chewed meat with broth. "Must
we go already?" I whimpered, barely able to sit up. The younger women
moved slowly, doing necessary chores. The older group lay as though they
never wanted to move again. Sammik was already gone, running to explore with the men. My body ached and I still craved sleep. "Padloq, don't
you think Qisuk will allow us to rest here one more day?"

"He already said so. He knows how hard we women worked during the
crossing, so he decided to let us refresh ourselves. The men are exploring."
I sank gratefully back among the bundles and pulled the furs up over myself and the baby. Padloq said, "The crossing took longer than we expected. I'm ready to crawl back under the furs myself." She soon did so. In
a very short time, the gentle rise and fall of her blankets told me she slept.

We slept all through that day and half the next. It was so good to be
still. I felt secure, knowing there was land under me. The solid beach
would not break apart to send us tumbling to a cold, wet, airless death.

Several cracks like thunderclaps shook the beach. I threw off my furs
and jumped to my feet. The sun continued to beam. No clouds in the blue,
untroubled sky produced that awful sound, but the deep rumbling continued. What was it? "Mikisoq!" Padloq screamed. The children had jumped
up first. The rest of us scrambled to our feet and grabbed up our belongings.

"Look!" Someone pointed to the ocean. I heard more screams and felt
a scream ready to leap out of my own throat at what I saw. The sea had

pulled back from the beach and a great green wave was forming out on the ocean. The ice sheet had separated into huge chunks, each larger than a house. The waves, so long held back, were preparing to rush to shore. The large seabirds wheeled above us, shouting obscenities at the noisy sea. I grabbed for Qalaseq. "Sammik!" I shouted. "Where are you?"

"Here!" He and the boys had rounded up the frightened dogs and chased them with their puppies up to the highest of the fallen rocks at the base of the cliff. We raced across the black sand to the fallen and broken boulders, carrying furs and pots and babies in our rush up the scree. I carried Qalaseq on my hip and climbed with one arm, afraid to look behind me. Qisuk hauled his empty sledge up onto a high, flat rock while Padloq crowded as many of our bundles as she could carry over her shoulders and in her hands.

"Hurry!" Qisuk reached out a hand to her, grabbing away the bundles and heaving them higher so he could pull Padloq up to him. "Get higher. Lean against the cliff. Mikisoq!" he shouted. I extended my hand and he pulled me up, as well. I looked back to see the wave. It had swelled to three times normal height and crested. With foam frothing white against the dark surge, it poured and raced like a living thing toward the beach. The sound of the ocean roared, loud and long. I wondered if it would be the last thing we would ever hear.

Maki sat high against the cliff, her still-lit oil lamp protected between her legs. Ululik crouched beside her. He had rescued his spears and harpoons. His bow remained tucked into his shoulder carrier and his quiver with its precious arrows rested on his hip. I believe he always slept with them within reach. He uncoiled his rope and lowered one end to Aama. Braced against the taut rope, she climbed, using it for guide and support. Taaferaaq, right behind her, pushed. He helped her keep her balance while her infant daughter rode on a sling under her anorak. She had not regained her strength completely from the birth.

"Are we all here?" Qisuk demanded.

"We are." Minik gestured toward the churning sea, a magical gesture, I assumed, to beg Sea Woman's mercy in the face of the flood. We waited high on the boulders and watched. The wave crashed like rumbling thunder against the rocks, sending a flume of white water upward. The foam cascaded halfway up the scree. "What is happening?" I screamed above the noise. "What made the great wave come?"

"The ice field fell in on itself," Ululik explained as we watched. "I didn't think it would happen so soon." After the one big wave receded, the following waves advanced more normally. In the distance, ice floes swayed and crashed against one another—churning, turning the water white, creating eddies and whirlpools when they pulled apart again.

Another wave, not as big as the first, but large enough, rushed up the beach. Padloq lifted Qalaseq from me and turned to the cliff wall. "I don't want to look!" she screamed. Qisuk covered her body with his as all the men protected their women. I felt alone half a moment before Qisuk seized my arm and pulled me closer. He was my protector, too. I nursed his son.

The waters pulled back, leaving the black sand glittering like tiny stars under the sun. A boom and then another sounded to the north. "That will be the glacier dropping off pieces of itself into the ocean," Ululik explained. "It won't affect us here. I think the worst is over."

Great sheets of ice rose sideways and slipped down, sending more waves hurrying to the shore. We had saved the sledges, the bundles, the kayaks, and the dogs. Nothing more could be done while we waited for Sea Woman to stretch.

I could scarcely force my eyes away, thinking how we might have been out there. A shiver ran down my back and spread until my toes trembled in relief. "Thank you, Sea Woman, for waiting," I murmured.

Minik held his arms out toward the water, chanting a much longer invocation in the shaman's tongue. Another din arose. More birds than I could count, gray birds, white birds with funny yellow-and-red beaks, birds like gulls but twice their size, flocked toward us, screeching curses at the angry sea.

"They lived on the ice until it broke up beneath them," Minik said, his hands still overhead. "Sea Woman shook them off and told them to come to us, to welcome us to our new land with food. Thanks be to Nerrivik. Shall we accept her gift?"

"Birds!" Sammik exclaimed. "Get the nets." The children unpacked the small long-handled nets the women used to harvest seafood from the tide pools in the old land. With them, they caught birds on the wing, happily broke their necks, and reached out for more. It was almost impossible not to put out a net and have a bird fly into it. "My boy is a hunter already," Qisuk exclaimed proudly.

Padloq lit her stove from Maki's. The older woman managed to keep hers lit in spite of the spray. Sammik skipped up the boulders. "Look what I did!" Two long-necked birds hung limply from his hands, their heads swinging as he jumped from rock to rock. "I killed them myself."

He held them out for me to take. "I told you you'd be a hunter before long, didn't I?" I said as I relieved him of his prize.

Sammik's small eyes glowed with pride, his small teeth white in his wind-darkened face. "Pretty soon, my father will give me my own team. Padloq will make me my first *nanus,* my man's pants before next winter. Won't you, Padloq?" He smiled at his aunt, then at Qisuk. "Do you think I'll be ready to take your kayak after seal this summer, Father?" He blinked his eyes winningly and cocked his head.

"Pretty soon, you'll have your own kayak and take over from me as leader." Qisuk laughed easily at his own joke, hands on his hips. "We will all take your orders." Sammik laughed, too, and so did everyone within hearing, especially Ululik. "But give me a year or two first, my small brave hunter," his father said. "I'm getting used to doing it right. For now, go catch more birds. Then get out of the way while Padloq and Mikisoq cook them for us."

We ate and slept again while the tide drew back. In the morning, the ocean looked like itself again, with normal waves and floes gathering in the distance. Qisuk declared we needed a council meeting. We settled ourselves as comfortably as possible on the most level of the rocks, with legs folded beneath us or dangling down. Everyone gave Qisuk, Minik, and Ululik our attention.

With his back to the sea, Qisuk cleared his throat several times before he began. "We arrived in time. Our thanks for this are owed to Nerrivik, our dogs, and Ululik. Minik says we journeyed almost due east. Ululik remembers our fathers and mothers traveled mostly due west when they left this coast to go to the village where we were born. Therefore, it's reasonable to think we are near the old village built by our grandfathers, but half a day south of it. Our fathers and grandfathers followed a herd of caribou south when they first arrived in our western land. My grandfather was leader then. He and his *angakkoq* chose that site to make our village because of the caribou and the good harbor.

"Ululik says to find our grandfathers' village, we must walk north and watch for a notch in the cliff. The trail begins near that landmark. What remains to be decided is whether we shall attempt to return to our old village. Minik will know if the danger that drove our forefathers away remains a threat."

Everyone spoke at once. "That was years ago." "Why would evil remain in our igloos?" "Better build a new village and stay away from there."

Qisuk held up his hands. "This is why I wanted this council. Everyone must say what they think and ask their questions before I decide what we will do. One at a time, so we can hear. You first." He pointed.

"Does Minik expect the *tupilat* will prevent us from going home?" Aama asked, her hands over the bulge in her anorak, where she carried her babe. "I never understood how it happened. Will Ululik tell us?" The children ceased looking away and crept closer.

Ululik looked over the upturned and anxious faces. "Many things might have changed since we left. Even if our land and homes are clean of evil and jealous spirits, other Inuit may have taken over our igloos and hunting grounds. The *tupilat* were angry at *our* ancestors. Another village was mixed up in the story, but I don't think they suffered as we did. The spirits were mostly punishing us because that is where the taboo was broken."

Salluq protested. "All that happened so long ago, nobody even remembers what the ghosts were angry about. They must have long since departed. Who has more right to live in our igloos than we do?"

"We are not sure of anything yet," Qisuk said, "except that the crossing has made us weak. We have too few hunters to risk losing them in a battle over a few stones. This land is big, big enough to choose another site if the old village is haunted or taken over by others. Ululik, please tell everyone what made the ghosts angry, so we will all know."

Ululik looked toward Qisuk and nodded, saying, "The women should portion out food while we talk, so that we will be ready to leave as soon as we reach a decision." Maki and all the others did so. I took Qalaseq into my lap. He leaned against my chest, sucking his thumb seriously, and looked up at his grandfather like all the others, waiting expectantly. The child was close to a year old. I chewed some meat into tiny bits and fed them to him.

The sounds of the ocean and the birds faded as we listened. "You've heard of the fallen star, but few of you know why it fell where it did and how the angry ghosts used it to force our ancestors to leave their village. When our fathers lived here, summer birds nested in great multitudes on the cliff ledges, just as you see them today. The ocean teamed with fish and beluga. Bear and herds of musk oxen passed each summer within reach of our hunters. No one remembered a famine coming to our people until the time of the curse.

"There was a village a long day's walk from ours. We traded and visited them often, sharing celebrations and arranging marriages. A sister and a brother lived in our village. The brother married a woman from the other village, but the sister stayed and found her husband in ours. The sister gave birth to a boy in our village. Her brother fathered a baby girl in the other village. Both children were born in the same season of the same year. The young cousins did not know each other well growing up, for their parents did not visit often. When the children were grown, they found each other pleasing in a way cousins must not be pleased.

"By that time, their parents had died. A few old folks whispered that the two were growing too close, that they were cousins and ought to be separated, but young folks don't like to listen. Toothless old men tried to pull them apart, but the cousins laughed, saying they were only playing. A few more years went by, until the boy and girl were a man and a woman.

"The cousins went for long walks together and decided that they liked each other. They told our village their intentions. A few of the older people protested, but by then, there were not many of them left. Other things took the place of these children in the villages' memories. Their *angakkoq,* who had joined them recently, asked for a vision. The next day, he spoke, saying that cousins might not know each other as man and wife, that it was an enormous sin. 'We are asking for trouble if we let them make an igloo together. I forbid it.' He ordered the cousins to separate, telling the boy to go to a far village and look for a wife there. 'This man and woman must never see each other again,' he declared. 'They must avoid each other. The girl must have another husband selected for her as quickly as it might be done, before the cousins give in to temptation.' The *angakkoq* warned them that if the cousins copulated, it would surely bring destruction.

"The cousins ran crying to each other, declaring that they would not be forced apart, scoffing at our taboos, daring the gods. When the elders dragged them apart, they finally pretended to give in. The boy promised to go his own way, but in the night, they ran to the small hill near our village and copulated in the sight of the moon. The next day, they returned and told what they had done, daring anyone to part them now that they had declared themselves a family. 'Kill them,' the *angakkoq* advised, but no one did. That is why all were punished, instead of only the two sinners.

"So, the children of a sister and brother built their own igloo. By copulating, they committed incest, a crime the gods don't forget. The sun was once raped by her brother, the moon. She's been chasing him to punish him ever since, but that is another story. The *angakkoq* took his wife and children and fled. He didn't want to wait for the gods to punish the village, sure that their vengeance would be terrible.

"No one knew where the trouble would come from. Then one night, a white terror came hurtling out of the sky. It made a terrible sound when it plunged into the earth. It landed on the very spot where the boy and girl had lain together the first time. Since the star did not hit the village itself, Sorqaq's father took it for warning. He predicted if we did not punish the sinners for their evil, the next star would destroy the entire village." Ululik stopped to wet his throat from the water skin Maki passed to him.

After he drank, Minik continued. "The star fell because our grandfathers did not kill the sinners immediately. The proper punishment would have been to place large stones at the entrance to their igloo. The villagers should have guarded it so the couple could not escape and would finally starve to death."

"You are right," Ululik agreed. "Instead, the headman pulled the cousins out of their igloo that very night and sent them away to starve on the glacier. We don't know to this day whether or not they died, but afterward, many people dreamed of *tupilat*. Their heads were huge, their ears pointed, and their teeth too long and sharp to close their mouths, so they slobbered at all times.

"Hunters became afraid to hunt, thinking every howl belonged to an angry spirit waiting to sink those teeth into their necks. Both men and women fell into fits. Children were born dead. The fallen star frightened the animals away, too. After several unsuccessful hunts, we knew we had to leave.

"Sorqaq's father told his people to gather what food we had, and then the entire village set out over the ocean in our umiaks, to escape as far as possible from the angry spirits sent to punish us. The tale is done."

Before we had a chance to discuss this history, Minik spoke of how the unfortunate incident that drove the Inuit away from their eastern village affected the concerns of the villagers today. "Because our ancestors allowed the couple to live, they were punished. Their error was in not keeping them from going to the hill together. Because of that, we lost our homes. If *tupilat* yet reside in the old village to guard it against our return, we will turn aside and build elsewhere."

"I would at least like to see the village where our fathers were born," Qisuk mused. "Let us try to find it again. Minik, after so many winters, we may find the angry spirits have forgotten us. What do you think?"

"Perhaps it is so," Minik allowed. "If we find it again, we will learn more than we know at present."

"Who sent the star, Grandfather?" asked Sammik. "It could not have been the cousins. They were still alive when it came."

"Our *angakkoq* said it was likely the spirits of two other cousins or even a sister and a brother who had sinned and been properly suffocated or starved."

A thought came to me that made me tremble. In my homeland, no one might choose a mate from her own clan. But our clans consisted only of our mother's family. If we considered our father's clan as cousins, we might be guilty of incest the way the Inuit understood it. My own father and mother might have been cousins! I held out my arms to steady myself against the rock.

"What are you thinking?" Sammik demanded. "You look like you're going to faint. Your eyes turned all white."

"Nothing. Speaking of cousins made me think about my home." I would not speak my thoughts to any of them. Even in my reaction to stories, my differences from the Inuit were obvious to me.

"So now," Qisuk said, "the question about whether to find our old home is settled. The next question is whether Ululik can find it for us. We must certainly go somewhere, soon."

"Did anyone go to see the star after it fell?" Salluq asked.

Ululik answered him. "Half our hunters went to look for it while the rest remained to defend the village if the first group died. My mother tried to stop me, but Sorqaq and I, and also my friend who died during the storm on the crossing, ran after the men."

"Weren't you scared, Father?" Padloq asked. He ignored her question and the other women stared her down. She covered her mouth. You do not ask an *inuk* if he was scared, although it was no shame to be afraid of ghosts.

"We found the fallen star still red and glowing in the great hole it made when it fell. Before we left it, the red faded to black. The air close to it smelled like soot and lightning. The part that showed above ground was large as a headman's igloo."

The men whistled. Minik said, "I would like to behold the fallen star again to discover if any evil intent remains near in it."

The men carried the sledges back down to the beach. We lugged down the furs and bundles and strapped them in while the men harnessed the dogs. The snow was washed away, which would make driving the sledges difficult, but we could not carry them without the help of the dogs. The men carried their kayaks to lighten the weight, and we set out. The children who ran ahead were first to spot the notch in the cliff face.

We halted while the men combed the uneven cliff face, trying to detect

the trail Ululik said existed. Ululik leaned against the boulders at the foot
of the cliffs, looking at them as if they were his old friends. From the location of the notch and his memory of the land, he was first to spy the path
himself. "Here!" he called. "Bring the sledges."

It was a dangerous climb. We got out and pushed, carrying the remaining bundles up the mostly mud and ice path. It took all of us, with much
effort and heaving, to haul the sledges past birds' nests balanced on
precipices. The braver of them flew at us with sharp beaks and claws outstretched, warning us away from their nests. The dogs sprang after them,
snatching a few on the wing and gobbling them down, feathers and all. The
rest of the birds veered away.

From the heights, I looked back the way we had come. The ocean
shimmered pale blue, with floes drifting apart and jagged ice mountains
moving farther out. In the north, the ocean still seemed to be locked in
ice. Such a great body of water could not melt all at once. The land
stretched both ways along the high cliffs, but several narrow inlets carried
choppy water inland between the islands and cliffs. Soon, my view was
blocked by the cliff we ascended and I could see no more than the path
and the headland.

Finally, we reached the wide, flat plateau. Farther east, rounded hills
rose here and there. Inland, white-capped mountains soared. Light snow
still covered the earth, but yellow and red flower heads poked up between
clumps of green sedge grass. "Just look at this country." I heard Maki sigh.
"What a land! Pray Nerrivik will let us keep it."

"This way," Ululik said. "It is not very far now." The women pointed out
familiar herbs and lichens. Grazing beasts would find all they needed here.
Even the children stared at the wonderful panorama as we trod the unfamiliar terrain.

After awhile, Ululik stopped and looked about, listening and sniffing.
We drew up beside him, waiting for him to speak. "There! Do you see it?"
He pointed his gloved finger. South of us were two mounds. "Near the farther one lies the star that fell." Before I could quell my fear of the heavenly
weapon, he added, "We shall look at it later, without the women. Our village is this way."

We proceeded northward. A long inlet, probably the one I had seen
from the steep path up the cliff, penetrated the land. The water was dark
and still. It would not be long before the men could go out on their kayaks
after seal. Ululik led us toward a slope partway up a shallow hill. There,
we saw the igloos, some of them built halfway into the hill. Low piles of

stones remained partially constructed, but many more lay broken and stark against the partially frozen earth.

No smoke hovered, no smells came to our noses, and no dogs barked. The roofs supports and sod had caved in and the entry tunnels were top-less. Ululik's attention focused on one igloo in particular. His sharp intake of breath hissed between his teeth. He blew out harshly, shaking his head, his chest heaving.

"What?" Minik demanded.

"My house. My parents. It is too much to see it again." His hoarse voice, gruff from too much tobacco, became hoarser. He turned away from it. "There is Sorqaq's father's igloo. It is where he was born."

"My father's house!" Qisuk's jaw dropped. "It is real," he said at last. "This land is real!"

"You doubted the land was real, but you brought us here?" Padloq exploded. "You took us across the ice field and through all that danger when you weren't sure?" Her eyes flashed and she did not lower them when the others stared at her. I had never seen her so angry.

I thought Qisuk would raise his voice to her, but he had changed. The crossing had made all of us steadier. "My father was sure, and Ululik was sure, too," he answered calmly. "It was like a fantasy to me, but I trusted them."

At that, Padloq relented. "Forgive me, my husband," she said formally. "It was my fear that spoke."

He nodded his forgiveness. The others, who had pretended to inspect harnesses during the brief confrontation, looked at Qisuk again. "We can release the dogs and feed them now," Qisuk said briskly. "Minik must inspect the village before we enter it. He will learn whether the stones are still cursed and if danger awaits. This may take some time."

While the men attended to their dogs, we women sat and looked down at the village. Minik walked to the largest igloo. He touched the air above the stones with open palms. Shortly, he ducked into the passageway. He remained inside for some time before crawling into each of the others. The old stones had fallen in from wind and two generations of winters.

Finally Minik returned, a pleased smile distorting the design of his chin tattoos. "I feel nothing evil in the stones or in the air between," he reported. "It is safe to stay for one sleep at least. In the morning, I shall go with Ululik to inspect the fallen star. If evil forces hover nearby, we may yet need to look for another site for our village. That shouldn't be so difficult. I notice there is no shortage of stones in this country."

The men chose their houses. We stayed in the same groupings as on the ice field, but Minik selected a house alone. Qisuk picked his grandfather's, of course, since it was the headman's house and therefore largest. We carried the bundles in, then repaired the entrance passage as well as possible. We laid hides over the empty spaces on the roof. If Minik decided we could stay, more repairs would be done. A few of the sledges could be dismantled to make supports for the igloos. New sledges would not be needed for months.

Maki and I made even piles of the rubble, producing high lamps to better warm the igloo. When the wicks had been lit and the evening meal warmed, we built up the *illeqs,* smoothing them on top and covering them with hides for our bed platforms. "This looks more like a village for the living now," Padloq declared. She carried the extra furs outside to air out over the sledges and standing kayaks in the brisk spring breeze.

"This village won't be a bad place to live once we close in the igloos better. *If* we stay," her mother hastened to add. I sat on the new *illeq* and nursed Qalaseq. "I want to see that star for myself," Padloq said. "It isn't fair that the men make the decisions, then laze around while the women do all the work."

"You are just noticing that?" Aama asked with a mocking laugh. She had come to see how we were progressing. "In my next life, I think I shall be a man. Taaferaaq can have the babies."

Qisuk checked over his weapons, his kayak and sledge, and fed his dogs while we got the village in order. We slept snugly behind rounded stone walls that night, far enough from the moody ocean.

The next day, most of us set out. We walked south along the rim of the cliff, in the direction of the twin hills. Aama, Meqqoq, and the other young wives remained behind with their infants. Before we left, Maki, Padloq, and I packed meat for our relatively short trek. We expected to get there by midmorning.

Qalaseq remained behind in the women's care. He was heavy to carry now, nearly ready to walk. We found a clear stream tumbling down a ravine. Snowmelt still poured out of the mountains. "Here is our freshwater," Maki commented. "Our ancestors chose well when they built here."

Taaferaaq said he hoped we would remain in the area. "Caribou will be drawn to eat this hardy grass. My mouth waters for roasted caribou meat. A few good leg bones would shore up our entry tunnel nicely."

"We'll know if we are staying soon, Taaferaaq," Minik said. We paused near the rim of the cliff. When I looked down, I could not see the beach.

We were too high for that, but I could see the ocean. The ice field was in the process of breaking up, as it had where we made land a few days before. We heard the booms of ice clashing and the crashes of waves as they escaped the shroud of winter. "It happens again," Minik said, "but this time, we are well out of it. The women have gone far enough. Wait here for us," he commanded.

The men continued down the trail. They rounded the rocky hill, Sammik and the two older boys trotting behind. Naturally, Sammik would not want to miss anything. The other boys, being eight and nine, vied to be first to show their courage to each other.

We waited pleasantly for a while, looking out over the ocean to see if the tumult produced waves such as those that drove us to take shelter on the scree. I heard the *boom-boom* of the glacier meeting the moving ocean. We were safe on the heights, but the noises intrigued me. Inuteq had handed out food. I was in the process of lifting meat to my mouth when I heard the first cry, and I jumped, almost dropping it.

"It's an auk; they sometimes sound like that," Inuteq said, her tone attempting to comfort. I did not believe her.

"That's no bird," Padloq said. "It's a *tupilat*. The spirits know we slept in the cursed village. Oh, what will we do?" The squawk came again in two parts, sounding like words.

"It speaks!" My eyes bulged. I retreated, pulling my *ulu* from my waist pack. "We must defend ourselves. The men won't return in time."

"Can women fight against spirits?" Inuteq asked.

The squawk repeated, sounding more human. "It cries in a man's voice to lure us over the cliff to our deaths," Padloq guessed. "Let us hurry after the men."

"We must remain and wait, as they told us to do," Maki insisted.

Again, the sounds repeated from the cliff, even more desperate. "What can it be?" Covering her eyes, Padloq rocked on her heels.

"Hush," Inuteq commanded. "Remain still. It knows we are here."

The rocks gave little foothold, since the cliff dropped steeply to the beach. Nothing human could climb the cliff wall, so it must be a spirit, I told myself. If it took to the air, we were done for.

"Padloq!" Sammik ran ahead of the men. In my concern, I had almost forgotten about them. How long had we remained like this? "I saw it," he yelled. "I saw the fallen star! It's all right. Minik says we may stay!"

Padloq jumped up and ran to her husband. I could not hear what she said, but he gripped his harpoon and rope more tightly at her words. We backed away when the men ran to the edge of the cliff to confront the danger. The scream or cry rose again, sounding like a tired bird trying to make human sounds. "Is it really a spirit?" someone asked Minik.

"I felt no presence in the star rock or the crater it made. Perhaps a solitary lost spirit remained behind. It sounds like it needs help."

Help? A spirit can fly, I thought. How can it need help?

"Let us go closer and try to see it," Qisuk said. "I have my harpoon and a long rope." He approached the edge, Ululik crept after him, and the others closed in behind. Qisuk stretched out to look, his legs flat behind him, head hanging down over the edge. "That's the most peculiar spirit I ever saw," he said. "I may be wrong, but I think it's a man. Let's help it up and see what it is."

While he lowered his rope, the sounds from the cliff face changed from a cry for help to a shout of astonishment. "Grab hold of the rope," Qisuk yelled. "Grab on, I said. Climb up. What's the matter with you?"

"Wait," cried Ululik. "He might be too weak. Make a sturdy loop. If he can lower it around his legs and tie the rest around his waist, we can haul him up. A few more ropes would be better." Qisuk pulled his rope back and tied a strong loop into it. He lowered the rope again, bawling directions to the thing on the cliff. Some of the others lowered their ropes, too, looping them around surface boulders to anchor them.

"They're bringing the spirit up here!" Padloq screamed. "It will regain its strength and eat the children." Minik stared at her. Padloq shut her mouth at once, but she continued to tremble.

The spirit made more sounds, shouting something. Its voice grew weaker, as though it had been calling for help for a long time, perhaps trying again when it heard our voices. Minik stared over the cliff without speaking. Perhaps he communicated with the spirit, signaling that it must cooperate with the men for them to free it, to drag it up to the plateau.

"It is tying itself into the ropes," Qisuk shouted.

"Good," Minik said. "We'll soon know what we are dealing with. Pull carefully so the ropes won't snag on the rocks."

I was bothered by its lack of comprehension. I understood my ghosts because they knew my language. A *tupilat* might have understood Inuit words, but this spirit knew no human words. What if it were no spirit or ghost who once was human, but, instead, one of the strange monsters of legend. I recalled winters beside my grandmother's hearth when storytellers spoke of granite men and flying heads with flaming hair.

"We have it!" Qisuk yelled, his rope coiling at his feet as he worked to bring in his prize. Two granite arms, then a pale stone head with flames surrounding it rose above the edge. I saw no more than that before I screamed. I could not have imagined what I saw rising from the abyss. "It's not a spirit. It's only one of those Big Eyebrow men, the Qallunaat my father warned me about. I knew they were nothing to fear."

Chapter 24

I lowered the furs from my face at the sound of Sammik's gleeful laughter, my face suffused with hot shame. The stranger, still tangled up in the rope, lay on the ground, looking up at all our faces. The women, who had feared to see a spirit brought over the ridge, seemed reassured by his solidness and confusion.

I stepped closer to study the stranger, who lay helpless and shivering in ropes on the turf. Under my inspection, the orange "fire," which covered his neck and the exposed part of his chest, became hair. Orange hair covered most of his face, as well. The hair of his head remained the color of wood flames at night.

Qisuk insisted the poor creature was as human as the rest of us. Sammik continued to grin at my foolishness. While Minik bent over the man to retrieve his rope and those of the others, the odd-faced stranger struggled to untangle himself. At last, his broad chest and neck free of binding, he stretched. Against the blue sky behind him, he appeared to be a giant. The tallest Inuit man among us, Meqqoq's husband, Salluq, seemed short next to him. My eyes came level with the stranger's chin. The pale-skinned man's teeth showed like a grimace, white as ivory between his mustache and beard. I realized he must be trying to smile at his rescuers, while his eyes calculated our numbers.

His forehead and nose were light as granite, with small brown specks sprinkled over his nose and the backs of his hands. The nose was well shaped and rather long, like mine. Our glances met. I thought his eyes the green of leaves underwater. To my dismay, I found that I could not pull my gaze from them. His were the oddest features I had ever seen. Embarrassed, I turned away.

"It seems the tide and the waves forced him to seek shelter on the cliff," Minik said. "One may be sure he dropped his water bag and has become very thirsty from calling." I wondered whether Minik probed the stranger's mind or only guessed at what seemed reasonable. Inuteq lifted her water bag to the stranger, who took it from her hand with a thankful nod, then downed its contents thirstily. He said something to her when he returned the empty bag. The words were foreign, but the voice pleasant and full.

With a toothy grin, the stranger held out one hand to Qisuk. It seemed as if he were asking the smaller man to extend his. Qisuk did so, warily, and the stranger took it with both of his.

"What's he doing?" Qisuk asked Minik, squinting at their clasped hands.

"Thanking you for saving his life, I think."

Qisuk disengaged his hand, poked his own chest, and said, "Qisuk. I'm Qisuk." Then he pointed to the stranger's chest. "Who are you?" He waited for the man to speak his own name.

"Halvard."

I repeated the name in my head.

"I sense no danger in him," Minik said. "Let us take Halvard back to the village to rest. Then, I will question him. We must learn where he came from. Where's his tribe? We have to find out if there is a Qallunaat village nearby. Remember your father's warning, Qisuk."

"Don't forget he comes from an enemy tribe," Ululik said. "I remember a time our men encountered a group of them. There were deaths on both sides. His kind is warlike and not to be trusted."

Qisuk appeared to consider both men's advice before he replied. "I know Sorqaq warned us about the Qallunaat, but this one is alone. He appears harmless. He's not so frightening after the first shock of seeing his hair and red beard, and the strangeness of his skin. Since we saved his life, I suppose we ought to learn what we can about him. Minik is right. We must take him to the village."

"What if he is a decoy?" one man asked.

I asked Padloq to explain, not knowing the word. She whispered the meaning. I had seen decoys the Naskapi made of reeds to resemble ducks. The decoys lured real ducks close enough to kill. They were so cleverly constructed that, from a distance, I couldn't tell them from the real thing.

"If the man has been hanging on to the cliff all this time, how did he know we'd come by and the women would wait exactly here? Could he see

them from the cliff?" Qisuk asked. No answer was necessary. "Where are
his companions? They aren't on the cliffs, too, are they?" The other men
had peered over the edge themselves while they pulled Halvard up. No
one hid there.

"Are they around the other side of the hill, then, waiting to attack us?
I don't think so. They would have done so by now. Let us bring him back
with us for now. We'll figure out what to do with him later. Minik?"

"*Iyeh.* Do it," the holy man concurred. "I'll go to your igloo tomorrow
to help you talk to him."

The stranger appeared bewildered at the unfamiliar words around him.
I knew quite well how that felt. Minik beckoned for him to come, a gesture anyone would comprehend. We could ask about what the men had
found at the star stone another day; this was just as interesting.

Padloq pulled me toward the back of the line so we could speak. "What
about him scared you like that?" she asked. "You're usually not skittish."

"He is white like stone, red like fire. Like Inuit fear *tupilat,* we in my
tribe fear forest monsters." I said the word in my language. "He has such
colors, white skin, red hair, green eyes. How can he be a man?"

"Well, he is big and odd-looking," she agreed, "but he's human enough.
You saw how he finished Inuteq's water. I hope Minik will be able to learn
something about him. I'd like to know what he was doing here by himself.
If there's one Qallunuk near, I'm afraid his Qallunaat tribe can't be very
far away. Maybe this isn't a good place to settle after all."

"I don't think Qisuk wants to leave our new village," I said, doubting
our headman was likely to be swayed. He would think his courage was in
question, which would only serve to increase his resolve. "He only just decided to stay. You know what he's like."

"*Iyeh,*" she replied, smiling faintly. "I know."

Qisuk took Halvard to his igloo and motioned him to duck down and
crawl in. Once we were all inside, I thought he should have let the man
rest after his harrowing experience, as Minik suggested. Because I had
been a stranger myself in too many places, I felt sympathy for the tall Qallunuk. Qisuk was too impatient. He tried to communicate with hand signs
that the man could not have understood, although he appeared to try. Halvard attempted to hold back a yawn. The man needed sleep and food, yet
he displayed a very unmonsterly human politeness to his rescuer, even in
his exhausted and confused condition.

After awhile, Qisuk realized the stranger might do better if allowed to
refresh himself. "Padloq, while you care for him, see if you can get any in-

formation from him. If you can't, Mikisoq can try. She's a stranger, too. Come with me, Sammik." So saying, they left the igloo.

So. In spite of my year among the Inuit, in spite of sharing their hardships and helping to cook their food, in spite of the magic pictures I had made at Minik's behest, to Qisuk, I remained a "stranger." Never would he or any of them, even Padloq, think of me as one of them. That made me pity the Qallunuk and resolve to feed him and tell him to rest. From our place on the *illeq,* I told Padloq my intentions. She signaled me to go ahead.

I dipped some soup from the cooking bowl and gave it to the stranger, offering my mug to him. My dark fingers touched his light ones. Unlike granite, his skin felt alive and warm. Our hands and arms contrasted, dark and light, slender and burly. Small orange hairs poked sparingly out of his white knuckles. I slowly drew my hand back and discovered I was gawking rudely again at his oddness. To cover my confusion, I backed to the *illeq* and took Qalaseq into my lap while Halvard sipped his soup.

Padloq crawled forward, her shyness gone already. "My name is Padloq, of the Inuit," she said, pointing to herself.

"Padloq," he repeated. "I am Halvard," he said, pointing again to himself.

"We know his name," I whispered. "Ask him his tribe."

"Your tribe? Qallunaat?" she asked.

"Qallunaat?" He had asked what it meant. Padloq pointed to his furry eyebrows. "Halvard? Qallunaat?" he asked, saying the words together. Surely that was not the word they knew themselves by.

"*Iyeh,*" she agreed. "Halvard is a Big-Eyebrow man."

"I am a Greenlander," he insisted, seeming not to like the name we gave his tribe. "Padloq is a Skraeling."

"Skraeling?" She said it back to him, requesting an explanation, but none came. He seemed to be at a loss to translate the word.

"I am *Inuit*, of the true men," Padloq informed Halvard proudly. To me, she said, "He doesn't know how to explain his word, Skraeling, but I don't like the sound of it. It sounds like something dirty."

I never told her the Naskapi called her tribe Eskimo, raw meat eaters, or the Algonquin word for my tribe, Mohawks, man-eaters. It was better not to explain certain things.

We were not yet finished with introductions. "This is Mikisoq." Padloq pointed to me where I sat on the *illeq,* still nursing Qalaseq. Halvard repeated my Inuit name. "Mikisoq is not Inuit; she's Naskapi." I let that stand.

She knew I was not Naskapi, but she did not know the name of my tribe. There had been no point in telling it. The name Naskapi would mean as much to Halvard as the real name of my tribe—nothing at all. He must have assumed Qalaseq was my baby. It was much too confusing to explain without words. Even if we spoke a common language, I could not have explained that I was not one of Qisuk's wives.

"Mikisoq no Inuit?" Halvard repeated, taken by surprise. He stared at me. "Baby? Whose?"

He did seem to know some Inuit words. Until that moment, I had not guessed. I wondered where he had learned them.

"Qisuk's baby. Baby's mother is dead."

"Not yours?" He looked to me.

"No. My baby and her father are dead," I said, signing. He nodded, but his eyes revealed his confusion. How could he understand, since I nursed Qisuk's child? "I have no man," I said, again signing. What must he think? "This boy, Qalaseq, his mother is dead. My baby is dead." I signed and said the words, not knowing if he knew the word or the Inuit sign for *dead*. He gazed at me strangely. I flapped my arms to show their souls ascending out of their bodies, not sure if the symbol for birds would confuse him further. He nodded, though, and appeared sorrowful, so perhaps he grasped my meaning. I could not be sure.

After Halvard put the mug aside, he indicated he wanted to rest. I pointed to the *illeq* and lifted the fur. With a small smile, he sat and took off his boots. He pulled the fur over himself on the foot of the *illeq,* one arm curved over his eyes, and fell instantly asleep.

The next day our guest had been refreshed by a night of sleep and the morning meal. Sammik took him outside to show him where the men relieved themselves, holding him by the hand to lead him, talking all the time. "Just like he used to take you," Padloq murmured. We walked arm in arm to the women's squatting ground. "Maybe Sammik will teach him our words like he taught you, so he can speak the tongue of the true men."

"He won't have two seasons to do it in," I reasoned. "The stranger must go home to his own land."

Qisuk attempted to question Halvard again when they returned. Slowly, the story came out. Halvard had gone hunting with many companions in boats. In the search for seals, he had become separated from the others and had come upon the ice sheet. He decided to seek out the coast alone. He continued north, farther away from others of his kind.

When the water ended and the ice field began, he pulled his boat high up on the beach. Before he left it, he weighed it down with stones to keep it from being discovered or floating away. He found no trail to the top of the cliff, but continued to walk along the shore. When the ice broke and the tide rushed in and covered the beach, he climbed to save his life. The water made the footing too slick for him to climb back down. If he stepped off the small ledge that supported him, he would fall and be killed.

Halvard demonstrated this in pantomime, not having enough words. He seemed to enjoy doing this. His playacting fascinated me. Halvard made climbing motions in the air, looking down, creases worrying his face and his down-turned mouth. He had grown weary on the ledge. He had called for help from his gods until his voice became gruff. He expected to die. At this point in his story, he pointed to himself and made hand-flapping motions as I had before to demonstrate the word *dead*. So he had understood my made-up hand sign.

Then he heard voices. He called again for help. When he looked up, there was a rope hanging down for him from the top and Qisuk yelling directions to him. His gods had sent us to help him, to bring him up the cliff to safety.

Qisuk seemed to like the part about himself. "I don't know any Qallunaat gods," he said. "Wait. What's he showing now?" We returned our attention to Halvard, who, giving a high-pitched, feminine yelp, threw a piece of fur over his face and ran to cower at one side of the igloo. He pretended to be me the moment I saw him. Qisuk got the joke and hooted a huge laugh. Tears rolled down Sammik's round cheeks. Even I giggled at how funny I must have looked.

Halvard lowered the fur and looked toward me sympathetically. He had caused my original fright, and now he was making all of them laugh about it. His smile showed me he intended it kindly. He was alone in an unfamiliar world. And again, I felt drawn to Halvard, as a fish caught in a net pulled by invisible cords.

Before the others stopped laughing, I noticed something sad about Halvard. It showed in his eyes. I knew then what he had not told about why he set off alone, leaving his companions behind. He grieved for someone dear to him whom he had lost to death. I, of all people, knew that expression. I had seen it on my face when I returned to my body from the spirit world twice. I lost everything—my home, family, friends, and, last of all, my daughter. His eyes possessed a haunted look, a memory of being stranded. Somehow, I felt it was neither child nor parent he had lost, but a wife.

"Halvard," I whispered. He saw, then lowered his lids and turned away, as a man hides emotion among my people.

After awhile, the conversation drifted to the fallen star. Sammik wanted to know if Halvard knew about it. The men had not spoken about what they found or how it looked after Minik checked if evil emanations still hovered in the star or near it.

"I want to hear about it," Padloq insisted. "We women didn't get the chance to see what it looks like. Qisuk. Tell us all about the star that fell." I was as curious as she.

Qisuk did not mind talking about his adventure. He was in a good mood now, after the laughter. "We found the crater after we circled the second hill, just as Ululik said. The star appears like a boulder half-buried in a big hole. If we could dig it out, it would be big as an igloo. It's good that the *tupilat* only meant to warn the villagers when they threw it white-hot from the sky. If it fell here, many people would have died."

"Is the star dead now?" Padloq asked. "Completely dead?"

"Cold and dead. We were a little concerned to get too close at first, in case more *tupilat* were around. Minik climbed into the depression and touched the stone. When nothing happened, we all climbed down to get a better look. It is darker than rock, so gray that it's almost black, and it has holes in it, some big, some small. It doesn't feel like a rock, either. It is cold from all those winters it spent in the sky. When I struck it with my flint, it sparked white flashes like stars. It remembers its nature. I wish we could quarry it. A piece to carry with us would be good for making fire. If we can shape it, it would make excellent spear and harpoon points. I'd love to have a knife made of star stone."

His description reminded me of the knife the storyteller woman had given me. I touched it through my hide shirt, where it lay still encased in its buckskin sheath, and wondered if its bright blade might be made of star stone. Cold prickles made my arm and neck hairs stand up.

"A small piece of star lay beside the big one. It must have cracked off. I brought it home to show you, Padloq, but after we found the Qallunuk, I forgot. Here it is, in my anorak pocket." He took it out and held it on his open palm.

Although Halvard had been listening, I don't think he understood much of what Qisuk said. I was wrong. "A star? Fell?" He motioned, pointing upward and fluttering his hand to the ground like snow falling.

"*Iyeh,*" Padloq explained. "A star."

The dark chunk, about the size of a fist, did indeed resemble a rock.

Halvard seemed just as curious and impressed as we were to see such an unusual object. Apparently, stars did not fall every day in the south, either.

Qisuk took out his flint knife from its pouch in his boot and struck the grip against the gray surface of the star stone. Sparks flew. A ring, not a clunk, sounded in the stillness of the igloo. I had heard such a sound when I struck the storyteller woman's gift knife to my flint fire stone. I had marveled at that sound every time I made my lonely fires during my trek north.

"What's bothering you, Mikisoq?" Qisuk asked, seeing me back away, my hand over my chest, touching my knife through the leather. He might have seen the sheath before, and assumed, as most did, that I touched my protective amulet for protection against the sound and the sparks. "This piece of star can't hurt you."

The time had come to show them my knife. Minik might be able to explain how a knife could come from a star. Before I could pull it out of my shirt, Halvard drew his knife out of a sheath tucked into a pouch below his knee. When he placed it naked beside the piece of star, I squelched back a scream.

What was happening? What were the gods trying to tell us? His knife was the same as mine; they could be twins. Even the handle was the same, ivory, with black carved designs. The blade was lighter in color than the star stone, just like mine. It caught the glow of firelight. Before anyone intervened, I stroked the knife and found it cold, the same as mine. The two might have been cut from the same living star.

Qisuk barked at me. "Mikisoq, a woman does not touch a man's knife. You know better." I backed away obediently, but I opened the neck of my shirt and drew out the cord-held sheath.

"Your amulet? What about it?" Padloq asked.

"It's not an amulet. Look." I lifted the flap and withdrew my knife, holding the ivory grip flat on the palm of my hand. I laid it beside Halvard's. "This one is mine. They are the same," I whispered, too struck by the miracle of finding my knife's mate to speak louder.

The Inuit, all of them, froze in place, staring with widened eyes. Halvard grabbed up my knife and his own, then moved into the beam of light slanting in from the window. It reflected brightly off both blades.

"You own a steel knife," Halvard said slowly, his eyes glinting like the knives. "Steel. It's of Norse design. How did you get it?" he demanded. His green eyes accused me, although none of us understood his outburst.

"No one move," Qisuk commanded. In an instant, faster than the bigger man could follow, Qisuk seized both knives from Halvard and backed up. "Don't move, Qallunuk," he repeated for the foreigner. "Get back, there, over on the *illeq*. Women, get Qalaseq away from him." He gestured and Halvard obeyed. Qisuk set both knives down beside the star stone and pulled out his flint knife to enforce his authority. "Mikisoq, do not talk again until the *angakkoq* comes. Sammik, go tell Minik we need him now. Hurry! *Assut!*"

The boy ducked to crawl from the igloo. I heard his running footsteps on the hard ground as he set off. No one said a word while we waited for him to return with Minik. There was frightening magic going on here. While we waited, I could not keep my eyes from Halvard, the Qallunuk who called himself a Greenlander. When Halvard met my gaze, my breath quickened.

Minik entered before Sammik, taking in the scene in the igloo, his eyes glancing in turn at the knives and the gray star stone where it lay on the floor. Sammik must have told him the situation. "You should have waited for me to question him. This is my responsibility," he said. "I allowed you to bring a Qallunuk into your igloo."

He bent to inspect the objects. Halvard tensed when Minik took up his knife to examine it. Minik lifted my knife next and looked at them together. "The markings are not the same, but they might have been carved by the same hand. Where did you get your knife, Qallunuk?"

Halvard was weaponless and alone in an Inuit village. There was a chill in the air that did not come from the outside. He answered fearlessly with words and signs. "My knife. From my father. His father."

"Did it come from a star like this?" Minik pointed.

"No. From rock and fire. From Norway." He pointed east. "Very far."

"There is more land in the east?" Minik inquired, pulling on his thin black beard. Halvard did not answer. "I have heard rumors of that. There are more mysteries to solve, then. Mikisoq, where did you get your knife?"

"A friend gave it to me. I don't know where she got it." Before he asked, I volunteered, "Except for Halvard's knife, I have never seen another like mine." I was as anxious to learn about the knives as the shaman.

Minik closed his eyes for a long moment, seeming to consider. "Mikisoq, do you know if Tobacco Growers ever visit this side of the ocean?"

"We do not know it is here."

"Qallunuk, do your people ever go to the Tobacco Growers' land?" Somehow, with a magic only Minik could command, he made the Greenlander understand his question.

Halvard looked up to the dark, smoke-stained ceiling. Perhaps he understood part of the question, but not all of it. "Tobacco Growers' land?" he repeated.

"The land across the ocean. West." To clear Halvard's confusion, Minik motioned him to follow down the passage and out of the igloo. Padloq, Sammik, and I crawled after them. The sun's glare after the dimness blinded me for a moment. Through watery eyes, I saw how Minik grasped Halvard's shoulder and turned him toward the west. He pointed down to the cliff and the bright water beyond it, blue to the far horizon. "West. Land. Land with trees."

Confusion. Minik asked Padloq to fetch a scrap of uncured leather and the spare oil lamp. He pointed to the smudge around the rim. "Mikisoq, make a picture of a tree. We have to make him understand." I had described trees to Minik when I described my land and my foods to him, and drawn pictures to better explain our forests, the tall pines, maples, and oaks.

Halvard watched over my shoulder as I made a simple tree. "Markland?" he asked, astonished. When I was done, he dipped his own finger into the smudge. He made small circles hanging in clusters from a vine in the tree, like grapes. "Mikisoq," he said. Do you know what this is? his expression seemed to ask, for he did not know the Inuit words. His life might be at stake.

"He makes pictures, too!" Sammik and Padloq exclaimed at the same time.

"Grapes," I said using my Ganeogaono word.

"What?"

I pretended to pull one off a vine and eat it.

"Vinland!" He leaned back against the stones of the igloo wall as if dazed. He shook his head and stared at me in horror. "Skraeling!" he cried out again in anger and frustration. "Vinlander Skraeling! Vinlanders and Greenlanders fought," he said, motioning to make Minik understand his meaning. "Many died. This knife"—he pointed to mine—"is a Greenlander knife. Skraelings killed Greenlanders for our knives and iron spears."

The gist of what he meant came through a little. Men died over such weapons. To be sure we understood, Halvard acted it out, like the story of his rescue from the cliff face. This time, his expression remained grim. It seemed he accused my people of killing his for such weapons. If I understood, Minik surely did. Why did Qisuk have to find him? I did not want Halvard to be my enemy, although I could not tell why it should matter.

Suddenly, like the sun's appearing from behind a black cloud, the solu-

tion appeared. I was startled by its simplicity. His tribe and mine had not
been enemies. His tribe had never fought mine; Halvard was wrong.

"No, Minik. Tell him an Algonquin friend gave me this knife. It must
have been passed down to her from the man who took it. Algonquin warriors fought Halvard's people for the weapons. Not Ganeogaono warriors.
My tribe and his don't know about each other. We are not enemies, he and
I. Make him understand what I say. It's the truth. Ask Nerrivik."

In my excitement, I had spoken more in my own language than in
Minik's, but the *angakkoq* had powers of understanding greater than
speech. He nodded to me, appreciating my logic. "I know you speak the
truth, Mikisoq. He is not your enemy. Nor does he wish to be. I think I see
something else here."

He ushered us back inside and approached Halvard, who flinched ever
so slightly. "Be still, stranger. Do not fear." Putting the knives beside the
star stone, he approached Halvard, who sat still on the *illeq,* not withdrawing, but solemn. Minik rested one thumb on each side of Halvard's
temples, with his fingers spread over the thick red hair. He held him fast
and stared past his eyes, into his mind. There were few secrets from Minik,
only those he did not trouble to learn.

Padloq moved closer to Qisuk, and Sammik came to stand between
them, leaving me alone. At times like this, even Qisuk was in awe of the
angakkoq's powers. They whispered together so softly, I could not make out
the words, but I gave them less mind than what Minik was doing to Halvard.

Minik lowered his hands and backed away from Halvard. I think something strong must have passed between them entirely without words, as
though they had spoken at length and in full trust. There was a sudden release of tension when Minik smiled. "There is no problem here," he said.
"I shall explain and it will become clear."

I rubbed my neck. Minik took Halvard's knife from Qisuk and handed
it back to him. "This is yours," he said, laying it down beside him. Halvard
did not put it away. Instead, he closed the space between himself and
Qisuk. He stopped a foot away, reversed the knife, and extended it, handle first.

Qisuk seemed not to know what he was intending. "Take the knife,"
Halvard said, taking Qisuk's hand and wrapping it around the ivory grip.
Qisuk looked to Minik, questioning.

"He offers his knife to you. A friendship gift. He wants you to have it
for saving his life," Minik explained.

Qisuk grinned. He took the knife from Halvard and stroked the cool gray steel blade. "It's good. A knife with star power. We are friends for always now. What can I give you to seal our friendship? What is in my igloo with so much worth as a star knife?"

"Ask," Minik commanded Halvard. "Tell him what you want. Your dead wife wants you to let her go and be happy again."

Halvard turned to look at me shyly. He hesitated, seeming to look for words. What did he wish to say? "I want the woman. Give her to me, Qisuk. Give me Mikisoq."

I could not believe I had heard correctly. The Greenlander asked Qisuk to give me to him? I shook my head and moved back. "No," I murmured. This could not be happening. For one thing, Qisuk couldn't give me away; I did not belong to him. I was a guest in his house, a friend, not a possession.

Minik said it better. "He wants to know if you will give her permission to leave your village. He does not have the words to phrase the question properly." They waited for Qisuk's answer. I did not know if this was what I wanted, for it was happening too fast. To have a man lie with me again? How could I respond to him? I thought in panic.

"She has my permission to leave if she wishes to go with you," Qisuk replied after some hesitation. "But I will not tell her to go. We Inuit do not give a woman against her will."

Padloq grasped my hand and pulled me back to whisper in my ear. "He seems like a good man. You don't have to decide right away. You can think first. If you choose, you can live and laugh with him in a private igloo for three days. See if he pleases you. If you don't enjoy him, come back to us and send him on his way back to his people alone."

Halvard waited for the others to stop talking. "What do you want, Mikisoq?" he asked. "I have two sons but no mother for them. I want you to come home with me, help me, live in my house." His words were aided with gestures, and Minik helped so I would understand. We had just reached this land, yet there had been so many omens—the star stone and the knives. He made pictures to explain things, just as I did. Did Orenda send him to me to restore my harmony? I wondered.

I could hardly see myself as the wife of an *inuk*. If I stayed, I must certainly become someone's second wife. A woman in her childbearing years could not be wasted. I guessed they only waited for Qalaseq to be weaned to tell me. Something half-remembered from a dream came back to me, a message about finding what I needed across water. Could Halvard, the

Greenlander, mourning for his dead wife, and I, who was mourning for my lost world, console each other and begin a new life together?

"He asks for me, but he did not say to be his wife. Is he trying to own me as Qisuk owns the knife Halvard gave him? Make me understand what he intends, Minik," I said.

He asked Halvard in such a way that he could not fail to understand. "Yes, he asks for you to be his wife. His ways will be strange to you, but not as strange as ours were at first. This man does not ask you to be his possession. He will protect you as your husband and will provide a home for you."

An impulse came over me. I picked up my gift knife from where it lay next to the piece of star stone and returned it to its sheath. "Take this," I said, offering it to Halvard. "Since you gave away yours, you will need a knife to provide for me. I agree to go to your land as your wife." I left it to Minik to communicate my meaning to this stranger.

"Are you sure?" Padloq's tears dripped down her cheeks.

"I think I must. Nerrivik desires it."

"It's like the end of a story," she said. "A good ending. The Qallunuk and the Tobacco Grower go away together to a land of mystery, where people make knives out of stars. I like it. We will tell the story over and over for years."

"Mikisoq is not going yet," Minik said. "Halvard must prepare an igloo for their first days together. We will show him. Mikisoq will sleep in Qisuk's igloo tonight. The women will prepare her, wash her, and fix her hair. Tomorrow, after our feast to thank Nerrivik for her blessings to us, Mikisoq will go to the igloo of her new husband."

"Halvard, you must please your new wife if you expect her to tend to your needs and those of your children and father."

Halvard's mouth dropped at the last of Minik's words. Somehow, he understood. With Minik's help, I understood when the red giant muttered in shock, "How did you know about my father? I did not mention my father."

"Minik is an *angakkoq*," Qisuk said. "He can speak with spirits and enter the minds of men. Do you have anything like him in your Qallunaat country?"

"No. Nothing."

"Then see that you remember Minik when you return to your people. Tell others to beware of the Inuit when they go north. We do not possess star-stone weapons, except for this one." He lovingly displayed his new knife. "But we Inuit have men of great power among us."

"I shall remember," Halvard said, and then turned to me. He reached out for my hand, and when he smiled, it seemed I must give it to him. When his big fingers wrapped gently around my hand, I felt a blush spread from my cheeks to places where I had not known I could blush. The net had closed and I discovered I no longer wanted to escape.

Chapter 25

Qisuk ordered the men out of the igloo, since they had much to prepare before the ceremony and feast. Sammik ducked into the passage, but he turned his head back, then reversed himself and ran toward
us. Pouting, and suddenly shy, he sidled up to me possessively. "Are you
really going to marry the Big Eyebrow man and go away?"

I looked to Padloq as if she could help me understand how this had happened. She only smiled her encouragement through moist eyes. My own
emotions remained jumbled and could not be easily explained. "*Iyeh,*" I admitted.

"Do you want to leave us?" he persisted.

"I think I must." I hadn't answered his question, and I knew it. "It looks
like Sea Woman sent him to me. We all saw the omens, so I suppose I must
go with Halvard to see the land where the Qallunaat live. Minik said so,
too. He always knows best, doesn't he?"

The boy nodded thoughtfully. "For a Qallunuk, Halvard's not so bad.
He can laugh and tell a story without words, but I still wish you could
stay." A new light came into his eyes. "Maybe, before you go south with
him, I can teach Halvard to talk, like I taught you. That would make living
with him easier. Imagine a husband and wife who can't talk to each other!"
He chuckled at the absurdity of it, then ducked and crawled out of the
tunnel to run after his father and the others.

"I am imagining it," I responded dully, but only Padloq remained to
hear.

"It will be all right." She took Qalaseq and stood him on the *illeq,* both his chubby fists wrapped around her fingers. He got himself to his feet and arched his back, pulling his arms taut for balance, smiling proudly and turning his head to make sure I watched. It was sad to realize I would not see the child grow up. I had become fond of him, but he was of his people. Neither would I see Sammik go off on his first hunt and then return to the village with his first seal. Both boys were Inuit. I had no family, no people at all anymore, unless I counted Halvard, who, for whatever reason, wanted me.

"It's frightening to go to a new home and a new family, where I don't know the customs or the gods of the place. I hope Halvard's family will like me. He has sons who will think their father brought me to take their mother's place." My reservations gnawed away at my courage. Sharing them helped.

Padloq put the tips of her fingers under her chin and looked at me over them. "Sammik remembers his real mother. I would never let him forget her. He knows I will provide for him and sew his clothing as his mother would have, but he also knows I would not try to take her place in his heart. Time will teach Halvard's sons you don't expect more of them than the status of their father's wife. When you cook and sew for them, they will be grateful. Status must be important to the southern people, just as it is in every tribe. From their chiefs down to the orphans, everyone has their status. Yours will grow with them over time, from stepmother to maybe Auntie, like I am to Sammik. You see?"

I could find no argument with her assessment. My status had changed many times. Once, I had the status of chief's daughter and clan matron's granddaughter. When I was taken away, I was nothing. A slave has no status or rank at all. After that, I was a stranger. Soon, my status would be changed to both wife and stranger at the same time.

Padloq pulled her hands toward her, causing Qalaseq to hang on tighter. He put one foot in front of the other, taking steps. She laughed, bringing giggles to the child. "It's this boy I almost think of as my own baby, although my sister bore him, and you have nursed him."

"If I don't expect too much of Halvard's sons, maybe I won't be disappointed, but—" I lowered my voice, not liking to hear the words. "I fear they shall hate me."

Padloq eyed me with amusement. "Who could hate you? You ask for so little. You only give." When I said nothing, she went on. "In Qallunaat villages, probably the women manage the houses and the men do the hunting, the same as everywhere. I suppose you can expect new gods, and

maybe they have a new way to make fires. You didn't know ours," she reminded me. "You'll need to learn to make his clothes and boots, too. His
clothing is oddly made. It does not appear to be of animal skin, but of animal hair. Possibly their dogs have long fur. You can figure it out, or some
woman of his village will show you. It reminds me of a mat I would make
out of dried grass. I wonder how they make the hair so long. I couldn't see
the joinings." I nodded, having noticed that. Since then, with all that had
occurred, I had barely had time to think of how Qallunaat clothing was
made.

"Of course, there is the Qallunaat language. That will take effort, but
before that, you will have other things to learn."

Suddenly, I felt shy, even with her. I cleared my throat politely. "How is
it with you and Qisuk? Does he hurt you when you come together under
the furs?"

She let go of Qalaseq's hands abruptly, seeming to flush under her
brown cheeks. The boy dropped to the furs, startled, but he caught himself on his knees and hands. He lifted his head to me.

"What, Qalaseq?" I asked. "What do you want?"

He crawled closer and pulled himself up, tugging at my shirt. With his
chubby fingers, he gestured toward my breast. "Uh. Uh," he demanded
stridently.

"An *inuk* must be obeyed." Dutifully, I lifted my shirt and took him
under my arm. His lips and tongue made happy sucking sounds while I
kept my eyes on my friend. Had I embarrassed her in asking about Qisuk
and their activity under the furs, when she had been so ready to speak of
mine and Halvard's?

"Don't you know?" she asked at last. Her question conveyed more significance than the words alone indicated. I must have missed something
important. What was she really saying? My mouth grew dry. Had I violated
a prohibition, asking such a question of a married woman? Halvard and I
were betrothed, not married. "No, Padloq; I don't know. What should I
know?"

"Qisuk and I are only half-married. We live together for the sake of his
sons, who are also my sister's. We have never copulated."

I could hardly credit what her confession revealed. For almost a year,
they had slept side by side, yet he'd never mounted her. She was still untouched in the way of a married woman. Inuit prohibitions went beyond
my poor Ganeogaono understanding. Astonished, I could think of nothing
to say.

Padloq continued to explain. "We mourned for my sister for half a year. After that came the poor hunts and the hunger. We could not take the time to couple during our trek on the ice field. My sister barely hinted to me what it was like. I hoped you would tell me what it is like to have a man poke into you the way men do, and how it feels. You had a baby yourself, so you must know." I looked down, memories flooding in. I could not answer her.

Padloq blushed so hard, her cheeks turned crimson. "Oh, I am sorry, Mikisoq. I bring up bad memories. Your baby. The man who hurt you. No wonder you asked me what it is like with a good man. I wish I could answer you." Her voice shook and she turned her face away from me to compose herself, rocking back and forth on her heels.

"I cannot believe it!" I exclaimed in amazement.

She turned back, almost in tears, but her small mouth trembled at my outburst. "No. You don't understand," I hurried to add. "I don't imply that you are lying. It is that it is so strange. You never copulated with Qisuk! I never suspected such a thing."

She jutted out her chin. "It's our law," she told me softly. "But now that it is allowed, I'm a little afraid. Even though I wished Qisuk could have been my man since I was a girl, he chose my older sister. You saw how I wanted only him on the voyage to the traders' island, but he never noticed me. I was only thirteen then; but I had already had my first woman's blood, so I was entitled to choose a husband. That is," she added, blushing, "if I could get one to accept me. But as often as I looked at him, Qisuk thought only of Aleqasiak."

Padloq's hand flew to her lips, a look of horror crossing her face. "We aren't supposed to say the name of the dead. It's forbidden." Another prohibition, I thought. Even the Inuit could not remember every one. Thank Sea Woman, I would not be required to learn them all.

Padloq glanced toward the ceiling fearfully. "Forgive me," she murmured to the air, just loud enough for me to hear. She must have been speaking to her sister's spirit. Since nothing happened, it was safe to assume her breaking the taboo had caused no harm. "I planned to wait until the new baby was born and ask my sister if she would ask Qisuk to take me for his second wife. But then she died to give her second son life."

With Qalaseq's arms wrapped around me, I closed the distance between us and hugged Padloq warmly. She returned my embrace, clinging to me for the comfort of our closeness with the child between us. To him, we were his two mothers. I said, "We will discover how to be real wives tonight. It can't be so difficult, if they don't hurt you." I hoped it was true. "In any case, men still have to do most of the work, don't they?" Instead of Padloq comforting me, it had turned around and I was trying to comfort her.

Padloq giggled and patted my hair. "This will be your marriage feast, yours and Halvard's, but it will be my first night as a real wife, as well. We can compare how it went afterward." She laughed, her old self again. "Maybe more than one baby will be made this night. May they be boys," she added.

"I hope mine will be a girl, but whatever they are, may both our babies be healthy. Most of all, may they be born easily to a village full of food."

"That's the best blessing of all," she agreed.

I changed Qalaseq, thinking that I would miss this little boy. His curious brown eyes watched me impatiently while I cleaned and rubbed seal oil into the creases of his skin. After I tucked fresh moss into the leather diapering and closed his small trousers, he crawled to the tunnel and pointed, babbling with excitement. "He hears the birds. Qalaseq wants to go outside and play," I remarked.

Before she could comment, we heard a high-pitched cough just outside. "Come in, Mother," Padloq called.

Maki crawled in and stood up. "I heard the news." Worn hides for towels and double-sided water bags hung over her arms. Aama, Meqqoq, and Minik's wife, Inuteq, crawled in, one after the next. Aama and Meqqoq appeared radiant. A small boy and a girl poked their heads from the long hoods of their mothers' anoraks.

"We have to make our Mikisoq ready for her husband," Maki directed, assuming control. "Yesterday, while you were running after stars and finding the giant, we found the hot spring Ululik had told us about. We'll bring back some water to wash your hair. If we hurry, we won't have to warm the water again. We might as well bring rags to wash our arms and faces, and the babies, too." I took up our seal-bladder water bottles while Padloq cornered the crawling baby.

Maki said, "I'll carry Qalaseq. Give him to me." She lifted him up, swinging him and making him laugh. The picture of a grandmother with her happy grandson riding her hip reminded me of my mother the last time I saw her play with my sister's son. I suppressed a momentary longing and smiled to my companions. "I am ready to go now."

The sun sparkled off the inlet's water. From the heights, we could see the waves far out on the ocean. Overnight, more grass had pushed up amid the broken stones of the new village. On the way to the spring, I was amazed to see large clusters of flowers had opened their cups. Blue-winged flies hovered and buzzed between the red and yellow cups. The earth must have created the flowers overnight. Small white butterflies sipped from the flowers.

From the slope's rim, I looked back at the village. Clothing had been spread out to freshen in the clean-smelling breeze, winter anoraks, caribou *qalitsaqs,* with hoods lined with seal or fox fur, men's trousers and knee boots, and women's thigh-length *kamiks* hung over the skeletal sledges. Below the village, several Inuit worked on mending kayak coverings. Two women fished on the shoreline of the narrow beach with long-handled nets. Children played with the large dogs, chasing them and rolling over the new grass and flowers. The ghost village had returned to the living just as the world returned to life after the long winter.

We walked toward a craggy cliff. The water splashed down, falling into a moss-lined pool whose contents poured into a meandering stream. "Not here. This one is glacier runoff. It's cloudy. Look there, Mikisoq," Maki said. She guided us to another pool, smaller, with a black stone lip where ferns and moss grew in the warmth, only steps away from lingering snow in the cliff's shade. Where it bubbled up, the water clouded and steamed. The spring smelled very faintly like the yellow earth my aunt used to brew preparations for fever.

"Can we wash in this?" Padloq asked suspiciously.

"It smells a little queer from the rocks underneath, but the water's fine. It is too hot to use on the other side, but here it is only warm. You have to be careful. Let us dip our rags and wash ourselves. Then we can fill our water bottles in the fresh stream to take back to the village for cooking and drinking."

While the women dipped their rags and washed their babies beside the spring, I crouched opposite the bubbles and steam and dipped my hand. I had never seen a spring such as this one with hot, bubbling water. I had heard rumors that such springs existed south of my home on Turtle Island. The land was called Saratoga of the Bitter Waters. Ganeogaono tribes who lived there had their sick people drink the water to cure them.

The water felt warm to my fingers, but not hot. I tried to peer into the pool's depths. The darkness cast back the breaking, shimmering reflections of the hill behind us. I lifted my sweat-stained shirt over my head and tugged off my *kamiks.* I was nearly out of my loin apron when Aama pointed at me and yelped, "Don't do that, Mikisoq!"

"You can't go into the water," Maki warned. "It has no bottom. Take your feet out of there. You'll turn into a fish."

"A fish?" I queried. "Really?"

"Well, at least you'll grow scales. People don't go all the way into springs. There may be hungry monsters underneath."

"It is boiling where the water came from," I pointed out. "Monsters wouldn't live in hot water, would they?"

"Inuteq, make her stop," Padloq cried, fearful for me.

"Our people don't do this," Minik's wife said firmly.

This logic would have worked on the rest of them. "*Mine* do." I am a stranger, I thought. Even though I love these people, I have remained a stranger to them. If I cannot be Inuit, I shall be myself, I reasoned. Since I would marry Halvard the following day, then go and try to be a Greenlander, as Halvard called his people, I determined to start my new life clean, purified in living water. I gave myself into the protection of Mother Earth.

Holding on to the pool's rocky lip, I lowered myself slowly into the warm spring until the water came up to my chin. The bubbles flowing across the pool soothed and caressed my skin. I sighed at the pleasure of it.

"What do you think you're doing?" Padloq shouted, frightened for me. "Come out before something bad happens to you."

I pulled the leather strips from around my braids and, using the fingers of one hand, loosened my hair. It cascaded around me and rested on the surface. I had to push it down. Disbelief and disapproval showed on all their faces. I ignored the stark disapproval, treading water.

"You're not holding on. Why are you not sinking?" Maki asked, astonished and not a little afraid.

"The water holds me up," I explained. A breeze tickled the surface of the pool, blowing up clouds of steamy vapor.

"Fire monsters will come through the steam to swallow you," Inuteq warned, dismay crossing her face. "Have a care for us. If you don't hurry out, you may never leave the spring at all."

Being Minik's wife, she might know more than I, but I was not ready to move. For just a little while, I had cast off all restraints and exulted in my freedom, laughing inside at their disapproval. I did not believe Orenda and Sea Woman would have taken me so far from home merely to satisfy the hunger of a water monster. I laughed in delight at the tickling bubbles, then rubbed away the grime and sweat of a year's making.

The spring renewed me, giving me what I needed to begin my new life cleansed of my many sorrows. I took a great breath and plunged underneath, diving headfirst, with wide-open eyes. Light penetrated the surface, making the water appear pale green, but the lower rocks were cloaked in darkness. I noticed bubbles rising, but no monsters swam into view. Nothing lurked in the depths but warmth and peace. If I were not growing short on air, I might have stayed longer. The world and my new life awaited me. At last, I reversed, kicking strongly for the surface, until I broke through to the air, laughing and scattering drops of water over the faces peering downward.

I squeezed out my hair, then pulled myself onto the grass and wrapped myself in a wind-scourged and freshened hide. Wrapping the first hide around my wrung-out hair, I grabbed another to dry my skin briskly. In a few moments, I had pulled on my loin apron, my *kamiks,* and long shirt again. "See!" I told them. "No scales. I saw no monsters."

"Nerrivik favors you. She must have sent them away," Inuteq muttered. Maki continued to shake her head. The younger women looked from me to their sternly disapproving elders, but if I read their expressions right, thoughts of trying the pool themselves tempted them.

"I am sorry. I should not have made you worry," I apologized, immediately contrite for making little of their customs. I hoped it was possible to obtain their forgiveness at least, if not their approval. I hurried to explain. "Back in my country, one begins a new life clean. I ought not to give offense to my hosts, but I must not ignore my tribe's teachers and shamans, either."

"I suppose you did what you felt you must. It is over," Inuteq said, partly mollified that I had apologized and explained my outrageous actions with humbleness and respect. "You ought to obey your teachings when you can, but you gave us a fright. How could we enjoy your marriage feast without you?"

Maki gathered us together and shooed us back toward the village. "The hunters must have returned by now. We'll prepare the meal. All must be ready for our feast in the morning. Padloq, comb Mikisoq's hair when you get home, and see she gets enough sleep." All the way back to the village, my damp, loose hair swayed around my hips.

Padloq set Qalaseq on the *illeq* and went to look for her ivory combs. I let him nurse again while she combed the tangles from my hair. The preparations and changes in his routine had made him anxious. I crooned to him, using the lullaby my mother had sung to make my brother sleep when he was small. It was a little tune about how he would grow up to be a great warrior. I substituted the word *hunter* and rubbed this small boy's back to soothe him. He rested his head against me and stuck his thumb in his mouth. "Poor Qalaseq," I whispered softly. "Will you miss me?"

Padloq arranged my hair. She twisted its locks into ringlets around her fingers, allowing it to tumble down my shoulders. When she was done, she fastened in combs to hold the curls back from my face. "Such thick hair will take half the night to dry, Mikisoq," she said. "What made you decide to go all the way into the hot-spring pool? Why weren't you afraid?"

"My people are not afraid of inland water," I said. "The cold ocean is different, although I've been in the ocean several times, too, farther south, where the water is not so cold. The water in this spring called to me. I heard it saying, 'Come in and wash yourself, Mikisoq.' You ought to try it, Padloq."

"When water talks to me, I'll try it. You look as you did the day you came to us, except your middle is flat. In the morning, we must dress you in the clothes you wore on the traders' island—the Tobacco Grower dress and the pretty little shoes." She spoke with her back to me as she looked through the clothing packs. I had not seen the Naskapi dress, leggings, belt, and moccasins since before my illness. During all that had happened since then, I hadn't thought about them.

The men slept away from Qisuk's igloo that night. With so many thoughts swimming in my head, I thought I would not sleep, but when next I opened my eyes, the sun had returned to the east. I smelled caribou roasting and crackling over a driftwood fire.

As soon as we had attended to our morning duties, I nursed Qalaseq for what might be the last time. Padloq washed my face carefully, anointing seal oil into my brows and hair. She arranged my hair in two braids, then put carved ivory combs at my temples to hold them back. Maki came inside while Padloq held up my doeskin dress for me to slip my arms into the sleeves.

"What are these?" Padloq asked, holding up the leggings.

Maki realized what they were in a glance. "She won't be needing them," she stated firmly. "Put them away. Here are your small boots, Mikisoq. What do you call them?"

"Moccasins," I said, pushing my feet into the enveloping soft leather.

When Inuteq arrived, she handed me a small piece of ivory carved in the shape of a gull, wings at rest. Its feathers looked tiny in miniature. This was a work of great skill. It was pierced cleanly and strung on a leather thong. "Minik made it for you. You must not go to your new life without an amulet. Even if this is not your custom, do it for us so we will have less reason to be concerned for your well-being. The gull will connect you with the wind and the ocean."

"How perfect!" I exclaimed, and hugged her hard. "Thank you; I will do just as you say," I added, wanting to make amends for my small rebellion of the day before. I tucked my gift amulet between my breasts, where I used to wear my magic knife.

All the women came to escort me to the feast, nodding appreciatively at my costume. There were more people strolling about the village than I knew. Our hunters had encountered others of the nearby village and invited them and their wives to attend the feast. Outside Minik's igloo, the driftwood fire burned, roasting the sizzling carcass of a spitted caribou.

"The men found a small herd near the mountains," Maki said. "Halvard killed this doe for your marriage feast. We'll prepare the hide for you to take as our gift. For now, you must do no work. For your first three days and nights, you're not to do anything but learn to be happy with your husband."

The smells of burning wood and the roasting venison were only the beginning of the good smells. Fish and seal and bird meat roasted on slabs of rock alongside the fire. The women tended the cooking, pulling away the birds deftly with their fingers when they were done, laughing and licking their fingers. They quartered them with their *ulus* and arranged them on mats.

I looked around, wondering where Halvard was. "Go into Minik's igloo," Maki directed me when she saw my confusion. She pointed to the tunnel. "They are waiting for you."

I ducked down and crawled through. All talking inside the igloo buzzed to a stop. By the dim light, I saw many people seated on both *illeqs* and on many hide mats between them on the floor. As soon as my eyes adjusted, Inuteq appeared at my side. "I will guide you in the woman's proper performance for this ritual," she commanded, handing me an empty bowl.

She gave me my instructions. "Select food from all the serving bowls. Fill an eating bowl and take it to your man." She pointed to the serving bowls set out in neat rows. They contained meat, fish, green herbs, and roasted roots.

Halvard sat on an *illeq* across the room. His expression had turned solemn. I gathered up a little of each food into an eating bowl and poured water from a storage skin into a mug. With these offerings in both hands,

I walked across the room to the red-haired man. I held out the bowl and mug.

In spite of its oddity, his face no longer appeared so frightful. He had been filthy and frightened on the side of that cliff. The men had bathed him, then oiled and combed his hair and beard. What does a man think about at such a time? The two of us could barely speak to each other. He knew little Inuit; I knew no Greenlander words. Did he question his gods' intentions, as I did, in throwing us together? This day would change both of our lives.

Minik must have schooled him in his part of the ceremony. He lifted a meat chunk to his mouth and plopped it in, closing his lips around it. Then he pushed a morsel into my open mouth. As soon as I had swallowed, our hosts cheered and the feasting began in earnest.

After the ceremonial first bites, everyone ate. In a short while, we exited the igloo to the sunny green meadow between the igloos to enjoy the rest of the food and the games. There were more bowls set about around the cooking fires. I knelt down to select more meat for Halvard, choosing the best slices of venison. The sea wind and the tantalizing odor of crisp venison fat made my mouth water again.

While we ate together from the one bowl, the men and boys participated in games of strength and skill, wrestling, aiming their spears at a set mark on the grass with a throwing spear, racing. The boys wrestled first among themselves; then the men competed. The warmth of so many people and the high-burning driftwood fire cheered everyone. Such games and high-spirited fun reminded me of the midwinter's festivals we held in my own land when I was younger. The Inuit clapped the winners' backs, then bounced them high on a white bear hide to the cheers of all present.

The women played a rope game, making pictures out of large hanks of twisted sinew. I could not tell what they were doing at first. They started with cord loops around their wrists and held the sinew on their fingers, passing it back and forth. Each time the sinew loop was passed from one woman to the next, the design changed. I stared, fascinated, at the strange configurations until they got to the last design. The women laughed uproariously, but my face burned in embarrassment.

The Inuit enjoyed their fun and even the children giggled. Nothing remained hidden from them in this small village. Sammik winked at me. Such lewd pictures as were made by this cord game were like nothing I ever drew with charcoal or paint. My people would have been shocked.

Minik and his youngest son, whom he was training to be *angakkoq* after him, danced to the music Inuteq played on her white bone flute. Qisuk pounded the beat on a skin drum stretched over a caribou antler, using a thighbone for his drumstick. The dancing men swayed and turned, moving their hands and heads in time to the music, amulets flying as they whirled. Some of the hand movements to the dance were as suggestive as the rope pictures. "This dance is to show you what to do so you will make a baby," Maki explained to me.

"I can see that," I assured her, my face burning. The dancing and the music had their intended effect. Couples disappeared toward their igloos. In one way, I found myself looking forward to being alone with Halvard. Yet my fears persisted as well. After Hawk Feather, how could they not? Would I tense or flinch when he pulled me close to him?

At first, he merely watched the others. Then, to my amazement and to the villagers' amazement as well, he impulsively jumped inside the circle of dancers, moving to the pulsing beat in a dance all his own. He moved his hips suggestively and pranced around the circle, jumping high on the drumbeat. In a great voice, he sang a song in his foreign words. The Inuit cheered him when he was done. "For *Inge!*" he shouted and bowed, acknowledging their whistles and stamps. At the dance's conclusion, he grinned to me and waved, sweating and breathing hard.

I raised an arm to return his wave, but I could not meet his eyes. My throat felt too dry to swallow, as though sand filled my mouth. I needed all my concentration not to be overwhelmed by memories of Hawk Feather forcing me to my knees and slamming into my hurt body, trying his utmost to make me scream and admit defeat. I resolved to be brave this time. Halvard could not hurt me more than I had been hurt before.

Qisuk and Minik led us to the small isolated igloo on the hillside. They had helped Halvard prepare it for our first days away from the others. "You will become husband and wife now, Mikisoq and Halvard," Minik said before they made ready to leave us. "I will not help you with this ceremony." The children watching him give us our instructions giggled at that. He ignored them and went on. "Laugh together and make children with your laughter." Qisuk winked at Halvard before the Inuit went down the hill to return to the ongoing festivities.

I entered the igloo first. It was difficult to see Halvard inside the small igloo, which seemed to be quite dim after the brightness outside. There was a bare window in the carefully placed stone wall that allowed light and air to enter. It did not take long until my eyes adjusted. Someone had covered the *illeq* with furs and left one oil lamp burning. A good supply of ren-

dered blubber waited for when I needed to refill the lamp. A stiff hide basket of meat, along with bundles of roots and shoots, stood against one side
of the tunnel, keeping cool. We would not need to leave the house. For
three entire days, we were to be left completely to ourselves.

He walked up behind me and turned me around so that our eyes met.
His hands rested gently on my shoulders, as if he wanted only for me to be
still so he could look at me. I think he was as tall as my father, but I was
smaller the last time I saw my father alive. I tilted my chin to look up into
Halvard's white face and his odd green eyes and tried my best not to tremble. He was not in his first youth, but he was not really old, either. I
guessed him to have thirty years. Double my age. Halvard appeared uncertain at how we ought to proceed.

"What is Inge?" I asked. Perhaps trying to talk would make both of us
feel more at ease. Besides, I had not forgotten his energetic dance and
what he had cried out at its conclusion.

"Like the others danced for." He arced one hand over my belly to make
me see myself pregnant, then curved his arms to show carrying a baby. At
least he did not use hand motions to demonstrate the act of conception, as
the Inuit had done, so I assumed his word *inge* meant "fertility," or its
spirit. "Good?" I assumed from his motions and his questioning tone that
he was asking if I wished to begin making a baby, as well.

It affected me that he should ask, although the matter was not entirely
mine to decide. "If we make a girl baby," I signed, "will you be angry?" I
made a circle with my thumb and forefinger, the sign for a female, then,
pointing to him, frowned. I raised my eyebrows to ask the question.

"I have two boys," he signed, twice making the sign for a small male, the
forefinger curved downward. "A girl is good." His lopsided smile eased my
concern. He would not reject a daughter. He hesitated then. "Mikisoq, I
want to call you Astrid," he said. "Astrid."

He seemed to offer me the new name ceremoniously, the same way I
had offered him meat before the hunters. "Astrid?" I asked, pronouncing it
after him. "I am Mikisoq."

"For me, be Astrid. New name. My mother was Astrid," he managed to
say, and then added our sign for the word *dead*. "Name Mikisoq is Skraeling. Not for Greenlander woman. Astrid means 'gift of a star.' " He motioned to show me we met because the Inuit went to find the star. His life
had been saved on the cliff because of the fallen star. I smiled to say I understood, without attempting to convey my complicated thoughts.

I did not understand the name Skraeling, but I gathered that he preferred I use a name his people would know. He motioned further to indicate that he honored his mother, as my people honored the females of their line. "Astrid. Good," I said, giving him my approval for the change. If he had been one of our people, his mother and mine would have arranged our marriage, as my mother and Plum Stone's had arranged my sister's. Mothers always arranged the weddings of their daughters, with the concurrence of the warrior's mother. Men never did the asking, but Halvard and I were both foreigners, with no knowledge of each other's customs. My heart beat more steadily.

While he watched, I drew my arms from the sleeves of my dress and let it slip to the floor. When I had folded it, I removed my moccasins, laying them neatly beside the dress on the hide-covered floor. Warmth rose from his aroused skin even before he walked close enough to touch me. His hand, which had been ready to remove his clothing, dropped, his expression changing to one of anger. What was wrong? I shuddered, trembling. Had he changed his mind? Seeing my dark skin, did he no longer desire me?

"What? What is this?" He touched the grooves on my back, legs, and breasts, the deep scars of the whips. The marks of my captivity, of my status as slave, spoke louder than any words. If my scars disgusted him, he was not the man Sea Woman thought him to be. Deciding he might as well see them all, I turned, exposing my entire back for him to see. This woman was once a despised slave, the scars proclaimed. With disappointment, but without consequence, he might withdraw from me before we consummated our marriage. He spun me around to face him. "Who did this? Father of dead baby?" he demanded angrily.

"*Iyeh*," I replied. How much more could I explain?

"Bad husband!" he exclaimed

"Not husband. Algonquin!" I spat out the word, hoping my expression and action would convey that he had taken me against my will.

He made a sympathetic sound. Then, light as down on a gosling, his fingers touched the places where Algonquin lashes had left their marks. Warmth spread from his fingertips like a friendly fire on a cold night, reassuring me. When his lips pressed into my shoulder and neck, my resistance faded. I closed the space between us, meeting and welcoming his embrace. Compared to the Inuit women, I stood tall. The crown of my head reached his mouth, so he did not have to bend much to hold me. It was not much more of a reach for our lips to touch in the new way he showed me.

He backed away just long enough to remove his Qallunaat clothing.

Then he climbed upon the *illeq* and reached out his hand, inviting me to join him. My heart beat like a tom-tom. I wanted to take his hand, to lie beside him, indicating I trusted him, but my body betrayed me. I flinched just a bit. He held back then, gazing at me sadly. "I won't hurt you." I did not understand his words as much as the sympathy he demonstrated by his reserve.

Words can lie, but Halvard proved he would not take me until I was ready. I took his hand then and moved down beside him onto the *illeq*. With great gentleness, he had me turn onto my side. With one large hand to the small of my back, he supported me. He touched his lips to my throat and my breasts, teasing them with small kisses.

Could there really be such joy as that which welled up inside my woman's flesh? Was this the longing Mother Earth/Sea Woman gave to all her free creatures? It was a drive to override memory and anxiety. The differences in the tones of our skin, as well as our lack of a mutual language, became as nothing. The only difference that mattered is that he was male and I was female. The surge of my blood warmed me and welcomed his advance. I no longer shied from his total embrace, only wondered how my earlier fears appeared to fade in the face of such an urge to join with my husband.

He placed me on my back and cupped my breasts, barely touching the tips with his soft tongue. I had never experienced such a sensation. His tiny touches sent feelings I could not comprehend down my legs. I felt warm, as if in the throes of a fever. Thought vanished. I wanted to hold him so close that no space might remain between us. His clean male sweat, even the curling red hair on his chest and body, excited me, until I could wait no longer. With a soft cry escaping from my throat, we came together.

I had not known what to expect, beyond what I had learned from Hawk Feather's savageness. With Halvard, copulation was more than what male and female flesh may accomplish. His tenderness erased those awful memories as the ocean's waves wash away a drawing on the sand. Safe and protected in the arms of this stranger who was my husband, a thing happened between us I had never anticipated. At last, I knew what had eluded me, what I did not know existed until Halvard showed me. With this man, I felt cherished as a wife should be cherished. I believe we conceived our daughter Ingrid under the bear furs that first night together, when Halvard taught me about love.

Chapter 26

How do you begin to communicate with the one fate gave to you? What do you say? Between the furs, no words were necessary. His tenderness spoke to me more truthfully than another's words might have done. He cried on my neck, without sound, but I felt the hot tears of his emotion. He was bidding peace to the memory of his first wife and thanking her. How I knew this, I could not say, but I learned there was more to this sort of communion than I had imagined possible, because of love. We discovered trust and an openness that allowed the transfer of feelings. This created a joy I could barely contain.

After our first passion was spent, Halvard held me tenderly. His mind spoke to me without words, as it must have done to Minik, with magic provided by our respective gods. I felt the undercurrent of his remaining pain and knew how close he had come to madness when his wife passed away. If not for his remaining family, he might have done as my people do when life becomes unbearable, simply stop eating and wait for death. He had tried to accomplish the same thing in his escape to the solitude of the northern lands. Men have died hunting since the beginning. If he failed to return home, who could give blame? He was in the hands of fate, but instead of death, his gods had guided him to me.

With the sun beating down on the village, it was warm enough to cast back the furs. During my previous anxiety and our first rush of passion, there was not the leisure to see with our eyes as well as our hands. At last, I had time to explore his body slowly. Sweat dampened his hair. Drops of it gleamed on his chest and neck. Hair the color of wood fire covered the top of his chest, surrounded his brown nipples, and continued downward to form a line to his navel. From there, it spread around his male part and down his legs. Only the soles of his feet and his palms were bare. He seemed to glow with sunset.

He did not mind that I wanted to study him. It seemed my curiosity amused him, but he was indulgent. He must have known I had never seen a man like him before. I touched the hair of his chest and legs tentatively to see how it felt, finding it almost soft as puppy fur. He laughed deeply and playfully. My touch must have tickled. "Stop it, Astrid," he complained, wriggling away and pulling my hand up to his mouth to kiss it. I noticed his male part harden again, and he was aware that I did so. When he drew me close again, he had stopped laughing.

No newly formed couple among my people had been left alone like this for three days, but I could not complain. We had so much to learn about each other. Later, I picked up the pieces of his clothing and examined them. His jacket had been tailored from hide with the fur left on, but not from any animal I knew. I could not determine how his shirt had been made. It seemed to be woven, as Padloq had surmised, like one weaves baskets, but I marveled at the tightness of the weave. Animal fur is not so long as grass and straw. Each strand must be longer than the longest human hair. I could not see how they joined or how one could hold the pieces to weave. When I asked, he used words I did not know. I hoped there would be a woman in his town or village who could show me.

He tried to tell me about himself in a way I could comprehend, then had me repeat his sentences in Norse. "I have two sons." He laughed at my imitation, for I said it exactly as he had. So I learned his words for *I* and *you* and how to make my tongue and teeth go into the positions to speak his language. But there were too many strange sounds to remember. We used our hands for signs to demonstrate our meaning. He had made me understand that he hoped to retrieve his boat. We needed to be able to speak in words. When he paddled his boat, his hands would not be free to help him speak to me.

He laughed the first time I tried to say, "Are you hungry?" telling me how to say it correctly. I am not sure what I did say. It might have been "Are you food?" instead of what I had intended. He corrected my wording indulgently, but it made me indignant. I, after all, had learned to speak my native language, then Algonquin and Inuit, and now I was being forced to learn yet another way of talking. Had he needed to learn my words, he might have made as many mistakes or more.

"*Aii,*" I said, stamping my foot. "I'd like to hear you speak my language," I said in Haudenosaunee. "Repeat," I ordered, using his word. "My wife is Gahrahstah. She is from the town of Doteoga, which is in Ganeogaono Country on Turtle Island." I wagged my hand. "Well? Repeat." He actually tried and, in doing so, discovered he was worse at my words than I was at his. I laughed, hoping he would see my frustration. Life was too difficult without humor. With it, we would find a way.

"Enough for now," he said in Norse, which meant we could stop. "No more talking." He pulled me toward the furs. The remainder of our conversation that day did not need words.

We did not spend all our special time alone together learning and eating, or even playing games on the *illeq*. The sun slanted through the window into the igloo, warm and bright. The smell of greenery penetrated the tunnel and air vents with every breeze. We decided to go walking. I took a bag over my arm to gather shoots and berries, if I could find any, to cook with our meat.

Children played, climbing on the slope, running with the big dogs. The animals ran close to greet us. They knew Halvard from the hunt and accepted him, nosing into his hand to see if he had brought something for them. Seeing he had not, they bounded back to the children.

We passed Sammik as we walked. "Where is everyone?" I asked, glad to be able to speak without thinking of the words first.

"Qisuk and Padloq told me to get out and play. Qalaseq is here. I'm watching him. I guess all the mothers and fathers are busy making new babies for the village. Did you get tired of doing that?" There was laughter in his eyes. The girls and boys listened to hear how I would answer. A boy of my village was not so impudent; even my younger brother at Sammik's age would not have been so blatant.

He seemed to wait for me to rebuke him, ready to see if he could make us chase him. Instead, I said, "We are done with that for a while and so decided to take a walk." I smiled as if I possessed a secret I was not prepared to share, lifted my chin, and walked us away with dignity.

"What did he say to you?" Halvard asked as I walked with him down the meadow and past the children.

I tried to explain but soon gave it up. "Come. Walk. I want to see the star." I knew that the word for it was a part of my Norse name, *asta,* like Astrid. He complimented my wording. We continued south, forgetting about the children soon enough.

"Look, there are berries growing." I stopped to pick the tiny red things.

Summer had taken winter's place so fast, the snow had hardly melted before the earth put forth its bounty. I tasted the unfamiliar berry, which looked like a tiny strawberry, hardly the size of my smallest fingernail, and found it tangy but sweet. I put several into Halvard's mouth. If only I had known his words, I would have asked him if corn and beans grew in the south. I wanted to ask what his people used to make their cereal and bread, but I had no way to explain my words. "What do you eat in your Greenlander village?" I asked, hoping to learn at least something of the foods I would need to prepare.

"Not a village. Just farmsteads," he replied. "We eat meat and fish. Also milk, cheese, and yogurt." He had understood my question, but I had no idea what he was telling me. It would take seeing the foods and how they grew. For all I knew, these were his words for corn and beans.

Wisps of high clouds blew like ice floes in the sky. This land held more contrasts than the western islands that belonged to Sorqaq's village. The cliffs were steeper; the inland mountains reached the sky, still topped with white, even though it was spring now. The meadow was wide. Around us, bright colors mixed with the green of the new grasses and bushes. Pink lichens decorated boulders, which poked up from the grounds like the plants. Scant snow remained in the shadows of the hills.

Although Halvard's tribe hunted for seals north of their own country, I believed this land was foreign to them. Halvard knew it no better than I knew the ocean when I beheld it for the first time. His eyes explored the terrain, too. I followed his gaze to the foam-flecked waves of the channel and the melting ice floes. "You and the Inuit came from Vinland. Very far," he commented, seeming to ask me how.

"Dogs pulled sledges over the ice from Inuit land there. My land is Turtle Island, not Vinland." I realized by then that when he referred to Vinland, he meant Algonquin Country, so I wanted to separate it from my country in his mind.

"Vinland is place where grapes grow," he reminded me, knowing we had discussed this before.

I wished he would use my name for my land, not his. "My land. Not yours. I say Greenland, your word. You say Turtle Island, my word." He nodded, giving in to my demand, and repeated it my way. I could not be as submissive as an Inuit woman.

As we walked, we discussed the name he called Padloq's and Qisuk's people. "Skraelings means all men who are not Greenlanders?"

"No." He waved the subject away with a motion of his hand. Only later did I grow to understand the name meant "savages." To Greenlanders, we were more like a pack of wolves than like people. I wondered if all Greenlanders had Halvard's coloring, or if they varied like dogs of the same litter. Perhaps it was merely a matter of strangeness, of not knowing the other's customs. If he knew my people, he would not consider us savage. We had laws and respected Mother Earth and the Creator, her son. I hoped his Greenlanders would accept me and realize I was ready to be adopted into their tribe.

The sun rose higher than ever. Halvard and I ran through the sweet-smelling meadow, avoiding lichen covered boulders and bush-high trees, until I could not think, but had to give my attention to our path, the smells of the wind, and my husband's warm hand. We stopped near the ridge of the cliff. The afternoon wind came cool off the mountains and billowed my hair in front of me, blowing it out toward the ocean. "Ga-oh," I called to Wind Spirit. "Tell my mother I have taken a husband, a Greenlander man from a new world across the ocean."

Halvard saw me holding my arms out to the ocean wind, talking to the nothingness. I could not stop to explain until I had given Ga-oh all of my message. "He is called Halvard. His hair is the color of fire; his eyes are green like leaves under the river. Hair grows on him like a bear, but he talks like a man."

"What are you saying?" he asked when I paused, deciding what else to tell the wind to convey to my mother.

"I speak to Ga-oh, the wind," I explained, gesturing with my fingers and puffing my cheeks out to show a wind blowing. "I gave him words about you to tell my mother." As I spoke, I recalled how Hawk Feather forbade me to speak in my own language even to talk to Wind Spirit. Halvard watched me curiously.

I continued. "Ga-oh, tell my mother the Inuit shaman made magic. He sends me with Halvard to his land in the south. My husband's tribe fought Algonquin long ago, so that makes the two of us allies. Blow west to my mother, Glad Song of Doteoga, and tell her. Do this for the woman who used to be Picture Maker of Wolf Clan, in Ganeogaono Country."

When I turned back to Halvard, he said, "Tell Ga-oh I send greetings to your mother." Joy washed over me at his regard for my family over the ocean and happy tears blurred my vision.

I turned away to hide my emotion. "Halvard sends greetings to my mother!" I called, "Tell her that, too, please." I pulled down his head to press his lips with mine, as he had taught me. "You are polite. It is a very good thing." I used the Inuit word for *polite*.

We walked inland, past the first hill. The star stone lay in the crater, half-buried. It seemed to be only a large boulder, but the rock was grayer than flint. Many holes curled through the rock like termite burrows in a fallen log. I once thought stars were the campfires of spirits, but perhaps things were different on the western side of the ocean. The Inuit showed no surprise at this one being a stone. I tried to picture it glowing white up in the night sky before it fell.

Halvard looked into the clouds, frowning and searching the blue as if another star might decide to follow this one. I climbed down carefully and touched the stone. It was cold, like the steel of the knife blade, but much darker, gray mixed with black. It did not feel or smell like a rock.

He came after me, touching and inspecting, even peering into the holes. One curled all the way through, so a person could put one hand on one side of a tunnel in the rock and meet it with the other. "Iron," he said. "Stars must be iron. My people say when a star falls, it means someone will die soon."

"Yes," I replied, making a motion of one hand coming down out of the sky to crush the other, like a star on a man.

"No. I mean an omen. To warn us or explain something."

I understood. A sign from Greenlander gods. Perhaps stars spoke to Greenlanders like dreams spoke to my people. Halvard climbed back up out of the crater first, then extended his hand to help me climb out. It was time for us to return to the village.

As much as I wished it could, time would not stand still for us. Our three days ended. Halvard went away with the men for one last hunt before we left the village for his home. While they were gone, I visited Padloq's igloo.

"So?" she asked. It was the first chance we had had to speak alone since my marriage feast.

"His hair tickles, but it went well," I answered. Padloq laughed, as I knew she would. It was good to have a woman to speak to again. Men are important, but most of a woman's life in a village is spent among other women.

"So then it was not so bad as you feared," she concluded. "You are a real wife now. He's not a bear under the furs, but an *inuk*?" I agreed with that. Halvard was surely a man.

"And Qisuk?" I would not have asked if she hadn't asked me first. "How was he?"

She giggled. "A man as well, in all respects. I'm a real wife now, too."
My friend appeared satisfied; her face glowed with fulfillment. She had fattened up since the famine last winter in the old land and the crossing. I
hoped that good hunts would continue in the new land for Qisuk's village.

Aama and Meqqoq crawled in with their babies to visit and gossip, too.
We all sat close together on the big *illeq*. I had taken the tiny boy and girl
on my lap, one on each knee, when Qalaseq crawled up to me, his eyes
filled with resentment. He must have thought I had deserted him. Worse,
I had returned to his house, but I held the smaller babies. "Take your babies back, and I'll nurse him once more time," I suggested to Aama and
Meqqoq.

"No, wait." Meqqoq called Qalaseq and opened her shirt. He crept over
to her, plopped himself down, jammed her nipple into his mouth with
both hands, and sucked noisily.

"Well," I said, insulted. Then I smiled at his full cheeks and his eyes ecstatic with the pleasure of feeding. "He makes me think of Ululik sucking
on his pipe." The women tittered at this. When will I have a group of
friends to laugh with again? I wondered.

Padloq turned the conversation. "We ought to gather herbs and see
what we can find for making tea while the men are hunting. My mother
taught me some good plants to soothe stomachaches and heal wounds, but
we don't know all the plants here. We'll have to try them and see what
they are good for."

"I wonder when we'll visit the other village. They would know the local
plants," Maki said. She had recently crawled inside. So the talking and
speculation went on. In the meantime, Qalaseq, sated but still awake,
crawled back to me and pulled himself up to lean on my shoulder. "Mik-
soq," he said clumsily.

"He said your name, Mikisoq," Maki shouted. "He's trying to talk." I
hugged the boy, tears in my eyes. I did not try to hide my emotion this
time. The Inuit laughed and cried more easily than my people. Perhaps that
explained why I found myself doing it more frequently. Qalaseq would
miss me after all.

The men stayed away overnight with the dogs. When they returned,
there was much meat in the village. We learned they joined their numbers
with a group of hunters from the next village. Half the men cut off and
drove a group of musk oxen from the main herd, stalking and herding
them slowly toward men waiting with spears. When the animals realized
they had been separated, they tried to rush through the line of men, but

by then, the second group had taken their places in the ambush. Between both villages, four oxen were taken. Each village had two of the fat long-haired animals to share.

Finding the other hunters had been lucky. They must have been from the second village mentioned in the story of the fallen star. We ate well that night and went to our beds early. The next day, we were to begin our journey south.

I prepared bundles of musk oxen and dried seal meat, enough for many days of travel. With my Naskapi dress folded and packed away, we had enough bundles to fill two large packs. I decided to wear Inuit clothing for the trek. Halvard carried a spear as well as the knife I had given him, which he tucked into the sheath above his boot. In addition to the *ulu* at my belt and my old flint knife in my sleeve, Padloq gave me a short-handled net.

Qisuk presented me with a quiver of twenty Naskapi arrows and a short bow. He believed me when I told him our women hunted in our lands when our men stayed away for several moons at a time. "It's not our way, but you are used to Tobacco Growers' customs. Remember to look about you in the south. I hope your husband's people don't object to your hunting."

"If I need food, I will hunt. Children mustn't go hungry." That satisfied him, but I owed him a grateful response for his warning. "I'll try to learn his customs and follow them whenever I can, Qisuk," I said. He gave me a one-sided smile. Someone must have told him how I had bathed in the hot spring.

The others gave us presents, too. I wished I could have done more to show my gratitude, but Minik said the pictures I drew for him would bring them good hunts for many seasons, so it was enough.

Ululik had become like a father to everyone in the village, and Maki like a mother. Even so, if a bad winter came to the village, bringing a shortage of food, they would be first to go out on the ice. It was the Inuit way, that the old must make room for the young. Their experience and counsel had helped the others survive the crossing and earned them respect for their final years. I hugged them both warmly. Halvard adjusted the straps of the frame carriers they gave us, shortening mine, adding strips of leather to the one Qisuk gave him, while I packed fishhooks and lines, bone needles, awls, and sinew thread. We worked outside in the sunlight. I noticed Qisuk taking long strides up the slope toward our igloo. As soon as he reached us, he said, "I decided Padloq and I will go with you as far as Halvard's umiak. My wife wants to see the land, and I want to see how Qallunaat make their boats. Halvard, you've had Mikisoq to yourself long enough; she was ours first. Four will travel more happily than two."

To be polite, Halvard could not object. I had tried to impress upon him how important it was never to offend one of Qisuk's tribe. It was a complicated matter to get across, and I did not know how well I had succeeded. Thankfully, he appeared quite glad to share the next two days with our friends. Of course, I was glad to keep Padloq with me longer.

Sammik, who pretended to be playing nearby, ran to us, bawling. "Don't leave me behind. I want to go with Mikisoq and Halvard, too. I'm not finished teaching him how to speak. I'll help carry. Let me go with you, Father."

"*Iyeh*," I agreed. "Please let him."

Qisuk pondered his request, pursing his lips, not willing to give in too easily. Finally, he nodded, but he said, "You must obey me in everything, Sammik. Every time. No arguing."

Sammik danced from foot to foot, eyes sparkling. "I will."

Fairly soon, the village was gone from sight. Qisuk and Halvard walked faster, forcing Sammik to trot to keep up. Padloq and I followed more slowly, keeping along the land's edge. Although we could not see them, we heard the waves breaking on the rocky beach. From the heights, it was a light, bubbly sound. The ocean had calmed, and I hoped it would remain so while we traveled on it. Birds flew busily between the ocean and their nests in the recesses of the cliff, fish dangling from their bills.

My short Inuit breeches, soft leather shirt, and thigh-length, double-soled sealskin *kamiks* protected me from the morning cold. I opened my fur-lined anorak with its woman's hood when the morning sun strengthened.

Padloq and I laughed when a gang of seabirds, all white-bodied and orange-billed, squabbled halfway down the cliff over a crab one of them had dropped. One took off with the morsel in its mouth. Another pulled it from the bird's mouth, but then lost it. A third flew underneath to snatch the crab before it reached the water. Padloq rested her head against my shoulder. I hugged her impulsively. We had been through much together. "We must hurry to catch up," she suggested.

We found the men waiting for us. They sat on the grass, close to where Qisuk had fished Halvard off the cliff face, trying to converse. Halvard was the teacher this time. Sammik grasped Norse words readily. Even Qisuk repeated them, giving Halvard their Inuit names.

The men discussed winter hunts over the ice field. Qisuk continued his description about a time he had cornered a bear with his dogs. Halvard was suitably impressed at the lone kill before the other hunters caught up.

"How do you hunt seals in winter?" Halvard managed to ask.

Qisuk jumped to his feet, signed, and acted out so Halvard could follow. "I dress warm, find *allu*. Then I wait. Long time, all day, I wait." He moved his hand like the sun to indicate all day. I read his words from his hands and actions, wondering how much Halvard understood from words and how much from gestures. Sign speaking needs to be much simpler than word speaking. Soon, Halvard and I would have to rely on words only, for we would be paddling.

Qisuk hunched down into a waiting position. "Sometimes a whole day goes by, sometimes two," he said, continuing to sign. "I wait like this. I don't move, so the seal will not suspect. Seal comes to breathe at his *allu*. The water ripples; then . . ." He heaved an imaginary harpoon like a bolt of lightning and yanked on an imaginary rope. "Meat." Both Halvard and Sammik were rapt, absorbed by the story.

Qisuk accepted their admiration as his due. He pointed outward over the ocean. The ice floes had blown out to sea, but ice mountains still floated southward. Ululik had told us these were remnants of glaciers, frozen rivers that pushed to the ocean and broke off, making great splashes and waves. "Watch out for them. Nerrivik does not need Mikisoq to keep her company down there."

The ice mountains were threats, but they could be seen and therefore avoided. I thought of us paddling southward in Halvard's lonely boat with whales below us. They could push us over for a meal.

We opened our packs and Padloq handed out chunks of the musk ox cooked the day before. I ate my food, then swallowed a long drink of water. Qisuk crinkled his eyes when I did not reach for more. "You stop eating too soon when there's food. That's why you don't get fat and pretty like Padloq. It's better to fill yourself, make some fat here to use later." He touched his belly and arms. I had fattened some since we had arrived. Although I remained slim, my muscles were strong. "Don't be so sure there will always be more to eat soon. Sometimes, there is a long time between meals."

He was right. I took another slice and then another. The last famine had been hard, and I did not know what to expect as far as hunting in Halvard's country. Halvard matched Qisuk for eating at first, then gave up. Whether in fasting or in eating, the Inuit did everything best.

Halvard peeked over at me when the other man bent to pick up some more, and he rolled his eyes heavenward. Without words, I knew his mind. He thought we must manage our food carefully when we were alone so that it would last the journey. Hunting was chancy, and he feared we might not find more.

Qisuk must have noticed his expression, too. "You'll find food on the way," Qisuk assured him. "This land is full of birds. Before you go, we'll make up for what we eat now. Mikisoq can hunt for you, so you won't go hungry." I had not told Halvard that women of my tribe are taught hunting, so I hoped he would not take offense at Qisuk's joke. Instead, he laughed.

While we ate, Sammik asked, "Halvard, why do you keep looking at the sun? It will hurt your eyes."

"My sons must think I am dead after so long." He was obviously worried how they were managing. If their old grandfather was too frail to hunt for them, the other villagers would take care of its boys, wouldn't they? I wondered.

"Some hunts take long. Sometimes a man needs to be alone. A family must know to wait for their man and not give up so soon. You'll get there as soon as you can. Making long faces will not help, and watching the sun will not take you home faster. It will be a good surprise when the people of your igloo see the gift you bring them—Mikisoq."

I lowered my eyes as Inuit women do when they are praised, but I noticed Halvard's weak smile. He must be wondering how to explain me to them, I thought.

"Iyeh," he agreed. Padloq turned from one serious face to the other. "No frowns," she insisted. "Halvard, you must think of nothing except for walking and eating and laughing to keep your Mikisoq happy with you."

He brightened at her words, smiling broadly. "Laughing with Mikisoq. Good." I turned to hide my face again, for he had learned that word overly well and knew its double meaning. Sammik grinned, then skipped ahead to chase a pair of lemmings through the tall grass. Our friends were determined to keep us happy. Brooding was for winter.

Padloq changed the conversation abruptly. "Look. There are the two hills together where the star rock fell. It's only a short distance out of our way. I want to see what everyone was talking about. Let's go there before we turn back for the trail to the beach."

I hoped Halvard would not be upset at further delay, but to my delight, he agreed. It would have been discourteous to complain, after all they had done. Halvard and I would be on our way south to his country soon enough.

We turned inland again. It was a short walk to the hills, especially with Padloq chattering. She said, "When I was young, I used to think stars were small in all that blackness of a winter's sky, but Ululik said the star was bigger than an igloo. They must be farther than they seem to be. A man seems small when he's far out on the ocean in his kayak, but he grows bigger to our eyes when he comes close."

I had been disappointed by the star boulder but kept silent. Sammik took Halvard's hand, not wasting a moment when he might be talking to him. Norse words floated back to us.

"Do you notice Sammik learns Halvard's words faster than you do?" Padloq asked, concern for me softening her voice.

"You are right, and it worries me. I'll be alone in a strange place, unable to talk. Halvard has no women in his household to teach me women's crafts."

"There must be a friendly neighbor who will be curious about you and will teach you. Any one of us would have taught you our ways for the curiosity of learning about a stranger. I was the lucky one who had you to myself for a while."

"I'll never learn to speak his language. He points to something to explain and I don't know if he means the color or the thing. He calls his country Greenland."

"Greenland," Padloq repeated. "Does the name mean something?"

"Grass, or the color of it. I'm not sure which. Do you see what I mean?"

"Yes, and I agree it's confusing, but you'll learn his language. You learned mine without trying. No one could believe it wasn't magic when you started to talk so suddenly. You'll do the same thing there. You'll wake up one morning and you'll be a Qallunaat. You'll know everything."

"Without the red hair and big eyebrows, I hope," I added mischievously.

Padloq grew pensive. "Was Qisuk right? Do you think you have a baby in there?" She patted my middle after looking me over one more time and stroking my cheeks. I shrugged. "How many winters do you have? You look young to be growing your second baby."

I had to think how old I was when I was taken from my home and how many winters had passed since then. Twelve when I was captured, thirteen when my menses began. The Algonquin who had attacked Doteoga gave me to Hawk Feather shortly after that. I escaped just before winter and reached the Naskapi village just as the real cold of the season set in. When the strawberries turned red, I reached my fourteenth year. It was then that I came to the Inuit and my child was born and died. Almost a year had passed since then.

"It is the moon I was born, I think." I recalled the berries I found and fed to Halvard. They were not the same, but they were berries. Therefore, I must count myself as having begun my fifteenth year. Not knowing her words for numbers, I held up both hands, fingers apart, then my right hand alone.

"Me too," she said, "Pretty soon, we shall be old. Our teeth will wear out from chewing hides to soften them. Then we must throw ourselves over a cliff so our husbands can get themselves new wives." She grinned and I grinned back at the thought of being old.

"Look. Here we are!" We had reached the crater. "So that is the star! My father said it whistled when it fell and made a noise worse than thunder when it struck the earth. It's nothing but a boulder," she said, pouting.

"It surely is old and worthless now," Qisuk agreed from the crater. He had been inspecting it. "Nothing to be afraid of. See?" He thumped on it with his new knife. There was a clang, deeper than the song of the small piece he took away from it to the village. "The same sound your knives made," he exclaimed, striking the star stone again.

"Shall we go now?" Halvard asked.

"I'm having an idea," he announced. "Wait." Padloq put one finger over her lips while Qisuk's face scrunched in deep thought. We stood around the edge and waited, not speaking for fear of disturbing his concentration. When he was done with his figuring, he smiled. "Listen to my idea. This is good. I think the old star is not useless after all. Some of its spirit remained behind. We can chip out pieces and make knives and harpoon heads with star stone. Ha! What do you think, Halvard? Our weapons will be as strong as yours. With my harpoon point of star stone, no bear or walrus will escape. Orca will not be safe. I will ask Minik how we must do it," he added, as though that were the simplest part of the plan.

I don't know if Halvard really understood the name Qallunaat or that it meant "Big Eyebrows." One of his orange brows lifted while he tried to piece Qisuk's words together. If enmity arose between the Greenlanders and the Inuit over hunting grounds or anything else, both sides would be more evenly matched if the Inuit also had weapons of iron.

He responded cautiously, using discretion as well as good manners by tapping his head and nodding approval of Qisuk's good thinking. Then he jumped down, too, and pointed out the reddish bumps on the dead star to Qisuk.

"This is rust. Rub seal oil on your knives. It's good for star-stone iron."

"Why?" Sammik asked.

"So your knives won't rust." He used Norse words, but his meaning came through. Fat would protect any knives they made from the chipped star, so the knives would not get more of the red bumps, which made iron crumble. I knew this because the knife the storyteller woman gave me had the smell of squirrel grease and no rust. It was good for Halvard to tell Qisuk this, but then he knew Qisuk and the distance of his village. The two men would never have to face each other in war.

Sammik did a victory dance around the crater's edge, strutting and jumping as if the fallen star were Nanuk, the white bear, and he had killed it himself. He gave a high, melodious yell, like a Ganeogaono war cry. "Star-stone spearheads and knives will make us strong hunters," he crowed. "This is our star, and I claim it for my father's village."

"Good," his father said, "but come away now. We must still descend to the beach and find Halvard's boat before we make our camp for the night."

While we walked, small clouds floated high in the deep blue sky. Flowers burst forth all around. Yellow flies buzzed from one bright cup to the next, flying heavily laden to their underground nests. Padloq and I gathered buds and onion bulbs and stalks to cook with our meat when we camped for the night. She stopped to inspect a white rock as big as my two hands together. She crouched, licked her finger, and touched it, tasting thoughtfully. "Mikisoq, this is salt. It makes your meat and fish taste better." She scraped at it with her *ulu* blade, grating off small bits. She dropped them into my hand. "Taste."

I licked the flakes off my palm. We had a different word for the same thing. I wrapped the rest for later use in a scrap of hide and tucked it into one of my inside pockets to use later.

We caught up to the men. "Time to stop," Padloq insisted.

"My wife must be breeding," Qisuk said, moving a hand over his middle to make sure Halvard got his meaning. "Breeding makes women bossy. I think yours is breeding, too. Look, now, how she smiles. Are you?" he asked, turning and asking me directly.

I shrugged. "It's not time to know yet." Men in my land did not ask such questions; it would have been rude. It was the woman's choice whether to tell her man before she was obviously showing. I was far from home and getting farther.

"There will be more babies in the village," Sammik shouted before a dark look suddenly crossed his face. He must have remembered how his mother had died.

"We must keep the women cheerful while they are breeding," Qisuk replied, nodding back and winking. "They'll be more likely to make boys. Tonight, we will camp early. You and Mikisoq will make up the time later."

Chapter 27

Halvard was first to sight the narrow path from the headland down to the beach. Since the floods, the descent had become treacherous, forcing us to pick our way down slowly over the broken and slippery scree piled up against the base of the cliff. Birds swooped at us and screeched, guarding their chicks. I might have caught one with my short-handled net, but they kept just out of reach. The farther we descended, the more strongly the air smelled of brine and bird droppings. We left the green world behind us on the plateau.

The rocks led down to seaweed-covered pebbles and black gravel. When I shaded my eyes, I could just about make out the pale remnants of floating ice mountains far away from the coast. We continued along the beach until the sun lowered. It did not set, but hovered above the horizon, where it tinted the bottoms of the clouds the color of my husband's hair.

Halvard motioned for us to stop at a mound of rocks, sand, and seaweed, which looked much like the rest of the storm leavings piled against the cliff. I wondered why he wanted us to stop there, but then Halvard pulled away the first stones, scattering them behind him. "My boat," he cried, working harder to uncover it. Although he had left his boat over on its side and covered it with stones, it was obvious he had feared the storm might have pulled it out to sea when the waters receded.

Qisuk and Sammik helped dig out the boat until the gray form underneath emerged. By the time we had set down our packs and begun the fire in the oil stove, the men had uncovered Halvard's boat and propped one side of it up with the rocks to make us a shelter. Narrower than an umiak

but wider than a canoe, this Greenlander boat was unlike any I had seen in
the past. It had not the look of bark nor the texture of walrus skin. When
I touched the unfamiliar surface, a gray splinter came away and stood
against my skin. The boat was fashioned of long pieces of wood, cut into
planks and shaped. The pieces were held together by some means I could
not fathom. Although weathered, the lumber did not appear to be driftwood. Each section had been stripped of its bark and coated with something dark and tacky. I could not imagine how such pieces could be cut and
formed so evenly, but I began to suspect and even hope that trees, real
trees, grew in Greenland.

True driftwood had washed up on the sand down the beach. Qisuk sent
Sammik skipping off to fetch it for us. "We'll make a bright fire tonight,"
he said. I thought a wood fire would be perfect. The smell of burning wood
reminded me of my homeland, and the fire it made waved and crackled
the way fires ought to.

While I prepared the fire and got it going well, Padloq climbed silently
back to the boulders lining the cliff base. From below, I watched how she
crept up on a large crab. She yanked it up as deftly as my cousin Wolf Cub
Mother caught fish. "Perfect," she said, holding it well out by its back so
the waving claws had nothing to grab. "Look at these legs; they are enough
to feed us all." She smashed its head with a hand-sized rock. When she
reached us, she washed it in the surf and wrapped it loosely in damp seaweed to cook.

Soon, steam rose through the cracked shell. With Qisuk's appetite to be
concerned about, I decided to add to our meat supply. I took up my short-
handled net. Hearing the tread of my *kamik* on a rock, a gray web-footed
seabird gathered its wings to take flight. Before it could lift up out of my
reach, I had it. A sharp twist to its neck and it went limp. I carried my prize
back to our camp to gut and wash and feather.

Qisuk's prediction proved true: We had more meat than when we had
begun. While I worked, the small feathers floated in the air above us. The
fluff was caught up in the fire's wind currents and whipped about in
sparkling circles. Between Padloq's and my hunting, we had enough meat
for now and tomorrow's breakfast without dipping into our reserves.

"Watch out, Halvard, for women who catch their own food," Qisuk advised. "They can manage without us." I rubbed some of my salt onto the
bird's flesh and propped it beside the fire. Pretty soon, the duck's skin
crackled and turned golden. My mouth watered at the delicious aroma.

"Come eat," Padloq called. Her face had flushed from tending the fire.

I handed out the empty shells to hold our food and placed our water skin between us. We pulled apart the crab legs, breaking them open against rocks to get out the succulent flesh. I tore the legs off my duck for the men, then gave the wings to Sammik. Padloq and I plucked portions off the still-sizzling breast. The salt I had rubbed in increased the goodness of the crisp brown skin. Little of the duck would remain for breakfast, but I ceased to worry. Everyone licked their fingers and smacked their lips. We still had the dried meat in the bundles, and I could fish while Halvard paddled. We would not go hungry in Qisuk's land.

The food left me feeling mellow, comfortable, and a little dreamy. Sammik found more driftwood, enough to keep the fire burning during the night so the smell of food on the air would attract no roving white bear to our camp. We washed our greasy arms and faces in the clear water where the waves lapped against the beach. Soon, dusk deepened the sky bowl. It would not get darker than this. Only the brightest stars burned in the sky. Whatever stars were—whether spirit campfires, or the points of godly weapons, as they were to the Inuit—it was good to see them.

Against the flickering fire, Padloq, Sammik, Qisuk, and even Halvard became silhouettes. The firelight shut us in from all the world, leaving the five of us together to savor the night. The half-moon floated directly overhead.

Halvard chanted a Norse song. I picked out a few words but had no idea of the sentences' meaning. Qisuk took his turn, singing an Inuit hunting song that told of long nights on the ice. I had not known his voice was so pleasant.

Padloq touched my arm. I must have looked as far away as my thoughts. "If you had remained with us in our village, if Halvard had not come, Qisuk agreed with me that you ought be his second wife," she said. Her voice lowered as she whispered so only I could hear. "I told him I would not mind sharing. You see, I wanted you to stay with me, but I made him think it was his idea." It was generous of her to say so, and I squeezed her hand to tell her.

Qisuk heard at least the first part of Padloq's words, because he moved closer to me. "If you weren't going, would you have agreed, Mikisoq?"

If I were not leaving, the answer would have been easy. I had no longhouse clan to hunt for me. As the headman's second wife, my status in the village could hardly be higher. My children would be allowed to live, even though they'd be only half Inuit. These thoughts flashed through my thoughts before I replied, although I could barely have refused with politeness. It would have insulted Qisuk's offer. "If I were not going away, I would be pleased to become your wife," I lied courteously. Saying the right thing was more important than the entire truth. I would truly have accepted. I did not know how much I would have liked to have Qisuk as my husband. "I would say yes." Qisuk grinned at my flattering response. Why ask me now, I wondered, since I *was* leaving?

Halvard turned from one to the other of us, trying to understand our conversation. I lifted my hands to show him I could not explain. Padloq and Qisuk shared a knowing smile. I could see their teeth gleam by the firelight. She nodded and his cheeks puffed out so that even I, who understood their words, if not their thoughts, wondered what they were planning.

"My good friend Halvard," Qisuk began, which told me he was leading up to something significant, "we have known you only a short time, but in these few days you have become like a brother of my own igloo, like a son of the same parents." He spoke slowly and used some signs so Halvard would understand.

Halvard had learned enough to get the gist of what Qisuk was saying. "Yes. Very good friends," he replied.

"When parting for the last time, it is our custom to offer good friends comfort and joy, to mark how close we feel to each other. I would like to give you Padloq for tonight and you can give me Mikisoq." Had I heard correctly? "This sharing means we are brothers, although of different tribes. Of course, our wives must agree. What do you have to say to my offer, my friend?"

Obviously, Halvard's agreement was taken for granted, although at the time, I was sure he did not know it. I had the right to refuse, but that would be impolite. Besides, it would pain Qisuk and Padloq if we rejected their offer. What if Halvard did not know this and refused? His tribe's customs might differ. I felt dizzy. My heart raced while I tried to gauge Halvard's reaction, for he was not answering. Too long a silence might be taken for a refusal. Perhaps it was only that he had not understood.

Sammik followed the conversation with great interest. He rested his puppylike eyes on me, as if I was the one who had not consented and was holding up the proceedings. Now I understood Qisuk's hesitation about bringing him with us. Qisuk must have guessed this might prevent us from being at ease.

"Say yes; Mikisoq, you must say yes," Sammik said, crossing over to me. "You are our family now."

Inuit children were seldom rebuked for what they said or did, but that was too much. "In my tribe, children were taught manners enough not to interfere in grown-up decisions. This has nothing to do with you," I said. I made the corners of my mouth turn down and glared at him severely, hoping he could see by the firelight that I was displeased with his behavior.

Sammik backed away from me, but turned his face to Halvard. "My aunt will make you laugh under the furs, won't you, Padloq? Why is your face changing like that, Halvard?"

Beside the fire, Halvard's face had turned an odd shade of pink that did not look well with his orange hair and beard. He realized this was a difficult situation and knew he had not the words to respond as he might wish.

Padloq and Qisuk had put us in an awkward predicament, neither seeming to realize how awkward. It became quite clear to me that this was not Halvard's custom. I wanted to smooth things out, but I, too, could not think what to say.

"Sammik has no manners," Qisuk said. "Boy! Keep your mouth closed. You embarrass my friends."

"I think his customs differ from yours, Qisuk," I replied at last. "He does not understand your offer of friendship." I feared Halvard was about to refuse, angrily perhaps, and that Qisuk would take offense.

"Poor Halvard," Padloq murmured. "I will explain better so you will understand. This is our way to make good friends better, so you won't forget us." Was it embarrassment or confusion that made his face so red and his hands tighten on his knees? He was aware, I hoped, that he must not give offense to the man who had saved his life and given me to him.

Padloq rose from her place beside Qisuk and sauntered over to Halvard, moving her hips more than was necessary. Her summer tunic moved, swaying against her bare legs. Her open jacket barely covered the swell of her breasts. She had taken the combs from her hair when we washed after eating. Now her loose shoulder-length hair and womanly smile made her seem more attractive than she really was.

While I learned how to be a wife, she had been learning, too. Her stance held new confidence, and it seemed to me she took pride in her recently acquired ability to please. The next moment, she stood behind Halvard, massaging his shoulders and neck with her strong thumbs and fingers. Whether he sighed or moaned, I could not tell. "Your back is tight," she remarked, although he wouldn't know her word. "Let me help you to relax." The air near the fire grew warmer. She started to tug off his shirt.

Qisuk continued to coax us by speaking to Padloq. "Our friends do not know how to express their joy that I am so generous. They are speechless. You must help me show them that we are all one family tonight."

Padloq bent to whisper something in Halvard's ear. Whatever she said, his hands, which had been clutching his knees, relaxed a little, but his mouth still hung open, round like the mouth of a cornhusk mask.

"Astrid!" he said, turning to me in desperation. Although it was unlikely we would see them again in this lifetime, I knew we must not part from our Inuit friends on bad terms. With this realization, I came to a decision for both of us. Halvard and I would have to forgive each other later. I lifted my hands in resignation. Padloq was almost in Halvard's lap by then. At least he had the sense not to push her away. When I smiled coyly to Qisuk, it was all the answer he required.

"Will I have a big hairy man to keep me warm tonight, then?" Padloq asked happily. Halvard said nothing at all, only watched while Qisuk guided me to the side he had chosen under Halvard's boat.

I knew I would have to sort this out with Halvard later. In spite of my initial reluctance, I tried to behave in accordance with our hosts' customs as I understood them. Under the shadow of the boat, I helped Qisuk remove his boots, as Padloq would have done. Then I drew off my own boots and undressed, creeping between the furs. In a moment, Qisuk was bare and had crawled in beside me. His skin was smooth as a woman's compared to Halvard's. He smelled clean and his breath felt warm against my cheek.

"Little wife of the night," he murmured tenderly. "I know we confused Halvard, but he will understand. I'll miss having you in my igloo. You don't know how long I have wanted to wrestle with you. Now we will be one family until you go." His hands warmed me as they cupped my breasts.

He was strong but patient, and more gentle than I would have expected, for he was ready long before I could relax to his unfamiliar touch. His smooth body pressed against mine in the dark of the boat's shadow. He laughed in pleasure when he opened my legs and stroked my inner thighs. To my surprise, an inkling of desire traveled up my legs and tightened the small of my back.

The idea of coupling with Padloq's husband while she opened her legs to mine was so absurd that I laughed softly, too. Soon, Halvard would enter into the shelter with Padloq, unless they were already wrapped together by the fire.

I tried to feel jealous, to imagine Padloq stroking Halvard's broad back and chest, feeling how the hair grew on him, smelling his skin and sweat, tingling to the sensation of his strong fingers touching her in intimate places. Although I could not have explained why, I discovered I didn't mind. Sharing like this made us sisters. It would not have been so at home or anywhere else in any world, but perhaps the Inuit custom had merit. Being close to Qisuk made me feel closer to Padloq.

There was no use thinking too much. Soon, I found I could hardly think at all beyond the furs and Qisuk's exploring hands. He did not hurry as he stroked my breasts, my hips, and my long hair, which fell over my buttocks, until I arched toward him in spite of myself. Then he moved to cover me. Prickles of pleasure crept up my back and insides the way they did with Halvard, but without the surge of love. The pleasure he gave me was real nonetheless, but in a teasing way. Qisuk was a friend. We had shared a home for a year, and at this point, perhaps he understood more of who I was than Halvard did.

Qisuk was soon spent. He grunted his satisfaction, then rolled off me. "That was very nice, wife of the night," he said. "Did I please you?"

"You pleased me very well." He stroked my hair with affection once more at the compliment, then closed his eyes to sleep.

When we awoke, I rejoined Halvard, as if last night had not occurred. Halvard ate with me again, and Padloq served Qisuk and Sammik before taking any food herself, as always. I felt my husband's look of betrayal, and although he tried to conceal it, he could not meet my eyes. I knew I must make him understand, although I did not know how I would do so.

Padloq chattered happily and smiled at both men. Of course, her customs were right for her. The kind of sharing we had participated in meant only what it was supposed to mean, no more.

I felt shy with Qisuk, but both of our friends were warmer to us than ever. When it was time to go, Padloq pressed her cheek against mine. "Remember your time with us," she said.

"I shall never forget you or any of the friends I have made here," I assured her. I pressed her hand to my lips, then whispered words just for us. I told her I hoped Qisuk would make her happy. "Let him give you sons, if that is what you want, although you have your sister's two to raise. You would be better off with a girl, who could help you with all the work you must do. Your mother was glad enough with her daughters."

"You make me cry," she replied, hugging me tightly. "I love you, my sister Mikisoq. Be happy in your new life."

While she hugged Halvard good-bye, Qisuk wrapped his arms around me. "Good crossing, Mikisoq," he said. "I will pray to Sea Woman to watch over you." I returned his hug easily, glad for his kind words and hoping his prayers would be answered.

"Good hunts to you and good knives from the star," I responded. "I shall miss you." I smiled tenderly at him, a brief reminder of the one night we had shared. His response told me it had been special for him. When he touched his temple and his heart, I did the same. It was a good way to part.

Sammik suddenly became shy. "Come here, young *inuk*," I commanded. "You were my best friend when I was sick. You cared for me and you taught me how to talk." I caught him and hugged him tightly before he could escape. He squirmed a moment, then hugged me back so hard, I gasped. Regretfully, he released me. In spite of my training, tears ran down my cheeks. I wiped them away.

"I *will* visit you," he declared. "I'll travel on my kayak or with my dog team. When I'm a man, I'll bring bear and seal meat to your family in winter. You will see what a good hunter I shall become."

"You'll be the best," I said. Qisuk grinned and nodded at my prediction. If an *inuk* ever let anyone overshadow him, it was his firstborn son.

Lastly, Qisuk grabbed Halvard and hugged him, slapping his back. "You are a lucky man," he said, using Halvard's word for luck. It was a word I was to hear often, a word the Greenlanders depended on as much as their gods. Padloq and Sammik hugged him, too, one after the other. "We are friends for always now, Qisuk of the Inuit and Halvard of the Qallunaat."

"Friends," Halvard repeated in an oddly shaded voice, but he returned the hugs. We righted the boat, tying down the bundles. "Take extra ropes," Qisuk said, pulling one out of his pack. "Keep safe in Sea Woman's care." We pushed the boat into the surf, until its bottom no longer touched gravel. Halvard and I climbed in and Qisuk gave us a powerful shove. We were on our way. They watched Halvard pull both oars to take us over the waves.

He turned the boat southward and rested one oar by his feet so he could look back and raise his hand in farewell. I also waved to our friends. As we moved south, they seemed to grow small. The cliff and the mountains loomed up behind them. After awhile, I raised my arm again and wondered if they had seen.

Padloq's tiny figure waved in response before the three of them turned back down the beach to make their way home. My time with the Inuit had ended, and now, I would discover why the gods had sent me across the water and given Halvard to me.

BOOK IV

Inuit

GREENLAND

➤ Qisuk's Village

Sorqaq's
Village

Inuit

➤ Western District
Halvard's
Greenland

➤ Trader Island

Pine Tree Woman's
2nd Village

Pine Tree Woman's
1st Village

Naskapi

LABRADOR

Hawk
Feather's
Town ➤

Algonquin

Gulf of
St. Lawrence

Algonquin

Wide River

Doteoga

Ganeogaono

← to Oneida

← to Onondaga

▬ ▬ to Halvard's home by sailboat

A flock of birds flew overhead, snow geese, honking. They flew southeasterly, not a sign of winter yet, but their flight en masse was sign enough. They were not finding the abundance they expected. Odin's messengers, the black birds known as ravens, were silhouetted against the sky for a brief moment. They ducked between clouds, chasing one another, diving and gliding over the blue and glittering fjord. Their flight took them over the distant hills, until they were gone from sight. Each bird had its flock, each deer its herd, but I had nothing. I was exiled, like the lone mountain lion, or the lone wolf, my clan's namesake. What had I done to my husband and children by losing my temper?

Halvard's Greenland

Chapter

Halvard pulled back powerfully on both oars, propelling us through and then beyond where the water piled itself into waves. The sun glared off the foam and mist, sending up sparks like a spray of fire. Once we passed over the swells, the boat perched more securely, and I was able to release my clutch on both sides of Halvard's boat. I opened my pack to retrieve the wide-brimmed grass-woven hats Maki had given us for a wedding present, then held one out to Halvard. He took his from me without a word.

"Like this," I said, showing him how to secure it. We cut through an unruly wave I had not seen coming. The cold spray splashed my face and the smell of salt tingled through my nose until I tasted it in the back of my throat. Tears sprang to my eyes at the shock, and I coughed.

Halvard spit out the water that splashed down his throat and secured his hat, which he had managed to hold on to, but he said nothing. The slap of the waves against the boat and Halvard's creaking oars were the only sounds. Then, with a sudden move and a slam, Halvard pulled in the oars, letting their handles fall beside his feet.

The forward movement of the boat soon ceased and we drifted, bobbing up and down. "Why, Astrid?" he demanded, his voice full of pain and confusion. "Why? Why did you go with Qisuk? You are my wife." His eyes accused me of faithlessness.

My plan had been to make sure he realized the reasons for what had happened between us the night before, to explain as soon as I had enough words. I hoped we might speak about it calmly. Instead, anger flooded through me, causing me to respond more harshly than I wished to.

On the chance that it would help, I moved my hands in the sign talk as well. "Qisuk is your friend, your brother, who saved your life." He had to understand. "You do not say *no* to a friend. He made you a closer friend last night; he gave you Padloq." He knew most of my words, if not all of them. In any case, he could hardly fail to see my anger. How did he dare to accuse me, when I had saved him from the terrible blunder of refusing to share with a sworn friend?

His ragged breaths whistled through his clenched teeth. His eyes blinked before my onslaught. As soon as I had finished, he shouted back at me. "You are angry with me? Me?" he asked, as if he found it absurd. "You think I'm in the wrong here; don't you? Am I crazy?" He moved his arms around like winter branches in a storm. His breath wheezed like gusts of wind.

"Listen to me now," I shouted, willing him to understand. In the heat of my excitement, I no longer cared whether I mixed up words. "You would make Qisuk your enemy if you said no. He saved your life. He let me come away with you." I threw my hands up in exasperation. The next part was most difficult to say, for I did not know his Greenlander words for it. I had to show him what I meant with hand signs, making my face burn. "I copulated with him for you. Only for you! We are in Qisuk's country here. You must be Inuit polite—not insult a friend."

He stared at me, thumb jabbing his chest. "For me? For me?" He threw up his own hands as if asking his gods to explain it to him, since my words had failed to do so. Then quite suddenly, he covered his mouth and his cheeks puffed out, no longer questioning. His eyes squeezed shut a long moment before he looked at me again, anger gone, but hurt remaining.

I nodded. "*Iyeh.* Yes," I repeated, saying it in his language. "He made you his brother. To say no would humiliate him. Inuit polite." Whether he understood me or not, I had to say it. One does as one must among foreigners. We both owed them and dared not reject their generosity.

His eyes cleared and the good sense I believed he had reasserted itself. His lips came together, thinking. "Not Turtle Island polite?"

"No." I quivered like a bowstring just released, and grimaced to show him it would rankle me to lie with another had I not been trying to protect him from social blunder. "Not polite in my country."

"Not Greenland polite, either," he warned me.

"Good," I replied with a small smile of relief. It was difficult enough to have to contend with one Greenlander.

He lifted his oars, but then allowed them to drop again. As yet, it was easier to speak with the help of our hands. "Astrid. Mikisoq." He said both names tentatively, listening to their sounds and cocking his head first one way, then the other. He directed his gaze to me. "I hope you don't mind that I call you Astrid?" We drifted while we spoke, bouncing gently on the rolling green water.

"No. I like. Greenlander name good," I responded. "Your mother's name." Besides, since Mikisoq meant "little one," it was never a proper name at all. I hoped my new name would help me fit in. If all his tribe had hair the color of fire and brown specks on pale complexions, they would know me as a stranger on sight. I hoped it would not prevent them from accepting me.

He smiled at me, glad I liked my new name, then gestured toward the north with a sweep of his arm. "I don't belong in Inuit country."

I echoed the words. "I, too, don't belong there."

"Where do you belong, Astrid?" He knew where I had come from, in a manner of speaking, but I think his questions asked more than that.

"Back across many waters, many lands, many people." When he said nothing, only gazed at me sadly, I added, "Sea Woman says I belong with you." He pulled in the oars and leaned to me in the small boat, until the brims of our hats touched and our lips came together. The boat rocked under us.

Halvard reached under the inside edge of his boat and pulled up something slim and long, wrapped in fabric like his shirt. I waited for him to explain. "We're far enough from land to put up the sail now." He unwrapped the staff, laying the wrapping at our feet. The boat bobbed while he affixed the staff somehow though a hole in the plank down the center of the boat. Soon, it stood upright like a narrow tree. Then he turned a crossbeam on it. This done, he fastened the wrapping with cords to metal hooks at both sides.

"What are you doing?" I asked. "What is that?" I looked up at the strange staff and the material flapping against the dazzling blue of the sky.

"A mast and a sail," he said, touching each when he pronounced the words. I gasped when the material billowed out like a leaf in the wind. Halvard knelt by the pole and shifted the sail to the sea breeze. The boat pushed forward, blown by the wind over the rolling green water. The line of the coast fell more swiftly behind as Halvard turned the sail to catch the wind.

How many more marvels would he show me? "You make Ga-oh your slave," I cried. "You make magic like Minik." He had to guess my meaning, for I did not know his word for *magic*. "You are an *angakkoq*. Like Minik. You make wind row for you."

"It works for anyone with a sail," he said. "We go fast now, with no work." I crawled up to touch the magic sail. I could not guess at how Greenlanders made such a substance for clothing or for sails. No animal produced fur like long, soft strands of human hair. My people twist inner bark into cordage for our fish lines and bowstrings. The Inuit twist wicks of moss or dog hair and braid leather into rope and harnesses. The strands were so soft and thin, I could barely see the individual woven lines where they crossed.

The sail blew us steadily over the waves. Between Halvard's boat and the coast, a gray whale spouted and jumped, arcing out of the ocean and diving back down, waving a great black tail. The double slap of his dive and tail caused a wave that rocked us, but we continued to skim the surface while Halvard managed to steady our course, adjusting his sail to best catch the wind.

We continued our talking lessons while I baited a line and tossed it over the edge of the boat. So many Norse words filled my head and mouth that I held up my hands. "Stop," I complained. "I get them mixed up. It makes my head hurt."

In a few moments, my line had snagged two fish, and I gutted them quickly. More fish swimming beneath us jumped and snapped up the innards almost before they fell back into the water. This gave me an idea. The next time, I would have my net ready to grab them and we would have enough fish to last the trip. Halvard made a face when I bit into the raw flesh. We had far to go and could not land to make a fire. The fish would soon go bad if uneaten. I held out a piece for him, saying, "Eat." After awhile, he accepted what I offered. I also preferred what fire does to the flesh of fish, turning it white and tender, but it was more important to be practical.

While the wind pushed us farther and farther south, I leaned against the bundles, resting my head under the wide-brimmed hat, and slept. When I awoke, the snowcapped inland mountains had changed and the sun had lowered.

Halvard brought us though a narrow bay into a long estuary, away from the ocean. High, sloping banks of stone without beaches bordered the water. I dipped my hand and tasted the water on my fingers. It was still salty, a part of the ocean, and not a river as I had expected. "Fjord," he said. "The ocean water comes in."

Halvard released the ropes holding the mast and pulled up his sail. He turned the sail-laden crossbeam even again with the mast, then picked up the oars. He rowed us to a grotto, where the low sun illuminated stony shallows at the base of the cliffs. The water flowed and ebbed over rounded rocks, wetting the webbed feet of seabirds standing there.

"This looks like a safe place to come ashore," he said, climbing out into the water once he had guided the boat over a smooth stretch of gravel. I did the same. The water came over my knees, but the *kamiks* kept me dry. We hauled the boat high onto the rocks, out of the tide's reach.

There was no freshwater at this landing place, nor any driftwood in sight. "Better to have no fire so close to Skraeling villages," Halvard said. He handed me his pack and mine for us to make our fireless camp. "There's bad blood between Skraelings and Greenlanders."

"Bad blood?"

"Anger. War." He grimaced and pretended to lash out. "War. Killing." Like Ganeogaono and Algonquin tribes, I thought to myself.

We found a large rock, which was lying on its side and flat enough to rest on for the night. With Halvard's cape spread beneath and over us, we watched the sun descend to the west while we practiced more Norse talking. The repetitions made me yawn. "Enough words," I pleaded again. At last, the sun rested. Although the sky remained a pale blue, the crescent moon and the brightest stars showed themselves, floating and bobbing against the gray wisps of clouds.

"Enough words," he agreed.

"You no more angry?" I ventured to ask.

"I'm not angry anymore," he repeated, saying it more correctly. Surely the Norse custom of not sharing a mate was strong among Halvard's people. I could just see the white of his teeth. He drew me close, and with a kiss to my nose, he made me understand all had been forgiven. I touched him under the furs. The short summer night passed quickly while the stars spun over us.

The next day, we passed small islands, the neck of another fjord, a long shore, then a bay. With my hat brim shading my eyes, I discerned hump-like shapes, stone igloos. "Look, Halvard," I said, pointing landward, "Inuit village."

Several women worked the tide pools on the beach with their nets. A woman noticed our boat and gave the alarm. "Strangers. A Qallunuk and a woman in a boat!" she yelled. "A cloud sits on the boat."

Halvard turned his head, first to the beach, then behind and west to the horizon, looking for an escape route. "Do you see kayaks?" he asked, scanning the water for them.

"There," I said, pointing south. "More setting out now from the beach."

The men paddled their narrow skin boats, using powerful racing strokes. I remembered them from the old Inuit country, north of Turtle Island. During the first few days I spent with them before my sickness, young men practiced using the double-blade paddle, shifting with easy motion from one side to the other. They plied their paddles so swiftly, they blurred, propelling the light kayaks faster than a warrior can run. I used to think no craft could move so swiftly.

Halvard pulled the ropes that held his sail, shifting our course to the west. One *inuk,* close enough to throw, lifted his harpoon to take aim. "No!" I shouted. "Don't do it! Go away."

The *inuk* shook his head as if there was water in his ear. "I will save you," he bellowed. "Don't fear. I will kill him."

"No. He's my husband. Please go." I held out both arms in supplication. The man lowered his harpoon slowly and waved the others back. Mystified, they drifted to a stop.

"Thank you," I called. They let us go, but they made a wide half-circle on the water, making sure we would not come too close. Soon, the wind blew us beyond harpoon range, far from the village. "Danger over."

"They left," Halvard exclaimed. "What did you tell them?"

"I said you belonged to me."

"Oh." If Halvard had tried to return without me, these villagers might have killed him. Perhaps that is why his gods gave me to him. He swallowed thoughtfully, as if imagining how it might have been. We turned south again.

To my disappointment, I saw no forests on the southward journey, which made me wonder again where the wood of our vessel had grown. I asked, "Trees? Wood? Where did the wood grow?"

Halvard perceived why I asked, for he answered me gravely. "Not in Greenland. In the old land of my people, in Norway." So there were no trees. I did not know how to ask about corn, and, fearing the answer, I refrained. I would learn soon enough what Greenlanders ate.

"We need freshwater," he said, weighing our water bags. Only one remained, and that was only half-full. We drew up a short way into a fjord and found a stopping place where the bank dropped gradually. Halvard moored the boat with a stout rope to a rock, leaving the boat bobbing while we climbed over the side. My legs almost buckled, not used to the steadiness of land, but soon I found my balance again.

We shrugged on our packs for our trek inland, carrying food and furs to make shelter if we decided to sleep on land that night. Only fish remained in our sealskin containers. We took our weapons, Halvard his spear and knife, and I my bow and quiver of arrows, my *ulu,* and my old flint knife from Turtle Island.

We proceeded warily, picking our way toward patches of green among the rocks. The earth and the fresh smell of herbs and ferns seemed to extend a welcome to us and beckon us close. They could only grow near water, I knew. "This way," I said, leading him. A trickle, splashing over rocks, came to my ears. The stream sparkled, inviting us. We lay beside the bank, cupping water to drink our fill, savoring, splashing, and laughing. The cool freshwater tasted delicious. I emptied our bags, then rinsed and filled them again.

"Let's see where the stream begins," Halvard suggested playfully. "I've almost forgotten how to use my legs." We followed its meandering, making a nearby stony hill our landmark. We climbed, keeping the stream in sight. Soon, we were high enough to see the ocean again. "Listen," Halvard said, looking around. "There it is! I see the spring!"

Clear water bubbled out of a bluff, then fell over a ledge into a shaded green pond which led away into the stream. Thin, small-leafed brambles and ferns tangled close to the water. While we circled the pond, I felt a faint breeze blow from the bluff. "Look." Taking Halvard's arm, I pointed. The breeze moved the fern fronds.

"Where is that breeze coming from?" Curious as a boy, he loped to the hill and pushed the leafy vines aside with his spear. "It's a cave," he said, telling me his word. "I want to see. Come with me."

"Bears sleep in caves," I cautioned, but he waved me closer. The brush near the opening had not been pressed down by heavy paws. I crouched to inspect the new leaves. The branches had been nibbled back recently, as a deer would browse after it had been to the spring or the pool to drink. Grazing animals would not go so close to a bear's den as long as there was other greenery for them. I judged the cave to be safe, so I followed Halvard.

We entered into the semidark and sniffed. There was no animal smell, only warm dampness and the splash of running water. Maybe the pool was connected to the water outside, dripping through rivulets inside the rock. A faint limestone smell wafted to my nose. The sound of water dripping became louder. The echo bouncing off the walls confused our ears, making it hard to locate the source.

We walked farther into the cave, moving cautiously, bending low to avoid the damp rocks above us. Another turn and the light from the entrance faded entirely. Halvard tapped the ground ahead with his spear before we advanced. I wished for a torch, hoping the ground remained solid beneath our feet as we continued in the darkness. We could no longer see each other, but Halvard's tapping and his boots sounding solidly on the stones guided me.

"The wall turns here," he said. He grasped my hand while feeling along the wall with his other. The trickle and splash of falling water grew louder. He stopped. "Here, Astrid." By the sound of his voice, I realized the cave's walls must have drawn apart again. "Don't move. I found the pool." He tapped around the rocks, then knelt to splash the water. "Warm," he said. He cupped it to taste, allowing it to drip through his fingers.

"Good?" I asked. He made a noncommittal sound.

I felt around the lip above the surface of the water and dipped my hand into the blackness, feeling the peculiar warmth.

I felt and tasted the steamy mist rising from the water. Three days of salt and sweat coated my skin. It would be good to make myself clean again. "Come," I said, "the water is not too hot." I proceeded to rub my face. When he reached for me, I took his hand and lowered it to the water. "I'm going in. You come, too. Bathe," I suggested. I did not know the Norse word for it, so I said the word in Inuit. Halvard would guess my meaning. I could not gesture, because we could not see each other in the blackness.

I shrugged out of my pack, then removed my *kamiks,* trousers, and shirt, leaving them on the rocks. The water enveloped me, welcoming me into its warmth. I prayed Mother Earth and Nerrivik would keep me safe if water monsters lurked underneath.

Halvard hesitated. "Come," I said again. In another moment, he stripped and climbed in beside me. There was no bottom under my feet, so I held fast to the rock edge with one hand. Without soap plant or sand, I did my best to rub away the salt and grime. I scrubbed my hair, ducked, and scrubbed again. When that was done, I stroked Halvard's broad back with my free hand, massaging with my fingers. When I turned my back, he returned the treat with smooth, hard fingers and gentle strength.

We emerged, hair dripping, into the warm air around the steaming pool, and retrieved our packs, drying ourselves partially with the furs. We gathered up our clothing, packs, and weapons, then backtracked until we could see again. The stone walls seemed to glow with pale green light. It must have been sunlight passing through the ivy and ferns by the cave's entrance.

"Well," he said. "We have freshwater now and our fish. Let's sleep here tonight." I nodded. He laid out his fur cape for us to rest upon. I opened our container and handed him fish. Even near the entrance, the inner pool kept the cave warm enough that we were comfortable with just the one fur. I spread the others to dry nearby.

After we had eaten, Halvard stroked my hair. When I moved back to lean against him, he cupped my breasts under my wide leather shirt. Bumps rose on my skin at his touch. "Are you cold?" he asked.

"No. Not cold."

"Then take this off," Halvard said. I did as he urged and turned, to find he had stripped, as well. Benevolent spirits must guard the cave, since they had kept us safe in the pool. I pressed against his hands and moved my legs around him. To my surprise, he wriggled us around so that I lay on top of him, my breasts touching his cheeks. He tongued both tips, one after the other. "This is a Greenlander way." I laughed. He laughed. Soon both of us laughed according to the Inuit meaning.

Before we reached our boat in the morning, I spied a pair of snow hares, mostly brown now, with patches of old white in their pelts, sniffing the air. Before Halvard could disturb them, I cautioned him to stillness with a gesture. We were upwind, where they could not smell us. Before they turned, I had loosed two arrows, one after the other. My shafts had pierced their throats from behind. We had meat enough for another two days.

We sailed out of the fjord and continued down the coast. After awhile, we glided past several houses, more angular than igloos, with broken stone walls. There were no uncovered tunnels like those we had found at Qisuk's deserted village. No women fished on the beach; no children played. It was empty and forbidding. "What is this place?" I asked, shivering, feeling the wrongness there.

"It is part of the Western Settlement. Skraelings pushed the Greenlanders south. Only ghosts are here now. We must keep going." Grass grew over what was left of the fallen roofs and broken walls.

"So sad!" I remarked. "The ghosts will be lonely."

He smiled at me with a crooked smile, as though I said something funny. "I suppose they are. These ghosts won't be used to humans after all this time." He seemed to try to shake off the melancholy of the deserted houses as a dog shakes off water. He studied the sky before saying, "If the winds continue steady, we will come to my homestead and farm in another day and a half."

After we passed the houses and meadows, another house came into view, quite alone. It seemed to be in better shape than those behind us, with most of the walls still upright. "The house and all this land must have belonged to a rich man once, with many fields and animals." Perhaps dogs belonged to men, but I wondered how other animals could belong to a man.

The sun reflected pink off the clouds. We looked for a place to put in for the night. Halvard began to pull toward shore. We glided south, spied a likely place to make our camp, and started toward the beach.

As we approached the wave line, a gust of wind suddenly turned us around. The large puffy clouds that had followed us most of the day had grown together and turned gray. The sun disappeared behind them. It seemed night had descended without warning. Lightning bolted out of the sky, followed almost immediately by a loud thunderclap. The waves rose, and whitecaps splashed across the boat's prow, covering our legs with salt water.

The most dangerous place to be during a thunderstorm is on water. Halvard tried to regain control of the boat, struggling to roll up the sail while it whipped and snapped loudly, lashing at his face and shoulders. I feared the wind would lift the sail and carry away the mast. The waves grew higher, spilling over onto us. A heavy wind-pushed rain hid the shore from our view. Halvard grappled with the flapping sheet, managing to roll and tie it, then yanked back the mast, which threatened to lift out of his grasp. He got it stowed at last, but while he worked, the wind and waves pushed us farther from land.

I found it hard to hold on. "Sit in front of me," he ordered, and stretched a rope across me to help me hold my seat. He left my hands free to reach my *ulu* if I needed to cut the lines in case the boat overturned. We were both drenched. His teeth chattered as he strained, muscles bulging while he tried to propel the boat to shore. Under the driving rain, I could barely see the land.

The boat rode up a wave crest and balanced on the summit. A flash of light illuminated a beach before we plunged down. I hooked my legs around the tied bundles and prayed to Sea Woman, begging for our lives as we slid down into the gully and up the side of the next black hill. Halvard shouted, "Hold on to an oar if you wash overboard. If we're separated, I'll find you."

My scalp prickled. A moment later, a streak of light flashed down beside us and thunder covered my scream. We bailed water with our hats to keep the weight from submerging Halvard's boat. Between the wind and the waves, I could not hear Halvard's shouted words. I shook my head to tell him. The next moment, his mouth pressed against my ear and he said, "I love you." It took me a moment to interpret the Norse phrase. When I did, I squeezed his arm and returned the words to him. The next flash showed me his face, more full of sorrow than fear that we were going to die. Our time together had been so short.

Thunder followed the flash. "Don't take us yet, Sea Woman," I pleaded. Whatever the gods intended for us must come to pass, but we continued to bail. I do not know how long the storm continued, but finally the wind died down somewhat and the waves grew smaller. We remained afloat.

"There's land," Halvard shouted when the rumbles of the last thunderclap died away. "I think we can make it." We neared the shore and jumped into the surf. The breakers brought the water higher than Halvard's head, threatening to pull us back out, but then I felt gravel under my feet and the rope still in my hand. The wave subsided, almost throwing me off balance. Halvard held me tightly against the strong undertow, pushing me forward, helping me hold the rope.

The suck of the tide lowered the water to our ankles. I could make out the white surge of the next wave. We had only a moment before it would crash down on us. Halvard yanked the mooring rope strongly. I feared the boat would break away from him with all our equipment and food. With feet dug into the slippery sand, we managed to haul the boat far enough along. The next wave wet us and pushed us forward, until we were beyond the reach of the backflow.

We were used to communicating without words. Fear gave us strength. While the cold rain lashed at us, we pulled and pushed, dragging the boat higher inland to the scree, those fallen rocks at the base of the cliffs. When we reached it, we could haul the boat no farther.

I untied my pack from the bundles. The food and rendered seal fat would keep us for a few days if the boat washed away while we figured what to do. Halvard took up his spear and my bow, as well as his pack. We climbed over the fallen rocks, feeling our way to high ground. I tripped in the midnight darkness, for the sun was smothered by black clouds. Halvard's arm held me steady. We clung to each other like lost children when lightning streaked nearby, illuminating an angular pile of stones.

"This way," Halvard shouted.

We found the shelter and crawled inside. Wind gusts drove the rain against the wall, but we were out of the wind and had found a measure of refuge. The storm had pushed us back the way we came, to the lonely half-fallen house.

Old beams, stones, and sod still covered a portion of the roof. "Watch out," Halvard said, pulling me back to a wall. "Lightning may strike even here." We huddled close in the lee of the wall to wait, wet and shivering, with no dry furs to crawl between. Although the night was not very cold, my teeth chattered as I thought of our circumstances and our narrow escape from the water. Halvard had taken the hide he used for our shelter when we made camp. He hung it from the wall behind and tied a corner of it to the next section of wall to make us a tent in the ruined house.

"What about the ghosts? Will we anger them?" I asked when he returned. He had gathered me close, but I had to shout into his ear to make my voice louder than the renewed storm. Where the water gushed through the stones of the farther wall, I could almost hear the ghosts gurgling through the water. Halvard shrugged, which I took to mean he would rather wait out the storm here and deal with the ghosts than with the lighting and blinding rain.

After awhile, I stopped shivering, gaining warmth from Halvard's closeness. Perhaps the ghosts were glad for company after so many lonely years. In the dark, I sang them a little song of my homeland to tell them we intended no harm, only that we required a safe place while the storm blew itself away. With Halvard's arm for my pillow, I tried to keep watch, but even the streaks of light across the clouds could not keep me awake.

In the morning, I thanked the spirits of the house and its stones for their kindness before we left. I was afraid for Halvard's boat, fearing that it had been destroyed or washed out into the ocean with the waves. We found it farther inland, covered with strings of seaweed. "It's not damaged," Halvard called excitedly as he checked it over. "The mast did not blow far. The packs are still here, and the oars, too." He ran to the mast, which had caught between two boulders, and brought it back. "We can still use it. This could have been much worse."

"Nerrivik has kept us safe," I said to Halvard.

"Someone has," he agreed. We carried our belongings down to the beach and set off again. We had lost a day's travel, but we were still alive.

After a long while, we turned into what Halvard told me was the mouth of his home fjord. Around the bend was a boat similar to ours, bobbing on the water, with two men inside, trailing a net. I stared at them. One man was barefaced and young, the other bearded. Neither bore the same fiery red hair I had expected. Their hair was more the color of dried cornstalks or ash trees, brownish.

The older nudged the younger. Before we had pulled close enough to exchange words, Halvard rolled his sail, then held the boat steady with his oars. "How is the fishing in the ocean?" the elder man asked.

"Good enough. How is it in the fjord?"

"We do all right. You must have been caught in the storm." He pointed toward the ocean with his chin.

"We were lucky," Halvard responded. "I'm anxious to get home now."

Although they talked to Halvard, both men's eyes flitted to me. The younger man said, "The cod are running in from the ocean. A longship is due from Norway with supplies for Iceland and then for us. I hope they made it through the storm. The ship is supposed to bring us wine and blessed wafers for the church from Nidaros. Bishop Alf has a standing order for them so we can have a proper Communion at Gardar again."

Halvard said nothing to the man. I shuddered, knowing my reaction had nothing to do with cold. I had not understood most of what the fisherman said, but I did not like the way the two of them looked at me.

"The bishop needs wine, not milk, for Christ's blood and wafers of ground wheaten flour for the body, not seal meat. We must observe our sacraments properly to obtain help from the Savior."

"What do you mean?" Halvard said when the man had finished speaking.

"To hold back the Skraelings, of course, those minions of the devil. Are you sure you want to bring one of them into your house?"

"She's mine," Halvard said somewhat forcefully, the way I had told the Inuit we encountered in the kayaks that he belonged to me.

They shrugged their shoulders as if to say possessing me was his misfortune and none of theirs. "No ship has come since last summer. This will be the first of the year, so everyone is fishing. We're catching all we can. The captain will want wind-dried cod for the trip home. They'll take fish for wood and nails, but if you have hides and tusks, there are many other treasures to trade for."

Halvard let the oars rest at his feet, suddenly curious. "What else will they be bringing?"

"Iron tools and pots. More horses. A rich farmer in our parish ordered a new stud bull for his cows. The bishop asked last year's captain to have the archbishop of the cathedral at Nidaros send us more ordained priests."

When Halvard made no reply to this, the father, if that's what he was, nudged the son. "That may be none of his business. Are you a Christian, man? Or do you persist in the old ways?"

"I serve our Norse gods, not the dead god nailed to a tree. That upstart saps a Norseman's strength and turns him into a fool. What do you need with such nonsense? Iron, wood, and animals are worth trading for, which is more than anyone can say about Jesus priests." Halvard bellowed out his words, for we were floating farther from the fishermen. I felt glad for the stretch of water that had grown between us, feeling unrest because of the dangerous stares of the fishermen. Sorqaq had been right when he said that the Big Eyebrow people were warlike. It seemed they liked to provoke fights even among themselves.

"The ship's captain will trade with old-god people, too," the older man called before we were out of hearing. "Sailors aren't fussy who they'll deal with. That Skracling female should be good for a few wooden boards or maybe a pot. She can keep the sailors happy on the voyage back."

Halvard raised a fist, then lowered the sail to put more distance between us. I lifted my chin and bit my teeth together at the man who spoke. I would never be a slave again, to be taken at the will of someone who loathed me. I would kill again if I had to in order to remain free. Halvard did not speak until we lost sight of them. "Some Greenlanders are not polite," he explained through clenched teeth.

We passed islands with small dwellings built upon them, until I noticed a steep path that came down to the water. All I could see from the boat was the house's sloped roof, covered with thatching and tucked up against a hill, which accounted for one of its walls. From halfway along the steep path, a woman watched us. It might have been a trick of the sun that confused me about the woman's appearance. I shaded my eyes, trying to pierce the water's glare. "Look there," I said, pointing. "Do you see someone standing on the hill? It looks like a Qallunaat woman."

The closer we approached, the more I was sure this was a woman. She beckoned, indicating the landing and the stone walkway that led to the base of her hill, where it met the fjord. Halvard took down his mast. "She's inviting us to her house. It would be a good thing for us to sleep under a real roof tonight and to reach my steading in the morning, after we have rested," he said. He looked into the distance for a moment, as he did each time he tried to put words together for me. "The woman will not understand what you are, dressed in that clothing. Remember to stand behind me until I can explain."

Halvard waved his acceptance to her invitation. We tied up beside another boat at the landing, then took up our packs while the woman waited above us on the stone walkway. "I want to bring my bow and quiver," I stated.

"You won't need them," Halvard said, but when he saw my face, he nodded. "Keep the bow over your shoulder," he said. "I don't want to frighten anyone." I did as he directed and slung my quiver around my waist. The quiver hung lower than my anorak, but I could reach my arrows with either hand if necessary. Halvard took up his spear before we started from the boat. "We can't leave them on the boat to tempt anyone who might come along."

As we ascended, the woman appeared in a curve of the path. I was startled all the more at her appearance. Her hair blew in the breeze like corn tassels, pale yellow, almost white. Her eyes reflected the blue of the sky. The sun lit her complexion whiter than Halvard's, making her cheeks the color of blushing clouds. Most startling of all to me was her clothing. It was not the grass behind her, as I had thought when first I saw her from the fjord, or even a trick of the sun. The woman was clad in the deep summer green of growing cornhusks.

Chapter 29

The woman's wide blue eyes darted to my bow and quiver of arrows. She stared at me with a combination of fear and loathing before centering on Halvard. "I—that is, my father—we thought you captured a Skraeling." She stepped between us as though to use him for a shield against me. "But he's carrying weapons. How could you allow a Skraeling to bring weapons into a Greenlander steading?"

If I did not comprehend all of her words, I could not fail to see that she despised me. Her pale hair and green garb were not of the spirits. Was this how all of Halvard's people would receive me? I felt my skin crawl and longed to leave, to run back to the boat and return to Qisuk's village. Although they were cautious of me at first, although they never made me truly one of them, they had never looked at me with unconcealed hate.

Fortunately, Halvard spoke before I moved, placing his hand softly on my arm and bringing me forward to stand at his side. His light touch brought me back to my senses. "My wife and I won't leave our weapons unguarded in the boat. She is not of the northern Skraelings, even though she wears their style of clothing for travel. If your father objects to her clothing or what we carry, we have wasted our time stopping at your landing."

She looked at me more closely. "Your wife?" It took her more than a moment to compose herself. While she inspected me, I studied her. Her face seemed young and her teeth strong inside her partially opened lips. Her tongue flicked out, impatient, it seemed, at this odd situation. Her hair, pale as corn silk, and her blue eyes no longer evoked my reverence, for I realized it was only one of the many shades of these multicolored Greenlanders.

In the time it took me to sort this out, I had regained control of my reason. Her dyed green dress was an oddity to me, but so were all aspects of Greenlanders. Halvard moved closer. "Yes. She is my wife," he responded. Some explanation was needed if this was to be a peaceful encounter. "Astrid's people live west of Vinland. I'm Halvard Gunnarson. My steading is on the west bank of Eriksfjord, south of Gardar."

"I'm called Helga Thorvaldsdottir," she said, then backtracked, realizing what Halvard had just related. "You say this Skraeling woman comes from beyond Vinland, that country of legends? How could she?"

"It's a long story. I'll tell it to your father, if he asks courteously."

Helga lifted her chin slightly as though annoyed, then said, "Follow me. I think my father will want to see her for himself, rather than hearing it from me. He'll also want your news. My mother has the evening meal prepared." We exchanged a glance. I shrugged, trying to look casual. If Halvard thought it was safe, I would trust his judgment. We were in his country now.

"I'll be glad to exchange our stories for food and shelter this night. Please announce us first, Helga Thorvaldsdottir. Say who and what we are to be sure your father will want to admit us." She bounded up the path, leaving us alone.

"So far, you haven't seen much Greenland courtesy," Halvard said, looking after the woman with regret. "The Greenlanders you have seen thus far were not polite," he added, using the Inuit word to be sure I understood.

"Will we still go to the house?" My face must have shown my confusion, for though they had been speaking quickly, I thought I had followed most of it until the yellow-and-green Helga woman departed alone.

He repeated the exchange in simpler terms. "If her father says yes, we will go to the house. There are bound to be questions and challenges, Astrid. Let us see how it goes and learn from how this family treats us. I think it will be safe. I'd rather arrive at my house rested and fed than not."

I touched his arm lightly. "I follow where you lead," I said, still unsure of my welcome, but trusting Halvard to choose what was right. I patted my dark braids, hoping they had remained neat over my shoulders. Shortly, Helga appeared at the top of the hill and beckoned.

Two young animals with deerlike hooves grazed on the roof, cropping the grass and chewing their cud. They were the beasts Halvard called "goats." Small beards, like those of the Inuit, sprouted from their chins.

Halvard did not seem concerned or amazed these animals would browse on a dwelling, nor did he expect them to have a fear of humans. The planked wood door opened inward and a slim man ducked out. His beard held gray hairs among the yellow. The hair on his head was not as pale as that which covered the head of Helga Thorvaldsdottir. At our approach, two boys sidled around him to gawk at me. They all had shades of yellow hair.

Helga turned smugly from the others to us, holding out one hand toward him. "My father, Thorvald," she announced. A frightened-looking older woman peered out. "My mother, Gudrun. These are the strangers."

"Halvard Gunnarson," said Halvard, bowing slightly, "and my wife, Astrid Vinlander. We are on our way home."

Thorvald blinked several times. Gudrun stepped outside, patting down the apron that covered her stomach. She repeated our names, noticing my Inuit clothing and weapons. Helga had prepared them for us, but even so, the sight of me appeared to startle her.

Thorvald's voice held a hint of humor when he remarked, "No wonder my daughter took you for a man, dressed like that." He watched my expression. I nodded to him. "Strangers don't stop here often. The seal hunt has been over for a fortnight. Why did you not return with the others, Halvard Gunnarson?"

"I remained longer in the northland than I expected to." It was a brief answer and told nothing.

The other man did not take it amiss, but nodded, stroking his beard. "A Vinlander woman in these parts is most unusual. In fact, I daresay it's never happened before at all. Well, if you're both peaceable and hungry, and willing to talk about your travels, we'd enjoy your company for supper and lodging this night. I'd like to discover how a Vinlander woman connived to come to our country. Last I heard, the western Skraelings don't build longships."

When Halvard put this in words I could understand, I had to smile. "We don't," I admitted.

Gudrun approached me shyly. When I smiled, she took both my hands into hers. Several of her teeth were missing, but she seemed not much older than my mother would be. Her pale blue clothing matched her eyes. The coarse sand-colored apron tied over her garment covered all but the toes of her dark leather shoes. "You are welcome in our home, Astrid," she said in a kindly way. The two younger boys advanced with a show of bravado.

"Thank you," I said, grateful she had decided not to be frightened of my bow or my Inuit clothing.

"Come inside," Gudrun said. "Food is ready." We began to enter, when suddenly, from the hill, there came the sound of dogs barking and the clatter of hooves prancing over fieldstones. Two dark, short men with wisps of beards approached the house in the midst of a herd of animals. With them bounded a pair of thick-coated spotted dogs, which drew back their black lips and charged toward us. I spun and reached for my bow, strung it, and had notched my arrow before Thorvald faced the dogs and commanded, "Down, Ruff! Down, Spot! These are friends. Get down!"

At their master's voice, the dogs whimpered, tails whipping. "My dogs don't care for Skraelings much," Thorvald offered in explanation. "Your clothing fooled them like it fooled us. When Skraelings come this far down the fjord, it's usually to steal our beasts or burn our houses."

The dogs growled softly, waiting while the two dark-toned men ran up to them. I lowered my bow and unstrung it, but I could not take my eyes from the men, who returned my rude gaze. If we were in their land, I would not have held their eyes and risked their annoyance. What were Inuit doing here, and why were they dressed like Greenlanders? If Thorvald was so afraid of *Skraelings* killing his animals, why did he have two guarding them? The only explanation that occurred to me was that they were slaves.

"It's all right," Thorvald explained to them. "This man and woman are my guests. Go on, both of you, and put the beasts into their fold and water them. I don't need you now."

Their small, sharp eyes bored into me another moment before the slaves turned away, driving the flock with short whips. The dogs jumped up and followed along to help. They led the beasts to a sod-covered shelter of planks and stones, then closed them inside. One shoved a long bar through iron loops. From there, they turned to look at us again with a mixture of curiosity and distrust before sauntering away to a small stone hut behind the main house.

Gudrun ushered us inside. After the sunlit field outside, my eyes needed to adjust to the darkness. Smells other than those of cooking penetrated my nostrils, odd and sour smells. I tried not to sniff. It was vastly impolite to sniff about a bad odor in an Inuit home. Halvard did not appear to notice.

The low and soot-darkened ceiling was supported by wooden beams. Several wicks flickered in bowl lamps around the main room. The tallow had not the pleasant aroma of seal or walrus oil. I wondered what the Greenlanders used for fuel. The beams and wall stones were damp where condensed lamp grease had settled and congealed.

"You may leave your weapons and packs on the floor," Thorvald said, gesturing to show us where. Halvard did so at once, so I did, too. We removed our outer clothing and left it there, as well.

Gudrun brought us to a bench. "Sit here by the table," she suggested. I had never seen a bench such as this, which was made of wood planks like the boat. I lowered myself as gracefully as possible to the bench. The planked object taller than my knees must be a table, I thought. Halvard sat down beside me. Gudrun bent to pull a heavy black cover from a steaming pot hanging over an oil stove. She spooned food into a bowl for Halvard and placed it before him on the table. He snagged up a piece of meat with two fingers and popped it into his mouth while Gudrun portioned out the rest.

"Have you not brought your spoon with you, Halvard?" Gudrun asked.

"I seem to have lost it," he answered, grinning meekly.

"Here," she said, and handed him a small ladle hanging from a hooked shelf of the thick stone wall. "Here is one for Astrid, too."

I used my spoon as Halvard did, blowing my meat carefully, dipping the spoon for broth, rather than sipping it from the bowl. "What meat is this?" I asked her curiously.

"It's mutton," she replied. "Take all you want; there's plenty. Here's a mug of water to wash it down." The meat tasted like boiled caribou. I licked the juices off my fingers and ate until my bowl was empty.

When the meal was over, Thorvald invited Halvard to speak. "It would interest us to know how you fared in the northland and how you found Astrid. We've seen Skraelings with bows, of course, but never any of their women. The woman of Vinland must be different. How did Astrid arrive on our shores without a longship?"

Halvard invited me to speak for myself. I knew I would make mistakes in front of these strangers and I did not want Helga to despise me more for my ignorance. "You tell for me," I suggested. "I cannot say so much."

Halvard described in a few sentences how he was rescued and about his meeting with me. He never made mention of Minik or his magic. "Astrid's country is farther south and west than the Vinland of Leif's Vinlander Saga. The land across the western ocean must be huge, more vast than our Greenland, from how far Astrid traveled. It took nearly a month over the ice. You must remember that no one ever found Vinland again after Leif and his party were overrun by hostiles. Eriksson's men barely escaped to their ships to make the voyage home to Greenland." The family nodded. It seemed everyone here knew about my world, but they considered it too far and the men there too warlike to visit again.

Halvard continued. "Leif Eriksson wrote about the land, how mild their winters were, but he said the Skraelings were too numerous to subdue. Astrid's people have fought against those inhabitants of Vinland, as our people have. She visited a northern country. When they decided to cross the ocean looking for better hunting, she went along with them."

I liked Halvard's way of telling my story. If only it had truly been so simple. "When I found her, I needed a wife. She agreed to come south with me." He made that simple as the rest.

"But how did you talk to the Skraelings, Halvard? Do you speak their language? Why did they not kill you?" Helga demanded.

Thorvald interrupted his daughter's rush of words. "I admit I'd like to know the answers to her questions, but I'd be a poor host to demand more than you are prepared to tell." He refilled Halvard's mug with water.

Halvard took a long swallow. "I don't mind. I learned some of their words from slave boys I used to play with, near my father's steading years ago. The Skraelings who rescued me had never seen white men. Remember, they just arrived in the north wastelands from over the western ocean."

"Did they come so far in those little skin boats?" one boy asked. Before Halvard or I could answer, he added, "How could they have just arrived? The ocean was frozen."

"Their big dogs pulled them on sledges, loaded up with all they needed, their skin boats, too, their stoves, everything."

The family members looked at one another and back to Halvard. "That means," Thorvald said slowly, "that they came over on the ice field. Is it possible to cross the ocean on foot and sledge? How long did it take?"

"It was a long trip!" Halvard exclaimed. "The Vinlander Saga says the ocean is narrower if you sail north first, but still, about a month—on sledges!" He whistled. "Did I mention the ice field melted the day after they arrived?"

When the silence had gone on for several heartbeats, the smaller boy asked, "But how did you talk to the Skraelings with just your few words. How did you ask Astrid to marry you?"

"There is a child, a little Skraeling boy who taught me enough to ask for Astrid. Sammik is as big as you." He looked the boy over. "How old are you?"

"Eight."

Very softly and with wonder, Gudrun said, "You know those people might so easily have killed you, Halvard. How unlikely it is that they lowered a rope and helped you up the cliff, instead of feeding your flesh to their dogs. What possessed you to go into their lands alone?"

Halvard did not seem to object to her question, but his eyes peered into the distance as if looking past the wall. "Sometimes, we have no idea why we do things. I supposed, then, that I simply wanted to see it, but, in fact, the Norns had spun my destiny on their spindle of fate. Their plan for me pulled me north the same way a bird's nature makes it travel when the seasons change."

Gudrun showed us to a small space off the main room. Inside stood a raised bed, shelves, and a curtain to block off the bed from the main room. "You will sleep here," she said. As I thanked her, an Inuit woman came in from the field, carrying vessels on a wooden support over her shoulders. Her sand-colored woven dress covered the woman from her neck to ankle, but she was Inuit as surely as I was Ganeogaono.

Her mouth went slack at the sight of my hide shirt, trousers, and *kamiks*. I think she wanted to speak, but she closed her lips abruptly and made a bobbing motion to the Greenlanders. As soon as she had set down the containers, she escaped.

Helga lifted one of the vessels, poured a white liquid from it into mugs that waited on the hearth, and handed one to each of us. Halvard raised his to his lips, gulping down the contents noisily. I stared at mine and sniffed, forgetting to be polite.

The boys and their sister laughed at me. "Go ahead. Drink. It's only goat milk," Helga explained. "Drink it while it's warm."

"*What* is it? What is *milk*?" I asked.

"Milk. From goat teats." The boy grinned and pointed out the window to one of the beasts he called a goat. He moved his clenched hands as though he were pulling on something.

"Ugh," I exclaimed, realizing at last what he meant. "Are we babies?" I asked in Inuit, pushing the offensive mug away. I wanted to be courteous, but this was too much. How could they drink it? The children laughed at me again, but I had not thought I was making a joke. "She's never tasted animal milk," Halvard explained, as if embarrassed by my behavior.

"Skraelings like milk," Helga interrupted. "The Vinlander Saga says so. They wanted more milk every day. It's in the book."

"*Who* said so? Who is this Vinlander Saga?" I thought they had been speaking of a storyteller.

Her brother lifted something from a shelf. "Here," he said. "This is our copy. Father, read the part about the milk."

I stared at the thing. What new wonder was this? When Thorvald sat on the edge of his bed, his sons and wife climbed up and sat beside him. Helga reclined comfortably on hers to listen, and Halvard pulled the benches closer so all could hear in comfort. Thorvald took both sides of the thing and pulled them apart. The object split down the middle, resting flat across his knees. Both sides contained designs such as those engraved on the hilt of my knife. Thorvald moved his fingers across the marks and turned over some of the sheets while he searched for what his boy called "the part about the milk."

"I had better explain," said Halvard. "The marks are called runes, Astrid." Thorvald searched through the designs while he did his best to make me understand. "Each mark means a sound. When we say the sounds together, they make words. Writing is like speech, to tell histories about people who lived before us. Leif Eriksson wrote this saga so everyone who came afterward would know what happened to him and his people in Vinland. I have a copy in my house. Many Greenlanders keep this history, and several others, as well. We read these stories by firelight to help pass the long winter nights."

All of this was difficult and peculiar. Words in marks? People telling stories without being there? "When did the man go to Vinland?" I asked. That much should not be so confusing.

"Three hundred years ago," Halvard said. I never heard of such a number. I looked to him for a better explanation, but he shrugged. "Many more fingers than are on all the hands in Qisuk's village and the next village, as well."

Thorvald found the place he wanted. "Listen," he said. "I'll read, but I must explain what went before so the milk part will make sense." So saying, he began to talk about longships rowed by adventurers from their motherland, which was called Norway. The adventurers had long names.

"Here is a picture, Astrid. Look!" In the book was such a picture as I could not have imagined to draw. It showed a longboat with a high, wide sail, much wider and taller than Halvard's. The hull of the boat could have contained two companies of a war canoe. Many oars descended from both sides. The prow rose high like the neck of a swan, finishing in a long-snouted monster face overlooking the waves.

Thorvald related how sailors from Norway settled in Iceland, a country with fiery mountains, east of Greenland. They found it a good land with trees, grass, and great amounts of fish in its fjords. Deciding to stay, men cut down the trees to make homes and boats. Their animals thrived on the good meadow grass. "Each man took a piece of land for himself and his family. The Icelandic farmers traded with Norway and life was good, but after some years, Iceland became crowded, and all the best land was taken. Its young men wanted to see what else there was to find across the western ocean.

"Their leader, Leif Eriksson, and his father, Erik the Red, discovered Greenland and decided it was worth settling. They went home to Iceland to tell people of the good pasturage for their flocks. It was true in the early days. Erik led boatloads of settlers west in many longships. When they looked for a good place for their settlement, they discovered Skraelings living here already.

"Leif's brother, whose name was Thorvald, like mine, found men sleeping under their narrow skin boats. The Norsemen killed a couple of them, but one managed to slip away. He returned with more of his kind while the Greenlanders were chopping down trees for house beams. In the fighting that followed, Thorvald and several others were killed. The Norsemen left for a time, but they came back. With iron weapons, they drove the Skraelings to the northern wilderness and the edges of the fjords, where they live to this day." Thorvald's son clapped his hands at the conclusion of this part of the story.

I did not like this at all. It was little wonder the Inuit killed Greendlanders on sight. Halvard was lucky indeed that Qisuk and his villagers did not know of these happenings firsthand.

"You haven't read the part where the Skraelings liked milk," Helga said from her bed.

"Yes, I thought I would tell Astrid the history of our land first. Here's the part you wanted her to hear. I'll put it into easier words. You see, Astrid," he said, turning to me, "someone reported seeing a long coastline farther in the west when a storm blew him off course. That spring, Leif and his friends pointed their longship over the western ocean again.

"The first land they came to was barren, nothing but rocks. They called it Helluland. The next land had so many trees, they called it Markland. Some of those very trees produced the beams of our houses and planks for our boats. Markland had its uses, but it did not provide for our animals, so they continued south. Lastly, Leif and his men found the best land of all, with meadows of grass for our cattle, our goats and sheep. There were few trees, but grapes grew wild. They called this land Vinland, because of the grapes.

"Little snow fell that first winter. When the water was free, Leif sailed his longship home to Greenland to gather settlers as his father had done with the Icelanders. He brought families, along with their sheep and goats, to this mild, good land. The Skraelings of Vinland were friendly at first, trading furs for cloth. The next time, however, they demanded the Greenlanders trade their iron weapons and tools for permission to stay. The Greenlanders refused, knowing they could not survive without their weapons. A few days later, the Skraelings came at them, screaming like demons. They killed several Norsemen. The rest ran for their longship and set sail while the Skraelings loosed arrows at them.

"They tried again, building a settlement south of the first, cutting trees to build houses and clear pasturage for their animals. Skraelings of the same sort as the first came to drive them out. One man's wife thought fast. She milked a goat and offered some to the Skraeling chief, who liked it very well. So milk bought peace, and the Greenlanders stayed the winter.

"By spring, the new Skraelings noticed our iron weapons and tools. When the Greenlanders refused to trade for them, milk was not the peacemaker it had been. Few Greenlander families escaped. Leif returned to Greenland and wrote his saga." He lifted the book. "It has been copied many times and read every winter, so every Greenlander child knows the story." Thorvald looked at his children, who were ready for sleep. He closed the book, returning it lovingly to its special place on the shelf.

"Vinland has never been found again. That is why it seems a land of legend now. Good night, Astrid of Vinland. Sleep well."

We thanked Thorvald for the story and Gudrun for the food and hospitality. The story had given me very much to think about. Finally, I knew how a Greenlandic knife came to be in the possession of the Algonquin storyteller. When it came to her, it must have been old, seldom used, and handed down carefully through the many generations since the Algonquin drove the Norsemen away.

It must have been kept as Greenlanders keep books, to be taken out to remind them of the events of a battle and a strange people with foreign weapons. They told it from the opposite point of view, so each new generation would remember how they bravely drove away the invaders. Perhaps the storyteller woman considered it lucky, since her ancestor had taken it from them. After thinking this over, I decided to hate the Algonquin a little less. Except for those who invaded my home, and Hawk Feather, none had actually done me harm. The storyteller woman had made it possible for me to escape. I realized, finally, why she had given me the knife.

"Sleep now." Gudrun rose to usher us to our bed closet.

Thorvald stopped her. "First, Halvard must give thanks to Jesus for his safe return." He pointed to a small carving of a man stretched onto an open mast. I walked to the wall to look closer. Curious as I felt about the meaning of this odd object, I was interested in the workmanship. An Inuit child could have carved it better. Halvard had not followed me, but stood rooted to the ground.

"Are you not Christians?" Helga asked.

"Astrid has her own gods and my father is Odin's high priest. He speaks to the god for those Greenlanders who are still faithful."

Something awkward hung in the room like black smoke from an ill-trimmed wick. I, however, had a larger concern. I whispered into Gudrun's ear.

"Follow the path behind the house. You'll smell the place."

Things seemed to have returned to normal by the time I let myself back into the house and found my way to the bed closet Gudrun and Thorvald had assigned us. The mysteries of the dusky night and the words in the book washed through my sleep like lapping waves. It was the first time a vivid dream had come to me in many moons of time.

I found myself in a canoe made of birch bark, paddling through the dark waters of a tree-shaded stream. The spicy scent of earth, moss, and ferns thinned when the close banks drew apart to become a river. Shadows of people paddled war canoes on the river, enough to turn the river black with them. They paddled through the water, hurrying to escape their mortal enemies. I felt no fear of capture, but I feared the shadows in the canoes beside me. When I looked west, fog filled the river, rising until it covered the forest.

Splashes of sunlight peeked through the fog, exposing maples, oaks, and elms. Moose swam through the river, but no man hunted. The river became a bay and then widened until it reached the ocean.

The shapes beside me were no longer feared or hated. They had changed again and become the shapes of Inuit in their hooded, fur-lined anoraks. The boats, no longer canoes, had become umiaks. The last hump of land disappeared. The ocean rolled and its briny mist filled my nose and eyes. Our faith-keepers tell us there is a message hidden in vivid dreams, but I could not discern what my dream meant to tell me. Qisuk's villagers crossed the ice field in winter with dog sledges, not in boats.

In the dream, the sun and the moon were two bright eyes in the blue summer sky. There was an enormous cloud resting on the waves. As we approached, the cloud became an ice mountain, blue and white. Shadows created a woman's face with deep-set eyes and a jagged nose. Below the icy head hung pendulous breasts that touched and descended below the surface of the ocean. The rest of her body remained below the surface.

I heard the name Nerrivik in the chanting. Sea Woman's face glistened benevolently at those of us who passed over her domain. In my relief, I reached out my hands to her, thanking her for her bounty and care, when, suddenly, I returned to the semidark bed closet. My breath came too fast and my pulse beat a tom-tom in my ears.

"What is it, Astrid? What woke you?"

I shook my head, not knowing how to explain in his language. I did not know the word for *dream* or if Halvard's people understood the significance of dreams. This was not the time for a discussion. "Sleep," I suggested. "Shh." I needed to discover the remainder of the message. In my half sleep, I tried to return to the place of my vision. Sea Woman, Nerrivik, Sea Woman. Please come back. Tell me what you wish me to know, I implored.

The clouds changed again and the wind blew harshly. Nerrivik's mouth opened like a cave. Winter wailed forth in white sheets of cold, but not upon us. We, who rode in walrus-hide umiaks, knew her power and deferred to it. Waves of wind billowed icy gusts against the land. Sea Woman had gathered her fury. She had seen and remembered every slight to her people. Then, I knew the Inuit would have their land returned to them again. The last of the prophesy faded, but, before the dream ended, I remember wondering what would happen to the Greenlanders. Would my beloved Halvard survive?

I awoke before anyone else was stirring. Halvard slept too deeply to hear me rise this time. Thinking that his family must not see me as an enemy when we arrived at his steading, I decided to put off my Inuit clothing and change into my Naskapi dress and leggings. I did so, barely making a sound. Then, stealthily, I crept from the house, shutting the door soundlessly behind me.

The sun hung low just over the inland mountains, casting deep shadows down toward the fjord. I returned from the privy, to see the Inuit woman waiting outside her hut, as if she had summoned me to come to her. "Who are you and what are you?" she asked me in Inuit. "You are not one of theirs. Though you wore the clothing of our people yesterday, neither are you one of us."

I answered in her tongue. "You speak true. I lived with the Inuit for four seasons and learned your speech. When the village grew too large, we crossed the ice field on sledges from our western islands. This is the clothing of my own people who live on the mainland." She stared at my beautiful Naskapi dress and leggings and at my small moccasins.

"You are more of a stranger than I supposed," she said.

"Yes," I admitted. "But, I have a friend-sister in a northern village. My husband is friend-brother to the headman there."

The men of her house had slipped outside and now sat beside her, crossing their legs and listening. "He is my man, and he, my brother," she said, pointing. I nodded but did not lower my eyes.

"I am called Mikisoq in Inuit, Astrid in Norse. I come from the western land where tobacco grows. It is over the western ocean."

The woman put a hand to her mouth. "I have heard of your country! Who can believe it is possible to make such a journey?"

"I came with the Inuit, to whom anything is possible," I said. I believed it to be true and still do. All of them nodded at that.

"I am called Oona," the woman told me. "Tell me how you came to be living with a Qallunuk."

"Halvard, my husband, was lost and in danger. The Inuit of my village rescued him from the flood. They had never seen Qallunaat and did not know their ways and their crimes, having always lived in the west. The village *angakkoq* said I must leave with this one." I stopped, waiting for her to speak, but she looked to her men, who scratched their heads at this unusual tale. "Now, you know who I am and why I am here. Why do you serve Qallunaat?"

Oona told me they had been captured when they were children. Greenlanders had killed their parents. They had been traded to the owners of this farmstead for a horse. I did not know what she meant. "An animal for riding on. We were too young to run back, too young to survive alone. Now, we have been away so long, they would not take us back."

I wanted to say something but did not know what. This was wrong, that they accepted their servitude. Oona spoke again. "It's all right. Thorvald and Gudrun are good masters. Do you know you carry a female child inside?"

"I do?" The suddenness of this revelation stunned me, so that I squeaked out, "How can you know that?" I had not missed even one moon flow.

"My father was an *angakkoq*. Some of his seeing power came to me in my blood. Sometimes, I know things that will happen. I feel your daughter's presence. It is strong. She will live long and be a comfort to you."

I thanked her for her prediction.

Oona's two boys came up to me before I could say more, feeling the soft leather and fringe of my dress. The smallest tried to taste the colored porcupine quills sewn into the sleeves and shoulders. "We call the boys Han and Kettil. Han is oldest. They are both curious about your dress. It is tanned in a way I do not know. It's pretty."

"Thank you. We smoke the leather over dampened wood fire to make it strong and watertight. That and twisting, pulling, and washing make it supple." I complimented her on her sons, expressing hope that they would become good hunters. The boys stared at me blankly and turned to their mother, who translated my words into Norse. "How can they not know their own language?" I asked.

"We speak in Norse to them," Oona confided. "Before they are men, they must learn to live as the Big Eyebrow people live. They will dress and speak like Greenlanders, and when they are grown, perhaps they won't be slaves."

I didn't believe it. My voice had deepened and the words seemed not to be the ones I intended to speak. I did not know what was happening. "Teach your sons to speak like true men speak, like Inuit," I charged her, as well as her husband and brother, who had listened to all our conversation without speaking.

Oona's husband spoke up at last. "Who is this Tobacco Grower to tell us how to raise our sons?"

I looked into his face. Something he saw in mine made him waver. "I tell you this because this land will return to its first owners again when your sons are grown. Teach them to hunt like Inuit. The next winters will be long, and so cold that the Greenlanders will die or go away, back to their old lands. All this will be left to you as it was before they came." Although these people and their stone hut were close enough to touch, I looked down at them as though they were far beneath me and small. Everything seemed to swim for a moment. I felt giddy. Then abruptly, I returned to where I had been, on the bench before a small hut with an Inuit family who looked at me with a mixture of awe and disbelief.

Oona backed away from me as though I were possessed. Perhaps she was not wrong. "What are you saying? How can such a thing come to pass?"

"I don't know, but Nerrivik said it! She was here. Didn't you feel her power? She frightened me." I reached out to lean one arm against the hut.

The men had sunk to their knees. "But *you* said the words!" They exchanged a meaningful look and returned their attention to me. "Will she do this wonderful thing for us? How many winters will it take?" Oona demanded.

"I don't know. I don't know anything." Suddenly, my knees weakened. Had I been speaking nonsense? What had I said? The words still echoed in my head, something about winter destroying the Greenlanders. It was what I had seen in my dream. Now, Nerrivik spoke through me to warn the Inuit!

The people backed away from me, as frightened as I had been myself by the strange experience. "Let me return to the house. They will be looking for me." Shaken, I ran all the way back, afraid to look behind me.

When I returned, Halvard sat awake in the bed closet, yawning and watching for me. "It's almost time we were on our way," he said. "Gudrun is a good hostess. In spite of our differences, they have both shown us hospitality. I think they will give us something to eat before we go."

Gudrun came up to me, smiling. "You were outside a long while, Astrid. What an interesting dress! It is so different." She felt the quills on my shoulders and gestured to the fringe at the seams. "Is this something special you brought with you from your home?"

"Yes," I replied weakly. "It is something special to me."

"Before you go down to your boat, eat some sour milk. It set so nicely during the night. See how well it lumps? It will strengthen you for your journey home. Now that you will be living here, you must learn to eat like a Greenlander."

I had eaten worse in my travels. I took the bowl and spoon from her hand, nodding my thanks before I spooned up the horrid mess.

Chapter 30

The sun rose above the ice cap, illuminating the meadow and home field in rays of brightness. Helga Thorvaldsdottir and her brothers managed to be out of the house when we were leaving, but Gudrun and Thorvald walked us to the path. "A good summer to you, Halvard Gunnarson and Astrid Vinlander," Thorvald said. Gudrun added, "Good luck," a phrase I had learned to understand. We thanked them both for their kindness to us and wished them the same.

Our visit had been good, in that we had learned better how our union might be approached by Greenlanders and how best to counter inevitable questions. We descended the steep path to the landing and Halvard's boat. I meant to tell Halvard about the strange thing that had happened while I spoke to the slaves. It had all seemed dreamlike, part of the dream that had come in the night. Both held urgency. I couldn't doubt Oona's prophesy that I was pregnant with my second daughter, but I wished I had been able to understand the rest.

Had Nerrivik put words in my head to speak? I had heard them with as much amazement as the Inuit servants. I felt sorry for Oona's sons, Han and Kettil, and hoped that she and her husband would teach them Inuit speech. I was more sure than they that the boys would never be accepted as other than servants, at least not as long as Halvard's people remained on the land. That led to more worries.

Halfway down to the water, we entered into a white mist so thick, we could barely see each other. Halvard walked first, feeling ahead with his staff. Cold gray water slapped against the boat's wooden hull while swirls of fog clouded both banks. Halvard said fog was common in early summer, when the cold of night gave way to the day's warmth.

The damp salt smell of the fog extended around us like cold fingers. I could hardly see Halvard. "Is it safe to leave?" I asked.

"We are near the ocean. The fog will rise farther inland when the water warms." He took the bundles from me and tied them down into the boat. "I'd best row until we can see better."

We listened for the splash of other boats, since we could make out little through the gloom. Halvard peered intently into the gray mist that swirled about us. As Halvard predicted, the fog began to thin as we progressed. "You will see your home soon?" I ventured cautiously, hoping he might continue the topic and warn me what to expect. How would his boys react to a new wife replacing their mother when she had so recently died?

"Very soon," he repeated somewhat absently. A single green-tipped feather floated down from the sky and landed on the pale water beside the boat. The current caught the feather, pushing it along with bits of driftwood into a vortex, where it spun until it disappeared behind us in the misty ripples.

A faint thump repeated at intervals, sounding like the beat of a distant tom-tom. The sound snatched my attention from the fjord. I lifted my head. The rising fog still shrouded both banks. It magnified and confused the sound, so I could not pinpoint its location. "What is that?"

Halvard looked around, straining to see. With each thump, the booms became louder and closer. "It sounds like a longship's rhythm drum," he said. "This year's trade ship from Norway must be arriving. If I'm right, we'll see it soon. It will have to pass us on its way to the cathedral at Gardar. We'd best keep close to shore." As he spoke, he adjusted his oars to redirect our course, pulling us toward the rocky strand on the bank.

There were too many new words. I chose the first to ask about. "What does a rhythm drum do on the longship?"

"The rowers pull to the beat so the boat rides smoothly. I'm surprised they are sailing in this weather. They must be in a hurry to make their trades and get home again before winter. They'll have a sail, too, much bigger than ours. You saw a picture of a Viking longship last night in Thorvald's book. Now you'll see a real merchant longship."

I understood the idea of copying what I could see and drawing what I could imagine. My own pictures had amazed the Naskapi, but the pictures in the Vinlander Saga book were like nothing I could have imagined. The sails were decorated with vivid colors, and the hull of the boat was lined with a thin yellow metal Halvard called "gold." I remembered the picture. The longship's prow rose like a serpent facing forward, but it curled, whereas the ship in the picture had a face with open jaws. "Will this longship bring warriors?" I asked.

"Not quite. The dragon head was to frighten enemies. This will be a steady merchant ship coming to trade. It's rowed by sailors, not fighting men. They will have wood beams and iron for our farmers, and perhaps more settlers. In trade, we will give them codfish and woolens. Greenlanders haven't been Vikings for many years. We are farmers and fishermen."

"Vikings?" Were they a different tribe? How could he know they were not returning? Halvard tried to explain his answer in easier terms, but he soon gave up. Fragments of speech and the sound of creaking oars drifted over the gray water, and then the hazy boat appeared out of a patch of fog. High above the deck, a thick mast, tall as an ancient fir tree, carried a taut square of red-and-white-striped cloth that was almost as tall as itself. The sail billowed square and wide. The fresh wind hurried the great ship over the wavelets. From midway down the ship's side, two lines of oars worked like a many-legged insect.

The prow approached from the rising mist, cleaving the water as the longship glided down the center of the fjord. Its oars pushed the water behind, creating a wake. Halvard's boat was like a cygnet bobbing in the wake of its mother, the swan.

"Where did such a tree grow that made that mast?" I asked, looking up to where it disappeared in the lifting white swirls of the remaining mist. We had passed no trees as yet in our travels.

"In Norway or Iceland, our countries in the east. You won't see any such tree on this Greenland of ours. Merchant ships used to sail to Markland in the west, near your world, to bring us lumber, but that was long ago. It's too bad no ships sail west now. Lumber is worth more than gold to us."

The longship's oars reached out and pushed the water behind it. Its broad side drew even with us, wide and deep as a longhouse. The sun came through the clouds and lit the mast and sail. A man, who stood in a basket lashed against the giant mast, spotted us in our boat against the bank. He called to the other men and pointed. Several men ran to the side rail to stare down at us. I kept low, as I did not care to be noticed by a boatload of men.

Halvard pushed his oar against the granite cliff and unfurled his sail when we reached the current. The sun brightened and glimmered off the water. Although we did not come close to the longship's wake, we sailed close enough to hear the voices on board. Two dark-robed passengers stood by the stern rail, looking back at us. Gold necklaces in the shape of two crossed bars suspended by thick chains gleamed upon the dark cloth of their robes. The taller man stretched out his arm from his hanging sleeve to point at us with one long finger. The second man pushed back his hood and leaned over for a better look.

"Halvard!" I cried, disturbed at what I saw. "They have young faces but old heads. Look, no hair on top!"

"Jesus priests!" he said, his voice tinged with anger and resentment. "We don't need more of them. We need wood and spears!"

I looked toward the men again, trying to discern if they were evil, as Halvard seemed to think. Aside from the bald circles, one man's hair was ash brown and straight, the other's blond. He squinted at us. "The taller man's eyes are old, too." He was too distant to do us harm, but my neck hairs rose at his scrutiny.

The wind carried their voices over the water. "That must be a Skrael-ing, Poul," said the yellow-haired man. "I didn't expect to find one so close to settled land. Our reports say they live among the seals and the white bears along the ocean and the northern fjords."

A scowl marred the face of the squint-eyed one. "I thought they wore furs, not cured hides. It looks like a woman, although it's hard to be sure. Imagine Skraelings in their native clothing sailing up our fjord, free as birds. It's a blessing we were ordered here to help our bishop. He grows old to govern this parish, if this is a sign of it. Skraelings in Norwegian land!" I heard the disapproval in his voice. They continued speaking, but as they drew further ahead, their words no longer carried back to us.

"It is as the fisherman said," Halvard said. "The king sent more priests to strengthen his bishop. Soon, the last of our freedom will be gone." Not taking his eyes from them, he leaned closer to me. "My father leads us in prayer and sacrifices to the gods of our fathers. Keep far from men such as those you just saw. They will take your spirit and try to own it like men own slaves." He used signs and words to make sure I understood, as most of what I heard was meaningless to me.

Halvard pointed to the longship. We watched it disappear behind an is-land, until even the sail was lost to view. "They'll sail south, then north again at Eriksfjord. We follow the same route. We'll see the longship again before we get to my house. The captain will have his goods unloaded at Gardar's landing, by the cathedral. We have to pass it." Again, his words left me behind. He wanted what was in the longship, but the place it would go, the cathedral, whatever that was, brought a grimace to his face. Halvard talked all the time, like Sammik. Perhaps if I listened hard enough, the words would come clear.

When we reached Gardar's landing, the longship's striped sail had been rolled tightly to the mast's crossbar. A horde of men swarmed from the land and crossed a plank up to the deck. The men worked like ants, unloading and returning empty-handed to fetch more, carrying beams of wood. Many dark-robed men stood at the side of the lines. They shouted directions to the workers to take this or that first and march with it where they were bid. "So many priests," I murmured to Halvard, assuming all men dressed thusly were priests.

"Far too many," he agreed. "And yet they bring more."

The hill was dominated by a tall stone and wood structure. Smaller buildings clustered around the massive one. Halvard noted my face as I stared in amazement at the enormous building. It was like three longhouses piled on top of one another. "That's their cathedral, king of churches," Halvard said. "It's where Christians hold their rituals. Take a good look. If you're lucky, you won't have to see it again."

We sailed past the moored longship and the cathedral. Herds of animals grazed in green-walled fields. Some of the animals were different from those I had seen before, much larger. Halvard told me their names: cattle, horses. "Their sheep and goats will be up with the herdsmen in the high meadows. In late summer, men will cut and dry the hay in their fields. This will feed their stock through the winter. We have to do so for my animals, too. My father is too old and my sons too young to help much. It's time I was back. There is work to do at my homestead, repairs I should have done sooner. I can't wait to see their faces again. It will be good to get home, Astrid."

After the fields, a shimmering blue lake sparkled in the sun. "Look ahead. Those are my hills, there on the right, in the shadows of the far hill, just before the fjord splits again. I can almost see my house." His excitement almost overshadowed my apprehension.

We sailed past more houses, each with its own surrounding land. I kept my thoughts to myself, but I wondered how people could live so apart from one another like this. Not to have villages or towns would make each family easy prey for enemies.

Halvard furled his sail and rowed us the final distance. He slipped the rope loop over one of the rocks below his hill and we climbed out. "Only take your pack, Astrid," he said. "I'll come down for the rest with my sons while you get acquainted with my father." Heaving our packs to our shoulders one last time, we climbed the slope. No animals grazed in the fields as we crossed them, and no dogs barked out a welcome.

Halvard's home was small compared to Thorvald's, a low house of chipped stones fitted together in straight lines. The turf-covered roof hung almost to the ground on both sides. A pen for his animals leaned against the house, but no hoofprints pressed the grass. No smoke came from the smoke hole. It reminded me of the ghost village of Qisuk's grandfathers. Halvard had been gone for more than two moon cycles.

It was too quiet. Halvard must have felt the silence of our arrival more profoundly than I. He gestured toward the high meadows with a casual wave of his hand. "The boys took the dogs," he explained too loudly. "They're away grazing the sheep. My father let the fire go out; it's too warm for a fire today."

The wind blew through the long sedges, exposing the pale underside of each patch of grass. A gull winged by, flapping to catch up with its mate on a current of wind. Together, the pair flew, gliding easily to the other side of the fjord. "Leif, Ole! Father!" Halvard called. "Where are you?" The dark-planked door remained closed. He pounded the rest of the way to the house and pushed open the door. It creaked on iron hinges into blackness.

Halvard rushed inside, his wide shoulders almost touching both sides of the narrow door. I followed him. It was too dark to see inside, and the house smelled musty. In a moment, Halvard had pulled away curtains of hide that shuttered the windows. Rays of light slanted into the room, illuminating each empty corner. With a moan, Halvard knelt by an empty bed closet.

The house was deserted; even the bed closets were bare of furs and blankets. "What happened here? My tools are all taken." He paced back and forth, mumbling his sons' and father's names as if he could make them appear out of the empty air.

Fear for Halvard clutched at me, but I forced myself to reason out what might explain his family's absence. Anything might have happened to them while he searched for oblivion or adventure in the north. I took both Halvard's hands and clasped them firmly in mine, willing calm into him. "Who would take them and all your belongings?"

"Skraelings, of course, in a raid. They come in their skin boats for children. My father is too frail to defend my boys from them." This sounded backward, from all I had heard from Oona, but I let that go. I had to help my husband.

"There is no sign of a struggle. Your father's body is not here, and the animals are gone. If the Inuit killed them, there would be blood. If they drove them away, a few of the beasts might have returned, but there are none." I did not know if this meant anything, but I tried to put the picture together from all the parts, especially the parts that were missing.

Halvard took a deep breath, as if he were preparing to dive underwater. He let it out slowly. "Say what you think."

It took more words than I knew. I used hand signing to help me, but I feared Halvard did not understand. He watched and listened carefully as I said, "Your family thinks you died in the north. Your father is too old and your sons too young to care for themselves and your animals, so they took everything from your house and went to ask someone for shelter. People will know what became of them. We must ask."

"You are right," he said. "We'll find them at Osmund's steading. That's what my father would decide to do. Minik spoke truly when he said to take you home with me. I needed you." He pulled me into a close embrace and kissed my nose. His eyes were less troubled when he pulled back, with hope in them, when there was none before.

Chapter 31

I hoped my guess was right, for I had no other idea. Halvard dragged the door shut behind us. "Which way? Water or land?" I asked.

"Land." The trail led between fields and over a hill. We strode at a half run, splashing across a shallow stream. Down a gentle slope stood another house, this one with a line of smoke rising above the roof. Sheep bleated in the meadow above the house and children played tag in the home field. They had not noticed us on the rise, looking down at them. Halvard raised a cautionary hand. "Thank Odin, there they are! Wait here for them to see us. I don't want to frighten them."

A long-skirted woman with braided light brown hair walked back and forth before the door, twirling something. The man worked on top of the house, throwing down the old sod roofing. A pale-haired boy of about twelve lifted the sod and stacked it into a pile nearby. A dog barked, its muzzle pointing up the hill. The woman paused and glanced our way. With a shrill cry, she dropped the thing that was in her hands and screamed.

The man looked. "Halvard!" he yelled. He slid down off the roof and ran to alert the children. Two of them, boys with flame-colored hair, stopped their game to peer up the hill.

"Father?" The dog's snarls turned into bays of welcome. Leaving me alone, Halvard ran down. One of the red-haired boys separated himself from the others, shading his eyes. "Grandfather! Hurry outside and look!" he called into the house. "Father is back! He came home to us!" The boy skipped up the hill like one of the goats, racing toward Halvard.

Halvard knelt and the child threw himself into his father's outstretched arms to be lifted up in a fierce hug. "Leif, I missed you so much." The bigger boy ran up after his brother, long red hair flying behind him. He stopped short when he saw me. Halvard set Leif down and turned to his other son. "Ole! Let's go down to your grandfather and our friends." He went to hug his older son, who shrugged out of his father's embrace and backed away.

"Who is *she?*" the older boy demanded angrily.

"I'll tell you about her soon, when we're all together. Don't be angry at me for being away." Halvard ran down the hill and clasped his father in a bear hug. I descended most of the way, enough to see and hear, but not too close. A person did not enter a town or village without being invited.

"The house was empty," Halvard said, pulling back to look at his father. The bent gray-bearded man stepped back from Halvard slowly, using a staff. Deep hollows cut into his cheeks and under his eyes. He leveled his chin at Halvard, saying, "When Osmund brought us meat from the hunt, the seals you killed, he told us you went exploring the northern wilds alone. I did not expect to see you again. Only a man who wants to die goes into enemy lands alone."

"I needed time to be by myself. You know why."

"Your sons depended on you. You had no right." His voice was reedy, but I could imagine it strong as it once had been.

Halvard shrunk at the rebuke, not arguing. I had thought the same thing many times since I learned that he had sons. "Enough! You are right. I should not have done what I did. The Skraelings might have killed me, but they helped me instead. They allowed me to go home, and with gifts." I waited, neither moving nor speaking, for Halvard to tell them about me and for someone to invite me to come down the hill and join them.

"It doesn't matter. Nothing matters except that he's home again, at last," the younger boy exclaimed, pulling Halvard down and kissing his father's cheeks loudly. "Grandfather, stop being angry. I don't care where he went, as long as he's back. We can go home again. Shall I cut our animals out of the herd?"

"Soon, Leif." Halvard beckoned to me at last. "Come here to me, Astrid." When I approached, he took my hand and led me down to the others. His neighbors' children stared at my unfamiliar clothing. One was a girl I guessed to be eleven or twelve. I was no more than three or four years older than she, but I was a woman. "Stay close," Halvard whispered. Curious looks bored into us.

"All of you, this is Astrid, whom I found in the north country and

brought to stay with us. Ole is my elder son, and Leif is the younger." I inclined my head. Leif made no sound, neither of welcome nor anything
else. Ole's lips pressed closed in an angry line. "This, of course, is my father, Gunnar."

"Gunnar," I said. The old man did not speak, although he raised a questioning eyebrow when Halvard said my name.

"This is Osmund," Halvard said, embracing his neighbor. I repeated the
name, hoping I would remember. Norse names sounded strange to me and
I had not yet begun to know men's names from women's. "This is Birgitta."
The woman lowered her eyes, enough to acknowledge that we had been
named to each other, but no more. She looked more at my foreign clothing than at my face. I nearly wondered if this was the usual Greenlander
courtesy, not to look into a person's face, although that had not stopped
others from staring at me.

"Thank you both for taking in my family, Osmund, Birgitta. I owe you
more thanks than I can repay. If there is ever anything I can do for you,
name it and I will do my best."

Halvard seemed about to turn away when Osmund said, "In that case,
don't leave yet. Take some milk with us and stop making us guess what is
going on. You've been gone so long, another short while won't matter. I
hope the north cured you of your melancholy."

Osmund gazed at me squarely. "Where is Astrid from? She doesn't look
like the others. Her clothing is like none I've ever seen. Tell us, Halvard."

"Yes," repeated Gunnar, his mouth set. "Tell us."

Halvard closed his eyes painfully for a moment. "I wanted to explain
this slowly to my family at home, but all right. I got myself trapped on a
cliff when the sea ice broke up. Skraelings pulled me up the cliff and took
me to their village, not realizing their people and ours are enemies. They
had just come over the ice by dog sledge from the west, across the ocean
north of Markland."

"That's incredible," Osmund said. He had allowed himself to be distracted from the first question. "But what was this girl doing with them?"

"Her country is west of Vinland. That part of the story is confused.
She'll tell me more about that when she can speak our language better. As
far as the Skraelings were concerned, we were both strangers. Their holy
man told me to take her, so I did. That's all."

They seemed partially satisfied, perhaps enough to let us go. Leif sidled
up and clung to his father's hands as if the wind might blow Halvard away
again.

Birgitta said, "The rest can wait, Osmund. They've only just arrived. Halvard, wait while I bring out some cheese and fresh milk so you can wet your throats. Don't say another word until I get back. Come help me, Ludmilla." The girl followed her mother into the house.

Birgitta emerged several moments later with a board of cheese. The girl held a pitcher and several mugs. As she poured milk into mine, she said, "I'm Ludmilla. Are you a real Vinlander? Can you speak?"

She meant in Norse. I answered the last question first. "Yes, a little. Halvard says my land is near Vinland."

He interrupted to explain better. "Well, Vinland is our name for it. Her people have their own names for their countries. Astrid says her land has trees, and grapes grow there, too."

Osmund spoke. "Well, it is amazing to see a Vinlander here. No one thought to lay eyes on one, here on our side of the world. How did she get a Norse name? Why was she with Skraelings if her home was west of Vinland?"

"Until she can speak better and tell me, I don't know. I gave her the name, and it is a good name." He was ready to leave and had turned to speak to his sons, when Gunnar turned to me.

"Welcome, Astrid. We can surely use a servant," he said. Dismay filled me and I backed away from the old man.

"I have not finished explaining," Halvard said at once. "Father. All of you. I didn't bring Astrid home to be our servant. She's my wife."

I lifted my head. Gunnar had turned his back on Halvard, and Leif screamed out his disbelief.

"Is this a joke?" Osmund asked.

Ole raised his eyes to his father first, then looked past him to me. He drew himself to his full height, breathing hard and fast. His voice emerged shakily at first, but he gathered it into a snarl. "Grandfather said you lost part of your mind when my mother died. Now you tell us you took a Skraeling to be your wife and gave my grandmother's name to her. You should have stayed in the north." His feet pounded the grass through the field and continued up the opposite slope until he was out of sight.

"Father, it can't be true," Leif pleaded. "How could you do it?"

"Halvard! By all the gods! Sigrun is hardly cold under her burial mound!"

Halvard withdrew my gift knife from its sheath. "Look at this!" he demanded. "If you think I was wrong to bring her, look at this. Go on! It will convince you the gods sent her to us. Astrid brought it with her from the land of her enemies, the Skraelings who enslaved her. She escaped them and ran north to live with the people who crossed the ice."

He handed the knife to his father, ivory hilt first. Gunnar took it, squinted over the marks carved there, and looked up at me. "By Odin's lost eye!" Gunnar shouted. "Look at what the runes spell out! This must have been one of our ancestors who lost it there." For a long pause, he said nothing, turning the knife over and over.

He handed the knife back to Halvard and walked toward me. My people taught me to honor elders. With an outstretched hand, he beckoned me closer, his gnarled fingers bent and fluttering. "Come to me, Astrid," he said. It was the softening of his voice that drew me to go to him. His wide mustaches looked like walrus tusks. "Astrid," he said, as if tasting the name. "Did my son tell you he gave you my wife's name?"

"If you are angry, I will ask Halvard for another," I offered.

"No, don't. Please forgive us for our thoughtless words." I looked at him, saying nothing, trying to comprehend. "We were wrong. It will be good to have another Astrid in the house again after so long." He held out one hand to me. I took it, finding his grip stronger than I had expected. "Give me the knife," he requested, holding out his hand for it. Halvard gave it to him again.

He indicated the design on the knife's ivory hilt to me. "Do you know what these runes mean?"

"Halvard says the design makes a name."

He traced them with his forefinger. "The runes spell out my forefather's name. Now I understand why the gods sent Halvard north to find you. The name written here is Ole, his name, and my grandson's, too, who was called Ole after him. One of my ancestors sailed to Vinland with Leif Eriksson. It is said his knife was the only iron knife the Skraelings captured in their attack. There were a few axes, too, left in their heads. The Norns gave us a puzzle to figure out, teasing us with missing pieces. Now, it all fits together. Our fate has been sewn into the threads of our lives. Take back your knife."

I could not understand what he said then about these creatures called Norns. I learned much later, after I could speak and understand better, that the Norns are three sky sisters who spin out the destinies of humans on their distaff like yarn. They measure the length of our years and cut the threads when our time is over. Gunnar nodded to both of us and stretched out his arms to us, smiling. Halvard had told me his father was a priest who could see these things. It appeared the spirits of my world, the Inuit's, and Halvard's had conspired to bring us together.

Halvard reached for my hand and pulled me to him. I leaned my head against his shoulder. Gunnar said to Osmund and Birgitta, "Odin's blessings upon you for what you have done for us while my son was healing from his melancholy. Halvard, don't fear for your elder son. Tend to your wife and her needs. I will explain it to Ole when he comes back, so that he will understand. Leif, go ahead and separate our animals from the herd. We're ready to go home."

Chapter

Gunnar and Halvard unloaded Osmund's pony cart of all their belongings. The cart moving on circular wooden disks was another one of the miracles these Greenlanders commanded. I was still getting over my shock at seeing a pony, an intelligent and strong beast of burden, much bigger than a dog. She had gentle eyes and a patient manner, and she let humans hitch her up like a dog. She resembled neither dog nor deer, but was a new form of creation completely. A different Creator must have thought this sort of beast into existence than He who created the men and creatures of my world. Leif touched my sleeve to get my attention. "It's only a pony pulling a cart," he said. "Come with me, Astrid. We have to do the milking."

He led me over to the low stone-walled enclosure he called a "fold," the place where they had secured the herd. The goats' long ears twitched and their oddly-shaped pupils followed me with what seemed like suspicion. I had trouble remembering the names for these manner of creatures. First were sheep and goats. The sheep were taller and had down-curving horns and long hair. Most of them were female, with young standing beside them. A couple of males, one of each sort, wandered between the herds, sniffing and snorting. Leif pushed them aside, naming the animals for me, ewes and does, rams and bucks. I assumed these were the names the animals responded to as we name dogs, but it turned out they were only the gender names of each sort. It would take me moons of time to keep so much in mind.

Leif explained about milking as we walked, but as my knowledge of his speech had a long way to go, he soon came to understand that showing me was much better than talking. He took what he called a "bucket" from a corner of the fold. "Watch me now." He picked up a handful of fodder, then cornered a ewe and shoved her into a corner. "This is how you milk."

While the animal was distracted with food, he demonstrated, suiting action to words. "Catch one and get your legs over her so she can't move. Bend over her side, curl your hands like this around her teats. Be careful not to get a ram, or you won't get milk." He laughed at his own joke. It took me a moment to figure out what he was saying, but then I laughed also, my anxiety forgotten.

Instead of it being a detriment with Leif, my ignorance of Greenlander skills had become an asset. I was the newcomer, unsure of words and of myself. I had no knowledge what demands my new life would make of me. Even speaking was a challenge. Except for that first moment on the hill above Osmund's steading, I don't think he feared I would try to take his mother's place in his life. That would have been absurd, since I was not old enough by far. Halvard must have been close to thirty, more than twice my age. He would have been married to Leif's mother more than ten years. He could have been *my* father, too. I would be content if his sons came to think of me as their elder sister.

Gunnar helped us carry in the bucket of milk. "It's almost time for sleep," he said as we poured the milk from bucket into bowls already lined up on the stone and wood bench beside the lamps. "This will set overnight and be ready for our breakfast. We should go to bed soon."

Halvard had been staring out the open door. "I'll wash out the bucket and carry it back to the sheepfold for tomorrow's milking," he said. "I want to take a look around. Don't wait up for me."

Gunnar knew exactly what he was thinking. "Ole will come home when he decides he's ready," he said sensibly. "Just like you did." Halvard turned on him for that, but wisely, he said nothing. "Don't stay out there long. You'll have to begin the shearing tomorrow if you want anything to trade. The expected longship drew up at Gardar's quay earlier."

"We saw it," Halvard said softly. "You are right about that as about the other. Go along to bed. It's been a long day for all of us. I have a few things to do outside." He closed the door silently behind him.

I waited beside the lamp, thinking of everything that had occurred since Halvard brought me into his family. Leif and Gunnar had become my allies. Ole saw me as an enemy because his father had taken me for his wife. I could think of nothing I might do that could change that. By the time

Halvard returned, Leif and Gunnar had gone to their beds. "Did you see him?" I asked.

"No," he said, unhappily. "We might as well rest." The sleeping places were laid out as they had been in Thorvald's house, recesses in the walls, with curtains for extra warmth or darkness in summer.

Before Halvard came to bed, he pulled a garment from a leather chest stored under the bed and slipped it on over his head. "We wear these for sleeping," he explained. It was loose and hung a little past his knees. I had never seen a gown for sleeping before. He dug deeper within the chest to retrieve a smaller one for me. The fiber was loose to the touch, napped and blended together, making the material quite soft, like well-worked doe-skin. The sleeping gown must have belonged to his first wife.

"This is wadmal," he whispered in response to my question. "It's felted loose weave to let air through. The boat sail was tightly woven to catch the wind so the wind could push us over the water. That would have been your next question. No more talking. Put this on and come to bed." It seemed odd to change clothing for sleep, but everything seemed odd. I folded my deerskin dress and laid it on the chest next to Halvard's clothing.

I moved over to the wall to make room, but Halvard did not come into the bed. Instead, he sat beside me, his feet on the floor. His breaths came close together. He was alert, listening. I could almost hear his heart beating. He would blame himself if anything happened to Ole out there. I wondered how close wolves prowled to the steadings. They would be tempted by the scent of easy prey. No wonder they closed in the herd for the night, but it concerned me that they left the dog to sleep with them. The dog must be trained not to eat his master's animals. An Inuit dog would have made short work of them.

I could not sleep, either, wondering what my new life held for me. It seemed Halvard was going to sit up until morning, or until Ole came home, whichever came first. He changed positions now and then, crossing a leg, stretching his neck. He was worrying and listening, but finally, his weight shifted. He moved in and stretched out on the soft bedding. "Are you awake?" he whispered. I took his hand and pressed it to my cheek first, then to my lips.

With the tip of his fingers, he felt the side of my eyes, my ear, and the line of my jaw. I turned over on my side, thinking he needed comfort, but I had no words. None were needed. When he closed the distance between us, I forgot everything but the rushing of my blood in my ears, and in more intimate places. It was as easy to slip off the sleeping gown as it had been to slip it on. If it comforted him to lose himself in my body, it gave me comfort, as well.

We were wrapped tightly around each other when the door opened and footsteps sounded lightly across the floor. Halvard lifted his head, exhaling in a vast release of tension before burying his warm lips in my hair again. I was glad he had remembered to draw the curtains.

Before he left our bed in the morning, Halvard said he needed to take Leif and do the milking. I heard Ole speaking with his grandfather in the old man's bed closet. Gunnar's voice came softly from within, his deep voice pitched for closeness. I could not make out the words, but I recognized the higher tones of Ole's sullen complaints and resentment.

I dressed again, went outside to take care of my needs and wash, then returned to the house. I ladled out some of the sour milk for myself. When Ole and Gunnar finally emerged from Gunnar's bed closet, Halvard's father smiled in a friendly way and wished me a good morning. Ole turned to look me over. His shoulders hunched, but his hands were no longer curled quite so tightly. His previous hostility had shifted to resignation.

"Grandfather told me about the knife with my name written on it," he said. "He says you brought it to us all the way from Vinland to return my ancestor's knife to my family." This was not exactly my intention at the time, but if it served to gain me a grudging acceptance, I would not gain say his interpretation or Gunnar's. "My grandfather says he can tell that Odin, king of the gods, sent you to my father's house to live with us." I had learned by then that Odin was Great Spirit to those who worshiped the "old gods."

During his speech, Ole could not or would not look me in the eye. Finally, he lifted his chin to look into my face. I held his gaze for a long moment, searching there for any glimmer of warmth or welcome. There was none. "I shall call you Astrid," he added, "since that's the name my father gave to you." It had been his grandmother's name as well, of course. I wondered if he remembered her and if he resented that I had her name as well as his mother's place with Halvard.

"I shall call you Ole," I replied in response. This was not a welcome on his part, but the terms of our truce. Under the circumstances, however, a truce was preferable to open hostility. With a quick glance over to his grandfather for permission, Ole retrieved his cloak from a wall hook and left the house.

Halvard returned from the sheepfold. While he poured the morning milk from the bucket into the two vats, he said, "We need to prepare cheeses to put away for the cold months. It will last longer than fresh or soured milk." He ladled himself some thickened milk from the bowls set on the hearth the night before. "Father, Astrid has to be shown what to do. People don't make cheese where she comes from, or drink milk, either."

"I know." Gunnar put his hand to his cheek in mock sympathy. "Poor Astrid," he said, commiserating. "You have so much to learn. You might have been happier in the north." My mouth turned down at his words, although he said them sympathetically. Did he, too, not want me? When he added, "But I'm glad you came," he smiled, showing his few remaining yellow teeth. "My son's disposition has improved noticeably."

There had been tasks put off during Halvard's absence that needed his attention now. Halvard spent the mornings of the next several days in his boat, fishing with Leif. The afternoons were given to shearing his sheep with Ole. Gunnar and I wind-dried the fish and prepared cheeses for winter storage.

I came to understand the Greenlanders had names for their days and counted them in a series of seven, which they repeated when the first series ended. Just as each day had a name, so did each month. We had been back a week and a half when Halvard took up several sacks of dried fish and two sacks of cleaned and combed wool. He had given the cart and pony back to Osmund, so with the exception of Gunnar, all of us walked to the cathedral to see if these goods could be traded for beams of wood, or iron pots and tools.

On the way, Halvard pointed out another sort of animal to me. It was called a "cow." We saw a herd of them grazing in the stone-lined fields of the priests, their young ones beside them. Halvard and Ole went forward to greet friends and make trades while Leif and I waited nearby. Many people moved through the small structures around the tall building, working at many of the tasks that were becoming familiar to me. We passed smokehouses, where fish hung to dry over fires of seaweed and damp sod, the former roof coverings. We passed dairies where women and girls worked to make cheese. More stood under porch hangings, working to weave cloth on what Leif called "looms." Others spun yarn and still others cut seaweed, using the sun to light their work.

Leif explained as much as he could, considering my limitations. It was only one moon—month, I corrected myself—since Qisuk had pulled Halvard, tangled in ropes, over the lip of the cliff. My knowledge of Norse speech had improved since our first days together, but it was far from complete.

Boys led in the cows from the stone-lined meadows to the sheltered dairy. Men in brown robes and sandals sat on stools at their sides to milk them. Halvard returned with a new bucket and a sickle. He left them with us and was about to return to the trading, when he saw me staring at the cows' angular rumps and great teats. "Cow milk has different qualities than that of ewes or does. Maybe we can trade for some butter and thick cream." He walked off again.

I looked around, in awe of everything. The male of these huge animals, black-coated and larger even than the cows, was kept in an enclosure of his own. Leif told me this was a bull. I had seen it alone, in a special pen behind the cathedral. His weapons were horns, instead of antlers. The male was nearly the height of an elk, but stouter at shoulder and rump. Men emptied sacks of cut brush and grasses over his enclosure wall. It would take a great deal of grass to fill a body that big. The beast swept this field regularly and warily with his small eyes, even while he ate. Sometimes, he scraped the ground with his front hooves and bellowed indignantly if anyone stepped too close. If there had been another male nearby, his bellow would have been a challenge.

Children shouted and ran about. Carts pulled by ponies like Osmund's gentle female brought up bolts of woven cloth, much finer than I had seen so far. Someone traded for a bull calf from the Norwegian merchant ship, offering two narwhal tusks and dried seal meat. Someone else led a half-grown and muzzled white bear cub by a leash. He made it dance on his hind feet to amuse the crowd. Everyone applauded and guessed at how much it would fetch, saying that the cub was a gift fit for kings. The captain would be unable to resist the beast. The man walked through the crowd, leading his bear. Before we left, he had returned with two bolts of cloth as red as strawberries.

Leif pointed out long lines of boys sitting cross-legged, with ink jars beside them and pointed quills in their hands. They sat away from the crowds and were not interfered with. Men dressed similarly to the Jesus priests walked between the boys, checking over their work. "The men with the short whips are friars, Astrid. Those are poor boys and orphans who were loaned or given to the priests in exchange for food or supplies. The friars teach them to write so they can copy out the priests' books. I can read and write a little, but I wouldn't want to be doing it all my waking day. Other boys scrape and dry the sheepskins into parchment and they use that to copy out the words on."

I was surprised Greenlanders would keep boys of their own in such a lowly status.

Some of the boys were hanging cleaned hides in the sun to dry as the other boys struggled over their copying. "They are allowed to rest and visit their families on Sundays."

It would have pleased me to have such a sheet of parchment to decorate with pictures of all the new animals. I enjoyed drawing pictures for presents or when Great Spirit Orenda urged me, but to be forced to spend their youth hunched over, struggling to make words, seemed worse than working in our cornfields at home. There was no joy in such work and nothing to look forward to but a beating if they made a mistake. I was glad to turn away from the unhappy children and look back to the crowds to watch for Ole and Halvard.

A man walked a long-maned small horse past us, leading it by harness straps on both sides of its long muzzle that fastened behind its neck. I remembered seeing these animals walked off the longship, when Halvard and I sailed past Gardar on our way to his steading. The horse was larger than the pony, with a longer mane, but not as shaggy. The man tied it to the supports of one of the small buildings while he haggled over his trades.

I pulled up some tufts of grass and tried to make friends with the animal. The horse stepped back on her delicate legs, snorting nervously. I made a friendly snort back at her. When she raised her long nose to take a better look at me, I stepped closer to offer her the grass. It amazed me, all over again, how easy these strong beasts were to tame and how they did not fear to be handled by people.

Leif stood by, enjoying my delight. I leaned over the mare's neck, stroking her thick gray coat, her strong shoulders and back. She pressed against my hands like a dog when it wants a scratch. I would not have done so, knowing it belonged to someone, but I wondered what it would be like to climb onto her back and ride her the way several men rode their beasts to the trading grounds, instead of hitching them to carts. I leaned forward, resting my head against her neck and inhaling her sweaty fragrance. I could almost see a picture of myself mounted on this wonderful beast, the two of us, she running free, me holding on with my knees, my hair blown behind me by the wind. Suddenly, the owner strode up and pushed me back. "Get away from my horse, Skraeling!" he shouted angrily.

Although he startled me, I kept my balance and looked around. The crowd parted a little to see what was happening. "I only . . . like her," I began to say, wondering how best to apologize. "I am not taking it," I said in my poor Norse, the words getting confused in my head, as they tended to do when I needed them most. "I only like her."

"She wasn't hurting your mare," Leif said in my defense.

The man ignored him. "I said don't touch what's mine. Who do you belong to anyway? What's a slave girl doing wandering around loose?" He looked around, standing on his toes to look behind me. Several of the Jesus priests and friars, who carried short whips, began striding toward us to investigate the commotion. Other people made way for them.

Fortunately, Halvard and Ole noticed the crowd gathering around me and came running up before anything more could happen. "She was not going to do anything to your horse," Halvard said. He stood almost a head taller than the horse's owner.

"Is that yours?" he half-snarled, pointing to me.

Halvard did not answer. Instead, he turned to me. "Come away, Astrid. Our business here is done." He held out his hand. When I came forward to take it, Ole and Leif closed in on us so we presented a united front to the stranger. Several of Halvard's friends came to stand between the man and us. When I looked back over my shoulder, the man was still standing beside his horse and complaining to anyone who would listen about impertinent Skraelings. Finally, he mounted the mare and rode away in the opposite direction, making his way through the crowd.

We gained a bucket, two wooden roof beams, a black iron pot, a small wood-handled scythe, and a handful of nails. The planks had all been traded for. I was glad to go home, having had my fill of Gardar, its animals and people.

I lacked women's conversation in this house of men, but in some ways, Gunnar made up for what was missing. Since he could not go about easily, he livened up his days by teaching me. He helped with my work, advising and simply talking to me. It helped me hugely to have him listen to my speech and patiently correct me when I said something wrong. One morning, we sat comfortably on the bench outside the door overlooking the home field while the others tended to their work. "Gunnar," I asked, "what do you use for your cereal?"

"What do I use for what?"

"To eat. Like sour milk, but . . ." I tried to explain cereal, but I could not think how to convey what I meant without knowing the words. I asked him instead about Greenlander foods, hoping he would mention it. "You have meat and milk, sour milk and cheese, but no cereal." He continued to look at me blankly. "It grows like grass. We cook." I gave up and looked for something to use for a surface so I could draw a picture for him.

It did no good. He knew nothing about corn or even lake-grass seeds like those the Naskapi cracked over their fires and later winnowed, ground, and cooked in water. No seeds were harvested and nothing was planted. Tall grasses grew near the banks of the fjord, but no one planted them. Did they harvest their seeds when they were ready, to make into cereal for winter?

I had learned of most Greenlander foods by then. Berries were added to the milk. Herbs and shallow roots were sometimes cooked with the meat or fish. I gathered fragrant leaves to simmer for tea, but aside from meat and fish, I ate clumped sour milk and cheese for breakfast, as the others did. It seemed this was all they had to eat.

The next day, I walked in the hills with snares for catching ptarmigan and puffins, the common birds that nested in the back hills. Their meat was good, a welcome change from sheep and goat. Gunnar advised me to put on Sigrun's dresses and boots when I wandered from the house, so no one would take me for a Skraeling and capture me or shoot me from behind.

The skirts reached to my ankles. After wearing my supple moccasins for a moon, the Greenlander leather boots felt stiff. I pulled and chewed the leather to soften it, as I had learned from the Inuit. I enjoyed exploring the hills and small valleys in from the fjords while Halvard and Leif fished the fjord and Ole took the herd to the high meadows to graze. It was good to be outdoors and to walk over the firm earth again, knowing protection and rest awaited me no more than a morning's walk away. I could see Osmund's house and several others far in the distance. How odd it was that Greenlanders were not happy to live close together and share the work of guarding their beasts. Possibly, they lived apart because their race was so argumentative and jealous of each patch of ground and belonging.

Birgitta promised to teach me spinning and weaving. One morning, she came to get me. As we walked back to her steading, she told me I had much to learn. "Ludmilla has known how to card wool and use a distaff since she was five. Maybe I'll let her teach you that. Afterward, I'll explain the weaving and the dying. I'm glad to see you dressed like a decent Greenlander woman, but you ought to put your braids up with combs and cover your hair properly."

At her house, she fastened my braids, as she said, and tied a swath of cloth around my head. It covered my ears and felt peculiar, but I allowed her to do as she desired. The loom hung from a ceiling beam. The long yarn was held tightly by stones, and sticks of wood separated and held the strands even, yet apart. Yarn was drawn between to do the weaving.

"You have to learn to make the yarn first. This is a distaff. Show her how to use it, Ludmilla, while I tie off and finish the bit I'm working on."

So we went on with my learning. For the next several days, I walked to Birgitta's house and learned by observing and doing, glad of Orenda's gift of skill to draw and work with my hands. As I learned, Birgitta spoke sometimes about the bishop and the cathedral, repeating the stories he had told to her and the other Christian women. They had learned from the high Jesus priest that Odin and Frigga, the old Great Spirit, his wife, and their children, the other gods, were false.

I listened politely. Her stories held my interest, for they increased my store of words. It seemed Jesus was the son of a very powerful god who was jealous of all those others who lived beyond the clouds. Jesus was sent on a journey to live as a human to teach them about his father. Many liked him, but others felt sure their gods would be offended if they ceased to worship them. A powerful tribe destroyed this Jesus god and sent his spirit back to his father. I would have expected the father god to be angry and bring great destruction to the world for the evil done to his boy, but it seemed he had expected this. I found it all very confusing, partly because I had thought gods lived forever. No wonder that Gunnar cautioned me not to believe what I heard from Christians.

Halvard and Leif found and killed a seal on the fjord one day while I learned under Birgitta's supervision. They gutted it at the fjord, dragging it up to the house for me to butcher. I used my *ulu,* making thin slices to dry in the wind for winter. I cured the seal hide, rubbing and stretching it to make it soft enough to make a blanket for my second daughter. I had not yet told Halvard I carried her, although soon, he and Gunnar would be sure to guess.

After a rain-filled night, I took my gathering pouch over my arm and walked inland to see what I could find. I brought my quiver of arrows and my short Inuit bow in case I had a chance for a duck or goose on the wind. The air smelled fresh and spicy with summer herbs. A breeze caressed my face as I strode briskly along the path, my long skirts brushing my legs. Inuit trousers were much better for walking.

I had not gone far when I felt danger. I pulled my short bow from my shoulder and retrieved an arrow. There was nothing to aim at as yet, but I was prepared to defend myself. Although I could see no one, the feeling that someone was watching remained. When I came to a boulder, I stepped behind it, alert for anything unusual. A human footstep drew my attention.

It was Ole, who had followed me. Stepping out from behind my hiding place as he passed, I asked, "Why are you hiding and following me?"

He collected himself quickly. "I wanted to go into the hills with you," he said. "You left before I could ask."

That was a lie. He might have called my name. "Come, then," I said, putting away my weapons and continuing into the hills. I watched the ground for ferns and familiar shoots to add to my pouch. Plants grow very fast in this land, I thought to myself, noticing the many herbs and feathery leaves.

"This is a good place," I said, expecting no response and receiving none. I crouched and began to dig out some shallow roots. Here and there, I dug, picked, and tasted, comparing the leaves and root shapes to those I knew. Thanks to the instruction of my mother and aunts, Pine Tree Woman, and Maki, I had become an excellent forager.

Ole disappeared around a bend, but he soon returned with salt leaves and mint for my pouch. The sun warmed my face as I foraged. Yesterday's clouds had thinned, chased by the wind. Breezes stirred the grasses.

Honks and passing shadows alerted me to a flock of low-flying geese. With a smooth motion, I strung my bow, nocked an arrow, and let fly. A goose dropped out of the air, landing with a thud nearby. Ole watched while I hurried to twist its neck and drive away its mate.

"I never saw a woman use a bow," Ole exclaimed. "Greenlander women never do." I pulled my arrow free, gutted the goose at once, and tucked it away. "Where did you learn to shoot and aim like that?"

"In my country." In spite of the balmy air, I shivered and hugged my arms around myself. When geese fly in arrow formation, cold weather is not long behind them. I remembered my dream. "Winter comes soon," I said. "We must hurry back."

"I'll carry the pouch for you," Ole offered, "if you want."

"Thank you," I said slowly, handing it to him. Perhaps he was trying to make friends. I was grateful for any sign of a thaw in his coldness. In response, I offered him information. "You ought to learn to use a bow. When your sister is born, I won't have time to go into the hills."

He halted stiffly, suddenly cautious. "You are having a baby? How do you know it's a girl?"

"I just know." I had not spoken of being with child even to Halvard, and I now regretted mentioning it to Ole. His expression changed from caution to suspicion as he backed away from me.

"Are you a witch?"

"I don't know your word. An Inuit woman told me."

His voice grew shrill and accusing. "You mean a Skraeling? You're all witches, aren't you? You look into time to see what is yet to come. You tricked my father into marrying you because you had a Norse knife with my name on it! You tricked my grandfather, too."

"I did nothing," I said, horrified, as his words became clear.

Ole raised one hand with clenched fingers, as if to deflect evil. "You are making a child to steal our inheritance from me and Leif. Your family murdered Norsemen. You came across the ocean to steal our souls. I wish my father had never met you. I wish you were dead."

I yanked my gathering pouch out of his hands and ran, without looking back. What bitterness he must have inside him to throw such hateful words in my face. Bitterness like this throws the world out of kilter. It spits in the face of the Creator and Sea Woman.

I did not know how to make Ole understand that he was mistaken, but even as I ran from him, I realized I must keep Halvard from learning of his behavior. It would hurt him to know how much his son hated me.

When I reached the home field, Halvard was busy securing the house for winter, filling the cracks with mud mixed with dried grass. I bolted through the open door, flung down the food pouch, and ran to my bed. "What is it?" he asked, coming to stand over me. I huddled in our bed, shaking, trying to slow my heart, taking deep breaths. Halvard knelt and pulled me close against him, trying to soothe me. "What is wrong. Tell me. Did you see a wolf up there?"

A wolf would have been a comfort. "It's nothing," I lied, hating the necessity to do so. "It is a woman thing. A memory like a bad dream. Only let me rest for a while."

Halvard looked at me doubtfully. "This is not like you," he persisted. He felt my arms. "You're cold. You shouldn't be cold." Gunnar watched from across the room, rubbing his mustaches with thumb and forefinger. His faint smile told me he had guessed part of what I had not said.

Suddenly, Halvard's face lit up in a huge grin. "You're with child! That is what this is all about! Isn't it?" I returned his smile, glad for the excuse to say nothing about Ole, and admitted to what I had known for some time.

"Yes. I am with child."

"Thanks to Freyr and Freya, who give *inge* to men and women." It was the word he had used in his dance at our marriage feast. I learned these were brother and sister gods who drew men and women together with the magic of shared desire. *Inge* was their gift of fertility.

"They blessed us that very first day. I was almost sure we would make a baby." He lifted me up off the bed and swung me around in a great hug, then set me down more gently. "The baby," he said, his eyes twinkling. "I must be more careful of you. Don't be sad or worried." He piled the quilt around me. "You're warming up already. I'll make you tea."

Ole returned in time to see this display. I wondered what he thought as he set about some task or other, not speaking.

If Halvard had taken a Greenlander woman for his second wife, I doubted Ole would have thrown such words at her, but I was foreign, dark of skin and eyes, and I spoke his words poorly. I had skills he knew nothing of, but not those of Greenlanders. Perhaps Ole blamed me that his father could find joy in life after his mother's death, while Ole, as yet, could not. My only hope, until I found a better solution, was to construct a kind of stockade, a kind of spiritual shelter, around myself and my daughter that the boy's resentment and hate could not penetrate. However he felt, I would not allow Ole's misplaced jealousy to harm my child.

Chapter 33

"Let's work outside, where the light is better." Birgitta detached her bare loom from its ceiling beam and loom weights, which she left on the floor. "We'll get those later. Ludmilla, help me carry the warp bars and the batten to the porch. Astrid, if you would get the heddle and the combs and the yarn"—she pointed these things out to me—"we'll set this up under the outside rafters."

She opened the door that led to the sunny home field. I followed her with the objects she mentioned and a sack filled with hanks of yarn. Birgitta had us drag over the bench. She and Ludmilla climbed up on it, while I handed them the bars and hooks. Together, we tied on the bottom weights to hold the warp strands taut. While Birgitta worked, she explained how everything was going to work.

I examined every loop holding the strands to the bars. I examined the strands, too, still not grasping how sheep fur became long fine strands. I supposed it was similar to how we make cord from the inner bark of basswood. Ludmilla looked from me to her mother and then back. "Don't they know anything where Halvard's wife comes from?" she asked with a chuckle. "It's only yarn. A three-year-old knows that."

"But I don't," I protested. "Please, Ludmilla, let your mother tell me everything she can. I have very much to learn."

"If Vinlanders know nothing about spinning and weaving, that must be why they wear hides. Is that right, Astrid?" the girl asked, her tone incredulous, rather than demeaning. "Is that why you wore a hide dress when you first came?"

"We like hide dresses," I said, compelled to defend my wedding dress. How could she not see its beauty? "We weave fine baskets and mats, but we make nothing like this because we have no animals such as yours." I stroked the cloth of the Greenlander dress I wore, a purplish gray double layer of wadmal. Touching it made me think of its first owner, Halvard's wife, Sigrun. These people were undoubtedly comparing me to her.

Ludmilla took her place at the loom, attaching the strands as her mother demonstrated. She shifted the upright bars containing the warp back to separate each strand, then slid the shuttle containing the weft yarn crosswise. Another shift, another pass, and tamp down with batten and combs. Pushing a shuttle of green yarn every few rows, she was making a design with the different colors. Sometimes, my mother did the same with her baskets, using bark of a different color or a row of knotted weave.

The girl had twelve winters and stood almost as tall as her mother. Her light, loose hair framed her young face, cascading over her shoulders and newly growing breasts. She laughed easily as she worked, still a child in the safety of her mother's house. "Astrid, it's your turn," Ludmilla said.

I brought my attention back to the loom and took the yarn. The work was not difficult, once understood. While we practiced, Osmund and his boys raked up the home field Osmund had already scythed. They spread the grass to dry in the sun for winter feed. The swishing of the rakes and the knocking of the shuttle reminded me of home. Before winter closed in, we all worked, aunts and cousins, to the crackling sounds of braiding cornhusks while the strongest women ground the corn in hollow stumps.

One day, about two months after I arrived, Birgitta sent me into her house for milk. The hangings were pulled back from her bed closet. While I waited for my eyes to adjust to the inside light, I found on the wall there a wooden cross with a man figure carved upon it. "What is taking you so long?" Birgitta had come in and was standing behind me. A quick memory of my cousin Brown Otter flickered through my head. I had not been alert, or I would have heard her footsteps.

"This is your god, is it not?" I asked.

"Yes. That's a likeness of Jesus." Gunnar himself did not believe it was proper to keep images of his gods. When I said no more, Birgitta added, "I decided to accept the Christian faith. It will bring us luck and better harvests. Bishop Alf says those who don't accept Jesus' sacrifice for our sins will be punished after they die, but we who do will go to live with him in the sky."

"The elders tell us that all spirits go to live in the sky with Great Spirit Orenda," I said. "They know best." Ludmilla giggled.

"It would take a priest to explain it to you," Birgitta replied. "You were raised among Skraelings not to know any better."

I forced all expression from my face so as not to betray my anger and hurt. Because Greenlanders could make cloth and tame sheep, that did not mean they knew more about spirits than my people. "Gunnar says it is not right to make a god's image, that it angers them."

"I notice you wear a seagull amulet around your neck."

How could she compare the two? "This is not a god. It's a seagull and is also a luck gift from a friend."

"The bishop knows better than Gunnar. Bishop Alf gave me this to wear around my neck when he sprinkled holy water over my head." She showed me a small copy of the man on the cross that hung from the wall. The wood was oiled and quite attractive, but the carver's craft was better represented by the Inuit. The statue had a loop over its head, through which was passed a thin braided cord. "Do you see the beauty of it? It was carved out of linden wood by monks in a monastery in Bergen. That is in Norway, the old country of our people."

"What does Osmund say about having Jesus in this house? Has he stopped believing in Gunnar's gods also?"

"Years ago, King Haakon ordered all his people to worship the Christian god and his son. We are behind the times, so far from the rest of the world. In Norway, mothers use pagan gods to frighten children into behaving."

She smiled sweetly and clutched my arm as though to whisper a secret. "Tell Gunnar and Halvard you are coming to visit me tomorrow, and I will take you to the cathedral with me. The bishop will explain Jesus to you. You and your child will be saved from your sins so you can go to heaven with me. Say you will."

I pulled my arm away from her. "I don't want to go to a place where Halvard will not be welcome. Gunnar and my husband keep faith with their own gods. They know them best. I must go home now."

When I did not return to Birgitta for some days, Gunnar asked me why. I explained as well as I could. "What shall I do?" When Halvard entered with his sons, whistling after his work in the field, he found his father and me in serious discussion.

Gunnar rubbed and twisted his mustaches as he did when he was puzzled or thinking deeply. "When did this happen?"

Ole answered him. "When we stayed there while Father was away, I saw her amulet of the dead god hanging in their bed closet. I didn't want to tell you, Grandfather. At the time, we had nowhere else to go." Halvard looked to his father, waiting for his reaction.

"If I knew what they were thinking, I might have talked sense into Osmund, if not Birgitta. Women have a weak spot for a god who suffers, especially if they can be convinced he did so for them. I assume Osmund went along with it to keep peace in the family. If he ever expects to be a judge at the next Althing, he will have to ascribe to the popular gods. This is what happens when the wrong people come into power. They decide for everyone else."

"And what do you propose we do about it?" Halvard asked Gunnar. "They're still our neighbors and friends."

"What shall I think about a god who couldn't protect his son while he was on a mission for him?" Gunnar asked. "Obviously, the son was weak and the father god not much better. From this, we learn that those who put their faith in weakness will be destroyed if evil times come. We have faith in the strength of Thor's lightning and Father Odin's wisdom. The gods will turn their backs on Greenland when good men are seduced by stories priests tell to their wives."

"It's more than stories," Halvard said. "They do rituals to celebrate the death of their god by eating his body in effigy. Perhaps they feel they are taking in his strength. When I went to the trading, I met our friend Skaddi, priestess to the goddess Freya. She told me she went to the church in her district to investigate. She wanted to see how the Jesus priests served their god."

"It is worse than I thought. They pile horror on top of sacrilege with such a celebration," Gunnar stated coldly. Leif and Ole sat beside him. He rested one hand on each of their heads. "Skaddi should have told me." I did not know the meanings of all his words, but I felt sure that Jesus' priests must have misinterpreted their dreams to think any god might desire such a ritual. "In any case," Gunnar continued, "there is little strength in such worship for them to digest, to eat a god who was killed."

"Gods can be killed. Baldur died. He was the son of Odin," Leif reminded his grandfather.

"He was the god of beauty and joy. Since his death at the hands of the traitor god, Loki, all good men have mourned the loss of these things with tears and the cutting of hair and beards. We don't celebrate his death."

"You might as well hear all of it," Halvard said. "Skaddi says the Jesus

priests threatened us, and you especially, with hellfire for our commit-
ment to the old Norse gods. That's why she didn't tell you. They knew her
for a priestess to goddess Freya. They won't be content until all of us who
pray to the old gods come to them and beg forgiveness. They want to pour
water on our heads so we will be like newborns, clean of sin."

Gunnar rested his hands on his lap and smiled. "Newborns indeed. With
as much sense. They will not be content until they have destroyed all of us
with their nonsense."

"Skaddi told us that for permission to partake in their priests' grisly
feast, worshipers are required to give them a tenth of their dried and
salted fish or seal meat, fleeces, walrus tusks, and cloth. The cathedral has
more food and wealth stored in their treasure houses than Old Harold
Blue Tooth, greatest king of Viking days, when men acted like men."

Gunnar turned to Leif and Ole. "What do you say, boys? Norsemen
have always valued their freedom. If they give allegiance to a good king or
wise and helpful gods, it is by their choice, not because they are sheep.
Shall we desert Odin and Thor to please a foreign king or his bishop? Shall
we make our souls filthy with gruesome meals, or do you stand with me
for Odin and his children?"

"I'm with you. You know that, Grandfather. I'll never bow to their statues and crosses," Leif asserted very seriously.

"I'm with you, too," said Ole. "May Odin strike me blind and Thor fling
his hammer at my head if I forsake the gods of my fathers."

"Good boys. I am proud of you," he said. "My grandsons won't shame
me, Halvard. You can count on your boys."

I walked over to Gunnar and stood before him. Leif looked into my
face, but Ole backed up just a little and tried to disguise a scowl from his
grandfather. "I will follow your rule in this," I said. "I will continue to learn
weaving from Birgitta, but I won't go with her to listen to her bishop's stories about his gods."

"I know you won't," he said, grinning at me. "Our Astrid won't be
fooled by priests and bishops, no matter what they promise or threaten." I
kissed Gunnar's wrinkled cheek, then rested my head against his bony
shoulder before I went back to bed.

The next time I visited Osmund's stead, Birgitta did not bring up her
new religion to me. Instead, she invited me to look into a vat she had
steaming over a driftwood fire a short walk from the house. The fumes
smelled awful. It was good that it was outside, where a brisk wind carried
away the stink. "What are you cooking?" I asked.

She laughed. "It's dye to color my gowns and Ludmilla's, and the breeches I sewed for Osmund and the boys. It won't be as fine as the dye in Norway, where the right plants grow, but we can get a decent blue from snail shells. I have other dyes for yellow, and we can mix them to make green. In Iceland, women wear gowns and headdresses stitched with many colors of yarn and embroidered with beautiful designs."

All of a sudden, a cloud drifted in front of the sun. The creeping shadows chilled me as they spread over the straw-colored field, turning the grass gray as Birgitta's dyes turned gray sheep wool to blue. Mist lifted from the fjord. It drew together and thickened into a cloud bank that rose and began to roll up the hill toward us.

A sudden wind blew cold off the ocean, like an exhalation from the mouth of an ice mountain. My dream. "Winter comes. You must hurry to take in the hay and be sure of your food. There is no time to make colors for your clothes."

"What are you talking about? We have another month before winter. It's a summer storm." The wind carried the smell of the dye to our noses, making us cough. She doused the fire and pushed the vat against the house, covering it. "It will be fine again tomorrow. Bring clothing to dye."

She did not believe me. I could not say why I felt so sure myself. "Please bring in your hay and secure your house," I begged her, for she had been good enough to teach me weaving. "Tell Osmund to bring your animals into their byre before the snows begin. I must go now to warn Halvard."

"What Skraeling god told you this? Winter in September. This is nonsense," she insisted. Even as she spoke, I hurried to the path between Osmund's stead and Halvard's. Fog rose over the fjord, covering all but the masts of the fishing boats, which were putting in to land while they could still see.

I ran, trying to keep ahead of the creeping fog, watching out for every root and rock so as not to fall and injure my baby. As I ran, a vision came to me. It was not like a dream, nor was it entirely clear, so it might have been only a vivid memory. I saw Doteoga and its stockade behind the cornfields on the curve of the Wide River. Brown leaves blew from the trees on the breath of the north wind. Snow was already beginning to fall and ice to form on the puddles of summer rain. Were the men home yet? My little brother would be nine. In a few years, he would be old enough to walk the paths of war with the men. My cousin, Laughing Girl, would be a mother by this time. Did she ever wonder whether I survived and what had become of me? Was the rest of my family well? I found I even wondered if the squirrels had time to stash enough acorns in their hollows in the trees, and if the harvest had been secured. All over the world, Sea Woman made winter, and this would be a winter such as the world had not seen for a long time.

In the year that I was stolen, winter ended the season's battle in time to force our warriors home early. With war happening in my land and such gruesome sacrifices in Halvard's as the Jesus priests made, all the world's harmony surely must have been lost. How could it be restored? How could I save Halvard? Such thoughts swam through my head as I ran.

"Halvard," I called breathlessly. He stood in the home field, holding his new sickle. He had been mowing down his grass, but now his back arched like a drawn bow as he watched the threatening clouds. They raced on the wind to cover the last of the sky's blue and the wind blew the grass around his legs like a field of water. He turned in time to see me running into the home field. "You saw the fog coming up from the fjord in time," he said, running to meet me. He threw his arms protectively around my shoulders and put his jacket over me. "I was worried you would get lost in the fog. Summer storms can be brutal when they blow in from the north like this."

As soon as my breath caught up with me, I blurted, "We must not wait to bring in the hay. Winter is almost here."

He looked toward the fjord and the rolling fog. "It may rain and the wind will blow, but there is time to gather the harvest. We have another month at least before first snow. You don't know the weather this far south."

"This time will be different."

Gunnar hobbled out, leaning into the wind. "I've seen the geese, too," he said, "and my bones agree with Astrid. The weather is going to change."

"Take in all the hay now because of a few birds and a summer storm?"

Gunnar nodded. "As much as you can. It will be difficult to dig it out from under the snow. When her dreams and my bones agree, don't argue, but do as Astrid says."

Halvard shrugged. "Between the two of you, you've made up my mind for me? Well, I'll work until my arms are tired. It can't be done in one day. Let's see how it goes tomorrow. I hope the rain won't rot the standing hay. Ole!" The boy ran up, leading the herd. "Put them in their byre for the night. A storm is coming. Get Leif to help you. Then help me bring in the hay."

The next day, the fog was gone. It had not rained, but low clouds hung

from the sky. Halvard and Leif worked on the harvesting. Halvard warned
Ole not to take the herd far. "If the sky gets worse, bring them back home
as fast as you can. I don't trust this weather."

Ole glared at me for a moment, but then he went off. Leif and the dog
trailed behind, keeping the animals together. The sound of the lead ram's
bell grew faint as they disappeared into the distance. The pale sun penetrated the clouds enough to tint the straw of the home field pink. I strung
out the last of the fish to harden on my drying frames.

In the house, I checked over our supplies of dried meat and fish. There
were enough round cheeses packed in strips of moistened wadmal to fill
two shelves. If I were wrong, Sea Woman had no power here, and my
dreams were not to be believed as they were in my own world and that of
the Inuit.

The sun hovered in the west that evening. It looked like the full moon
instead of the sun, white instead of yellow, and small, as if in retreat. The
wind ceased. When I looked toward the fjord, the water might have been
slate-colored ice, although there had not yet been a freeze. Halvard
gripped my arms and turned me around. "We'll be all right," he said.
"We're ready for whatever happens."

"Look." I pointed at the first light flakes as they fell to the cut home
field.

"It will melt," Halvard said doubtfully. "The sun will come out tomorrow."

"Perhaps," Gunnar said. "We shall see." I pulled my shawl closer around
my shoulders. Like scouts, the first flakes drifted lazily from the low-
hanging sky, before the multitudes that followed. In the white haze of the
falling snow, I heard the lead ram's bell and the clatter of hooves over field
rock.

"Thank Odin, the boy has sense," Halvard said. We hurried to help lead
the animals to the byre and close them in. The dog nipped at the sheep the
way the wind nipped at us, booming and howling around the byre while
we fastened the door shut behind the frightened animals. At last, it was
done.

By the time we reached the house, we were covered with white. Gusts
of frigid air drove the snow thickly enough to blanket everything in sight.
Gunnar got a driftwood fire burning on the hearth. We had rendered fat
enough to light the house and warm us for months. I hoped it would be
enough. We held our stiff, wet hands over the flames to dry them.

Cold followed the snow, freezing it. More snow came, then more cold.

We were buried in Halvard's steading like groundhogs or brown bears in their burrows and caves. When the snow was half as high as the house, we exited through the window to dig out the door.

What was once a short walk became a great one. We no longer visited neighbors. I learned to use skis, but I missed my snowshoes. Winter dragged on slowly. My pregnancy advanced, making my back ache. We never saw the sun at all. To make our food last, I insisted we ration our meats and cheese. Often, I felt fatigued and willing to give in to the lethargy of sleep. Halvard went to the byre each day to feed and water the animals.

During winter's darkness, Gunnar told us what his gods and heroes did to fend off the frost giants, their constant enemies. These giants were tall as mountains, so big that in one legend, Odin, Thor, and Loki, the god who later killed Baldur, god of joy, took shelter in a frost giant's mitten, mistaking it for a cave.

Six moons passed with little change. Halvard dug through the snow for fodder. Few of his stock remained, for we had eaten them.

"My stomach hurts," Leif complained. "I want something else to eat. We'll have birds and fish soon, Astrid. It's nearly April." It hurt me as much to hear the boy's complaints as to feel my own pangs.

Halvard gave him another chunk of goat meat, taking less for himself. "There are no signs of spring yet, Leif," Halvard explained. "Sleep and be brave. You'll have your piece of cheese and a dry fish in the morning. Hot water will help fill your stomach. Warriors don't complain of hardships."

"They don't go to bed hungry like we do. My stomach hurts. Maybe tomorrow you'll kill another goat."

"I suppose I will, but if I slaughter any more, we won't have a herd to feed us next winter." The boy suggested his father spear a seal through the ice the way the Skraeling do.

It was not as easy as that. He had tried once, sitting on the ice most of the day at what he thought was an *allu,* the way Qisuk had described it to him. He might have frozen down there. Ole and Leif could barely help him back up our hill. Sometimes, the boys fought mock battles, but they were usually too tired to keep it up for long.

"Look what we've forgotten," Halvard said one day. "Here's our old chessboard." Halvard set carved pieces upon colored squares of the game board.

My head swam, so I could not follow the game. Gunnar explained it was like a war between countries. Each side had a high priest, a king, and

a queen. "Grandfather against the bishop!" Leif hollered. "I'll take Grandfather."

I moved to the other side of the room, away from the evil priest carving. I thought of Tododaho, the evil shaman who had tried to destroy the
world I knew. In my mind, he became mixed with the frightening aspect
of the man Gunnar referred to as the bishop, who was the sorcerer of the
cathedral. When the game was over, I hid the sorcerer doll so the bishop
could not harm us.

Halvard and Ole dug under the ice for seaweed to feed the remnants of
the stock. Under a snowdrift, they happened upon a nest of sleeping white
hares. We were hungry enough to eat the first of them half-cooked. Their
meat and broth fed us for three days. The moon waned and grew full again.

Halvard heard me moan under the quilt early one morning. He turned
me to him in time to see me grasp my middle. "Is the baby coming,
Astrid?" he asked. I nodded, glad that the wait for my daughter was near
to over.

Since I could not go alone to a birth hut, I closed off a section of floor
beforehand and lined it with rags. I did not intend to push out my daughter in the bed closet I shared with Halvard. "I will wait in here," I said, and
entered my makeshift version of a birth hut within the house. I had prepared clean clothes, water, a sealskin for swaddling, and I kept my
woman's knife close beside me to cut the cord. A strong contraction
squeezed and tightened my belly. I doubled over, suppressing a groan.

"What must I do?" Halvard asked. Why should he do anything? I didn't
know if Greenlander customs were like Inuit customs. I only knew I would
be most comfortable with my own, and this time, I was ready. Bringing a
child into the world was women's work. I only wished Halvard and his
sons would go away and leave me to do it. "Shall I bring you Birgitta? She'll
know what to do."

I nodded and let my breath escape. "Yes, go." It would take him out of
the house. "Take Leif and Ole with you," I added weakly. They got into
their heavy coats and strapped their wide skis onto their thick boots. I did
not want them to hear me grunt and heave, squatting to push my daughter into the world. I hoped she would arrive before they returned.

While I paced, Gunnar waited in his bed closet, chanting prayers to
Freya, leaving me to do my work undisturbed. Another pain grasped me,
holding me tightly. My upper lip dripped with sweat. I lowered myself to
the straw.

When Birgitta and Halvard returned on their wide skis, Ingrid was already lying beside me, wailing while I wiped her clean. Gunnar called my name softly and asked for permission to enter. I pulled a blanket over me to cover my bottom and told him to come in. He looked down at the squirming infant. "Inge is in her spirit. We shall call her Ingrid," he said. I nodded, accepting that the spirit of fertility resided within her. Ingrid would be her name. "I'll have Birgitta come in to attend and clean you before Halvard sees you," he said. I thanked him for my baby's name before he padded out.

I heard the door open and close again, and Gunnar tell them there was a new girl in our family. He thanked Birgitta for coming and directed her to the alcove where I lay. "You didn't need help after all," she said. "That girl cries lustily as any boy. She sounds robust enough to live." Birgitta wiped the sweat from my face and cleaned me of blood with hide rags, wrung out with the water Gunnar had heated. With another, she wrapped the afterbirth, which she would dispose of under the snow on her way home. "You are good to do this for me," I said.

"Let me show you how to hold the baby to nurse her." Of course she would assume this one was my first. In a normal year, winter would have been gone and the berries would be ripening. I had begun my sixteenth year. She bent over me to adjust Ingrid at my breast, at the same time whispering in my ear, "Your infant's soul is in danger. In this cold, she could die. We must get her named and baptized by the bishop."

I shuddered at her words, feeling as if she tried to curse my innocent baby. "My daughter already has a name. It is Ingrid. She will live or die as the Creator and Freya and Sea Woman decide."

Birgitta straightened up and cleared her throat. "Ingrid is a name for pagans. Better name her Mary or Marguerite, or maybe Martha."

"Her name is Ingrid, as Gunnar said it should be. Thank you for your help." I clutched my child. Thoughts of Maki and Putu came to my mind, reaching for my first daughter while I slept. I had forgiven them, but I would never forget. When Birgitta had covered me, she returned to the main room. Halvard walked her to the door and thanked her again for coming so far.

More than anything, I hoped that Halvard would accept this girl child we had made together, that he would want her. He entered my alcove hesitantly, watching me nurse Ingrid for a long moment before he came closer. When her sleepy mouth fell from my nipple, Halvard lifted his daughter and rocked her gently in his strong arms. He sniffed her new baby smell. Ingrid did not resemble my first daughter, being fair even at birth. Her hair, even damp and pressed to her head from her passage, held sparks of sun like her father's.

"You are well?" he asked me, concerned, for I had not spoken since he entered. I awaited his reaction to this person we had made.

"If you are pleased, I am well."

"I never had a baby girl to love." He leaned over and kissed my forehead, still cuddling the baby. "My father wants to call her Ingrid."

"It is a good name," I said. Inwardly, I thanked Freya for *inge,* the gift of fertility, and for making sure I had conceived before our last night on the beach with Qisuk and Padloq. Thanks to Freya, the Norse goddess who presides over birth and babies, our daughter had fair skin and light hair, and *no* blue spot in the small of her back. There was only so much Inuit "politeness" Halvard would have accepted.

Halvard called Gunnar to hold the baby while he carried me to our bed closet and propped the pillows behind me. "I'll get you some water. You must be thirsty." As soon as I was comfortable and leaning high on my pillows, Gunnar gave her back to me. "Is it all right to bring Ole and Leif to welcome their new sister?" he asked. When I nodded, he called them.

Leif approached shyly, first looking at me. He stroked and patted Ingrid's cheek. The baby awoke and tried to follow his finger with her lips. Ole observed her, but he made no attempt to touch her petal-soft skin. His pale green eyes blinked, and he nibbled his lower lip. Leif backed away and motioned to his older brother. Only then did Ole come closer. "It's a girl, as you said it would be," he whispered. "She can't have my inheritance and Leif's."

"She is of Wolf Clan. She inherits from her mother, not her father. Though she lives here among you, she is of my people, Ganeogaono." He could not have understood me, but it did not matter. I thought of my foreign blood and the inheritance Wolf Clan gave me. It was not a thing to hold. My inheritance was part of me, no matter how far I traveled from my people. How could I impart this pride and feeling of belonging to my child? I would sing her children's songs from my land, songs of pride. I would speak to her of Great Spirit Orenda, who keeps all life within his own. Perhaps she would see our land in her dreams.

Ole backed away when Halvard came over with the promised mug of water. I took it and drank deeply. With a tender, shy smile, Halvard stroked his daughter again. He would protect and love this girl. I would not wake to find another newborn in my arms and my own dead.

Sleep pressed warm fingers over my eyes. The last I remembered before I surrendered to it was confusion in Ole's face, delight in Leif's, and pride in Halvard's. It was good to let the world fade away, to feel my middle almost flat once more, to be safe and snug in my bed closet. I lifted Ingrid so as to memorize her face. She yawned and stretched, arching her tiny back. Her small pink tongue curled and her blue eyes gazed fuzzily into mine.

"My daughter." I sighed, wishing I could protect her always, but knowing I could not. "You are so trusting, so helpless. What lies in your future? Will I always be there when you need comfort or protection, or the wisdom experience brings?" Such questions occurred to me as I nestled down to sleep, the infant tucked into the curve of my arm. The rest of them already loved her. I was less certain about Ole, but I hoped that someday even he would protect and love his little sister. He *will* care for you, Ingrid, I thought. He's your brother.

Chapter 34

Gunnar said that according to his calculations, it should have been spring, but frigid winds still howled like ghosts around our isolated house. Of Halvard's herd, only three ewes and two does remained, each with young. If we hoped to live through another winter, we did not dare slaughter any more.

Halvard brought the animals inside. He and Ole chopped up the frozen sod that roofed the byre, bringing it inside to feed them. The does and ewes had barely enough milk to keep their young alive. We did not take any.

The first night while we slept, the dog jumped the half stone wall that separated us from the animals. Claws scratching on stone and a terrified yelp told us he had brought down one of his charges. Hunger drove him to it, of course. No dog could withstand such temptation. He wolfed down chunks of the newly killed lamb's flesh, his muzzle red with fresh blood while the ewe and its companions bleated in terror.

Halvard jumped the wall, knife in hand. "No, Father, not Blackie," Leif begged. The boy hid his face in his arms when Halvard pulled the dog's head back and slit its throat. Halvard climbed back, cradling the dead dog like a child while its blood dripped on the floor.

"I had to, Leif. When a dog learns to eat what it's supposed to protect, it has to die. I know he did it for hunger, but he has the taste for lamb now. He'd kill the rest of them in time. I choose our lives over the dog's." With tight lips, Leif patted his dog's matted fur as Halvard carried it outside.

I butchered the dog and cooked it together with what was left of the lamb. His flesh would make up for the lamb's and keep us for another few days. Leif remained in his bed and would not look at me when I called him to eat.

"Talk sense into him, Father," Halvard said. "You know I had to do it."

The old man nodded. He seldom moved from his bed closet anymore, but he walked to Leif, sitting down lightly on the boy's bed. "I know you cared for your dog," Gunnar said. "You grew up with him. Blackie was your friend."

"Do you expect me to eat a friend?" the boy asked.

"At least his hunger died with him," I said. "Don't let his death go for nothing. He wouldn't want you to die, too. He'll be helping you. Eat." Leif looked at me steadily to determine if I was serious. "Thank Blackie's spirit first," I said. "That's what my people do when we kill any animal for food. Maybe he'll be born again. The Inuit think everything comes back."

"Do *you* think so?" He lifted his spoon doubtfully.

"I do." The chunks were small enough to be unrecognizable as the animal they were. While I sipped the broth and chewed, I could not help but remember the feast after our warriors returned from war, when man, not dog, gave nourishment to my village. I had not recognized which part of which enemy warrior filled my bowl that autumn. Our war with the Onondaga Nation had faded in my memories. That long-ago victory feast had happened in a different world.

More days passed. Frigid gusts of cold came through the cracks and even the wall hangings, chilling us. The animals bleated and cried for food, huddled together neck upon neck for comfort and warmth. Wet straw rotted under the animals on the other side of the room. Ole and Leif raked it into piles to keep rot from spreading to the animals' hooves. The piles of soiled straw steamed and added warmth to the room.

Although the sun glared off the ice, it gave no warmth. Ingrid's tightly sewn baby carrier hung empty beside our bed closet, for I kept her with me. She slept between us, sharing our warmth.

Halvard returned from collecting water at his spring. He stamped the ice off his boots, removed his heavy coat, and shook it off. Ice crystals sparkled like tiny rainbows in the light before he shut the door on the white world outside. I brought Halvard a bowl of thin mutton soup.

"Thank you, Astrid," he said. He flung down his mittens and cupped his bluish hands around the mug to warm them while he inhaled the steam. "There has not been a winter like this in anyone's memory. Have the frost giants killed the sun? And is that pale disk in the sky only its ghost? Tell us, Father."

"I don't have an answer for you," Gunnar said, "but in all my years, I never saw winter hold on to Greenland like this. It's like the story of Idunna, this death of the sun. When the frost giants stole the goddess of spring and youth, the gods were helpless. They began to get old, and they knew they would have to go down to Hella's cold underground world in death if they could not find a way for Idunna to return with her basket of apples. The apples held youth, and only they could save the gods from old age and death. Finally, they sent Loki to trick the giants and bring Idunna back to them." It sounded to me like this Loki was both good and bad, depending on his mood. He killed one god but saved another.

"What are apples?"

Gunnar shook his head. "How do I describe apples? Even Halvard asks. It is something good to eat and it grows on trees."

I thought of plums, which made me think of home. Gunnar's world in the east with trees and apples might be more akin to mine than this strange Greenland.

Sea Woman shared her ocean with no other, although the ocean itself had many moods. I thought of her warning to me. Why had she bothered to show me the future if there was no hope? She must have known I would try to save my family. I adjusted Ingrid more comfortably against my bony ribs, where she immediately latched onto my nipple, sucking strongly. Somehow, I still produced milk for her. While she suckled, I tucked her seal-fur blanket under her chin and pushed the red-brown curls from her eyes, which had changed from blue to the color of seaweed.

"Ingrid is all Norse; she looks like her brothers," I remarked to Halvard. "Her hair holds the setting sun and her eyes are the color of spring. She is getting bigger, isn't she?" Before he could answer, I said, "She will live to see summer. Won't she, Gunnar?" Why did we always think he knew the answers to our questions?

"We can only pray," he replied softly. His faded blue eyes looked at us. "We can't spare any more animals for sacrifice."

My eyes grew heavy. I must have fallen asleep without knowing it. Something banged and scratched against the door, startling me awake. "Open the door!" Halvard's voice called hoarsely from outside. "Hurry and let us in." Gunnar rose at once from his stool to pull open the door.

Halvard, Ole, and Leif were covered head to foot in their long coats and shawls. Thick scarves hid all but their eyes. They kicked out of their broad skis, leaving them propped just inside the doorway. White light filled the house for a moment, hurting my eyes, until Halvard pushed the door closed again, sucking in the warmer air. He and his sons were loaded down with brush. The skeletal branches scratching against the wooden door were what I had heard.

"Did you find food?" Gunnar asked. "What's that?"

"The wind uncovered the bushes and dead reeds that grew on the banks, near the fjord. There's more down there. The dead twigs may nourish the beasts, if they'll eat them. There may be green life hiding inside the bark."

Gunnar added, "If it does nothing more, it will fill their stomachs." Halvard crossed the floor to pitch the icy brush over the half wall to the animals.

"After we warm up, we're going back to the fjord," Halvard said. He backed away when the does and ewes struggled up on their spindly legs to sample this offering. The goats nosed at it curiously. The bravest snapped off a mouthful. While she chewed and crunched the twigs between her strong teeth, her kid butted between her legs for milk.

"I wish we could eat twigs," Leif said. "Look. They're filling *their* stomachs."

Ingrid fell back to sleep. A small white bubble formed in one corner of her slack mouth, pulsing with her breaths. I tucked her into her hanging cradle. There was something about the stalks of the dead grass and brush. I reached for the brittle branches. Their small leaves were dead, having surrendered to the frost long before, but there were tiny seeds clinging. They were like the grass seeds Pine Tree Woman's people harvested from the marshes and lakes. She had hulled the seeds with fire. These were cracked with cold. "You *can* eat the bushes, Leif. There is food here for us, too."

Leif looked at me as if I had lost my mind. "What are you talking about?" Halvard asked. "Is your mind wandering from hunger? When the animals eat, they'll make more milk. That will suffice for our food until the ice melts and we can fish the fjord again."

"No. The seeds are food. Get more. I'll show you how they can be eaten. Naskapi women make gruel and cakes from water-grass seeds like this. I can make gruel for us if you get more brush and reeds. We'll eat before long."

Whether or not he believed me, he bundled back into his long coat and closed the door behind him. In the meantime, I pulled a milking bowl down from the stack and drew the clinging seeds off the thin twigs with my fingers. Leif jumped over the half wall to get me more branches; Ole watched my efforts silently. With a prayer to Orenda that my plan would work, I fed the flame with twigs to make the water boil in my hanging pot.

When I had accumulated a fist-sized pile in the small bowl, Gunnar and my stepsons came up to see what I would do. It seemed incredible to me that Halvard's people had survived this long without knowing the goodness that resides in seeds. Those in their old land might know more than the Greenlanders, but these beside me appeared completely baffled by my actions. "What are you going to do?" Leif asked.

"Watch." I spread them out on a flat hearthstone, then crushed them. I used the round fist-sized stone I sometimes used for stretching and softening hides. When I sprinkled the ground seeds into my pot of simmering water, the hulls rose to where I could skim them off the surface of the water.

"What are you doing now?" Gunnar asked.

"Hulling the seeds."

"Astrid, do you know this as food? Is this what the Skraelings showed you in the north, where Halvard found you?"

I had to admit the truth, for I did not know the seeds or the plants of this world. "The Inuit ate no seeds that I know of. The Naskapi ate food like this. They are another tribe of my world, on Vinland, as you call it. If I am wrong, if this food holds danger, it will be better than starving. I'll try it first."

"No, you won't," Gunnar insisted. "If you die, who will nurse Ingrid? I'll be the first to taste your seed broth. At my age, how much longer can a man expect to live anyway? If I die, it won't matter so much."

"Grandfather!" Leif exclaimed. "Don't say that."

Halvard returned with more brush. Another few days of food might bring us to a change in the weather. Eventually, the ice in the fjord would have to melt, and then we could fish. Spring has to come sometime, I thought.

The goats and sheep wagged their tails briskly as they sniffed the brush Halvard had brought in. "Don't give them more yet. If they try to fill their stomachs too quickly, those twigs may not stay down." He spoke as if he knew what was in my mind. The boys laid down their bundles beside me and did as I had done, pulling off the seeds with their fingers and dropping them into the bowl.

The water bubbled again. I fed more sticks to the fire and stirred, breathing in the steam as I sprinkled in the crushed seeds and skimmed away the hulls. "Watch and see if the water becomes thick. Only a little makes much."

When it was done, I thinned the gruel with milk and ladled it into five bowls. It was not much, but we were used to eating little. Halvard, Ole, and Leif took their spoons, then waited, as if expecting me to give directions. "Let it stop steaming," I cautioned, feeling I ought to say something.

Mouthing a prayer, Gunnar lifted some to his mouth and sipped. Eyes closed, he pushed the gruel around with his tongue. "Mm, mm," he said, and swallowed noisily before sucking in more from the edge of his spoon. "Nearly as easy to swallow as sour milk. I believe my stomach feels less empty. Go ahead and eat yours, Ole. It won't make your disposition any worse." He ignored his grandson's face and took more. Soon, all of them had tried it. The flavor was better than the dry twigs would have been. At least it was warm, and if the seeds still contained life, it would provide nourishment.

The next day, the wind changed, blowing away the accumulation of snow from the fjord ice. Halvard took his ax down the hill. While he and the boys were out of the house, I made more seed meal and thickened it into gruel. When it was done, I left several cakes to harden on the hearthstone. "Try this, Gunnar," I said, holding it out to him. "We call it bread in my country." I used my word for corn bread, knowing no other.

"What now? What is this?" He took it from me and held it flat on his hand. Gingerly, he bit off a piece and chewed.

"This reminds me of the wheat bread I tasted as a child in Norway. It is bread, although it's a different grain. No one here ever thought to harvest the reed and bush seeds."

"Bread," I repeated, liking the sound of the word. "Hard gruel is bread." It took longer for it to dry into bread. I made more, enough for another meal for us, leaving the remainder on the hearthstones to harden.

The next morning, I decided to visit Osmund's stead. Since Birgitta had come to help me when Ingrid came, I thought to give her a present of my small breads. "Don't stay away long," Gunnar advised. "The weather could change again. Is it wise to take Ingrid?" he asked when I lifted her from her hanging bed.

"I'll keep her warm under my anorak," I assured him. I had taken to wearing the Inuit long jacket again. "I won't be gone long."

The ice crust remained hard enough to support me on my skis. With my small breads wrapped in wadmal in my back carrier, I made my way carefully over the snow. My skis were wide and flat, not very difficult to learn for one who knew snowshoes. The sun climbed higher in the sky. I supposed the exercise of thrusting my skis forward was what made me feel warm. I pushed back my hood, and for once, the tips of my ears did not smart with winter's bite.

The hills remained buried, but small trickles dripped down the slopes. I sniffed a new smell in the air. I looked up to the sound of water. In the hills and mountains, streamlets tumbled and fell over precipices, catching the sun's light and making rainbows. The high sun glistened on the snow and reflected back. I had to squint. Inuit sun protectors would have been helpful.

"Do you feel it, Ingrid?" I asked. "Spring is coming!" I paused and opened the front of my anorak to uncover her eyes, her tiny nose, and pink mouth. She also squinted. She stuck out her tongue to taste the air, then pursed her lips and sucked in the almost balmy air as if it were milk.

I progressed, crablike, down the slope to Osmund's stead. The idea came to me that I should be able to glide effortlessly. The impulse to hurry took possession of my feet. I placed my boots together, bent my knees, leaned in the direction I wanted to go, and pushed myself forward.

Ingrid's shrill wail announced my lack of foresight. We glided faster, cutting through the air swiftly enough to create our own brisk wind. It took all of my balance to stay upright. "Birgitta. Osmund," I shouted with all the strength left in my lungs when we were close enough that they might hear. "Ludmilla!" I managed to turn both skis to one side, aiming us back uphill, which slowed my progress ungracefully, but enough to stop.

Ingrid's mouth remained open from the rush of wind that had entered it. She did not make a sound. "Breathe!" I screamed, rubbing her with my mittened hands. To my relief, she coughed and wailed indignantly.

Osmund appeared at my elbow. "It is good that you called our names. When I saw you in those clothes, I thought Skraelings were attacking."

"It is warmer," I said, thinking the Skraelings had no reason to attack when they had all they needed. Winter had attacked Greenland on their behalf. "The snow was slippery. I came to show you my baby and I brought you bread."

"Bread?" He said the word as though he did not know it.

In the small warmth of the house, Ingrid's cries changed to whimpering. "What possessed you to come over the hills in the snow?" Birgitta asked while Osmund built up the fire with brush. He, too, had discovered patches of brush under the softening snow and harvested it for fuel. His family was huddled in their bed closets when we went inside. They roused to see me, but feebly.

Birgitta's pale hair lay stringy and lifeless and the skin hung on her arms, but she, Ludmilla, and the boys fondled Ingrid, who by this time had ceased to cry altogether and looked around her at the new faces.

"Eat this," I said, pulling pieces of soggy bread from my pouch. "I made it from seeds. Gunnar said it's called bread."

"What seeds? Let me see this bread you made," Birgitta said, taking it from me and sniffing it. "The only bread I ever heard of is the bread of the sacrament. We have to use dried seal meat for the ritual instead because you can't grow wheat here." What Gunnar related about Christians is true, then, I thought. At least my bread had no magic imposed upon it and was not disguised god's flesh.

"You'll find these seeds in the brush you feed your goats. You can make some yourself." I explained how I prepared it. Birgitta shook her head, but she ate and licked her fingers when the bread was done. The little fire flickered below her hearthstone. Ludmilla fed it more twigs. It seemed too quiet in the small room. "Where are your dogs?" I asked.

"We had to kill them," Osmund said. "My daughter said you warned Birgitta winter was coming early and hard. How did you know?" The suspicion in his face should have warned me.

"On our way home from the north, the Inuit god, Sea Woman, told me so in a dream." Osmund and his wife exchanged a long look between them, then thanked me for my visit. It seemed a good time to go home.

Osmund took up his ax. "I'll walk with you as far as the fjord. The ice is still hard enough to walk on. There will be more brush there to feed our remaining animals. Bjorn and Jon, both of you, come along." He and his sons dressed warmly while I closed my anorak over Ingrid. The ice wouldn't melt for several days and ought to be better for traveling than the slippery snow. At least it was flat.

We crossed their home field together and descended. A sound like the rustling of dried leaves came up the hill before we reached the frozen fjord. I looked to Osmund. "What is that?" Then the curve of the path showed us.

Such a sight as appeared before my eyes was almost too much to take in all at once. Like the day I saw endless warriors filling the path to Doteoga and endless canoes encroaching on our river, I beheld Greenlanders. Men, women, and children trudged over the frozen fjord. In shawls and coats, they came. On skis and skates, they came, closer and closer, until they passed Osmund's landing, not stopping, but speaking among themselves.

Osmund rushed over to the nearest, exchanging greetings and words. When he returned, he spoke to his son. "Bjorn, chop some of these standing bushes and reeds. Take them up to the house for the stock. Jon, go tell Mother I'll be back later. We're going to the cathedral to get back our tithes."

The boy's mouth dropped. "Will the priests let us?"

"That's what it's for," Osmund said. "To help the poor and feed the hungry. Who is hungrier than we are? After you take the brush up to the house, Bjorn, come too. It will take some time to gather our shares. You can help me carry food home. Bring Ludmilla and your mother, too, if they'll come."

The procession continued to pass us while Osmund gave his directions. He and I walked along, adding to their number. My trousers and warm anorak drew stares, but Osmund reminded them I was merely Halvard's wife, who had once lived among the Skraeling.

I intended to go directly home, but Osmund suggested Halvard and I join them. "We'll be at his steading soon and we'll ask him." I had not seen so many people assembled since I had arrived in Greenland. As we walked, more folk streamed down the hillsides. I tried to make myself insignificant and remain close to Osmund's side, for I knew none of them. We kept along the bank, plodding forward on our broad skis.

"This is Halvard's wife," Osmund informed someone else who asked about me. "Stay close to me, Astrid, until we reach your hill."

The warm weather must have drawn them out of their houses to make visits at first, simply to see who remained alive, to discuss their food reserves, and learn who had died of hunger or sickness during the winter. The curious mumbled when they saw me among them, asking questions of one another.

Fortunately, they had other things to discuss, more important than the woman so strangely dressed in trousers and anorak who walked with Osmund. Like a village, with its people spread apart, they came together in their need for food and lamp fat. I heard snatches of conversations, words like *cathedral* and *priests, food* and *dogs, cheese, new fodder,* and *stock.* "We will begin again with new dogs, more stock."

"The church has full storehouses."

"It's time for the priests to give back what they took from us."

I wondered how the priests and monks would react to the demands of this multitude. It would take a lot of food to feed so many.

Halvard waited on the landing. Gunnar must have seen the mass of people approaching along the fjord from the hill. When Halvard saw the crowd, he plodded down his hill and ran out to meet me, carrying his ax in case I needed defending. Gunnar and the boys stood behind him at the edge of the ice. I raised my arm to show them I was safe and called out Halvard's name.

"What's all this?" he asked when he reached us. "Osmund, where's everyone going? What's happening?"

"Look! It's Halvard, and there's Gunnar, Odin's priest," someone exclaimed to those nearby. "The old man made it through the winter. Who would have thought it possible?"

Halvard took me in his arms briefly. "By all the gods, I was beginning to worry. I thought you'd come home this way, but I didn't expect you'd have such an escort. You must be frozen. Take the baby back up to the house."

"Let me go along. There are other women here, too," I implored. Halvard looked doubtful.

"Halvard! Over here!" Osmund shouted. "Come with us. We're going to the cathedral to get our tithes back from the priests, if there is anything left."

"Come, too, you old pagan," someone shouted to Gunnar. "See how Christian priests help the helpless."

"Yes, do," another Greenlander added.

"Father? Should we go?" Halvard asked. "We have no right to the tithes, for we have given nothing."

"I'll give you part of mine," someone offered. "If the truth be told, Gunnar's prayers have kept us alive for years."

"He's helped me, too," another added. "I'll give Gunnar and his family part of my share for all the favors I owe him. You've been good neighbors."

Gunnar scanned the crowd, stroking his mustaches. He straightened up to his full height, drawing his great coat around himself like the robe of a chief. Folk milling about awaited Gunnar's decision. "Yes," he said, agreeing at last. "I believe I shall join you." He looked over his neighbors gravely. "I would like to see for myself what answer you'll receive when you ask for help. Perhaps I shall learn something new before this day is over." Leif and Ole, their red hair blowing around their heads as always, were his champions. They flanked their grandfather like two torches shining in the dark.

"To the cathedral!" someone called loudly. The others took up the chant. "To the cathedral!" In the forward surge of the multitude, Halvard forgot he had ordered me back to the house.

Chapter 35

The hungry and weak rabble dragged itself over the uneven ice. We were absorbed into the middle of the mob, listening to the discussions and grumbling on all sides. Someone assured his neighbors that the priests could be counted upon to see our plight and give succor. "We've been faithful. It's what Lord Jesus would have done. He fed the hungry multitudes." Some women called upon their god's blessed mother and the saints. It seemed to me that these Christians implored help from more gods than did the old Norse.

Gunnar echoed my thoughts to Halvard. "Is there no end to the amount of gods in the Christian heaven? They say they worship only one, yet each time I listen to them, they have more." Gunnar walked slowly. Halvard, his sons, and I kept back with him, falling behind in the great press of people.

Along the way, others joined up with us. As we passed each landing, people, their gaunt faces tempered with hope, came down to the frozen fjord and swelled the procession. From both banks and from other fjords and islands, people came. The word must have spread, but it seemed the warm air drew them together just as the snowmelt from the mountains is drawn to the sea. It trickles into streamlets and then streams, moving faster and faster, until the streams become torrents. We were as many as could have filled Doteoga by the time we reached the landing at Gardar and saw the cathedral on its rise of land.

No ships or boats lay encased in the winter ice. The landing was bare until the people climbed up the bank. Husbands helped their wives and children up over the packed gray snow. Ingrid lay strapped in her harness under my coat, replete with her last nursing. During all the tumult, she continued to sleep.

A serving boy atop the hill spied us first. He cried out a warning to others behind him, then hurried off to inform his masters. Servants scattered as we ascended the stone steps. A small circle of space separated our family from the others. The Christians did not avoid Gunnar, appearing to give him a courteous respect instead. When we reached the broad area in front of the cathedral's high double doors, one of them opened from inside. A man emerged wearing an impressive multicolored headdress. Ermine fur bordered the purple winter robe he wore. He smiled compassionately from the high step, well in view of the people.

"It's the bishop himself!" a nearby woman shrieked, reaching for support from her man. After this first outburst, a hush came over the multitude. Two younger priests, wearing simple gray robes and fur caps, emerged to flank their master. They looked out over the crowd, swiveling their heads as they tried to gauge the number and mood of their visitors.

"God's blessing to you all on this fine spring day." The high priest raised his arms as though blessing and embracing his listeners at once. His voice carried loud and strong. "We have been praising and thanking our Lord for subduing the winter. Christ has driven back Satan's minions at last, allowing the sun's strength to return to this good Greenland of ours."

The people muttered at this, many of the women saying such things as "I told you" and "We must thank the holy fathers."

The bishop's words were repeated and passed down the hill like waves following one another, until the farthest in the crowd had heard. "If you have come to join us in prayer and thanksgiving that spring has come, I welcome you to this holy place. In the name of the Father, the Son, and the Holy Spirit, I welcome you. We will hold a Mass tomorrow, several, so all of you may attend."

There was no clear sound, only much mumbling. One man cleared his throat and spoke up loudly, taking heart from those who thrust him to the front. "We thank you for your prayers and we thank our good Lord for his help, although it's taken somewhat long and many of us have died during the waiting. The Mass will be fine, but before tomorrow, we have a different concern."

The bishop frowned and his protectors glared at the speaker. Undaunted, the man continued. "Spring comes, but we aren't saved from winter yet, for the grass has yet to push through the snow and we can't fish until the ice melts. As you know, this winter has eaten into all of our stores, until many of us were forced to go hungry. Not a few of us have lost our children. We've done our best to make our supplies last and prayed to our merciful Lord. We implored his mother and the saints on bent knees, as you taught us. We made sacrifices, turning over a tenth-part of our cheeses and dried meat, our animals, and fodder to feed them with, too. You must make up for our losses."

"I must?" The bishop's tone remained gentle, although guarded. With such simple words, he had cowed those who felt his authority.

"I ask, with respect, for all of us," the speaker persisted. "Give us back from our tithes what we need to survive until we can fish again and the grass grows."

When he had finished speaking, there was no sound, not even a cough to break the silence.

The bishop's calm, reasonable voice reached out to the people. "We, here at Gardar, at every parish church, every monastery and convent, have suffered right along with you. We had more animals to keep and more mouths to feed. We are God's servants, men and women, fishermen and dairymen. The children who copy out the Holy Gospels on parchment need to eat just as you do. All of us have devoted many hours each day of the winter to prayer on your behalf.

"At last, we have succeeded in procuring our Lord's blessings. You should not need to be reminded that is why you give your tithes to the church. It is to support those of us whose job it is to pray for you while you work your herds and grasslands and fish the fjords."

"How well did you pray, if it took this long for the sun to grow warm again?" someone called from the back.

"You've made servants of the destitute," said another, adding, "My brother became yours when he lost his farm and his lands after the vomiting sickness claimed his family. Is our Lord too far to observe our needs?"

The bishop raised his hands for silence. "I will forgive your insolence. As you know, we have not been able to pray properly and conduct a proper Mass since we ran out of real bread and wine from Iceland. We do our best. Even if it takes the good Father and his Son longer to hear us, Jesus has shown his love for us now. The sun's warmth has returned. God forgives us and will hurry to give us sustenance."

One of the priests whispered to him. Then the bishop said, "We might have enough spare fodder to provide each household with what its master can carry. Soon, spring's warm rain will make your hills green. We must take our chances along with you, trusting that soon there will be enough grass to save our herds."

Folk shuffled uncertainly, but no one came forward or answered. "We might be able to bring out bowls of milk to feed the young ones, and trenchers of dried seal meat for the rest." Silence again. The people crowded closer to the steps. "What more do you think we can do? I'm the Lord's servant, not the Lord, who can make fishes and loaves multiply. Take what I offer you and return to your homes to pray."

"See what they have hidden in their byres. See if their ponies still live. Do they yet have their dogs and sheep and fat for their fires? See if dried meat and cheeses line their storeroom shelves and whether hay remains to keep their stock alive. What is there belonged to you first. If they hold back, make it be yours again."

My mouth opened in astonishment, because the strong voice that stirred the people beside us belonged to Gunnar.

I wondered whether the Christians dared do as he advised, but the man who had first addressed the bishop smiled. "Yes, I think that is good advice. We ought to do as you suggest. Forgive us, Holy Fathers. In famine, people do what they must to survive. Friends, search the storehouses and the kitchens. Look into every outbuilding. Don't be greedy; take only what you need to keep souls in your bodies until the grass grows. The sin is ours if we leave our priests to starve, but if food and fodder remain, these belong to those who gave it. Go!"

At his word, people swarmed around the main building, away from the three men on the steps of the cathedral. Some pushed into the storage houses, others into byres and stables and cookhouses. The dairy door was nearly pushed down before someone inside unbarred it. Many of the women had gone there to search for food for their children. I remained close to Gunnar.

Halvard was one of the men who pushed open the dairy. Men led ponies out of their barn. "There's fodder in here," someone yelled. "Fodder to keep our sheep and goats alive until the grass grows!"

"Gunnar!" I tugged at his sleeve to move him out of the way. Priests and monks were running everywhere, trying to protect what they had stored away so carefully. "We must get out of the way," I said, leading him to one side. "Folk are driving animals through. Let me find us a place to wait while they pass."

In the rush to open the storehouses, Leif and Ole had been shoved from our side. After the long walk, Gunnar lacked the strength to go far, but I guided him to a small place where the crowds and animals would not trample us. "Thank you, Astrid, for your concern. Halvard told me he felt your kindness before he ever shared a word with you, in the Skraelings' country. All is as it should be now. You and the others won't go hungry, so my work is done."

"We?" I asked. "But nothing of this is ours. We never gave them anything." I grasped his hand and squeezed it, trying to encourage him. His outcry seemed to have drained his strength. "We'll be home soon."

"Yes," he agreed. He gave me a half smile. "It will be as the gods foretold." He turned his attention to the cathedral, where the bishop stood helplessly while his storerooms were raided. The Christian high priest leveled his gaze to stare at Gunnar as he and I waited, isolated from the movement around us like an island in a stream.

Men passed us by, their coats bulging with straw, cheeses, and other good things. They pushed by, herding animals and young dogs to drive home to their steadings, while the priests and servants watched, unable to resist. Brown- and black-robed men gathered to wait upon their master. The bishop pointed to Gunnar. He appeared to ask his men to name the old man. A shout went out from his faithful servants. "Why, that's the unconfessed priest of Odin."

I feared to move from our spot. At last, Ole, Leif, and Halvard rejoined us. "Let's go home, Halvard," Gunnar said. "I've seen enough." We turned away to start for home, so we never saw who flung the spear. There was a thud and Gunnar faltered. He started to collapse. Ole rushed past me and caught him before he fell, easing him down to the pressed snow.

"Father!" Halvard screamed. "Someone has killed my father!" There was an uproar around us. Halvard jumped and pushed through the crowd, trying to see whose hand had been poised, who tried to blend back with the crowd. A spear stuck out of Gunnar's side and blood seeped through his coat.

People shrieked and scattered and ran. I knelt in crushed snow and blood, doing my best to cradle Gunnar's head so he could breathe. His heart still beat. "He's not dead," Leif yelped. "His eyes are open."

"Astrid, Leif, Ole." He struggled to make the words. "It's all right."

"Maybe he will live," I cried. "Ole. Help me get him away before someone steps on him." Ole was only nine, but he had grown tall and strong enough to help. We half-dragged, half-carried the dying man.

As soon as we had settled Gunnar in the open doorway of a small outbuilding, Ole sped to lend support to his father. Halvard had split the skull of one of the monks with the ax he had brought to cut brush for our stock. "He's killed him," men screamed, reaching out for Halvard, trying to pull him off his victim, but Ole and Osmund, among others, would not let them interfere. One of the priests cried out that Halvard must be judged for murder, now, before the Althing.

Halvard turned to face his accusers. "Serpents who claim to speak for a loving god! Such courage this so-called man of god displayed, to murder an old man! It was a revenge killing. No Althing, no court of judges, would convict me for it. He killed my father!"

"He's right," Osmund asserted. "Accuse him at the Althing if you think you have a chance, any of you!"

"It's 'an eye for an eye.' The Holy Book demands such justice," a man shouted to the priests. "Your monk murdered a good man who was friend to many of us. Justice has been served."

"He was a heathen," the bishop yelled. "Is a heathen worth a Christian?"

"What about 'Honor your father'? Did you not teach us that?" someone screamed. Another man shouted that no man would dare to level charges against Halvard at the yearly court. "He did no more than avenge his father."

Halvard only half-listened to the talking. He held both of Gunnar's hands, tears dripping into his beard. "Father!" He gave a wailing moan, for Gunnar's blood stained the snow and his chest labored to draw breath. Other voices rumbled around us. One, the bishop's, sounded louder than the others, and thundered for an end to violence on consecrated ground.

At last, Ole convinced Halvard that Gunnar still lived and might be taken home. Someone warned Halvard that if he pulled out the spear, the old man would die more quickly. I wrapped my scarves around Gunnar to stanch some of the blood.

Someone shouted, telling his listeners to look up. A thick gray cloud settled over the cathedral, billowing out as we watched. Black birds descended from the cloud to the field, cawing like the crows I remembered from our cornfields, but they were not crows. The birds settled all around Gunnar. Had the cloud brought them? I might have reached out and touched one had I wished to. People mumbled fearfully. "Odin's ravens!" Some made the cross sign.

The birds encircled Gunnar as though to protect him, facing outward and cawing with open sharp beaks. They did not interfere when Halvard gathered up his father into his strong arms. When we moved, the ravens leapt up and hovered above us.

We had almost come to the edge of the crowd when a woman's voice shrilled, "The bishop attempts to speak. Hear him." A hush descended. I hardly cared, but Halvard paused to hear what the high priest would say.

"We are all Greenlanders here," the bishop said. "A great evil has happened on consecrated ground. I will pray for your souls. May our Lord Jesus forgive us all for today's deeds. Go home and hope our Lord and his mighty Father accept these two sacrifices. Let the faithful come back here on Easter to commemorate the day our Lord rose from his death, so we may sing praises together and ask for his forgiveness. Don't let Satan enter your hearts. Pray God has been appeased. Let there be no more bloodshed. Pray that our Lord will soon cause our valleys and hills to grow green again."

Many shouted "Amen" to these conciliatory words and hung their heads. A woman near us sobbed, begging her husband to return to the church what they had taken. "Don't be a fool," the man said, hurrying his wife along. "Of course he speaks of forgiving. Without it, the church would have no worshipers."

Halvard turned back to us. "Let's take my father home."

Gunnar barely made a sound, but I heard a sharp intake of breath when Halvard shifted him. "I'll get you home safe, Father," Halvard said, his mouth trembling.

"No, Halvard. Don't try." Halvard exhaled in a sigh as realization came. He still hoped. Ole blanched, but he managed to control himself, standing ready to help. There was a level shelf of land before the ground dipped to the fjord.

An elderly woman's voice called us from amid the people milling about. She bid us wait for her to join us. "It's Skaddi, Halvard," she said, hurrying up to us. "Don't try to carry him any farther. Let him rest where he is." The woman wrapped herself in her cloak. Her blue-fox furs made a snug hood around her face.

"Skaddi," Halvard said. "I had not thought to see you again in this world, after this last winter. Freya preserved you. Astrid, this is Skaddi, Freya's priestess, an old friend of my father's."

"Do as she says," Gunnar's weak voice commanded. We put down his cloak first, then set him on his side because of the spear. Halvard took off his great coat to lay it over him. I added mine, folding it several times under his head. Skaddi crouched down and the two old friends spoke together softly. When she rose, Halvard took her place at his side with Ole.

"Where is Astrid?" Gunnar asked. His pale lips formed a toothless smile. "I can hardly see you. Ole, Leif, take my hands. Dig in your fingers. I want to feel you." They did as he said. "Your grandmother Astrid waits for me. I see her now more clearly than I see you. Ole, look after your sister as she grows. Protect her. Give me your word." Ole hesitated, but Gunnar found enough strength to hold his grandson's eyes. "Do you hear me?"

"I hear you, Grandfather," Ole replied. His hazel eyes glittered with unshed tears. So did mine, for the fact that in his dying moments, Gunnar thought to extract this promise of the boy. "If it is what you want, I will do it." For once, I did not try to stop my tears from falling.

"I will, too, Grandfather," Leif said.

"Of course you will, Leif." Leif would have done so in any case. That is why Gunnar had not extracted the promise from him. After awhile, Gunnar closed his eyes and did not open them again. The birds shrieked and flapped their wings noisily, circling twice before they ascended the wind into the cloud again.

A moan escaped Halvard's lips. "He's left us." The cloud covered the sun, casting a shadow over the entire hill and all its buildings. It drifted by, uncovering the sun again. A golden ray slanted down to illuminate Gunnar's peaceful face.

Skaddi said, "Odin's ravens came to carry his soul to its rest."

The birds' flight had not been lost on what was left of the assembly. "Those who die in battle share the glory of the gods," Ole said. "My grandfather will go to Valhalla. Won't he, Skaddi?"

"If that's where he wants to be, the gods will find room for him in their golden halls. They'll give him Idunna's apples to eat and he will be young and strong again."

Halvard bent to lift his father's corpse into his arms to convey it home, when a party of men approached us gravely. "With your permission, my brothers and I will help you carry him." Four men stepped forward. Halvard nodded. I learned later these were sons and grandsons to Skaddi. They walked up and gathered the edges of the cloak to carry Gunnar.

Skaddi walked beside us all the way back, while others drove the sheep and dogs and carried food and fodder. As we progressed, Skaddi said, "I, too, came to observe Christian charity. My children came along to protect me. Up in the stone house of their god, the bishop would prefer all of us who remember the old ways to die. The bishop lost some of his sheep today, the human kind, thanks to Halvard's father. Undoubtedly, they will be drawn back with fine words and promises, while we who keep to the old ways disappear. There won't be another like Gunnar to make them remember the days when Norsemen bowed only to the gods of our fathers."

Ole, who was walking beside us, had been listening. "I promised Grandfather I would be faithful."

"I did, too," Leif echoed.

She put one arm over each of them. "The gods will know who we are."

Skaddi's sons and daughters-in-law walked back to the house with us and helped carry Gunnar inside. While Halvard sat heavily on his bed, Skaddi directed her sons. "Lay him out on his bed. Folk will want to pay their last respects." They draped his coat over him to his neck and propped up his head. His eyes had already sunken and his lips were bloodless, but even in death and at rest at last, his features evoked a connection to his gods. I wondered if Odin looked a little like Gunnar. "We must prepare his burial mound," Skaddi said.

I went back outside and looked over the fjord as people trudged toward Halvard's stead on their flat skis, driving their new animals and carrying their bundles. Two more days of melting would make it unsafe to travel. Halvard came out of the house and found me there. "Why are you outside?" he asked, turning me toward him. "You should be in the house with us."

"To give you time alone with your father," I said. "He was good to me, but you are his family."

"You were his daughter. Don't you know that?" I raised my eyes to his. I had come to love the old man. "My father told me this. Come inside with me now." His cheeks were damp. Before we went inside, he pulled me close and kissed me deeply, as if life could negate death.

Gunnar lay on his bed, half-covered in his robe, his bed hanging drawn back. Skaddi stood near his head and beckoned me. She took my hand without speaking and gazed into my face. I felt her consoling presence strongly through her touch. She seemed almost to enter into my thoughts and heart as Minik had done. I invited her in and did not hold back. "What will become of us all?" Until I heard my words, I did not realize I had spoken aloud.

"In the end, we will all be ghosts. The winters will continue. I think this land no longer wants us here. I'll die soon," she said.

I could accept that for myself, and Halvard was older than I. If Sea Woman truly intended to destroy the invaders of her people's land, my only fear was for the children. "What about my daughter? Halvard's sons? What of them?"

To my surprise, she smiled. "Dear Astrid. Do you think I really see into the future? I speak as an old woman who has been through too much loss and the worst winter our people have seen. You are the one who has been given a glimpse into the future. Gunnar told me."

"I don't know what's going to happen," I protested. "Visions come to me when it pleases the Great Spirit. I expected this winter, but I don't know what will happen to us now."

"You have kept your family alive so far. You used what you have learned in your travels and you share your knowledge freely. Maybe some of us will survive. Trials and dangers can be overcome with strength and determination. I speak from many years' experience. Teach your children what you know and give them part of your spirit. We may yet change the intentions of the gods."

"Thank you." I hugged her. "You give me hope." After awhile, I excused myself to fill the lamp with new tallow and to warm milk for our remaining guests.

Others came during the long spring evening. Each set down a piece of cheese or dried fish or seal meat, or a container of tallow by the hearthstone before he left. I arranged slices of the cheese and seal meat in the dry milk vat, inviting visitors to help themselves, but no one did. They said it was for us.

I had changed the packing in Ingrid's wrappings and was nursing her behind our bed hanging when a voice startled me. "Astrid, may I enter?" Ole's voice squeaked, perhaps a measure of his uncertainty. Most times, I nursed his sister in full view of the family, but strangers were present. I pulled a corner of the blanket up to cover my breast.

"Yes," I replied.

He pushed the hanging aside and stepped inside. "Those things I said to you when you first came . . ."

I remembered every word. I was the Skraeling witch who made a child to steal his inheritance away. In the small light that seeped around the bed hanging, Ole was white as birch bark, except for his red-rimmed eyes. His hair framed his face like fire on snow. "I was wrong," he admitted. He ducked out as soon as the words left his mouth, leaving me staring at the swaying bed hanging.

The following day, while we piled the stones over Gunnar's shallow grave, cracks appeared in the fjord's ice. Booms and cracks sounded as the water rushed back into the fjord from the ocean and the ice field broke apart. Above the thunder of spring, seabirds screeched, swarming up from the ocean to roost in the relative safety of the cliffs. The next day, grass was sighted. Whatever Sea Woman planned, it was not going to be accomplished in one winter.

A New Home

Chapter

We gave our small herd plenty of dry straw and what seeds we could manage. When the grass grew in the meadows and hills, they received water and sunshine, as well. The goats and sheep grew sturdy and even put on some fat. Finally, even in the shade, the blanket of white gave way to green. Halvard told me a funny thing. The men who founded the Greenlander colony, Erik the Red and his son Leif the Lucky, wanted families to follow them to the new land and settle there. Leif returned to Iceland and told the folk there he had found a green land, capable of nourishing many flocks. For perhaps three months out of a cycle of moons, the story was true.

So the frozen ground had put forth new growth, turning the hills into a rainbow of colors. Still, folk remembered the day at the cathedral. A good number of them had visited us at Halvard's stead to pay respects at Gunnar's grave. As often as not, someone came leading a lamb or carrying a round of cheese to appease Gunnar's spirit. They gave these offerings to us, his family, to do with as we saw fit. I wondered if folk expected to buy goodwill and protection from Gunnar's gods by doing this. In my view, it never hurt to respect the gods of any place one happened to be.

Halvard and our visitors often discussed the weather. The Greenlanders never stopped hoping that merchant ships from Iceland or Norway would renew their annual visits, bringing them much-needed wood beams, nails, flour, and other supplies. There had been no ship, no contact at all, from the eastern countries, not since that longship that sailed proudly down the center of the fjord to Gardar the day I arrived. Everyone agreed the winter had been bizarre. They never wanted to see and feel its like again. I could not help but agree.

During the green days of summer, I wind-dried fish Halvard netted in the fjord while the boys pastured the herd. With Ingrid watching from her hanging cradleboard, I milked the animals and made cheeses for winter. We lived mostly on fresh fish with thick sour milk. I learned to be grateful for it.

In the month Halvard's people call August, he and other men left the district for four days. The priests, who owned Hreiney Island, where their reindeer wintered, asked every able-bodied man to help round them up for the yearly kill. Halvard went along with the others and returned with venison.

Ingrid was crawling about the day one of Skaddi's sons, a man called Steinthor, summoned us to help bury his mother. The old priestess's daughter, Freydis, was older than Halvard. Freydis took my hand and held it after the first stones were laid. She thanked me for coming to see Skaddi properly covered. "My mother told me your land is west of Vinland, that you never saw a white man before Halvard. She said you did not know of us. It must have been difficult for you to learn our ways," she said.

I agreed. "It is very difficult. You are so different."

She asked me to explain. I shrank back a little, fearful of offending her. Seeing my hesitation, she added, "I ask only because I'm curious. What was most different? Our food? Our woolens? Don't be afraid to tell me."

"That, as well as your iron and your planked boats, your sails. The way you think. The different gods!" She had not turned cold eyes upon me yet. Perhaps because she was Skaddi's daughter, I could speak comfortably to her. "Most of all, you are different because you don't live in villages, but in separate houses away from one another. If Greenlanders moved after the game as the Inuit do, you would have more, not less to eat. Go where the animals go; learn their runs when the seasons change. You should live as Sea Woman directs her people. They grew fat this winter while we went hungry. I wonder if their Sea Woman would be appeased if we learned this."

She did not answer as I expected, but instead, she smiled a crooked smile. "Do you really trust the Skraeling god's power?" I lowered my head, not wanting to meet her eyes. "If your Sea Woman thinks she will change Norsemen, she doesn't know us. This is how we've always lived. One harsh winter won't convince us. We've been here in Greenland three hundred years and more. We're proud of what we've accomplished."

"In my country, the spirits send dreams to instruct people. I have dreamed Sea Woman wants you to go away, as I told Halvard. Do not expect any mild winters."

"Perhaps that is true," she said. "But how does your Sea Woman expect us to leave? Greenlanders have no ships that can cross oceans. There is not the wood to build them, and even if there were, we are forbidden by our king in Norway to make our own trade ships. Whatever comes, we will have to make the best of it, as we have always done." I had no reply for her.

It was good to see how many folk turned out to honor Skaddi. I began to think that under the surface, many people felt uneasy trusting the church's god to care for their needs. We did not see Freydis and her brothers often, even during the warm months. They lived across the fjord. Besides, there was work to do. Winter was coming and I feared Sea Woman had not exhausted her anger.

Before winter returned, Halvard took one of his yearling rams and sacrificed it on Gunnar's grave, leaving the haunches and the head on the stones, giving the blood to the earth. Birds came to eat the meat and fly back to the clouds. "They take our offering across the rainbow bridge to Asgard, the city in the clouds where the gods live," he said. "May our gods do better by us this winter than the last. Let old Sea Woman try her hardest."

"Don't say that," I begged. "You have not seen what she can do when she is angry, even against her own people. I have." He seemed to want to laugh at my fears, but the laughter would not come.

We estimated the amount of fodder we had stored and how long it would take the herd to eat it. Afterward, he slaughtered all but one ram and buck. I cut the meat into strips and dried it in it sun. At the same time, I rendered fat for two days outside over a driftwood fire. When it cooled, I poured it into cleansed stomach bags and stored them in the larder under the floor.

I did not trust the summer to remain with us very long. No merchant ship came that year. Instead of spinning yarn, weaving, and tailoring breeches and shirts, I rough-tanned the buck hides, stretching and twisting them as I would have done at home. When we found driftwood against the banks of our fjord, I smoked the hides as well to make them shed water. I used the toughened leather to sew new winter clothing and moccasin boots for myself and Halvard. I made Leif and Ole shirts and trousers long enough in the legs and shoulders for them to grow. Their old clothing was already too small.

The following winter was not as brutal as the last has been. By her second summer, Ingrid could speak. The next few years hurried by. No one winter was quite as severe as my first in Halvard's land, but each summer there was less grass to harvest, less milk to put up enough cheeses. More folk died in the outlying areas. Of those who survived, many moved south to take over empty homes in the more populated fjords. The churches took lands and properties, collecting up the deserted steadings.

As the years went by, people continued to hope for the sight of a longship, but this did not happen. Folk wondered what to do. They asked many questions, but all the talk in the world could not give them answers. They wanted to know what was happening to their motherland, Norway? What about their parent country, Iceland, and the many people of Europe? It seemed we were alone.

Each winter, the Greenlanders lost more land; each winter the Skraelings' villages drew farther south and closer to the southern district. We often saw their sea hunters in kayaks, looking well nourished and strong as they plied their double-bladed paddles. It seemed all the gods, both new and old, had deserted Greenland, except, of course, for Sea Woman. Perhaps because of Gunnar's intercession for us with Odin in Asgard, the home of the old gods, we survived each winter. I couldn't say.

Although Ole and I had made peace, he never warmed to Ingrid. His promise to Gunnar that he would look out for his sister did not include liking her. One day in early summer while I worked outside, stretching the hide of a reindeer Halvard had taken in the last hunt, I heard weeping. I followed the sound and found Ingrid curled up on the piled hay, her face buried in her arms. Even when my shadow fell across her, she did not lift her head. "What's wrong?" I asked her, crouching to stroke her loose red curls back from her face.

Her hazel eyes were rimmed with red. Tears furrowed lines down her dusty cheeks as they dripped to her chin and fell into the hay. "He hates me," she whimpered. "Why does he hate me?"

During her four long winters, Ingrid had learned to go to bed with too little in her stomach, and too little company, but not Ole's rejection. "Is this something new?" I inquired. "What did your brother say to you?"

"I named the new lambs Buttercup and White Wing. He chased me away when I tried to play with them. Why is Ole like that? Can't you tell me?"

I had no answer for her. "Ole is one of those people who is more sour than sour milk," I admitted. I pulled her up onto my lap and kissed away her tears. "Don't cry. It's a sign of weakness, and you must be strong. Do you want Ole to think he is winning?" She shook her head.

"Good. Don't let anyone see when you are unhappy. I wish I could take you home to play with your cousins. You have many of them, in their home across the ocean." She pointed westward. "That's right. You know the ocean. We took you to see it when the birds were nesting. I go every spring to steal some eggs for us."

She pressed her lips for a moment and looked at me sideways. "Mama! I'm a big girl now. You talk about my cousins, but it's like telling a story. Nobody really lives on the other side of the ocean." She sounded older than her years. "Don't tease like Ole."

I tilted her chin to make her look at me eye-to-eye, willing her to believe me. "I would never lie to you. My people do live across the ocean, near a wide river. Unfortunately, it is too far to visit. Your father doesn't want to leave his land. We could be happy there." While I told her about the people and places she would never see, she listened, fascinated. If nothing more, it distracted her from thinking about Ole.

How I wished for the company and the wisdom of older women. In my country, no mother had to deal with a child by herself. We had elders to advise and teach, cousins for a girl to play with and learn from. I told Ingrid about maple trees and the syrup we made from their sap, how we made candy sugar in the snow. I told her about our festivals and how corn grew. I told how we listened to storytellers every winter night around my grandmother's hearth.

"What's a grandmother? Do I have one, too?"

I swallowed my emotion to be able to answer her. "My mother is your grandmother. She would hold you on her lap right now if she could. She would feed you corn cakes and the sweet, thick syrup of the maple tree."

She did not accuse me of teasing again, but she looked doubtful. "Is it like that when you're dead, where the gods bring you?"

"What? Why would you think that?"

"Leif says the gods take us to live with them when we die and they feed us until we're not hungry anymore. I won't mind dying if I can go there."

"No. No." How awful to think my child thought a normal childhood was something only the dead could achieve. "I'm talking about a real place, Ingrid. It is my home, the place where I grew up. On Turtle Island, winter is fun. We have winter games and feasts. No one goes hungry and friends are everywhere. Maybe you'll see for yourself someday, so my mother can hug you and feed you corn cakes."

Ingrid closed her little mouth in a way I knew. She still supposed I was telling her a tale like other winter tales, to divert us from hunger and hopelessness. Soon, she began to yawn and doze in my lap, sucking her thumb. I carried her in the house and put her onto her bed. If only my worries could be put away as easily as my work when it became too dark to continue.

That night, when Halvard came to lie beside me, I planned to talk to him about Ole, but the tangy smell of his sweat gave me thoughts of another kind. The children's problems could wait for a while. I spread my fingers lightly over his hairy chest. He looked at me in surprise, then lifted my palm to his lips and bit my knuckles playfully. "Yes," he agreed. "It has been much too long." We made love happily, tenderly, giving strength to each other. It was good. Afterward, we lay in the warm afterglow, content.

"What are you thinking, Astrid?" he asked, gazing down into my face by the pale light from the unshuttered window.

I gathered my words carefully before I spoke. "Leif enjoys his little sister. I think he'll like the new one, too," I whispered.

"Yes. He seems to like babies. Will the new one be a boy, do you think?"

"This time, I have no feeling either way. Something is troubling me. Perhaps you can help me understand why Ole treats our daughter the way he does. Do you notice?"

He twisted a lock of my long hair around his fingers. "Of course I notice, but I can only guess," Halvard whispered. "It's not a thing I can speak to him about, but I think he's jealous."

"Of what? And why?" My voice came out louder than I intended. Halvard pressed his hand gently to my lips.

"Because he lost his mother, but Ingrid has you."

I thought how different it would be if Ole had been born Ganeogaono on Turtle Island. "In my country, Ole would be training to be a warrior. He would have many age-mates and cousins to run with. He would not have the time for brooding over a small sister."

Halvard continued to play with my hair, running his fingers from my scalp down the strands until they reached my hip. "Ole needs time to work out his feelings. He's a lot like me."

"Did you never make up your mind swiftly? What about the time you traded a knife for your woman?"

He laughed deep in his chest, a comforting rumble. "Yes, there was a time when I made up my mind swiftly. When a man is hungry, he doesn't think too much. I was very hungry." He pulled me close against him to nibble my shoulder, then moved his lips from my shoulder to my neck, and soon we were joined in a long, deep kiss. Shortly afterward, his even breathing told me Halvard slept.

I lay with my head resting against his broad chest, just thinking, when I heard soft footsteps rustle the mats I had laid over the hard-packed floor. The boards squeaked under Ole's and Leif's bed closet. My stepson had been listening. Afterward, I always stayed alert for the small sounds that told me Ole was listening. The sharp hearing my aunt had drilled into all of us remained. Instead of guarding my words, I used them skillfully, weaving good thoughts into them, like yarn on a loom, for him to hear.

Our new baby was another girl, born in late winter. There was not enough food. Before spring came, her cries grew weak. When my milk dried, I chewed meat for her and mixed it with broth. I squeezed it into her mouth through wadmal, but she died.

Ingrid took her small sister's death badly and became withdrawn. All of us became grim, as if a dark cloud always hung above us. We spent much of our time sleeping to save strength. If not for my living daughter, I hardly would have minded following the infant to her small mound next to Gunnar's.

When it happened again the following year, Halvard stopped sleeping with me. We did not speak about it. I knew he feared that the next time I lost a baby, I would follow it to the land of the spirits. Without our joining in love, there were times I wondered why I lived and suffered. Halvard hurt, too. Neither of us could bear to lose another child.

My memories of home and forest, along with memories of my mother and aunts and grandmother, dimmed. It began to feel as if the ocean *was* the end of the world and nothing existed east or west of Greenland. When winter came again, the entire world seemed a place of whiteness and howling wind, hunger and cold. What if my memories of early, happy times were only memories of dreams? Could there really be a place with tall trees where leaves blocked the sun? Did there ever exist a tribe whose women brought corn from the earth and rendered sweet syrup from trees?

The sun finally returned. Somehow, we had managed to survive another winter. I had perfected my porridge making. Usually, the bush and tall grasses that grew at the water's edge had set their seeds but had not yet dropped them all when they froze under the snow. My crushed seeds simmered until they expanded and made gruel. Eaten with a little milk, we managed to fill our bellies and stop our hunger from consuming us. The new lambs and kids were scrawny for days after they were born, too weak to stand. They suckled lying down while we fed their dams seaweed and twigs by hand until the grass grew again. "This isn't going to work," Halvard said. "We might as well make up our minds to die. Another year like this will destroy us."

I remembered all I had learned and heard. Skaddi had bidden me to give part of my spirit to my family. "Halvard, I think we will live as long as the children need us. Sea Woman is spreading her anger over several winters to give the Greenlanders false hope. Come back with me to Qisuk's village. They'll take us in. If we live as the Inuit do, our children will live."

Halvard's face grew red, as if I were blaming him for the death of our children. "This is my land! You never understood about what land means to a Norseman. Slaves don't own land. Men do. Without his own land, a Norseman is a serf, which is worse than nothing!"

"Halvard! Qisuk and his people are not slaves." I had never heard him so angry since the day after I slept with Qisuk under the boat. We had accepted the differences between ourselves, but not until this day, had I realized how strong a hold his land had upon him. Instead of the land being his, he was the land's.

He saw how I pulled back at his words. "I'm sorry, Astrid. How could I expect you to understand? It's different for me. I'm a Norseman! I will not leave the land of my fathers and spend my life on the move. Try to understand this. We farm and fish. That is the way Greenlanders have lived for over three hundred years." It will also be your death, I thought, but there was no point in saying so.

Ingrid ran over the home field, bursting with something to say. When she was close enough, I saw one of her eyes swollen shut and her cheek scratched. She started to talk even before she reached me. "Olga said you make sure we have enough to eat, because you're a Skraeling and Skraelings always find food."

"How did you answer her?" I asked.

"That you're not a Skraeling and that we don't always have food. I pushed her down and hit her until her nose bled. I don't want to play with her again."

I tried to comfort my daughter, but I wondered if she were going to have trouble because of me. I had never discovered how to contend with such twisted hatred when I encountered it. All I could do was to try to make Ingrid strong, teaching her how to live within herself. After this, I preferred to remain at home so the neighbors did not have to see me and flaunt my darkness in my daughter's face.

One day, three men came home with Halvard from the fjord where he had been fishing, Osmund, Steinthor, and another, whose name was Oskar. They had rowed up and left their boats bobbing in the water. I offered them tea and moved into a corner to get out of their way.

"The stomach ailment is spreading again," Oskar said. "I had word from my wife, who attends the church. The priests say God sent trouble to test us, to make us worthy to be saved. We must bear our trials as our Lord bore his suffering when he lived among men on earth."

"Put that in terms a pagan can understand," Halvard suggested.

"The priests want all of us to examine ourselves for sinful thoughts, since these open the door for Satan." At Halvard's question, Osmund explained Satan, who seemed to be like the Creator's evil brother. He enjoyed destruction.

"You holdouts are probably the problem, although we like you well enough. Come on. Let the priests baptize you and your wife and children, Halvard. It's not much to ask," Oskar said. "Some of us have taken Skraelings for slaves or for wives. I can understand the attraction of a docile wife. Even the priests sometimes take wives." Without turning my head from my work, I smiled. Would Halvard consider me docile? I doubted it.

The conversation continued. "Those who keep to the old gods are just as much at fault if Satan gets his grip into us. Coveting and lusting can't be so awful. We did that in good years, too. I think it has to be the pagans."

"Have you gone over to them, too?" Steinthor asked Oskar sadly.

The man nodded. "I'm not saying it's men like Steinthor and Halvard in particular, but it's obvious our old gods deserted us. We live on the edge of the world. Odin doesn't care whether we all die. I'm willing to give our Lord a try. Maybe he'll bring us better luck. Why won't you try him?"

"Your god has helped no one these last few years," Steinthor replied. "Are we lambs to be herded by the bishop's dog-priests, or are we Norsemen?"

"We are hungry and sick Norsemen."

Halvard rose from his bench angrily. "Do you expect me to desert the gods of my fathers? Maybe our gods could defeat the frost giants as they have before if only so many of you had not turned away from them. You deny them their sacrifices and prayers. If we drove out the Christian priests—"

"It's too late for that. You can't make time run backward like sand going up an hourglass, Halvard," Oskar shouted. "Stop living in the past, you pagans. The old gods are dead."

"I agree with Halvard," said Steinthor. "Why should our gods bother with you, since you've turned away from them?" Both men glared at each other.

Osmund had grown frail in the last few winters. White streaked his hair and beard. He spoke quietly, as if sharing a confidence. "Astrid predicted our winters would worsen. She said the Skraeling god, Sea Woman, warned her in a dream. I wonder if we could placate her."

"I thought you were a Christian now. Whose side are you on, Osmund, the Skraelings'?" Oskar turned to me next. In a snarling voice, he asked, "Do the Skraeling gods continue to talk to you, woman?"

I rose from my corner, angry. "Do you suppose I bring the long winters and the sickness? Would *my* babies die if I had power? Instead of arguing about your gods, work together the way the Skraelings do." My voice had grown loud, or else it was the silence around me that made it seem so. Leif and Ingrid crawled into one of the bed closets, but Ole walked over, coming to rest behind his father.

"You still have Skraeling friends, don't you?" Oskar asked.

Halvard answered for me. "I don't want to hear any of that, and I don't like your tone. You are speaking to my wife. Neither of us has been north these seven years. Our losses are as bad as yours."

Oskar said, "It seems to me that our winters have been getting worse for exactly seven years. Isn't that when you first brought Astrid here?"

"It's also the year the priests came on the last longship," Steinthor countered. "Perhaps the priests are doing it themselves, to bend us to their will. They still have their ponies and a small herd of cattle, while their converts go hungry and watch their babies die. If this Jesus or Christ or any of your gods can defeat Sea Woman, let them do it."

"Don't argue about it!" said Osmund, trying to be the peacemaker. "Let us act like reasonable men and agree that we are in this together. Try to reason out what to do, rather than quarrel among ourselves about who is to blame and which gods are strongest."

"All right," Oskar said. "You've always been the voice of reason in our arguments. Do you have any ideas?"

Osmund shrugged. "I already made them. We must work together."

"Men can only control so much," Halvard added. "We need to replenish our food and fodder and build up our supplies. How many of us are going on the seal hunt tomorrow?"

"I'm going with my brothers. Set your tent beside ours, Halvard,"

Steinthor said. I was glad when they invited Halvard, and that he agreed to go.

"Take Ole," I suggested. "He's nearly a man already." Hair had already begun to spout from his chin.

That cheered Ole and brought Leif running from his bed closet, with Ingrid right beside him. "What about me? Mayn't I go, too?"

"Next year, you will come with us," Halvard said. "We need to have at least one man remain here at home to protect Astrid and Ingrid from danger." Leif accepted that.

"Ole and I will be ready to join you in the morning. Come by in your boats. We'll be waiting." Halvard walked the men to the door.

I mended the hides Halvard used for his tent. This year, I drew seals swimming to decorate the outside. Ingrid bent over the skins to trace the sun design over the water. I prayed good weather would accompany the hunt, so I included no clouds. "Those are seals your father wishes to hunt," I said, sitting back on my heels above my work. "Notice how the water is calm."

"What is it?" she asked, indicating the designs. "All of it?"

"A picture," I replied.

"But why did you make it?"

"Pictures may give hunting luck." I handed her the charred bone dipped in sooty lamp grease. "See if you can draw a seal." She took the bone and stared at the hide. "Go ahead. Take it and think *seal*."

She tried, very intent on the task, to copy what I had done. For a first try, it was fairly good. She even remembered the whiskers. "If Grandmother's spirit is watching from the clouds, she would be proud of her great-granddaughter." Ingrid looked up at the sky as if she expected to see someone looking down. She saw me watching her fondly as she searched the clouds. Her grin lit up her face.

When the men returned from the hunt, the slaughtered seals were divided among the hunters after the church had claimed its portion. The next day, I sliced the meat into strips to hang on racks to dry in the wind. I charged Ingrid to keep it from the dog, but I could not help wondering if it would be enough.

Chapter 37

A council of landowners with great tracts of land and servants offered support for the next winter to the first ten stalwarts adventurous enough to sail east to learn what had become of the Icelanders. In return, these men must return with tidings of the eastern countries. Bright sunlight and bubbles of foam danced over the wavelets of Eriksfjord the day the three boats sailed. They carried enough dried fish and freshwater to last them two weeks.

We descended halfway down the hill from Halvard's house to watch the boats glide past our landing. Halvard explained it to me. "They'll have to sail around Cape Farewell and then north up the eastern coast before they turn eastward and head for the open sea. If they don't go down in a storm, they should reach Iceland in five or six days." I studied the three small boats and their brave crews, wondering if we would see them again. We could not remain watching long. There was work to be done.

After supper, the sun remained low in the western sky. The herd had been put into their fold for the night when visitors came. While the men talked on the porch bench outside, Ingrid and I breathed in the flower-scented air and listened by the open window. It was the usual sort of conversation, but this time we had greater hopes of learning the truth. "If there's plague come to the eastern countries, I don't want the sailors bringing it home," Steinthor said.

"Perhaps the winters there are as bad as ours," Halvard said. "That might explain the lack of merchant ships. I hope our men are being cautious, but even if it is the plague, they can't find it out without landing and asking the Icelanders."

"And yet, we must know," Osmund continued. "It is interesting that we've seen Skraelings paddling in and out of our fjords in their skin boats without fear of reprisals. They offer to trade seal and walrus meat for Norse-smithed iron tools and spearheads, and our lads do it. Those Skraelings are armed with iron weapons now, while the food we received is eaten and gone. They live as well or better than before these hard winters began. Have you noted how they grow fat while we waste away? I have, and it makes me angry. I hope the Icelanders are decent enough Christians to send food back with our men."

While they spoke, Ole walked out of the house and leaned against the wall next to the men. He spoke as if to no one in particular. "It seems to me that if the Icelanders have food, they wouldn't be so free with it. They will want something in exchange. Shall we offer ourselves to be servants in order to be fed?" Since his first hunt, he had gained respect among the men of our acquaintance for his skill with a spear and the strength of his arm. He was growing into a powerful young man. Ole had made a valid point. No one cared to answer.

Steinthor lifted his eyes to the clouds. After awhile, he looked back to Osmund and Oskar. "Maybe your Christian gods and our Norse gods have deserted us. What if the Skraeling Sea Woman really does hold sway over this land? Maybe we ought to go north and throw ourselves on Skraeling charity."

Osmund growled and glowered at him. "That is not funny."

Soon the men departed for their steadings and their own beds. Before we slept, I told Halvard, "Steinthor's idea may be the best of all. We have friends in the north. Our family doesn't have to starve."

Halvard sighed. "Not again. Please, Astrid. Our sailors will discover what has happened and why no trading ships have come. This is my land and I intend to hold tight to it. It will belong to my sons. If we leave it, I will have nothing and be nothing. Sleep now." He kissed me and turned to the wall. All I could think was that the boundary stones that walled Halvard's land from his neighbor's would do well to bury us. I did not say so, but remained silent and tried to sleep.

The sailors were gone three and a half weeks, as Halvard counted time, between one Odin's Day and the next three times, and a few days more. A lookout in the cathedral bell tower first sighted their sails coming up Eriksfjord toward Gàrdar's landing. The brass bells of the cathedral were sent to ringing until they echoed through the hills.

Groups of homesteaders gathered and began to converge on cathedral land. There were fewer walking the trails than on the day Gunnar was killed. Many had died in the winters since then, but people came dressed in their finery as if it were a holiday. The men wore their best woolens, dyed or embroidered with many fine colors of thread. The women wore their best embroidered headdresses and their fancy-worked bodices with sleeves, belted over their long skirts. My weaving was neither dyed nor embroidered, but we too, put on woven clothing to greet our explorers and hear the news.

We proceeded cautiously, for the only meeting place large enough to hold this assembly was the cathedral hall. I worried about bringing Ingrid inside those walls, but she could not be left alone. She pointed out every new face and colorful headdress, excited and eager to share in this adventure. Every church from Brattahlid, the first, to the most eastern monastery, rang its bell. Each bell alerted the next farthest, until all the Greenlanders knew that our sailors had returned. The peals echoed like a summons through the valleys and across the fjords to the islands and beyond.

Masted sailboats thronged the fjord. I hadn't thought this many people remained alive. The fields and hills along the way were full of spots of color, like bits of rainbow. All three boats were tied up at Gardar landing when we arrived on the cathedral grounds. We passed servants' houses, the dairies, kitchens, and sewing rooms, all deserted because everyone wanted to hear the sailors' tidings with their own ears. Looms hung from ceiling hooks, unworked, and spindles lay unspun. Scythes and rakes rested against the walls.

In the priests' and monks' residences, doors hung open, displaying scrolls of parchment left on narrow planked tables beside earthenware bottles of ink and feather quills. Stones had been left to hold the parchment pieces down against stray breezes.

A pair of priests pushed both carved wooden doors outward. Between them, the great inner hall appeared cold and forbidding. Two boys swung from ropes in the bell tower, enjoying themselves hugely. Another priest climbed up to make them stop for no one could hear another speak over the clamoring.

"Shall we go inside?" I asked Halvard.

"Why not? This meeting is for everyone. No one will notice us among all the others. I want to hear what the sailors found."

Even Ole entered, but he muttered below his breath to Leif, "I don't like being in here." Leif nodded his agreement and looked around. I clasped Ingrid's hand more tightly so as not to lose her in the shuffling crowd. Sunlight slanted in golden rays through high, narrow windows. The rays illuminated woven tapestries hanging on the walls. When my eyes adjusted to the dimness, I saw that these weavings contained pictures. It was a new form of art to me, and I could not help but stare. In colored threads on golden backgrounds, the artists had pictured people suffering dreadful agonies.

What is there about suffering that so thrilled these folk? "Look, Halvard," I said, pointing to the nearest wall hanging. It showed a blind woman, quite young and pretty, but her eye sockets were raw and empty. She held out a trencher on which sat the two globes of her eyes like plums. It was as though she were offering food. "How does this help them worship their god?"

He also appeared disturbed at the picture. "I don't know. I had no idea Christians worshiped atrocities. I've heard the terrors of the Vikings of former times. This is worse than what they did when they ransacked a town or a city."

Ingrid tugged on my sleeve. "Do they really nail gods to crosses and tear out women's eyes, Ma?" I regretted coming at once. We might have waited for the news.

"I don't know. Try not to look." I held Ingrid's hands tighter. Her attention shifted from one picture to the next. It was shameful for such skillful artistry to depict these terrible pictures. They might give Ingrid bad dreams.

Halvard spoke into my ear, to make sure I heard him above the buzz of conversation. "Our stories say Odin sold one of his eyes to buy wisdom from the Norns who assign our destinies. Who knows what the girl expected to trade for both hers? I've heard the bishop is full of stories, but this goes beyond any explanation I can imagine. Let us hear the sailors' report and get out of here." I could not agree more strongly.

"Ma," Ingrid said, squeezing my hand, "I don't like it here. There are too many people and the pictures scare me."

"We will leave soon," Halvard told her.

I bent to speak in Ingrid's ear. "Stay close to me and nothing will harm you. We will go right after the sailors tell us what they found in Iceland." While we waited, I noticed the picture of the next tapestry. It made my flesh crawl. Men in metal shirts and caps wielded iron axes against defenseless people. Hacked and bleeding limbs lay upon the green grass. Stumps and torsos poured into puddles of scarlet thread. On another, a young woman on the tapestry beheld her own bleeding tooth, which had just been extracted. A man, cruelly leering, held a grasping device, covered with blood. Great tears poured from his victim's heaven-gazing eyes while her hands clenched in pain or in prayer.

In a further display, a steel-clad warrior aimed a glowing red iron tool at the eyes of a gentle-faced victim. It disgusted me to see such behavior displayed. Doteoga's bereaved women never inflicted such tortures, which is not to say that they wouldn't if they had thought of them. How could Birgitta and Ludmilla's god be as gentle and loving as they thought him to be? No good god would permit those who served him to suffer such torments.

"What's the matter with you?" our neighbor, Birgitta, asked. I wondered how she managed to approach us with all the folk milling about.

"These weavings! How can people do that? How could you turn from Gunnar's old gods to this?"

"You don't understand," Birgitta said, trying to explain. "Those are our saints who suffered for Christ. The pagans who harmed them are burning in hell for the rest of eternity. Can't you see the halos around the saints' heads?"

"I see. Such glows are always visible around ghosts. My father appeared to me with such a halo, not only around his head, but his entire form. My first daughter's spirit, when she appeared to me, also shined with such light."

"How can you compare Skraeling ghosts to saints?" she asked, shaking her head at my ignorance.

There was no point in saying more. I raised my eyes from her to the last wall hanging. It depicted a family, the mother and father with a naked son on his mother's lap. This picture was different in that it was happy. Birgitta explained. "That's Jesus when he was a baby, sitting on his blessed mother's lap. Her husband is standing behind them."

In spite of myself, I asked, "Then, is the man with the black beard your Creator, the god who made your world?"

"No. Saint Joseph is a man. You can't see Jesus' father. I can't explain. Wait! One of the sailors is ready to talk." The murmuring ceased.

The ten sailors huddled in their coats, their eyes gleaming and haunted-looking in their gaunt, wind-tanned faces. It seemed to me as if they had not expected to set foot on land again, as if they'd visited the places of the dead. One of their number, a bedraggled man with sun-yellow hair and beard white with sea salt, came forward. He held his coat close, to keep warm, although it was almost stifling in the hall with the press of so many sweaty bodies.

He cleared his throat and began to speak in a clear voice that spread through the hall. "Small boats like ours aren't made for ocean crossings. We hoped at least one of our number would make it to Iceland and back. Our mission was to learn if the world still exists. We found Iceland and got home again. That is the good news. The rest is not so good. We are truly cut off. I'm thirsty."

Someone brought him a mug of water. He lifted it to his lips and drank noisily, then wiped a grimy hand across his dripping mustaches. He looked out over the folk filling the hall. "Iceland's mountains are belching fire. Smoke and fire fill the sky above them. Villages are buried in lava. As if that was not enough, it is true that plague runs rampant in the remaining cities. It's like the end of the world."

Several men and women made the cross sign over their chests. "Satan is winning. He's winning," someone shouted.

One of the other sailors came forward. He must have been well known because someone called out his name. "Olaf! What do you say? Is there really plague? Did you see it there for yourself?"

Before he could reply, another yelled, "If there is plague, they've brought it here to us! We're all going to die!" Folk looked around for the best way to run, but before anyone moved, the man spoke again.

"No, you are not! Not of plague. Listen to me. We turned our boats around and came back. We never stepped foot on land." The shouting died to confused and whispered murmurings.

"Olaf, if you saw no people, how do you know there was plague?" Halvard bellowed. The people quieted to hear the reply.

"I'll explain if everyone will stop interrupting. We were off the coast when we first saw the light through the soot and ash. It was like a false dawn. The closer we sailed, the redder the sky flamed, and the more thickly the ashes fell. Finally, we saw the mountains. They were spitting fire and towns burning, up and down the coast, three volcanoes, all erupting together. The mountains roared and lava flowed down to the houses and the beach. Earthquakes and high waves washed away the low lands. Where streams of lava flowed into the water, the ocean itself was boiling."

"How can mountains be on fire?" I asked.

Halvard answered me. "There are certain mountains with fires deep inside them, where fire gnomes forge metal. Thor's Hammer was forged in such a mountain. When a volcano erupts, it hurls out melted red rock that burns everything in its path."

The people ceased their questions and listened when the sailor continued. "A small group of Icelandic sailors saw us and put out to sea, coming close enough for us to exchange words with them. They begged us to wait while they got their wives and children. They had forgotten us, but now they wanted to follow us home.

"They said that before the mountains exploded, one last longship had come to anchor in the town's harbor. It wasn't a trade ship, but a ship of refugees, trying to escape the plague in Norway. They thought all aboard were well, but before they landed, one of their number became ill. They threw him overboard, but the others landed. It is that ship that brought the sickness into Iceland. No longships lift anchor now. Perhaps they have all been destroyed. In any case, there's nowhere to sail one to, and not enough well folk for a crew.

"Priests were doctoring the sick in the villages when the volcanoes erupted. Hundreds of folk and their animals with them are under lava and ash. Poison air seeps from vents in the ground and fires burn out of control. Animals are left to rot. Those who tried to eat their flesh sicken and die."

"You bring us the plague," Oskar shouted a few feet away from us.

"No. I ordered the Icelanders away from our boats. We had no food to spare, only enough to get back. They wouldn't believe me when I told them about our trouble here. One man tried to get too close to us. Bjorn was forced to spear the poor fellow to keep him off." The crowd breathed heavily, probably in relief that at least this one particle of information was favorable.

"That is everything. Expect no longships and no succor. We have been forgotten by the world, just as we suspected. We might as well go back to our houses. Death rains down in fire from the sky in the east. Hot or cold, we'll soon be just as dead."

"Lord, no!" A woman fainted and her family had to carry her out. Folk began to scream and to rush outside to tell the waiting crowds.

One of the priests, who had been standing by a wall, hollered to get people's attention. "We need holy wafers to offer at our Lord's Mass, so Christ will hear our cries. We've had none since the last trade ship. To save ourselves, we need to hold a proper ritual. What will keep our children from starving, Bishop Alf? How will our prayers help us, when God cannot hear them?"

His anguish spread out from wall to wall. The laments of the people increased until it seemed the roar of a storm. At last, I perceived what a mistake I made in allowing our family to come here. Ingrid held my hand more tightly and looked at me. "Can't we go yet, Ma?"

"Yes. We are going home, right now. Halvard, Ole, Leif. Let's leave, please." We tried to force our way toward the open doors, all of us holding on to each other. "Don't let go of my hand, Ingrid." We had to push against the tide of people since folk outside pressed inward. We made some small progress toward the open doors, but it was like swimming upstream.

Around us, the desperate cries and wails continued. "We'll starve and die. Without bread for the Mass, our Lord won't know. Christ has deserted us. Satan is let in upon us."

"What are our priests doing to protect us?"

The bishop and his priests tried to calm the people, calling upon men by name, telling them to remember they were in the Lord's house.

"It's the ride of the Four Horsemen. This is the end of us." A frightened priest tried to drop to his knees, but could not.

"Ragnorak!" a man shouted. "Great Odin! It's the end of the world." Folk cried and screamed to their god and their families. All around us, women were wringing their hands. Some of the priests lifted their voices to pray.

We were almost to the door, but more people started to press inward from outside to determine the reason for the wailing. While we searched for a way through, I asked Halvard, "What did that man say? What is Ragnorak?"

"Ragnorak. That is the twilight of the gods," Halvard answered bleakly. "The final war between Good and Evil. The end of days." Fear had become panic. Others pushed toward the doors as well. I feared we would be crushed.

"It is as I have told you," came a powerful voice. I looked back. The shouts stopped and people turned to see a purple cloaked man with a high white headdress and golden chains circling his chest. People pointed and exclaimed that the bishop was speaking.

Everyone turned to the high platform and the big room began to hush. "Quiet. Quiet, I say. All this means is that Jesus is conquering the old gods. He's toppling them out of the sky and casting them out of the bowels of the earth where they have hidden. Come back and bow to Lord Jesus. He will soon reign over us in victory with his Holy Father. All other gods are dead and must be forgotten."

"God has already forgotten us!" an old man yelled from the side of the hall. "We must have a proper sacrament with wine and bread, not milk to substitute for blood and dried seal meat to take the place of the body. Satan will claim our souls. There's no forgiveness for us, here at *Ultima Thule*."

The bishop lifted his hands again, palms out. Cries and laments ceased long enough to hear his next words. "Our Lord understands the substitution. There are Odin worshipers in this land. That is why He doesn't help us."

"They're not just in the land; they're here in our cathedral!" shouted the frightened priest. "Kill them!"

Others took up the cry. Knives flashed and women shouted. Someone thought to climb up to the steeple and ring the bell. I was prepared to believe it was truly the end of the world when men of one nation fought like this over gods, and mountains brought forth fire. "Let us hurry away," I implored Halvard. "Stay together." We tried to move again and were almost to the outside when suddenly, a woman's voice pierced the tumult.

"That woman knows how to make bread." It was Birgitta who spoke. Faces craned to see where she pointed. A hush fell over the great hall as folk turned around to look at me.

Chapter 38

Halvard held my hand, but it was too late to escape. The great open doorway of the cathedral was blocked with observers. Ole stood before me and Leif behind, while Ingrid clung to my sleeve. "What do they want, Ma?" she asked, frightened. I wished I could comfort my child, promise her that all would be well, but I could not, because I didn't know.

"No one is going to hurt you, woman. Bring her here to me," the bishop commanded his monks.

"Let me go," I said as several young men with shaved heads closed in.

Halvard and his sons made a circle facing outward, with Ingrid and me inside. "Don't you dare touch my wife," Halvard shouted, spinning about.

"Why, look at that. That is the Skraeling woman who dresses like a Greenlander," a young man remarked. "It's the pagan Halvard Gunnarson with his Skraeling, the one who predicted the winters."

"She knew the cold was coming," a woman shouted. "She warned some of us not to dye our clothing, but to store more food."

A clear path opened between the bishop and me. Halvard still stood by me protectively, but I could see past him. The bishop had put off his high headdress now, and his purple cloak. His black robes covered his arms loosely and fell like drapes to his feet. A hood framed his face. His gold chain bore a golden cross with a small figure displayed upon it, like the wooden statue of their tortured god.

"Perhaps this woman can be of help. No one harm her. Bring her to me gently. I only want her to answer some questions," the bishop charged his followers. He showed us a kindly smile. "Please step aside and let her come to me," he said to Halvard. "I know you follow the false gods, but today, you stand in the Lord's house. This is a house of peace." I remembered when servants of this house of peace had killed my father-in-law. Men laid hands upon Halvard, but he stood fast and would not be budged.

"Come now. Serious problems threaten us, and your woman may have some knowledge that can help us. I give my word to you that no harm shall befall her." To me, his voice oozed like rancid maple syrup. I did not trust him, but the crowds were too thick to penetrate; we were trapped. I decided I might as well answer the bishop's questions so they would let us depart.

"We came to hear the sailors talk, not to hear you," Halvard protested, tossing his head from the bishop to those in the crowd. "Allow me to take my family home. It is no crime if my wife warned the women to store up food instead of dying their clothing. Which would you prefer when the wind howls around your house in April, dyed clothing or cheese? Would she have warned people if she wished them harm?"

"Halvard Gunnarson, come now. Think of your neighbors," the bishop repeated. "You may stand at her side."

Halvard hesitated. "We have no choice," I whispered. Ole stepped up beside us as we walked forward. His shoulder brushed mine. He was fifteen, broad across the shoulders, and had been practicing with knife and spear. I felt confident that no threat to me would go unchallenged. I smiled as bravely as I could. Whether or not Ole and I had become friends through the years, we were family. Ingrid clenched my hand. When I looked down, I saw her proud bearing. She looked right into the bishop's face, as if to say he did not frighten her.

"What do you want to know, High Priest?" I asked politely.

"Tell me, woman, what is your name?"

"It is Astrid," I answered

"What is your entire name? Say it properly, with the name of your father."

I gave him my identity and my father's name in my language. "Garah-stah of Wolf Clan, daughter of Dehateh of Doteoga, Ganeogaono." Since my father was dead, an enemy's knowledge of his name could do him no harm.

"What kind of gibberish is that?" Halvard's fingers moved to the hilt of his knife. The monks and priests saw the move and started toward him. The bishop gestured with his hand. "There is no need for violence. I only asked the woman a question. I will settle for the name Astrid. Now, woman, are you a Skraeling or aren't you?"

"No, High Priest," I replied. "If you mean the people who belong to this land, I am not one of them. I am from Ganeogaono, over the ocean. It is west of the land you name Vinland." A few people gasped and exclaimed. A man by the door called out the news to those outside. Few here actually knew me, even by sight, but word or rumor moved faster than wind.

"Well, I shall call you Astrid Vinlander, then. I cannot say your father's name. This is the first I've heard of Vinlanders from over the ocean coming to civilized lands. Perhaps you can tell me why you predicted such long winters."

"I dreamed it." I would not tell him about Sea Woman, whose name is Nerrivik, nor how she appeared to me as an iceberg, while the cave of her open mouth blew gales toward Greenland's coast. It appeared my understanding of my dream was correct. "My people believe dreams are messages from gods."

"I see." The bishop lowered his head in a courteous nod. His hood had fallen back and I saw the bald circle on his head. The rest of his hair came to his shoulders and was mostly gray. "Do you think the gods of your land over the ocean can send you dreams when you are here in my land?"

His land? I did not know how to answer him, so I remained silent.

"This is not the land of your gods," he instructed me smoothly. "You have no gods. Only the Father and the Son and the Holy Spirit rule the world. There are no other gods." More people were pushing forward. From the corner of my eye, I saw them gathering and recognized some of them as Skaddi's sons, Steinthor and his brothers.

The bishop spoke again. "Perhaps we need to teach you about Heaven and Hell. I see you have no knowledge of what awaits those who are unsaved. Because of your ignorance, it would be wrong to blame you for your error. We mean you no harm, as I said. If you know how to make bread where no oats, millet, wheat, or barley can grow, please be good enough to explain your method, so that we may have bread for our ceremonies."

If that was all he wanted of me, there was no harm. I would tell him so we could leave. "It is just reed-grass seeds, separated from their hulls, ground, mixed with fat, and baked on a hot, flat stone. The seed meal is much better boiled in water and made into gruel than baked. The other way, it can hurt your teeth."

A priest laughed, but he stopped when the bishop frowned. "You poor ignorant child," he said kindly. "Don't you even know what a Mass is?"

Perhaps I had misunderstood. Why would Gunnar know everything about a Christian ritual? Birgitta herself admitted that many things of a religious nature were difficult to comprehend. The high priest of the Christians should be able to explain it best. "No, I don't," I admitted. "Please tell me."

He proceeded to do so. Everything I had been led to believe was true. Christian magic words turned spoiled grape squeezings and bread into the flesh and blood of their god.

"How terrible," I said when he was done, "to eat a god's flesh and drink his blood." Halvard touched my arm to remind me of our danger, but all caution had deserted me. I could not keep myself from saying, "No wonder luck is gone from your people in Greenland."

"What do you mean, Skraeling?" I winced as though he had called me that name the Algonquin gave me: Mohawk Girl.

"You say you love him, but you eat your god's flesh as if he were your enemy. Naturally, he deserted you."

"Are you telling me that your people eat the flesh of your enemies?" The bishop's voice came out of his throat oddly and his eyes bulged.

All caution deserted me in my anger, leading to my disrespect in front of the others. "They are half-cooked anyway when we are through with them," I said. "We don't waste meat."

His pale face flushed pink, as though I had slapped him. "Demon woman! Abomination! Idolater!" he ranted. "She's the tool of Satan!" With one shaking hand, he pointed at me while he held tightly to his gold cross with the other. "She brought these winters upon us with her evil deeds. She's a witch!" he cried. "Take her outside and throw her over the cliff."

Two priests closed the distance between us and tried to lay hands on me. Halvard kicked one away, and, crouching, he drew his knife. Ole yelled for his favorite god, Thor, to witness, and he raised his fist in the sign of Thor's hammer. Skaddi's sons and grandsons rushed at the priests who were rushing at Halvard.

Roars and screams of repressed rage and pain made me frantic. Where was my Ingrid? I ducked away to avoid the grasp of one priest who lunged for me. He looked familiar somehow, something about his nose and the way he squinted his eyes. I remembered. He was the priest from the longship who had pointed me out to his companion when we sailed up the fjord.

Someone grabbed Halvard and held him while another tried to wrestle away his knife. Another seized Ole from behind. The boy kicked back strongly. The blow must have connected, for I heard the priest groan. Ole escaped his grip, pulled a knife from his boot, and threw it. There was a thud and a scream. I turned and saw a priest writhing on the ground, blood spurting from his shoulder.

Ole calmly retrieved his bloody weapon, warrior's fire lighting his face with serene strength. For a moment, he reminded me of my father in his last battle. "That blow was for Thor," he shouted. "Who wants to be next?" He was off, looking for another fight.

Above the shouts and taunts of "Kill the Christians" and others of "Kill all Skraelings and Odin lovers," Ingrid's high voice screamed. She was somewhere in the back of the great hall. "Mama! Father! Where are they taking me? Let me go. I want to go back to my mother."

Those were my very words as the Algonquin grabbed me from the gates of Doteoga. I have been where she is, I thought. I was dragged away from my people, screaming for my father and help that came too late. I began to sway. I fought to control myself, refusing to faint. I would not be helpless. She was my one child who lived. No one would harm her while I breathed.

I dove to the floor. Somehow, I avoided the twisting and grunting bodies that hovered over and around me long enough to retrieve Halvard's fallen knife. He still struggled with the man who had tried to grab me. Rage and fear for my child poured strength into my arm. The knife edge was sharp and cold. Suddenly, I knew what I must do. Let me be truly Mohawk Girl, I thought to myself. I would become what the hated name meant and have the blood and flesh of any who threatened my daughter. "Nerrivik," I begged. "I need you. Help me."

I lunged at the bishop. It would have been so easy to kill him, but I refrained. He was the purchase price for my daughter—her life for his. He deserved to die, having ordered my death after promising no harm would befall me if I answered his questions. Instead of pressing my chance to drive the blade home, I yanked him off balance, pushing him to his knees. I held him securely with one arm. The edge of the ancient knife touched the skin of his throat. It would take little pressure to slice his windpipe. There was one other I had killed the same way. I whistled a high warning note. The sounds of battle died and people turned. "Stop!" I cried. "Or I shall kill him."

"Do it!" Leif shouted, standing nearby. He made a fist like Thor's hammer, as well. "He deserves to die." I was glad to see Leif safe, but I shook my head. A dead hostage would do me no good. There were screams and a great rush of air as half the folk in the hall gasped.

"She's got the bishop!"

"The Skraeling's got the bishop! She's going to kill the bishop!"

As if the moment were a picture I had drawn on bark when I was Picture Maker of Wolf Clan, the scene froze. It seemed to be waiting for the next stroke of my charred twig. Folk were poised in midstroke, midcry, midrun. All faces had turned to me. I was frozen as well, with my knife at the high priest's throat. Even Halvard regarded me with a combination of horror and awe. We might have been one of the tapestries within the cathedral. No one moved or seemed to breathe.

"Where is my daughter?" I demanded. "Let me see her alive and well. I want to see her *now*, or this shaved-head priest will die." My words brought them around again. They parted between us and the light from the open doors. A woman at the back of the crowd, near the door, rushed outside and returned with my daughter. She lived. The woman standing beside her was old Freydis, Skaddi's daughter.

"I'm not hurt, Mama," Ingrid called to me. "Freydis and Sigrid, Steinthor's wife, took me away from the fighting." My heart beat again. Ingrid was safe.

"I'm sorry, Astrid," Birgitta cried to me. "I just wanted you to teach them to make proper bread. I didn't want anyone to hurt you. Oh, please, let him go. Don't kill the bishop."

I found I did not want to kill him. Touching him made my flesh crawl, as though I touched the water snake that had once threatened my brother's life. In fact, I'd almost forgotten the man I held captive. I looked at the bishop. He trembled, no longer so arrogant. "What shall I do, Halvard?" I asked. "I leave it to you."

Before Halvard answered me, he addressed my captive. "Bishop, will you rescind your order if my wife lets you live?"

"Wife? You dare call her your wife when no proper priest united you? Fornicator!"

At this, I pressed in my knife just enough to make him squeak.

"Do you think it is fitting to bargain with the bishop?" the squint-eyed priest screamed. Halvard glared at him for a moment, then turned back to the bishop, not lowering himself to reply to the insolent question.

"It is fitting to kill you for breaking your word," I reminded my prisoner. "If you wish to convince me not to, then answer my husband."

"Let me go," he demanded.

I pressed the knife closer. It made a line on his throat. No one dared move to try to pull him from my grasp, for fear I would slay their high priest. If I lived past this day, someone would be sure to kill me later, and probably Halvard as well for bringing me to live among them.

"If I let you live, will you give us your leave to walk out of this hall in peace?" I asked, loudly enough for all to hear.

"Yes," he whispered.

"Say it louder, so everyone can hear," Halvard demanded.

"In the name of the Son and the Father, I order that no Christian man or woman is to harm you in this hall. If you do not leave our lands, however, I cannot guarantee your safety."

I knew that, and it might be for the best. If I died now, it would mean little. Halvard and his sons would care for my daughter. "You will not harm my husband, his sons, or our daughter?"

"I gave my oath to Jesus and the Father."

"You spoke so before. You must answer to every Norseman here if you go back on your word," Halvard said.

I pulled up my knife a little, but before I released the bishop, I said, "I will certainly go away. Tell your people to let us walk away from this cathedral now and return to our home in safety so that I may prepare."

"Will you really go and never return?" the squint-eyed priest asked.

"I will," I said. Halvard groaned. I needed to make him understand I made the promise for his sake, so he would not have to leave his house and the land of his fathers. I could not leave him in danger, not on my account.

"Go, then, Skraeling," the bishop said. "As God is my witness, I will not hinder you or harm your man or his children."

I looked around, wondering whether to simply hand Halvard back his knife and walk away. It might have been safe, but how could I trust the oath of a man who could lie. To my people, our given word is our honor. "Hold him," I said when Halvard took the knife. "Even if he can be believed, I fear we must take him with us until we are on the trail, or one of his men may do us harm even yet." We had a mob to walk through, and it frightened me that someone would plunge a spear into one of us before we were gone from the building.

"That will not be necessary." Steinthor stepped through the ranks of the people, but it was Oskar who said, "I will take good care of your captive." He raised his voice until it reached every corner of the cathedral hall. "Astrid and her family must be permitted to go in safety. I won't be led to God by a man whose word means nothing. Many of us within this hall and outside of it agree. Bishop, take back your former decree of execution against Astrid. You said no one might kill her here. I want you to add that no one is to follow her and kill her later. Say it now and say it loud if you want to avoid a war in which you will surely die."

The bishop gasped at such effrontery, but he retreated long enough to yell, "I make the witch free of my order, then, but I do so only to save Christian lives. My order stands for two days. If she does not leave the Eastern Settlement, I'm not responsible for what God-fearing men may do. I still believe she's an emissary of Satan, the Skraelings' god!"

"Don't forget she eats human flesh! She admitted it," the squint-eyed priest added loudly enough to be heard halfway across the cathedral. It started off more muttering, which others carried on, but softly.

"I will go, as I agreed to do. Please, take me home, Halvard." He put his arm over my shoulder like a shield and walked me outside.

Our friends pushed open a path to the doorway. Leif and Ole followed us out into the sunlight. Ingrid's arms flew around me, her wet face pressing into my neck. "I thought they were going to kill you, Ma. You were so brave!"

"I thought I was going to lose you. That's why I was brave." She let go of me and ran to Halvard, hugging him fiercely. He lifted her up, letting her ride on his shoulders. I turned around and smiled to our friends, who had gathered around us. "Thank you for defending me and for keeping Ingrid safe. Let us hurry away from this place. I want to go home."

Chapter 39

The crowd parted to allow us to walk through, pushed back by others who shouted the bishop's decree. "No one harm this family. The woman leaves the district in two days." The monks walked through the assembly, repeating this phrase over and over until everyone knew. Each curious stare added weight to the burden I carried. By my given word, I had become an exile once more. I had two days to put my life in Halvard's house and Greenland behind me forever.

How blue the sky appeared over my head, and how soft the lying summer breezes, with their false promise of growth and life. All too soon, the breeze would turn to a drying wind, which would kill the grass and crumble the protective roofing turves of byres and houses to dust. Rain at the wrong time would rot the hay.

A flock of birds flew overhead, snow geese, honking. They flew southeasterly, not a sign of winter yet, but their flight en masse was sign enough. They were not finding the abundance they expected. Odin's messengers, the black birds known as ravens, were silhouetted against the sky for a brief moment. They ducked between clouds, chasing one another, diving and gliding over the blue and glittering fjord. Their flight took them over the distant hills, until they were gone from sight. Each bird had its flock, each deer its herd, but I had nothing. I was exiled, like the lone mountain lion, or the lone wolf, my clan's namesake. What had I done to my husband and children by losing my temper?

Pictures of my life swam past my eyes. I was seven, and Grandmother told me I should be known as Gahrahstah, Picture Maker. In my mind, I saw the painted medicine masks of the False Face Society. Their carved wooden grimaces and huge eye sockets had frightened me and my cousins all those years ago. I could still picture the men under the long masks shaking their turtle-shell rattles and dancing away bad spirits from the sick.

My mother's and sister's faces nodded to me. My four-year-old brother froze to stillness on the riverbank, threatened by the water snake. Again, I crept up silently and smashed its head with a rock. My father, in his war regalia, his paint, with two turkey tail feathers tied to his scalp lock, lifted me up and hugged me against his chest.

I recalled faces and places, pain and loss, moons of walking and moons of plying a paddle upon rivers and over the great open sea. The years and their pictures flew by in the time it took for us to traverse the fields. Sea Woman, Nerrivik, came into my mind as she appeared in my dream, a great ice mountain floating on the waves. Her deep brow directed her gaze toward me where I stood alone on a cliff above the sea. She knew my distress and grieved for me.

Halvard knew my past now, what I had not considered evil when I lived among my own people. He knew why the Algonquin reviled me and named me Mohawk Girl. Every Greenlander in the district must know by now that I had partaken in my people's grisly victory feasts.

Halvard strode silently by my side while Ingrid and her half brothers ran ahead of us. When we came to the home field, he called his sons and Ingrid aside to remind them to attend to their tasks. It was as though we were returning from an outing, instead of the day that severed my future from his.

We had barely ducked inside when Ole got a packet of dried meat from the larder, along with a water bladder. "I'm going into the hills to check my traps," he said, heaving a large carrying sack over his shoulders. "Leif and Ingrid will do the milking." He walked off in one direction and the younger two entered the fold with the milking vessels.

Halvard guided me in, away from the door. He closed it against the green fields and the summer sun. He had arranged for us to be alone, so he could tell me, away from the children, how my presence revolted him.

"You are angry," I said, understating what he must have been feeling. I readied myself to face the brunt of his abhorrence. We had no time for silences, for I would have to hurry to prepare the few possessions I would take with me. I had no intention of waiting out the two days since Halvard would want me out of his sight as soon as possible.

My poor daughter must be without her mother. There was no protection for her where I was going. I might beg sanctuary of the Inuit, but I knew what they thought of girl children who had no father to hunt for them.

It hardly mattered what became of me. Whether hunger took me or I threw myself over a cliff into the ocean to save time, my life might as well have ended. Once I entered the desolate northland, it would not be long before the wolves would come to tear the flesh from my unburied bones. If such was my fate, it would be an honor to mingle my spirit with that of my beloved wolves. I would not count my life as wasted.

Halvard sat me down and paced the room several times while he gathered his thoughts. Finally, the wrathful words exploded from his mouth. "Naturally, I'm angry. I'm furious! I should never have allowed us to go where I couldn't defend you." My mouth fell open in disbelief as he ranted. I had seen my white bones, pale against the snow. Halvard's words pulled me back. "Was there ever a woman who stood up to the bishop and threw his words into his face the way you did? If it were me, with my knife against his throat, I would have killed him. Then and there, I would have destroyed any chance for all of us to get away with our lives. You saved us."

I shut my mouth and looked up into his face. The ruddy anger had drained away with his words, and he was smiling at me tenderly.

How could it be? Had I misunderstood so much? In my confusion, I must have sounded like a little girl. "You mean you don't hate me?"

"Hate you?"

"But . . . but," I stammered. I had expected his revulsion, not his praise. "You cannot have understood what happened back there or what it meant. I must go."

"No." His strong arms came around me and his warm, good smell filled my nostrils. "Don't you see? The priests have lost their hold over the people. Folk aren't afraid to speak out anymore. We have nothing to lose. Perhaps the old ways will return. People stood up for you today because of the care you gave to my father, and because of your courage."

"If I stay here, there will be a battle in which everyone will lose. Then there would not be enough Greenlanders left to go on. In any case, I gave my word. I must go."

He stroked my hair and put his lips to my neck. "You can't leave us. Without you, this house would lose its soul."

I tried to pull away, but only succeeded in turning my face. "My presence is a danger to you, no matter how many of your friends support us. Do you not understand what I said before he condemned me? My tribe tortures the captives we take in war. The women do so more viciously than the men. Although I was young before the Algonquin dragged me away, I participated. We burned our prisoners and peeled the crackling skin from their flesh. We did as bad and worse than the evil pictured on the tapestries, what was done to the Christian saints, because we ate the bodies after. I have done so myself."

I had made it as plain as I could so that he could not fail to take my meaning. Since Halvard did not reply, I continued to press my point. I would not put my husband in jeopardy by staying. "You and your sons are in danger as it is, but this is your land, where you were born. You told me how very much your land means to you. I've suffered exile before, when I lost my land and my people. I walked for months without seeing another person. My time among the Greenlanders is done. Now that you know the worst about me, you must surely want me to go. How can you bear to touch me?"

My voice rose as I spoke so many words, but it fell when I finished, because I wanted him to touch me more than I could say. For one last time, I wanted to be close to Halvard, to feel the rush of his blood, for our pulses to beat together in the rhythm of love. That memory would keep me warm when I wandered among the shifting winds of the spirit world. I sighed deeply, looking away so my longing would not show in my face and humiliate me.

Halvard grasped my shoulders and turned me, lifting my chin to look into my face. His teeth clenched and the pulse in his neck beat so hard below the vein, I could see it. "You will go nowhere without me," he said.

I could not pull myself from his grasp. "I don't belong here; I never belonged here. You say this because of the magic. Minik's magic, the *angakkoq* magic that made you love me."

Halvard shook me, roaring as though I had wounded him. "It was never his magic. It was you."

My mouth opened in astonishment. Even when he pulled me close and tenderly wrapped his arms around me, I was speechless. His voice spoke softly in my ear, explaining, consoling, and erasing my lingering doubts.

"It was my loss and yours that brought us together at first. The wildness in you spoke to me. I felt it the first time you touched my hand. Don't deny it. It was not Minik. We made our own magic. Do you think I would have returned from the north without you? It was you who gave me back my life after my Sigrun's death. Without you . . ." He did not finish what he was going to say.

"But you know me now," I reminded him. "Everything."

He stroked my hair and my hip. "I come from the seed of Vikings. If you killed the bishop and cut out his liver after he ordered your death, I would have eaten it raw. My ancestors were as fierce as any of your people. The gods saw how much I needed you, and they brought you to me." His teeth bit softly into my ear. Heat coursed through my body.

His lips and teeth worked down to my neck while he opened the ties of my dress. With his hand cupping my chin, he kissed me deeply. As though in the newness of our first passion, we fiercely pressed our bodies together, as if we could blend them into one. When he pulled back a moment to touch the pads of his fingers to the tips of my breasts, I felt them reach toward him. Shivers of joy darted through my veins, transforming my objection into an irresistible yearning.

The sweet kisses of his mouth made magic indeed. My dress fell at my feet and I stepped out of it, kicking it aside. A moment later, he stood naked as I, beautiful as a chief in his strength and the glory of his manhood. He lifted me and carried me into our bed closet.

"Astrid," he whispered as he lowered me to the softness. His kisses lit me on fire, from my breasts to my belly, and down to my toes. Nothing else mattered but his raging desire and his body. The world, which had been empty and desolate a few moments before, became complete under his loving weight. There were no words. Nature ruled us, making us one with her.

We came together like wolves. We swam in a warm ocean of love, letting the waves carry us down and then up to even greater heights. We were together at last, after so long. Halvard gasped just as we reached the crest. Delight and love as irresistible as a great wave welled up inside me, until I could no longer wait. I cried out like a she-wolf, unable to keep silent.

Slowly, slowly, we came to the surface, still joined, holding each other close and savoring the final ripples of the bliss we experienced. Halvard's eyes were moist. I touched his damp cheek with a finger.

"What is it?" I whispered. "You are sad. Are you sorry?"

"No," he answered, giving me a tender kiss. His passion had passed and his lips were soft again. "I will never be sorry for one moment of our time together."

"It's what I wanted, too. Now I can take the memory of your love with me into the wilderness."

Halvard lifted himself with both arms and looked down. A good many thoughts seemed to be crowding behind his eyes. "You still don't understand. Do you imagine you're going alone? Do you think so little of my love for you?"

"But your land! The land where your fathers are buried. I won't take you away from it."

"If I can't keep my woman safe and my children safe, this isn't where I want to live. Maybe your dream is true and the winters will bring us all death. We can't fight the gods, but I won't go to war with my own country because of them. When the storm pushed us north on our way home, we came to land near a deserted house. The rain came hard on the wind and there was lightning. We climbed the hill and slept in the shelter of its walls. Perhaps you remember?"

"I remember. I sang for the ghosts."

"We can go there, Astrid. We'll take our herd and live off them as long as we can. There should be enough time before the wind changes to make the house secure for winter. If it becomes necessary, we can hunt and gather like the Inuit, you and me and our children. You can teach us how. We'll make our own world. Never again speak of leaving me."

It was difficult for me to speak, but I sought to understand. "We'll live alone, not with the Inuit, who make so little of their women?" I asked. "I don't want Ingrid to think she is worth less than a boy." I spoke dreamily, scarcely believing.

"Ingrid will never think that. My Astrid. What would I do without you?" My heart beat faster. Our lips met, hot and strong as before. I drank his sweet desire, strong and powerful like the good West Wind. I felt light as a bird, as a cloud. He was the rain, and I was the land. Our love chased other thoughts away as the shepherd chases his sheep home. Together, we were alive and home, wherever we were. After all this time, I finally knew he felt the same.

It would have been so good to sleep, but there was too much to do. Leif and Ingrid were still with the sheep, but they would return soon. There was supper to prepare and eat, and the planning of our journey. Halvard intended to ask his sons if they wished to remain. "This steading is theirs if they want it, but I believe they will choose to go with us. When the priests come to see if you are gone in two days, they'll find all of us gone. I hope they don't desecrate my father's grave."

"His spirit is with Odin. They can't hurt him." He nodded at my words and went to call in the children.

The shadows grew long as I worked to finish the last piece on my small loom and to pack it. Ingrid ought to know Greenlander skills. For all I could guess, she might need them someday. Only the Norns knew what the future held.

I was deciding what to take and what must be left, when I heard bells, not the loud, ponderous bells of the cathedral, but tinkling, singing bells. I looked through the window. Just outside, running through the home field, were many animals. Ours were safely in their fold. The dog Halvard got from Osmund barked, then howled most peculiarly.

We ran outside to make sense of what was happening. Birgitta rushed out of the mass of sheep, goats, and dogs. She caught me up in her arms and embraced me, mumbling apologies into my hair.

"Why are you here? What is all this?" I asked in confusion, as the animals bleated and Birgitta and Osmund's dogs barked at them and howled their greetings to their old comrade.

"Astrid, my poor friend," Birgitta gasped. "I can't tell you how sorry I am for what happened. I never thought it would end in you having to go away. Let me try to make amends."

"What are you saying?"

"These animals are yours now, to take with you. I'm giving you two more dogs to help herd and guard them. They're three months old, from our last litter, fully weaned and half-trained. I never meant any harm to you and your family. I only wanted you to show them how to make bread."

I squeezed her hand. "I believe you. I really do," I said. "But how did you know Halvard was going with me? He just decided."

"He would never let you go alone. How could *you* think otherwise?"

So I had been half-blind. I hugged Birgitta, wishing that we had become better friends over the past years. She was a good woman after all.

Osmund clasped Halvard's arm. Although he spoke to Halvard, his eyes turned to me. "Will everything come to pass as Astrid's dream foretold? Will we all die, or will life return to the way it was? The children of this land have done no wrong to anyone. Will they have to suffer for the sins of their fathers?" Halvard also looked to me for the answer.

How could I answer them? "I dreamed we would have one bad winter, long and cold, with great winds. After that, I cannot say what will be. Some winters have been warm, with no snow, but the hay rots with late rain. If I could always see truly into the future, I would never have left my house the day I was stolen from my people." I shook my head and shrugged, not because I didn't care, but from helplessness.

I wanted to leave Osmund and Birgitta hope. "Perhaps the Icelanders will take some of you in when the illness stops and the mountains rest.

Perhaps some of you will go north to live with the Inuit. Only the Norns know the future for certain, isn't that right?" At that, Birgitta grimaced and looked toward her husband, but Osmund had nothing to say.

"Or perhaps your children will build a longship out of the old boats, wide enough and strong enough to take them back to Vinland again. Perhaps the Skraelings won't chase them away this time. A wise woman told me my child will live. Others must live, too, then, or how else will Ingrid find a husband?"

We hugged and thanked them for the sheep, knowing it was to be our last farewell. In the morning, we must leave. We left the new herd to graze overnight in the home field. There would be no harvest this year, not for us.

Before we returned to the house, Halvard asked Leif and Ole their intentions. They knew why we had to leave, but the exile did not include anyone who did not want to go. "I won't return as long as Astrid is not welcome," he said. "There is a deserted house several days' travel north. On our return from the Skraelings, we sheltered under its walls. I expect it won't take very much to make it livable again. You two are men now, and grown enough to make your own decisions." He smiled at their expressions.

When they did not reply at once, he went on, watching them to see if his arguments were swaying them. "With three men and two women"—he looked at Ingrid, who grinned at being called a woman—"we'll have a better chance. We'll be able to take the boat. Otherwise, we can take only what Astrid, Ingrid, and I can carry. We will have to drive the herd inland to avoid the fjords, and the journey will take longer. I would hate to leave our boat behind, but if you stay, it is yours. Remember, we will have no one to count on but ourselves. Do you want to sleep on it and give me your decision in the morning? Ole? Leif?"

Neither Leif nor Ole spoke up right away. Halvard said, "This house is yours to have and hold, if you remain behind. I'll deed it to both of you legally, so the bishop won't add it to the cathedral's lands when they discover I have gone. If you decide to stay, we'll split the herd, half for you, half for us."

"You're my family," Leif said. "You don't go north without me." His freckled nose stood out over his white teeth. He had become a handsome youth, this boy with the gold-red hair. Girls followed him with their eyes when he passed them. He would want to choose a wife in a few years.

"And you, Ole? Are you willing to leave this land behind? You're a man now. What do you say?"

He did not hesitate. "I would hate to miss the expressions on their faces when they find all of us gone. Deed the house over to Osmund. Leif and I will load up the boat in the morning." He looked at Leif, who nodded. "You say we can see the house from the coast?"

Halvard grinned. "Yes, but we'll see you before then. We'll look for you where the fjord empties into the ocean. If you fish as you go, and we have any luck with my spear and Astrid's bow, we'll save our herd during the journey. With you to ferry us and the livestock across the fjords, it won't take more than five or six days of travel to reach the outskirts of the old Western Settlement." He went inside for parchment to deed the house over to Osmund.

There was dew on the grass in the home field when we awoke. I looked over our supplies. We could not pack the milking vessels until Ingrid and I did the morning milking. We drank what we could and put the rest into stomach sacks to turn to rough cheese as we traveled. I did not mind leaving the chess pieces behind or even Halvard's parchment sagas. There was only so much we could carry. Halvard knew the stories already and could tell them to us just as well on winter nights, without the books.

I carried a special bundle with me from the house to the stone-lined ditch. I removed my long woven dress, together with my stockings and bulky leather shoes, so that I could wash before we began. The water felt good, even when I rubbed my body and hair with the coarse soap we had made from grease and ashes. I poured bucket after bucket of water over my hair to wash away the smoke and grease that adhered. I dried myself briskly with rags and stood bare a long moment in the summer sun.

Grandmother Moon hung low in the east, over the blue glaciers and the ice-capped mountains. At least a moon was there. I do not know by what name the Greenlanders called it, for perhaps they had a different name. The only thing that was certain was that we must leave.

When I was through drying my hair, I opened my bundle. The under-belt went around my waist first. I drew the fringed leggings up to my thighs and I tied them to the belt. After that, I slipped the Naskapi dress Pine Tree Woman had made for me over my head and pulled it smooth. I wore this dress when I left Turtle Island to meet the Inuit, and also on the day I wed Halvard. I wore it the day I came to his house to meet my new family, as well. It was a dress for changes—endings and beginnings. I found the leather still soft and supple, the colored quill designs as beautiful as before. Lastly, I slipped my feet into my ankle-high moccasins.

Instead of braiding my damp hair, I tied a band around it, leaving it to hang in loose, wavy ripples. Halvard's eyes widened when he saw me walking back to the house. Ingrid had never seen me like this. "You seem so different, Ma," she said, coming close to touch the fringes and stroke the soft doeskin. "It is beautiful, but it's like you're someone else."

"I am someone else," I said, and laughed at her confusion. "I'll tell you what I mean someday. Are you ready?" I hoped she would not carry the scars of yesterday's terror in the cathedral. Perhaps the memory had begun to fade. She had not witnessed or heard the worst of it.

"We're going on a journey," she said, eyes sparkling with innocent enthusiasm. If she regretted leaving the only home she knew, I could not see it. "Father and my brothers are coming, too. We're going to see new places, climb new hills, and see new fjords. It will be an adventure."

"Yes. It will be an adventure to make ourselves a new home," I agreed. It would be a struggle, too, and she would have no girls her age to play with as she grew up. Away from any world but the one we could make for her, it would surely be lonely. The family might return to live among the Greenlanders again when I died, for I did not believe many years were left to me. I wondered how the next few years would affect my daughter.

Her face grew serious. "We'll all be together. I'm not afraid."

"Good girl," Halvard said, his voice deepening with emotion. This was the house he had been born into, the home he hoped to keep for his sons. His load was already in place on his back. He wore his warm coat so as not to have to carry it. His spear and knives were tucked into their holders and he carried his ax under his wide leather belt. He sheathed the steel knife I had given him in a pocket in his sleeve.

We returned to the house for a last look, then helped Ingrid fit her small back carrier into place. I slipped my arms through the straps of mine. Our knives were tucked in our pockets and we carried staffs to help the dogs manage the livestock. I carried my small bow and quiver over one shoulder. "Let us go," I said.

I released the sheep and the goats from their fold a last time and waved them west to the path near the cliff's edge. The plan was to follow Eriksfjord north past Brattahlid, then west to the coast. The dogs worked well together, the older seeming to train the pups. It was in their blood to herd.

Ole and Leif climbed down to Halvard's well-loaded boat. We saw them row out, turn the boat north, and unfurl the sail. A brisk breeze came up to push them over the rolling water. They would take the deed to Osmund first. Then, they would sail north to where the fjord joined the ocean. I sent a silent prayer for Sea Woman to protect them.

Before we began, Halvard and I knelt at the small cemetery near the house, at Gunnar's grave, and the graves of our children who never lived past their first birthdays. Sigrun and her dead children were covered there, too. Too many dead children break a mother's heart. I felt a connection with Halvard's first wife and shed a tear for her. Few of us lived long, and for those who did, like Gunnar, there was only a wider bit of earth to lie in.

Halvard saw me whispering to Sigrun's shade when he knelt beside me. I heard him tell her he would take care of their boys. With his free hand, Halvard traced the wing sign of Odin's raven before he stood. "We're all destined to lie under the earth someday, aren't we?" he said, not really needing me to give him an answer.

I did so anyway. "Our bodies are. I've never understood why men fight over land. Everyone will have as much as they require at the end. They would save themselves a lot of grief if they remembered that."

Ingrid ran ahead of us between the dogs and the goats and sheep, skipping and jumping with the lambs and kids. Every time we passed a boulder half-buried in the wild grass, she climbed it to look back. When we were too far to see the house, she climbed the next rock just to see the hills she knew.

Her arms and legs were sun brown from chasing after goats since she could walk. She was almost as dark as I, but her hair held the sun's red light and her eyes were sea green like her father's. Her auburn braids flew behind her as she bounded forward with youthful energy. I hoped she had a few glad memories to hold her through the years to come. The bell hanging from the lead goat's neck rang back to us. Halvard took my hand and we hurried to catch up.

I had my man beside me, the sweet smell of trampled grass, and the glorious colors of the nodding flowers. The salt breath of the ocean filled me with gladness while we two walked over the tilting and rock-strewn land. There were still pictures to be made. Our children, Ingrid and her brothers, would have to make their own pictures as the gods and their fates guided them.

Glossary / Characters

aama—Again
Aleqasiaq—Qisuk's first wife, Sammik's mother (the nice older sister)
allu—Breathing hole in the ice made by seals
amaaq—Hood
Angakkoq—Sorceror
anorak—a heavy, hooded jacket, a parka
Doteoga—Ganeogaono Town, birthplace to Garahstah
Ga-oh—Iroquois Wind Spirit
Garahstah—Picture Maker; female artist in Iroquois
Heno—Iroquois Thunder Spirit
igloo—Inuit house with stone walls, camp igloos made of snow blocks
illeq—Platform
Inuk, Inuit—Man, Men
Inuteq—Minik's wife
kapatak—Jacket
kayak—Narrow boat for sea hunting
kamiks—Boots
longship—Large Norseman wooden boat with one square sail
Maki—Not found, Padloq's mother
Manitou—Algonquin Great Spirit
Meqqoq—Salluq's wife (the hairy one)
Mikisoq—The little one (Picture Maker's Inuit name)
Minik—Qisuk's sorceror

nanu—Bearskin pants or trousers worn by Inuit

Nanoq—Bear

Nerrivik—Inuit spirit of life (Sea Woman)

Orenda—Iroquois Great Spirit

Padloq—Qisuk's second wife (the one who stretches out on the stomach)

Putu—Sorqaq's wife (hole)

Qalaseq—Qisuk's younger son (navel)

Qallunuk, Qallunaat—Big Eyebrows, singular, plural (Inuit name for Norsemen)

Qisuk—Wood

Salluq—Meqqoq's husband (liar)

Sammik—Qisuk's older son (left-handed)

Skraeling—Norse for savage, applied to natives of Greenland and America

Sorqaq—Headman of Baffin Island village (whale bone)

Taaferaaq—Aama's husband (seagull)

Toornaq—Human's ghost or roving spirit

Tupilat—Spirits; not necessarily human

ulu—woman's knife with rounded edge

Ululik—Padloq's father, Sammik's Grandfather

umiak—Big boat used by Inuit

Author's Note

This is a work of fiction. I researched each of the cultures and places where Picture Maker lived and tried to represent as accurately as possible these cultures as background to my characters' history. Concerning the Algonquin use of the name Mohawk: From interviews I conducted, this name truly did concern some of their practices during war.

During the latter years of the fourteenth century, the western hemisphere was little affected by European influences. In the eleventh century, Norsemen led by Leif Eriksson landed and lived for two years somewhere in Labrador. Remains of a settlement have been found in L'Anse aux Meadows, but recent archaeologists think this was merely a base easily found by ships sailing southward along Labrador's coast—a place from which short expeditions could be mounted for timber, walrus, or furs for trading.

Encounters between the Norwegians and the Algonquin turned violent when the Norsemen refused to trade their iron tools and weapons. The settlers returned home, but not before discovering the Algonquin liked milk. Imported Greenlander sheep and goats would have turned wild. No animals were herded in the New World except for turkeys in the North American Southwest and llamas and their cousins farther south.

The Inuit had sorcerers like Minik who did unbelievable things. French geomorphologist and cartographer Jean Malaurie, in his *The Last Kings of Thule,* reports about them and their powers still existing into the early 1950s. Canadian Inuit have crossed the Arctic ice by dog sledge. Malaurie repeated this journey to Canada and back with four Inuit companions.

The star stone in the story is a large meteorite found near the coast in northwest Greenland. I saw it on display on a class trip to the Hayden Planetarium in New York City. The names for the Inuit used in *Picture Maker* were the names of real people mentioned in *The Last Kings of Thule*.

The Norwegian Eastern Settlement of Greenland thrived for more than four hundred years, the Western Settlement for slightly less. Archaeologists tell us a small ice age occurred during the late 1300s, which made the settlers' way of life impossible to maintain. Ruins of their homes and cathedral were found in the nineteenth century. I have seen the tapestries I described on walls in museums. Jane Smiley's version of the last years of the Norse colony in her novel *The Greenlanders* inspired my interest and led to my research.

The sagas were written in Norse runes, not Latin. These sources survive in Iceland to this day. It is from them that we know about the Norse gods, and about Norse seafarers' battles and explorations. It is assumed these sagas were embellished. Latin was the language of scholars during the Dark Ages, and only priests were allowed to learn it. The Norse settlers of Iceland and Greenland could not be controlled so easily, due to their distance from "civilization." Most adults were literate and proud of it.

Most of the stories and legends in *Picture Maker* came from Iroquois and Inuit sources.

Penina Keen Spinka is the author of many award-winning novels for young adults about Native American culture. She lives with her husband in Glendale, Arizona, where she is at work on the sequel to *Picture Maker*.